I couldn't believe my e~~~~lia
decrying and describing~~~~is
main characters in new~~~~

From earliest time,~~~~the re-telling of stories, bardic traditions have re-told tales and entertained people with stories of mystery, myth and magic. For us, as a race such things are inbuilt; they're locked into our genes and will never disappear.

When a new author comes on the scene to take up the reins, to refurbish and polish the ancient; to explore new avenues for well loved actions bringing new heroes and strong characters to the Fantasy Genre, they should be applauded.

When they do it well, with style and good language command, they should be feted.

So it is with this author, Melissa A. Joy. She has totally immersed herself in creating the fantastic world of Aeldynn, breathing life and emotions into her characters. Her stories within the Saga are immeasurably magical. The hint of sorcery warring with nature hangs and drifts through the air, filters through each page. Heroes and heroines battle with dark forces; with always the influences, the shadows, of the nature of the world they inhabit. These influences reflect real life but are enhanced, magnified and used to add to the stories of Legend. They are expounded, analysed and set within this saga, bringing colour, vibrancy, emotion and knowledge.

You cannot help but be impressed with the world of Aeldynn; Book 1, The Keys of the Origin, The Scions of Balance.

A brilliant new entry to storytelling at its best; I commend it to you.

Terry G-F editor 2016.

Keys
of the
Origin

Book 1: The Scions of Balance

Melissa A. Joy

books.aeldynnlore@gmail.com

Keys of the Origin
ISBN 978-1-911368-11-3 Hardback
978-1-911368-07-6 Paperback
978-1-911368-01-4 ePub.

For more information on the author, please visit
www.Aeldynnlore.com

Supported by

BLACKHEATH DAWN
Hafren House, Blackheath, Wenhaston, Suffolk. IP19 9HB

*For Amanda; because you've been there since the
foundations of Aeldynn were laid, and you have played a
fundamental part in its development.*

*And for my parents for putting up with me all these years.
I can only hope that this is the start of something, whereby I
can repay all the support they have given to me.*

ACKNOWLEDGEMENTS

I had dreams of being a published fantasy author for as long as I can remember, but without a number of key individuals, I wouldn't have come this far. I would like to thank Amanda, who has been a part of this project since its very beginning, and I must also thank all those who have given their input and support in my endeavours to mould this story, which has served to shape the world of Aeldynn.

Further thanks go to Terry Gilbert-Fellows and Linda Perry, who have served with avid interest and support as my editor and proofreader. Without the two of you, this wouldn't yet be happening. I am also grateful for the assistance of David Cooper, who formatted my cover design and maps, and Frostnight Illustrations for all the artwork she has produced for me thus far. I am eternally grateful to you for all your hard work in helping me to get this book finished and published.

And not forgetting all others who have partaken of my writing on some level and given me positive feedback, I thank you also (you know who you are). It is immensely encouraging when others give praise to work that has seen seemingly endless hours of writing, rewriting and editing, especially at times when I lost confidence in myself, for it breathed new life into my creativity, and allows me to take up the pen once more. It has happened many a time, but now that you hold this book in your hands, all of you who have been involved on some level, whether great or small, will know that you played a part in finally making this book a reality.

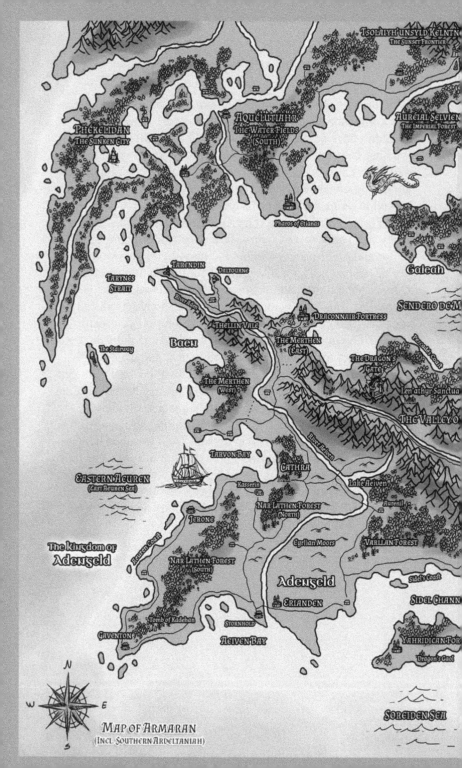

TSOLAIYH UNSYLD KELNTN
The Sunset Frontier

AQUELUTIAHH
THE WATER FIELDS
(SOUTH)

AURELAL SELVIEN
The Imperial Forest

PHEKELIDAN
The Sunken City

Galeah

Pharos of Etianas

TARENDIN
DALTOURNE

SENDERO DE M

TARYNES
STRAIT

THELLIN VALE

DRACONNAIR FORTRESS

The Stairway

Baeu

THE MERTHEN
(EAST)

THE DRAGON'S
GATE

Len'athyr Sanctua

THE MERTHEN
(WEST)

THE VALLEY O

River Arden

TARVON BAY

EASTERN ACUREN
(East Acuren Sea)

CATHRA

Kasserin

LAKE AEIVEN

Aurenil

VARLLAN FOREST

NAR LATHEN FOREST
(NORTH)

JERONE

The kingdom of
ADENSELD

Cyrlian Moors

NAR LATHEN FOREST
(SOUTH)

ADENSELD

Sidel's Coast

SIDEL CHANN

ERIANDEN

Tomb of Kadehan

STORNHOLE

YAHRIDICAN FOR

GAVENTON

Dragon's Gaol

AEIVEN BAY

N

W   E

S

MAP OF ARMARAN
(INCL. SOUTHERN ARDELTANIAH)

SOREIDEN SEA

PART I

"The properties of Altirnathé were recorded in ancient Nays texts. It was said to have the power to make our ships more efficient so less manpower would be required, and stability would be vastly improved. Most intriguing, however, is that timbers soaked in it are toughened and tend not to rot easily. My question is; why is the archetype so much more powerful than her sisters?"

– Admiral Traven Wendale.

"The world has changed. We are aware, even as we sleep. To the Everlasting, no change goes unnoticed. Power has shifted, people have failed, and the world suffers. Long ago we ended war, and peace was brought unto Aeldynn. Empty though, are the promises of mortals.

Forgotten are we who brought justice down upon the Aurentai. Long forgotten are those who came before even us. Not even the deities remember the truth about the Origin. Did the Origin simply abandon this world to our charge? Or did they leave us with no answer to fall back on but the power of the Taecade Medo?"

PROLOGUE

Dazzling shafts of sunlight broke through the fractured canyon walls, permeating the depths of the Niradessian Vaults buried in the heartlands of Ardeltaniah. Segments of the ancient sepulchre were carved into rock faces displaying a constellation of hues between vermillion and amber.

The sun had begun its slow descent into the night as a lone figure wearing a slate grey cloak approached the rear chambers, stopping only for a moment next to an ornate altar inscribed in an ancient language. A glyph seal marked its centre.

The figure drew back the hood of his cloak, took a stream of snow white hair out from within and tossed it over his shoulder. With his long pointed ears, alabaster complexion and piercing aquamarine eyes he could be recognised as a member of the Kensaiyr; the elves of White Silver. He stood in silence, waiting.

A glimmering white light surrounded him. Its pleasant warmth lasted perhaps a few seconds, washing over him like the early morning sun after a cold starlit night. He closed his eyes.

"Madukeyr Saierkýn," a soft female voice whispered. "You have woken at last from your long slumber. Proceed, and summon the Kaesan'Drahknyr from Valdysthar." Madukeyr bowed his head in acknowledgement.

"As you command, My Lady." He rested his right hand over his heart. Opening his eyes, he looked toward the expansive chamber that lay before him.

'It has been an eternity,' he thought, breaking into a run. *'A little over three thousand years I believe. Well then, I*

wonder whether or not I should be looking forward to seeing what civilisation has made of itself since then...'

He slowed to a brisk walk as he approached the vast central chambers, glancing back and forth at the ornate craftsmanship of the walls, vaulted ceilings and statues of the winged Drahknyr in remembrance of the last time he wandered these hauntingly beautiful yet so often empty corridors.

The walkway to the central chamber of the Kaesan'Drahknyr came into view. The chasm below was deep, and at its bottom ran a narrow section of the largest river in western Aeldynn, the Aquelar. It was wide and deep enough for a large warship to sail through.

Madukeyr stopped to look over the rail at the rushing water below. *'There will always be something about this realm that makes it all worthwhile...'* he mused. *'What about you, Melkhar? You appreciate Mother Nature don't you? However, you do not think the same of civilisation. You and I are more alike than you think.'*

Soon after reaching the end of the bridge the resonance of the Naturyth pricked his ears. It was a quiet but almost mechanical natural sound, occurring roughly every five seconds or so when the crystals glowed. The resonance itself was characteristic of power flowing through any such crystal larger than the palm of the average hand; these crystals, like the Altirnathé, grew directly from Aevnatureis itself. In most mortal tongues, the giant crystalline support pillar was widely known as *The Foundation.*

Madukeyr was well aware of the nature of those he encountered. He was in fact as old as those he was about to awaken, and he had always assisted them in more ways than one. Advancing, he looked up into a vast chamber filled with ice-blue crystals that stretched up the cavern walls and hung from the ceiling.

Seven towering crystal monoliths enshrining the Kaesan'Drahknyr were the source of that glowing, pulsing resonance; a rhythm of surging high density energy. Each of the Kaesan'Drahknyr was sealed separately; their arms folded across their chests with their palms resting against their shoulders, their colossal white-feathered wings perched authoritatively upon their backs. He came to a halt standing in front of the central crystal, gazing up at the flame-haired woman sleeping within.

The Nays were known for their finely angled features, and smoky black lines framing their eyes that were often mistaken to be cosmetic by most mortal races. Their ears were notably pointed, though they didn't extend as long as those of an elf. This one was in many ways different from the other six. Her early experiences in physical life drove her to almost complete detachment from others, and with it came a great hatred for the unjust.

"Melkhar," Madukeyr whispered. "I am looking forward to speaking with you again." He closed his eyes and smiled faintly, "but first you need to wake up and regain your strength and ability." He stepped back, spreading his arms wide and called out: *"Ye'nah veauh aeu'te Kaesan'Drahknyr arth ce'lleth maren Ye'nen nemadas, vaehr Ye'nen émitas séi kamen. Éyn, Madukeyr Saierkýn, ce'llen Ye'nah makh'e vhar Aeldynn."* [1]

---

[1] You who are the Master Dragon Knights of Valdysthar are called from your sleep, for your time is come.
I, Madukeyr Saierkýn, call you back to Aeldynn.

LORE
Aeldynn's Creation & the
Prophecy of the Kaesan'Drahknyr

*For balance to falter, it only takes one small
measure to tip the scales.*
Nays Proverb

In a year and era unknown, the world of Aeldynn was built
upon a celestial crystal foundation, a pillar system called
Aevnatureis. As it is written, it is the source from which all
spiritual and magical energy originates on the middle and
higher planes. Far below it, beneath a passable mirror realm
called Dyr'Efna in the netherworld of Ne'Vedanhyr, exists
its counterpart – Phandaerys. Both pillars form the shape of
gargantuan obelisks, though their crystals spread outward
from their base across the realms above and below, from
ethereal Valdysthar down to unholy Dhavenkos Mhal.

Nays lore states that the Origin called the gods into
existence; those who first descended upon the surface of
Aeldynn, along with the two original dragons bound by
scriptures of balance called the Taecade Medo. As all forms
of life above Dyr'Efna were born of the energy of
Aevnatureis, so did Phandaerys mimic as a bitter and
corrupt reflection.

The first races on Aeldynn were either immortal or
significantly long-lived, having descended in succession
through the Thean Hierarchy of Deities. There were three at
the peak: Raiyah, Lyte, and Velhana. One after the other,
Raiyah was given charge of the Nays; Lyte; the elves – of
which the first were the Kensaiyr – and Velhana; the Fey.
The first of the Fey were the Aurentai. As the Nays began to
flourish, the Origin were said to have made their plans clear
to Raiyah, and bestowed upon her the gift of the Drahknyr.

The Drahknyr, empyrean warriors bearing colossal
white-feathered wings, were born into physical form via the

Nays. It is said the Origin claimed it was the only way in which they could acquire a physical existence, but the power they harboured often took its toll on the mothers who carried them for a year.

Records also mention that following the Drahknyr's original trial, they have since been born infertile as it is believed Aevnatureis was once forced to bestow too great a power upon one such offspring. There is balance in all things, but if that balance wavers, control can easily be lost to one extreme or the other. In addition to this, their existence is inextricably bound to combat, meaning it is their lifelong duty to be engaged in or ready for combat. The legend of Alymarn supports these claims as it is written his birth and subsequent actions brought down catastrophe upon Aeldynn.

Legends also state that once the Drahknyr's weapons and armour are forged, they are soul or perhaps spirit-bonded to their user, so only they may use them. This also means such armour and weaponry, along with their wings, may be summoned into their corporeal form or banished from wherever they may be.

At that time, there was a prophecy passed down from the Origin to the Sun Goddess Raiyah that foretold seven greater Drahknyr; the elite of the elite. They were the Kaesan'Drahknyr. It was to be that their maximum efficiency could reach the very limit of Aevnatureis' natural power. They would govern all other Drahknyr, serve as guardians of Aeldynn and of the Nays, and rain down destruction on the chaotic forces that threatened all life.

In the War of the Black Sun that followed generations later, the Nays and the Drahknyr engaged in an all-out battle with the Aurentai, the Star Goddess Velhana's prime Fey race. At the climax of the war, Aevnatureis suffered a rupture. All of nature was disrupted as a result, and the Kaesan'Drahknyr laid down their lives to restore it. Now more than three thousand years have passed.

CHAPTER 1

I
Senfirth

The chase was well underway by the time Zehn joined in. He knew he was more likely to succeed than the average city guard, though having them around was useful for the inevitability of flushing his target out from under cover.

Senfirth was one of the larger mercantile ports on the Coast of Eresta, and was therefore prone to pirate activity due to the flourishing market selling fresh produce from the nearby farms and many other varieties of merchandise. Branches of the Hunters' Guild in almost every other port across the region had their notice-boards plastered with wanted posters of pirates on both outside and inside walls, but it was common practice among many to collect them as trophies.

Most of Senfirth's buildings were constructed from whitestone, half-timbered beams and rust-coloured roofing tiles; and at the centre of the bustling town square was a tall clock tower now about to strike noon.

Flocks of seagulls laughed and wheeled overhead. It was market day and considerably busier than usual, meaning there would be plenty of easy pickings for the mischievous birds. Additional stalls including merchant caravans selling rare spices, trinkets, exotic clothes and fabrics were lined up either side of the road outside the gates.

Various odours drifted through the streets; some pleasant, others not so. In the mix was everything from roasting meat and fresh vegetables, to perfumes and incense from the continent of Manlakhedran to the east, along with the pungent smell of horse manure and waste wafting down from the stables at the edge of the town. The very distinct whiff of sewage occasionally drifted out from the alleys.

A lookout standing on the mainmast crosstrees of a large renegade naval ship in Senfirth's harbour signalled to the rest of the crew as they manoeuvred to pass close to the protruding quayside, ensuring they would be well on their way by the time their captain arrived back on board.

Unlike most other ships, this one had been the archetype of a new class of man-o-war that turned Faltainyr Demura's navy into the most powerful naval force in all of Armaran, and perhaps even the whole of Aeldynn. Research on Aeldynn's great crystals had given rise to a diverse system allowing such vessels to be built with archana that ran on a fluid made from altirna crystal, a substance the ancient Nays used on their own ships to improve steering, mooring, and the working of the capstans.

At the next alley, the mercenary paused for a moment to consider where his quarry may have been heading. He ran a hand through his shock of windswept brown hair, but kept his hand on his sword; always at the ready. It had become a habit; trouble was usually never far away. The striped purple bandana he wore was already half soaked with sweat after his first job of the morning, which involved a small group of bandits, and his blue-grey tunic displaying Faltainyr Demura's osprey insignia was covered in dirt.

In less than a year he'd attained the respect of almost all of Faltainyr Demura. Many considered him even more proficient than his father Rajan had been, which had given him a great boost of confidence. Additionally, the number of professional mercenaries was growing and only those with an established reputation were likely to be accepted for the best jobs.

He didn't have long to wait; a flash of red dashing out of the alley into the next street caught his eye and he took up pursuit. The commotion of the prisoner's escape soon flooded the main street and the market district.

The young pirate captain rushed through the busy streets and alleys sporting his full-length scarlet military coat and matching cavalier hat, the right side pinned up and a large white plume of feathers dancing in the breeze. Two elaborate scimitars hung at his waist along with flintlocks, daggers and throwing knives attached around his waist. He tore one of the posters bearing his image from the Hunters' Guild notice-board as he ran past, stuffing it untidily into a pocket as he engaged the busy crowd. Somewhere nearby a guard dog started barking.

"Sorry! Comin' through, no time to wait, beggin' your pardon ladies," the runaway said hurriedly as he dodged the many busy townsfolk to keep as much distance as possible between himself and his pursuers. *'Where's that ladder?'* he mused, stopping for a moment to look around. *'Ah!'*

The ladder he searched for was propped up against the wall of a nearby house and led up on to the rooftops. Ignoring his newfound audience, he wedged himself between a pair of stalls and climbed up, then pulled the ladder on to the roof. When he stood upright, he noted there were more guards on his tail than before, as well as the mercenary who had captured him the previous day. He brushed a hand through the underside of the layered, sandy-blond hair that fell to his shoulders and gave them a cheeky smile, which in turn brought a mischievous twinkle into his sprightly blue eyes.

"There he is!" he heard one of them shout from another street. "Bloody scoundrel!" He made a dash across the rooftops with an accuracy that could only be kept up with speed and precision. This inevitably made things difficult when the time came for him to come down, but it was something he'd quickly grown accustomed to. It wasn't until he saw the mercenary running almost opposite on the rooftops two streets away that he began to worry.

'He's no ordinary mercenary,' he thought. There was no need to discern what his opponent was up to. *'Fancy that, mastering the thieves' highroad.'* He wasn't about to let the

same mercenary get the better of him a second time; it didn't matter how professional he was.

The fugitive saw the next network of back alleys was clear save for a few beggars, and decided dropping to the ground again was the better option seeing as this mercenary was about as determined to catch him as he was to avoid being caught. He ran down the slope of a roof on to a pile of unevenly stacked crates and barrels, which then collapsed underneath him, sending him crashing down amongst them. Picking himself up with a groan, he quickly dusted himself off before placing his hat back on his head and dashing into the next alley leading toward the harbour.

Two streets later he was on the quayside, sprinting as fast as his legs would carry him toward the magnificent warship motioning close to the protruding section of the quay wall. At a distance, it looked as though the ship had three gun decks, for along the ship's broadside were black stripes under both the capping rail and along the two lengthy gun decks with a cardinal red stripe below each of them, carved golden vines winding through the middle. The black stripes cleverly hid all the gun ports.

"Larkh Savaldor!" Zehn yelled as he ran, "surely a smart and flamboyant ruffian such as yourself wouldn't want to be seen as a coward!" Larkh gritted his teeth. Crossing his arms over, he drew his scimitars and skidded to a halt, turning on the spot to block Zehn's elaborately decorated longsword.

It was of a rare single-handed variety, with a hilt that appeared to be white dragon ivory; the intricate draconic detail could have only been Nays design. The deep red jewel in the cross section, however, made Larkh even more curious. His own blades were slender, but grew thicker toward the tip and curved upward. They were single edged save for the wider tips that doubled back at an angle with a concave curvature. The handles were also ornately decorated akin to Zehn's sword, but in black dragon ivory.

"I must thank you kindly for giving me extra work to do here today," Zehn smiled, adding more pressure into his sword.

"Good pay?" Larkh hissed, returning the pressure with equal force.

"Men like you keep me fed and sheltered with enough left over for a few good rounds of self-indulgence," Zehn retorted, stern despite the caustic remark. "And I do my homework: you're twenty-four, born Jenne 10th, naturally left-handed but self-taught to be ambidextrous, and *formerly* the sole heir to the Savaldor fortune, since you turned pirate. You've quite the habit for targeting wealthy merchant ships, of which several had been heading for Saldour from ports in Enkaiyta or Manlakhedran. You also like to show other pirates who's boss on the high seas. Need I go on?"

Larkh arched a brow in interest, their blades still locked together. "My my, you have done a bit of diggin' haven't you? Give me a list of dates of every raid in at least the last three years an' I might just be impressed! Now how 'bout you stop talkin' eh?" He ducked out to the side, making his opponent stagger, blocking swiftly as Zehn made his second swing, responding with a heavy spin that knocked the mercenary back, giving him a light gash on his right arm.

Larkh's style of sword combat was commonly known as a dual sword-dance, but this variant was ancient and known by few in the present day. For anyone to know the original name of the style meant they must have studied the Nays, and when used by someone who'd mastered the technique, it was more difficult to defend against than any other dual-wielding style.

He threw Zehn off balance again, but jumped back, allowing him to recover. With a wry smile, he sank into a light stance, arcing his left arm over his head and extending his right. He cocked his head to one side.

Despite having caught him the day before, this was the first time Zehn had actually duelled with him. With a single weapon, his kite buckler served well as a light shield. He knew Larkh was going to be a challenge, especially having heard numerous stories about him, which for him was a change from the norm. The downside was this quayside was too narrow for either of them to utilise their skills effectively.

Growling, Zehn launched himself at Larkh. The grating sound of metal grinding against metal, rapid and continuous, encouraged a number of spectators to gather around the quayside, and neither of the two showed signs of giving up.

Raeon, a Silver Mage and a close friend of Zehn's, watched from the sidelines, analysing Larkh's every movement. *'It's been some time,'* he thought. *'You've come far since then, albeit on the wrong side of the law.'* The long strands of his sweeping dark brown fringe drifted across his noble face while he stood as motionless as a statue in silvery-white robes, arms folded neatly, expression thoughtful.

He also wondered if Larkh happened to be the pirate Zehn had complained about when a friend of his had apparently befriended one. It wasn't until he was able to get a good glimpse of the blades Larkh wielded he was able to tell both his and Zehn's had probably come from the same maker. Both were evidently of Nays origin, and he had discerned that something about them was shrouded in mystery.

Zehn deftly stepped aside as he was driven to the edge of the quayside. "What do you take me for, pirate?" he laughed. "I'm not slow-minded as you believe."

"I beg to differ, you were rather close," Larkh winked, glancing briefly toward the warship drawing closer where someone on board waved wildly at him. "Never mind eh? Maybe next time." He released the tension that held Zehn at bay by lowering his scimitars suddenly in the midst of turning and fleeing at full speed in the opposite direction.

Larkh sheathed his blades as he ran and bolted for the ship with his blazing red coat trailing out behind him. He became caught up in an obstacle course involving city guards, cargo awaiting dispatch and crewmen from other vessels docked nearby. A line was thrown out to him off the stern as all thirty-six gun ports opened on the port side, with numerous crew also stationed by several cannons on the weather deck. This was a clear warning to anyone who dared assail him now.

Zehn ceased his pursuit and skidded to a halt. Larkh caught the line, held by several men on board to take his weight, and allowed it to drag him off the quay to dangle over the ship's stern. He braced his feet against the windows of the sterncastle and climbed up and over the taffrail. With a beaming grin he tipped the brim of his hat to Zehn, who shot him a dangerous glare.

The mercenary watched in anger and disbelief of his own bad luck as the enormous rogue ship sailed out of the harbour. As she neared the harbour mouth, the gun ports closed again, making him wonder if Larkh had really intended to attack in the first place. Thwarted, he turned and made his way back across the docks. The crowds had already begun to disperse, but amidst them he saw his white-robed friend holding two parchment envelopes.

He and Raeon had been close friends since the incident involving the Yahridican Fortress on the southern island of Ehyenn. However, research had always been Raeon's obsession since becoming an apprentice under the direction of the old mage, Vharik Walfein, at the Archaenen in Aynfell. After his graduation, Raeon had joined the Order of Silver.

Raeon had an idea where Zehn's dreams were leading him, and it made him feel awkward that he was under obligation not to speak of them until the right time, nor could he speak of the sacrifices that came with being a Silver Mage. He suspected it would eventually cause a rift between them, but he didn't intend to give up his life's ambition.

"Raeon?" Zehn asked, looking his friend in the eye, "are you alright?" Raeon shook his head and laid a hand on his friend's shoulder.

"Yes, I'm fine," he replied. "These two letters are contracts for you, should you choose to accept them. The first is an extension on Savaldor's bounty, meaning you have no time limit on catching him – that is unless someone else beats you to it – and the other is about a particular woman. She has long fiery red hair, a somewhat curved scar on the right cheekbone, and stands about two inches taller than you." Zehn's brow arched.

"So she's around six foot three, has red hair, and a scar on the right cheek..." he mused aloud. Raeon nodded. "They can't be thinking........? But they're a myth aren't they? If not a myth then they're certainly dead."

"You don't know much about the Nays do you?" Raeon said in a whisper, handing Zehn the contracts and tightening his ponytail. "It might explain something about your dreams. I think we should head back to the inn, give these a good read and you can clarify acceptance – or not – with the guild in the morning." With a reluctant sigh, Zehn nodded. He glanced over his shoulder at the departing warship. *'Not much I can do about him right now...'*

II
Coast of Eresta

A loud roar of appreciation erupted from the crew of the *Greshendier* as Larkh stepped on to the quarterdeck, along with several shouts of good cheer. He raised a hand and closed his eyes, smiling smugly to himself. "Now, now my good men, this has happened many times before," he said, as if trying to show some modesty, "an' each time we've foiled them, not just I. It wouldn't have been possible if it weren't for you lot. You still have the items from the chapel, don't you?"

"Aye sir," said one young man, "but if you don't mind me askin' how are we goin' to get what we want off Her Ladyship?" Larkh chuckled, dropping his left hand on to the boy's shoulder.

"You've not been in this business long have you Reys?" Reys, roughly eighteen years of age, wore an expression of uncertainty. He shook his head. "Put it this way, if she doesn't give me what I want, she doesn't get what she wants. If she gives me what I ask for without complaint, I get what I made the deal for, you lot get paid, an' she walks away with her precious statues, got it?" Reys nodded. Larkh gave him a wink and strolled across the deck, looking up into the rigging.

"Alright lads, let's get goin' shall we? Krallan, set a course heading north along the coast to the Ene Canal, an' then bear north-east through the canal to the Sendero de Mercader." The burly black-haired quartermaster nodded and strode briskly astern to the helmsman. Larkh continued, "all hands to your stations to brace the yards sharp to port! The wind is favourable, we ain't gonna miss it!"

"Aye sir!"

"Show off," a husky voice grumbled in jest as he followed Larkh across the quarterdeck. It came from a brawny blond man with heavy stubble on his chin; his name was Larsan. He already knew what kind of reply he was going to get.

"Why thank you Laz," Larkh replied, looking over his shoulder grinning broadly.

"Narcissist."

Larkh brushed his feathered hair from his face. "Naturally."

"A fine day, don't you think so brother?" Larsan asked wandering up to his friend, watching him intently as the crew rushed back to work. Larkh lifted his eyes to the cloudless sky.

"Aye," he replied, relieved. "I wonder how long it'll last though. This time of year tends to bring unpredictable weather to where we're headed."

"What about now though?"

"Now?" Larkh asked, following up with a dreamy smile. "Now I'm goin' to find somethin' ever so slightly better than cold gruel to eat an' have a nice long nap."

"I'll second that," Larsan chuckled in response as both of them made their way toward the great cabin.

"Nath!?" Larkh called down the galley's chimney. There came a grumble from below. "Whatever you've got on the go'd be great thanks!" Another grumble followed.

"Cheer up!" Larsan yelled to the cook.

"Yeah, yeah," came an apparently sullen reply.

"I find it difficult to tell what frame of mind that man's in half the time," the warrior mused.

"He's in a good mood," Larkh replied. "If he was in a bad mood you'd soon know the difference." He unlocked the door to the great cabin and proceeded to ensure the rolled up hammock above his regular canvas pipe bunk remained secure.

The floor of the spacious cabin was largely covered by a large hand-woven tribal rug, and around the cabin most of the furniture was made of polished cherry wood. There were a few rosewood chests of various sizes, with golden designs painted along all the edges. There was a bookshelf lined with charts, historical and mythological texts, and a few recognisable novels.

The smell in here was pleasant in comparison to the rest of the ship below deck. It carried with it a whiff of ancient oak, old books, along with the faint scent of musk and spice that undoubtedly came from the direction of the rug.

Larkh took a seat at the chart table. He let out a long sigh of relief and slouched as Larsan sat down opposite. "So, the goods are for that girl are they?" Larsan couldn't help but ask. Larkh glared back at him having already guessed where the conversation was going.

"Aye, they're for her," he answered, "an' I told her that she'd not get them from me unless she gives me somethin' valuable I've been after."

"You've yet to tell me what that something is."

"I don't need to," Larkh tapped the side of his nose, "but if she wants what I've acquired an' almost been hanged for, then she'll have to give it to me."

"What was her name again?" Larsan seemed intrigued.

"Meynra," Larkh said with a yawn, "usually known as Mey."

Above them the crew on deck started singing, shortly followed by those below deck. It was a short-haul shanty called *'The Captain is Back'*, though the identity of its author was unknown. They repeated both verses twice, and in seeing the self-satisfied smirk on Larkh's face, Larsan sighed and shook his head.

> *Way a-hey ay lads, slackin'*
> *–NO SLACK!*
> *Heave away, haul away*
> *–The Captain's back!*
> *Way a-hey ay lads, you slackin'?*
> *–NO SLACK!*
> *No slackin' lads!*
> *–'cause the Captain is back!*
> *Way hey, way a-hey ay,*
> *Heave away, haul away*
> *Way hey, way a-hey ay,*
> *Give it one more*
> *–HAUL!*
> *No slackin' lads!*
> *–'cause the Captain's back!*

The *Greshendier* was once an elite class ship-of-the-line of the Faltain Navy based in Saldour, but while she was a magnificent slender giant cutting through the water gracefully with a captivating figurehead of an eagle, wings spread, with a blood red orb in its clutches, she was under the command of pirates, and boasted at least ninety guns.

Despite her size, *Greshendier* had been built to a sleek design with an altirna system that granted maximum efficiency in how she could be manned and manoeuvred. Without the proper training, she was a ship that could prove to be difficult to handle, but she was sturdy nonetheless. Having studied the ship extensively to his grandfather's specification during his childhood, Larkh knew every inch of her and how she would respond in each and every situation.

"The Faltain Navy wanted a design of ship to be faster and more manoeuvrable than the standard classes of ships-of-the-line," his grandfather once told him, "so I designed something that still has all the necessary specifications but is a bit more streamlined – something between a first rate, a third rate and a frigate, but better than all three with the grace of a clipper. The altirna system will enhance that. It should give her manoeuvrability at least equal to that of a frigate, if not better."

This was something he'd taught his crew very early on so they would come to know her almost as well as he did. What most of them couldn't fathom, however, was how he knew so much about the complexities of sailing at such an early age when he'd first become their captain nearly seven years earlier, and how his prowess in dual-swordsmanship was so formidable. As a result, he'd been deemed a prodigy.

The altirna system was also something that took extensive explanation to crew. There were networks of pipes inside the ship through which a special fluid flowed. They were connected to the rudder and capstans to make their operation smooth. That was why she had the standard helm in which two large double wheels were connected for back-up, as well as a main helm situated on the poop deck using altirna that allowed operation by a single helmsman.

III
Coast of Eresta

Nathaniel came through with bowls of soup and bread, singing along with the shanty, and set them down on the charter table. Larkh gave the cook a nod of approval as the stocky man turned to leave the room. Nathaniel gave him a deliberate dopey smile and wandered back to the galley humming the song to himself.

"So, what's she like?" Larsan proceeded with the conversation almost too eagerly. Larkh picked up his spoon, arching his brow suggestively. He watched this muscle-bound warrior's body language shift from casual to very comfortable in an instant.

"She has better taste," Larkh snorted. "Call her a rival if you will."

"Better taste than you?" Larsan laughed. Larkh lifted one brow this time as he took a mouthful of soup.

"Look in the mirror," he said with a wry smile. Larsan smirked.

"Go on."

"Put it this way, she's not the sort I'd want to try an' tame," he admitted, smiling wryly. He heard a snigger. "I'm serious, it ain't worth tryin'."

"If you say so my brother," Larsan said, watching the reaction on his friend's face – and taking great pleasure in doing so.

"Y'know I wonder if people actually think we're brothers when you say that," Larkh mused.

"Do you think we look like brothers?"

"No."

Larsan conceded the point with a nod, and although the rest of the meal was eaten mostly in silence, once it was over both of them resumed conversation that went from serious to almost nonsensical in a matter of minutes. Larkh was quite content sitting with his hands planted around the back of his head with his feet up on the table, vowing that

the next member of his crew to enter the room without
something important to say was going to regret it. When
Larsan asked in what manner they'd regret it, Larkh simply
grinned and told him that embarrassment was usually a good
punishment for minor offences, rather than breeding
contempt and hatred by resorting to flogging when
something as simple as a useless piece of information was
brought to him.

He brushed a hand across his jaw as if in thought, then
regarded Larsan with mock sincerity and said, "by the way,
I have cargo to pick up in Almadeira, so dependin' on when
we arrive there'll be some time for you to go an' sniff out
the local alcohol trail."

"You mean smuggle," Larsan offered as an alternative
description of the forthcoming operation, "and what are you
implying?"

"Absolutely nothing, I'm simply givin' you the chance
to try out what they have."

"Is it good?"

"I'm not sayin' a word."

Judging from this response, Larsan gathered that the
spirits in Almadeira were indeed very good. He knew Larkh
well enough now to know the meaning behind many of the
hints he dropped. At twenty-four he was a more experienced
sailor than many who outlived him by a good number of
years, and there was a lot more to him that met the eye. He
was a clean-shaven, dashing young man overflowing with
charisma, who was well-loved and respected by his crew.
Larsan had come to realise very quickly that he'd certainly
earned it. He'd also come to know a few of the many
reasons behind some of Larkh's more drastic actions, and
his plundering techniques.

"Keeping secrets as usual," Larsan remarked, picking
up his hip flask and taking a long swig of brandy from it
before offering it over. Larkh took it, did the same, and
passed it back.

"It's always healthy to keep a few secrets," he countered.

"True," Larsan agreed, somewhat thoughtfully, "depending on what said secrets are. Care to tell me what Almadeira is like?"

Larkh gazed up at the ceiling of the cabin and lowered his arms to rest them over his lap. "Like many places in Faltainyr Demura it has the half-timbered architecture of the western kingdom of Adengeld," he replied. "However, it has an ancient Nays Kathaedra with an astronomical clock perched under the spire, and the place is laden with underground tunnels."

Larsan offered the flask once more, and again Larkh accepted. It wasn't in his nature to refuse unless there was a very good reason. He could see the urge to explore was building up in Larsan, although what time they would get in Almadeira depended entirely on how Larkh's plans went.

"Smugglers' tunnels," Larsan ventured.

"And they have been for a very long time," Larkh added, smiling wryly, "and one of the more favourable spots for the black market."

CHAPTER 2

I
Lonnfeir

The Vlaedranistas Amečana was an undersea passageway that served as the most indirect route between Ardeltaniah and Armaran. A network of caves and tunnels had been integrated into the structure for the creation of a shrine to the aquatic deity Ireiya many aeons ago, but life down here had never ceased to exist. Over time, the doors, walls and seals had degraded, allowing all manner of different creature to move in. Even though the longevity of Nays constructions was always much more durable than average architecture, they still only lasted as long as their upkeep was monitored regularly.

The pungent smell of damp stone and rusting metal was strong. Various types of moss and fungus stretched up the crumbling walls and through the numerous cracks in the floor. They'd spent a few days travelling through this place, and yet Arcaydia found she still couldn't get used to it. She had been assured it wouldn't be much longer before they would surface on the continent of Armaran.

Out of one of the many cracks in the passage walls crawled five skinny lizard-like creatures standing about two and a half feet tall with large almond-shaped ears and frills framing their jaw lines. They were amphibious beings, displaying fins as well as arms and legs, their slimy mottled skin a bluish-grey colour. Their yellow-green eyes were huge in comparison to their heads, and in their mouths were rows of small but very sharp pointed teeth. The claws on the ends of their fingers and toes were equally vicious in appearance.

Foolishly, they approached. The leader of the group stopped, regarded the intruders, and made a rasping snarling sound. Taking a step forward with arched arms, it bared its teeth as the frills on its jaw stood on end and vibrated. The rest of the group mimicked him, and then all began to snarl and hiss as a foul stench like the smell of rotting fish filled the air.

What seemed like a single flash of silver in their midst saw them all sliced to ribbons and scattered across the flooded shrine floor. Arcaydia flinched.

"What were those things?" the young woman asked as her companion stepped forward and bent low to examine the corpses. "They looked like....gremlins...?" She tossed back her long, cascading frosty blonde hair over her shoulders and looked toward the strikingly tall winged woman in ebony leathers standing beside her. The woman flicked blood from her demonic-looking sword and returned it to its scabbard.

Arcaydia watched her for a moment. Her slender yet exceptionally well-defined musculature, and chiselled otherworldly beautiful features were enough to tell anyone she was a force to be reckoned with, even without her fearsome eyes. Flame red hair fell straight to the lower edge of her shoulder-blades, but it was those wolfish emerald green eyes framed with natural smoky black lines – often mistaken for cosmetic paint in the wider world – that struck fear in to the hearts and souls of many.

Under her right eye along the cheekbone was a slightly curved scar. The enormous white-feathered wings perched upon her back towered, arcing over her head by several feet from the shoulder blades before curving downward to her ankles.

"They are Aquétha Empas," she replied. Her voice was deep in tone, but so rich and vibrant her authority was unquestionable. She spoke with an accent that hadn't been heard anywhere else on Aeldynn for over three thousand years. "Water Imps. They should not be lurking about this place."

"Melkhar?" the blonde woman asked. "Is something wrong?"

"Quiet," Melkhar firmly recommended. "It has been a long time since anyone has been down here, even for the purpose of maintenance; anything could have taken up residence. Those creatures are partial to damp cavernous habitats, but worse things have crawled up from the darker places of the world."

Arcaydia stared at her in awe. She tilted her head to one side and reached out to touch the feathers. Melkhar arched a brow. "What are you doing?" Arcaydia pulled her hand away.

"They're just so...beautiful," she answered, "and how—"

"This is not the time for admiration," Melkhar interjected coldly, moving forward through the great vaulted passageway. "Anything could attack at any moment." She looked back at Arcaydia, narrowing her eyes. "Save the rest of your curiosity for when danger is of no concern. We are a short distance from the exit now," the lofty flame-haired warrior answered abruptly. Arcaydia's head sank toward her shoulders. This woman was so intimidating.

"Yes ma'am."

As she followed along behind the lofty winged stranger, Arcaydia thought back to their first meeting, and the conference she had attended before embarking on this journey.

'I don't know who I am,' she thought dolefully. *'I've spent so long away from my homeland that I don't know anything about it, and then I discover I am of Nays lineage. Now I am sent on this trip not knowing what I am doing! I meet this warrior and I am both terrified and fascinated, and....'* Memories of her first meeting with Melkhar flickered through her mind.

~ *"You're asking me all these questions,"* Arcaydia had said in the private interrogation room rich with the smell of incense. *"I don't know the answers to any of them. I don't remember anything before I travelled with the gypsies."* Melkhar's intense stare made her quiver as icy dread ran down her spine, as if her stature wasn't intimidating enough. *"I'm sorry."*

"You really do not remember anything about who you are?" Melkhar had enquired.

"No, I'm very sorry," Arcaydia sighed, lowering her gaze momentarily.

"That must change," Melkhar declared, rising from her seat. She turned away, furrowed her brow, and took a deep breath.

"You're in a lot of pain right now," Arcaydia observed, standing up. *"I can tell. Please, let me help you."*

Melkhar shook her head, waving her off. *"Sit down,"* she ordered through gritted teeth. A man matching her height rushed into the room. He had medium-length platinum-blond hair, and strangely, brown eyes. *'Unusual,'* she thought. He urged Melkhar to head to the infirmary, suggesting her old wound ought to be checked over again. *'And her wings weren't visible then...'* ~

'That old wound...,' Arcadia thought presently as she walked. *'Could that be the wound that killed her once? I don't know much at all except a few legends. With wings like that, perhaps the legends really are true. They really are from ethereal Valdysthar...'* She shook her head. *'And what about now? Where are they sending me? What am I supposed to do? This is a test of some kind, they said so in the meeting. Melkhar left the room briefly too...even now she's still getting pain sometimes from that ancient wound after waking up.'* Her mind drifted back again.

~ *The conference chamber was brightly lit with alchemical chandeliers, a few sconces on the walls, and a brazier in each corner. There was a long grey-white table, carved and decorated with gold chasing in the centre of the room and matching chairs either side with deep red cushions. She guessed the set was made from the great towering albequa trees of the Silverwood on the continent of Armaran.*

The walls of the room were ornately decorated with murals, tapestries or sculptures set around golden friezes, and on each of these walls was a tall, arched mirror. Behind the head of the table a large orb sat on a pedestal, the colours of red and gold swirling within it. She had learned that this was known as a seikryth, and it was used for communication over great distances.

The Atiathél Arkkiennah, ruler of the Nays, and high priestess of the Aeva'Daeihn was seated at the head of the table. She was clad in a cream dress adorned with golden drapes and jewellery, wearing an aureate headdress with feathered wings spreading out behind her, the head of a dragon perched on top; clothing befitting of an empress. The strands of dark hair draped in front of her shoulders were braided; the rest was tied together behind her knees.

Hours after Melkhar had been taken to the infirmary, she had returned to attend this meeting, but it had grown eerily quiet after her pain had forced her to leave again. They had patiently awaited her return, and she'd even heard others suggesting it was a result of the wound she'd sustained at the climax of the War of the Eclipse when Aevnatureis had ruptured and she was run through with a Phandaeric weapon.

This topic was abruptly cut short. The Kensaiyr known as Madukeyr sat nearest the door dressed in black leather traveller's gear, his stream of white hair hanging loosely over his shoulders. He made it plain that all of the Kaesan'Drahknyr had fallen in that war, that all of them had injuries they were recovering from that were incredibly painful to endure, and it would delay the recovery of their full strength. The other six

Kaesan'Drahknyr in the room had remained silent, but all had given Madukeyr a solemn nod in thanks for his respect.

The Atiathél lifted her head toward the door as Melkhar had walked back in. "How are you feeling now, Melkhar?" asked the woman at the head of the table.

"It shall not hinder me, Your Majesty," Melkhar replied. She took her seat, looked to Arkkiennah, and nodded in confirmation that the meeting could proceed.

"First and foremost, I have already discussed matters with the others as they were departing for their respective regions at the time. Right now, as you know, the balance of civilisation among Aeldynn's many mortal races is once again falling into chaos," Arkkiennah explained. "You will have felt it during your sleep these many ages. We have been called the Guardian Race for a reason, and that is to keep Aeldynn's balance in check."

"What, however, is the answer to our fervent hopes of success in this endeavour? Aevnatureis, the very pillar of nature itself is feeling the effects of its counterpart, Phandaerys, which has already been used in wicked endeavours by mortals for selfish gain. Let me say this though; I have no control over you, the Kaesan'Drahknyr. You are a part of this race as much as you are your own kind, and a part of ethereal Valdysthar; you lead your Drahknyr legions as a part of the Nays army, but you still have your own free will. Your loyalty, as always, is appreciated more than you can imagine. This world needs your presence, but you are still free."

"Your Majesty, if I may speak?" Madukeyr asked, rising from his seat. Arkkiennah regarded him softly.

"Go ahead, Tseika'Drahknyr," she replied.

"Forgive me for saying so, but you know what the Kaesan'Drahknyr are. They are inextricably bound to Aevnatureis, and are therefore never going to be completely free to do as they wish," the Kensaiyr explained. "Everyone here may have their own opinions on the world, *and add to that a range of passions that cannot be denied, but ultimately there are jobs to be done, and the Kaesan'Drahknyr are the only ones chosen and born to accomplish them."*

"Perhaps you are right, Madukeyr," Arkkiennah said solemnly as she lowered her gaze to the table. "I am perplexed I am unable to grant you all the freedom you truly deserve. You are forever bonded to your duties."

"Every honourable person makes a living by working in a role central to a particular trade," the man with the platinum-blond hair intervened. "We may not have a choice in our line of work, but we are free to decide how we live." He pointed to the tan-skinned man beside him dressed in brown leathers with a long river of black hair that draped over the end of the seat he sat upon with a large eagle's feather clipped in at the top. "Kalthis here is a prime example."

"Zairen...," Kalthis said with a modest smile. Under his tan skin he may have been blushing. At this, Arcaydia felt her own face suddenly flush warm.

"I'm sorry," Zairen chuckled, "but it is true."

"It is true, when I have the free time to spend at home with my tribe in the forests of Marlinikhda," Kalthis countered. "However, what is existence without purpose?"

"Meaningless," Melkhar stated, narrowing her eyes. This was an expression she often wore, especially when she was irritated or simply didn't want to justify giving an answer to a question she deemed pointless. She leaned back in her seat, and folded her arms neatly across her chest. "We exist for a purpose, but it is indeed our choice in how to live that makes us unique." ~

Arcaydia snapped back to the present again in time to walk straight into Melkhar's back between her colossal pair of wings. Melkhar was standing still, observing the sealed exit to the continent of Armaran.

"Welcome back to the here and now." The sarcastic remark came while Melkhar examined a towering arch that resonated with a veil of lilac-coloured energy rippling through the space in-between. "You were lucky there was an absence of enemies. Your lack of attention could easily put you in the ground were I not sufficiently capable of covering your backside."

"I...I'm sorry," Arcaydia apologised sheepishly. "This is a part of why I am on this journey right? I'm here to learn." Melkhar stiffened. Her lips pressed into a thin line, and her wolfish eyes followed suit. She advanced toward the exit, and with a shimmer her wings faded and dissolved into faint ripples in the air. Arcaydia lowered her gaze to the floor ashamedly, and followed her through the watery film out into the open air. They had reached the continent of Armaran.

II
The Valley of Daynallar

High in the Daynallar Mountains stood the Drahkouenýs Kahgathis. Known to most as the Dragon's Gate, it was a gargantuan archway large enough to accommodate any size of draconic species; the only gateway that connected directly to the Lhodha Drahvenaçym, the realm in which all dragonkind had first originated.

Nays expertise was the only explanation for this architectural phenomenon. Only one of many archways across Aeldynn, but by far the largest and most magnificent, it was fashioned from black and white dragon ivory; decorated all over with sculpted images telling stories of the world's major dragons. At the peak of its arch was a large jade-coloured crystal with two smaller red orbs mounted to each side.

Next to it stood one of its smaller counterparts. It was crafted from the same materials, but it stood as tall as one of the Drahknyr with their wings manifested, and almost wide

43

enough for one to pass through with a fully extended wingspan. The difference in size between these two gates was astonishing.

A flash of electric blue energy sparked and surged through the centre of the smaller arch, forming a rippling film like the surface of calm water on a sheltered lake. Two streams of hair, one white and one black sporting a mottled feather were swept back with a brisk easterly breeze as both figures emerged from the gate one after the other.

Kalthis breathed in the fresh mountain air that brought with it stronger scents of life rather than death. He turned his head to Madukeyr. "This place has recovered well," he said, smiling. His voice was calm and precise, befitting of his tribe. "Nothing has changed." The gate's energy surge dissipated behind them.

"The cycle remains undisturbed here," Madukeyr observed, nodding at Kalthis' comment with approval.

The landscape that lay before them was little different to how they remembered it before their awakening. It was a valley where dragons had dwelled for aeons, and it also served as their graveyard. Much of it was still green with life; various draconic species made their home here, but the amount of skeletal remains stretching across the mountains shaped much of the region.

There was one major route that ran directly through the centre of the valley between Adengeld and Faltainyr Demura where the River Nidhan ran eastward. This road was not recommended for ordinary folk to travel upon. This land belonged to the dragons and their kin; venturing into the open in their territory made typical passersby fair game. There were other roads to take, but they were indirect and it took considerably longer to cross. The positive side was that those routes were largely hidden by other mountains or cliffs, which would make it difficult for a dragon or wyvern to attack, but there were odd sections of even those passes that were still exposed. One had no need of worry, however, if they were a natural ally.

"Do you remember the arrangement?" Kalthis asked, turning his head to the Kensaiyr. Madukeyr smiled wearily.

"I know you have the pleasure of listening to the ramblings of the old sage," he replied with a wry smile. "Lésos has located both of the Keys, but only one of them currently has the dreams. The one that hasn't yet begun to dream, however, is spiritually stronger. I am to intercept the one who dreams to ensure that he doesn't interfere with Melkhar's mission according to Lyte Warden Saiyinn. He should at least live long enough to play his part."

"You make it sound like theatre," Kalthis said, peering over the cliff.

"Not at all. All people have a role to play in life," Madukeyr corrected him. "All characters in a story must also play their parts. Sometimes their significance cannot be realised until the time is right."

"You have a point," Kalthis conceded the truth of his observation. "Come, the sage's hut is not far from here. He expects us tonight, and I really hope he has made cake."

"You're obsessed with cake," Madukeyr sighed. "Wait.....us?" His indifferent expression morphed into concern.

"Yes. Vharik was informed that you would be resting the night, and leaving in the morning," Kalthis explained. "I was not the one who told him that, though I think it is a good idea to eat and sleep well before you continue on your way." Madukeyr covered his face with his palm. "Don't tell me you would rather go hungry and spend an extra night sleeping on rough terrain than put up with him talking awhile?"

"He never stops talking," Madukeyr pointed out.

"Hahaha! That is true!" Kalthis laughed, tossing his hair over his shoulder as he made his way down the mountainside. "At least it is not you who has to remain in his company for too long. If it were you, I would probably find him tied up and gagged in his cellar." He laughed again. At first Madukeyr found he was unsure of how to react to such a comment, but soon relaxed as a faint smile crept upon his lips. Shaking his head, he followed Kalthis down the dragon bone strewn mountainside.

The two journeyed east, following the mountain trail deep into the Daynallar Valley, keeping close to the shade provided by the many enormous skeletons. The bright afternoon sun beat down on them relentlessly, but the basking drakes by the river didn't seem to mind one bit. Those that noted their presence bowed their heads in respect – to Kalthis in particular – in acknowledgement of his return to Aeldynn. Without hesitation, Kalthis returned the gesture.

Long grasses swayed in the carefree winds, stirring meadow sprites into an excitable frenzy. The pair walked the path, eagles and wyverns soared together across the sky. It was a place where many different species were able to live and co-exist, where many draconic beings comfortably laid themselves to rest. Not all draconic species were immortal. Once it had been a battlefield and many dragons and their kind had fallen here.

An almighty roar reverberated through the air and ground underfoot, followed by an enormous shadow passing overhead. From the nose to the tip of its tail, this dragon looked to be at least the full length of one of the vast Kathaedra built by the Nays.

"Dehltas!" Kalthis breathed.

Despite the enormity of his size, the dragon perched quite gracefully upon the outcrop of rocks above them. Jet black scales and sharp ridges gleamed in the sunlight, and a sinuous tail draped and coiled about the rock face like a colossal python with jagged blades rising out of its back.

The dragon snaked his head slowly toward Kalthis and Madukeyr, staring with fierce flame-coloured eyes as he lifted his torso and arched his neck to reveal his robust underbelly. All activity in the vicinity seemed to cease.

"Kaesan'Drahknyr Kalthis of the Ashkelleron tribe of Marlinikhda, and Tseika'Drahknyr Madukeyr Saierkýn of the Kensaiyr," the dragon rumbled; his voice deep and guttural. He lowered his head. Despite his fearsome appearance and resonant tones he sounded almost despondent, though his manner certainly betrayed anger.

"What's wrong?" Kalthis asked, showing concern. He searched the dragon's eyes to find wounded pride and restrained fury and hatred.

"The red hybrid, Rahntamein the Renegade, may soon be free," Dehltas hissed. "It appears the King of Adengeld wishes to attempt striking a deal with him."

"No!" Kalthis gasped.

"They must have a very desirable promise for him to agree to do that," Madukeyr observed.

"Who could possibly free him from the prison beneath Ehyenn?" Kalthis asked.

"I do not know," Dehltas replied, "but no ordinary mortal could break that seal. King Ameldar sent men to seek my assistance in waging war against Faltainyr Demura. I refused, and am now accused of betrayal. My oath is all but forgotten."

Kalthis shook his head, running a hand through his hair. "Protecting a country does not mean waging war on others," he said, gritting his teeth.

"If I am to fight, then the battle shall come to me," Dehltas assured him, his tone darkening. "Mark my words, if that time comes, I will show no mercy."

Kalthis looked away, furrowing his brow. Then he turned his attention back to Dehltas. "Do what you must, old friend," he said, bowing his head. Dehltas nodded graciously and took to the air again, his great leathery wings blowing gale force gusts of wind across the cliff and long grasses of the meadow. With another loud roar aimed at the heavens, he disappeared into the distance over the peaks.

For several moments, Madukeyr became lost in thought. He brushed his snow white hair away from his face, a crease forming upon his brow. Kalthis too now wore a disquieted expression. Nevertheless, birds continued to twitter in the nearby trees, the river still continued to flow eastward, the wind still carried fresh scents through the valley, as the afternoon sun still shone in the sky. Kalthis looked upward and took a deep breath.

"Do not forget this, Madu," he said as he closed his eyes and smiled, the sun warm against his face. Madukeyr glanced over his shoulder. "This," he gestured to their surroundings, "is what we want to remember. Remember all that is natural. Our purpose may be to fight, but we should not lose sight of what we are fighting for."

"And perhaps the sage will be able to shed a little light on the troubles of this day and age," Madukeyr mused as he too closed his eyes, and smiled.

Evening had fallen by the time Kalthis and Madukeyr arrived. The hut stood next to a small lake in a secluded area of the valley surrounded by dense coniferous forest. Each of them had become subject to the sage's overwhelming banter before either of them were able to set foot through the door. Madukeyr's unimpressed glare prompted an apologetic shrug from Kalthis.

The slowly aging older man had already taken advantage of the opportunity to talk at great length, and exploited Kalthis' weakness for confectionery. In generations past, Vharik's lineage had once connected with the Nays, giving him a significantly longer lifespan than most mortals. He'd also acquired a varied collection of items across the years.

The most interesting items were displayed in wooden cabinets, but the rest were in chests that were stacked one on top of the other. The truly rare objects, such as ancient relics of whatever race one might care to name, were locked away in one of three very large oak chests that had been saturated with altirna fluid, which made certain types of wood either resilient or impervious to rot.

Vharik's hut was otherwise cluttered with bits and pieces he'd collected over his long years, and it was obvious he didn't intend to part with them any time soon. Across the room a small kettle sat over the hearth of a well-stoked fire, and in the corner a small bed covered with old linen sheets and animal furs.

While Kalthis didn't seem to be bothered much by Vharik's incessant ramblings, Madukeyr's eyelids were beginning to sag as he gazed lethargically out of the window into the dusky forest.

"It seems you are still fond of the sponge variety," Vharik laughed. "You never change Kalthis." Kalthis shoved the plate aside. They sat in the sage's tiny kitchen which barely accommodated a table with a set of four chairs.

"Nor do you," he said with a beaming smile. "I've not been able to get a word in sideways all evening."

"I thought that was the deal. You stuff your face, and I do the talking," Vharik taunted him. Kalthis arched a brow. "I'm kidding of course." The old man smiled. Kalthis simply smiled back, interrupting Vharik before he could say another word.

"Anyway, Vharik, what can you tell us about the changes across Aeldynn?" he enquired.

"Well now," Vharik said thoughtfully, stroking his white beard. "I've been awake for the past fifty years. Before that, I slept as you did and awakened at regular intervals to keep an eye on things. My naturyn coffin is in the basement. I shroud the hut in glámar before I go into that kind of sleep." Kalthis lowered his head and fixed an expectant stare on the old man. This information was blatantly obvious. Vharik coughed.

"What I do know, is that peace in this world did not last very long at all. Most mortals, long or short-lived instinctively covet trivial things that others have and they do not. I do not want to say that your efforts were all in vain, but chaos will always rebel against order. The renegades are on the rise, and our enemy is ever stronger."

"Some immortal races are also guilty of this," Kalthis pointed out. The sage nodded.

"Do you have an idea of how long it lasted?" Madukeyr asked, disdain plain in his voice. He was still staring out of the window. "I can think of a couple of races that would have been the first to give in to such petty temptations." Vharik shook his head.

"Zaern'Kairnell's kingdoms saw three civil wars in the first five centuries, Icetaihn saw two in the same time span, and another two wars between its kingdoms of Reivalohn and Kreldt in the last two thousand years," Vharik explained. "Ceruait seems to have stayed out of most of that. All have fought against the rise of the Vhaeoul though. Armaran's mainland split into two kingdoms that are now close to opposing each other. The nomads of Manlakhedran have fought repeatedly over territories during the second millennium and still do so to this day. The Shäada have been plotting something for quite some time, and the Aurentai quarrelled among themselves repeatedly very soon after the War of the Eclipse. They often tend to keep to themselves these days, but even though many realised the error of their ways, there are still those that harbour resentment. The Shäada have been much the same, generally speaking."

"I thought so," Madukeyr sighed, tilting his head to look at Kalthis. "Mostly human nations. That is no surprise to me, and I know it isn't to you either."

"And the people of the world said they wanted peace? I do not understand them, but I do not believe we are out of options yet," Kalthis thought aloud.

"I wonder how long it will be before Melkhar loses her temper though," Madukeyr mused. "That volcano is long overdue a major eruption."

"You shouldn't say such things," Vharik told him. "I may be a talkative old man, but..."

"But what, good sage?" Madukeyr asked. "It has happened before, and it could happen again. I've never known anyone else with such a powerful sense of morality as her." Vharik shook his head.

"Don't forget, Madu, that such morality is also mirrored with intense hatred," Kalthis pointed out. Madukeyr acknowledged him with a brief nod and rose to his feet.

"I'm going to bed," he said gloomily. "I must leave early if I am to reach the Altirnathé in good time." The Kensaiyr rose, bowed, and left the room before either Kalthis or Vharik could respond. After Madukeyr had left the room, Kalthis turned back to the sage and leaned forward.

"Do not worry about him," he assured him. "There is nothing wrong in his words. You know he speaks true, though he could lighten up every once in a while."

"Hahaha! Kalthis, you know how to make someone smile," Vharik laughed. "I've always admired that about you. Funny isn't it? You have a strong heart but a weak stomach."

"Sensitive," Kalthis retorted, arching a brow as Vharik retrieved a cream bun from the nearest cupboard and waved it in his face, "not weak—" he paused. "You already have my attention Vharik, and if you are implying this as the weakness, we're on a completely different wavelength." Unable to refuse the offer, Kalthis took the bun with a grin.

"Back in Atialleia, on what days do you not visit the bakery?" Vharik chuckled. Kalthis let out a heavy sigh, his shoulders sagging.

"If I'm honest, I only go there a couple of times a week," he shrugged. "Anyway, this isn't about me and my love of cake, or the few food intolerances I happen to have despite being one of the Kaesan'Drahknyr."

"It's because you're an easy target, Kalthis," Vharik laughed again, "but yes, you're right. Would you like some more tea?"

"Perhaps just one more," Kalthis smiled. "I'll have lavender this time if that is alright?" At this, Vharik beamed and shuffled across the room to the fireplace.

"I have plenty of everything," he said. "Whatever you want, you're welcome to it."

CHAPTER 3

I
Ene Canal & Sendero de Mercader

"It's what you live for isn't it?" Larsan asked him as he approached and leaned on the starboard deck rail.

Larkh snapped out of his reverie. He stood on the quarterdeck beside the double wheels serving as the ship's standard helm, which would require at least four crew members to steer – were they manned; they stood almost as tall as him. Instead, the single smaller wheel located astern on the poop deck was the helm of choice. Larkh's crew were well aware of the mechanisms within and how they functioned, but there were secrets even they weren't aware of.

"Sorry what?" he asked.

Larsan laughed loudly, slapping him on the back. "You, you're in your element now," he pointed out. "It's what you live for."

"It's all about bein' free," Larkh winked, turning away. He strode across the weather deck and followed his friend's gaze across the landscape. "Could you appreciate life when you're tied down to the law and work?" he asked. "If I'd betrayed my rescuers an' succeeded my father, then I'd be tied down to the aristocracy in Lonnfeir an' be shacklin' myself to the Admiralty. I'd be Lord of a manor while bogged down with tedious politics."

"Fair point," Larsan conceded. *'What would you have done if your family still lived then? Would you still have run away and chosen this life?'*

Larkh slapped him on the back in return. "Now who's off with the fairies?" he laughed. "Think about it Larsan! By this time tomorrow you'll have your nose under every keg in Almadeira!"

For the better part of the day the sun's rays showered the ship with warmth, and either side of the canal the scenery was breathtaking. The North Mazaryn Peaks and rich farmlands of the Aranise Plains could be seen to the east, and the rolling hills of the Vairfell Downs to the west where tendrils of mist crept out of the Silverwood clinging to the South Mazaryn Peaks. It was a sight Larkh never grew tired of so long as the sun shone in the sky.

The Ene Canal, was a stretch of water a mile wide that could take less than a day to sail through provided the wind blew swiftly in the right direction. After the somewhat awkward departure from Senfirth, Larkh set a heading for Almadeira that took *Greshendier* northward before turning north-west into the canal. Much to Larkh's approval the wind followed in their favour as the ship turned west out of the canal.

He tilted his head back to look at the fore and main masts, watching as the sails filled out in the brisk yet gentle breeze, driving them onward toward the looming expanse of whitestone that was the Great Thannen Whitebridge. Closing his eyes, he took a deep breath as his mind drifted freely with contentment. No ship could be prevented from passing beneath the towering arches; besides, even if pirates could be detained here, they could easily enter the Sendero de Mercader via the Mabriltar Strait – except that would take at least a day or two longer from here with the right weather.

II
Sendero de Mercader

The pleasant weather wasn't to last. A violent storm struck late at night along the eastern stretch of the Sendero de Mercader almost as soon as they had emerged from the Ene Canal. The ocean's swell had continued to rise for some time, and black, roiling clouds had darkened the horizon in a matter of minutes.

Larkh had taken up the helm to see them through the worst of it. He'd given the orders to hand sail early enough to avoid potentially disastrous consequences, and that had been the least of his problems. The lookouts on deck had noticed that early on during the storm's onslaught, one ship veered sharply off course, and another ran aground.

"Krallan!" he yelled through the driving rain and howling wind, "get two topmen up there to secure the port side of that sail!" The quartermaster looked up. The topsail on the foremast, though it had been furled like all the others had loosened and fallen off the yard, and was flapping wildly in the gale. Someone, in their haste, hadn't tied the gasket on to the jackstay properly.

"Hakett! Reys!" the quartermaster called.

"Aye sir!" young Reys and Hakett responded.

"Reys, if you think you're clever enough, get up there wi' Hakett an' secure that sail," Krallan challenged the boy. "You're always lookin' for ways to prove yourself to the Captain an' the rest of us. Now's your chance." Reys' jaw fell open.

"You can do it Reys," said a dark-skinned and long-standing crew member named Daron. This was intended as an offer of encouragement. Reys wasn't so sure, but respect was hard earned aboard any ship, let alone a pirate crew. He glanced at Larkh, who was clearly beginning to grow weary from his exertions after having held the ship steady since the foul weather had struck. *'I hope he sees me…and that I live for it to matter,'* he thought, grimly. Taking a deep breath, he wiped his brow and began the treacherous climb, following Hakett.

Larkh flexed his stiff, icy fingers and grasped the wheel tight, turning it with determination into the next rogue wave as it hammered into the starboard side across the bow, drenching him and everyone else, but the sea heaved again before anyone could recover their senses. The ship creaked laboriously, rolled suddenly and unwillingly on to her port side, sending several men sprawling across the deck; one man tumbling overboard screaming, leaving others scrambling for something – anything – to hold on to. Krallan lost his footing, fell sideways, his head slamming against the capping rail. Reys and Hakett clung to the ratlines for dear life. Larkh held on to the wheel tightly lest it spin and the sea drag them under. He gritted his teeth as he regained his balance, forcing his aching joints and muscles into keeping the ship as steady as possible.

"Krallan! Shit! Larsan, see to him!" he bellowed. "The rest of you, stop dilly-dallyin' around an' get to work! I don't need to be tellin' you what to do in this mess!" He squinted through the downpour, his bedraggled hair plastered to his face and his oilskins all but saturated. "Make fast anythin' loose, bail out water an' stop any leaks, you know the drill!"

At once, all hands rushed around in a wild frenzy, seizing any job they could find. Some argued among themselves, but Larkh didn't care about their personal complaints. All he cared about was that the chores that needed doing were done properly.

He glanced up briefly at Reys and Hakett as they climbed the mast to adjust the ends of the flapping sail. His brow creased in deprecation of Krallan's decision to send the newest and most inexperienced member of the crew to perform such a dangerous task, especially in such a livid storm. It was known to him, though, that the boy was desperate to earn his respect. He guessed it was probably why the quartermaster had chosen him. If he made a good job of it despite the conditions, he would be praised, yet if he ended up badly injured or even dead, Krallan's punishment would certainly not be light.

"Oi! Daron, Laisner!" Argwey, shouted. The elven boatswain thrust his arm toward the ship's forecastle. "Grab a team an' tighten up the foremast braces!" Obediently, Daron and Laisner did as instructed.

Larkh had experienced many storms, and one of the worst had been when he'd served as a cabin boy long ago in a crew he loathed as much as the gods. He frowned at the sky, having stirred a sleeping maelstrom of hatred that lurked within his soul. "You didn't get me then, an' you'll not have me now," he growled under his breath.

Larsan wiped the blood from his own stubble-flecked chin, having split it on one of the iron cleats, and stumbled and slipped across the quarterdeck as he held the barely conscious Krallan up as best he could. He made for the door and headed below with considerable difficulty. He laid the quartermaster down on the cot in his cabin, took a handkerchief from his pocket and held it against the open cut on his forehead.

Krallan groaned as he opened his eyes to the violent rolling of the ship as she battled the tumultuous ocean where the yardarms periodically made contact with the surging water. He blinked a few times and took the handkerchief from Larsan's hand. A sudden swell beneath them lifted the ship higher once more.

"Hold on to somethin'!" Krallan sharply advised; his voice hoarse. Larsan grasped hold of one of the bulkheads as another wave crashed into the hull, forcing *Greshendier* over on to her starboard side. Amidst all this chaos, the warrior realised it was only Larkh's hands at the wheel holding the ship against the waves that prevented them from being swallowed by those fearsome waters. Several shouts and cries rang out on deck, one being Larkh barking orders through the din and heavy rain.

"I'm glad you just said that," Larsan laughed, "though, I am concerned about Larkh taking a beating out there. It's him who's holding all of her weight against the waves alone."

"He knows what he's doing," Krallan assured him, and although he smiled back at him there was still worry in his eyes. "The man's quite a rare prodigy; he knows as much if not more'n most sailors who've been at sea years longer than him. That storm was a sudden one though." He sat up.

"You should rest," Larsan said, examining the cut on Krallan's head.

"I'll be alright," Krallan assured him, adding pressure to the wound again. He brushed his soaked black hair aside. "Feel that?" he asked.

Larsan nodded. "The sea's calming. It seems the storm is almost over."

Back on deck, Reys had made it safely back down from the main mast, but Hakett had lost his footing as he was stepping down when another rogue wave struck, which had sent him sprawling, breaking his right arm in the process. Daron and Laisner were tending him, and other members of the crew on deck assisted the injured.

Parts of the rigging were in a shambles and needed repairs, and bits and pieces of the deck rails were dented and splintering. The sky had begun to quieten and the sun was now a hazy orange disc in the cloud in the distance behind them. That at least was a small blessing. Larsan ran astern to where Larkh was slumped at the helm, saturated and barely conscious against the wheel. He'd been fighting against the storm since it had begun, and now the sun had almost fully risen on the horizon.

"Argwey!" Larsan yelled. The boatswain looked up through long bedraggled locks of dark hair. "Would you take the helm for a moment? I need to get him down from here." Argwey nodded, first giving instructions to the crew members present on deck, then making his way aft and taking the wheel as Larsan held on to Larkh and prized his rigid fingers from it.

Larkh slumped sideways, though Larsan kept a firm hold of him, laying him gently down on the deck. The warrior tapped his cheek twice and thumped him over the back. Larkh spluttered, rolled on to his stomach and coughed up a mouthful of seawater. He shivered and slowly pushed himself up on to his knees, letting out a soft groan of fatigue. "Is it over?" he croaked.

"More or less. A hot bowl of soup and a good rest is what you need now though," Larsan said, taking out his hip flask and holding it to Larkh's lips. Gladly, Larkh accepted and took a good long swig of the brandy before passing it back.

"Aye," he agreed. "I'll be glad of it." Larsan stood up and held his hand out. Larkh grabbed on and allowed his friend to pull him to his feet. He continued to hold on, feeling dizzy and exhausted. "I don't think I can..."

"Don't worry yourself about that, you've had one hell of a night," Larsan said with a grin.

III
Sendero de Mercader

Out of his drenched leather oilskins into fresh, comfortable clothing, Larkh threw himself down on his usual seat at the chart table on the port side of the great cabin nearest the door and wearily ran both hands through his damp, straggly hair. Now that it was starting to dry, the layers were already beginning to flick up at the ends.

Larsan entered the room with a warm bowl of soup and bread for them both. "Do you want to know how difficult it is to bring soup up here without spilling it in this weather?" Larsan asked. Larkh arched his brow as he rubbed his aching wrists. *'Silly question,'* thought Larsan. "Never mind."

"At least it wasn't a necessity for you to bring it earlier," Larkh remarked. Larsan lowered the food to the table and shrugged as he sat down. "Although sayin' that," he added, picking up his spoon and watching the soup gently sliding from side to side, "if Nathaniel had put it in shallower bowls most of it'd have ended up everywhere other than where we want it."

Larsan snorted in amusement at this as he picked up his spoon and ate. "Have you any idea whereabouts we are?" he asked.

"I've a fair idea," Larkh replied, blowing on the soup. He seemed too tired and troubled to say any more.

"Is something wrong?" Larsan knew the expression on Larkh's face well enough now to know there was more behind it.

"We're still in the Ennerth region," Larkh said in reply to the initial question, ignoring the second, "but we've gone a bit astray because of the storm." Larsan knew there was little point in trying to force it out of him; he'd only get angry and demand to be left alone. His reaction, however, prompted a response anyway.

"I know what you want to ask," Larkh gave an exasperated sigh, "but I'd rather not hit too many of the low notes right now. I lost a few good men last night. That's all. Leave it there."

Larsan conceded the point. The subject was more than a little sensitive. He remembered Larkh telling him that he had lost his entire family to a group of bloodthirsty pirates many years ago who'd been hired by the Duke of Lonnfeir. The group he belonged to now had saved him back then, and so he repaid them honourably while thinking of them as his new family.

"We should be fairly close to Almadeira by now," Larkh mused, leaning back in his seat. "Gresh is going to need at least a couple of days for repairs. There'll be ample time for you to get ashore to enjoy yourself." Larsan lifted his gaze to him.

"Larkh, I—" Larsan faltered.

"I'm fine, really," Larkh smiled briefly, glancing over his shoulder at the dismal weather outside as he placed a piece of bread into his mouth. "We've been through storms like this before, but this one was definitely different and somethin' about that gives me the willies."

"It was a little *too* sudden. I suppose we can only ponder on that right now, but something hasn't been sitting right with me since I boarded this ship from the very beginning," Larsan admitted. "I've always wanted to ask, but after seeing you last night in particular, it made me want to know all the more." Larkh turned his attention from the window back to Larsan.

"Oh? What's that?"

"How is it that a single man can steer this ship?" Larsan asked, all the while keeping his eyes fixed on Larkh's body language. "You have a secondary helm wheel that allows this. I'm curious as to how it works."

"Ah I see," Larkh said, then chuckling despite his fatigue. "I wondered when such a question might crop up from you." He sat forward, picked up his spoon and considered which hand to use it in. Quickly settling on the natural left, he leaned on his right elbow and allowed his hand to cradle his jaw.

"So...?" Larsan prompted.

"Greshendier has a few wonderful little secrets," Larkh gave his friend a cunning smile. "She's certainly befitting of her name too."

"And what does her name mean?" Larsan leaned forward.

"Aura of majesty," Larkh replied, stirring the soup. "My grandfather designed her an' named her, an' she was built in his shipyard near Saldour. But back to your question; she's a ship of mysteries, at least to those who don't know her very well. She was built with an altirna system; however, she's more efficient than her sister ships. The Faltain Navy's always been confused over why, an' even I'm curious about the underlyin' truths. She was also the archetype. All the others of her line have the same altirna-related archana, but this here girl's a bit different. I first saw the blueprints durin' her construction, though I was still very young at the time, mind."

"I've never been on board a ship with an altirna system," Larsan thought out loud. "In any case, do you think it relates to the Nays, perchance?" He watched his friend manoeuvring every spoonful of soup in an almost expert fashion.

"I believe there's somethin' about the archana itself that's different," Larkh replied. "If I knew any more, I'd not say anyway lest the information fall into the wrong hands; even by accident."

"You're a shrewd man Larkh," Larsan remarked with a smirk, "and watching you juggle your food with such precision is both amusing and intriguing."

"And?" Larkh prompted with a grin despite the fact he was struggling to keep his eyes open.

"And, I'm not going to pressure you into giving me a full answer," the warrior sighed. "I don't fancy sleeping with the fish. Besides, you're about ready to drop after that hammering you took out there."

"Don't worry, I'm goin' straight to bed shortly after I finish this," Larkh assured him. He yawned. *'Something certainly isn't right with the world.'*

IV
Ennerth

Zehn began to grow concerned about his sanity as he lay in his bedroll under a clear sky that night. He watched the silent twinkling of the stars and the eerily glowing disc of the full moon while he wondered agitatedly about the series of strange dreams he'd been experiencing night after night. Each of them somehow linked to the one previous.

Raeon had come to suspect it had something to do with the remnants of ancient magic dating back to the time of the Nays, and that it could have something to do with the sword he carried. He wasn't sure why he would be having such vivid dreams linked to an era that ended over three thousand years ago or how his father's sword could possibly be relevant, but he wasn't denying the possibility.

When Raeon then told him that the leviathan Guerin had been spotted in the Wahren Sea – in the middle of the favoured passage to the island nations of Enkaiyta no less – that worry increased. There had been no reports of Guerin attacking any ships sailing in that direction, however. Something roused his suspicion that it wasn't just a coincidence for there had also been sightings of Adengeld's revered protector, Dehltas, becoming more active than usual in the Daynallar Mountains.

His mind drifted as he listened to the trickling sound of the nearby River Silven. It would only be a matter of another day and a half before they reached Almadeira if they kept up their current pace. He couldn't help but feel he was already out of his depth, and as if the confusing dreams weren't enough, the contract regarding the lofty red-haired woman was signed M. *Saiyinn*. That was the name of his instructor in swordsmanship; Marceau Saiyinn.

"Thinking too much again?" Raeon asked, tossing more wood on to the fire. "I can understand how strange and confusing this must be for you, trust me I do, but if you allow yourself to fret too much you will make yourself unwell."

"I think I am already unwell," Zehn sighed. "Marceau is usually in Kessford Academy, but he's currently using his house in Almadeira. I can't fully accept this contract until I have more information, but it's these dreams. It's as if they're telling me some kind of story."

"From my studies and experience, dreams always show us something," Raeon answered with an air of indifference. He reclined in his bedroll and let his dark brown hair out of its ponytail. "Finding out who you really are is never an easy task." Zehn turned his head to his friend.

"What do you mean by that?" he asked. "I know who I am."

"You know exactly what I mean," Raeon chuckled. "We learn more about ourselves every day. It's what one chooses to do with their knowledge and beliefs that defines them. Sometimes we find ourselves searching for something very specific, and it's usually a demanding question that takes a very long time to answer."

Zehn turned his head back to the stars. "Trust you to always bring depth to words." The silver mage simply laughed. Zehn frowned and looked at him again. "What?" Raeon looked back at him, momentarily straight-faced, and burst out laughing again. Zehn closed his eyes and shook his head.

"I'm sorry," Raeon said. "It seems I'm easily amused tonight. You spoke so seriously that I couldn't help but laugh; but Zehn, it's because I just think that way. You've known that since we first met on that ship all those years ago, and secretly, I think you appreciate that in a friend."

"At times like this, yeah I suppose I do," Zehn smiled, "but not when I'm looking for a straight forward simple answer to something."

"It's a bad habit."

"Don't I know it!"

Zehn turned on his side and pulled his bedroll up over his shoulders. "Enough banter for now. We'll be there soon, and hopefully Marceau will have some answers regarding this damned weird contract. Goodnight."

"Goodnight Zehn," Raeon replied, now turning his own attention to the night sky.

~ *The thick, roiling mist slowly dissolved, clearing a path ahead of him. Zehn found himself standing before the ruins of a shrine atop a mountain. He knew not where he was, but the gentle whispering of the trees managed to subdue any ounce of uneasiness.*

The shrine itself had been built out of a silvery-white form of stone known as whitestone. Small murals and statues of winged warriors and dragons were sculpted into sections of its walls. Time and conflict had ravaged the place; walls had collapsed and debris was strewn haphazardly across the mountainside.

Behind the shrine, however, was a towering crystal formation. It looked as though it had gushed out of the top of the mountain as water does from a geyser, and then solidified like a frozen fountain. Strangely though, it looked as if it were in some way dead. It had a grey weathered look about it, but it piqued Zehn's curiosity.

Could this be the Altirnathé at the summit of the North Mazaryn Peaks? It would make sense with the altirna mine at its base, but he'd never heard of a shrine being up there. If this crystal was, for all intents and purposes, dead, then it would explain the recent shortage of altirna. What or who was this shrine built to honour though?

He felt a presence behind him. He turned to see a shadowy male figure dressed in close-fitting black leathers matching him in height. He couldn't make out the features through the mist, but the ears were pointed and almost twice the length of those of a human.

A Kensaiyr. The hair was long and pure white. This person was definitely a white-silver elf. In each hand the Kensaiyr held a curved sword with a thin blade. Again, he couldn't make out the details, but he didn't have time to think. The figure lunged at him, and in that moment Zehn noted the incredible determination in a pair of striking aquamarine blue eyes framed with milky white skin. A great shadow then arose from the side of the mountain, and blackness claimed him. ~

Zehn sat bolt upright in his bedroll sweating. He wiped his brow. Taking long deep breaths, he ran a hand through his unkempt shock of wavy hair and stared into the distance where the faint glow of sunrise crept softly over the horizon. 'Dawn already?' He laid back again and heaved a sigh.

"Another dream?" Raeon asked, opening his eyes and staring worriedly at Zehn, who nodded, rubbing his face.

"This one was different," Zehn replied.

V
Sendero de Mercader

Having slept for the better part of the morning, Larkh stirred in his bunk. He rubbed his eyes and took a deep breath, staring up at the ceiling swaying to and fro above him. His own cot, and those of his officers, were fixed to the ship's bulkheads though they still resembled hammocks. They also had access to hammocks, but unless the sea's swell was extreme, something more secure was preferable.

He blinked, stretched, and rubbed his eyes again. *'Damn, I could have done without this headache,'* he thought as his mind raced over the events of the storm and the various parts of the ship that were damaged. *'Alright, make that two headaches.'*

Forcing himself out of the bunk, he peered out of the nearest window. They were near Almadeira alright; he recognised the coastline. The sea was far less choppy now, and the weather had brightened considerably. Krallan and Argwey would need to speak to him as soon as he emerged, so he made for the door, but stopped. He looked down at himself to see nothing but a nightshirt and underwear. *'What are you doing?'* he asked himself, narrowing his eyes sleepily.

He found a pair of black breeches and pulled those on first, then rummaged around for a shirt. Thankfully there was a fresh one in the drawer. Most of the others needed a good wash, and that was something Mrs. Menow at the Silver Gull would be able to help with. He thought for a moment, smiling as he remembered the mouth-watering cooked breakfasts she made. He would have one of those as soon he went ashore.

With a contented sigh at that thought, he unbuttoned his nightshirt and pulled it over his head just as Larsan burst through the door, to which he yelled, "haven't you ever heard o' knockin'!?"

"Sorry for the intrusion, but I have some bad news." Larsan's rugged face was solemn. Larkh swallowed hard and turned away. There had been two other men who hadn't been lost overboard in the storm, but they had been seriously injured. He didn't need to ask for the details.

"You don't need to tell me; thanks for lettin' me know," he sighed, his handsome face now a picture of sadness. "We'll bury them at sea before we make port." He threw the nightshirt aside on to his bunk and picked up the white shirt he'd taken from the drawer.

"Forgive me for prying, but how did you get *that*?" Larsan was pointing to a somewhat faded circular scar on Larkh's stomach to the lower left of his navel.

"You mean to tell me you've not noticed that before?" Larkh asked dubiously.

"Afraid not, and to be honest it's not all that obvious," said Larsan. Larkh put the shirt on and buttoned it up before turning to the mid-calf boots. He sat on the bunk whilst he put them on.

"I was shot with a flintlock," he told him. "It was a deep wound as well. Many of the crew thought it a miracle I survived."

"You're a lucky man then," Larsan thought aloud. "Maybe the go—" he saw the shadow of disapproval fall across Larkh's face and thought better of finishing the sentence. "Ah, never mind." Larkh's brow knit as he rose to his feet.

"Maybe the gods...what, Larsan?" he snapped. "The gods can give my family back to me an' kiss my arse millions of times before I'll even consider forgivin' them." He touched the locket that hung around his neck as he strode to the door and opened it. "Perhaps I'll tell you about how I got shot when we have a bit of time to ourselves."

"I'm sorry," Larsan apologised. "I didn't mean to—"

"Let it go, Larsan," Larkh shook his head and went through the door. "I know you didn't. Sorry I snapped. It touches a raw nerve, that's all."

They emerged on to the quarterdeck. Larkh wandered over to the port side where Almadeira was gliding slowly into view. He could see the astronomical clock on the towering whitestone walls of the ancient Nays Kathaedra already. The sun shone, reflecting off its golden rooftops. There was scarcely a cloud in the azure sky.

It was almost noon as he had predicted. Larsan joined him. He waved a hand at Krallan and showed him five fingers. The quartermaster nodded and instead turned his attention to the elven boatswain, Argwey.

"So, you recommend this place for fine booze then, do you?" Larsan enquired, remembering his recent conversation with Larkh after they'd swiftly departed Senfirth.

"You don't hold back, do you?" Larkh chuckled, smiling faintly. "There's good ale, good spirits, and good wine. You'll have a couple o' days to get as plastered as you can on as many different variants as you can."

Larsan rubbed his hands together. Larkh's brow promptly arched response. "I don't think I've ever known anyone quite as enthusiastic about alcohol as you, not even the crew. You fancy yourself as a connoisseur then?"

"Call it a hobby." Larsan leaned on the deck rail. "It's not so different from your hobbies; thieving, smuggling..."

"Point taken." Larkh said, pulling a face and shrugging as he turned to approach Krallan and Argwey. They would now discuss finding a suitable berth for the ship.

CHAPTER 4

I
Lonnfeir

Dawn broke across Faltainyr Demura, pale sunlight filtered through the branches of the lazily swaying treetops. Enriched by the twittering sound of birdsong, a golden illumination spread across the southern entrance of the Vlaedranistas Amečana. Melkhar and Arcaydia packed away their bedrolls. They had left the underground passage shortly after midnight and Melkhar had sealed off the opening, but there had been an air of disquiet about the place shortly before dawn. The western stretches of the hills flanking them were blanketed by the coniferous Lennale Forest; a perfect place for an ambush.

Following a winding gravel road south, they would eventually join up with the D'etrun Highroad leading through the small village of Foristead to Almadeira. Arcaydia was now paying more attention to the way Melkhar walked. Her long limbs gave her an unusual gait, but strangely it contributed to her fearsome reputation. Her body was incredibly lithe like a snake, but she was sturdier on her feet and more grounded than anyone else she'd ever met.

Melkhar scanned the trees back and forth. Her lip curled into a sneer. "Stay on your guard at all times."

"Are we being watched?" Arcaydia said, glancing in all directions.

"A clever observation," Melkhar remarked.

"Th-thank you," Arcaydia replied as they made their way toward the road.

"I see you don't yet understand sarcasm."

"What?"

"...Never mind."

The reason for their uneasiness finally became apparent. Along the western and eastern hillsides, and the forest edges, several rows of soldiers belonging to a single troop emerged from the forest. Melkhar stopped, holding a hand in front of Arcaydia. She glanced around in all directions, the expression on her stern face remaining ever calm and indifferent.

"What is this?" she called out. "An entire troop sent out to capture two travellers? Surely this cannot be common practice in these times."

"We know what you are!" the captain shouted. "We do not want the Nays returning and interfering with our affairs. It is none of your business. You must return to the land from which you came, or else—"

"Or else what?" Melkhar interrupted. "If you truly had any idea of what I am then you wouldn't be attempting such folly." *'How could men like this have known...?'*

"Such arrogance," the captain snarled. "The Nays shall not dominate us again."

"Dominate?" Melkhar asked, almost as if she were surprised. She frowned. "It seems you have taken a stranger's words far too seriously."

"I don't think so. It was prophesised long ago that the Nays would return to reclaim the world they once dictated!" He appeared apprehensive, but lifted his arm nonetheless commanding his soldiers to attack.

Melkhar's eyes flashed with menace as a wry smile spread across her lips. "Have it your way then. Arcaydia, please look after our belongings." Arcaydia watched her for a moment. *'Her eyes...'* A chill ran straight up her spine and across her shoulders. *'They look like they should belong to.....a dragon.'* She grabbed their belongings and ran to hide in a secluded spot between a cluster of crags as a ghastly aura began to emanate from Melkhar. Arcaydia froze, fear etched into every line of her face. It was an aura laden with ill-intent, and so terribly thick with a darkness that could only be known by someone who truly embraced hate.

The Kaesan'Drahknyr took her draconic sword into her left hand, leaving her other blade in its scabbard, beckoning with her right. The head of the black dragon on the hilt clasped the slender blade in its mouth, its ruby eyes gleaming brightly in the morning sun. She drew it back ready, bloodlust fuelling her ferocity. The captain signalled to attack.

Some hung back, frozen in their tracks as the majority charged; she met those head on. She swung her sword with such speed and grace it could have almost been a whip, slicing through her enemies as a scythe felled wheat in a bloody display of otherworldly skill and agility while her finely sculpted countenance remained emotionless, the murderous intent only showing in her eyes. Arcaydia and the captain watched in awe and horror, but only Arcaydia knew this was the very least Melkhar was capable of. There was a fire in her very soul that once lit would turn into an unstoppable blaze.

The entire troop was strewn in a grisly crimson mess across the hillside in a matter of minutes. Their executioner stood spattered with blood and gore, her expression unmistakeably demonic. She breathed slowly and steadily, though clearly not out of breath. She was on a high, maybe even a thrill. As she turned, she fixed her chilling gaze upon the captain; the man was quivering. He saw nothing but raw determination and malice in those fierce eyes, and for a moment he wondered exactly why he and his men had been sent on such an impossible mission. Totally in agreement with his king that the Nays had no business returning to the world they had left to its own devices, there were the beginnings of doubt as to King Ameldar's intentions, and those of the people he now opposed. If the Nays truly wished to dominate the world, would it not still be so? It was too late now though. He had to see this through. He lifted a shaking arm. Dozens of archers rose up and aimed their bows at both Melkhar and Arcaydia.

'A wise man to bring reinforcements,' she thought with nonchalance, *'it's a shame I already knew they were there.'* What she didn't expect was for half of them to aim their arrows at Arcaydia. *'Damn you! Anyone with any sense would have hidden out of sight.'* They fired.

Melkhar threw herself sideways, blurred, vanished, and then reappeared in front of Arcaydia mid-roll and deflected or sliced through the majority of the arrows with her sword as she landed. She caught one in her right hand as another slammed into her belly with a wet thud, and another crunched into her left shoulder. Without so much as a flinch, she clenched her teeth, shocking her assailants. Arcaydia was about to run to her side, but a hand signal soon stopped her.

Before the captain could think himself victorious despite the almost instantaneous loss of almost the entire squad, the lofty flame-haired warrior rose to her feet. She flicked the gore from the blade and sheathed the sword, then broke off the ends of the arrows as she advanced toward him. Her right hand was poised with her fingers slightly curled; a burst of flame shot up from her palm and danced. Archers daring to raise their bows against her now burst into flames with a single flick of her wrist as her fingers guided the trajectory of her magica. The rest of soldiers attempted to flee, searing bolts of lightning flashed from her fingertips; the shock killed them almost instantly. The captain found himself frozen to the spot as if he'd been turned to stone.

She approached him with the same chilling gaze she shared with all who dared challenge her, unflinching despite the two arrowheads still embedded in her flesh.

"I commend you for your effort, sir," she said nonchalantly. "Whoever gave you orders to attack me certainly had some tact behind their stupidity." Clenching her jaw, she wrenched the arrowhead from her shoulder, followed by the one protruding from her stomach. He swallowed hard as he watched.

She studied him for a moment. He was human, perhaps in his late thirties with unkempt brown hair and some stubble around his chin. "Might I know your name, soldier?"

"F-Falthen," the quivering man replied.

"I'll not forget it," Melkhar assured him. "Who do you work for?"

"K-King Ameldar DeaCathra, o-of Adengeld," Falthen stammered. Melkhar frowned.

"Cathra is far to the west, what are Cathran men doing in the regions of Faltain?" she demanded.

"A-Ameldar wishes to conquer all of Armaran to make it an empire, his empire." Beads of sweat were running down Falthen's face. The Kaesan'Drahknyr's expression darkened further. "Th-they're secretly p-planning a coup d'etat to overthrow King Jaredh. Please l-let me go. I won't tell them I've told you about this!"

"You can go and tell your superiors that you have failed in your mission to strike me down – if you truly know who I am – and you may also tell them that another attempt will see the capital city of Cathra destroyed. Any word of this breathed to anyone else will be heard by the Adels. We will find you. That is a promise. Now I suggest you get out of my sight before I have second thoughts about allowing you to live."

Falthen forced himself to make eye contact with her. His eyes widened as profound realisation washed over him; without further delay he heeded her warning and took off in the direction from which she and Arcaydia had come, running as fast as he could. She watched him go, her eyes narrowing. Turning away, she slowly walked back down the slope toward Arcaydia who was about to open her satchel to access bandages and healing aids. Melkhar grabbed her by the collar, hauled her to her feet and slapped her hard across the face, almost knocking her to the floor again.

"Ow! What was—" Arcaydia started to say. Melkhar tightened her grip, pulled her closer and leaned in.

"Never before have I met anyone so *stupid*!" she snarled. Her accent was noticeably more exaggerated when she was angry. Arcaydia shivered, saying nothing. "Did you really think that crouching down there in plain sight was a wise plan? These wounds mean little to me, but I did not need them before my task at Mt. Dorne, and if I had been an ordinary member of Aeldynn's society, I would be dead if not close to death. Learn fast, Arcaydia Na'Sairdun, because you cannot afford not to."

"I-I'm sorry," Arcaydia sighed into her breath.

"You shall be if you continue the way you are now." Melkhar released her. "We need to be moving, now."

"What about those wounds?" Arcaydia asked.

"Not here," she said. "We'll find a secluded area to patch them in the Lennale Forest."

"Are you sure?" Arcaydia asked. "It'll be—"

"How old are you?" Melkhar asked.

"Twenty-three," said Arcaydia.

"How old do I look?" Melkhar continued.

"Late twenties to early thirties by human reckoning?" Arcaydia answered reluctantly, "but I know you've lived for many centuries; millennia even."

"Then you will understand that I know very well what I am doing," Melkhar concluded, edging down on to the road facing north-east in the direction of Almadeira. "I don't see anyone on the road near where we're going, so we need not worry about me being seen like this."

"What about that um...mess?" Arcaydia failed to fight off the nausea as she cast a glance in the direction of the troop's bloody remains. Leaning forward into the bushes, she retched violently. *'So much death.'*

"Does it trouble you that much?" Melkhar's eyes seemed to bore into her very soul.

"What troubles me is that I sense you're capable of much worse," Arcaydia replied weakly. Melkhar grunted dismissively and walked away.

"To answer your question, have you ever heard of bandits? Groups of them appear almost anywhere, so any passersby may assume that is the case and a bounty will likely be posted for mercenaries. They won't find anyone, but that isn't my problem. The soldier is likely to have orders not to divulge information about me to the general public anyway, so he will return to his superiors and inform them. They obviously already know about us from someone, but if they have any sense at all they will also blame my actions on bandits. They are planning a coup d'etat to overthrow the king of these parts, so they will not want their cover blown just yet."

Arcaydia had to mull this over for a moment. She didn't really understand politics, but a plot to overthrow King Faltain? People with political power were astonishing. And why were the Nays being dragged into something like this? There must be something else at work for them to be targeted. Did they think the Nays were allies of Faltain or something?

"Shouldn't we send out a warning though?" Arcaydia asked. "Surely we don't need to keep quiet about this. We might be able to prevent a lot of bloodshed if we—"

"It would only cause more bloodshed at this stage of their game," Melkhar interrupted caustically. "When their king finds out about it he will wage war on Adengeld. That much is a certainty. Either way, you aren't going to stop them. Ameldar may be taking a back door right now, but it will turn into an all out war eventually. They are mortal, Arcaydia. They thrive on their own selfishness and will stop at nothing to get what they want. We do not need to involve ourselves yet. Should you speak up, you could land yourself into a greater and deeper hole than you can get yourself out of, and that will then blow our own cover. You are to remain silent on the matter, do you understand?"

"Yes ma'am," Arcaydia said obediently, lowering her head. *'You're so cold,'* she thought. *'What will it take for me to understand you?'* She followed along behind Melkhar wondering how anyone could turn away from such carnage as if it meant nothing, and walk with such wounds without indicating they were in pain. There was no denying that she had seen it on her face when Melkhar had been hit, but this warrior concealed pain with such skill that one wouldn't think she felt it at all if they hadn't witnessed what Arcaydia had when she was interrogated only a matter of weeks ago.

Melkhar located a set of stone steps belonging to the ruins of an old human settlement, and signalled for Arcaydia to come down. "We'll take them out here," she said, glancing westward toward a copse by the side of a small stream nestled in the hills at the edge of the Lennale Forest, shrouded in early morning mist. "Could you retrieve those bandages? I shan't need them on for too long, perhaps only a day or two."

"You know, before that strange man rescued me that day and returned me to Ardeltaniah, I wouldn't have guessed that one day I'd be travelling alongside one of the legendary Kaesan'Drahknyr," Arcaydia told her, rummaging in her satchel. Melkhar watched the water trickling over the rocks beside them.

"Life often takes many unexpected turns," she replied in contemplation. "Sometimes there is nothing you can do about it."

"Yes, that's true," Arcaydia said, casting her frosty blue eyes downward, finding the bandages. "What about the times that you expect something to happen, and it doesn't?"

Melkhar's eyes narrowed. "You wish to enter into a philosophical discussion with me right now?" she asked, remaining almost perfectly still whilst the wounds were cleaned and the bandages applied. Arcaydia shook her head. "Wise choice. Still, something is not right."

"Isn't that why you and the others have returned?" Arcaydia asked, tying off the second bandage and stepping away to sit on a patch of grass.

"It is relative to my purpose," Melkhar confirmed, "but it is a force separate from the capabilities of mortals. It is anyone's guess how long it will be before we must reveal ourselves to the world at large. I would be willing to wage it will be sooner than we would like." Arcaydia conceded the point silently as she looked up at the smoky blue ridges of the North Mazaryn Peaks to the east.

'The first of them is very close, and the other near Almadeira,' Melkhar discerned. Furrowing her brow, she cast her attention toward the mountains. Further back beyond the road they had just travelled, a malignant presence took form and stood among the scattered remains of Falthen's troop, trying to shield itself from her senses. The Kaesan'Drahknyr stopped to look over her shoulder.

"Is something wrong?" Arcaydia asked, following Melkhar's line of sight. Melkhar turned away, brow furrowing.

'That presence appeared and disappeared so quickly,' she thought. "No, not yet in any case."

II
Ennerth

Now beyond the mists emanating from the Silverwood, Zehn and Raeon crossed the River Silven on to the road toward Almadeira below the North Mazaryn Peaks. It was by far the shortest route to the second largest port in Ennerth, save for a short climb before reaching the pass entrance.

When they arrived at the pass, they were greeted by the great Blue Emperor butterflies, famous for the range of shades of blue dazzling their wings like an optical illusion. All around them the smoky blue mountains were streaked with mazarine blue layers of rock in-between meadows littered with dozens of different kinds of flower, but notably lavender and bluebells.

Zehn had been here many times before, but something else now caught his eye; the large crystal structure on top of the nearest peak. *'The Altirnathé?'* he thought. *'Could that be the place?'* He knew of a path that led up that mountain, and as a consequence, curiosity was going to get the better of him.

Raeon stopped for a moment to look up, raising his left hand to shield his eyes from the sun, pondering over the task he'd been given by his mentor. His white-silver robes billowed in the swift breeze, carried westward toward Lonnfeir. He took in the fresh air, and set off again at a brisk pace to catch up with Zehn.

"You wished to look at it too, eh?" Zehn asked looking to Raeon, who ran a hand along the flowers and grasses growing alongside the mountain path. Raeon slowed to lift a Blue Emperor on to his right index finger from one of the few crimson flowers blooming nearby, watching with admiration as it flexed its wings.

"It fits the description of the crystal you saw in your dream recently, doesn't it?" Raeon asked, lifting the butterfly to eye level.

"It does, from what I can see of it down here," Zehn agreed, suddenly curious about Raeon's affinity with nature. "How in the world do you do such things?"

Raeon wiggled his finger. The butterfly took flight. Turning to his friend, he smiled. "I suppose it just comes naturally," he chuckled, dispelling the glámar that made his ears appear round. They now appeared naturally pointed; they were definitely elven, but slightly smaller. "Have you never tried getting closer to nature though?"

"Forgive me; I often forget you're a half elf because you use the glámar to hide it. I enjoy the great outdoors, but no, I don't think I've ever tried to pick up wild animals or insects before," Zehn shrugged, and Raeon simply smiled and nodded.

They continued onward along the rocky path with Raeon close behind, but neither seemed to be in the frame of mind to hold much of a conversation. Thick, rolling white clouds drifted across the azure sky above them as they hiked up the mountainside. There was no indication of the weather suddenly turning as it had the night before along the northern coastline.

As they climbed, the shimmering cerulean waters of the Sendero de Mercader spread out below them, and to the east was the bustling port of Almadeira. Zehn's brow dipped into a frown as he caught sight of a familiar ship anchored in the port. "That would be one way to put a damper on my day," he muttered half to himself. Raeon followed his gaze.

"Savaldor's ship is it?"

"There's no mistaking the flag, or that elaborate decor for that matter." Zehn turned and looked up the path toward the crystal formation at the summit. "The man is a master of exaggeration and I can't fathom why so few people attempt to rein him in. He's hard enough to bring down without nearly everyone else making it that much easier for him to slip by."

'He certainly doesn't exaggerate with his skills though. Those are genuine.' Raeon knew he had to be careful with his words when it came to topics such as Larkh Savaldor. Zehn was so steadfast in his opinions and set in his ways that trying to coerce him into considering the surrounding facts was a sure-fire way to getting his head bitten off. When dealing with Zehn, it was necessary to apply tact to the conversation, and even then it didn't always go to plan.

"A question, if I may, Zehn," Raeon said thoughtfully. "Do you really know as much about him as you let on back in Senfirth? There is no question that he is a lawbreaker, but in my experience he is tolerated more because he does not kill indiscriminately, and because his father was an admiral. I am not out to change your mind, but I think there are far worse pirates out there who deserve to be put behind bars." Now Zehn was lost for words. Did Raeon know more than *he* did? If he did, he wondered how. Perhaps he'd ask him later.

"He is a pirate, Raeon, and therefore an outlaw. I don't need any other reason for him to be put away." That made the subject closed for discussion, at least for now, but Raeon was content in the knowledge he'd made his friend think.

The silver mage secretly smiled to himself. *'You're kidding yourself Zehn. He annoys you because he's just too clever for you really. If only you knew the truth, you'd change your mind, at least to a point.'*

When Zehn and Raeon arrived at the mountain's summit, the majority of the peak was now obscured by clusters of slowly drifting cloud. The tip of the crystal structure was visible, but the path before them was almost completely obscured. Despite the density of the fog here, Zehn could just make out the outline of an old building. Raeon signalled for him to move aside, whispering unfamiliar words; *"arofenh al varthen vaehr ýs."* [2]

The cloud rippled and dispersed, revealing a safe path leading up to an ancient shrine. Many of its walls had collapsed, pieces of broken statues lay scattered, and yet it appeared not to have lost much of its original splendour. For a fairly small structure it looked much larger than it actually was. The roof stretched upwards as if pulled toward the heavens; tall doors, aisles and windows formed pointed arches at the top and were etched in gold to match the peaked rooftop. There were intricately detailed sculptures of winged people, dragons, artefacts and symbols carved into the pearly stonework of its walls in the same style as the Kathaedra standing in the centre of Almadeira.

"There is no doubt about it Raeon," Zehn shivered. "This is definitely the place I saw in my dream." He wandered around the statues close to the front of the shrine as if entranced. He turned and wandered inside. Raeon

---

[2] Open a path for us.

followed, but allowed his friend to investigate without disturbance.

Murals of events long since passed had been painted in designated spots along the inner walls, and more stone sculptures loomed beneath the vaulted ceiling. At the back of the room were life-sized statues of seven winged warriors, all wearing extravagantly pointed armour and draconic masks covering the top half of their faces. They were standing around another statue of a woman. Unlike them, she did not bear wings, and was draped in a long dress with her neck, waist and arms covered in jewellery. Her hair stretched down to her knees. In front of her was an altar bearing an inscription in a language and alphabet thought to be long forgotten. The wings on the warrior statues were folded, but each pair rose up several feet above the head before they curved downward, ending just above the ankles. Four of the winged figures were male, and three were female. Raeon gazed upon them in awe, and it didn't take Zehn long to notice. He wandered up to the silver mage, staring at them.

"Incredible," he thought aloud. "Raeon, were you suggesting from the contract written by Marceau that one of these is the woman I am looking for?"

Raeon nodded. "From the description, I certainly believe that to be the case, and there's no mistaking that she's tallest of the three females. I think we should take a look outside at that crystal formation and eat before we head back down to Almadeira though. It'll be evening by the time we arrive."

"Yeah, not a bad idea," Zehn mumbled, momentarily gazing at the loftiest winged female statue. Another shiver ran up his spine. *'The statue even looks formidable,'* he mused.

The two wandered back outside the shrine, only to glimpse a figure cloaked in the mist. Zehn stopped in his tracks. The figure stepped forward. Just as it had been in his dream, the male figure was dressed in black, carried two swords and had long pure white hair that streamed out behind a pair of very noticeably pointed ears.

"You," he said under his breath. "You were in my dream." He laid his hand on his sword. "Who are you?" Piercing blue eyes stared at him long and hard.

"My name is Madukeyr," the other answered after a significant pause. "I appeared in your dream because I called you here to allow the one you pursue to do her job unhindered – for now – and to test your abilities as one of the Keys."

CHAPTER 5

I

Almadeira

It was just past noon the next day in Almadeira when Arcaydia arrived alone bearing both sets of luggage. Melkhar had given her a note with the name of the inn at which they would rest, a map and instructions to find a man named Marceau Saiyinn. She looked around and sighed.

'I don't know what I'm doing!' she thought gruffly. *'What if something happens to me again? I'll never hear the end of it. Well, she's the one to blame if that happens. She left me on my own to go and do something that's "too dangerous" for me.'*

She wandered through the streets in admiration. It was a pretty port town with half-timbered houses lining most of the cobbled streets. Potted plants and flowers in hanging baskets dotted about the houses of the more wealthy folk. From what Melkhar had told her, the underground sewer here was originally built by the Nays, and the same applied to the naval port of Saldour. The air was much more pleasant as a result. The Nays had been the first to create them, and the people of Aeldynn had followed their designs if the coin was available, which in most places of the world it either wasn't or the governments didn't care enough to spend money on doing something about the squalor in which many lived.

Arcaydia approached the inn, the Silver Gull, tucked away behind the town square. The sign swinging outside had a picture of a silver bird on it with a tall sailing ship on water in the background. As she approached the door, it opened unexpectedly, and she collided with the person making an exit. She tilted her head back.

The figure she had bumped into wore a long red coat, with a matching red hat on his head. The right side of the hat was pinned up, holding a set of thick white feather plumes in place. She stepped back awkwardly; her right ankle buckled. The young man caught her by the shoulders and steadied her.

"Thank you," she said, looking him in the face. He was strikingly handsome; sandy-blond hair fell in layers, flicking out and hanging loosely around his shoulders. She felt her cheeks flush red. "I-I'm so sorry!" she stammered. His brow arched.

"Well, aren't you a fanciful young lass," he observed, leaning toward her. "You need not apologise; I was the one who left the place without lookin' where I was goin'."

'Fanciful?' she thought.

"Are you alright there?" he asked. "You've a fair bit of baggage there, would you like a hand in gettin' them to your room?"

"My room!?" she exclaimed, "what kind of a perv—" Both his hands shot up in defence.

"Hold up!" he broke in, taking a step back. "I know my reputation precedes me, but I've never made the assumption that I'll be takin' a girl to bed seconds after I meet her."

"But the thought did cross your mind," Arcaydia interjected, pointing a finger at him.   Pulling a wry face, he put a finger to his temple. "I like to think the part of my mind that resides up here has more common sense than that. Now, before we make any more assumptions, may I assist you in gettin' your bags to your room?"

Arcaydia thought about this for a few moments. She was on her own, and this man seemed like he knew the town well enough; perhaps he could show her around? He didn't seem all that bad.

"How about we introduce ourselves first?" she suggested. "I'm Arcaydia."

"Ah, how silly of me," the young man laughed and offered his hand. "I'm Larkh, captain of the *Greshendier*."

"Captain?" Arcaydia enquired, accepting the offer of a handshake.

"Aye that's right," he smiled. "Don't worry; you're not the first to give me such a look. I may be young for a captain, but where's the fun in bein' ordinary eh?"

That was true, but there was something else about him. What kind of captain was he? How many captains dressed, or spoke for that matter, like he did, she wondered. He assisted her with carrying the bags inside.

The first thing Arcaydia noticed was the musty smell of old wood, smoke and alcohol. It was cleaner and probably a lot older than many taverns. There were few customers at this time of the day, who glanced up from their tables. Larkh received a sideways glance from the innkeeper. "Back to raid the larder already?"

"I'm just helping the lady get her bags through the door Elsie," he assured her. The middle-aged woman regarded him sternly. "Stop lookin' at me like that! You're makin' me nervous."

"Larkh Savaldor, you are a scallywag," said Elsie Menow as she dried off a set of tankards. She set them back down on the shelf. Larkh suddenly looked like a scolded puppy, but his bright blue eyes danced with lively mischief. "And don't you give me that look. I know you're a kind soul, and valued customer though you tend to diminish my larder whenever you make an appearance."

"You're all the more better off for it ma'am," Larkh countered with a smile and wink. "I don't give generous tips to just anyone in business."

"Filling you up is like trying to fill an abandoned mineshaft," Elsie muttered. "I have to keep buying in new stock whenever you're around." Larkh closed his eyes and sighed, scratching the back of his head.

"Scallywag?" Arcaydia enquired.

"You've not told the girl, have you?" Mrs. Menow observed. "Most of the folk around here know you're a pirate, so if she didn't find out from you or I, she would from someone else." He looked over his shoulder at Arcaydia, whose eyes had suddenly widened, then angled his head to glance back at the innkeeper.

"Thanks Elsie, I wasn't *quite* ready for that." Elsie stuck her tongue out at him, drying another tankard.

"You certainly don't come across like any pirate I've read about," Arcaydia admitted. "The tales I've heard about are all about men who pillage indiscriminately." Larkh arched a brow, surprised that she wasn't more annoyed with him – or indeed afraid – for refraining from telling her about his dishonest occupation.

"You might say I'm a rare exception, but I do what I must," he said with a shrug. "The kind of stories you'll have heard reflect the truth, but y'see, we're all tarred with the same brush no matter what the circumstances."

"But you still plunder," Arcaydia pointed out.

"A little obvious, no?" Larkh said dryly. The corner of his mouth quirked up into a knowing smile. "Justice isn't always on the side of the law. You'll often find the authorities can be often just as dishonest as outlaws; even more so usually."

Arcaydia opened her mouth to speak, but any words that might have been there refused to come out. She'd remembered hearing something else that reminded her of this. He seemed to understand a lot more than he let on, and she was curious to know more.

Weary and hungry, she sat down at a table by one of the building's dusty casement windows covered with a thin film of old tobacco smoke. Her mind drifted back to the talks she'd had with Kalthis. His deep-rooted connection with nature made him appreciate the world on a level most simply didn't understand.

'If everyone took the time to take a walk outside to smell the fresh air and gaze upon the forests and mountains,

then maybe people would bond with serenity more often and be less inclined to divide, conquer and destroy. Sadly people are too caught up in their own selfishness to even consider doing anything about it. It is not within the nature of the majority,' he'd said to her. A forlorn expression crossed her face. Larkh's words also rang true in her mind. The law could often be as unjust as the actions of the criminals it sought to put behind bars. As she looked up, she jumped.

Larkh now sat opposite her, cradling his jaw in his right hand as he leaned forward, staring at her. "We have a daydreamer," he said.

"It's no reason to stare at me like I'm some ornament though," she objected.

"On the contrary, I regained your attention," Larkh retorted. "Shall we get your room an' your luggage safely out of the way? If you've nothin' better to do, I've the mind to show you around if you'd like the company."

"That sounds like a good idea," Arcaydia agreed, "I wouldn't mind having a bite to eat before I go out though. What about you?" Larkh shook his head.

"I've already eaten," he replied. He heard Elsie snort and mumble something like *"wait five minutes"* as she wiped the bar with a cloth. He rolled his eyes. "I finished up, then we walked into each other as I was leavin'."

"Aren't you busy though?" she asked. "I mean, you're a captain and—" Again the dashing captain shook his head.

"Not really," he shrugged. "My crew know me well enough. I come ashore when we make port to have a little time to myself. They know if I'm not back by a certain time, somethin' has likely grabbed my attention." Before she could speak, he lifted a finger and continued; "indeed that somethin' would be you, but I assure you that not everythin' I say is as you initially think it." Arcaydia glanced at the innkeeper.

Mrs. Menow gave a heavy sigh. "He's alright lass," she told her. "He is a renowned ladies' man, and the girls flock to him like seagulls to a tasty morsel, but he has a heart of gold...for a scoundrel." Larkh's grin spread from ear to ear. "Still, feeding him is like trying to fill a bottomless pit." The grin faded. Arcaydia chuckled.

"That sounds like Kalthis!"

"Who's that?" Larkh enquired.

"Oh...someone I know from home," she replied.

"Can I get you anything girly?" Mrs. Menow asked. "I've got plenty on the menu, but not sure how my stock levels are faring due to—"

"Stop blamin' me!" Larkh cried out. The innkeeper smirked. Elsie leaned over the bar.

"By the way, he's easy to wind up," she said with a wink.

"Don't I know it..." Larkh muttered.

"The soup I think," Arcaydia answered with a smile, chuckling at the playful digs Larkh was receiving. Mrs. Menow nodded, and disappeared behind the bar. She returned a moment later with a key and threw it to their table. Larkh was the one who caught it. "The key to your room," she said to Arcaydia.

"What about the payment?" Arcaydia asked, holding out her hand for the key. It did not drop into her hand.

"No worries girl; we'll sort that out later." She disappeared again.

"So," Larkh said, turning back to her, "why don't you tell me what brings you to Almadeira? Oh, an' why your friend has left you with all the luggage."

"Give me the key please," Arcaydia said with a frown.

"Answer my question first," Larkh pressed. He swung the key around his finger a few times as he leaned back in his seat.

"I never mentioned a friend," she replied in an attempt to avoid telling him as much as possible. If she did let slip too much information, especially to an outlaw, Melkhar would not be best pleased.

"That's too much luggage for one person to travel with lass," he observed. "If you were movin' in you'd have come with a carriage an' porter. You were travellin' *with* someone. Almadeira is a nice port, don't get me wrong, but there are a few areas that are host to the unsavoury types, especially after dusk. There's always a dark side to a place no matter where you go." He looked at the key before handing it over anyway. "Ah, room four. You're right next door to me."

"My companion is more my master than anything else really," Arcaydia admitted. "She's off on a mission at the moment and told me to find this inn to wait for her. She could be away a few days. And I thought you had a ship?"

"Aye, but as much as I love travellin' on board my old girl, life on board ship is never easy, so it's nice to take a break from it every once in a while," Larkh explained. He stood up and picked up two of the bags. "Come on, we'll get your stuff secured in your room. Then you can eat an' I'll show you around town. I'll even show you my ship as well."

Arcaydia couldn't deny that seeing the ship sounded like a wonderful idea, and if the city wasn't entirely safe, having someone around to look out for her would prove to be a good idea. She was still in training under Melkhar after all, so her abilities hadn't yet come to fruition. He obviously knew what he was talking about, and he'd probably been involved in many skirmishes with others of his kind as well as the authorities. It made her wonder though, why was he so well tolerated here? The innkeeper, Mrs. Menow, had said that most people in the city knew who Larkh was. Perhaps she'd find out eventually.

II
Cathra

Castle DeaCathra stood overlooking Tarvon Bay and the sprawling city of Cathra, capital of Adengeld, located west of the Valley of Daynallar. It had once been a Nays palace, but had fallen into disrepair and been rebuilt by the monarchs of more recent generations. Fierce turrets jutted upward on almost every corner, coupled with great flying buttresses on the elongated sections of the building, suggesting, according to Nays lore, that it had also once served as a holy fortress. Though it was quite the spectacle to look upon, it was still a shadow of its former self, the whitestone having dulled to a pale grey and its golden rooftops weathered and tarnished.

An adumbral mist manifested and swirled adjacent to the colossal main doors inside the entrance hall. It stretched upward and expanded into the form of a woman. A flowing black cloak with curved, barbed pauldrons fell from her shoulders and spilled across the floor, and long blonde hair hung straight and free down her back. She was beautiful except that her right eye was clouded and white, but she bore the Nays smoky kohl eyes.

One of the nearby attendants approached her; he seemed to be quivering. "Lady Zerrçainne, the King has awaited your return," he said, trying desperately to hide the shakiness in his voice. "He is ready for you in the audience chamber. Please go in."

With a stern nod, she proceeded through the marble hall toward the ornate golden doors at the far end, the soft clicking of her boots on the marbled onyx floor echoing throughout the towering halls. Instead of opening these doors, she walked through them. They rippled as still water does when a stone strikes its surface and reverted to their solid state once she had passed.

King Ameldar sat idly on his throne at the far end of the audience chamber flanked by statues and huge tapestries of

Adengeld's history. His dark brown hair hung in unkempt waves to his collar, and there was a little stubble around his chin which he periodically scratched with his left index finger. He was tall and muscular, though ran a slight paunch around the middle, and appeared to be in his late forties. Though he seemed disinterested in his surroundings, his attention shifted to Zerrçainne as soon as he caught sight of her. He quickly straightened his posture.

"What news?" The question sounded more like a demand. Zerrçainne tilted her head.

"Good afternoon to you as well Your Majesty," she remarked caustically. "The two I am searching for are in the same area at present, so with the *Noctae Venatora* on the prowl Kradelow's operation should run smoothly."

"I see." Ameldar scratched his chin again. "What about the soldiers we sent to intercept the Dragonmaster in that area?" Zerrçainne's expression darkened.

"They are dead." Her voice was deadpan. "Falthen lives, but the brigade was 'scattered' across the area in quite the literal fashion. I warned you that it is not wise for mortals to engage the Drahknyr in direct combat, let alone one of the Kaesan'Drahknyr without the right kind of power."

"Dead?" the king muttered under his breath. He didn't seem particularly surprised or concerned. "Hmm, is there any other way we can—"

"For mortals, unfortunately not. Not yet anyway," Zerrçainne interrupted. Ameldar frowned deeply. "The archana I have developed has not yet been fully implemented into your new weaponry. Patience is a virtue." His brow furrowed deeply.

'How dare you talk to me like that!' he thought. Zerrçainne smiled wryly.

"While I cannot read thoughts directly," she told him, "I *can* sense the intent behind them from looking into your soul with this eye. You cannot hide the truth from me." His expression darkened and became withdrawn. "Yes, you are right to withdraw that opinion now. To better explain the power of a Kaesan'Drahknyr, you may as well declare war on the very forces of nature. You should leave tackling their kind to me."

Reluctantly, Ameldar conceded the point. He would have no choice but to let her deal with them as she saw fit unless he wanted to risk losing more soldiers needlessly.

"For now then," he said, crossing his legs and folding his arms as he leaned back, "I will further the plans in operation with Duke Kradelow for the coup against Faltain within Lonnfeir's aristocracy. As a part of the plan we will rein those two troublemakers in and make a move on Sherne." A cruel smile spread across Zerrçainne's lips. She could see Ameldar was thinking much more deeply now. The ideas she presented to him were almost too good to be true. He couldn't have dreamed for a more cunning ally to assist him in conquering Armaran, and one who could travel across great distances in the blink of an eye, even if it did happen to be spiritual projection most of the time. It took a considerable amount of energy to make such journeys physically, especially considering her soul and spirit were now bound to the Dryft rather than the astral world of Nira'Eléstara.

"I trust you are continuing to work on that red dragon?" he enquired. "Since Dehltas failed to honour his sworn allegiance to Adengeld, I need a more compliant dragon in our ranks, and the promise I make to him I will uphold." Zerrçainne suddenly laughed loud and shrill, unable to stop herself. "And what do *you* find so amusing?" Ameldar frowned.

"Never before have I heard Rahntamein spoken of in the same sentence as the word 'compliant' much less heard it associated with him; or any dragon for that matter," Zerrçainne said darkly. "I require more time with him. He is ill-tempered at the best of times, and has only recently been roused from his long sleep. He is not yet in the right frame of mind to honour any pacts you might attempt to make with him. Do not worry though; I have been making gradual progress."

"Are the Nays not in allegiance with dragonkind?" Ameldar enquired.

"Strictly speaking it is the Drahknyr who make that possible," Zerrçainne replied in a disinterested tone. "It is true, though while that allegiance is unshakable there are still many draconic species like Rahntamein who refuse to be bound by any oath. Any beast that poses a significant threat to civilisation is destroyed. Besides I no longer associate myself with them. I, like the dragon, am also a renegade."

"He will have the entire Valley of Daynallar once we have conquered Armaran," said a young male voice. Prince Rannvorn stood against one of the marble pillars. His dark hair curled about his chiselled square face, coming to rest on broad shoulders. He bore much likeness to his father. Resting one foot against the pillar, he gazed assuredly at Zerrçainne, ambition burning in his determined slate grey eyes.

"Rann, you should not be here," Ameldar snarled, gripping the arms of his throne tightly.

"Pardon me, Your Majesty," Zerrçainne interjected coolly. "I was aware of his presence; forgive me for not saying so. I think he was right to hear it. He will be king one day after all; perhaps you might consider it a learning curve for him?" Rannvorn confidently brushed a hand through his hair, turning his head to hide the smug smile on his face from his father. The sorceress inclined her head a little toward the prince.

"Prince Rannvorn," she said, "I must remind you now that Rahntamein is a greater hybrid, and he will take whatever he desires whether Adengeld gives it to him or not. Have you ever faced a beast the size of this building with teeth the half length of your arms? Dragons are not easily bargained with. Not even Dehltas is as soft of heart as he has been made out to be. Unless you wish for your flesh to be melted from your bones, exercising caution is key to your survival." The smile fell from the young prince's face, to be quickly replaced with a scowl. She focussed on his core with her pearlescent white eye, reading his soul.

"No need to worry Your Highness," she assured him. "There are great tasks that you may yet be involved with, if your father will consent." Surprised, Rannvorn looked to his father, as did Zerrçainne. Ameldar considered this for a few long moments, drumming his fingers against the armrests. Finally he nodded.

"Very well," he agreed. "I understand Zerrçainne's thoughts regarding this. There are a few possible duties I can think of that you might well be suited to, but for now you are to go and begin your preparations for your training today. I will consider how you might fit into my plans for Faltainyr Demura and I shall discuss them with your tutors. Right now, I have further *private* business to attend to and so you will take your leave now." He gave the sorceress a sidelong glance.

Rannvorn bowed low, clenching his jaw to hide his resentment. He should be allowed to listen; he would be king one day after all. At a brisk pace he left through the western door, barely managing to contain the anger threatening to burst out. Ameldar watched him leave, noting Zerrçainne's attention was keenly fixed on his son.

"What do you see in him?" Ameldar asked. He now leaned on his left elbow with his chin cupped in his hand. Zerrçainne looked down her nose at the departing prince as a wry smile spread across her lips.

"He has potential," she replied matter-of-factly. "However, he is not an easy one to pin. He is loyal to you, of that you have nothing to worry about, but certain events may have forced him to call his feelings and objectives into question." Zerrçainne could read the truth in this man's heart without needing to look into his soul, although she had done so for clarification. "The Prince can be guided down the path you deem most favourable."

"This is most pleasing," Ameldar acknowledged, absent-mindedly stroking his chin again with a self-satisfied smile. "And I look forward to your efforts regarding the new archana."

"Just one question if I may, Your Majesty," Zerrçainne ventured. King Ameldar reclined and crossed his legs.

"Go on," he agreed, his brow lifting with interest while Zerrçainne's narrowed thoughtfully.

"How is it that I have never before met your son?"

"Ah, that would be because he has been in lessons or combat training when you have visited me," Ameldar replied. "Until today that is. He has spent most of his time recently in our barracks town, Kasserin. I will be having words with him later about his interference in my private meeting with you this afternoon."

"Might I ask that you let this one slide?" she enquired, the corner of her mouth curling up slightly.

"You have something planned for him?"

"I do."

Later that night, Zerrçainne made her way silently through Castle DeaCathra. Prince Rannvorn, crown prince of Adengeld, had piqued her interest.

She marched through the tall, vaulted marble corridors, past row upon row of statues depicting the DeaCathran royal family lineage. The ceilings were decorated with gold and ivory friezes and painted with classic murals of all the wars Adengeld had won. There were sculptures of dragons etched into some of them, and there were enormous tapestries depicting parties, battles and other events over the course of the nation's history.

The Prince's quarters lay at the top of a wide staircase at the end of a long corridor decorated with red carpet, more statues, and more royal tapestries hanging from walls lit by alchemical sconces; a basic form of archana taught in all magi academies and by alchemists that anyone with at least some skill in arcane arts could use. Alchemy was, in fact, one of the few kinds of magica she discovered she could still use freely without her newfound energy warping it.

Zerrçainne approached a mahogany door with a carved wolf insignia mounted in the centre. Slow and steady she knocked three times, and waited. It didn't take long for Rannvorn to respond. "Who is it?" he asked.

"Just a friend," she answered.

Rannvorn opened the door more out of curiosity than anything else. He wore little more than his black breeches and a matching unbuttoned tunic; his hair was wet. He felt his heart skip a beat as he looked upon the sorceress, trying hard to avert his gaze from her milky white eye. Zerrçainne guessed he was perhaps in his mid-twenties, though his demeanour reflected that of someone younger.

"Might I come in?" she asked. "There are a few things I'd like to discuss with you." Reluctantly the Prince stepped aside.

"What do you need?" he asked disinterestedly, sitting down on the edge of his large four poster bed. "It had better be something worth hearing; I'm not sure my father would be too happy to hear about you venturing into restricted areas of the castle."

"As if your father could stop me if he wanted to," Zerrçainne snorted in disdain. Rannvorn's brow knit. "To begin with, I'd like you to tell me a bit about your past at the Kessford Academy in Faltainyr Demura," Zerrçainne answered with a wry smile as she stepped inside. She was looking at a graduation plaque hanging on the far wall between two arched windows. "You knew a rather skilled young man there, didn't you?"

"And what would you know of that?" Rannvorn's frown deepened. He folded his arms. "Do not forget you're speaking to a member of the royal family in line to the throne."

"I have not forgotten," Zerrçainne replied coolly, "but if you wish to move up and take your father's place, then you will unfortunately have to at least look upon me as a social equal." Her white eye flashed. "I can see the very essence of who you are, Prince Rannvorn DeaCathra. I do not *see* memories, but I can feel them radiating from within those I happen to look at, and that in turn is enough to grant me enough information to pursue the answers I seek. That is the gift I have been given."

Rannvorn's confident demeanour vanished. His face was ashen as if all the blood had drained from it, and shivers shot up his spine like forked lightning. The hairs rose on the back of his neck, and suddenly he felt as if he wanted to flee, but there was something holding him there. Was it pride? Or was it something else? It was neither. He found himself oddly attracted to this woman.

"Tell me what I want to know," she insisted. "You were forced to train with someone who bested you, someone who made you feel small." How could she know all this? Her eyes widened with eager interest. "Tell me about him."

The Prince's expression darkened. These were memories that were rife with ill-feeling, and it was exactly what she was looking for. He took a seat by a table next to the arched windows at the back of the room and leaned on the table, resting his chin on top of his fist. Thunder rolled outside, accompanied by the occasional flash of lightning. And then the rain began to hammer against the glass behind him.

"My father sent me to the Kessford Academy about thirteen years ago," Rannvorn explained. "I didn't know of his plans then, but this academy was rumoured to be the best in Armaran for swordsmanship training. I was the top of my age group until a boy called Zehn joined about a year later; he rose in the ranks at least twice as fast as anyone else. He won every tournament he was entered into in single-handed sword combat, and he—" his fist clenched "he always showed me up in front of everyone else."

"Ah," Zerrçainne mused. "For someone of high social stature such as yourself I understand that must have severely wounded your pride." Rannvorn snorted.

"I heard he was sent to the academy a few years after the incident on the island of Ehyenn where his father was killed by a powerful sorceress—" The wicked smile creeping on to Zerrçainne's lips was enough to stop him mid-sentence. He felt his jaw slacken. "Don't tell me—"

Zerrçainne procured a swirling indigo-coloured orb from under her cloak. It was set in black dragon ivory shaped like some sinister-looking flower. Shivers ran throughout Rannvorn's body as she approached. The air around him suddenly felt heavy and oppressive, the candles went out and the flames in the alchemical lanterns flashed and turned blue. All he could see of the sorceress now was a silhouette with two eyes, one purple and the other a blinding, lurid white.

"Prince Rannvorn DeaCathra, I believe Zehn Kahner may be one of two keys that stand in the way of your father's ambition; an ambition that will come to rest upon your own shoulders," the black spectre whispered, her voice echoing eerily around the room. "I sensed something in the boy back then, but his power was clearly suppressed. You told me he rose in the ranks of swordsmanship rapidly, which can only mean one thing. They have tried to hide the truth all this time. Stand with me and I will not only give Adengeld the strength to conquer Armaran before it spreads across Aeldynn, but I will also grant you the power to take the throne and bring your enemies to their knees."

Rannvorn's gaze was fierce, and fixed upon the spectre of the sorceress in front of him. What she was offering was an opportunity he could not afford to refuse. He would take his father's place as king and rule all of Armaran, and he would have his revenge on the boy who humiliated *him*, a member of royalty. His father had never been a monarch fit for rule; he was too soft around the edges although his strength of will and ambitions implied otherwise. He knew the truth though. It was laughable Ameldar thought himself organised and formidable enough to become a prosperous emperor. Rannvorn rose to his feet. "What must I do?"

LORE
The Laws of Aevnatureis

*The ebb and flow of the tide joins past and
present so the future may be decided.*
Nays Proverb

Aevnatureis, the crystalline pillar supporting the world of
Aeldynn, is nature's governor, and the source of spiritus and
magica. Were it to malfunction, the whole of nature would
fall into disarray. Even the immortals would be affected.

The behaviour of Aevnatureis, otherwise known as the
Foundation, was studied long ago by the Nays and the
Kensaiyr. It is they who became fully aware of how to
harness its power and how to respect it, particularly via the
mining of its most multifarious form of crystal, the
Altirnathé.

At the appointed time of a child's growth following
conception, Aevnatureis bestows upon it a spirit, a soul and
an essence appropriate to its race. It will automatically
attune the spiritual aspects of an individual to itself, thus
anchoring them to it permanently with a limitation on the
prowess of each race's tolerance for magica, except for a
handful of races. The magica of the Nays, for example, is
said to naturally reach a little less than three quarters of
Aevnatureis' output capability, but those who are proficient
and developed in their magica may reach a somewhat higher
percentage.

The Galétriahn Mages of the Nays, however, are
exceptionally gifted individuals, born with a full three
quarter anchorage, but are capable of reaching the point
where the Drahknyr's natural levels begin. Drahknyr magica
levels begin at around eight tenths of Aevnatureis power,
but they may reach for up to almost nine tenths. So what of
the abilities of the Kaesan'Drahknyr?

Ancient texts state the Kaesan'Drahknyr are gifted with
a minimum of ninety-percent anchorage to Aevnatureis, and

may reach ninety-five effortlessly. However, if the correct conditions are in play, it is said they can draw upon its full magica output. The raw power of this kind of magica has the destructive potential of the most devastating of natural disasters, and could potentially cause such disasters to occur when and where they otherwise would not. It has been said, that with this kind of power, the Kaesan'Drahknyr are primal forces of nature in their own right.

Each race of Aeldynn bearing a natural anchorage to Aevnatureis has a lower degree of power in the amount of magica they are able to harness, positioned in a hierarchy of magical ability. Humans are included among a few races that have no natural anchorage, and so must tether themselves to it temporarily each time they use magic. The physical and mental repercussions are dependent on each individual's level of skill. A skilled human mage will be able to endure a higher percentage of magica than others, although there are limits to the magical capabilities of all races. Pushing oneself beyond the natural limit can shorten one's life expectancy.

It is believed the cataclysm that opened the channel we now call the Ene Canal and redirected Mount Dorne's source of magma caused the collision of high density magica that ruptured Aevnatureis during the War of the Eclipse. Legends claim this occurred when Aevnatureis itself was attacked by the entity known as Alymarn while the Kaesan'Drahknyr and the Lyte E'varis attempted to stop him.

CHAPTER 6

I
North Mazaryn Peaks

Zehn, sword in hand, was ready to engage Madukeyr in combat. What did he mean by his ability as a *key*? It made no sense. The fact his opponent was one of the Kensaiyr was strange enough; that he had the ability to manipulate his dreams made it all the more unsettling.

"I don't know what you're talking about," Zehn growled, the fog gracefully lifting amidst an abrupt shift in the wind as the gentle breeze began to gust. "You say I am a key. A key for *what* exactly?"

Madukeyr arched a brow at Raeon. *'The silver mage must be the guide for this one,'* he thought. Raeon gave the Kensaiyr an awkward glance in return.

"You are still on the path to awakening your true self," Madukeyr said placidly, inclining back toward Zehn. "It is to be expected. There is a side to us all that we must discover for ourselves. I'm only here to play my part as directed."

The Kensaiyr fell upon Zehn almost before he'd had the chance to blink. Zehn blocked his blades just in time. Madukeyr's speed was unreal; he definitely held nothing back.

The flurries of flashing steel were blinding in the midday sunlight, their blades slicing the air. Zehn wasn't even sure how he was capable of keeping up his defence. Something inside him was calling the shots; he could feel it. There were precious few openings in which he could successfully land an attack, so he had to be patient. But the look in this opponent's eyes was something else. He'd met

Kensaiyr before, but despite their piercing aquamarine colour, Madukeyr's eyes appeared entirely devoid of emotion while he fought.

It had only been a matter of minutes, but it felt like an eternity since the fight began. Zehn felt himself beginning to tire against such a relentlessly formidable opponent. How much stamina could Madukeyr possibly have? He somehow managed to draw upon a small well of hidden strength that lay deep within, allowing him to gradually edge on to the offensive with well-timed swings and thrusts swift enough to knock Madukeyr off balance. It was only then the Kensaiyr's expression altered, displaying a smile of satisfaction.

It wasn't surprising to see him switch tactics at this point. Madukeyr used his natural acrobatic abilities to his advantage, diving and rolling sideways gracefully out of harm's way as Zehn's swings and thrusts were skillful enough to clash blades, but not quite quick enough to land further blows. Madukeyr had already mentioned he was there to test him; he was now judging how he fared against an opponent who could defend in any number of different ways. It was a style Zehn had seen before all too recently, though there hadn't been the space or the time for a proper fight.

Madukeyr leapt back, laid his right hand against his left shoulder and bowed respectfully. "You're better than I expected. You will improve further as you awaken."

"I still have no idea what you're getting at," the mercenary replied, shaking his head as he slid his sword back into its scabbard.

"And you probably won't for a while yet," Madukeyr said, sheathing his blades. "Unfortunately, I'm not at liberty to discuss the details. You'll learn more if you can speak to your friend there. Tread carefully though when you finally meet the woman you're trying to track down. I warn you that for the time being you must *not* get in her way." He smiled knowingly and turned his attention to the great

Altirnathé at the rear of the shrine. "You'd also do well to stay out of my way," he added making his way toward it.

Raeon saw the anger flare up on Zehn's face, and caught him by the shoulder.

"Do as he says Zehn," Raeon said, watching Madukeyr approach the crystal as casually as a man would wander up to a bar in his local tavern. "What he says is true; it is not wise to interfere."

"You know something, don't you?" There was cold anger in Zehn's voice. He ran a hand through his shock of hair. "Of course you do, the Order of Silver studies the Nays and all forms of magica and archana. What is he even doing anyway?"

They both watched as the Kensaiyr removed a large grey gem from a gilded recess at the base of the structure, replacing it with a much brighter turquoise stone, sparkling in the sunlight. There was a low rumbling sound that grew louder and louder until it relaxed into a resonant hum reverberating inside the chests of all standing within thirty feet of it. There was a brilliant flash of light as the enormous crystal's colour brightened to match the gem Madukeyr had inserted into its base. In moments it glistened and gleamed like the rays of the sun against the ocean. The raw altirna fluid was visible, coursing back and forth beneath the surface as if through invisible veins.

"He is reactivating the Altirnathé," Raeon replied. "They have been given other more casual names, but that is the correct one. You will know altirna fluid and gemstones have been in short supply recently. They have numerous properties, but their primary functions are a little complicated to explain. You've seen the mine at the base of this mountain, but Altirnathé fountains like this one cannot be excavated. Think of them like trees that cannot be felled, but resources can be mined from their roots. There are only a handful of these in the entire world."

"It seems I'm the only one here who doesn't know what the hell any of this is about," Zehn huffed, leaning against the crumbling wall of the shrine. "I know the Faltain Navy uses altirna fluid in some of their warships, and they season wood with it to make it stronger and more watertight, but I do not understand why any of this is relevant to me."

"Perhaps it isn't directly relevant," Raeon suggested. "Perhaps it is something you must understand later."

Zehn opened his mouth to speak as a low guttural roar echoed across the summit, interrupting his train of thought. His sword flew from its scabbard as the shadow of a wyvern flew over the Altirnathé, circling once before coming into land. The shrine's foundations shook as the beast landed, scattering dust and grit. Zehn recognised it as one of the larger breeds. Its scales were ivory-white, and like all others of its kind its wings also served as its forearms. It stared at them both for a long moment, its fierce amber eyes focussing on the man brandishing a blade.

"Is this the one you spoke of Tseikané Madukeyr?" the wyvern asked, its voice deep and gravelly. Madukeyr watched as the Altirnathé settled, and then turned to approach the wyvern. He leapt up on to its back and sat between the long ridges across its neck.

"He is," Madukeyr replied. "You have impeccable timing, Avlashrenko." The corner of the wyvern's mouth turned upward into what might have been a sardonic smile, flashing razor sharp teeth.

"Kenadekhna wuten eth," [3] . Avlashrenko said to Zehn before inclining his head toward Raeon. *"Vokar naroh elsvaa magekan."* [4]

"Your path will become clear," Madukeyr assured Zehn. "I am but a mere stepping stone on that path. The greatest truths lie atop the highest of peaks, and so must you climb to find them."

---

[3] Well met saviour
[4] Strong path Silver Mage.

"Your words merely stir up the silt further, Kensaiyr," Zehn said bitterly, his sword still poised for attack. "No-one can see through muddy water."

"Then wait for the silt to settle and you'll find what I've left behind for you." Madukeyr's wry smile almost matched the wyvern's, but before Zehn could say anything more, Avlashrenko beat his wings. "We will meet again!" Madukeyr called over his shoulder. Zehn covered his face with his arms and Raeon shielded himself with his cloak as the wyvern's wings scattered dust and gravel in all directions. The two of them watched as they swept up into the clouds.

"How does anyone understand anything when they're faced with nothing but riddles?" Zehn snapped. "And what in the hell did that thing say anyway?"

"He said *'well met saviour'* to you, and *'strong path silver mage'* to me," Raeon translated. "Study of the draconic language was also a part of my tuition at the Archaenen."

"Is there anything you *don't* know?" Zehn muttered under his breath. His sullen words were enough to make Raeon frown.

"You asked me a question, and I happened to know the answer," Raeon replied icily. "If my intelligence insults you so much perhaps I had better take my leave and return to Aynfell." The response caught Zehn by surprise.

"Raeon, I-I'm sorry," he stammered. "Gods damn it I'm just so confused with all of this." *'If someone would just shed some light into this dark place I'm in, maybe, just maybe I'd be able to relax.'*

"Let's talk more when we reach Almadeira," Raeon said, shrugging. "For now, I think much lighter conversation is in order. We've been up here some time, so it might be best for us to stop for the night somewhere on the way down." Zehn gave a heavy sigh. He had a point; though it aggravated him to have to leave Savaldor free another night.

II
Len'athyr Sanctuary

West of Faltainyr Demura, early afternoon came to the Daynallar Mountains. The sun had fully risen past its zenith, but despite its warmth the chill of the mountains clung to the air. Kalthis stood beside Vharik high upon one of the peaks, watching a peaceful landscape that had remained undisturbed for generations. Madukeyr had left well before dawn, and Kalthis guessed he would be in the middle of his assignment that very moment. Over there it would be mid-afternoon.

The wind was cold but refreshing; the breeze subsided, contrasting with the warmth of the sun. Kalthis closed his eyes and lifted his head to the sky. There was nothing better to him than being surrounded by the wonders of nature. He wondered if many mortals ever stopped to appreciate the finer things in life; they tended to be shorter lived after all, so wouldn't it make sense to make the most of it rather than wage war? He breathed deep, and spoke into the ether, *"tén'arel vasthúveyr vél Armaran, arofenh aeu'te waiyhs. Éyn vaesyč aeu'te haewanyr, Len'athyr."* [5]

About three miles ahead of them across the chasm the air began to ripple as a great building seemed to materialise on top of a hidden plateau jutting out from the mountainside. The Len'athyr Sanctuary, built from whitestone, was decorated with statues and turrets shimmering gold in the sunlight. A great viaduct rippled into view, connecting the pass over a vast chasm to the doors of the grand temple. There were statues of Drahknyr warriors all along it. Each of the two structures complemented the grandeur of the other, and neither showed any signs of falling into disrepair.

Kalthis turned to Vharik and smiled sadly. "Come on," he said, "we have another hour's walk ahead of us across

---

[5] eternal watcher of Armaran, open the way. I seek the haven, Len'athyr.

that bridge as you cannot teleport any longer. The Galétahr, Dreysdan, will be waiting for us."

"Your mood has changed suddenly," Vharik observed. "What brought this on?"

"You should already have an idea of what it is," Kalthis sighed, staring at the Aevan Sanctuary of Len'athyr. "I am afraid of what the Voice of Armaran will tell me, and it's just one continent of many. I also think about what the others might say."

"Your unique mission was never an easy one," Vharik remarked as he lowered his eyes to look across the valley below them as they began to cross the viaduct. "With your soul being the only one the Voices will speak directly to on such matters, time is lost."

"That might be true, but you know it is because my soul is the only one of all seven Kaesan'Drahknyr that is considered to be balanced," Kalthis reminded him. "I do not think it is though. I rarely feel balanced or at peace with myself, but I do wish they would speak to at least one other."

They arrived an hour later. The great viaduct alone was a mile long, and now the giant golden doors of the Len'athyr Sanctuary loomed before them, etched with designs of the Drahknyr, dragons, and the cloaked Galétriahn Mages. In the centre was a distinct symbol; a great crystalline obelisk with a dragon perched either side of it, their tails coiling around its base. One dragon had been given a pair of blue gemstones for eyes, and the other, red.

'Quaetihs of Alabaster, and Shaorodes of Obsidian,' Kalthis mused. *'I wonder if, or perhaps when, both of you will see it fit to intervene. As one of your representatives, I hope that we can avoid that for some time yet.'* He took a deep breath. *"Galétahr Dreysdan, Éyn mahr Kaes—"*

The door opened before he could finish his sentence, and at once Kalthis knew the man standing inside the expansive entrance hall. He was draped in a black cloak with a wine red lining, and raven hair hanging to his collar;

his fringe sparse and somewhat unkempt. His face was stern and unreadable, but his dark eyes brightened at the sight of Kalthis.

"It has been a long time, Kalthis," he said with a voice as smooth as the marble walls around him. "You too, Master Vharik." The old sage nodded, pleased that he hadn't been left out, though his mind had drifted into reminiscence as he recalled his previous visits to this temple.

"Dreysdan," Kalthis smiled. "You always did prefer a personal welcome." Dreysdan smiled faintly, gesturing with his right hand for them both to come inside.

"Why hang back there, Kalthis?" he asked. "You hold the highest rank here."

"It is not my residence," Kalthis replied, following his host's gesture. "My rank comes after common courtesy." Dreysdan nodded and made his way toward the back of the vast hall. Vharik wandered in another direction.

"I'm going to the library!" the old sage called to them. "I'll meet up with you later." Kalthis glanced over his shoulder, waving in acknowledgement. He turned his attention back to the Galétahr, but his mind drifted to previous visits to Len'athyr many generations ago.

Through the marble corridors on the way to the room known as the Chamber of the Voice, Dreysdan told him what visions the Voice of Armaran had shown him. It was one thing for the Voices to show visions, but it was quite another to converse with them. Holding a conversation with a continental spirit had many limitations unless you were Kalthis. He had also gathered information from other Galétriahn Highlords occupying the other Aevan sanctuaries across Aeldynn. There was unrest across many nations, but no major battles had yet unfolded. The next place to be focussed on following Armaran was currently likely to be Icetaihn and the Shäada territory of Caran D'aerken.

"So, Galétyr Maiyah Galdestiar picked up on hostilities inside Caran D'aerken's borders from the Icina'Theniya Sanctuary?" Kalthis enquired, mulling over the details.

"That is what I was told," Dreysdan confirmed. "We can understand what is happening in terms of what the mortals are doing because it is in their very nature to disrupt the balance, and only the Voices can elaborate in any depth. But the Shäada, like the Aurentai, are grudge-bearers."

"That may be so," Kalthis agreed, "but this world is as much theirs as it is ours. Still, I cannot ignore the suffering they cause."

"You're in a deadlock then Kalthis." Dreysdan's observation rang true. In fact, it was truer than he wanted to admit, and in time he knew he would probably have to come up with some kind of solution, even if it was only for his own peace of mind. "While your sentiments and intentions are admirable, it is impossible to please everyone."

"That may also be true." Kalthis heard his own voice drop into a murmur as his mind began to wander. "But it doesn't make the subject any easier to think about."

As they reached the doors to the Chamber of the Voice, Kalthis felt the sharp tightening of the knot in his gut that had formed well before he even entered the building. He was about to learn three thousand years worth of Armaran's history in the space of a few hours, and he dared not think about how he would feel afterwards. Dreysdan opened the door for Kalthis, and remained there until he had passed.

Kalthis entered the dimly lit corridor leading to the chamber. His soft leather boots barely made a sound against the marble floor as he walked with a determined stride despite his blatant anxiety. He was already anticipating the world's descent into chaos, but it was his level of empathy that was in an entirely different league to that of everyone else. It was likely that reason alone that had caused the Voices to keep their deepest thoughts for his ears only. Such as it was that it was mandatory he was alone when he was to have an audience with a Voice.

"Kalthis, you have been called the Centre of Balance," Dreysdan had once said to him. *"You have always known this, and it is why you are entrusted with the words spoken*

by the spirits of the very land we walk upon." He was right again, of course. Even if the news was worse than he first expected, he could not allow himself to falter. Nevertheless, this task with which he was entrusted was one of such magnitude the pressure of it could easily overwhelm him.

What made it harder to deal with was it would always be him to bear that responsibility. It would never pass from him to someone else. He would at least try to encourage the Voices to consider lightening such a difficult and arduous burden, but unlike knowledge that was passed down from generation to generation in the society of mortals, he was one of the Kaesan'Drahknyr. He was eternal.

The final door to the chamber now stood before him. The resonance from within instilled within him a great sense of peace, which at least eased his troubled mind a little. He now felt compelled to enter, and did so without further hesitation.

Kalthis pushed through the great ornate doorway and gazed upon a chamber with many murals of natural landscapes painted all over the walls and the ceiling, separated only by the marble and gold friezes of the Nays, the Drahknyr and Galétriahn mages, and the Kensaiyr. In the centre of the room there was a milky white circle on the floor resembling a mirror, and an altar at the far end. With a gentle sigh, he relaxed and released his colossal white wings, allowing them to spread out into physical existence from their ethereal prison.

"Kalthis Ashkelleron..." The whispering voice was feminine. Its speech was slow, and it echoed across the room. A pillar of light lifted from the white mirror in the centre of the floor. "Draw closer, child of the ether." Kalthis obeyed. He stepped slowly on to the mirror, and was instantly bathed in its radiant light. "Kalthis, dear one, you are very anxious; the weight of how the world suffers makes you weary so soon after you have reawakened."

"Éyn mahr arfeín, Anu Amarey," [6]
Kalthis admitted, speaking under his breath.

"You are afraid," said the Voice of Armaran. "You are afraid of the mortals continuing to cause their own suffering and the suffering of all of Aeldynn, and that the situation grows worse. There are many conspiracies at present, many all at once, and they all lead back to one problem."

"One problem?" Kalthis asked.

"A woman," the Voice answered. "A Galétriahn renegade."

The thought sent shivers through every inch of his body. *'She can't mean.....!'*

"She has changed considerably," the Voice grew stiffer in her tone. "She has dwelt and rested very close to the Dryft for a very long time."

"What is her name?"

"I dare not speak it," the Voice replied. "She is on this continent at this very moment. I feel her presence as you would feel a sickness within your body or an infected wound. If I speak her name anywhere else in Armaran, she may know. Only the Kaesan'Drahknyr have been capable of it until now, but she is changed."

Kalthis thought for a moment. He knew that the information was vital for the world's survival, but in many ways he wished he didn't know. "What if I said it?" he enquired.

"It should have no bearing on you," the Voice mused. "If I were to speak your name while you stood anywhere in Armaran, you would sense it, but your voice will be safe speaking of one such as she." Kalthis stiffened.
"It's Zerrçainne."

The air around him shuddered, vibrating with fear and anger. He did not need any more proof that the name he had spoken was indeed the correct one, and he suddenly felt quite sick. Zerrçainne had once been a Galétriahn Highlord,

---

[6] I am afraid, Anu Amarey.

but she had turned renegade aeons ago and allied with a great evil that had been one of the greatest catalysts of the War of the Eclipse, though she had met with a convenient accident that should have killed her. Kalthis guessed in some ways, it had.

CHAPTER 7

I
Mount Dorne

In aeons past Mount Dorne had been a mighty volcano, but it had been extinct for more than three thousand years and had created what was now known as the Dorne Shaft when the magma drained under circumstances only remembered by the ancients. It lay a short distance east of the North Mazaryn Peaks across the Ene Canal; a route favoured by merchant ships.

Melkhar stood atop the mountain, her blazing red hair streaming out behind her like the flames of a great torch. She stared down into the enormous shaft, watching as the infestation of phandaeric fauna began to grow. A cruel smile formed at the corner of her drawn lips. She was waiting for the number of unholy spawn to increase. Under other circumstances it would be too dangerous to allow such creatures to multiply, but this way meant there would be more for her to kill. For something like this to end in mere moments had never been her style. *'It is time.'*

Two leather flaps on the back of her outfit parted as a pair of arch-shaped beams of light streamed out from between her shoulder blades, stretching up several feet above her head and curving downward just shy of her ankles. Her great white wings were bathed in a shimmering aura as they materialised. Shining brilliantly in the sunlight, they were a bold statement of empyrean power to anyone who looked upon them.

Around her head a helmet with a half-mask took form, showing only the lower half of her face with the eyes blacked out to any onlooker. This elaborate mask took on the features of a dragon with horn details stretching back from the cheekbones and temples. A suit of ebony armour followed, manifesting around her elongated frame and long limbs. The pauldrons, bracers, and greaves all extended into sharp points for as much use for offence as defence. It gleamed like polished obsidian and was embossed with intricate silver patterns near the edges. It had been the final image in the eyes of millions of victims across the ages.

There was a powerful burning sensation deep in her solar plexus; a feeling she had yearned for during her long sleep within the Naturyth; the lust for battle and the destruction of her enemies. She thrived on that feeling. It was euphoric. There was nothing more thrilling than vanquishing her enemies. Casually removing her malicious draconic sword from its scabbard, she spread her colossal wings and leapt head first down the gaping hole.

Dozens of demons and mutated creatures fell in less than a minute, their dismembered bodies dropping into the depths of the lifeless volcano. They were a pernicious threat to all natural things, and must remain sealed away in the lower realms of Phandaerys and the demonic underworld of Dhavenkos Mhal.

It was unlikely there could be anyone who relished such carnage on the level she did. When that mask covered her eyes, none could witness the madness in her chilling gaze when she went into that bloodthirsty frenzy. Some had called this behaviour utterly deranged, but what frightened them the most was when they learned that her sanity was unquestionably intact.

Presently, she was relying entirely on her ethereal and astral energy stores. These energies allowed her to push on and on without growing physically tired. Eventually those stores would diminish, and she would require rest and nourishment in order to restore them, but it would take many hours of combat before she would become entirely reliant upon her physical energy at her current level of restoration. When she had regained her full power, the amount of power at her disposal would be unfathomable.

She stopped momentarily; her wings beat steadily as she hovered in one spot to survey the level of activity beneath her. There was little to see in the darkness of the shaft, but she deduced the caves would be crawling with Phandaeric fauna, so rather than run the risk, she thrust her right hand upward and cast a barrier around the entrance of the shaft to ensure none of the abominations could escape. Sensing the direction of the portal, she dived down further underground.

II
Dorne Shaft

The empty magma chamber sat almost two miles deep, but no-one knew how far the tunnels and caverns extended as a result of the incident that occurred here over three millennia ago. A great cataclysm had cut Mount Dorne's power source from the world's core, and parts of the stratum underneath had either collapsed or shifted, redirecting the magma and opening up the many networks of caves and tunnels. Somewhere in those depths there was a portal to Phandaerys that had to be closed.

Melkhar finally reached the bottom and surveyed her surroundings. The air was dangerously humid and moist, warranting a cool protective barrier to ward off the heat.

The walls were an amalgam of colours ranging from mustard yellow and red to purple and black. The remains of the magma that had once filled this chamber had left crystallised gems that would bring wealth to anyone who dared set foot down here, but Melkhar ignored them. She didn't need them. Besides, ordinary mortals wouldn't survive long in such temperatures without adequate protection. She turned, surveying every direction, sensing from where the dense, oppressive energy of Phandaerys emanated; the tunnel leading north-west.

Parts of the tunnels were too narrow and low for her to fit through with her wings, forcing her to dismiss them. Other sections required her to bend almost double. When she dropped into a larger cavern, she ploughed through any abominations that still dared to live. They were far fewer in number now; their mutilated corpses lay scattered all around her, but it wouldn't be long before the portal began to spawn more.

She needed to complete the task as soon as possible; as incredible as her endurance and stamina were, they were not infinite. The Drahknyr could withstand many hours of both physical and magical combat, but the Kaesan'Drahknyr harboured even greater amounts of energy. The miasma emanating from Phandaerys feasted upon the energy it took to maintain her own protective barrier; so it was appropriate that her kind had an ample supply of energy and magica. Despite the negative energy siphoning her power, Melkhar marched onward, free of concern.

Ordinary mortals and even some immortals wouldn't stand a chance if they came into contact with such a dense concentration of the toxic miasma of Phandaerys. It would kill the weak in a matter of seconds, the strong in a matter of minutes, or for those who were particularly tough, it mutated them instead. Even the crystals down in the depths had grown dull, and yet they resonated with a foreboding aura seeping out as a result of sinister energy absorption of the same miasma clinging heavily to the walls like moss. She was close; she felt the air growing fouler with every step.

Eventually, the cave opened up again and at the far end was the portal; a large Phandaeric crystal surrounded by a dense cloud of miasma. The indigo-black crystal jutted upwards into the cavern; a gigantic stalagmite resonating a low humming sound, its power circulating, rising up into the damp, stagnant air.

The ground around it had sunk as though melted by an acidic substance, and it was gradually turning a dark purplish colour. It was from here the plagued monsters crawled; some were humanoid, some had originated as beasts, and there were even those that were draconic. Others that emerged were entirely of the Phandaeric realms; even occasional demons originating from Dhavenkos Mhal broke through.

Melkhar's ears pricked up at a faint thrumming that very quickly grew louder and louder. It became a heavy throbbing noise that reverberated through the putrid air like a heartbeat. Her sword was already poised for the attack. The one who appeared before her was a blonde woman cloaked in black, one eye milky white. She stood amidst the swirling miasma, unfazed by the poisonous gases.

"Zerrçainne..." Melkhar growled beneath her breath. "How can you possibly be alive?"

"How nice to see you too my dear cousin," Zerrçainne said coolly, smiling thinly. "It's been, what, over three thousand years since we last saw each other?" Melkhar's brow knit into a frown. She said nothing. "Come now, remove your mask," Zerrçainne added. "I haven't seen those dangerous eyes of yours for so long."

The corner of Melkhar's mouth dropped, and rather than dismiss the helmet she lifted it off her head into her right hand while retaining her rigid posture. She sensed the change in Zerrçainne's power, but it wasn't enough to concern her.

"Just the same as I remember you," Zerrçainne said, her tone almost playful. "Do you still love Zairen?"

"That's none of your business," Melkhar answered with disdain, "but you are far from the same."

"The mortals say *'what doesn't kill you makes you stronger.'* That's certainly true in my case don't you think?" the sorceress laughed. "Not that you'd know anything about that though. You have the privilege of getting back up again."

"I wouldn't call it a privilege," Melkhar argued. "Your new soul-sight is an unquestionable benefit though, isn't it?

So let's cut to the chase. You're here to stall me because you know you cannot kill me. At the same time you're making an attempt at reading my soul." She placed her helmet back on her head, smiling thinly. "Tell me," she continued. "Did you see *anything* of interest?"

Zerrçainne forced back the sense of dread that leapt into her core. Melkhar knew she couldn't read her? How was that possible? The Kaesan'Drahknyr weren't mind readers. Could it be just a guess? She chuckled darkly in an attempt at remaining nonchalant. "You always were good at hiding your feelings, and it seems you're just as good at hiding your soul as well. You're right though, let's not waste time."

The sorceress thrust her left arm out to the side, casting bolts of black lightning that wound down from her shoulder and out through her fingertips, striking at the rock faces surrounding the only exit leading back to the main shaft. The cave exit and its tunnel shattered upon impact as Zerrçainne struck out several more times at the ceiling before fading into the portal just as Melkhar's sword bore into her flesh.

Melkhar looked down at the miasma attempting to wind its way up her legs. She stepped back, spitting the words *"estuhs makh'e!"* [7] The virulent mist recoiled and hissed as a minor shockwave forced it to recede. She looked up at the crumbling ceiling of the cavern, then back to the Phandaeric crystal. *'So, she wants me out of this region and will go as far as to either bury me or force me into taking a detour,'* she thought. *"Kécn velyh. Éyn qelna'the vhe felhna,"* [8] she uttered under her breath.

If anyone had stood nearby, they'd barely have had time to blink. Three blinding sword strokes carved the crystal into six pieces, shattering them instantly into a fine dust that drifted idly to the cavern floor. The resonance ceased and the miasma vanished, leaving the cavern floor

---

[7] Stay back!
[8] Nice try. I will not be far.

blackened as if it had been scorched. No more demons would be crawling out of there again.

As the ceiling caved in, Melkhar dashed for the nearest exit, moving at breakneck speed through the former lava tunnels. Many of these subterranean territories may already be sealed off; leaving the only physical exit the tunnel she had entered which had already collapsed. She ran, ducked, rolled and jumped while the earth continued to tumble down behind her until she flew off the edge of a chasm and spread her wings again as she plummeted. Despite the invisible forcefield keeping her temperature regulated she felt the heat rising from the depths of the ravine below.

Glancing around, she took note of numerous openings that could take her anywhere. Hovering in midair, she considered her rather limited options. There were two: the first was simply continue moving forward and hope that she would eventually find a way out – which was unlikely – or find the nearest astral rift leading into Nira'Eléstara, and then look for the next available one leading out. The second option meant that she could end up somewhere other than where she needed to be, but at least it guaranteed a way out and would save time.

Melkhar brought her right hand up and rested her index and middle fingers on her helmet between her eyes, concentrating. Her wings beat steadily, keeping her aloft as she concentrated. She murmured a few words under her breath, *"aeu'te waiyhs vhar Nira'Eléstara, svahth mhir."* [9]

A short distance south of her location, a pale blue glyph formed in midair over the ravine. It spread into an oval-shaped opening to reveal a dreamlike landscape rich in nebulous colours. At least she didn't have to go far to gain entry. Hastily she lunged for it and vanished.

---

[9] The way to Nira'Eléstara, show me.

III
Len'athyr Sanctuary

Kalthis emerged from the Chamber of the Voice, his face a picture of turmoil. His great wings still perched authoritatively upon his back, though it was obvious he was weary. He saw Dreysdan approaching as he left the entranceway. It was to be expected; he'd been in there a long time. Before the Galétahr had a chance to speak, the troubled Kaesan'Drahknyr shook his head. "I think I need some time alone Drey," he said.

Dreysdan caught him by the shoulder as he stepped past. "Kalthis," he said. "I wasn't going to ask you to yield the words of Anu Amarey the instant you left the chamber. I was concerned because you had been in there much longer than is usually necessary. Direct connection with the continent drains your ethereal and astral energies, which drains your physical body rapidly; you know this."

"It was necessary," Kalthis countered. "So, I happened to give up a little more energy to Anu Amarey. That energy will be used to nurture the world, so I do not mind."

"You'll still need to get a good amount of rest," Dreysdan argued. "I trust you are at least staying a few days? I hoped that you and Vharik would join me for supper this evening at the very least."

"I will rest after I have reflected on what I was told. It will be impossible for me to rest until I have processed it." This compromise was not negotiable. "Of course we will eat with you tonight. It would be unwise not to."

"Good," Dreysdan smiled faintly. "Now I must pry Vharik away from the library."

Kalthis stood and watched him go. He knew Dreysdan felt much the same way as Melkhar did about the societies of mortals. The Galétahr had awakened almost sixteen years before him and had spent some time among them as part of an assessment, but he never spent too long away from his appointed outpost. The Galétriahn Highlords and the

Drahknyr took turns resting in long sleep, but the Kaesan'Drahknyr had slept for over three thousand years this time.

It wasn't surprising Dreysdan belonged to the same order as Melkhar. It was called *Nauohdr vél Ahdonyr*, known to others as the Order of Ebony or the Black Order. They were known for their ruthless tactics when dealing with their enemies. Melkhar was their leader after all, and Dreysdan was second in command. Although the Drahknyr and Galétriahns were two distinct factions, they made up a single order in their respective colours.

A Kaesan'Drahknyr was always the head unless they were at rest; they were the generals of each legion of Drahknyr. Galétriahn Highlords were always second, governing all mages. The Galétriahn Highlords without legions acted independently when they were not at rest, or they would take over from another within the order of their affinity.

Kalthis eventually came to a halt standing atop one of the golden turrets on the northern side of the temple. The chill mountain breeze was refreshing. He tilted his head back, closing his eyes, enjoying the moment as it swept back his river of black hair and ran under the great arc of his wings. It was a moment of exultant bliss he truly needed. He knew how to find moments like this when times called for desperate measures. Despite this, his mind still raced over the network of information that had been passed on to him from the Voice of Armaran today. It was then he realised his cheeks were damp.

He drew in a deep breath, telling himself it was no use letting his weariness get to him when his mission had barely begun, but it would still take a plan of action to dispel this melancholy. The voice of Anu Amarey echoed throughout his mind and soul; *'you may well remember Kalthis, that though I am immovable I am also movable. I am still and yet I am restless. I am awake even when I sleep. The people in the west are readying for war. The kingdom called Faltainyr*

Demura doesn't know of an impending doom. I am but one Voice.'

"And I am but one of the Kaesan'Drahknyr, Anu Amarey," Kalthis had countered. "Time may be wasted simply because I am the only one the Voices will speak to. I would like for you to consider at least one other."

'You are the only one we can fully trust to listen to our cause without discrimination, Kalthis,' Anu Amarey protested.

"I can only do so much," Kalthis replied solemnly. "I have given myself the additional task of seeking out another you might be able to trust. However, I do not think it will be one of the other Kaesan'Drahknyr."

Following this reflection, he leapt from the turret and glided down into the nearest courtyard. That conversation had been as fluid as it had been tense, but despite Anu Amarey's silence at this proposal, she hadn't shown disapproval. There were several other duties a Kaesan'Drahknyr had to contend with, and war was the greatest of them all. Mortal and immortal races alike were of the belief that he and the other six could well be gods given their abilities, but it wasn't what they were, nor was it their aspiration.

The one thing he thought he might truly envy about mortals was their ability to die. The only way for most immortals to die was to be slain. The Drahknyr could die in battle albeit with incredible difficulty, but they would be gifted with a new body given time. The seven Kaesan'Drahknyr on the other hand simply had to endure. If death did take them it was only a matter of time before they regenerated and were on their feet again, but it took forces beyond reckoning for them to die. Their only true respite was hibernation within the Naturyth when their spirits would return to Valdysthar for the duration. He thought that perhaps it might be a little easier to bear if some real living came out of it. They were always called for a purpose, for duty. There was little time for luxury.

He quickly pushed those thoughts from his mind, telling himself it wasn't going to make him feel any better. He stared up at the blazing orange sky as the sun slowly descended behind the mountains, and dismissed his wings. With their weight lifted from his back, he re-entered the sanctuary and strode briskly toward the dining room. There was no time to nap before dinner. He would have to make sure he retired to bed shortly afterwards.

Wandering through these halls made him feel out of place. It didn't matter how many generations he spent in the company of the other Nays nations; he was still a Marlinikdhan tribesman and his heart would always be with the wilderness. He was still dressed in his tribal leathers; he avoided wearing his uniform or any smart attire as much as possible. *'How many others in the world feel this kind of separation from the societies they live in?'* he wondered. *'Far too many, I imagine.'*

Here, the extensive marbled halls and corridors were complemented by gold pillars, arches and statues crafted by the most experienced and highly skilled of Nays artisans. Nays architecture was always of the same calibre of craftsmanship, no matter the style. The sheer grandeur of the great buildings spoke for themselves, but what of the grandeur of the forests, the plains and the mountains? He rarely found the time to immerse himself in the landscapes where he belonged.

When he reached the dining hall, he found the far end of the long table laid out ready. He was just in time. If he'd been much later no doubt Dreysdan would have come looking for him again. The Galétahr respectfully offered him the seat at the head of the table, but he politely declined. His awkwardness always became apparent whenever he was expected to take the seat on formal occasions. As far as he was concerned, Dreysdan was in charge of the Len'athyr Sanctuary, so that seat was his.

Kalthis silently thanked the lives of the animals sacrificed for the meal and took for himself a reasonable share. He was glad Vharik's attention was on Dreysdan; he doubted he could withstand much of his babble this evening. The old man was wittering on at the poor Galétahr though, seemingly unaware his victim's eyelids were drooping. For a moment it looked as if the man was just as burned of energy as he was. He figured it was appropriate Madukeyr wasn't present; he wasn't built for idle banter and had about as much patience as a ravenous wolf. Vharik's endless babbling could dull the minds of even the most patient of people. In a desperate attempt to escape, Dreysdan suddenly sat upright and turned his attention to Kalthis instead.

"Kalthis," he said, interrupting Vharik. The old man was about to protest, but Dreysdan lifted a hand, silencing him. "Are you ready to shed any light on the situation that concerns all of Armaran?" Kalthis finished his mouthful and shrugged.

"I will admit I lost myself in thought over it and did not find the time to rest," he sighed, "but my mind is a little clearer now, and I will tell you what I can." Kalthis tilted his head toward the ceiling thoughtfully. He cast his mind back to the long conversation with Anu Amarey earlier that day, and drifted into a kind of reverie as he explained the details while he ate.

"We know the information given by the Voices is always vague. They cannot tell us the details of what goes on in the world. Just as a baby cannot tell you in words why it cries; it could be hungry, or perhaps it could be in pain. An animal cannot tell you in words what it wants. It might try to show you instead. Interpreting what a spirit of a continent says is not so different." Kalthis failed to conceal the turmoil that stirred within him.

"Anu Amarey told me there is great power welling in the west. This comes from Adengeld. She senses ill intent toward the east in Faltainyr Demura. This means Adengeld will wage war on the Faltain Kingdom. There is also malign intent linked to the west, and given the location I think it might be concentrated in Lonnfeir. I believe there are people who are working for Adengeld." He thought for a long moment, feeling a sudden tightness in his chest. "There is also an incredible power awakening on the island of Ehyenn. You both know what that power is. Much of this was mentioned by Dehltas, but I heard the story from Anu Amarey as well. I do not need to decipher the story since the Master of Daynallar has already shed enough light on it." His gentle face hardened. "That is as much as I can make sense of right now."

Dreysdan's expression darkened. He steepled his fingers and leaned on his elbows, glancing first at Vharik, and then to Kalthis. "You speak of Rahntamein, the renegade.....the *gal'etden drahkouen* chained in the underground of Ehyenn. And what of Dehltas? You say he has already spoken to you on your way here?"

"It was Dehltas who warned Madukeyr and me of his intended release," Kalthis answered. He shifted in his seat. "Adengeld's military approached him with a request that he join them in waging war on Faltainyr Demura. Dehltas refused, was branded a traitor, and thanks to an old enemy of ours they have access to Rahntamein. They wish to bargain with him."

"Zerrçainne..." Vharik muttered under his breath. Dreysdan's head snapped round to look at him.

"What!?" the Galétahr's shock surprised them both. "But she—"

"Didn't die," Kalthis finished. "Vharik, you look as if you might be able to shed more light on this."

The old sage chewed his lower lip thoughtfully. Putting his story into words wasn't going to be easy in front of this Galétriahn Highlord and Kaesan'Drahknyr. He tapped his left index finger on the table nervously.

CHAPTER 8

I
Saldour

Further west, on the meadows above the cliffs of Saldour, stood the manors and estates of all the nobility in Lonnfeir. The meadows here were vast; the majority of them owned by the highest ranking nobility, though they were otherwise open to travellers and the general public. There was an abundance of different species of flower, too many to name, all blooming at different times of the year. Here the rare blue rose grew; a flower scarcely seen elsewhere in Aeldynn.

The entire sprawling city of Saldour could be seen from the clifftop; its grand whitestone walls and pathways set upon tiers jutting forward like enormous steps a giant might walk upon. It was the home of the Faltain Navy, and boasted the largest harbour in all of Armaran, extending out from the bottom of the cliffs, embraced by a fortified sea wall.

The manor furthest east on the meadows almost backed against the North Mazaryn Peaks; it had once belonged to the Savaldor family before tragedy befell them. It has since been occupied by the most powerful family in the region, the Kradelows.

The Kradelow family already owned the greatest stately house in Lonnfeir, and there had been no arguments over who was going to take over the Savaldor home. Other bids offered for the manor had been outbid by the Kradelows tenfold. There was no-one to inherit the Savaldor fortune, for the sole survivor had relinquished his rights to it, having outlawed himself by the time the news that he still lived reached Saldour.

The Kradelow estate was located on the western side of the meadows. It was perched higher up on the hillside than any other stately house, and naturally afforded the best view of the city and the surrounding bay. Even the large island of Gaieah and its many islets could just be seen from there. The estate encompassed five thousand acres and incorporated almost half the land the meadows covered.

From a burgundy velvet armchair in a sitting room large enough to be a ballroom, Duke Jarlen Kradelow sat watching the city and its grand harbour. Of course, there was also a ballroom, three times the size of this room.

Jarlen was a tall, well-built man who once served in both the Faltain Kingdom's army and navy, though his figure was now giving way to the generous indulgences his wealth had bought. His hair was dark, cropped and slicked back but there was a considerable amount of grey at his temples with a short beard to match. In his right hand he held a glass of red wine and was smiling to himself; his plans were going well. An abrupt knock on the door interrupted these pleasant thoughts, making him frown. "Enter," he said sullenly.

A young maid stepped into the room. "Ambassador Leyal Al'Hallané, from Adengeld has just arrived sir," she said shyly.

"Send him in then." Kradelow gave an exasperated sigh and sipped his wine. The maid gave a nod, curtsied and left the room quickly. Moments later the ambassador walked in, and waited. "Come over," was all Kradelow had to say. The ambassador did as asked.

Leyal matched Kradelow in height, and was dressed all in black with a cloak draped over his shoulders. His wavy mousy brown hair was tied back neatly in a short ponytail but the loose strands falling unevenly across his lean face made it obvious he had stepped in from the road only minutes earlier. The funnel-shaped ears that might be likened to those of a long-eared bat told Kradelow to which race he belonged. *'Damned fey,'* he thought. *'This one must be Aurentai from the looks of him.'*

"What of His Majesty Ameldar's plans?" Kradelow asked, not bothering to offer the man a seat or to even look in his direction.

"There are several matters at hand milord," Leyal said coolly, quickly taking note of the man's lack of courtesy; "one concerning the Kaesan'Drahknyr, another relating to the movements of the King's forces, and of course the Artefacts of the Varlen."

"Go on."

"The Lady Zerrçainne has forced the Kaesan'Drahknyr known as Melkhar Khesaiyde into the astral realm by means of an escape from the Dorne Shaft. In theory, she shouldn't be close enough to have an impact on Rahntamein until the damage is done, but then—"

"Anything else?" Kradelow interjected, dismissing the thought of the Kaesan'Drahknyr. "You talked about Varlen artefacts." The impatient tone in the duke's voice made the ambassador clench his teeth in irritation.

"Your men should be made ready to move out to Almadeira to invade the city tomorrow evening." Leyal did his best to hide his aggravation. "The pirate you and the sorceress seek is docked there now. I received word from one of my men just as I arrived here. That odd storm we had left his ship with only a few minor repairs to be done, so if we don't move fast we shan't catch him—"

"You mean Saldour's ship, MY ship!" Kradelow snarled. "That little bastard stole it from the navy, and that ship holds secrets, I know it! I want to know what they are, and one way or another I'll have the answers out of that spoiled brat before I have him hanged." He waved his hand. "Continue." Leyal's cold grey eyes glared as the duke continued to stare out of the window. *'How I wish I could gut you here and now.'*

"According to my subordinate, he is searching for Varlen Artefacts too and may soon be in possession of one.

It seems a lady friend of his has something of that description to trade with him."

"That upstart gets me riled!" Kradelow snapped, his face reddening. "That artefact must be taken from him, you understand?" He then relaxed a little and drummed his fingers against the arm of the chair. Apparently he wasn't interested in any details, ignoring the fact he hadn't even said the pirate was yet in possession of such an item. *'Do you even know what the Varlen Artefacts are?'* Leyal wondered.

"Yes sir. There is one other thing though," Leyal said, pretending to sound disquieted. Kradelow turned his head toward him. "The unit His Majesty sent in an attempt to stall the Kaesan'Drahknyr, before the Dorne Shaft incident that is—"

"Yes yes, get to the point."

"They were annihilated."

"What!?"

"They were found quite literally in pieces just beyond the meadows close to the road leading to Almadeira. The sorceress says it is the work of one of the Kaesan'Drahknyr as they are properly called, and that the King was incorrect in sending anyone, out there to attempt to stop her. It was Falthen who found me on the road and informed me. He's very shaken by the experience. Zerrçainne has now stalled her though."

"Fairy tales. When did this supposedly happen?"

"This morning, a short distance from the entrance to the Undersea Passage." Leyal briefly closed his eyes to keep himself from rolling them. *'Fairy tales indeed,'* he thought sarcastically.

Kradelow shook his head. All he cared about was furthering his own plans with Ameldar's assistance and bringing down the one pirate that had caused him so much grief. Whatever had happened, he would have the matter covered up with a story, perhaps a report of vicious bandits in the area would suffice. There were ways of achieving this;

after all, he'd had the Savaldor family wiped out to conceal his plans – except the boy had survived. As if he cared about Ameldar's forces and fairy stories! His forces were more than adequate to take Faltainyr Demura with as little fuss as possible, but it bothered him that fables were being used to explain a field full of dismembered soldiers. There were bandits who could be just as vicious if they felt like it, they could take the blame.

He enjoyed war, but this way was much more effective for guaranteed success. He'd rallied up support gradually over the years, promising wealth and benefits to anyone who pledged their allegiance to him. Anyone who might have been loyal to King Jaredh had been dealt with in the most permanent way possible. Leyal might be one of the Aurentai, but he was still one of the *Noctae Venatora*, and they were a considerably useful faction to have on his side.

Of course, it had taken more than fifteen years to get to this stage of the game, but Ameldar's army hadn't been large enough to gain the upper hand so easily back then. Now it was something to be reckoned with. With Kradelow's men to back him up, Ameldar was sure to win, in theory. Kradelow had his own designs to think about; the King of Adengeld was a mere stepping stone, but why did everything have to be so complicated?

"It sounds like all is going well then," Kradelow shrugged, "though not for Ameldar's scout brigade of course. Shame, I could have made some use of them. I will send the word for our forces to start getting ready."

"Ah, I advise that you do not send them just yet sir, but do mobilise them," said Leyal, a hint of amusement rising up on his face. "I have a team already set up in Almadeira overseeing the town's activity; that's how I know something of Savaldor's whereabouts. I have some ideas to make sure that your operation runs as smoothly as possible." At this, Kradelow actually smiled.

II
Almadeira

Larkh lay on his bed in the Silver Gull Inn. Old cream curtains fluttered in the cool breeze swept in through the open shuttered window of the tiny room, just large enough to fit in a single bed, a bedside table, small wardrobe, chest of drawers and a chair. The fact it was plain didn't bother him; he found it quaint and comfortable enough. He had to be in the right frame of mind to stay in the kind of places Mey had a penchant for, but in Almadeira, if a room was available, he always stayed at the Silver Gull.

He brought his knees up and crossed them, wrapping his right hand around the back of his head, idly flipping a coin across the knuckles of his left hand. He thought he'd heard the roar of a wyvern earlier, but nothing had happened since; he shrugged it off. After showing Arcaydia around a small portion of Almadeira, she'd begun succumbing to fatigue after having been so long on the road, so he'd brought her back to the inn, telling her, as she closed the door to her room, he would take her to see *Greshendier* later.

On the way back, he'd pointed out where the man named Marceau Saiyinn lived, but he wasn't home. Some of the locals said they'd seen him leave the city in a hurry, but no-one knew why or where he was going. He found himself wondering why her companion had left her to drag all the luggage to the inn by herself; it seemed odd. Why hadn't her master at least helped her into town before leaving? It was just another question he couldn't hope to answer.

Just for a little while he enjoyed having a bit of time to himself while the repairs on *Greshendier* were being seen to, though he would have to inspect the ship soon. It was not good for him as captain to let his crew do all the work while he continued to please himself. He sighed contentedly, closing his eyes, and soon found his mind drifting back and forth between the past and the present.

He compared his mind to the waves of the ocean that washed back and forth along the shoreline, but it didn't matter how many times he tried to stop himself from being swept too far back. He knew it was the ocean's way to drag one out of one's depth should they swim too far from the shore, and that's when he would find himself in a state of melancholy. It was where he was headed now, and within moments the coin was on the bedside table and his hand gripped the gold locket around his neck. He swung his legs around the side of the bed and sat up, his stomach twisting into a knot. Tears welled in his eyes.

'Damn it! Why?' he thought. *'Every time.....after all these years, I still...'* Tears splashed into his lap as the beautiful multi-coloured meadows above the cliffs of Saldour invaded his mind. Then came the grand white manor house on the far eastern side of that meadow with its gravel boulevard lined with tall trees. Next he saw his father with his light brown hair cropped just above his collar, swept back tidily, befitting a man in the Faltain Navy's admiralty. His father spoke to his mother as he ran a hand through her wavy sandy-blonde tresses and gazed into her bright blue eyes. This was succeeded by his own little sister, barely five years old, chasing *him* of all people down the boulevard. He was almost nine years old then, and it was one of the last of his happy memories of them.

The knot in his gut tightened; he choked back the tears as he took a handkerchief from his pocket and wiped his eyes. Better that he get this over with now. His crew were aware of what had befallen his family. If a crew member didn't, it wasn't long before someone told them what they knew of the story; it wouldn't do for them to see such weakness in him. Even if some of them did understand, others might not; he still must maintain his standards as captain.

He sat for several long moments while he composed himself, remembering his childhood friend, a little girl with chestnut brown hair called Alirene. She was usually nicknamed Ali, or Rene, but after he'd once called her Liri, she preferred that he call her that from then on. She was the daughter of his father's closest friend, Admiral Traven Wendale. He knew Liri and her family were still alive, but would she forgive him for never returning? Would she understand why he couldn't return? There was no doubt she'd have received news of his survival several years ago when the pirate captain who'd adopted him had challenged him to prove he was responsible enough to reclaim his family's ship and worthy enough to call himself her captain.

He dried his eyes and rose to his feet, tossing the sandy-blond layers of his hair away from his face before slipping his coat back on and picking up his hat as he left the room. It was too warm to keep them on, so he would drop them off in the great cabin when he returned to *Greshendier*. He opened the door to see Arcaydia about to knock.

"Can I help you?" he asked, inclining his head to the side.

"I couldn't settle for long and I found myself getting a little bored in there on my own," she replied, blushing. "And, I had the feeling something was amiss, and wondered if you were alright." Larkh felt his heart jump at her words but couldn't hide the look of surprise that suddenly sprang on to his face. How could she have possibly known there was something wrong? "There is something, isn't there?"

'Curse you,' he reprimanded himself. *'Fail.'*

"Larkh?" Arcaydia poked him right in the floating ribs, causing him to yelp and recoil.

"D-don't do that!" he gasped.

"Now I know one of your weaknesses!" Arcaydia chuckled. "Anyway, how about you tell me what's wrong?" Larkh pulled a face.

"I thought you were tired?" he countered.

"I had a quick nap, then woke up and couldn't settle down again." She shrugged. "You haven't shown me your ship yet; why don't you take me to it and tell me what's bothering you on the way?" He smiled; how could he refuse?

The pair re-emerged on to the streets of Almadeira. Just around the corner was the town square where a large fountain dominated the scene. The Silver Gull was situated to the south west of the square, and though it was the closest inn to most of the best known shops, it was in an inconspicuous place, somewhat hidden around the corner of a backstreet, almost opposite the most wonderful smelling bakery. Arcaydia sniffed.

"It is rather good, isn't it?" Larkh chimed in. He smiled and waved at the portly middle-aged woman at the counter, who smiled and waved back.

"Definitely!" Arcaydia agreed.

"Well, you do have all the time in the world till your companion returns, right?" Larkh was wondering who this girl was more than anything else. "Enjoy yourself while you have time to. That's what I do when I'm not on board ship. Right now though, that smell is startin' to make me hungry."

"I heard," Arcaydia smirked, poking his belly. There it was again, that wry smile of his. There was something about it that was strangely alluring. "Shall I get some?"

Larkh gave the idea some thought. She'd certainly warmed up to him quickly; not that he'd ever had much trouble starting the fires of passion in the hearts of women. "Hmm, I was goin' to force myself to wait until the festivities started before I—"

"Festivities?" Arcaydia interrupted.

"Aye, the spring faire, Vàreia. They'll be puttin' the decorations up this afternoon as it'll start this evenin'." He winked at her. *'I'm pretty sure you'll know that word.'*

"Oh?" Arcaydia's eyes lit up. "Can we—"

"No need to ask lass," Larkh laughed. "I'm always here for Vàreia so long as the winds are in my favour." She smiled.

"I'll get some of that bread tomorrow."

They made their way toward the harbour through the cobbled streets displaying many decorative half-timbered houses with steep pitched rooftops, tall narrow windows with small panes, and large chimneys. Arcaydia admired her surroundings as she thought of something clever to say.

"Anyway, I thought you'd already *indulged* once already today?" she tried not to smile. In-fact, she tried not to laugh, but it was the look of disbelief on Larkh's face that made her release the giggles.

"What else has Mrs. Menow been saying about me?" the handsome blond pirate asked, tossing strands of hair away as the sea breeze flicked it into his face. He wore a cynical smile.

"That a standard fried breakfast is: two sausages, two rashers of bacon, one egg, one portion of mushrooms and a round of toast – and that your standard order of the day is double that on the same plate," Arcaydia told him. She prodded him in the belly again.

"Diets on board ship ain't fancy," he shrugged, "an' too often on long voyages there's not really enough to go around, so you can't really blame a man for takin' advantage when he gets the chance."

"She called you a human waste basket," she continued. His shoulders sagged.

"She said *'abandoned mineshaft'* earlier as well didn't she? An' she ain't wrong there either." He sighed. "She always succeeds in the end though."

Arcaydia laughed. "Maybe one day I'll let you try my cooking," she suggested.

"I like the sound of that," he grinned.

"I've been wondering something though." Arcaydia now seemed to be entering a state of contemplation as she watched the various people of Almadeira and their reactions to Larkh's presence. Some simply walked on by, some smiled and waved, and there were a few who simply glared, unhappy to have anyone infamous roaming freely around town. To those who greeted him, he would kindly return the gesture with a smile, a nod, a wink or a tip of his hat. "Why are you so well tolerated here?" Larkh directed her toward the left, following the road around where row upon row of masts jutted out of the bay.

"Ehhh, Almadeira is what we call a 'safe haven'." He explained. "It was an arrangement between King Jaredh an' an old acquaintance of my father, who was an admiral. In-fact, I think Traven Wendale still is. He was one of the few members of the Faltain Navy in Saldour – my hometown – who somehow understood why I chose this life after what happened. Here, as long as I don't plunder the town or otherwise deliberately cause a ruckus, I can do as I please so long as I carry my letter of marque. The smugglers tunnels under the mountains here serve as an autonomous district which isn't *exactly* unknown, but they aren't common knowledge, so that's where I tend to *'do business'* in these parts. In fact Ennerth is the only region that letter has any merit."

"What about your father? You said he was an admiral." Arcaydia's question was expected, but it still didn't allow for an easy answer. Larkh took a deep breath, side-stepped to avoid two small children running around the corner too fast at the bottom of the road, and turned left at the ocean market situated by the harbour entrance.

"That leads us into a painful subject for me," he replied matter-of-factly. "It is part of the very subject that your marvellous intuition picked up on. I'll put it simply; I am the only one left in my family."

"Your entire family? What h—" Another expected question. It irritated him that he was so easily able to predict what she was going to say.

"You know what's said about curiosity?" he interrupted softly. "It's a touchy subject, an' it'd be a shame to sour a good afternoon." Arcaydia cast her eyes at the ground. At least he'd worded his refusal politely. That was more than most other people were capable of. They had only known each other for one afternoon after all, so it was probably too soon to start asking too many personal questions.

As they wandered through the harbour, Arcaydia noticed a variety of crates and casks being loaded and unloaded from different types of ships, including: brigs, brigantines, frigates, barques, schooners and full-rigged ships. She was intrigued. She'd seen some of the beautiful ivory-white and gold ships back in Ardeltaniah, but these were just as magnificent. Eventually they came to a stop, and Larkh pointed toward what Arcaydia guessed was one of the largest if not *the* largest ship in the harbour moored at the corner of the quay on the western docks.

This towering full-rigged ship was the perfect picture of grandeur against the flame-coloured sky; rimmed with gold around her many gun ports and sterncastle where the name *Greshendier* was displayed. Arcaydia cast her eyes toward the forecastle. Her attention was drawn to the figurehead perched above a great ram jutting from the bow. It was a great eagle, golden and gleaming in the light of the setting sun, and it held within its talons a large wine red orb. *'The Nays ships have these,'* she mused. *'Why would this one have one?'*

"That's her," said Larkh. He approached the gangway, nodding to the two crew members on watch, and ascended it to the weather deck. The tide was in, so *Greshendier* sat high on the water. Larkh turned to face her. Arcaydia stared with her mouth agape at the ship. Her eyes scanned the full length, across the rows of guns she could see on the port side, and then her gaze shifted upwards to the masts and rigging.

"Th-this is yours!?" she exclaimed. Larkh took off his hat and bowed graciously.

"Please do come aboard." The invite was genuine and his manner was charming. He leaned over the gangway with his right hand extended. She found herself blushing again, and without thinking any further, boarded the ship, taking his hand as she stepped down on to the deck. As she did, Larkh leaned in and whispered in her ear.

"Just pretend you're mine," he said. He watched her turn even more red; his azure eyes sparkled.

"Why?" she whispered back. He glanced sideways, nodding towards the lustful eyes of several crew members. She swallowed hard.

"If you're not mine, you may as well be theirs." He was blunt and to the point. "If you're mine, they won't lay a finger on you if they've any sense." She nodded apprehensively.

"Gentlemen," Larkh addressed his crew quite casually. "This lady here is Arcaydia. We met earlier today an' have already grown close, so regrettably those of you who are free of duty this night shan't be musclin' in on my catch, alright?" There were a few disappointed groans. "Lads, c'mon, since when did I do your fishin' for you? There're plenty more fish in the sea, an' plenty more down the Camino del Lupanar." Only Reys piped up.

"What if we don't want to pay?" he asked. The rest of the crew on deck within earshot either burst out laughing or sniggered quietly.

Larkh turned and regarded the youth with a knowing smile, and though he maintained his composure, he only did so by a thread. "If you don't want to pay my friend, then you need charm," he countered. Reys had no comeback. "You're the newest member of the crew Reys, so I don't expect you to know it all just yet."

"Boy, y'gotta realise that the only man on this ship who gets to dip his wick for free is the Captain," Laisner taunted him. He was a man about the same height as Larkh with a lot of stubble and medium-length chestnut brown hair. "Well, perhaps if yer prostrated yerself to a whore she might be nice enough to give yer a discount!" There was another bout of raucous laughter. Larkh dropped a hand on to Reys' shoulder.

"Cut him some slack an' help get him some then Laisner, since you know those girls so well," he gibed. "He won't be innocent for long." He still wore that same smile.

"Though unlike you, he ain't a bad lookin' lad, so I'm pretty sure I can train him to cast his line to reel in a successful catch."

"Now that weren't nice!" cried Laisner as Larkh edged back towards Arcaydia. "Ain't many men on the high seas who 'av as many friends for cut like you do sir."

"Try makin' some friends then!" Larkh suggested, shrugging. "Don't be too quick to drop your trousers if you ain't visitin' a bawdy house; get to know someone, show some interest in who she is not *what* she is, an' consider the feelin's that reside above your belt rather than just the ones below it." He watched as Laisner began to mull this over, and then turned back toward Arcaydia.

"Sorry about that," he said quietly. "At least they know to not try anythin'." Arcaydia smiled nervously. "Thanks. Um, what now?" He could see she was uncertain of his intentions given his words to Laisner and the rest, and this was something he knew he needed to clear up quickly.

"Wander around a little bit, but not below deck. Stay up here. I have a few things to take care of, an' then we can head back into town for the festivities." He glanced around until he spotted Larsan. "I'll explain later. Here's not the place for it; too many ears listenin', you understand?" She nodded. "Good. Go talk to Larsan or somethin'. I won't be too long."

CHAPTER 9

I
North Mazaryn Peaks

Zehn and Raeon stopped to rest halfway down the mountain. They picked at a light lunch of cold meat, bread and fruit bought in Senfirth, but all the while, despite the serenity of the gently undulating hills below them and the fresh mountain air, Madukeyr's words rang out in Zehn's mind; *'Your path will become clear. I am a mere stepping stone on that path. The greatest truths lie atop the highest of peaks, and so must you climb to find them. '* If he remembered correctly, that last sentence was a Kensaiyr proverb. Had Madukeyr led him all the way up this mountain to prove a point?

The fight had challenged his stamina, provoking ideas that improving on his endurance would be a good next step if he were to have a chance at besting someone so skilled. He hoped Raeon would be able to share enough knowledge with him to allow him to understand the path he was treading, but Madukeyr's words reeked of destiny and prophecy; and that made him uneasy. What about his own desires? What about the paths he chose? Were they really his own, or were they all guided by fate?

'Some things happen for a reason,' he told himself, *'but I still have the right to choose where I go from here. I won't let myself be bullied into believing my destiny is not my own to create.'*

The large island of Gaieah could be seen beyond the rolling waves of the Sendero de Mercader. Thin wisps of cloud drifted idly, dappling the undulating waters with blotches of restless shadow. It was the first island of

Cerendiyll, heavily cloaked in forest; the kingdom of the Cerenyr elves ruled by King Faeronel, whom his father had befriended. He had been there once, many years ago. He remembered that beyond Gaieah, somewhere in the northern waters of the Sendero de Mercader, the Ghost Leviathan Albharenos was said to dwell.

"Thinking about the Kensaiyr again?" Raeon asked, handing over a wooden mug of herbal tea. Zehn took it gladly, nodding as he took a sip.

"I'm thinking about what his words mean," he answered with a shrug. "You know me, I've never been much of a believer in destiny or fate."

Raeon couldn't help but agree. Since they had first met, he had never known Zehn to agree to anything planned for him. He kicked against it passionately, always maintaining the belief he would do with his life as he pleased, and not even his parents were going to have a say in it.

Zehn's mother had been a successful merchant trading various goods from overseas, particularly from Cerendiyll and the north of the Sendero de Mercader, until she was assassinated one day when his father was away on a job. It was suspected the perpetrator was none other than a rival merchant jealous of her success, but there was no proof and no culprit had ever been found. She had always wished for him to take over her business when she died, but Zehn was keener to follow in his father's footsteps, and so the business was passed on to his uncle who still ran it to this day.

Stranger still was Zehn had never met any relatives on his mother's side of the family; she claimed to be an only child, and her aunts and uncles as well as her parents were all dead. His father, Rajan Kahner, was later hired to undertake a mission to the southern island of Ehyenn after there had been reports of a witch living in the Yahridican, an ancient Nays fortress. The very building itself had been corrupted; the once brilliant shining whitestone now blackened and rife with demons. Zehn, despite his age, had begged to go with him, but was restrained by his uncle and locked in his room. He'd slipped out of the house later that same evening and stowed away on the ship his father had embarked upon. That was how he and Raeon first met.

Raeon's mentor was asked by the Archaenen to seek out a renowned elite mercenary for the mission; Rajan was the one selected. Both Raeon and Zehn embarked on the same ship; so the stowaways kept one another company. As a result of fighting a powerful sorceress – not a witch – Rajan did not make it out of the fortress alive. It was something Zehn rarely spoke of, but since that day he'd sworn vengeance. Little did he know the sorceress had once been a Galétriahn Highlord, one of the most powerful mages of the Nays. There would never be a chance of defeating her alone. Even if he trained non-stop every day for a hundred years it wouldn't be enough, and yet one day he would face at least one of the seven Kaesan'Drahknyr, and probably all too soon. If he were to succeed in defeating the sorceress, he'd need the assistance of the Nays, who would likely insist he must first hold his ground against at least one of the Kaesan'Drahknyr for a minimum length of time.

It was then Raeon reflected on his mentor's instructions to watch over Zehn as they grew up. He said there was something sealed within Zehn, something of a spiritual seed, and that one day it would grow, bud, and bloom like a flower. During his training at the Archaenen, Raeon sensed exactly what his mentor had whenever he and Zehn met. The sensation was familiar, for he'd already met another boy who exuded the very same kind of aura.

"What about you, Raeon?" Zehn asked, sipping at his tea, a quizzical expression on his face. "You seem to be the one drifting off with the fairies now. Are you thinking about what you're going to tell me later?" Raeon rubbed at his eyes. Despite what he'd promised Zehn, he didn't know where to begin. His friend's scepticism was a tough barrier to break.

"I could give you a few things to mull over before we get back if you want," he suggested. "It might make the topic a little easier to slip into."

"Such as?" Zehn seemed interested in the idea. That was good. Raeon released his dark brown ponytail from its binding, casually brushing the hair over his shoulder.

"You know I am of the Order of Silver within The Archaenen," Raeon began, "but I'm not sure you know exactly what our studies or their purposes entail. You would be right to say we study the history and lore of the ancient Nays, but there is a lot more to it than that. We also practise the use of Nays magic, or *magica*, to be true to the term. It was the Order of Silver that researched and implemented the use of Altirnathé crystals in archana, thus giving birth to the altirna system."

"What has that got to do with me?" Zehn asked, puzzled. Raeon let out a shallow sigh as he took an apple out of his satchel. Raeon chewed his lower lip thoughtfully.

"We are attuned to anything relating to the Nays," he explained. "Something of the Nays resides in you, and I think you know it. You were drawn to that shrine, and you were obviously entranced when you went inside. You have unusual dreams, and I won't be surprised if you have more of them very soon."

Zehn could hardly deny this, but some part of him was still uneasy if not shocked. Even though Madukeyr admitted to having some part in guiding him through his most recent dream, there was something else that had drawn him to that shrine. Was there something he had missed? He couldn't think; he should have gone back inside again to take another look. Loathe as he was to admit it, his scepticism was beginning to split at the seams, and Raeon had already noticed.

Of all the questions now running through his mind, only one gnawed at him more than the others. It wasn't even a question about how he could possibly be connected to the Nays. What bugged him was a question about his closest friend who sat no more than a few feet from him. *'Who in the world is he?'* The possibility his friend held some real secrets chafed his nerves, especially when they were secrets associated with him.

"It happens at least once or perhaps twice a week now," Zehn shrugged, sipping at the tea. "You know I'm trying not to let it worry me too much, though I won't deny that it bothers me. I don't suppose you're going to tell me much more about everything you know though are you, particularly with regards to what you know about me?" Raeon ran his fingers through his hair and shook his head.

"I'm sorry Zehn," the silver mage sighed. "I can tell you a bit more later when I've had a chance to think about it, but there are two problems I face; telling you too much, which could change events drastically and for the worse, and possibly telling you something that still has the potential to be incorrect. It is you who must discover for yourself the truth of who and what you are. Whether you decide to eat an apple or not won't change the course of events in your life much, unless it was poisoned."

"I think I understand," Zehn thought aloud. "You don't want me to run away from my *destiny*, even if I don't believe in it."

"When you put it like that," Raeon said thoughtfully, "that's exactly how it comes across, except you missed something. Go back to the apple." He held up the apple in his hand. "If the apple is clean, whether you eat it or not doesn't make a difference. If it is poisoned, however, and you eat it, you may either die or become very ill and miss a very important event. Remember the last time someone made an attempt on King Jaredh's life at the summer banquet three years ago? What would have become of him if something had prevented you from protecting him, and what might have happened to this country?" Zehn's eyes narrowed.

"To put it another way, say you are definitely going to eat a cake tomorrow afternoon and there are three choices available. You will eat a cake regardless, but you have the choice of which one."

"So we're now comparing destiny to cake? Right..."

"You know what I mean!"

"Yeah I do, I just find your choice of metaphor slightly...unimaginative."

"Maybe I really just want a piece of cake myself, you know..."

"You're quite amusing when you're pretending to be offended."

Raeon opened his mouth, but quickly shut it again as he stifled a smirk. He wasn't sure his friend understood the point.

Zehn's brow quirked upwards. "What were you going to say?" he asked.

"Nothing!" Raeon laughed. "Absolutely nothing!"

II
Nira'Eléstara

The astral plane of Nira'Eléstara appeared to be forever locked in either the light of dawn or the shadow of dusk. It was impossible to tell when night and day began and ended unless one knew the realm well. The stars were forever scattered across a cosmic sky amongst blotches of colourful nebulae; the landscape like a painting of a vast dream world full of pastel colours with indigo hues stretched across the distant mountains. In fact, Nira'Eléstara was as much the realm where dreams flowed into the minds of people as it was the realm in which all spirits existing above the netherworld of Ne'Vedanhyr naturally resided.

Projection of the spirit on to this plane was possible through dreams or meditation, but such an experience separated the spirit from the physical body. Melkhar was more than capable of this connection, but her escape out of the Dorne Shaft required a more direct method that would transport her both spiritually and physically, involving crossing between both realms while fully conscious. Only the most magically adept were capable of such crossings.

As she stepped through the rift between planes, Melkhar's form shifted. Her helmet dissolved as she stood watching the shifting nebulous sky. A powerful aureate hue radiated outward from around her frame, from her fiery red hair and framed emerald eyes, right down to her ebony armour. Otherwise it seemed as though she were made entirely of white flames that spread outward into gold right through to the tips of her wings. Those colossal wings could not be hidden here, but they had grown in size, as had her whole form. In this realm, she stood nearly seven feet tall, shining like the sun, her wings arcing high over her head. The very sight of her was enough to force the lesser spirits dwelling here into submission. They either bowed in reverence or scattered and cowered.

"Lésos Taeren!" Melkhar called out, her rich voice echoing across the vast expanse of the surreal landscape around her. *"Éyn reqharias ye'nen deyeithra."* [10] *"Éyn auhdare ye'n Kaesan'Drahknyr Khesaiyde,"* [11] a male voice whispered back.

"I felt your presence," Lésos said coolly, appearing before her from a fine silvery mist in his own astral form. His ivory skin glowed, and his cloak flowed behind him like liquid platinum. There was a pearlescent shine about him, which complemented a pair of fierce azure eyes and pure white hair that trailed down to his thighs, tied halfway with the shorter lengths draped over his shoulders at the front.

Physically he sat in meditation in a private chamber of a temple in Kesar Nairéfa, the white-silver valley, homeland of the Kensaiyr, on the Nays continent of Ardeltaniah. He often spent many hours in meditation, keeping watch over Nira'Eléstara. He'd been proven as its next guardian when he directly channelled his consciousness into the realm at

---

[10] I require your direction.
[11] I heard you Kaesan'Drahknyr Khesaiyde.

will. Only when he meditated could he truly sense all that went on here, but he was always able to sense when something was amiss, or perhaps different, while fully conscious in the physical world. It was impossible for him to fail to notice the presence of a Kaesan'Drahknyr even when wide awake.

Every living creature of Aeldynn and the realms above owned a personal mind-space in Nira'Eléstara where their dreams took place, and while he could not see or feel their dreams, Lésos was still able to sense every kind of presence that wandered within its borders.

He gave Melkhar a pointed look. "You entered physically," he said easily. "There must be a most unusual reason for this. Are you trapped?"

"Zerrçainne brought part of the Dorne Shaft down on me as I moved to destroy a phandaeric gateway. She has the gift of soul-sight in one eye, and attempted to read me. I saw through the ruse, but she was quick enough to trap me down there all the same." Lésos' icy eyes flashed at the mention of Zerrçainne's name.

"I have felt nothing of *her* presence here." There was surprise in his tone despite his assuredly calm manner. "I was under the impression she was dead."

"You and almost everyone else," Melkhar conceded. "She has managed to disguise her presence all this time. It appears much of that time has been spent working in or around Dyr'Efna if not within the very borders of Dhavenkos Mhal."

"The Dryft," Lésos mused. "So, her spirit dwells there now. Why would she feel the need to trap you in the Dorne Shaft?"

"I believe you know the answer to that one."

"She wants you out of the way for something she is planning, and by forcing you to take the astral route she knows you'll be well away from anywhere you could access to intervene."

"Indeed."

This was troubling. If Zerrçainne had spent so long in the Dryft studying its spiritus and magica, and had transferred her own spirit there, she would now be using phandaeric magica. If she needed to stall the Kaesan'Drahknyr, then it was something to be very concerned about. He had worked with Zerrçainne once, along with other Galétriahn Highlords long ago, and she was not one to rush. Whatever she planned, it would be thoroughly thought through, and each part would be executed in stages, like the acts of a play. Worse still, she was Melkhar's cousin. Even Adjeeah, the goddess of the flame herself, had sworn by Melkhar's volatile nature when it came to anger. Her words were that if the spirit of a volcano could be incarnated as another kind of being, it would be incarnated as her.

"I believe she might be assisting Adengeld in waging war against the Faltain Kingdom," Melkhar observed, dangerous eyes narrowing in contemplation. "How close can you get me to Faltainyr Demura?"

Lésos scanned the vast expanse of the cosmic landscape around them. It was a bonus that in this part of the world most people were awake. There were very few spirits of the living wandering around, meaning he could see further without trying to navigate through them. Normally those who had recently died eventually passed through Nira'Eléstara on the way to their way to their afterlife.

"It would seem the closest rift is currently sitting within the Valley of Daynallar, approximately three miles from the Len'athyr Sanctuary," Lésos eventually replied. "As you know this place shifts all the time; that rift might not be there in an hour but then again it might still be there tomorrow."

It was difficult to read expressions on faces that shone so brilliantly on this plane, only the eyes seemed to give away an emotion. The more spiritual a person was, the brighter their spirit. Celestial beings shone brightest. Lésos guessed, however, that Melkhar was none too pleased, but he could tell she was thankful it wasn't even further afield.

"Let's go then." Her voice was sullen. This was to be expected. Bowing respectfully, Lésos gestured westward.

Melkhar believed her crossing into Nira'Eléstara had been somewhere between two to three hours ago. The rift lay just ahead of them. It sat stationary in the cosmic sky like a purple lightning bolt frozen in time. Landscapes here and in other planes differed somewhat from that of the physical world, but the basic geography of a specific area was similar and recognisable.

The basic structure of the Valley of Daynallar lay ahead of her, though it was significantly warped as a result of the continuous shifting of astral energies. She was a considerable distance from the Dorne Shaft now, but it was better than what might have been without the guidance of Lésos. She guessed she was now hundreds of miles away from Almadeira. Had the rift been much further away, she may have ended up as far away as the city of Cathra, or worse, back in the Nays homeland of Ardeltaniah. At least from here she'd stand a chance of countering whatever Zerrçainne was planning.

"I shall take my leave once I have seen you through the rift," said Lésos as a swift astral breeze gently lifted and toyed with the bound lengths of his shimmering white hair. "I shall report to Atialleia informing Empress Arkkiennah of what has befallen you. You have much to be concerned with, so I ask you, please leave this task to me." Melkhar stiffened. There was certainly no way of her reporting to Atialleia any time soon. It was essential some information be relayed, and Arcaydia had the seikryth crystal she used for communication with her in Almadeira.

"Very well," she agreed, her voice austere as always. "Make haste on it if you can when you awaken. The sooner Her Majesty is informed of the situation the better."

"I shall wake from my meditation when you enter the rift," Lésos said coolly, "and I will deliver a message to Her Highness personally."

"You have my thanks."

"Such is the way of Nira'Eléstara to carry us great distances in the blink of an eye. Take care, Melkhar."

Lésos met the fierce emerald gaze of the Kaesan'Drahknyr, his own eyes glimmering like ice in the intermittent light as wispy blue-grey clouds obscured the nebula above them. They studied one another for a moment longer. Melkhar's white-gold astral wings blazed outwards as she launched herself into the air and flashed through the sky like a shooting star, disappearing into the jagged purple line in the sky as it widened to accommodate her. There was a rumbling in the clouds as a shockwave burst from the rift's location, spreading over a mile in diameter as she entered. Lésos watched the astral sky for several moments while it returned to normal. When he was satisfied all was as it should be, he closed his eyes and vanished.

CHAPTER 10

I
Yahridican Fortress

South of Adengeld on the island of Ehyenn, lay the
Yahridican, an ancient Nays fortress, stood atop a rocky
outcrop between the Sidel Channel and the Soreiden Sea.
Most of it was still standing, for Nays architecture was
incredibly slow to degrade, but the colour of the entire
structure had turned charcoal grey, almost black. It was once
white or perhaps ash grey with golden rooftops and statues,
but over many aeons the negative archana used within had
corrupted the very stone. It towered menacingly over
everything on the island.

Varieties of red-eyed gargoyles, large and small,
perched themselves upon the many turrets and flying
buttresses; demonic sentinels from the underworld of
Dhavenkos Mhal keeping watch for any bold adventurer or
civilian who dared wander too close.

The air surrounding the fortress was chilling, and not
only because of the brisk winds often blowing from the
south. It was cold, sharper than any icy wind from the
frozen places of the world; an aura designed to ensure the
uninvited kept their distance. Sentinels would attack, maim
and devour any who strayed too close, but for the few
skilled enough to make it past, this aura was usually enough
to send them on their way.

Zerrçainne materialised within the walls, clutching at
her breast as blood seeped through her fingers, dripping
profusely on to the slate floor. Although she had acted
quickly enough to prevent Melkhar's sword from striking
her heart, the Kaesan'Drahknyr had come dangerously close

to succeeding. Zerrçainne knew she had taken a risk in attempting to read her soul, and an even greater one in meeting her directly. What she hadn't expected was failure, which had almost cost her dearly.

She half staggered and half dragged herself across the room, wondering why. Was it because Melkhar was one of the Kaesan'Drahknyr? Or could it be something else entirely? She was curious now; she would have to investigate the matter alongside all other projects. Perhaps it might even tie in with her overall plan. That would make more sense, but it still meant nothing could be done to stop the Kaesan'Drahknyr from interfering.

Granted they had been put to death, albeit temporarily, on the final day of the War of the Eclipse when she and the one she loved caused nature itself to be thrown into confusion, but it hadn't lasted long enough and now it wasn't possible to get close enough to try again. She had severed her connection to Aevnatureis by studying Dyr'Efna and experimenting within its borders for an extraordinarily long time. It could almost be called a miracle that she had retained her sanity and ability to maintain her humanoid form.

Over time, the power she had been given from Aevnatureis had become so tainted by Phandaerys her spirit was now anchored to the Dryft instead. She could no longer step into any realm maintained by Aevnatureis except Aeldynn; the realm in which balance was disturbed the most. Her beloved would also be unable to reach the Aevanythra if he were alive; *'in physical form that is,'* she thought, smiling. *'We'll work on that.'* With the assistance of the Warriors of Lyte working in unison, the one called Alymarn had been destroyed, his soul removed and his spirit dismembered. His soul, the God Aspect, had been cast into the very depths of the phandaeric abyss, the Abadhol, where she had eventually found it.

"Dhen—," she called weakly, dropping to her knees, "—taro." It would be impossible to heal naturally. Her body would no longer accept the natural flow of magica from Aevnatureis; Phandaerys had warped it. She required a different kind of method of healing originating from the underworld of Dhavenkos Mhal, especially with this kind of wound. She had been wounded with a weapon forged by the Nays, a weapon forged with the power of Aevnatureis, and therefore a power that was balanced. It hadn't been an ordinary Nays weapon; it was a specialised weapon forged for a particular chosen individual who happened to be Melkhar. It meant phandaeric power would be melted away by it, so the healing power of Aevnatureis was now toxic to her.

At once, Dhentaro walked out of a thick, coagulating black mist that swirled into the room. He was tall and lean, his skin raven black with red tribal tattoos covering several areas of his body. His eyes were like crystallised lavender. He was naked except for a black snake hide thong and matching loincloth bearing a lizard skin symbol on the front. Ears shaped like the jagged dorsal fin of a shark poked out from under a thick mane of red hair that thinned out and trailed into a fine line all the way down his back to join with a long tail at the base of his spine. He was one of the Fralh, one of many demonic races from the underworld of Dhavenkos Mhal.

"Zerrçainne," he said sensually, his voice smooth and gently warming like a summer breeze. "What happened? Ah, let me guess...Melkhar? You let your guard down." He stooped to kneel on one knee, watching the blood dripping from the hand she pressed against her chest. With no consideration of haste, or permission, he leaned forward, scooped her up into his arms and carried her to a stone table where he laid her on her back.

"I recommend that you do not attempt to fight me," he advised sternly. "I am aware this is going to be very personal, but if you value your life you will not give half a damn what I am about to do."

"The dragon," Zerrçainne winced, "Rahntamein. Is he—"

"He is getting rather impatient, and that may be an understatement," Dhentaro interrupted. Zerrçainne closed her eyes, grimacing.

He ripped open her tunic with long black claws, baring her pale breasts in the candlelight. The wound was vicious; she'd ducked out almost too late. If she lost her physical form to death now, she would not be able to complete her mission; she needed to retain her physical body for the tasks that lay ahead. Dhentaro ran his tongue across a perfect set of sharp pointed teeth as he bent down and set to licking the blood from the wound that almost pierced her heart; his saliva staunching the blood flow and working to calm the inflammation. He growled under his breath; *'I can taste the residue of Aevnatureis,'* he thought in disgust. Zerrçainne arched her back and whined in agony. *'That's what you get, my dear, for thinking you could best one the Kaesan'Drahknyr alone; that one in particular.'* His eyes flashed angrily as he worked, firmly pinning Zerrçainne's writhing form to the table.

Eventually he raised his head, blood smearing his razor sharp teeth and lips. He licked them clean, lavender eyes scanning the cleaned wound. Lowering his right hand over it, he began to chant, *"evos vandh ai do anha mero thalla Fandares o nadhos."* [12] . A violet light began to glow beneath his hand, followed by a thick indigo mist that laid itself over the wound, clouding it. Zerrçainne shrieked in agony. He removed his hand, watching as the gash in the sorceress' chest slowly closed, leaving a charcoal black scar; the skin a fierce livid red around it.

"It is done," Dhentaro announced. "Try to avoid that cousin of yours again for a while, but when you do face her, I wish to be there. I would know more about her. Stories are not enough. I would like to face her myself."

---

[12] Let the power of Phandaerys close this rift in the body

"I could not see her soul," Zerrçainne groaned. "I know not if that will be the case with the other six, but there was something else about her. I sensed a connection to something beyond even the Nays." Dhentaro's flame-like hair stood on end, his ears pricking up. "I think she is somehow connected to—"

"The Origin..."

II
Almadeira

Almadeira's networks of smugglers' tunnels leading to a small cove lay underneath the North Mazaryn Peaks, usually accessed either by boat or via a particular tavern. That tavern was known as the Mizzen Rest for it was located at the far end of the harbour against the mountainside. The innkeeper and his predecessors elected future candidates to succeed the role as a means to protect the black market within. Under normal circumstances they would be family members, but every once in a while the line would be broken, so potential candidates were chosen should a handover become necessary.

The tavern itself was packed to the gunwales with sailors, a good many of them pirates, among other types of swindlers and crooks of all kinds. Anyone looking for goods of illegal or dubious origin were pointed in the direction of the Mizzen Rest and told to speak to the owner. If they answered his questions satisfactorily, he would take them into the tavern's storeroom and open up a hidden hatch leading into the tunnels.

Larkh wrinkled his nose at the pungent odours of sweat, ale and smoke all mingling together as he pushed his way through the crowd with two crew members in tow. Somehow the smell was tolerable on board ship; perhaps it was down to how finicky he was about how often and how thoroughly *Greshendier* was cleaned and how he forced his crew to wash whenever possible. Regardless of the reason, it was always worse in crowded taverns.

Voices called out to him from across the taproom, some of them his own men, some of them acquaintances he'd not had the fortune or misfortune of meeting for quite some time. It had certainly been a while since he'd last seen some of these local scoundrels.

"Ey! Larkh my good man, how're ye doin'!?" one man called out. "Can see you comin' a mile off in that coat an' hat Savaldor, come 'av a drink will yer!" shouted another.

"Look boys! Cap'n Savvy's back!" yelled a third. Larkh cocked his head to the side, nodding as he tipped the brim of his hat to each man in turn. One of the serving wenches stepped past him, brushing his inner thigh as she went. He glanced at her; she winked at him. He gave her a knowing smile.

"Hallo lads," he said, edging and elbowing his way through. "I'll have a drink wi' you in a bit; got somethin' to take care of down in the tunnels, if you get my meanin'. Can't keep the lady firebrand waitin' much longer down there now can I?" All the men around the table sniggered. "I've not much time this evenin' though I'm afraid. I'm showin' a lass around town who's not familiar with the territory an' she's waitin' on board *Gresh* as we speak. I'm takin' her to the festival tonight."

"You're an extra lucky man t'night then!" said a portly man with thick, knotted biceps. He slouched in his chair, using his round belly as a table.

"This one's different," Larkh's mouth quirked up slightly. He shrugged. "Anyway, I'm in the habit of gettin' to know my ladies before I consider that sort of thing, unless I'm desperate. This new girl's a sheltered lass, but I don't need to tell you lads that Mey an' I go way back."

"Aye," said the big man. "I forget how long you an' that sassy girl've been fuck buddies."

"That's not for you to know anyway," Larkh smiled wryly.

156

"Lemme guess, you were fourteen?" said another man. This one wore a red bandana with straggly brown hair plastered over his face. More sniggering followed. The big man laughed so hard he had to take his tankard off his belly to avoid spilling his drink.

Larkh's brow twitched. "No," he replied, feeling something between amusement and irritation.

"Thirteen!?" a rather greasy looking man exclaimed. Laughter erupted all around them. This time Larkh gave them all a mischievous smile. He leaned forward and beckoned with his hand, inviting them closer. They all leaned in, eager for him to tell them the age at which he lost his virginity. Barely able to contain his amusement, he thrust two fingers up in a rude gesture at them.

"Fuck off," he said, turning and walking away laughing.

"Aw man! No fun!" squawked the man wearing the bandana. He smiled to himself; he could hear them all arguing over every possibility.

He approached the back of the taproom where Daron and Laisner waited. The innkeeper filled another tankard, slung it across the bar to a customer, and opened the door to the storeroom. Larkh was good friends with Mr. Loftan, and usually wound up somewhat worse for wear whenever he visited due to several free drinks being set in front of him one after the other.

No words were exchanged at this time. Harand Loftan, a tall and rather burly man with a thick dark brown beard and balding head escorted him, along with Daron and Laisner, through to the back of the storeroom. He shoved the crate blocking the hatch aside, and unlocked it. Entry and exit from the smugglers' tunnels via this route was always brief and discreet, no matter how many people in the room knew about what lay beyond. No-one asked any questions about why customers were taken into the storeroom because the Mizzen Rest had its very own brothel on the second floor of the three-storey building, the entrance cleverly positioned just behind the doors to the storeroom.

After dropping down the hatch into the tunnels via a creaky old ladder, Laisner took a lantern passed down by the innkeeper and followed Larkh toward the central cave where every black market dealer in the region gathered to sell and buy their ill-gotten gains.

It had been a long while since he'd last seen Mey, and he hoped she'd upheld her end of the bargain. Still, since the acquisition of the goods had proved tougher than he'd originally bargained for, resulting in a night in Senfirth's prison, he considered negotiating something extra for the trouble.

Moss clung to the moist walls of the tunnels; the further they ventured in, the more slick they became. The acrid tang of wet stone mixed with the salty odour of seaweed hung heavily in the air. This area was above sea level, untouched by the tide, but there was a lower section to the tunnels used by boats and small ships. *Greshendier* was more than a hundred feet too long and too tall to fit into this small space. Not even Meynra's brig could fit in here, though a two-masted schooner, sloop or ketch certainly could.

The sound of Mey's enthusiastic yelling echoed throughout the central cave as Larkh stepped in, though he stepped back out and around the corner just as quickly. She hadn't seen him yet. He glanced sideways at his two crew members, smiling faintly. Laisner and Daron were already grinning.

"When I see that scoundrel I'll give 'im a right punishin' that'll see 'im right!" she yelled. "He's always late, an' his ship's been in port nearly all day now. Damn it, he's always off doin' as he pleases when he's got business to attend to! Larkh Savaldor, I can see yer crew in the tunnel there, I know ya be listenin'!"

"Sounds like you're in trouble Cap'n." This comment came from the swarthy Daron, unable to hide a smile.

"Since when am I *not* in trouble?" Larkh chuckled. He shrugged, took a deep breath, and stepped back out into the cave, ducking as an egg flew at him and splatted against the edge of the wall, inches from Daron's head. Larkh pointed one finger at his hat, and the other at his coat.

"Rule number one, milady, take care to avoid the coat and the hat lest I keep the goods I promised you for myself an' you don't see a penny's worth," he warned. His smile was genuine, and he secretly always missed their banter, but there was an unmistakable sincerity in his eyes that told all that he wasn't bluffing.

"Just as quick as I remember," said she. "It could've easily been a knife."

"Aye, an' it could've easily been a knife that might've left me minus another crew member too," Larkh added, looking over his shoulder at his men. "An' you'd still be owin' me dearly." She smiled, sauntered up to him, tossing her long black hair over her shoulders and firmly planted a kiss upon his lips, which he returned gratuitously.

Meynra was a slender woman of medium height with tanned skin, wearing several plaits in the front sections of her hair decorated with a variety of coloured beads. She was dressed in a light beige blouse with puffed sleeves, a brown studded corset, black leather leggings with a long red sash tied around her waist, and a pair of knee-high overturned tan boots. She was perhaps a year or two younger than him, and to call her striking would be an understatement.

"It has been too long!" she chuckled playfully, breaking away from him. "I do hope you're free later this evenin'," she added with a wink as she ran her hands down his sides and over his buttocks. Larkh's brow arched; his eyes widening. He coughed.

"Ah, Mey..." his cheeks had turned a delicate shade of pink. "There's a time an' a place for this kind o' behaviour, remember? I've things to do an' I don't really want to be walkin' around with—" She gripped, and he jolted, biting down on his lower lip. To his embarrassment, his crew members and half the black market folk were sniggering.

"Oh but I do enjoy teasin' yer," she taunted, stepping away. Her voice was very nearly a whisper. "Shall we get down to business then?"

"Let's sort this out so we can head into town for the celebrations," Larkh said, waving a signal to his men.

Mey's request consisted of two elaborate statues, one male and one female. They were a pair of Kensaiyr elves fashioned from white pearl and gold with aquamarine gemstones as eyes. The small details, jewellery and name plates were pure yellow gold, and bore the names of Althaerin and Eoumisra, ethereal attendants of the Kensaiyr god, Lyte.

"I spent a night in jail for those," Larkh sniffed. "Got caught by that damned mercenary who's been huntin' me across the Wahren Coast." His eyes narrowed on noticing Mey wasn't paying the slightest bit of attention to him now. Her eyes sparkled as she stared at the statues as if there was nothing more precious in existence. "Y'know, you look at those with more interest than you do me wearin' naught but my hat." Mey shot him one of the slyest and most alluring sideways glances he'd ever seen.

"Maybe I'm just savin' the best till last, ya never know," she teased.

That shut him up. He felt Laisner's elbow digging into his ribs and Daron's fist thumping him lightly on the back of his right shoulder. He closed his eyes, knowing full well all of this would likely be reported to Argwey.

"Ah, Mey?" Larkh asked, leaning toward her. She looked up over her shoulder at him. Larkh opened his palm and stroked it with his other hand.

"Oh!" she exclaimed, quickly digging around in the many pockets attached to a belt beneath her sash. She brought out a small leather pouch and handed it over. "Here."

Larkh untied the pouch and tilted it. A shimmering pale jade-coloured gemstone pendant slid into his palm. The diamond-shaped gemstone was set in white gold with detailing that looked like ornate little vines winding around it to the ring at the top with a chain to match. *'So this is a Varlen Artefact,'* he mused. "The gemstone certainly matches the smaller stones on the pommels of those scimitars I acquired."

"What're those gemstones called?" he heard Laisner ask.

Larkh studied it a moment. "Varlenstones, accordin' to Nays lore. I believe they are fragments that have fallen from or been mined from what the Nays call a *Varleima*," he explained.

"Varleimas are supposedly giant tear-shaped gemstones the Nays used for various purposes includin' soul-bindin' themselves to weapons an' armour so they could summon them at will, an' so no other person could use them. The Drahknyr didn't require a varlenstone or any such artefact as this, they just called on the power of a Varleima by standin' right next to it – or so the legends say – but normal Nays required them to make the initial connection. They wore the artefact until their bond with a particular weapon or suit of armour was complete. I've heard anyone not of Nays or Kensaiyr blood is capable of makin' the connection, though it's said there may be consequences."

"Don't ya have to have some kind o' skill with magic though?" Daron asked, staring intently at the sparkling artefact in Larkh's palm.

"Not necessarily, it can an' has been done," Larkh replied, holding it by the chain, "though I'd stand a better chance of success if that were the case. It doesn't matter though, I'm still goin' to give it a try. You never know, right? It doesn't matter if they can't be used; they'll still bring in more booty than we could handle an' then some, just like our success in Elinda." He grinned broadly at his men, and likewise they grinned back. "Any kind o' relics like these are worth an absolute fortune, an' we'll find more of them."

Larkh noticed a gruff-looking man staring at him from across the cave. He was heavily tanned with a bristly brown beard, and was built like bear. His name was Burne; he had cargo for this man. Mey was too busy gawking over her prized ornaments to notice him slip away. Daron and Laisner followed.

Burne stood near the gangplank of a schooner named *Señorita Eliana* moored alongside the wall inside the gaping mouth of the cove. This was the perfect place for black market operations, for a small vessel sailing out of here wouldn't be noticed from the harbour or shore unless another out on the sea was close enough to spot it. The mouth of the cove was obscured by a handful of stacks, so a longboat would be sent out first to scout the area for any other ships in the area. If all was clear, the vessel could leave. On the way in, only lookouts were required. Almadeira's smugglers' cove was well-guarded.

"More interested in securin' yer anchorage fer the night were ya Savvy?" Burne asked, his voice hoarse. It was the voice of a man who'd smoked cigars for most of his life. Larkh arched a brow.

"I've no need to secure it," he smiled, glancing over his shoulder at Mey, "that anchorage has been mine for the takin' whenever I have need of it, should it continue to be on offer."

"Aye, ye've always got all the luck."

"Not always. Anyhow, your contraband is bein' unloaded an' taken through to Harand's storeroom as we speak."

Daron tapped Larkh on the shoulder. Larkh inclined his head as Daron whispered something in his ear then nodded. Both Daron and Laisner moved off to take a seat at a makeshift tavern for a drink, though they were still close enough to keep an eye on their surroundings, just in case anyone dared make a move on Larkh.

Burne glanced in all directions, giving Larkh a distrustful look. "Ye'd better 'av it all." Larkh's eyes narrowed.

"Had I now? Who'd you take me for?" the young captain asked, "some half-arsed lout who can't be bothered to do his job properly? C'mon Burne, you ought to know me. I'm not Pañoz for cryin' out loud; even I avoid dealin' with him."

Burne grumbled. "Those things ain't easy to come by; if I don't get 'em I'll be in serious trouble, so if you ain't got it all, I'll 'avta take yer in," he warned.

"Y'know, threatenin' me before you've even got your goods ain't exactly a diplomatic way of doin' business Burne," Larkh sighed, withdrawing a slip of stained and tattered paper from a hidden pocket inside his coat. He held it up and read it out. "Elindan tobacco, Avamont wine, Maceani rum, and Deka spice from Dekatta Vale." Burne gave him a long, hard stare. Larkh frowned. He thrust the piece of paper at the burly smuggler, his jaw tightening.

"Damnation Burne! Whatever you've written on that slip, you've got, providin' I've read your childish handwritin' correctly!" he hissed. "I assumed *t* was for tons rather'n tablespoons an' *g* was for gallons, not grams." The big man bunched his fists, looking like he was ready to throw a punch.

"How dare y—"

"You can pay me a third now, an' the rest when it gets here."

The muscles in Burne's big shoulders quivered as he hunched them up, his nostrils flaring as he exhaled noisily. "I can't do that," he said finally.

Larkh gave him a knowing smile. "Oh, I think you can."

"Ye already 'ad a third."

"An' I'm asking for another third before I hand it over. You want the goods, don't you?" Larkh shot an interested glance at the schooner.

It didn't take Larkh long to get what he wanted. Burne stepped aboard the *Señorita Eliana*, and returned a minute later with a large sack, which he grudgingly handed over. *'That makes about ten thousand soren,'* Larkh thought, giving Burne a hard glance. He felt the weight was appropriate to the amount. He noticed the man swallow hard, taking note of his nervousness. Burne and his captain both knew if there wasn't enough money in these sacks, the *Señorita Eliana* would either be at the bottom of the Sendero de Mercader when she was next spotted by *Greshendier*, or Larkh would disable her and take her as a prize he would later sell.

With a sly grin, Larkh thanked him, and made his way over to join Daron and Laisner. "At least ten thousand," Larkh said as he approached them. "That is, if Yurec's got any sense an' I'm a good judge of weighin' money." Both men beamed at him. "Now we wait for the others to bring in the rest, we get the final seven thousand, an' we'll be out of here. I'll divvy it later. We've done well for ourselves lads."

AD INTERIM
Reports to Atialleia

*The greatest truths lie atop the highest of peaks,
and so must you climb to find them.*
Kensaiyr proverb

Madukeyr soared over Atialleia, the sprawling white-gold Nays capital, on the back of the white wyvern; certain word of his approach had already reached the Atiathél. The city was so-called because of its architecture. The towering white Kathaedra, imperial district, royal theatre, amphitheatre, and the Atialléane Palace, stood in resolute splendour as their dazzling golden rooftops shone with unwavering glory in the afternoon sun. The sight of them was breathtaking, especially when viewed from the sky.

The Drahknyr, along with their dragons and numerous deities were sculpted out of the whitestone walls and flying buttresses; each of the grand buildings boasting towering archways to allow the Drahknyr easy passage with their colossal wings unfurled. Residential homes were built from several varieties of stone, often with whitestone framework provided the owners were wealthy enough; and for the wealthier still, courtyards and personal rather than communal gardens. In the centre of the city stood an extravagant fountain surrounded by life-sized statues of the seven Kaesan'Drahknyr, their folded wings towering high over their heads.

He heard faint shouts from below as Avlashrenko's draconic shadow swept passively over the city streets, gliding toward the great white palace standing atop a steep plaza backed against the mountains in the far north of the city. The people knew the Tseika'Drahknyr had returned with important news concerning one of the most ancient prophecies spoken of in the Taecade Medo. To the ancient races, prophecy was a widely accepted topic of discussion;

no-one need feel ashamed of mentioning events that had been foretold.

Avlashrenko banked as he descended, circling the vast palace as he came in to land on the wide open plaza. The warm glow of sunset rose up from the cinnamon-hued mountains, transcending the palace as the sun slipped toward the western horizon, bathing the city in an aureate light not seen anywhere else in Aeldynn. The Nays called it *Tsolàiyh'unsyld Kelntnéia*l, meaning Sunset Frontier. On the palace plaza stood another large fountain; this one depicting an empyrean sculpture of the goddess Raiyah wearing a two-piece set, swathed in cloth. In her hands she held a large Solneis Orb, its swirling colours of flame representing the sun. Madukeyr leapt from Avlashrenko's back, resting a hand against his shoulder.

"My thanks as always, Avlas," he said, running his hand across smooth alabaster scales.

"You are most welcome Tseikané Madukeyr," the wyvern replied with a gracious bow of his head. *"Anhavokh Ahzu me. Jheu'naa mekh nahvek wes."* [13]

"Go and rest now," Madukeyr told him. "I shall call when we leave again."

"As you will," Avlashrenko acknowledged, turning awkwardly on the wrists of his wings and once again taking to the air. He shrieked a roar in warning to his local kin that he had returned to feed and rest.

"E'verkéne, Madukeyr," [14] said a soft, calming voice. Madukeyr turned to see the Astral Overseer, Lésos Taeren, approaching astride a dappled grey mare sporting a black mane and tail. His rippling silver cloak hung loosely across the horse's back, draping over her flanks; his flowing lengths of white hair trailing after it, clasped together twice before it reached halfway down his thighs.

"Lésos!" Madukeyr gasped, "why are—"

---

[13] I am honoured. My service is yours.

[14] Greetings, Madukeyr.

"It seems Kaesan'Drahknyr Khesaiyde was lured into a trap, as loathe as she is to admit it," Lésos interjected. "Zerrçainne brought a section of the Dorne Shaft down, preventing Melkhar from leaving. She escaped into Nira'Eléstara and has re-emerged close to the Len'athyr Sanctuary."

"Zerrçainne? How can that be? And you guided Melkhar to the nearest rift, I see..."

"Correct. I am here to bear this news to Her Imperial Highness, the Atiathél."

"Then I shall listen to your report as well," Madukeyr decided. "I have returned from restoring the Altirnathé in the North Mazaryn Peaks, and bestowed insight upon the first key." Lésos gave a brief nod at this and smiled.

"Let us bring our news to the Atiathél," he suggested. The sunlight reflected brilliantly off the aquamarine eyes of both Kensaiyr like pools of water in a tropical lagoon. "There is much for us to discuss."

The entryway and lower levels of the Atialléane, Palace of Renewal, were a sight to behold; golden friezes, mirrors and colourful murals lined the walls; marble floors stretched from one end of the building to the other and crystalline chandeliers hung from the vaulted ceilings. The rich smell of ancient stone and fabric permeated the corridors, bringing with it a sense of familiarity.

A woven burgundy carpet edged with golden embroidery swirling down the edges lined the floor as they turned into the hallway that opened out into the vast audience chamber where the carpet spread across the entire room. At the far back of the chamber above the throne was a towering sculpture, a turquoise crystal obelisk with two dragons coiled around it. Both were fashioned from dragon ivory; one white and one black. The eyes of the black dragon were set with flame-coloured solneis gemstones, and the eyes of the white with icy blue luneis. Two female statues flanked it, and another was positioned directly above it on a ledge. The two figures either side had one arm extended; the one on the centre ledge holding both arms down with her palms extended up toward the ceiling. They were known as the Adels; they were the three high priestesses of Valdysthar, Raiyah's ethereal attendants representing courage, wisdom, and serenity.

Either side of the throne two tall braziers rose up beside the Adels positioned left and right, a small ladder attached to each at the rear for easy refilling and cleaning. Stretching outward to each end of the room from these braziers were enormous arched casement windows through which the glorious rays of the evening sun shone, dappling the carpet with shadow as wisps of cloud wandered idly by.

The Atiathél sat upon her throne between the three Adels. She wore her dark hair in the usual fashion; braided at the front, adorned with colourful accessories, the rest falling down to her knees, fastened together at the small of her back. She was clad in her cream dress adorned with flowing golden drapes and jewellery, her hands perched on the edges of the throne's armrests, her knees crossed. Her face was like the purest ivory, accentuated by cosmetics that made her look more like a sculpture than a living being, especially her lips, painted the colour of cherrywood. The Nays required no improvement to their appearance, nor did any of the elven races. Their beauty was ethereal, and coveted by other races, but some still attempted to enhance it, particularly royalty and nobility.

Arkkiennah rose abruptly from the throne. "Lésos!" she exclaimed. "Has something happened? Only Madukeyr was expected." Both Kensaiyr fell to one knee.

"Your Highness," Lésos began, "Zerrçainne has returned." Arkkiennah's gasp echoed through the hall. "Melkhar entered the Dorne Shaft as per her instructions to close the portal to Phandaerys, but Zerrçainne brought down the only route with an exit. She sought my assistance in navigating Nira'Eléstara to find the closest rift to Almadeira, which happened to be in the region of the Len'athyr

Sanctuary in the Valley of Daynallar." He glanced at Madukeyr. "I have also sensed a great disturbance in the direction of Ehyenn. A disturbance that is draconic—"

"Rahntamein..." Madukeyr growled, frowning. Arkkiennah stiffened, gripping the armrests tighter.

"Indeed, he has been awakened," Lésos confirmed, "but it would seem he is still confined at this moment, though his fury is great. I assume Kalthis will have met with Anu Amarey by now, so it will be he who breaks the news to Melkhar."

"Melkhar will see him as the priority over the Mindseer Oracle," Madukeyr observed. "The vendetta they share between them, however, is a cause for concern, is it not?"

Arkkiennah put a hand to her lips thoughtfully. "It's too soon for us to reveal ourselves," she mused. "And yet..."

"We have no choice," Lésos finished. "My guess is this is exactly what Zerrçainne wants. I believe it is she who has awakened him; the abandoned Yahridican is situated on Ehyenn, and very close to the Dragon's Gaol. I have no doubt Zerrçainne would have returned there and used it as her base of operations."

"Rise," Arkkiennah instructed softly, gesturing to them both. "Look at me." The Kensaiyr rose, fixing their eyes upon the slender figure of the Atiathél. While her words were soft, her face was stern. "The Mindseer Oracle was to meet with Lyte E'varis Marceau, but I received troubling news from him on the seikryth shortly before you arrived. He left Almadeira in a hurry to warn the king of imminent civil war in Faltainyr Demura. If Melkhar was delayed, and with yet another ancient enemy soon to be loosed on Armaran, we have a serious problem. Arcaydia needs to be found, and we must consider a means to mask our presence."

"We should try contacting Kalthis at the Len'athyr Sanctuary," Madukeyr suggested, glancing at Lésos, who nodded briefly in agreement.

"Len'athyr's seikryth has broken." With a solemn shake of her head, Arkkiennah sighed heavily. "Galétahr Dreysdan needs a replacement as soon as possible."

A deep frown knotted Madukeyr's forehead, telling of his disapproval of what was to come next. He knew exactly what this meant. He and Avlashrenko would soon be leaving again to deliver a new seikryth orb to Len'athyr. Tonight they would rest, and tomorrow they would be on their way again, but now it was his turn to give his report.

"I trust the new seikryth will be delivered to the palace plaza in the morning?" he enquired.

Arkkiennah gave a solemn nod. "You may rest a little longer in the morning though Madukeyr, so I shall ask you to leave by the first bell of the afternoon. Is this acceptable?"

"Yes, thank you," Madukeyr bowed respectfully. The Atiathél smiled meekly.

"Please tell me of your venture now Madukeyr," Arkkiennah leaned back, her long fingers laced and resting on her knee. Madukeyr placed his right hand on the left of his chest.

"The altirna resurgence crystal has been replaced, the Altirnathé revived. Its production rate should increase marginally in the next few months," he began. "It would appear it had been failing for some time; in recent generations it has been mined dry for the use in new archana, including use in warships in the same way we use it." Madukeyr glanced at Lésos, closed his eyes and folded his arms. "I discovered one of the two keys Lésos guided me towards, and projected myself into one of his dreams. I led him to the Altirnathé, and there we met in combat. His name is Zehn. Marceau has taught him well. He held back to begin with, but soon found his resolve to fight me." The Tseika'Drahknyr paused in thought.

"As for the one trained by Yahtyliir," he continued, "I sensed he was close by, perhaps in Almadeira. I have not yet met him as I am only able to focus on one at a time, but as the two are inextricably tied, he shouldn't be difficult to trace, especially if Arcaydia has anything to do with it. However, he does not yet *dream* as Zehn does. He could prove to be more spiritually adept, judging by the feel of his spirit; yet he guards his mind almost too well. I suspect this is why he is not yet open to the dreams of enlightenment, and it could be as a result of some kind of devastating loss. It will take something or perhaps someone to catch him off-guard for me to project myself into his dreams. I had considered the possibility of trying to make contact with Yahty to gain more insight into his mind."

Arkkiennah closed her eyes, slowly nodded, and then lifted her gentle yet firm gaze to the bright aquamarine eyes of both Kensaiyr who stood before her. She looked first to Madukeyr. "If the second key is a guarded soul, then meeting with his trainer may certainly assist with understanding his mind," she agreed. "Keep sight of them both, Madukeyr, for it won't be long before they will need to understand who and what they are, and be brought here to Atialleia." She shifted her attention to Lésos.

"Will you at least stay for the meeting of the council, Lésos? Your insight is much needed at this time." Lésos brushed his rippling silver robes aside and bowed graciously. "I shall stay for as long as you have need of me, Your Highness."

"Thank you. The road ahead may turn dark at any time."

Arkkiennah smiled again. "I trust Melkhar to do something about Rahntamein, and perhaps Kalthis may be able to locate Arcaydia. But what of Zerrçainne, have you not sensed her, Lésos?"

Lésos gritted his teeth and held his tongue steady, embarrassed. "I have not sensed her Your Highness; she has no presence at all in Nira'Eléstara." Arkkiennah's face turned ashen. She shifted uncomfortably, her chestnut brown eyes stared blankly at the red carpet in front of her.

"None?" she asked.

"None," Lésos repeated. "Her spirit has no existence there, not even a shred of resonance. The fact she lives means she is connected with Ne'Vedanhyr at the very least, or worse, Dhavenkos Mhal." Arkkiennah's brow knitted. It could only mean one thing. She clenched her fists, holding her head up high.

"I have decided," she declared, almost startling her subjects, "I will hold the council with whatever members we currently have in Ardeltaniah. They shall be summoned immediately. Zerrçainne's goal was always the revival of Alymarn, and it seems she's achieved much in these last few millennia, so we must begin preparing for the worst." She hesitated a moment, then continued; "we are not ready, and Aeldynn is not ready, but I am now convinced this is why the Kaesan'Drahknyr needed to be awoken earlier than we first intended. I will see to this after the meeting. Madukeyr, you are still to go to the Len'athyr Sanctuary with the new seikryth, but I will also send a letter outlining my plan for the council to Galétahr Dreysdan." The Tseika'Drahknyr nodded.

The sunlight filtering through the tall windows at the far end of the room dimmed and vanished as thick white clouds crawled across the heavens. If Zerrçainne truly was alive and had spent the last three millennia searching for a way to revive Alymarn under their very noses, masking her presence using the forces of Phandaerys, the chances were she was dangerously close to succeeding. No-one had any knowledge of what she was capable of now, which made her a force to be reckoned with.

CHAPTER 11

I
Len'athyr Sanctuary

The meeting between Kalthis, Dreysdan and Vharik continued, though the air of suspicion on the worldly affairs of Armaran was growing thicker by the minute. The vast marble dining hall was empty except for the three of them and occasional members of the temple staff milling about with little to do this time of the day.

"There was an incident about sixteen years ago on Ehyenn," Vharik began. "It was before you awakened, Dreysdan. There was activity in the abandoned Yahridican Fortress, and it was reported to me while I still worked in the Archaenen Academy in Aynfell. I felt it was my duty to investigate, but I needed someone with a good sword arm.

"There was a renowned mercenary named Rajan Kahner in the employ of King Jaredh Faltain. I thought he'd be the best man for the job. What we weren't to know though, was his son and my apprentice had stowed away on the ship we sailed on from Aynfell."

Dreysdan ran a hand through his hair, shooting Vharik an incredulous look. "Firstly, how are these boys relevant? And secondly, why was this incident not reported?" His voice had a caustic edge to it. "You—"

"My seikryth was destroyed during the attack on Zerrçainne before we knew it was her," Vharik interjected. "They're very useful crystals as long as they work, but they are fragile."

"Fair enough," Dreysdan gave an exasperated sigh. "My apologies, I wasn't thinking. Still, what of those boys?"

Vharik thought for a moment. He didn't believe those two boys had met by chance. Not in the slightest. And few people knew the details of his former apprentice's true lineage. The sage shook his head.

"I sensed something in Rajan's boy. It was something unmistakably of the Nays. His name is Zehn, and I believe he is one of the two the Nays are now searching for. My apprentice has since become the Second Archmage of Silver, so you will have an understanding of what is in store for him. He isn't entirely human either, and few people know it. His name is Raeon."

Kalthis showed no sign of surprise, but he thought carefully for several moments, then recited a section of an ancient passage foretelling events that had already been set in motion:

"When mortal folly passes the threshold of power,
the seven shall awaken and bide their time.
When mortal folly passes the threshold of greed,
the Centre of Balance will shift.
When mortal folly passes the threshold of malice,
the Keys of the Origin shall rise."

"Prophecies, Kalthis?" Dreysdan gave him a questioning look. "Prophecies are hazy even at the best of times."

"I know," Kalthis replied astutely. "We Kaesan'Drahknyr were prophesied, but the passages about the Keys of the Origin in the Taecade Medo are cryptic. Who last had contact with the Origin? They came and left long before us, but only they would know for sure what it means."

"We don't even know if they still exist," Dreysdan protested, "they are long gone, like you say. All we have are the books now. You'd be chasing rainbows trying to find the world's creators now when they left the Nays and the Kensaiyr in charge generations before even you were born."

A mass of black hair slipped over Kalthis' shoulder, spilling into his lap, covering his face as he looked down at his clenched fists. Perhaps the idea of it did sound like a fool's errand, but there was something nagging at him deep down. His mother had always told him to go with his gut feeling, but he couldn't pinpoint what it was he needed to do.

"Better to chase rainbows than do nothing," he countered. "I was given the title of *Centre of Balance* for a reason, or do you have a better plan for these riddles? We will need to answer them before we can move forward. How else are we going to restore balance to Aeldynn? All we did three thousand years ago was postpone the inevitable! We achieved what we thought was balance for little more than the blink of an eye! Zerrçainne lives; she will try to bring Alymarn back from beyond the Abadhol. Add to that the mortals playing their arrogant death games."

"It is in their very nature to behave as such," Dreysdan pointed out, shrugging. "They will always take what does not belong to them and hold prejudice against all who do not think as they do. There are even those who are immortal or significantly long-lived whose folly is just as wicked, if not more so. You've just spoken of one of them, and Melkhar's own father is another. You are one of few who know the full details of what he did to her, Kalthis, and that isn't counting all the hostile factions within the Aurentai."

Kalthis stared into his lap as Dreysdan spoke. When the Galétahr had finished, he closed his eyes and rubbed his face. "And that is justification to let things continue as they are, I suppose?" he asked.

"I didn't say that," Dreysdan objected, surprised though his expression betrayed none of it.

"They are the way they are, and nothing will change that," Kalthis fiercely reiterated the point. "If that is so, you say it is not worth trying to do anything about it? I disagree." He rose to his feet. "I have not forgotten my purpose. Perhaps true balance is a dream, but it is still worth fighting for. I will go now and sleep as you insisted earlier." He turned and left the room, not waiting to hear anything more Dreysdan might have to say. The Galétahr let him go, thinking it best to let him have his rest as he had indeed attempted to encourage.

"What do you think?" Dreysdan asked as Kalthis stalked out of the room, raven black hair swinging below his hips. Vharik solemnly watched the Kaesan'Drahknyr leave the room before he spoke.

"You both have valid points," the old sage mused. "Just remember he is caught in the middle of it all." He took a silver coin and placed it carefully on its edge on the table. Dreysdan watched as the coin stood perfectly upright. Smiling through his thick white beard, Vharik blew gently on it, toppling it. The faint metallic chink was enough to cause a faint echo in the otherwise silent dining hall.

"Balance is fragile, and when it breaks, it resounds as the effect of it expands and spreads far and wide. The trouble is, the surface Kalthis has to work with is not level and smooth like this table, and the world is far from being as solid as a coin."

It was the middle of the night when Kalthis awoke to the sound of thunder. He sat up in the regal four poster bed and brushed a blanket of black hair away from his face as he looked to the window, its white curtains billowing as a soft breeze blew in. The starlit sky, dominated by the shining eye of the moon, was interrupted only by thin cobwebs of cloud crawling across the vast expanse of the midnight heavens; so why had he heard thunder?

He slid out of bed and slipped into his leather leggings and mukluk boots, his face and bare chest bathed in the pearly moonlight as he approached the window. He scanned the valley, and then the chasm that stretched eastward, facing the direction of Faltainyr Demura. The bridge that connected the mountain pass was obscured from this angle; he could only make out the very end of it from his window.

Then he looked up to see a purple lightning bolt frozen in the sky above the mountains that soon vanished, followed by a familiar presence he knew all too well.

'Melkhar?' he asked, projecting the question in mind-speech to one who approached the Len'athyr Sanctuary.

'Kalthis?' Melkhar queried in return.

'You sound more weary than I am,' Kalthis surmised. *'Are you on the bridge?'*

'Approaching now.'

'I'll meet you.'

He picked up his leather beaded jacket and pulled it over his shoulders, making for the door. Concerned by why Melkhar was even here at all, he hurried down the spacious corridor and across the open walkway overlooking the entrance hall illuminated by the milky moonlight softly streaming through the tall arched windows. He opened the sanctuary's side door, stepped on to the grand viaduct, watching as his comrade landed.

Melkhar's feet touched the stone, great white wings folding after her. Her silver-embossed ebony armour dissolved as she strode towards him. A golden light glowed around her, gradually fading; she'd just returned from Nira'Eléstara.

For a moment he just stared at her, his mind suddenly cast back to Dreysdan's words earlier that evening, *'you are one of few who know the full details of what he did to her, Kalthis.'* Those events were as clear as the sun in the sky to him; why would anyone want to do as Nalehn Khesaiyde had done to his own daughter? Why did the man so desperately want to find out what kind of force would break the bones of the Kaesan'Drahknyr? Why did he want to find out what would make them scar? He'd found his answers alright; he'd found them at the cost of breaking her in body, spirit and mind.

She stood before him now, her face impassive as usual. It was difficult to get a smile out of her unless it happened to be either cynical or malicious, though she would often arch a long, thin brow in question, as she did right now. "Dreaming on your feet Kalthis?" she asked dryly. He blinked back into focus.

"Thinking," he replied, "and wondering how you came to be here. I take it closing the portal didn't go to plan?"

"I succeeded, but the section of the Dorne Shaft I was in was brought down upon me," Melkhar explained. "Zerrçainne is—"

"Alive, I know," Kalthis interrupted. Melkhar gave him a sidelong glance as he stared up at the clear night sky. "I have already met with the Anu Amarey. She sensed her, and the changes she has undergone."

"I want to meet with you and Galétahr Dreysdan in the morning to discuss it," Melkhar said with conviction. "Lésos guided me to the nearest rift, which happened to be here, and he will report to Atialleia detailing what occurred in the Dorne Shaft on my behalf. I also want to hear from you what Anu Amarey has said."

"I'm sure the Galétahr will be glad to hear it," Kalthis surmised. "I'm also guessing you have not eaten since you left Arcaydia."

"Concerned for me, Kalthis?" There was a definite hint of amusement on her face now. Those pressed lips had quirked into a wry smile.

"I know what you are like." Kalthis shrugged, brushing long strands of hair out of his face as the wind picked up. He regarded her with a hardened expression.

Under normal circumstances in the academy that trained the Nays military, the Drahknyr, and the Galétriahn mages in their respective divisions, Melkhar was known for working too much. She rarely stopped to rest and sometimes even neglected to sit down to a meal until she'd finished her work. She knew the look he gave her. "Fine," she snorted. Kalthis smiled.

II
Cathra

Rannvorn stood atop Castle DeaCathra's highest tower. It was almost three hundred feet higher than the natural slope it stood upon, and happened to be one of his favourite spots for losing himself in thought, if not simply to overlook the city whilst getting a breath of fresh air. His dark wavy hair was tossed back and forth in the brisk evening wind sweeping westward out of Tarvon Bay where Adengeld's fleet was being mustered, his face reflecting the events of the previous night. The same images kept swimming in circles in his mind; the dark spectre, the glowing white eye, the alchemical lamps flaring blue, and an aura so wicked he'd very nearly lost control of himself.

He took a deep breath, remembering the oath he made to Zerrçainne and the entity that now guarded and guided him. In exchange for assisting Zerrçainne in her plans, she would offer him protection, guidance, and a means to crush his enemies to make his dreams a reality. There was but one catch; his soul was at the mercy of a demon.

'Do you know just who I am, Prince Rannvorn DeaCathra?' a sinuous male voice oozed into his mind. *'There is no distance between us. You must tell me.....everything.'* Rannvorn shivered as thousands of icy pinpricks raced up his spine, dividing his mind in two.

"No, I don't think I do," the prince swallowed hard, his gaze flickering in the direction of the archana factory on the eastern side of the city. Next to it was the alchemy research facility and magi-academy. All together they made up the Magicista Akadema. "Why don't you tell me who you are before I tell me my story?"

In his mind's eye, Rannvorn saw a tall, dark humanoid shape with long hair. It was a perfect silhouette with pointed ears that protruded at an angle from its head, and colossal wings that appeared to be half feathered and half membranous like those of a bat. It stood amidst swirling blue and lilac flames, bolts of lightning in all colours dancing and arcing about in circles around it. It turned its head to face him with a pair of fierce gold draconic eyes. Rannvorn froze.

'We would never move forward if no risks were taken every once in a while.' The voice was dripping with menace, echoing through his mind as it read his emotions. *'I don't need to tell you who I am. Your intuition knows, even if you are not convinced. What I am is another matter.'*

"What are you then?"

'I am the arrow that pierces the very heart of life, the poison thorn in the side that seeks triumph. I am a myth, a legend, a character in the lost pages of ancient history.' It laughed wickedly.

"Stop talking in riddles! That doesn't tell me anything!" Rannvorn protested as the voice began to fade, his pulse quickening as if on the verge of panic.

'Think on it!' said the voice, amused. The silhouette threw back its head and laughed again, maniacally. *'The more I know about you, the more I can give you. I sense your anger and hatred, Prince Rannvorn DeaCathra, but it's the fine details that are elusive. Tell me all about what you told Zerrçainne...'* Then it vanished, and he was left alone in the starlit darkness.

In a single moment the oppression in his mind was gone, leaving him with a splitting headache. The residue of the power left behind by this entity was beyond comprehension. It was something he never imagined he would ever experience. His mind was torn. His conscience told him what he was doing was wrong, but he was incapable of ignoring it. What he'd been left with this night was an appetiser of such promise he couldn't possibly refuse the chance at going for the main course. Whoever this entity was, it was giving him a taste of the power that could be – no, *would* be – at his fingertips.

He turned his head back to the vast wall surrounding the towers of the Magicista Akadema. He didn't know exactly what kind of archana was being developed within its walls, but if Zerrçainne was behind it, it would be nothing short of incredible, of that he was certain. With the kind of knowledge and power she possessed, they would easily crush Faltainyr Demura, even without the aid of the Duke of Lonnfeir. He studied the towers intently, having never given them much thought before now.

Both towers rose like giant stalagmites from the city, supported by flying buttresses on all sides with enormous green or orange alchemical lanterns shaped like fuchsias. The factory had a huge rectangular building with a vaulted roof attached to its side. This was the warehouse where the completed archana was being stored. Rannvorn recalled that whilst the Magicista Akadema was second only to the larger and more prosperous Archaenen in Aynfell, the Archaenen was locked within its own world of rules and regulations, and appeared almost completely unwilling to explore the unknown.

Threads of grey cloud partly obscuring the eerily glowing white disc of the full moon drifted slowly by on a cool north-westerly breeze casting stripes of milky light across the alchemically lit half-timbered streets of Cathra. It might be spring now, but the wind could still bite back with the remnants of winter's chill despite the mountains of Aquélutiahr – the Water Fields of Ardeltaniah – playing a part in shielding Armaran from the icy winds of the frigid Niathenica Ocean sweeping down from the north. The northern and eastern regions of the continent in Faltainyr Demura territory would already be enjoying much warmer weather over the towering mountains of Daynallar with the tropical winds and ocean currents sweeping in from Enkaiyta and Manlakhedran.

The continent of Armaran was divided by the Valley of Daynallar from north-west to south-east; a territory not easily crossed, being inhabited by dragons, wyverns and drakes. The safest routes through those mountains where dragonkind could not easily pursue would be troublesome for an invading army marching on its enemy. Rannvorn realised the direct route would be necessary once they'd traversed the pass above Lake Aeiven. He doubted his father would get what he wanted; the fool always thought he could get his own way. Persuading a dragon to do his bidding? Rannvorn snorted.

CHAPTER 12

I
Almadeira

Since Harand Loftan had taken over the Mizzen Rest, Larkh had never managed to leave the tavern before he'd downed at least three tankards of something alcoholic, free of charge. He was partial to his evenings ashore being uninterrupted by business, so he always dealt with it before considering anything else. This time, before the innkeeper could pull another, Larkh hurried towards the door to avoid becoming further intoxicated.

"I'm seein' two ladies tonight Harand, I ain't gonna disgrace myself! Ta-ra!" he yelled over his shoulder. Daron and Laisner hastened after him smirking giddily to themselves. A roar of approval erupted as Larkh slipped away, grinning to himself. He wandered back to *Greshendier* with an extra step in his confident seafarer's swagger. Daron and Laisner were no better off than he was. Argwey spotted them.

"Seems it's happened again," the elven bosun muttered in Larsan's ear.

"Seems what has happened again?" Larsan scratched his beard. Argwey laughed and pointed.

"Look at him!" Argwey pointed to where Larkh shoved Daron into Laisner for making a joke, resulting in both crew members crashing drunkenly into a pile of crates on the quayside. "Whenever we make port, Captain Savvy has a little shore time to unwind, an' the rest of us take it in turns with the watches, see. Then he's back in his business frame of mind 'fore he even thinks 'bout dinner." Larsan rolled his eyes. "Mr Loftan always tosses him a few free drinks across the bar. Larkh says it's rude to refuse. The way to the smugglers' tunnels around here is accessed through the Mizzen Rest y'see; only small ships can fit into the cove."

"So he's half pissed already," Larsan sighed. "He obviously knows this happens every time, so why doesn't he—"

"The logic of Larkh Savaldor is that once he's had time to unwind, business comes first, an' then the rest of his leisure time won't be disturbed," Argwey shrugged. "That plan would be sound were it not for Harand Loftan. Today he'll have gone ashore, had his lunch, then pleased himself until he returned to Gresh to finish business."

"Lucky bastard," Larsan grunted.

"Buggered if I'm lettin' that happen again!" Larkh protested as he boarded the ship, balancing perfectly. He leaned against the capping rail, rubbing his eyes as the glow of the sun slowly morphed from saffron to terracotta, dying the clouds pink. *'How does he do that?'* thought Larsan.

"The accepting free drinks on an empty stomach part, or something else?" the big man asked, nudging Larkh with his elbow.

Larkh glanced over his shoulder arching a brow. "You my mother now or somethin'?" he grumbled. "And no, Mey just thought she'd embarrass me in front of every crook in the tunnels. She'll get what's comin' to her later."

"So does that tie in with your early drinking escapade?"

"You've been talkin' to Argwey haven't you?" Larkh gave Argwey a lazy glare. The bosun smiled innocently, shrugging.

Larkh rubbed his eyes again, realising it wasn't just the effects of the alcohol. He recalled the storm that had kept him up half the night, and groaned. There was a festival to attend, and then there was Mey. He yawned. "Anyway, we need to get to the festival so I can sober up an' enjoy myself."

"In order to get smashed again!" Argwey laughed whilst he gave the starboard side course braces on the foremast a tug, testing they were tight enough, "and to have your wicked way with Mey later!" There was raucous cheering across the quarterdeck.

Larkh glanced at Larsan again, whose grin spread from ear to ear. "Damn it Argwey," he muttered. "I'm not *smashed*; you all know full well when I am. I'm not even sure I will be later either, I need my wits about me wi' Mey for it'll be she who'll have her wicked way with me. If I was well an' truly three sheets to the wind I'd probably wake up missin' my tackle an' she'd only think of it as a prank."

"I thought you just said that *she'd* get what's coming to *her*?" Larsan reminded him. Larkh thought about this for a moment, narrowing his eyes.

"Ah yes, I did say that didn't I? Either way I'll be worse for wear."

He pushed away from the capping rail, gaily making his way up to the helm, stepping up next to Krallan. The quartermaster happened to be busy discussing with Arcaydia the details of how square-rigged ships functioned and how they were maintained. Larkh listened quietly. Neither of them seemed to have noticed him. Funny that; he'd recently been convinced he stuck out like a sore thumb in his long red coat and matching plumed hat. How could anyone *not* notice him standing there?

"Ah so the *yards* are *braced* for the sails to catch the wind," Arcaydia mused aloud. "I think I understand. I do have one last question though..." She looked up into the rigging where the blazing hues of the evening sky broke through the intricate network of ropes running up and down and across the ship, some of them dangling by the struts holding the masts in place Krallan had called the shrouds. The sails were neatly rolled and stowed on the yards, and somewhere up on the mainmast she saw two crew members working on repairs. She turned her attention back to the quartermaster.

"How do you...wash? And how do you, that is to say...relieve...yourself?" she hesitated. "You don't exactly—"

Larkh prodded Krallan in the small of his back, making the quartermaster jump and curse loudly.

"Shiiit! Don't do that!" he gasped.

"She's sayin' you smell, Krallan. Be thankful you're not sittin' on the deck rail," Larkh chuckled.

"Y'mean like that time you kicked Laisner into the sea when we were at anchor off the island of Anjeania?" Krallan asked, pulling a sour face.

"He stank more'n anyone else," Larkh smirked. "He had it comin'."

"Nah, I think ye just enjoy bullyin' the crew," Krallan countered. Larkh grinned, resting a hand on Arcaydia's shoulder.

"In answer to your question lass," he began, "when it's necessary, I have them sling buckets over the side an' haul up sea water, an' they'll scrub themselves down with that until we find fresh water. Can't buy soap at sea, an' we only have so much space in the hold, though I carry some when I can. If we're at anchor, they'll sometimes jump in—"

"Or get kicked in," Krallan interjected. Larkh didn't bother trying to hide his smirk.

"An' as for *relievin'* oneself, as you so politely put it," he continued, slipping his arm around her shoulders, "what you call toilets on land are called heads on a ship for they're at the bow under the fo'c'sle an' either side of the bowsprit. There're a couple of pissoirs as well down by the quarterdeck for the more open-minded lads. Those wi' ranks have chamber pots as well, an' on this ship we sort out our own." Arcaydia's upper lip creased in disgust. "Tha's the way it is lass. Privacy an' comfort aren't commonplace on board ship I'm afraid." He turned on his heel.

"Captain, are you drunk already?" Krallan asked. Larkh shrugged, held a hand flat and tilted it from side to side.

"Two words, Krallan," said Larkh, his eyes narrowing. "Harand Loftan. Y'know I don't get to walk away unless I've accepted a few free drinks." He yawned again, giving his belly a gentle rub. "Anyhow, I'm takin' Arcaydia here into town for the festival tonight, an' right now I need some grub. I'll enjoy the celebrations with her before Mey hauls me away an' gives me the screw for all glory."

"You enjoy it really."

"Aye, that I do!"

After stowing his coat and hat away in the great cabin in favour of keeping cool, Larkh left the ship with Arcaydia; he fell quiet instantly. Arcaydia saw he'd drifted into deep thought, and though his gentle face seemed indifferent; she could tell there was something bothering him.

For a while she remained silent while she tried to think of something appropriate to say. He'd been kind enough to keep her company for most of the day, and within that time she had already learned he was much like herself in many ways; completely alone despite nearly always being surrounded by other people. She had lost her own immediate family, but what could it possibly be like to lose them all? It also made her wonder about Melkhar's past; she had the feeling there was a lot going on beneath that rock solid exterior of hers.

She didn't know where Melkhar was, or exactly what she was doing, but she'd been told contact would be made when possible. She had also been told to seek out a man named Marceau Saiyinn, and though Larkh had known who he was, Marceau had apparently left town by the time she arrived. Her plan was to try again the next day to see if he'd returned, and if not to pass a note through his mailbox. Glancing across at the intriguing young man walking beside her, she silently wondered if he was still going to tell her anything more about his story.

Larkh was aware Arcaydia's eyes had been on him all along, and although he tried to tell himself otherwise, he resigned himself to the fact the young woman's curiosity was insatiable. It wasn't that he despised her questions, for she had obviously been sheltered, it was the agony of his past welling up to the surface he found impossible to control.

"I haven't forgotten about your question," he said eventually. While his voice was soft and calm, he was obviously tense. He didn't look at her as he spoke. "Please understand; every time I think about it, what happened to them, someone may as well be rippin' my guts out." Arcaydia tried to swallow a lump that suddenly appeared in her throat.

"You...you don't have to tell me anything," she said, shaking her head. "I suppose in some way I can relate. I lost my parents and my brother, and I've only recently discovered where I originally came from. I had severe amnesia, and though I've slowly been regaining my memory, it's still hazy in a lot of places." She showed him a long jagged scar on the right side of her neck. "I can't even remember how I got this." Larkh opened his mouth to speak, but found nothing to say.

"I've only known you for half a day, so I can't expect you to tell your life story to a stranger," Arcaydia continued, "although I suppose it was rude of me to have asked earlier. You might say I like to learn about others; I want to understand them." Larkh felt himself starting to smile. He stopped to look out across the harbour.

"Y'know, I'm not sure I've ever met anyone quite like you," he said, fixing his bright azure eyes upon her as she regarded him with uncertainty. "Don't look at me like that. It's not a bad thing. You take an avid interest in others, an' that means you're less worried about yourself. In some ways you remind me of myself. Still, you shouldn't forget about your own needs."

"In what ways?" she asked. Larkh chuckled. "What's so funny?"

"It seems that your appetite for information is just as insatiable as my appetite for a damn good meal when I set foot ashore," he laughed.

Then, without warning, he gently gripped her shoulders, leaned in and kissed her on the cheek before releasing her, strolling off back up the road toward the town centre. "You can't truly know a story if you keep skippin' from one chapter to another. You need to read it thoroughly," he added, tapping his temple. "One thing at a time. Always."

For a moment Arcaydia was stunned. He'd just kissed her. On the cheek, granted, but he kissed her! She didn't know quite how she was supposed to have received it, but she took a wild guess it was just a spur of the moment sort of thing, and he was tipsy. Still, she felt the heat rising on her cheeks again.

Whichever way she looked at it, he'd spoken the truth. She did ask too many personal questions without giving anyone time to think about their answer, and she was always thirsty for more information about someone. She was drawn more to certain people than others, and Larkh happened to be one of them. It was the way she felt about Melkhar, about Kalthis, and Zairen too. There was an energy about them that simply sucked her in, and it wouldn't let go. She lifted her eyes to the sky, her mind lingering on Kalthis a little longer, wondering what he was up to right about now.

As she turned her attention back to Larkh, she gasped as her vision blurred, switching to another form of vision, but only for a moment. In that moment, she believed she had seen Larkh's spirit, and witnessed something entirely unexpected. There were golden threads of energy weaving through him and around the pearly-silver form of his spirit, jogging her memory of a book she had read in Atialleia's grand library. She blinked, her vision returning to normal.

'That's happened a few times now,' she thought worriedly. *'It's different from seeing the pasts of others. I don't know what this means. Perhaps I should discuss it with Melkhar when I see her again...'*

"Hey, are you alright?" Larkh called after her. "You seem taken aback by somethin'."

"N-no, I'm alright," she answered. "I just thought I saw something strange. Do you believe in the spirit?"

"Yeah..." He sounded dubious. "My combat trainin' involved a lot of spiritual practices." There was a faint hint of suspicion in his voice. "Why?"

"It seems I have abilities that involve visions," she said, smiling weakly. Shyly, she added, "sometimes one might flash up in my face all of a sudden. I haven't learned to fully control it yet. I hope that this doesn't put you off talking to me." That was a lie. She wasn't able to control it at all.

"Why would it put me off?" Larkh asked, pulling a face. He watched her closely. Despite the fuzziness in his head he could see she was embarrassed, arriving at the conclusion she'd been rejected in the past. "Don't worry about that sort of thing with me," he shrugged. "I'm actually interested to know more when we're able to talk privately. Come on now, we're late." The next thing she knew, he'd taken her by the hand and was leading her up the road toward the lights and music in the town square.

There was something mysterious about him, she knew that much, but she couldn't quite put her finger on what it was. The book she had read in the library had been written specifically about spirits, including the behaviour, their energies and the deceased. *It's something to do with the Nays, I'm sure it is!* She was now racking her brain trying to remember. *Could he be one of the two she was talking about? I heard Madukeyr say they were both in this area at the moment. There's definitely something...'* Her thoughts trailed off, for Larkh squeezed her hand and pointed to the kaleidoscopic plethora of activity that had exploded into life in Almadeira's town square.

Arcaydia saw what she recognised to be a gypsy performance troupe with actors, fire dancers, and minstrels playing a variety of instruments. A trio of ladies danced while playing castanets. From the look of them, Arcaydia guessed they were sisters, for they were almost identical. They wore long pleated skirts, and their dark hair was tied back into braids. As was the custom for their performances, the eldest wore a single braid, the second sister wore two, and the youngest wore three so they may be easily distinguished. Every now and again one of them would stop and clap twice, initiating the next sequence. Occasionally, a sequence might involve only one of them. As they stepped back and bowed out, there was a loud round of applause, followed by the minstrels stepping in for their next piece.

It was then Larkh yielded to the smell of food, particularly of cooking meat. He looked left and right, scanning everything available in front of him – and that was only what was immediately in front. There were at least a dozen stalls on the other side of the square, but he was eager to make the best of the event. Still, choices had to be made. There was everything from roasted hams, spiced beef and venison skewers; to pies, grilled chicken, game and seafood. There were also sweet treats such as cakes and fruits glazed in sugar and honey.

Larkh ran a hand through his hair, scratching the top of his head. He was sorely tempted, but he didn't want to overdo it. Too much rich food in a day for a seafarer whose diet was basic at the best of times was a sure-fire way of making oneself ill. Trial and error had taught him that. An apothecary had once explained the details, perhaps a few too many details. It conveniently helped to narrow his choices.

They made their selections, paid the vendors, then moved to a vacant bench outside one of the taverns situated on the opposite side of the town square from the Silver Gull. This tavern was known as the White Sails; one of many half-timbered buildings, a white-sailed ship painted on an old square piece of sail canvas nailed to a sturdy wooden plaque dangling over the entrance. Arcaydia's eyes widened at the mound of food on Larkh's plate, watching him digging in.

"You know, I brought some other clothes with me," Arcaydia said suddenly. Larkh's brow arched in interest as he ate, earning him a kick to the shin.

"Ow! What was that for?" he protested with a mouthful of food. "You weren't exactly clear—"

"I said I brought some other clothes with me," she interrupted, tossing the waves of her frosty hair behind her shoulders. "After the deaths of my parents and my brother, I was taken in by a group of travellers, much like this troupe here. I still have the clothes they gave me. I've packed some of them."

Larkh licked his fingers. "Are you askin' me to dance with you?" he asked, giving her a sidelong glance.

"*Can you dance?*" She fixed her dark blue eyes on him intently.

"Yeah." He attempted to feign indifference, but failed. Instead, he was trying not to grin.

"Any favourites?"

"I suppose the Ena Canei version of the Pasaru Darvelle is one I'm good at," he suggested, unable to think of any specific favourites. "I can do a bit of folk dancin' as well," he added between mouthfuls. "You'll have to give me a bit of time to let all this go down first. You've no idea how often women expect me to get up the instant I push my plate away."

"Don't worry," she said, "I'll ask the minstrels about them in a little while." She beamed as she turned to face him again. "It's been quite a while now since I last danced like that. I hope I remember everything well enough."

"They know the music for all those kinds of dances," Larkh assured her. "I know this troupe. Besides, festivals like this include all cultures of Armaran; even Enkaiyta. Faltainyr Demura is more culture friendly than Adengeld though."

"It's wonderful to see different kinds of people gathered in a place like this," Arcaydia added, "especially when it's for an event like this." She watched as the sequence changed again, and the young woman wearing three braids stepped up to sing a ballad. Arcaydia's chin slid on to her palm, elbow resting on her knee as she listened, smiling appreciatively.

When the performance ended Larkh prodded her, having cleared his plate. "Are you going to finish that?" he asked. Arcaydia snapped her head round to look at him. His plate was already bare. Her eyes widened.

"What? I was hungry," he said defensively.

"No wonder you're called a bottomless pit!" she remarked, picking up a leg of chicken. "I'll finish it. You couldn't possibly eat any more though..."

"Give me about ten minutes an' I reckon I could," Larkh shrugged. He laid his plate aside, laced his fingers and leaned back. "It's not in my nature to let anythin' go to waste if I can help it. Oftentimes at sea goin' hungry is unavoidable; life has taught me to seize opportunities when I see them."

"Is that how your belly gained such an infamous reputation with Mrs. Menow?" Arcaydia giggled.

Larkh laughed as he looked up to the sky where the first stars dotted the heavens. "No no no, *that* reputation follows me wherever I go," he smirked. "People just like to wind me up about it, including Elsie Menow. My notoriety is otherwise related to bein' elusive an' just downright clever."

"You'll have to tell me some of those stories then."

"Indeed I shall!" he winked. "Don't forget you need to go an' change if you want me to dance with you in a bit though."

There was a distinct twinkle of charm in his eyes. Arcaydia felt her cheeks flush again, and quickly resumed her meal. While she wasn't looking, Larkh looked back to the gypsy performers, a smug expression crossing his face as the minstrels began playing a lively piece of music, enticing locals to get up and dance. *'How many times have I seen that look on your face today?'* he thought. *'You remind me of how Liri always behaved around me. Liri.....I miss you. I want to see you again. We spent the first nine years of our lives together after all. Too many years have passed since we last met.'*

II
Almadeira

Arcaydia dashed off to the Silver Gull, returning half an hour later wearing a light blue close-fitting low-cut blouse, and a long dark blue gypsy skirt with a white trim at the bottom. Her hair was left down but she had taken strands from either side of her face, braided them, and tied them together around the back of her head.

Larkh sat watching the three sisters dancing to a fast paced tune dominated by lutes, lyres, guitars and drums; Larsan, Argwey and a handful of other crew members from *Greshendier* now seated around him. All clapped and tapped their feet to the beat, some doing so as they attempted to down tankards of ale. Larkh felt someone nudging his arm. As he glanced over, Argwey nodded in Arcaydia's direction. Larkh quickly jumped to his feet and took a deep breath as he made his way over to her while Argwey approached an elven woman.

Larkh doubted his brow could rise any higher on his forehead as he admired Arcaydia. She smiled at him innocently. Like a gentleman he began with the face. She was beautiful. No, better than that, stunning. His eyes wandered down to her cleavage, and somewhat less like a gentleman his gaze lingered there a few moments longer before he finished his scan at the hem of her skirt. Then he looked her directly in the eyes. "What do you think?" she asked shyly.

"Breathtaking," he said, exhaling heavily. He wasn't quite sure if he'd just been holding his breath or not. "Quite literally. Better go an' ask if they'll do requests then, but I'm sure they'll accept." Arcaydia nodded and made her way over to the middle of the square to make her enquiry. He smiled broadly when he saw her wave him towards her.

He stood and inclined his head toward his crew. "Lads, get some grub an' watch the show." He smiled and gave them a wink before slipping between the tables out into the middle of the square.

The minstrels instantly recognised him. They either grinned or waved, but one in particular got up, throwing his arms around him. "Larkh Savaldor, I can't believe it's been a whole year!" he chortled. He was middle-aged of medium height with short dark brown hair and a carefully trimmed moustache and goatee. His theatrical mannerisms seemed to carry over into every non-theatrical situation. They gave each other a brotherly pat on the back.

"It's good to see you too, Arven."

"I've some news from the road for you later," Arven's tone darkened slightly. "Stuff you'll want to keep in mind." Larkh took note of Arven's expression. The information he held was serious. He nodded briefly. "Now though, your lady friend here's requested the dramatic *Ena Canei Pasaru Darvelle*, so get ready." He paused. "Hey, have you grown again or somethin'?" Arven tilted his head slightly.

"No, I don't think so," Larkh scratched the back of his head. "I was still six foot last I checked. Perhaps you've shrunk?" Arven pointed a finger at him as he returned to his position on the little makeshift stage they were using. He and another took up their positions followed by the three sisters, who readied themselves with their castanets.

Larsan, Argwey, and the small cluster of men from *Greshendier's* crew sat down to watch. Having not seen Larkh perform any kind of specific dance before, Larsan wasn't sure what to expect, but he found himself pleasantly surprised. Both he and Arcaydia were adept, and they were certainly nothing to be dismissed lightly.

The *Pasaru Darvelle* was a passionate theatrical dance requiring both participants – traditionally one man and one woman – to portray themselves as dignified and proud. It was a dance designed to be performed as though it were a competition, and there was no doubt Larkh and Arcaydia's skills were evenly matched. They complemented one another flawlessly; every move kept pace with the predominant one-two rhythm. Their steps were fast, sharp, strong and determined; the artistic use of their hands kept in perfect timing with their feet, adding to the drama that left onlookers speechless. Their performance drew even more spectators.

Arcaydia spun into Larkh's arms, her long skirt spiralling outwards around her. He caught her, lowering her as she leaned back. Her right arm held him around the back, her left trailing down the right side of his face as he leaned in, his eyes scant inches from her breast. She righted herself and spun out again, taking his right hand, allowing him to twirl her in circles before she let go, dropping to a crouch. A split second later she was upright again, alternating one arm high and the other low while Larkh made elaborate sweeping gestures with both arms.

Larsan almost wished he was in Larkh's position, but he admitted to himself he wouldn't know where to begin with a dance like this. That thought progressed to the realisation he wasn't sure that he could dance at all save for a few folk styles, and even then he was an amateur. Truth be told, he didn't really care once he'd had a good few drinks. Nothing else seemed to matter then. Argwey nudged him.

"He's a bit *too* good, ain't he?" the elf grinned. Larsan grunted an agreement.

"And he knows it," he added. "You'll have to tell me how he became captain. He's never mentioned it."

"That's a bit of a story," Argwey admitted. "When we have a bit o' time I'll tell you."

The dance ended with Larkh pulling Arcaydia firmly up against his chest with her braced against his shoulder, caressing one side of his face again as their lips almost met, her left leg lifted and supported by his right arm. There was a roar of applause from the audience. Slowly the two relaxed and stepped away from one another. Even the minstrels laid down their instruments and joined in the applause. Larkh and Arcaydia bowed to one another, then to their audience. They made their way back to their seats, Larkh receiving pats or light thumps to his shoulders. He found himself unable to hide the look of self-satisfaction on his face, but it was he alone who noticed the cloaks in the shadows.

CHAPTER 13

I
Almadeira

The full moon had climbed high into the sky, but the spring festivities continued, the lively folk dancing barely halting between songs. Those needing to catch their breath stood aside, clapping in time with the beat. The sisters took turns singing; each song prompting the townsfolk to partake in different varieties of dance, some frequently requiring a change of partners following each repetition of steps. The cheeks of every lady coming into contact with Larkh flushed a pale shade of pink, and judging from the scowls of a handful of men, it seemed some of them were already 'spoken for'. It was during one such dance Meynra moved along to be his partner.

"So who's the latest lassie ye've been lurin' into yer net my gorgeous heartbreaker?" she asked him, kissing him on the cheek as she linked arms with him.

"I met her today," he replied as they stepped back, clapped twice, and linked arms again to dance in the opposite direction. "I was leavin' the Silver Gull an' we walked quite literally into each other. She had a lot of luggage with her, so I offered her a hand in gettin' it all to her room."

Clap-skip, hop, clap-clap.

"It went down well then!" Mey laughed.

"Aye, but there were a few misunderstandin's to begin with," Larkh admitted, smiling sheepishly. "It seems she caught on right away."

"Well, she's certainly a looker ain't she?" Meynra said with a wink. "I saw ya dance the *Pasaru Darvelle* with her too. It's obvious she's travelled with gypsies before."

"I thought so too." Larkh's gaze flickered to where Arcaydia now danced with Argwey.

Clap-hop, skip, clap-clap.

"When're ye gonna come over to my room lover boy?" Mey's seductive tone was now kicking in. She usually sounded playful, but when she really wanted someone in her bed, she sounded like a true seductress. This kind of behaviour from her made it difficult for him to maintain his composure, but he didn't intend to leave the festivities just yet. There was time.

Clap-skip, hop, clap-clap.

"You want me that badly do you?" he asked, staring into her dark eyes intently. She smiled sensually as the music slowed and the dancing stopped.

"Aye," she said, stepping right up to him, pressing her hips up against his. "It's like a cravin' I get, y'know. Every now an' again ya get a cravin' for yer favourite food, an' then it drives ya *mad* until ya get a chance to devour it." Larkh swallowed and drew a deep breath, followed by a tense sigh.

"Hold on a little longer." He uttered the words into her ear under his breath as he leaned in. "Patience is a virtue. I want to make sure Arcaydia is safe at the inn before I leave her for the night. She's on her own while her master is away takin' care of some business. Besides, don't tell me you ain't havin' fun here too." Meynra glanced over toward where Arcaydia stood with Argwey.

"She's still hangin' wi' yer bosun," she shrugged, indifferent. "Methinks she's gettin' a bit weary though. I can see her eyelids droopin'. Hahaha! I bet yer glad ye'll 'ave someone who's still got some energy left in her eh?" Larkh shrugged.

"I was on the helm till the early hours so I'm gettin' a bit tired myself," he admitted. "Somethin' about that storm felt odd. Anyhow, that ain't gonna stop me from givin' you my all tonight. We don't see each other enough to take it easy do we?"

"Yer right about that," she winked. Then for a brief moment her face turned serious. "How about ye tell me more about that storm a bit later eh? It sounds like there might've been some magic at work," she added intuitively. "I trust ye've already recognised where that new lassie of yers is from?"

Larkh glanced in Arcaydia's direction again. She was now engrossed in conversation with Argwey and Larsan. He placed a hand on Mey's shoulder and gestured to a spot at the corner of an alley, away from the crowd. Mey nodded, following him until they came to stand just inside an alley.

"She fits the description of the Nays," he said quietly. "The lines framin' her eyes are a dead giveaway, though I don't think she's a pureblood; they're not dark enough, if the legends are true. Her kind of beauty is unmistakeable to those who know how to look."

"Are ye still investigatin' yer own lineage then?" Mey looked at him earnestly. Larkh looked away. "That artefact ye wanted was a part of it as I recall."

"Sort of," he confirmed, scratching his head, his eyes directed at the cobbled pavement. "I don't really want to discuss the artefact here. Anyone could be listenin'. It's also a tad difficult to investigate my lineage when I can't go strollin' back into Saldour on a whim. I do keep gettin' some very strange sensations every now an' again, an' not knowin' why is buggin' me." She ran both hands down his sides.

"Any other kinds o' sensations?" she asked. A smug smile spread across his face; he knew that one was coming.

"Like the kind of sensation that drives me to give in to my baser nature?" he suggested. His eyes narrowed suggestively. "All the time, especially with the likes of you."

"Tha's ma boy," she chuckled, running a hand through her hair while keeping the other planted firmly on his hip.

"Seriously though, things do seem to be a bit out o' place lately. Ye noticed anythin' odd about the city today?" Larkh whispered, leaning toward her and placing one hand against the wall behind her. She shook her head.

"I think I'm bein' watched," he added, his voice low and sincere. "I've got a sinkin' feelin' in the pit of my stomach that won't go away. I'm rarely wrong; you know that for a fact. Warn your crew before we slip away. There are those who know you're not really a merchant."

"Just like there are those who suspect that yer blood ain't entirely human?" Mey whispered back. Larkh glanced toward the festivities, then left down the dark alley.

"None of that's certain," he said in an idle tone, "but whether it's true or not doesn't matter. It ain't gonna change who I am either way."

"Don't get me wrong Larkh Savaldor," Mey said, brushing stray strands of sandy hair away from his face, "there are some gorgeous men out there, some really gorgeous men, but what you have tops all of 'em. There's no mistakin' it as far as I'm concerned." He dropped his hand from the wall on to her shoulder fighting to hide his embarrassment, and failed. She kissed him again.

"Mey..." he began as she pressed a finger to his lips.

"Shush," she said with a cheeky smile. "I know. Let's go back to the festival for a bit before we get lucky then eh?" Mey grasped his hand and pulled him back into the lively atmosphere, giving him a little push toward his crew. He returned to his seat where Arcaydia sat talking to Larsan. With a wink Mey returned to her table.

He watched her as she turned towards her crew, swiping a drink from one of them. She sat down and kicked one of the men in the shin for making an inappropriate comment. Larkh knew it wouldn't be long before she'd demand another dance with him, and he looked forward to it. He also looked forward to their meeting in her bedroom later. He saw Arcaydia turn her head toward him as he approached, and with a nod toward the square as the eldest gypsy sister began to sing a ballad, he gestured in the direction of the slow-dancing couples. Arcaydia nodded, her hand slipping into his as they joined in.

Larkh had barely taken his seat again before he almost fell off it as the next act revealed herself; a tanned woman with the lithest body he'd ever seen. She wore little more than a two-piece set made of gold, collections of jewels jingling as she danced, her perfect figure undulating laterally like a snake. Bangles held both ends of a translucent sash, which she held up above her head. Her wavy hair, black as midnight, was tied back in a high ponytail with a matching golden clasp behind jewelled attachments dangling either side of her face. Her ears, however, were the most notable thing about her. They were almost funnel-shaped, like a leaf curling in on itself from the bottom, pointing outward diagonally.

"What race is she? I've never seen anyone like her," Larkh heard Larsan ask, glancing towards where Argwey spoke with Arcaydia again, then across at the other crew members of the *Greshendier*.

"She's Aurentai," Larkh answered, distracted. His eyes were all over her voluptuous figure. Out of the corner of his eye he saw Mey giggling at him. He'd known Mey a long time; long enough to know that she never got jealous of other women so long as she deemed them worthy of him. He understood; he felt the same way when it came to her and other men.

The eldest of the three sisters began to sing again as four braziers filled with fuel were moved into position in a square around the dancer. As the Aurentai dancer raised both arms, the braziers flared, burning high and bright. She spun in circles, her long sash now billowing out behind her. As she slowed and stopped spinning, she began rotating her wrists up and down close to her body, her torso and hips seeming to undulate independently as the flames split, coiling around her.

"It seems she's also a bit of a sorceress," Larsan observed.

"She's an Adjen priestess," Larkh mused aloud, watching her intently. His eyes didn't move from her. "Adjeeah is the Lady of Flame, one of the elemental deities. Her priestesses double as exotic dancers, an' have extraordinary command over fire."

"You're certainly well informed..." Larsan trailed off, regretting his words instantly, for Larkh broke free of his preoccupation with the dancer, giving him a derisive look.

"If those who travel aren't well informed oh noble *bounty hunter* of the north, then who is?" Larkh hissed, reminding Larsan of their first meeting. "I've seen as many places in my young life as an experienced whore has clients, so I hope you'll forgive me for bein' in the know."

"Are you pissed off?" Larsan couldn't help but ask. Larkh turned his attention back to the performance.

"Nah," he said dismissively, slouching in his chair. As a wench weaved between the tables offering drinks, he waved her over, picked up a tankard and dropped a coin on to the tray. "I would be if any of you started anythin' though. It's been a long day an' I'm tired; don't forget I was on the helm half the night in that livid storm." He downed his drink in one draught. He'd had another two since arriving at the festival; that was enough. After his encounter with Mey, he would sleep very well indeed.

Larsan conceded the point. Since they'd tied up alongside the berth, *Greshendier's* crew had either been seeing to repairs or taking a well-earned rest. Larkh had been kind enough to put his own needs aside to assist a young woman on her own in unfamiliar territory. He hadn't noticed it until now, but fatigue was written all across the young captain's face.

"Why don't you go to bed then?" Larsan suggested. "I'm sorry I didn't realise earlier, but you look shattered."

"Promises to keep," Larkh said with a nonchalant shrug. "I'll wait until Arcaydia is safely back at the Silver Gull, then I'll pay Mey a friendly visit."

"Have you even got enough energy for *that*? There's always tomorrow."

"Scupper that Larsan," Larkh yawned. "You're whistlin' psalms to the taffrail. I'll get my second wind. There's no point in holdin' on to tension while there's an early chance to let go of it."

"Why haven't you—" Larsan stopped as Larkh nodded in Arcaydia's direction. "I see."

Arcaydia finished talking with Argwey and brought her chair up close. She sat and leaned against Larkh's shoulder. Larsan gave a nod and turned to begin a conversation with the bosun himself.

"Do you know her?" Arcaydia asked, following his gaze to the dancer. She too found herself entranced as the dancer made the flames roar and dance around her. "Her ability to control fire is....where have I seen this before?"

Larkh tilted his head. "This'd be the first time I've seen her in person," he admitted, "but I've heard about her before. I believe her name is Arieyta Ei Nazashan. She often travels with troupers around the world. Anyhow, what're you on about? You said somethin' about her ability to control fire."

"I feel like I've seen this before," Arcaydia said thoughtfully, shivering at the cool evening breeze against her bare arms. "I travelled a lot with my parents and my brother before they were killed, so I might have seen someone perform like this before." Her breasts pressed against his arm. Despite how interested he was in this dancer, he couldn't help but take notice.

Larkh straightened his back and cast his glance sideways and downward. He glanced back at the dancer, a dreamy expression crossing his face. "Ah, I see," he mumbled absent-mindedly, remembering her telling him she suffered from amnesia. He turned his head, watching her for a moment. "Are you gettin' tired?" he asked. Arcaydia rubbed her eyes; the world seemed different as if she were already dreaming. Arieyta was still dancing, but Larkh's eyes were on her now. He seemed worried. "I might be a bit tired," she admitted. Larkh shook his head.

"We've both had a long day," he said. "I know you tried to sleep this afternoon, but you told me you couldn't. I think it's about time you went to bed."

"But I'll miss the—"

"You idiot," Larkh chuckled. "You can't keep your eyes open. You'll fall asleep an' miss it anyway. There'll be more tomorrow."

He rose to his feet, gently pulling her up with him. He took her by the hand and looked over his shoulder at Larsan and his crew. "I'll be back in a few minutes." In seeing an expression of warning on his face, his men dared not tease him. "Come on," he said to Arcaydia. She rubbed her eyes again and followed him without argument.

He left Arcaydia in the care of Mrs. Menow and returned to the square to the sound of folk music playing once more, but he didn't consider rejoining the crowd or venturing back to the food stalls for a sweet treat despite the temptation being very real. He saw Larsan and his men laughing and joking, knocking full tankards together, sloshing the contents. Mey stood with them. When she saw him, the conversation ceased. She turned to face him with her legs slightly apart and leaned forward, one hand planted on her hip, beckoning to him with her middle finger, the most bewitching look in her eyes. The first three buttons on her blouse were undone, revealing her ample cleavage. He arched a brow, a wry smile spreading across his lips. He strode forward enthusiastically, taking a hold of her hand.

"Later lads," Larkh said dismissively, pulling Mey along with him. She waved at the men with her free hand, grinning at them. The crewmen whooped and cheered as they disappeared down the next street.

The door to Mey's room closed and Larkh locked it abruptly, turning the key one-handed as he worked at unfastening his trousers with the other. He'd barely turned around into the room when Mey shoved him hard against the oaken door. She was already topless save for her brassiere, but he dealt with that single-handedly as well. He snaked his left hand around her back under her silky black hair, unclipping it effortlessly. She kicked it aside as it hit the floor and pushed her breasts up against his bare chest while laying passionate kisses upon his lips.

Larkh pushed away from the door, dragging his shirt over his head, letting it fall to join the rapidly growing pile of clothing beneath them. He stroked her slender figure, keeping his mouth engaged with hers, running one hand across her smooth navel. He planted his hands solidly upon her hips, returning her kisses ever more gratuitously.

"Have ye taken the *thesilum*?" she asked in-between kisses. "Y'know I never take any chances."

"Aye," he replied, "an' you?"

"Good boy," she said fondly, running her fingers across the taut muscles of his stomach. "Don't worry, I've done my bit too." He shivered a little at her touch, recoiling only to yank off his boots and trousers while Mey slithered out of her leggings. Larkh threw aside what was left of his clothing dismissively and stood before her, waiting.

Their eyes met then, and for a long moment they watched one another intently, watching for which one of them was going to make the next move. The sandy layers of Larkh's hair danced in the warm spring breeze drifting in through the open window. Mey ran her tongue suggestively across her upper lip like a hungry feline; an invitation.

Larkh made his move. He grinned, grabbed her by the shoulders, guiding her backwards. With a gentle push, she fell against the bed and lay back, gazing up at him with lustful eyes, biting her lower lip. She stared at him intently, full of raw expectation. He breathed it in deeply, releasing the words "I want you," under his breath with a self-assured smile.

"I'll have you," she whispered back.

"I'll take you," he finished with firm assurance.

"Then take me," she said playfully. "Take me under full sail!"

He climbed on to the bed and crawled over her with the calm assertiveness of a cat, leaning forward, kissing her, lowering his body to meet hers. He brushed away the wandering strands of her pitch dark hair, and began caressing her neck with his lips. She smelled of wisteria and honeysuckle, which served only to further intoxicate him as their bodies became entangled.

II
Almadeira

The evening's festivities drew to a close, the folk still brimming with energy dispersing into Almadeira's many taverns. Larsan and the small group from *Greshendier's* crew retired to the Mizzen Rest, sitting around a table close to the bar while enjoying the music and song of a woman and three minstrels by the fireplace at the far end of the taproom.

It was a reasonable size for a tavern; it wasn't the largest nor the smallest Larsan had come across, but it catered for the majority of sailors whose vessels were berthed on this side of the harbour. It reeked with alcohol and the stench of old sweat and well-worn leather, though it appeared to be far more amicable than a lot of taverns he'd visited in the icy north of Icetaihn.

The innkeeper, Harand Loftan brought over their first round of drinks. The two maids he hired were busy serving other patrons. He was a big man with a paunch and a thick, bushy black beard. "Where's the Cap'n this evenin' then?" he asked, setting the tankards down two at a time. Daron and Laisner snickered behind their tankards as they picked them up. Argwey slouched in his chair, wrapping his arms around the back of his head.

"Right about now? Slackin' his main brace an' droppin' anchor I imagine," he mused, suggestively arching a brow.

"Ah," Harand said nodding. "I do remember seein' Meynra goin' into the tunnels earlier today. I don't doubt it's her he's with." There was more snickering from Daron and Laisner's direction.

"Aye, you're right on that one," Argwey confirmed. "An' he'll be with her the rest of the night I reckon. The man was about to nod off before he even left the festival. It was a hard night at sea; we lost a few men to the storm out there. Knowin' him though, he'll set every sail an' try to push for as many knots as he can before he loses the wind and starts to drift." Harand snorted a laugh and wandered back behind the bar.

"Anni! There're other customers to serve y'know!" Harand called out. Larsan and Argwey followed the innkeeper's stern gaze to where one of the serving maids sat on the knee of a handsome sailor. Blushing, Anni stood and stroked the man's faintly stubbled chin, leaving his table with the subtle hint she'd be seeing him again later. The bosun tilted his head back to his comrades with a lazy smile and turned his attention to Larsan.

"What's the matter wi' you?" he said, sitting up. The tall blond warrior stared into his tankard, his shaggy hair hanging loose and unkempt about his bearded square jaw. "If you looked any more miserable I'd say you were drownin' your sorrows into that drink."

"I'm not miserable," Larsan assured him, "just lost in thought I suppose. Do you think Larkh has been acting out of sorts today?" Argwey picked up his drink and rested his elbows on the table.

"You're worried about the Captain?" he enquired. "He always gets like that if he's been teased too much or if someone's prodded a raw nerve. How long've you been with us? Five, six months? You've got a lot to learn about him. I've never known a more complex man. There're more sides to him than a standard dice." He took a long draught from his tankard and set it back down. "An' you've seen him fight, so I don't need to remind you of that one." Larsan gave a sheepish chuckle.

"Yes, he bested me with his blades," he admitted, "and you're now going to tell me I've not seen him at his best, right?"

"To call him a prodigy would be an understatement," Argwey shrugged. "He exceeds that. I've known him since he was rescued; he was about nine years old. I watched him change from a terrified, mute little boy into our Captain, an' you're damn right you've not seen him fight his best."

"Argwey's told us stories from before we met him," Laisner chimed in, "an' after havin' experienced what he can do myself, I'd rather follow him into battle than fight against him. I was sceptical, an' as a result I got me arse handed to me."

"He may be young, but there ain't no other cap'n out there I'd rather sail under," Daron added.

"I've seen men approach him askin' to join his crew havin' fled other ships 'cause of how they been treated, 'cause he's fair," Laisner continued, leaning forward. "*Greshendier's* a big ship. She needs what hands she can get to sail her; but our crew's smaller than what she'd have if she were still in the navy."

"And what happens when the captains of other ships find out one or more of their crew have defected?" Larsan asked, waving one of the serving maids over for a refill.

"They tend to kick off o' course," Argwey smirked. "Then they learn their lesson, or some of 'em do anyway."

"It's normally settled between Larkh an' the other captain," said Laisner, "but sometimes they misjudge the size of their own balls an' challenge Gresh as well." The bosun leaned in, as did everyone else. "They think they're better 'cause their ships are smaller an' faster, but Gresh's got the best of everythin'; more speed than a first rate ship-of-the-line, a *tad* less firepower than one but hers is stronger, more effective, an' she has better manoeuvrability," he explained. "She can be a tough girl to keep steady, but once you know her, she makes sense. O' course Larkh knows her better'n any one of us, but it's strange, it's almost like he an' the ship are one."

Larsan was intrigued. Knowing a little more about how the crew saw Larkh and how efficient the ship was, gave him greater insight into his history. Something made him uncomfortable though; Larkh had denied him answers about the workings of the ship by sidestepping around them effectively, forcing him to give up the chase. He suspected the majority of the crew didn't understand all the details. He guessed Argwey and Krallan were likely to be well-informed, but they would undoubtedly be tight-lipped about it as well.

"I still think he's been acting out of sorts a bit." Larsan set his tankard down while the maid refilled it. Argwey, Daron and Laisner all shoved theirs forward as well. "I did happen to touch a raw nerve when I entered his cabin this morning, but it's been like he's been on edge about something. He seemed to be looking forward to arriving here, and yet seems stiff as a plank." Argwey mulled this over.

"Y'know, now that you mention it, I kinda agree wi' you," he said thoughtfully, looking at Daron and Laisner. "He has seemed a bit over strung considerin' this is our safe port in Armaran. Either me or Krallan will ask him if anythin's up."

"What kind of nerve did you strike then Larsan?" Laisner asked interestedly. "When that happens the offender usually ends up regrettin' it."

Larsan sighed heavily. "I noticed that scar on his stomach and was about to say something about the gods having mercy on him considering he survived, but he caught me as I thought twice about what I was saying," the big man grimaced. As Argwey was about to take a draught of his drink, he stopped, looking Larsan straight in the eye.

"Ah, then it's definitely not a surprise he snapped at you like an angry shark then." The bosun drank, slouching in his seat again. "You know he lost his family, but do you know anythin' more than that?" Larsan shook his head. Argwey continued; "some people think of the family as their mother, father and siblings. Larkh lost every relative he ever knew he had, an' all because the family went on a voyage on *Greshendier* to Enkaiyta. It was to test her handlin' on a longer journey, but once they arrived they were goin' to have a long holiday out there."

"How do you know—" Argwey held a hand up.

"Some had died within a short space of time," the elf continued, "so it was a means of copin' with their loss, an' who wouldn't want a holiday? It all *seemed* accidental to start with. They entered a bay to explore an island, an' then it happened; someone sabotaged the rudder, an' then they were attacked. Some on board the ship weren't who they were meant to be."

Larsan stared blankly into his drink, frowning, lost for words. One might lose some family, but all of them almost all at once? There was nothing accidental about that; of that he was certain. Who would launch a conspiracy to wipe out an entire bloodline?

"He doesn't see himself as lucky at all," Argwey added. "An' I'd feel the same were it me. He hates the gods with a passion, an' I don't blame him. Just do yourself a favour'n don't try to raise the issue with him. You may as well be settin' a ship's powder magazine alight; not only are you blown to smithereens but so is the whole damn ship."

This was sound advice from Larkh's bosun, though he knew keeping his mouth shut on everything he'd just been told was going to prove to be a challenge. He conceded the point, deciding the rest of the evening was better spent doing exactly as Larkh had suggested barely two days ago. He was going to try the different brews Almadeira had to offer, and would probably stagger back to the ship when the early hours of the morning rolled around, rather than the room he'd rented. Subject matter changed from one topic to another, and though mention of Larkh did creep back in on occasion, the stories told were of a more jovial nature.

III
Almadeira

It was late into the evening before Zehn and Raeon arrived in Almadeira. The Hunters' Guild would have been closed for hours, so they retired to the Silver Gull just as the last of the spring celebrations ended for the night; the townsfolk either slipping into the taverns or returning home. They ventured into the taproom shortly after dropping their bags to eat a small meal of leftover lamb and potatoes, finding a table in the quietest corner around the back of the room behind the stairs.

Zehn had refrained from asking anything more of Raeon until the silver mage was ready. Raeon saw it in his eyes though; the encounter with Madukeyr had sparked a number of questions he was sure the Tseika'Drahknyr would have been expecting. The possibility he might have to play a significant role that would affect the world bothered him. No matter how hard he might try to feign indifference, it was grinding away at him. It was never easy for him to accept the truth when he was set in his ways, refusing to change them to appease anyone.

Reclining in his seat, Zehn picked up his drink. He stared into it disinterestedly, eyelids drooping. "If you didn't really fancy it, why did you order it?" Raeon asked, running a finger around the top of his own tankard. Zehn's eyes slid up to meet his gaze.

"I thought I needed it at the time," he replied flatly. "I'll finish it though; I could do with something to help me sleep after today."

"That's understandable," Raeon nodded. "Now, I'm not quite sure what Madukeyr expects of me, but what I told you on the mountain today reflects what he was talking about." Zehn looked away, fidgeting in his seat, watching the other customers drinking, socialising and gambling. "Prophecies tell of key events and participants; they don't tend to state exactly how it will all happen. That's what I was trying to tell you earlier."

Zehn quickly drained his drink and set the tankard down on the table, giving his friend a pointed look. "You're saying that my choices aren't set in stone? Is that right?" he asked. As Raeon opened his mouth, he continued; "yet whatever choice I make will influence this prophecy of yours nonetheless? Not much of a choice if you ask me." The silver mage frowned.

"What will be, will be Zehn," Raeon sternly reminded him. "Every living being makes choices every moment of every day. You chose to order that drink; fate didn't make you do it. Whether you choose to acknowledge it or not is still your choice, but the outcome would be very different indeed, and as with all choices, you have to live with them." Raeon rose from his seat. "I would tell you more, but I think you need to do some thinking first."

"Raeon—" Zehn began to protest.

"No Zehn," Raeon hissed. "Until you're prepared to listen, there is nothing you will learn." Then he swept his robes away from the chair and ascended the staircase.

Zehn slouched in his seat and planted his face into his palm, elbow propped against the armrest. *'Don't you understand at all Raeon?'* he sighed inwardly. *'I'm scared, more than you can possibly know.'* He would approach the subject in the morning when he'd had time to rest and refresh his mind – if that were at all possible. Before retiring to the room, however, he would sit awhile in quiet contemplation to give Raeon a chance to cool down.

CHAPTER 14

I
Saldour

Leyal stood outside Duke Kradelow's estate scanning the soldiers that had been mobilised. All wore the white crest of Faltainyr Demura's osprey on their white and royal blue uniforms and armour. Officers wore navy blue cloaks on which the insignia was embroidered around the edges in gold, their helmets or hats sporting white plumes also decorated with osprey feathers.

The infantry wore body armour; cavalry wore dyed leather armour to ensure their horses were not overburdened; musketeers wore lapelled coats, and the handful of mages present wore their respective robes. He guessed mages who were to be involved with the military were sent to the Archaenen for their training, and then released to the king or their respective duke after graduation.

The Duke himself had yet to show himself, and they'd already been waiting a long time. Leyal was growing impatient. *'Filthy time-wasting racist bastard,'* he thought, eyes narrowing darkly as he glanced at the beautiful view of the Sendero de Mercader overlooked by the sprawling white port city of Saldour.

He found it hard to believe such a beautiful region, boasting the best views of the Sendero de Mercader, was home to men like Duke Jarlen Kradelow. The densely forested islands of Cerendiyll to the north reminded him of his homeland in Morkhaia in the south of Zaern'Kairnell, a continent far to the east. He even wondered if Albharenos the Ghost still guarded the waters north of Gaieah, the largest of the Cerendiyllian islands.

He guessed, and hoped, that by now the arrangements were underway in Almadeira. By now there should be no-one loyal or able enough to carry a message to King Jaredh Faltain; Kradelow was at the very least methodical and incredibly patient to have put this plan together over the course of sixteen years. It surprised him King Ameldar DeaCathra had agreed to wait such a long time. Sixteen years was not a short time for humans, that is, most humans. Still, it was the work of a genius. Ameldar had certainly picked the right man to do his dirty work for him here. There couldn't have been anyone better than one who had plotted the demise of an entire noble family and succeeded – with the exception of one troublesome individual – without being suspected.

He could see questions on the faces of the soldiers gathered before him. It was quite obvious some wondered who he was and what he was doing there, but others definitely wore expressions of racial contempt.

A thought crossed Leyal's mind; *'did any of them actually have any idea what race he belonged to?'* Some thought the Aurentai were related to the elves, but the truth was much more complicated. The simplest way of putting it was to say elves were as akin to the Aurentai as dolphins were to sharks; except perhaps for the Shäada, who despite being elven, displayed similar traits to his own kind.

The organisation he belonged to was an ancient one nonetheless; his predecessors knew all about Aurentai history, especially their feudal past with the Nays. That knowledge had been passed on to him twenty years ago when he had become a group leader within the *Noctae Venatora*, the largest network of elite assassins known across Aeldynn.

His gaze wandered over the edge of the cliffs down to the sprawling white tiers of Saldour below, jutting out toward the ocean with an enormous harbour stretching around the coastline to a fortified sea wall. There was a lighthouse at the far end of the harbour atop the cliff furthest from the city. Approximately half the Faltain naval fleet remained in the port; most of them sat at anchor with only handful of third-rate ships tied alongside the quay walls.

Finally, Duke Kradelow appeared. He was dressed in dark blue regalia with gold embroidery and patterned burgundy lapels with the same style of cloak as his officers, except the osprey insignia was much larger. His dark grey-streaked hair was slicked back and his beard had been trimmed, though it did nothing to improve his appearance, and certainly did nothing to improve Leyal's opinion of him. He resisted the urge to spill the man's guts, instead maintaining his composure with a straight face.

The fact Kradelow despised the idea of working with him was apparent on his face. Leyal was an Aurentai assassin, and Kradelow was probably wondering why King Ameldar considered anyone of a race other than his own worthy enough to work for him. The truth was, when one hired an assassin of the *Noctae Venatora*, they got who they were given, though Ameldar had actually been quite accepting of him. That was another reason why Adengeld's king had won his favour, even if he was otherwise a deluded fool.

"So what can you tell me, Al'Hallane?" This was a demand rather than a question. The way the man spoke his name as if it disgusted him made Leyal seethe. What had King Jaredh Faltain seen in this bastard to make him duke in the first place?

"Everything is in order sir," Leyal replied. "The mayor has been removed."

"What about the assistants and guards?"

"All in place sir," Leyal answered promptly. He'd learned very quickly Duke Kradelow was to be answered swiftly and directly and without ambiguity. "I have had no reports of resistance."

"That would be because traitors and failures were executed years ago."

Leyal straightened himself, pretending to match Kradelow's indifference toward manipulating or killing his own people. He feared he may lose his temper at any moment. This was, however, a man who had wiped out an entire bloodline through fear his plan would be discovered.

"Tell me though, Aurentai, is Leyal your true name?" the duke enquired. Leyal frowned.

"It is, but it is shortened," Leyal replied nonchalantly. "I thought my full name might be difficult to pronounce, so I kept to the shortened version." Kradelow scratched his chin. "And your kind are a breed of fey?" Leyal felt heat rising on his face. *'Breed? We are not dogs!'*

"Yes, sir."

"Hmm right. Are you ready to leave?"

'Am I ready to leave?' Leyal's jaw clenched tight. *'We've been ready to leave for nearly two hours bastard.'* "Indeed. We are ready to leave as soon as you give the word."

"Good," Kradelow turned to face his forces. "Honourable soldiers of Lonnfeir! Einar's unit will follow Leyal into Almadeira and seize control of the town. No-one is to leave either by land or sea. Whoever enters does not leave until I have given the word. Anyone who defies these rules is to be executed." His eyes scanned each row of soldiers standing in front of him. "You are all here because you believe Jaredh Faltain to be a flawed king who does not know how to lead his people; a king who allows pirates to do as they please on his seas, a king who fails to hang thieves. You would much rather see him off the throne, and see someone who knows justice replace him. Am I right?" The battalion roared with approval, causing a smirk of cruel satisfaction to pull at the corners of the duke's mouth.

"The rest of you will travel south with me," he continued. "Some will stay in Foristead, some will spread out along the D'etrun Highroad, and the rest of you will continue on with me to Almenden and Newlen Southsea where Duke Anthwell and Lord Verden will choose to side with me, or Jaredh. You know what to do should either of them choose Jaredh."

Kradelow made his distaste more than plain in his expression as he turned back to Leyal. "I have a few ideas you might be interested in," Kradelow smiled mirthlessly. "Don't worry too much if you lose Savaldor; I have other plans in place should he manage to evade you. In all other things, I'm counting on your every endeavour, understand?"

II
North Mazaryn Peaks

Leyal travelled alongside the soldiers of Lonnfeir considering the proposals Kradelow had in mind for him. Duke Anthwell was to be assassinated regardless of whether he chose to side with him or not. Kradelow certainly had something more than assisting King Ameldar DeaCathra up his sleeve.

It was mid-morning by the time they had left the estates of Saldour, crossing the meadows, heading north-east along the coast around the North Mazaryn Peaks toward Almadeira. None of the soldiers spoke to him unless it was absolutely necessary, and it wasn't until midday the commander spoke to him on what might be considered as friendly terms. He ate his lunch alone on an equally solitary boulder at the edge of the cliffs where the sea frothed as it crashed into the rocks below.

"So fella, where're you actually from then?" the commander asked. Leyal inclined his head toward the man. He was tall and broad-shouldered with a short moustache and beard, his shoulder-length black hair tied back. He held his plumed osprey helmet under his right arm. Leyal guessed him to be in his late thirties, perhaps early forties.

"Zaern'Kairnell," Leyal replied. "More specifically, Morkhaia, in the south."

"Ah," said the commander, "that's a densely forested area if I know my geography."

Leyal nodded. "I've not been back there for a long time though. I had an invitation to join the *Noctae Venatora* many years ago, and with them being based in Cathra, it was only a matter of time before something big came up."

"Aye. That plan has been in the works for almost two decades so I've heard. Not sure why it needed to take that long." The commander sat down beside him.

"More likelihood of success," Leyal observed. "That and the archana being developed in the Magicista Akadema is essential to the plan. Archana development is something never to be rushed, lest it go wrong at a crucial moment in the heat of battle. Why take a greater risk by declaring war outright, when you can slowly get under the skin of your enemy and tear them apart from within?"

"I suppose that makes sense."

The commander tilted his head back thoughtfully, then took the hip flask from his belt and took a swig of whatever was inside. He offered it to Leyal, who simply shook his head. The smell alone was enough for him to turn his nose up at it. Spirits made by humans had a tendency to intoxicate him more quickly than he liked, and he didn't particularly like the taste of it, though he was careful not to mention it. The stifling humidity of the afternoon didn't much put him in the mood for drinking any kind of alcohol anyway.

Leyal observed the man's body language as they sat in silence for several long moments; he clearly wasn't comfortable with what he was doing. He was doing his job, and that was all that mattered. Asking for reasons from Kradelow was out of the question, and even if he did enquire, his loyalty would be called into question and he might be executed.

"What do you make of all this?" the commander finally asked, feeling comfortable enough to discuss the topic with him. Leyal wondered on the intent behind the question.

"I am not at liberty to discuss too many details," he replied, "but at the very least I support King Ameldar's ideals for unity. I am also a member of the *Noctae Venatora*. I do what I am hired to do; abduction or assassination, sometimes both."

Leyal could see the man was troubled by these words. Glaring down at his feet, he was obviously considering his own position; doing as he was told with little or no regard for the reasons why or his own feelings about the orders he was given. The Duke had very clearly meant what he said about killing any who stood against him, yet many of his men, he knew, believed Jaredh wasn't fulfilling his role as king.

This fellow was an easy one to read. He didn't agree with the extreme measures Kradelow was taking, but probably couldn't think of a more effective way of putting matters to rights. It was doubtful he'd be leading the troops into Almadeira today if he allowed himself to falter. Anyone who made an enemy of Kradelow was a danger to his cause, and that couldn't be allowed. He would do what was necessary to see the mission through.

Leyal turned his head to watch the rest of the troops eating and drinking. They enjoyed their meagre rations of bread, cold meats and cheeses and ale or spirits as they openly and noisily discussed their personal lives and gossiped about the affairs of state. While his long, keen ears picked up a great deal of useful information, he still found their company more irritating and loathsome than he cared to admit. He wondered if they really gave a second thought to their own opinions when they were marching on a state that was still part of their own kingdom. He gazed lazily over at the other men, now laughing and joking about matters that bore no humour to him whatsoever.

"Mind if I call you Ley?" the commander asked. "I always call my men by either their surnames or nicknames they give one another. I feel less division with those I work with that way."

"I don't mind," Leyal shrugged. "What should I call you, besides Commander?"

"My name is Einar Carthiney," the man replied. "You can call me by Einar, or simply Carth when we're stood down like this."

"You have a strong name," Leyal observed and immediately sensed, a wavering feeling of uncertainty sweeping over Carthiney's aura at this observation of his name. *'Ah,'* he thought. *'One of those are you? Which way will you lean when this mission is over, I wonder.'*

"And a name I endeavour to live up to," Einar grinned. "I trained at the academy in Kessford. It's reputed to be the best combat training academy in all of Armaran. A lot of new recruits are sent there, and a fair few other swordsmen train there as well, including the elite mercenaries."

Leyal stared up at the clouds, enjoying the rich warmth of the sun and the tranquillity of the azure sky. "The Kessford Academy? Yes, I've heard of it," he mused aloud. "Even soldiers considered to be of exceptional quality from Adengeld have been sent there, including royalty."

"True enough, and now King Ameldar seeks to claim it for himself," Einar sighed. Leyal cast him a wary glance.

"Do you not approve?" he asked.

"I agree Armaran would be better off united under one banner," Einar explained, "but I'm not sure I approve of the espionage used to gain the upper hand. I feel it is dishonest and cowardly. Matters like this should be settled fair and square in a war."

Leyal considered these thoughts for a moment. "Do not all military factions have spies though?" he enquired.

"It's one thing to have a few spies to figure out your enemy's weak points," Einar countered, "but it's another to spend nearly two decades trying to whittle away at a kingdom's foundations from underneath it."

"Why do you suppose that is?"

"Stand beneath a roof as you try to bring down the pillar supporting it, and you yourself could be crushed."

He was right of course. The way the operation was executed was by far one of the most dishonest he had ever been involved in. Some might call it cowardly, but it was still the most effective means of making sure your chances of success were far greater than that of the enemy, but those involved were playing a dangerous game. Leyal was an assassin after all, an agent of the shadows; it was in his nature and expertise to bring down those who stood in the way of his employers in whatever way he was instructed. That was no secret, but was this Einar's way of trying to express his disdain at his involvement? If that were the case, he couldn't care less. The King of Adengeld hired him along with a careful selection of the *Noctae Venatora*, and his instructions were to assist Duke Kradelow. That was all that mattered. Why not be angry at the one who hired him instead?

The *Noctae Venatora* had strongholds all over Aeldynn, even in the Aurentai homeland of Morkhaia, but the faction's headquarters had always been in Cathra, the capital city of Adengeld. It was likely anything he said would be met with resistance, and it wasn't like any of the other soldiers would consider listening, so he spoke honestly without reproach. "It may be dishonest and cowardly, but it was the King of Adengeld who hired us. We do what we are trained to do, and what we are instructed to do. I care not about the details; a job is a job."

"I understand," said Einar, rising to his feet. "Well, we'd better get going. We've had a long enough break here, and we need to reach Almadeira as soon as we can." He strode over to the troops, ordering them to their feet and to be in line within five minutes. Leyal watched him disinterestedly. He would wait until they were all ready to move before he would rise; he only needed to stand and he would be ready to move on. Everything he needed was with him; only lunch had been brought in a small black leather bag he had attached to his shoulders. As the soldiers filed into line, he stood and made his way casually to the front to walk alongside Einar.

III
Dragon's Gaol, Ehyenn

After Dhentaro's intervention, Zerrçainne's wound was no longer life-threatening, although it would restrict her physical movements for a while. It would *not* stop her from furthering her plans for the continent of Armaran though, nor would it stop her from drawing upon her magica.

She was on her way into Ehyenn's underground; a deep and very dark place full of colossal caverns dripping with moisture and rife with fungi. The stench of damp clinging to the stone of the Dragon's Gaol was overpowering, and now Rahntamein had been awakened from his induced slumber, it would madden him. He was irritable enough already. The renegade was a supreme tyrant among his kind, matching Dehltas in size. They were two of the largest dragons in all of Aeldynn, excluding the leviathans under the oceans.

The wall sconces burst into life as Zerrçainne descended the staircase from the cavern's western entrance. Dhentaro followed closely behind, his tail gently scuffing the ground as his bare feet padded almost silently on the rocks beneath him.

Out of the shadows a large reptilian eye opened and stared, a thunderous growl echoing in warning as the creature raised its crimson head, snaking its neck around to get a better look. One great clawed hand reached forward, gouging at the rock effortlessly, followed by the sound of enormous clanking chains. The ground vibrated as Rahntamein growled again as he slowly crept into view. Pointed spikes rose up and angled backward from between his eyes, across the back of his brow, extending into two spear-like horns with jagged ridges all along his neck and spine. His eyes gleamed like molten rock as the remaining sconces flickered into life.

"Given any more thought to King DeaCathra's offer yet?" Zerrçainne asked. Rahntamein's upper lip curled into a snarl, revealing two rows of sharp ivory-white teeth, eyes narrowing.

"You test my patience Nays sorceress," the dragon rumbled. "When I am free, what I want shall be *mine* whether you or your precious king wish to give it to me or not." There was pure malice in Rahntamein's eyes as he gripped the walls of the cavern and thrust his beak-shaped snout within a hair's breadth of Zerrçainne's face. She smiled weakly, doing her best to ignore the smell of rotting meat on his breath. An entire herd of cattle had been delivered to him in recent days; there was nothing left but pools of dried blood and gore at the far end of the cavern. Dhentaro didn't appear to be at all bothered.

"What if you could be offered something you couldn't simply take by force?" she asked. Rahntamein snorted disdainfully. "What could you do with additional strength?"

Interest sparked in the dragon's eyes. Rahntamein sneered. "I do your bidding, and in exchange you give me such knowledge you *supposedly* know. Such a clever ploy that one!"

"I'll say it in your language then," Zerrçainne smiled wryly, reading Rahntamein's soul with her right eye; "I know how you can rival the Drah'kanos o'va Harkjuun." [15] Rahntamein's eyes widened, waiting for more. "If you do not make a pact with me, I shall not set you free from those bound chains. If you agree and then break your vow, I have the means to drag you into the depths of the Abadhol where you will be dissolved piece by piece over centuries if not millennia if you do not succumb to the mutation first. For such a large and resilient being it could take a very long time."

"You DARE to threaten *me*!?" Rahntamein boomed, his voice shaking rocks out of the cavern ceiling. His head reeled back, chest gleaming like the core of a furnace. "You...are...*nothing*!"

---

[15] Dragons of Origin.

His mouth opened wide, teeth illuminated by the growing orange light radiating from the back of his throat. Zerrçainne felt the blistering heat on her skin mere seconds before the infernal jet of flame engulfed the northern region of the cavern. She shimmered and vanished, reappearing behind a wall as flames blazed through the tunnel she and Dhentaro had used to enter, exploding out of the gaping main entrance like a fiery geyser.

"Are you still sure you can win him over?" Dhentaro asked dryly, bracing himself against the slick rock wall behind him. His upper lip curled up in amusement though he breathed heavily, trying to mask his fear.

Zerrçainne gently rubbed the wound at her breast. "He doesn't have a choice if he wishes to be free," she replied nonchalantly, closing her eyes, focussing as she spoke directly into the dragon's mind. *'The Drahkouenÿs Kahgathis is capable of connecting to the resting place of Shaorodes and Quaetihs that lies beyond the Lhodha Drahvenaçym.'*

As the flames gradually dissipated, the surrounding rocks were charred and smouldering; black and sticky like tar or glowing like the hearth of a furnace. After a momentary silence, Rahntamein snaked his head around the corner where they'd taken shelter. "I'm listening," he rumbled, snorting clouds of black smoke into the foul musty air.

"I told you," Zerrçainne said, her tone flat and emotionless. "When you agree to my request I will give you the knowledge you seek, and only after you return once the first deed is done."

"*Do not* play games with me sorceress!" Rahntamein spat, his sharp teeth snapping shut. He swung his tail heavily into the wall behind where Zerrçainne and Dhentaro stood, sending huge chunks of rock flying. Zerrçainne's form rippled and vanished again. Dhentaro leapt to safety as sections of the ceiling caved in.

"I don't play games," Zerrçainne replied, malice resonating in her voice as it filled the entire cavern.

A maleficent aura emanated from a roiling black humanoid shadow that wove itself together before the dragon's face. Its eyes were narrowed slits in the fabric of the shade, and while the one on the left glowed a fierce violet, the one on the right shone blinding white. The ground began to vibrate as if a great earthquake were about to tear the place asunder, and an unnatural turbulent darkness filled the underground prison, snuffing out each and every one of the alchemical sconces.

"Sometimes, Rahntamein, you need to consider co-operation in order to get what you want." Zerrçainne's chilling voice hissed throughout the spacious chamber. The wicked aura emanating from the shade ricocheted off the very walls. "Perhaps I *am* nothing to you, and perhaps I *am* what you'd consider mere prey, but know that I can set you free, and that I am capable of making a puppet of you if I so wish, despite what any Kaesan'Drahknyr may think, for I have been to the depths of the Phandaeric abyss and returned with my sanity intact. Not even a *dragon* has plunged into that world and returned with its mind still its own. You will be hunted by the Kaesan'Drahknyr until you die at their hands no matter what you do, and sooner or later they will succeed if you persist like this. Whether you like it or not, you do not have a choice in the matter if you wish to leave this god-forsaken pit."

Blazing reptilian eyes flashed angrily in the dim light of the super-heated rocks blasted by his fire, but there was something about this presence he recognised. "Where are you Alymarn?" he snarled. A foreboding resonance filled the space around them as Zerrçainne took a purplish-black orb from within her shadow and held it in front of the dragon.

"He can hear you, but he cannot yet respond with words outside the mind of his physical host," the sorceress explained. "He needed a compatible male vessel to be made whole again, and such a vessel had to be humanoid. I have already chosen someone to take on his initial physical form. This orb contains his deity aspect."

"And the dragon aspect?" Rahntamein enquired.

"I have yet to find it," Zerrçainne admitted. "It is strange; I thought the deity aspect would have been the most difficult piece to acquire. It was, in fact, the easiest if you don't count the toils of Phandaerys' underworlds."

"You knew where it was because it was cast into the bowels of Phandaerys where it was thought no-one could obtain it," the dragon's upper lip curled back in cruel satisfaction.

"Yes, and if you would be so kind as to do as I ask, I sense Alymarn will assist you in your ambitions."

"Does this include your search for the dragon aspect?"

"It does, but you must burn down the Archaenen and Aynfell along with it. Call it a trial."

Rahntamein considered this offer carefully. The thought of finally being granted the power to rule was too good to ignore, especially if there was a way to access Shaorodes and Quaetihs through the Lhodha Drahvenaçym, and with Alymarn on the rise again it made it all the more appealing. The flames of desire burned fiercely in his eyes. Zerrçainne saw in him the same kind of destructive force she saw not just in Alymarn, but in Melkhar as well. Rahntamein was never going to be content working for her, but it seemed he was at least willing to co-operate now he was aware of Alymarn's presence in the scheme.

"Do we have a deal, Rahntamein?" she ventured, watching the dragon mull over the proposal, weighting it against his current situation. "You have only to gain from working with me."

"I welcome the chance to have my vengeance so I might take my rightful place among dragonkind," Rahntamein growled. "Aynfell will burn, and I will fight if Adengeld's army should reach the Faltain Kingdom intact.

That will determine the strength of those passing through Daynallar."

What better way was there of determining the strength of Ameldar's army than forcing them to cross a valley swarming with all manner of draconic beasts without adequate protection? The dragon certainly knew how to gauge the strength of both foe and ally alike. What wasn't going to be pleasant was the king's reaction to Rahntamein's refusal to protect them.

Zerrçainne reverted to her natural form and spoke coolly in an ancient and forbidden tongue associated with the demonic races of Dhavenkos Mhal; *"evhas vhondas Aevanteis-o Fandares sjattha!"* [16]

The gargantuan shackles that bound the dragon to the cavern floor at his wrists and ankles glowed vicious red, then shattered into dust. Rahntamein thrashed his tail, threw his head back and released an almighty roar that shook the walls of the cavern and reverberated through the ground beneath their feet. Burning inside with violent anger, a fierce hatred ablaze in his eyes, he thundered to the cavern entrance, crawled out of it with some effort and stretched his wings out wide. He sniffed at the fresh air, hungrily licking at his teeth.

---

[16] Phandaerys shatters these bonds of Aevnatureis.

CHAPTER 15

I
Len'athyr Sanctuary

The meeting did not go according to plan in the Len'athyr Sanctuary the following morning; though all had anticipated Melkhar's reaction to the news of Rahntamein's impending release wasn't going to be good. The anger that flared in her emerald eyes had been brimming with menace. The mutual grudge between her and the dragon had lasted aeons, and none dared try to stop her in her pursuit; not even Kalthis. Initially they'd tried talking her out of it, but there was no reasoning with her once her mind was set.

She stormed out of the sanctuary; ebony armour knitting itself together around her as she strode briskly through the halls and corridors, the metal clanking louder as it materialised.

"Just be careful," Kalthis said, following her. "Your wound from back then—"

"Is slow to heal because of the Phandaeric poison," she finished for him. "I know. But Kalthis, you know we cannot allow Rahntamein to run loose. I left Arcaydia in Almadeira with instructions to find Marceau, but considering the circumstances you have described, she needs to be found quickly. I knew about an impending coup d'etat against the king of Faltainyr Demura, but I did not expect it to begin in Almadeira, nor so soon. I expected to have returned there by now."

"You want me to find her," Kalthis sighed, striding to keep up alongside her.

Melkhar's icy gaze was fixed down the ornate marble corridors ahead.

"You are the best person to guide her," she stated, the upper half of her face now masked. "Not me. The renegade should have been destroyed long ago, as I had originally argued with the council."

"The council won't be happy to see you shirk the duty given to you," Kalthis mused aloud, "but alright, I'll find her and return to Atialleia with or without Marceau and the guardians spoken of by the Origin."

"To the Abadhol with the council," Melkhar snapped, stepping out of the sanctuary on to the bridge. "It is not our duty to babysit fledgling warriors or oracles when Phandaerys reaches through distortions in its stratum, and when the world is on the brink of chaos." Kalthis opened his mouth, but found no words.

Melkhar turned briefly to look at him as her towering wings took form, spreading wide across the bridge. "You have my gratitude." Then she turned, and took off. Kalthis watched her leave, sighed, and made his way back inside muttering to himself, "stubborn as always."

He made his way back through the marble hallways, up several staircases, and knocked on the large double cherrywood doors of Dreysdan's study. These doors were ornately decorated, depicting winding branches with leaves and flowers carved into the wood with the *Dragons of Origin* gilded in the centre. Kalthis entered upon hearing a muffled and rather distracted reply.

Dreysdan sat at the back of the spacious room at a large desk, a wide arched window behind him. Rosewood bookshelves lined either side of the room, all filled with grimoires, historical tomes and encyclopaedias. Spread across the carpet was a rug spanning almost the entire width of the room, depicting the entwined forms Shaorodes and Quaetihs, the Dragons of Origin.

"She left then," the Galétahr assumed, looking up from the papers on the desk. "I'd have done the same were I in her position."

"Soon, all of Faltainyr Demura will know we are no ancient myth made up by Nays citizens who have since retired to Nalthenýn," Kalthis mused. "It is still too early; something must be done."

Dreysdan wiped his pen, dropped it into its well and leaned on his right elbow, his chin resting on the back of his hand. His thin brow furrowed, emphasising the black outlines of his eyes. It was the one look he could wear Kalthis had never been keen on; it could suggest a variety of things going on inside Dreysdan's head, and it was usually impossible to tell if it meant sincere thought, anger, or malice.

"What makes you think the world will ever be ready, Kalthis?" he asked, shrugging. "Whether it's done now or in another thousand years, the people's reactions will still be the same. The majority will still despise and reject us out of fear or for interfering, even when we have saved their lives. It has happened before, and it will continue. Now is as good a time as any."

Kalthis shook his head. "You misunderstand, Drey," he sighed. "We are not ready to make our move, but we have had no choice but to act. I believe this to be a deliberate act by Zerrçainne. She desires chaos and unrest, and she is orchestrating it behind the scenes by assisting a mortal king in his plans to conquer. We need a new plan of action, and when I have found Arcaydia I will return to Atialleia. I am certain Melkhar will do the same once she has dealt with—"

"Why did she leave without me? Why?" Vharik whined as he barged into the room, his face flushed red. "She could've taken me with her! I must get back to Aynfell! I received a mind message from the Archaenen that Rahntamein's attack could be imminent!" Dreysdan's eyelids sagged.

"Have you ever heard of knocking, sage?" the Galétahr muttered under his breath, slouching in his seat.

"No time for that!" Vharik exclaimed. "Melkhar left without me!"

"And how did you expect her to carry you?" Dreysdan frowned. "All Drahknyr are released from their earthly density when they take to the air and the biology of their lungs morphs for the accommodation of more oxygen so they may breathe at high altitudes." He pointed a finger at the old man. "You are not one of them; you are too heavy and you would suffocate. Secondly, the Kaesan'Drahknyr should not call their vassal dragons from the Lhodha Drahvenaçym unless they are truly needed."

The old sage turned away, his shoulders sinking; but Dreysdan continued. "Is it not enough one of the Kaesan'Drahknyr is making haste to defend Aynfell as we speak? None of them have recovered their full strength yet! Melkhar will not stop using power until she prevails."

"That's enough Drey," Kalthis growled softly, giving the Galétahr a long hard look. "He only wants to be there for those he cares about. There is no need to shout at him. It is Rahntamein we are speaking of, and we do not know if Melkhar will arrive before the dragon does." Anger flashed in Dreysdan's dark eyes, a look that was as close a match to Melkhar's own bone-chilling stare as anyone could hope to achieve. It would come as no surprise to anyone how alike they could be with Melkhar being one of the Kaesan'Drahknyr and Dreysdan the Galétahr of the Order of Ebony.

Vharik sighed as he scratched his beard, looking despondent. "It seems I spoke out of turn. Galétahr Dreysdan is right to be angry, as do you, though you do a fine job of hiding it Kalthis. I'll see to unearthing what I can about this prophecy. There must be some clues somewhere. I will place my faith in Melkhar." He brushed his robes aside and left the room at as brisk a pace as he could manage.

"I think it would be wise to link the gate near Vharik's hut to the sanctuary, Drey," Kalthis advised. "It would mean if he were in any danger when he returned home, he could make it back here immediately." Kalthis could almost feel the disdain rising out of the Galétahr. The gates had to be linked at both ends, so Dreysdan would have no choice but to return with Vharik to open the gate in the glade where his hut stood. Of course Dreysdan wasn't happy about the idea. "Drey..."

"I know it's essential that I do it," Dreysdan sighed, "especially considering you must leave this afternoon in search of Arcaydia. We can't have the old man dying on us just yet. As much as he angers me, he's still a good man."

"Thank you," Kalthis bowed his head.

"I look forward to the day Atialleia's gate is fixed," Dreysdan mused aloud, changing the subject. Kalthis lifted his gaze. "My second in command is overdue to take over, didn't you know?"

"No, I wasn't aware," Kalthis admitted, shrugging. "I don't know how long you've been on duty here."

"Almost twice as long as I should have been," Dreysdan said, rising from his chair, his black cloak spilling across the carpet as he strode toward the window. "Not that it can be helped; what with the Aeva'Daeihn clergy still training their new priests and priestesses and the gate being out of power. Sorry Kalthis, I'm just a bit tired that's all."

II
Almadeira

The sun had fully risen in the sky when Mey gave Larkh a soft nudge in the ribs. His face was pressed against her neck, and though she enjoyed the feel of his breath against her skin, it was time to get up. She brushed the sandy layers of his hair away from his face; it was tousled as if it had been through a gale. There was no response. She nudged him again, harder this time. A soft groan fell from his lips. Again she nudged him, digging her elbow in. "Ow..."

"Hey handsome, wake up," she said, then blew softly into his ear. He scrunched his face up at the unpleasant sensation. "Now, ye're not so handsome when you do *that*."

"Ehh... don't do that," he mumbled, slowly opening his eyes. "What time is...." he glanced at the window, seeing daylight had already forced its way through. He groaned again. "Crap."

"That lass ye were showin' around the place'll be wonderin' where ye are if ye aren't in yer room right?" she pointed out.

"Probably," he yawned as he rolled on to his back and stretched his arms up over his head.

"There's a little bit o' time to talk first before ye go," Mey said cheerfully. "We didn't get to before ye fell asleep on top o' me like ye'd just died. Not very romantic if ye ask me." A long sigh fell from his lips and he yawned again, rubbing his eyes. She slid her left leg over his as she turned on her side and traced lines across his bare chest with one finger.

"What did you want to talk about?" he asked, glancing at her, enjoying the warmth of her bare skin against his. "An' how can you be so lively after just wakin' up? I'll never understand you."

"Ye usually need to let a bit o' that sorrow out," she said dejectedly.

"Don't worry, I'm fine," he replied dismissively, slowly sitting up. He slid his feet out of the bed, and was about to rise when Mey's arms snaked around his waist.

"Larkh," she said quietly. There was sadness in her tone. "Ye're a bad liar when it comes to how ye really feel on the inside." He remained still, feeling her forehead against the nape of his neck and her breasts at his back. She continued, "I still remember the terrified little boy who was brought to Naredau that day nearly sixteen years ago. How long did it take me to get ye to talk? Ye'd say no more'n a few words every now 'n' again to anyone."

Larkh tried to think of something to say. He opened his mouth to speak, but nothing came out. *'I know, I was a wreck,'* he admitted silently to himself. *'I remember it all too well. For several days I couldn't eat without being sick, and even when I could eat it was very little. Everything and everyone I ever knew and loved was gone in an instant, but Mey...you were the one who encouraged me to come out of my shell again.'*

"I don't show you enough appreciation, Mey," he said finally, motioning to put some clothes on. "Eridan might've been the one who found me an' took me to Naredau, but it was you who brought me back from despair, an' Yahty who took care of Gresh an' trained me. Not once have I ever thought badly of you." Mey sank back on her haunches.

"How do ye do it?" she asked him. "How do ye manage to hide it so well? I know ye never really got over it, an' there's everythin' that went on after Gresh was laid up all that time when ye were sent off on other ships ..." Larkh turned to her as he fastened his trousers.

"Because I have to, Mey," he answered dolefully. "I have to. I'd go insane if I didn't." He leaned over and lifted her chin, planting a gentle kiss on her lips. "An' y'know I feel the same way when I think about some of the things that were done to you."

For a long moment she stared into his eyes and wondered exactly what made him so charming. The fact he was breathtakingly handsome was just one of the many factors of his overall charisma. She admired his iron will and determination to keep moving forward, and found some solace in knowing she had played a significant part of encouraging him to summon the strength to go on living. Likewise, there were times he'd been there for her when she'd been in trouble. They were both little more than thirteen years old when he'd stood up for her as a group of sweaty, vulgar men had tried to force themselves upon her. He'd ended up beaten, but was nevertheless content in the knowledge she was safe.

"Keep your wits about you more'n usual today," Larkh said once he was fully dressed. "Be ready to leave quickly. Things don't seem as safe for us as they ought to around here at the moment." Mey eyed him suspiciously as he brushed the tangled layers of his hair with her brush before checking his appearance in the mirror – for longer than was actually necessary.

He secured his belt to his waist, complete with daggers and flintlocks, confident he could make the two minute walk in daylight without needing a pair of scimitars. He'd left his most elaborate pair on board *Greshendier* and had taken one of the spare sets he carried on board instead, but they were in his room at the Silver Gull. Until he could be sure that no-one could ever take the pair he believed to be relics of Nays origin, he rarely used them, often carrying the more routinely forged sort most often seen in Manlakhedran. Only the design of the blades was the same. He hoped the Varlen artefact Mey had found for him would ensure the relic pair could only belong to him; he just needed to find a spare moment to give it a try.

"That gut feelin' of yers is strong ain't it?" she asked, sliding out of bed, starting to dress herself. Larkh's eyes took a leisurely wander over her delightfully naked form. If there had been enough time to spare, he'd have suggested they go another round. The look in her eyes told him she knew what he was thinking.

"It was strong enough last night," he admitted, "I definitely felt I was bein' watched yesterday. Find me on board Gresh after breakfast; we both know when there are eyes pointed in our direction, an' I want to see if I can dig up any info on anyone suspicious. It's also strange Marceau suddenly left town without a word." He thought for a moment. "Ah yes, I also need to visit Arven's caravan. He said he had news from the road for me. Just promise me you'll prepare for a swift departure just in case."

Mey chuckled. "Larkh Savaldor, ye worry too much," she said, pulling on her leggings and making her way over to him. She was still topless but her long dark hair hung loosely over her chest, neatly covering her breasts. As he was about to speak she pressed a finger to his lips, smiled, and winked. "But I *will* inform the crew they ought to be ready to cast off at a moment's notice."

"Thank you," Larkh said gratefully, though his expression was so sincere it almost scared her. "I'll see you later."

He moved to the door and unlocked it. Briefly smiling back at her, he winked and then left the room, shutting the door quietly behind him. He knew she would feel awkward, but she knew he would not forgive her if she failed to honour his request; and if something did happen there would be no consoling him. If something went wrong and she survived, she'd get the cold shoulder and for how long would be anyone's guess, and she wouldn't blame him. And if she died, it was anyone's guess what he'd do. After everything he'd lost, it was no small wonder why he'd ended up so protective of the people he now held dear.

Larkh made his way back to the Silver Gull, watching the streets and alleys he passed using his peripheral vision. At the end of the path he turned right on to the main street that led down a gentle slope to the town square where he could see every mast in the harbour.

Greshendier was moored on the western side on a berth that could provide a swift departure, particularly for a ship of her size. At present there was no other ship docked in Almadeira that could match her fighting prowess or size. At this truth, he smiled. He thought briefly on how differently things might have been if he'd not been able to become such a skilled swordsman; he'd likely have never regained Greshendier at all. It had actually been the coin and clever words of the female Kensaiyr warrior Yahtyliir that helped to keep her laid up for so long until he was ready. He remembered the conversation between her and Eridan clearly. In-fact, it hadn't really been a conversation at all. Yahtyliir had given Eridan a choice, the latter being engaging her in combat, which was never advisable if you knew you didn't have the skills.

"That ship is young Larkh's," she had told Eridan after he'd asked her to inspect it. "If you could crew her, you could try to sail her, but she's the sort of ship you really need to know before she'll let you handle her properly." A large sack of gold fell at Eridan's feet. "You can have all this in exchange for the *Greshendier*. If that's not good enough, you can fight me as well."

Yahtyliir, the governor of Naredau, wouldn't see Eridan's argument that they were all pirates, and they took what they wanted irrespective of who might be the rightful owner. *Greshendier* would be safest belonging to her heir, the one who already knew her best despite still being a boy, especially considering she was equipped with an altirna system. In case he needed any more persuasion of her authority, Yahtyliir had reminded him she was the only one in Naredau in possession of a dry dock pirates were permitted to use. Removing those rights would have caused an uproar, and he would have become the target. In addition, it was the only known renegade dry dock in all of Enkaiyta, and the only one capable of supporting a ship of *Greshendier's* size.

The deal was settled when Eridan said he would only agree if Larkh fought him for the right to claim the ship when he was tall enough and strong enough. He remembered Yahtyliir smiling at this in agreement. She taught him everything he knew about sword-fighting, particularly in dual-wielding. She had also told him about Nays lore, as well as legends passed down from her own people, and it had sparked a wild fascination within him; a fascination with artefacts and ancient technologies mortal races should never get their hands on. But he was different to everyone else around him. He knew he was different; he just wasn't quite sure how. Nevertheless, he was now in possession of a pair of relic scimitars, and a binding artefact, thanks to Mey. A smug grin spread across his lips as he wandered across the square to the Silver Gull.

"Here he is," he heard Elsie mutter over the bar as he entered the taproom. "Speak of a devil and it comes running." Larkh gave her his best wry smile and moved to take a seat by the window. As usual the place was considerably quiet this early in the day. It was just as well; he wasn't fully awake yet and noise grated on him until he was fed and not so weary. Elsie gave him a hard look and disappeared into the kitchen.

He relaxed into his chair, gave a long yawn and rubbed his eyes, wondering how the repairs on the ship were going. The storm had put quite a bit of strain on the rigging, but *Greshendier* was a tough lady and had been through worse ordeals. He was suddenly reminded of the venture to the Lands of Elinda where he'd sailed her through the infamous Maw of Elinda, the *Maidhrég*, where he had obtained the relic scimitars he now carried. He glanced across the bar as the pantry door opened again and Elsie came through carrying a wooden mug filled with coffee. The mouth-watering aroma of frying bacon that followed her out of the kitchen prompted his stomach to remind him he'd not eaten since the previous evening and it was already nearing midday.

Elsie patted him on the shoulder, placed the mug down on the table in front of him and stood opposite. "I take it you're hungry then?" she laughed.

"I figured you'd say somethin' like that," Larkh chuckled. He dug into his coin-purse and pulled out five silver coins. He slid them across the table toward her. Her eyes widened.

"This is far too much," she whispered harshly, lifting her eyes to look at him seriously. Larkh shook his head solemnly.

"You've got to keep this place runnin' for me Elsie," he appealed. "I never want to come back here an' find you closed down, y'hear me? Today's an' yesterday's brunch paid for with a bit of a tip, an' the rest is for the upkeep." He sipped at the coffee. "I like this place, an' I know you've been close to shuttin' down before. I'm givin' you what the government's wrong to take in the first place."

Elsie gave his shoulder a gentle squeeze. "What'll it be this morning then?" she asked.

"As much as I've the urge to indulge once again, I'd better not," he grimaced.

"How about a cheese bap filled with a generous amount of bacon?" the innkeeper suggested. Larkh's eyes lit up. "Just like an excited puppy," she snorted, making her way back to the kitchen. Arcaydia entered a few minutes later with his breakfast and set it down in front of him, Elsie following behind her.

"Thank you—" he began to say, but Elsie pointed to Arcaydia. "Arcaydia, you made this?" The frosty-haired girl smiled broadly back at him.

"Morning!" Arcaydia said gleefully. "Where did you disappear to last night? You didn't answer your door when I knocked, and when I asked Elsie about you, she said you never returned last night."

The bap was halfway to Larkh's mouth when he paused to give Elsie a questioning look. The innkeeper gave a faint smile and returned to the bar, and before he could speak, Arcaydia continued; "Elsie assured me you'd turn up eventually."

His expression was unreadable, but nevertheless suspicious. "I was...with a friend," he said. He was going to try to play this with some subtlety. Arcaydia cocked her head slightly. "The night before last we were sailin' through a storm; I was tired. I visited my friend, an' fell asleep before I could return here."

"I'm sorry," Arcaydia blushed, "I shouldn't ask about your private business." Larkh mumbled something with his mouth full. It sounded something like 'meh', so she guessed he didn't really mind. "Um, do you think I could speak to you privately when you've eaten?" Larkh arched a brow mid-bite. Was the look she gave him one of concern or guilt?

Definitely the latter. He chewed thoughtfully, swallowed, and regarded her with a questioning look.

"Such a shameful look on a pretty face. Now what could you possibly be schemin'?" he asked. Arcaydia shrunk back in her seat. Was it that obvious? "The most private place we can talk is my cabin," he continued between mouthfuls. "You never know who's listenin' at doors in places like this. You can follow me back to *Greshendier* when I finish this if you like, though I might grab a croissant from that bakery as we pass."

"If Elsie doesn't need any extra help I'll tag along," Arcaydia said, glancing across at the short woman behind the bar.

"You go ahead girl," Elsie chuckled. "Thank you for the help you've already given this morning. It's much appreciated." She turned to take the orders of a small group of weather-beaten travellers that stumbled wearily into the tavern. "You look like you've come a long way without a break. What can I get you?"

Larkh absent-mindedly glanced out of the diamond patterned casement window as he popped the last of the bap into his mouth. He stopped for a moment, observing the actions of two familiar individuals outside. They were heading toward the Silver Gull. Finishing his mouthful quickly, he downed the last of his coffee and tapped his fingers on the table to get Arcaydia's attention as he rose to his feet. The sudden noise startled her, forcing her attention on him. He nodded in the direction of the stairs with some urgency, then glanced outside again before making a move. They rose to their feet, briskly made their way to the back of the inn and ascended the stairs. No-one seemed to notice their hasty retreat, save for Elsie Menow, who understood his swift departure just as Zehn and Raeon stepped inside.

III
Almadeira

"A pain in the arse, that's what it is!" Zehn growled. "He just ups and leaves without a word before we've even had a chance to knock on his door."

"I'm sure he had a very good reason," said Raeon, leaning against the side of the doorframe. "It isn't like him to just disappear like this, is it?" The silver mage folded his arms, his brow knitting. "Something must have happened after he sent the note to the Hunters' Guild in Senfirth."

"If only we knew where he's gone, that would help," Zehn muttered, glancing out of the window. He couldn't see the harbour from here, but he'd seen *Greshendier's* masts again as they'd headed into town to Marceau's house. "You know what *would* make me feel better?" Raeon's eyes slid over to him.

"Don't even think about it Zehn," he warned. "If there's one thing we don't need it's a mob of angry pirates attacking us in self-defence because you couldn't wait for another confrontation with Larkh Savaldor."

Zehn ran his fingers through his thick shock of hair, exasperated. He was right here, and there was no way of telling whether or not he would be in violation of his agreement with the king if he attacked Larkh within the town. There was nothing to say he couldn't; his agreement with King Jaredh stated he could hunt his quarry wherever they went after all, but apparently Almadeira had been appointed a safe haven to Savaldor because he happened to have the privilege of privateer status in Ennerth despite not really being a privateer. He decided if he came across him, he would do that which his agreement said he was within his rights to do. The discrepancy was the king's own mistake, not his.

"I'm not going to go looking for him," Zehn muttered, glowering out of the window. "But if I see him, that's an entirely different story."

Behind him, Raeon sighed, covering his face with one hand, rubbing his eyes. *'Oh Lady Raiyah, why must these two hate each other? It would be so much simpler if they could have met and been the best of friends.'* A chilly draught rustled his robes, making him shiver, and then a woman's voice whispered, echoing through his mind. *'Aqeivalér, Te'les Arhcýn'Magían vél Kelsihva. Phasuthév drann naghestiiv.'* [17]

Realisation hit Raeon like a ball and chain to the skull. So that was it. This was how the forces of balance worked. While two opposing forces fought each other for dominance, there was also the potential for them to work in harmony with one another. The question was, how could he possibly get those two to see eye to eye? Perhaps it wasn't even his place to do anything of the sort; perhaps it would all happen of its own accord. Then he remembered what he had tried to tell Zehn, that all choices were personal, but people had to live with the choices they made. If they Keys of the Origin chose not to work together, what would eventually happen to Aeldynn?

"Did you feel that?" Zehn asked all of a sudden. Raeon instantly snapped out of his daydream.

"Feel what?"

"That sudden cold draught."

"Yeah," Raeon answered absent-mindedly. "This is an old building; maybe there's a crack in a wall somewhere..."

---

[17] Balance, Second Archmage of Silver. Positive and negative.

LORE
The Nays and the Kensaiyr

The warrior who strikes a dragon's tail
invokes annihilation.
Nays proverb

Of all races, the Nays and the Kensaiyr are the closest to the gods, with the exception of the Drahknyr and Kaesan'Drahknyr, who are closer still. They are immortal in that once they have matured, their ageing process ceases, but after spending many aeons living an entirely physical life, their souls grow weary and they move on to the next stage of their existence, gradually transferring themselves into a realm they call Nalthenýn. Only the Kaesan'Drahknyr are truly immortal; death for them is only a temporary release in the rare event they are slain.

The Nays and the Kensaiyr hold the closest bonds to Aevnatureis, and are therefore able to access and harness the highest forms of magica bestowed by it, except for the Drahknyr and the Kaesan'Drahknyr.

Expectant mothers carrying Drahknyr give birth one year after conception. When the child's spirit is bestowed, the mother experiences a surge of magica thought to be the result of the power the offspring holds. She becomes significantly drained both physically and mentally as a result, until the child is born.

It is said the spirit of a Drahknyr absorbs the spiritual life force of his or her mother while still in the womb to maintain physical existence until birth, which is why only the Nays can bring such a being into the world. No female of any other race could hope to survive the ordeal of birthing a child with such tremendous amounts of magica at their disposal. That, however, is relative only to the Drahknyr, and the Galétriahn Mages to a somewhat lesser degree.

Both races are typically tall; none shorter than five feet and seven inches have been known to exist, with the Drahknyr starting at five feet and ten inches. Differences in the characteristics and appearances between the two races, however, are unmistakable. Most Nays are pale, their complexions typically ivory and porcelain, but there are also the tan-skinned tribal peoples that hail from the Iylari Desert and the forests of Marlinikhda. Their features are always finely chiselled, and their ears, though pointed, are only a fraction longer than those of a human at their peak, but their eyes are perhaps their most notable trait. They are deep set and usually almond-shaped, framed with angled black lines once thought to be painted on, but are instead naturally occurring and therefore known to be a racial trademark. It is believed cosmetics originated from the striking natural beauty of the Nays and their Kensaiyr allies. The Kensaiyr, on the other hand, are always of ivory or porcelain skin; their eyes always either a striking azure or aquamarine colour, and their hair either pure white or silver. Their elven cousins are the Cerenyr, Thénya, and Shäada.

Nays architecture is known to be varied; they construct many buildings out of whitestone, including entire towns and cities, but they also use other designs that mix timber with various kinds of stone, some of which are now rare and precious outside Ardeltaniah. In the Nays capital city, Atialleia, only the grandest of buildings such as the Atialléane Palace, Kathaedra, colossal theatres and arenas, and the homes of nobility are constructed from whitestone. It is a mystery why towns such as Saldour are almost entirely constructed from it. One theory is only Nays nobility once dwelt in such places.

The Kensaiyr homeland is Kesar Nairéfa, the White-Silver Valley, in Ardeltaniah; a place well-known for the cascading waterfalls of the Great Aquelar with architecture bearing slight resemblance to that of the Nays in that they use some of the same materials and basic design, but generally bears a more delicate appearance with interwoven mosaic-like frameworks, arched bridges and smooth walls.

Dream-walking is a distinct ability of the Kensaiyr. It is a unique form of telepathic communication. Some may share their dreams with others, but there are a select few who can directly interact with others so long as they are able to make a connection with a person they wish to send a message to. The most skilled of dream-walkers are able to connect directly with the astral world, Nira'Eléstara. The most powerful may eventually become a new Eléstaelys Auvaesyar, meaning 'Astral Overseer.'

Like the Nays, the Kensaiyr bring another kind of ethereal being to Aeldynn's physical plane. They give birth to those known as the Lyte E'varis; Wardens of Lyte. Just as the Drahknyr represent the Sun Goddess Raiyah, the Lyte E'varis represent the Moon God, Lyte. However, there was once and only once a time when members of the Nays were born as Lyte E'varis, and Kensaiyr as Drahknyr. They were three each in number, and were to serve as auxiliaries between the Drahknyr and the Lyte E'varis, symbolising the balance and harmony between the two races. They were called the Tseika'Drahknyr and the Lyterané.

CHAPTER 16

I
Almadeira

Larkh quickly shut the door to his room and leaned against it. Arcaydia stared at him blankly. She opened her mouth, but he shook his head quickly, putting a finger to his lips, turning and pressing his ear to the door. Sure enough, he heard familiar voices ascending the staircase. They had a room here, and they could only have acquired it in the time he'd spent with Meynra.

"That bastard never gives up," he spat. His voice was almost a whisper, but there was enough anger in it to make Arcaydia step back.

He heard Zehn in the corridor. "We can't find out what Marceau was on about regarding this tall red-haired woman, and I do hope I run into that gods-damned pirate so I can put him behind bars once and for all. On the plus side, at least I have my long overdue pay."

Larkh ground his teeth. *'Yeah, I was damned by the gods alright,'* he thought sullenly, frowning. *'Nothin' like a bit of irony though, eh? But what's he got to do with Marceau?'* He glanced at Arcaydia, then back at the door.

"Zehn, I think you'll find the guild will do nothing about Savaldor here," Raeon reminded him. "He's got privateer status in this area."

"I'll do my job wherever I happen to be," Zehn growled.

"Even if it means violating the law you strive to uphold?" Raeon reminded him. "I didn't take you for the type to do such things. If he has special permission to walk

247

freely here then there's nothing you can do about it without making a criminal of yourself."

"Do you want me to get that permit out again Raeon?" Zehn snapped. "King Jaredh gave a pirate a letter of marque for a single region, but also gave an elite mercenary written permission to pursue his quarry wherever it may go? His Majesty has some explaining to do. I will not be arrested with this warrant, Raeon. If there's a problem, it's the king's royal fuck up, not mine."

"Zehn, please think about this—"

Larkh heard nothing more of the conversation as a door clicked shut. He took a deep breath and, exhaling heavily, pushed away from the door to gather the few belongings he'd kept in the room, including his scimitars. He strapped them to his hips and reached for the door handle.

"He said Marceau," Arcaydia said dubiously. "And, he also mentioned my master. I'm concerned about all of this." Larkh turned to face her.

"A tall red-haired woman, he said," Larkh recalled the conversation clearly. "And you're absolutely certain he means your master? That description could fit any tall female with red hair." Arcaydia shook her head. While this was true, she was certain the man was referring to Melkhar.

"If he mentioned Marceau," Arcaydia observed. "It could only mean Melkhar..." She trailed off, realising she had just spoken her name. Larkh's eyes widened.

"Did you just say Melkhar?" he asked. "*She's* your master? Well now, that's interestin'. It seems like you an' I need to have a good talk later. I'm most interested in matters concernin' the Nays an' the fabled Drahknyr."

Arcaydia clenched her jaw tight, now feeling incredibly stupid. There was no use worrying about it now. He knew. What she hadn't expected was for him to believe her, or know anything about the Nays for that matter.

"Come on," Larkh said, "we want to make a move before that mercenary leaves his room again." He opened the door and peered out. He could hear voices arguing from

Zehn's room. Good, they were occupied. Stepping out of the room, Larkh locked the door behind them. Arcaydia wondered if there would be any repercussions from her mention of Melkhar's name, though she didn't think many people in this day and age would believe the legendary Kaesan'Drahknyr still existed, or that they had existed at all for that matter.

It was a bright, sunny morning again in Almadeira. Barely a cloud could be seen in the sky, and there was a swift westerly breeze; Larkh breathed in deeply as he looked out across the ocean. In the same moment, the aroma of fresh bread from the bakery opposite the Silver Gull caught his attention. Moments later he and Arcaydia were enjoying freshly baked croissants while they made their way to the harbour at a leisurely pace, commenting on the many floral decorations and vendors selling charms and ornaments; meats cooked with traditional spring vegetables and seasoning; cakes, buns and bread, all decorated with flowers. Larkh mentioned there was a farmers' market up on the hillside where the gypsy caravans were pitched.

Arcaydia remembered Melkhar telling her that long ago the Nays built an underground sewer beneath Almadeira, but there were still open gutters running into storm drains connecting to the system in the lower class backstreets of the city. As a result, the stench of sewage was minimal. There were few settlements in the wider world these days that had been built on top of abandoned Nays towns and cities.

Arcaydia had to walk quickly to keep up with Larkh as he strolled briskly down the street. There was a light spring to his step, and he seemed to be in an even better mood than he had been yesterday.

"You're in a rather good mood," Arcaydia said, smiling.

Larkh laughed and put his arm around her shoulders. "It's a bright mornin', I had a damn good time last night an'

I slept like a log," he said with a beaming grin. "An' on top of that, I think I'm lookin' forward to pissin' off that fancy pants mercenary again."

'Again?' she wondered.

Larkh pointed toward the *Greshendier* as they rounded the corner into the harbour. "Now you see her in broad daylight in all her glory."

Arcaydia stared at the ship sitting at the end of the harbour; wide stripes of cardinal red paint, outlined and carved with gold vines running through the centre, marked the gaps above and below her black gun ports. Her regal stern gallery boasted the same kind of rich detailing; a carving of two eagles facing a phoenix in the centre dominated its peak, identical to the insignia on the red and gold flag flying atop the mainmast. The large eagle figurehead was a perfect match, complemented by the large ruby orb it clutched in its talons, making her wonder again why it was there.

Her eyes flickered to Larkh. He stood gazing at his ship, awestruck by her beauty, and rightfully so. She was a sight to behold. Even though she was already his, he still looked at her longingly as if he were yearning for something. She was his pride and joy; something he could never bear to lose, and she was all that remained of his family.

Larkh made his way along the quay, hearing the raucous cheers of his crew well before he reached the gangway. The fact he was beaming told his crew all they needed to know. Of course, Argwey would have spread the word the previous night, but nothing could hide the air of complete satisfaction radiating from him. Bawdy questions and compliments flew down from the weather deck as he approached. He replied by giving them a smug smile with one brow ever so slightly arched. He subtly glanced in Arcaydia's direction. As if he was going to discuss his pleasures in Meynra's bed with another young lady present!

Boarding the ship, he scanned the weather deck, failing to see Larsan anywhere. It was rare for the burly northern warrior to be seen below unless he was sleeping or perhaps playing card games with the crew if the weather wasn't bad. Arcaydia motioned astern of the ship to gaze out across the harbour, watching as the noon tide began to roll back out to sea.

"Seen Larsan about?" Larkh asked Krallan as the quartermaster made his way out from below deck. Krallan pursed his lips as he scratched his rough chin in thought.

"I think he went into town," Krallan replied, shrugging. "I ain't seem 'im on board for a while."

"Well, before we arrived, I did tell him to go an' sniff out the local spirits," Larkh reminded himself. "I wanted to ask him if he's noticed any suspicious lookin' folk lurkin' about. You know this lot; they don't bat an eyelid unless it's shiny or has breasts."

Krallan gave an agreeable nod. It was amusing when he refused to smirk; Larkh knew he wanted to, but it was far more humorous when he feigned indifference. "Dressed in black cloaks? Hoods coverin' their heads?" he asked, lowering his tone. "Not seen any this mornin' mind you, but they had their eyes on Gresh last night."

"The very same," Larkh confirmed. "They've been keepin' an eye on me from what I noticed yesterday."

"You think they're watchin' only you?"

"They might have eyes on Mey as well." Larkh's eyes narrowed as he spoke. "Round everyone up as soon as possible an' restrict shore leave as much as you can. We may have to depart swiftly at some point today or tomorrow, an' I don't want half the crew missin' if that happens."

"Aye," Krallan said blandly, chewing his lower lip. He gave Larkh a sidelong glance and moved to begin preparations, stopping briefly. "Hey Cap'n!" he called. Larkh leaned his head over his shoulder as he looked back at Krallan. "You gonna join us at the Mizzen Rest t'night?"

Larkh smirked at this but replied sincerely; "none of us can afford to get unreasonably drunk tonight, but a few rounds won't hurt – an' I don't mean a few too many."

"At least we'd have your company," Krallan patted him on the back and walked away grinning. Larkh smiled meekly, waving Arcaydia over as he disappeared inside the ship. Sure enough, Arcaydia followed without hesitation.

II
Almadeira

Arcaydia entered the great cabin, and was instantly mesmerised by its grandeur. Much of the decking was covered by a large hand-woven rug displaying tribal designs meaning it could only have come from the continent of Manlakhedran, and nearly all of the furniture was made from cherrywood. The entire room smelled of well-seasoned oak, old books, and a faint trace of some kind of spice that seemed to emanate from the rug. She also noticed a plaque in the shape of a family coat of arms bearing an eagle mounted behind the desk at the far end of the cabin.

The thought didn't cross her mind that Larkh stood by the door watching her. She didn't see the appreciative look on his face, or how it dissolved into despondence when her gaze lifted to the coat of arms, but when the door to the great cabin shut behind her, she spun around to see him leaning against the doorframe. All of a sudden she felt very helpless.

"Now we can talk in private." He locked the door and made his way over to sit at the chart table. He smiled knowingly. "You've come aboard twice now without hesitation. Is it Elsie's word that I'm a nice guy that put you at ease? She doesn't follow me wherever I go. I could've been playin' her for a fool all this time for all you know."

Arcaydia tried to swallow the lump in her throat, finding no words wanting to come out. Larkh slouched, crossing his ankles as he put them up on the table. He pointed a finger at her. "That shows how sheltered you are. It's well in your favour that Elsie knows for a fact I'm as good as my word. Now, tell me all about this little scheme you want me involved in. There'll be a price o' course."

"A price?" Arcaydia asked, suddenly more wary of him. Larkh stifled a smirk. He cast his eyes downward as he composed himself.

"What manner of pirate would I be if I did everythin' for charity?" he asked, arching a brow. "If your boss is one of the Kaesan'Drahknyr then I'm sure she has plenty of coin to her name." She saw the defiant glint of confidence in his eyes. When it came to favours, it was a business deal. He was a pirate; what was she thinking when she asked him for help?

"If Melkhar knew I'd even considered it she'd probably feed me to a dragon, let alone me actually giving away her coin," Arcaydia fretted, biting her nails.

"I do accept information as well," Larkh suggested, leaning toward the nearest cabinet and pulling a bottle of brandy from it. He took a long swig and put the cap back on feeling pretty sure it wouldn't be to her tastes. He relaxed as the warmth of it glided down his throat, easing the tension stirring within.

"What kind of information?" There was more concern in her voice. After what he'd said earlier when she let slip Melkhar was her master, she suddenly knew exactly what he was talking about. "You want information about the Nays." He flashed a broad grin in her direction.

'Crap!' she thought. *'I need to find out what happened to Marceau! What will he do if I refuse now? I don't know much, I've not been back with them for long, but whatever I tell him would violate the oath. He has some knowledge of the Nays already though, that much is obvious. Perhaps...'*

"Can you tell me what you already know of the Nays first?" she asked, now feeling there might be a way to play the game. Larkh took his feet down from the table and leaned forwards, locking his fingers together, resting his chin in the middle. He put on his business face and pointed to a seat. She took it willingly.

"Let's get down to business then."

"Well?" she prompted after she'd sat down and he didn't speak. Larkh regarded her thoughtfully for a moment, wondering whether he should give her the biggest hint of all. Yes. He decided he wanted to see what her reaction would be.

"What if I said to you...*Éyn kéiloh al yhet mahlé kalun ye'n nàide keh'na?"* [18] he asked. "What would you say then?" The picture of surprise on her face provoked laughter; he could clearly see she was lost for words again.

"I think... I would ask you where you learned that."

Larkh nodded; time to stop beating about the bush. "My grandfather, Ansaren Savaldor, knew the Silver Mages of the Archaenen," Larkh explained matter-of-factly. "He learned a fair bit of the Nays language as a result. My mother once lived with people who'd made their home with the Cerenyr elves, so she knew the language as well."

"So that's how you—"

"No," he interrupted. "I heard it spoken a few times, an' there were books in my mother's collection – I was never supposed to touch – that taught me most of what I know. That said, I learned most of the language from the one who taught me how to fight. I only really know enough to get by, though."

Various questions bubbled to the surface in Arcaydia's mind. Larkh could see it on her face. Even if she couldn't tell him all he wanted to know, he would still pursue the knowledge anyway, but he guessed now she'd dug herself a nice little hole she'd end up yielding more than she intended anyway. In some ways she already had. Her master was apparently one of the Kaesan'Drahknyr! No wonder Melkhar wanted her to train with Marceau.

"So you were always a bit of a rogue?" Arcaydia chuckled.

---

[18] I know a lot more than you may think.

He shrugged, giving her triumphant grin. *'At least she's relaxed a little.'*

"How did you get away with it?" she added. Larkh cocked his head.

"How do you *think* I got away with it?" he laughed. "I snuck 'em out an' snuck 'em back in before she could notice they'd gone missin', that's how."

"I should have known." Arcaydia rolled her eyes.

"Anythin' else you want to ask about before I ask you to tell me what you want?"

"There's this ship," Arcaydia said, glancing at her surroundings. "She has a red orb on her figurehead the Nays use on many of their ships, and I can sense power running through it that I'm not very familiar with." Larkh considered this new information carefully, then dipped his head in acknowledgement.

"The orb was a present to my grandfather, an' so were the plans for the archana inside the ship. Few know the truth about it though," he explained. "So, they're also on the figureheads of Nays ship? You've my thanks for enlightenin' me." Arcaydia clenched her teeth; something else she'd accidentally let slip without even thinking about it. She would have to try to be more careful. She regarded him earnestly, hoping he would continue. Larkh shook his head, aware of what she was suggesting.

"You realise there're those who're after my ship, an' they want her secrets. You've let slip to me more details than you should've already; so how do I know you'll not tell anyone if you end up in the hands of the authorities eh?" His expression was sincere. "You've a loose tongue lass, an' that's somethin' you'll have to start takin' control of."

"I'm suddenly aware of that; you haven't told me much of what you know about the Nays though," Arcaydia retorted, trying to ignore the fact she seemed to be making her situation worse. Larkh's eyes flashed.

"I told you I know a lot more than you may think by speakin' your language," he reminded her. "Consider these facts; I know enough Daeihn to hold a basic conversation, your master is supposedly one of the Kaesan'Drahknyr, you've told me the figureheads of Nays ships also have orbs of the same design as the one Gresh has, an' you inadvertently confirmed yourself as Nays without even thinkin' about it." Arcaydia swallowed hard. She hadn't thought of that! "How about you tell me what you're askin' of me an' then I'll name my price?"

Arcaydia wasn't sure about how to put her request into words. No matter how many times she considered it, her conscience tugged at her, but she wanted to know why Marceau had vanished, and it would help if she had some proof to show Melkhar of why she wasn't with him. "Do you have any idea why this man called Marceau has disappeared?" she asked. "I want to see if I can find anything out about where he has gone." Larkh leaned back in his seat.

"You're talkin' about me breakin' into his house for you." He was quick. "There's a predicament with this," he surmised. "Y'see, this is my only safe haven in the region. I've the rights of a privateer in Ennerth's waters so long as I don't cause any trouble. If I get caught, that's my safe haven gone. That doesn't mean I can't think of somethin' though, for a price."

"Do you enjoy doing this?" Arcaydia protested. "I didn't mean to land myself in this situation you know."

"Listen. I'd be puttin' the one safe port I have in all of Faltainyr Demura on the line, which would affect more than just my crew as well as my ship if I happen to help you break into the home of the most renowned sword-training instructor in the entire Faltain Kingdom," Larkh hissed. "A high price is only fair for what the risk is worth."

Arcaydia winced, biting down on her lower lip. There would be no backing down unless she dropped the idea completely, but it bothered her the man she was sent to for training had suddenly vanished when he supposedly knew she'd be arriving. Larkh was right. Why should he risk so much for anyone let alone for her, whom he'd only known for a day?

"I'm sorry," she sighed sheepishly. "I can't afford the risk." Arcaydia took a deep breath, telling herself it had been a stupid idea in the first place.

"Never mind lass," he said, his expression sobering. "You've just paid me with information for doin' nothin'. I didn't even need to lift a finger."

'How does he do it?' she wondered. *'He's right. He just got information out of me for nothing and I didn't even realise until I'd done it! Damn it!'*

"The alternative," Larkh continued, "would've been about five hundred soren." Arcaydia's eyes widened.

"Five hundred!?"

"Think about it," Larkh said, taking another swig of brandy. "How many men d'you think it takes to run a ship of this size? I've got to keep them all paid an' fed somehow."

Arcaydia's face said it all. She'd walked into a complicated situation, and it was obvious she truly feared what her master might do in retaliation.

"Look, it ain't your fault Marceau's done a runner," Larkh said, rubbing his forehead. Arcaydia's expression softened. "If he's not told anyone where he's headin' to, however, the only alternative is breakin' into his place to see if he's left any clues layin' around. I think you'll just have to let your master give Marceau a good tellin' off when the time comes. If she has sense, she's not goin' to reprimand you for his disappearance."

That was true. It wasn't her fault. Why was she trying to beat herself up about it, trying to find answers to cover her own back when she'd been in the right place at the right time? It was her mentor who was nowhere to be found.

"You're right," she sighed, looking down at the table. Everything seemed so complicated. All she knew was Marceau was supposed to be training her in basic empty hand and single-handed sword combat. Nothing could stop her from wondering what the reason for his disappearance was though, and who knew when Melkhar was going to return?

"I have something to take care of," Larkh said abruptly, rising from his seat and making his way to the back of the cabin. "As you're one of the Nays, perhaps you can help me." She didn't like the sound of that. He took a key from his pocket and knelt in front of a chest behind his desk. He unlocked it, lifted the lid and took out two elaborately decorated scimitars.

III
Almadeira

Arcaydia took note of the design on the scimitars; the handles looked like black draconic ivory with images of gold dragons heads carved into the pommel, and dragon wing designs on the guards, their edges set in white gold. Set into the eyes of the dragon heads were gemstones; on each of them, one gem glowed with the orange-yellow hues of a perfect sunset, and the other glittered blue and white like ice. Under the beak of each dragon head was a much smaller turquoise gem. Arcaydia gasped when she saw them.

Larkh gave her a sideways glance, then retrieved a pendant from the chest. This too was set in white gold, but it matched the smaller gems on the pommels. The blades themselves seemed to glide out from their hilts, gradually widening and curving upwards at the tips, markings carved into metal just in front of the hilt. He then removed the scimitars he already wore from their scabbards and placed them into the chest before locking it again.

"Judgin' by your reaction, you must know what these are then?" he enquired.

"Th-they're Nays scimitars," she stammered. "Where did you—"

"Even though it is apparent the Nays are still around," Larkh interrupted, regarding the scimitars with avid interest, "they still left an awful lot of ruins lyin' about in the world, including relics. Obviously they weren't that important. It's like they just left everythin' in a hurry, takin' little or nothin' with them."

Arcaydia shook her head. "I'm afraid I don't know much," she replied truthfully. "Either that or I don't remember. I didn't get much of a chance to study in the great library before I was brought here. I returned to the homeland only a matter of months ago, and I can't remember who rescued me." Larkh shrugged, though his eyes betrayed his interest.

"It's a mystery I intend to unravel in time," Larkh said, rising. "You do remember what these are though, don't you?" He showed her the gemstones on the pommels closely. "I understand the orange stones are called *solneis*, and the blue ones, *luneis*. The stones in the mouths an' on the pendant are all binding *varlenstones*. Correct me if I'm wrong." Arcaydia nodded. "Now to see if this works. I've not had the chance to try this out yet."

Arcaydia watched him with concern. Varlenstone artefacts hadn't been seen for generations, and if the legends were true – and she knew they would be – they could bind a person's spirit to a weapon forged with archana so long as a binding artefact itself was worn until the binding process was completed. That process could take hours to days or even months depending on the wearer. The bond was believed to be more effective if the items being bound were forged by a race naturally adept at using magica.

The Drahknyr, however, were exempt from using a binding artefact; they could temporarily bind themselves to a weapon bearing varlenstones, and then fully bind when they reached a complete Varleima. If a Varleima were present, they could bind the weapon even if it had no varlenstone attached at all.

"Now if I remember this correctly, these should react with me when I put the pendant on," Larkh mused.

"Do you have any idea what you're doing?" Arcaydia asked, her expression hardening.

"I've read the legends of such magica in books; that's where I learned of these things in the first place. That's about it really," he answered with a shrug of indifference. "There's always a first time for everythin'."

"But this is Nays magica!" she protested. "It can kill someone who doesn't have the natural anchorage to Aevnatureis!"

"Ah I see," he muttered dismissively, laying the scimitars on the table. "You've my thanks. At this rate you'll have paid me in full with knowledge well before mid-afternoon." Arcaydia grimaced. "Besides, you saw somethin' in me yesterday didn't you? You mentioned somethin' of spiritual matters."

"You could tell?" Arcaydia tilted her head a fraction. The corners of Larkh's mouth twitched upward.

"I'm observant," he assured her. "I've had suspicions about my lineage for some time but that's a story for another time."

"Are you not worried about what could happen to you at all?" The young woman's expression was gravely serious.

"I don't fear death," Larkh answered, his expression rueful. "I've no intention of dyin', but if I did, I'd consider it a release."

Arcaydia cast her eyes down at the table, knowing full well what he was referring to. It didn't matter what her opinion was, however, he wasn't about to back out of it now. He'd waited a long time to try this out, but he suspected the girl knew more than she was admitting to, just as he was so well practised in the art of keeping his mouth shut when it was advantageous. He picked up the pendant, secured it around his neck and picked up the first scimitar.

A sharp surge of energy exploded from the pit of his stomach, up through his chest, and then down his left arm as

260

if he'd suffered an electric shock. The solneis and luneis gems flashed brilliantly before quickly fading back to their resting state, though they hummed faintly afterward. Gritting his teeth, he reached for the other blade.

"Wait!" Arcaydia cried as she rose to her feet, but his hand had already closed around the grip of the second blade. Another burst of energy surged from his sternum, through his chest again, and down his right arm. He fell to his knees, dropping both scimitars, clutching at his chest and stomach, drawing in long ragged breaths. Arcaydia knelt in front of him.

"You shouldn't have done that," she said sternly. "You're supposed to let your body recover a little first." "What happened?" he gasped. His breathing was heavy, glancing toward the blades. Arcaydia knew it was her turn to impart some knowledge now. She knew she was uneducated in worldly affairs, but she did gain some knowledge of Nays artefacts during the time she had spent in Atialleia's library.

"I shouldn't be telling you, I know, but you should know what you're doing to your own body," she told him. She rested a hand on the left side of her chest. "The energy of your physical body is kept in motion by your heart." She placed her other hand over her sternum. "However, here is where your spirit's core is located. It is the centre of who you are. The heart of your spirit is your soul. That is why we have the sensations we call gut feelings. Very strong emotions are felt in the stomach." Larkh closed his eyes, nodding slowly. He took slow, calm breaths as his breathing began to stabilise.

"When you soul-bind, the energy from your very being is being forcibly drawn away from where it belongs," Arcaydia continued. "The energy connects with the varlenstone before it returns to your core. It leaves residual energy behind so that it recognises you and only you as the bearer for as long as you live; though for someone with Nays blood the binding process will be quicker. If the bearer dies, the artefacts will shed their energy, ready for a new user. Your core energy had not yet had time to resettle before it was ripped out again to connect with the second blade, so it's not surprising it made you feel ill. The Nays have more resistance to the unpleasant sensations you just experienced, but it's impossible to tell how much of your life force it took. Anyway, how are you feeling?"

Larkh placed his hands on the edge of the chart table to support himself as he pushed himself up to sit at the table. "Dizzy, like I've been ashore on a night of heavy drinkin' with the crew," he muttered, falling back against the seat. He pressed a hand to his belly. "That, an' my stomach is threatenin' to make me heave, but if I stay still I think it may pass."

"It should pass soon enough," Arcaydia said, giving him a disapproving look. "Do you have any water in here?"

"In the cabinet I got the brandy from there's a recently filled waterskin." Arcaydia approached the cabinet, retrieved the waterskin and passed it over.

"Take a few small sips every couple of minutes," she advised. She was lost for words at what he'd just done, and she had no idea why he'd done it, but perhaps she'd find out later. The scimitars still lay on the cabin floor. He'd pick them up and test them out the moment he felt better, no doubt. The link had been made now; they were slowly binding to him, and he still lived. Perhaps there *was* something more to him. Something told her he wouldn't require the use of the varlenstone pendant for long. She said nothing as she watched Larkh drink, secretly wondering who in the world he was. He was a famous pirate apparently, but there was a lot more to him than just that.

"I suggest you give yourself a little while to let your mind and body settle into this," Arcaydia advised. "Gods, you sound just like Larsan when you talk like that," Larkh mumbled, taking a breath of air before taking another sip.

Smiling, Arcaydia continued; "I know that the use of such magica has been reported to have killed people who don't have a direct natural connection with Aevnatureis, at least in ordinary people anyway, but to my understanding it takes a few days to fully bind." He regarded her through half closed eyes.

"You're more well-informed than you give yourself credit for," he observed, "but I'm not *ordinary*, I think that much is obvious," he yawned.

"Just rest for a little bit though, please?" Arcaydia pleaded, looking concerned. He tapped the table with an index finger as she regarded him worriedly.

"Aye, fine," he sighed in defeat, smiling faintly. "My mother used to worry like that."

CHAPTER 17

I
Kasserin

It was busier than usual in Kasserin the following morning as soldiers prepared for war. All the soldiers of Adengeld trained in Kasserin, a town in its own right. The soldiers' town lay close to the coast where the Nar Lathen Forest split, south of the city of Cathra. It was fortified with its own keep, and while all newer recruits slept in large half-timbered barn-like buildings, veterans shared houses, each accommodating up to twenty men. The only other folk living here were those who worked the taverns, stables, and other facilities.

The cobbled streets here were no different to those in Cathra. They were just as miserable and filthy as anywhere else, and sometimes a depressed soldier could be found outside one of the many taverns, slouching by the stinking gutters. Such soldiers were left to their own devices unless they failed to report for duty.

Kasserin's streets were cleared of horse muck on a daily basis by the stable hands. Once a day, a group of stable lads would be sent around with shovels and wheelbarrows to gather the manure, which they then transferred to a field outside the walls where farmers would claim it as fertiliser for their crops. The sewage of the military residents, on the other hand, was washed away into the storm drains either by grimy bath water tossed out of windows, or by heavy rainfall.

At the far end of the town were extensive training fields where combat training and horsemanship was undertaken in units, and marksmanship in both archery and firearms took place. It was all a part of the same academy where all forms of other weapons training were taught. Elite soldiers and royalty were, until recently, sent to Faltainyr Demura for additional training at the Kessford Academy where Prince Rannvorn had trained. The king had decided he intended to conquer his neighbour many years ago, but had kept up the charade of being King Jaredh's ally to further his own ends.

King Ameldar and his son reached Kasserin via a great stone underpass leading out from Castle DeaCathra. It was lit with alchemical wall sconces, its arched ceiling supported by thick columns. With walls over four feet thick, the underpass ran from the castle grounds under the city wall, and out beneath the countryside. Normally it would be at least a day's ride from Cathra, but Zerrçainne had somehow managed to shorten the journey with magic by placing what she called a *shyft* at several points within the corridor which should last approximately six months. How it worked was anyone's guess, but work it certainly did.

Cathra's walls were almost entirely surrounded by forest. The main entrance was accessed via a wide boulevard with half a mile of the Nar Lathen either side of it, the surrounding land taken up by farms or moors. Kasserin lay south-west of the city where the fields had been large enough to build a grand facility to train an army.

By the time they emerged from the basement of the commanding officer's keep, the sky was overcast, black with the threat of rain. Rannvorn remembered spending months at a time training in Kasserin before he'd been sent off to the Kessford Academy; so everything here was familiar. What he hadn't bet on was his father telling him he wanted him to command a battalion. The news had hit him hard as much as it excited him, but he suspected that was exactly what Ameldar wanted – to judge his fitness to lead. No doubt Zerrçainne had influenced him. Despite the feeling of dread hanging heavy in his gut, he felt confident in his abilities; there was now a force within him to guide him in every significant move he would ever make from here on in.

Male members of the royal family were usually put in charge of their own units once they had graduated and were capable of displaying adequate leadership skills. He had certainly graduated, and he had completed the training at the Kessford Academy in Faltainyr Demura as well. He would certainly prove he was more than capable. He'd dressed himself in his fine black studded leather armour today. It bore Adengeld's insignia of a dragon depicted in red, stepping forward with one claw raised, its head held up proudly. With his dark curly hair tied back into a short ponytail, he was sure to make a good impression.

And there they were. Lined up on the training fields were thousands of soldiers donned in black and red coats or armour, novice and veteran alike. This was roughly four tenths of the entire army; the rest being stationed elsewhere across Adengeld, Baen, Ehyenn, or abroad. If Zerrçainne had her way, that number would grow, though he guessed those numbers would not be made up of human recruits. There were also Duke Kradelow's forces to add to the equation, and the Noctae Venatora to boot.

Every soldier fell to one knee before their king and prince as the clouds burst and the rain surged from the heavens. Ameldar smiled meekly through the downpour and subtly gestured for them to rise, at which all stood to attention, slamming their right fist to their left breast. Rannvorn felt something in his heart stir and expand to affect all around him; that is, all except his father.

Ameldar spoke fervently to his soldiers; "citizens of Adengeld, you are among those who will change the course of history of this nation! Too long has Faltainyr Demura monopolised the best of everything; the best navy, the best training academies in both melee combat and magica, and the only altirna mine in all of Armaran! King Jaredh Faltain only allowed the best of your ranks to train at the Kessford Academy and at the Archaenen, and he refused us access to the altirna mine for us to further our own archana, instead offering us the dregs of what was left! What kind of alliance is that?"

He paused a moment, watching the faces of his men, then continued; "Prince Theran Faltain is a naïve young man who follows his father's ways without question, refusing to think and act for himself! He is not fit to rule! We will take Faltainyr Demura for ourselves for a unified Armaran where all can train at the Kessford Academy, where *all* can train at the Archaenen, where *all* can join the naval ranks of Saldour, and where *all* can benefit from the use of altirna with no restrictions on its development!"

The following roar of approval brought smiles to both Ameldar's face and Rannvorn's. "My son," Ameldar added, "the Crown Prince of Adengeld, Rannvorn DeaCathra, will be joining you alongside your generals when you leave for the invasion of Faltainyr Demura! Dehltas has forsaken us, telling us he will not assist us in unifying Armaran under one flag! We will make our move when an allegiance with the red dragon Rahntamein has been established. Together we will lead Adengeld forth into a new and prosperous era!"

Rannvorn was barely able contain himself. There must be some influence from his new guardian, if one could call it a guardian. He felt it stirring inside him like an ancient dragon just awoken. Again the voice spoke into his mind; *"fortune smiles upon you friend. With my leadership, you will prevail. I am here to share in your misfortunes, and to turn them into triumphs."*

Through the rain, a cruel smile spread across the prince's lips, and not one soldier appeared to notice. They were all busy listening to his father babble on. He would have taken his place as king already, but his power had yet to grow and it was too soon; much too soon. He had to be patient.

II
Yahridican Fortress

"What now?" Dhentaro asked, long tail bobbing gently behind him with every step as he approached Zerrçainne. He approached her as she stood on the tallest balcony of the Yahridican Fortress, looking out across the island of Ehyenn. It was an island covered with craggy moors and ravines, surrounded by numerous rocky outcrops where only the smallest of boats could navigate. There were many shipwrecks beneath the tumultuous waves of its shorelines, and plenty of hidden coves, though no pirates or smugglers used them; it was hard enough getting close with longboats and the tides always flooded them.

Rahntamein ruthlessly devoured a herd of deer on the moors a short distance east beyond the fortress gates; the grass stained red with blood and gore. The squealing doe clamped between his jaws suddenly disappeared down his gullet whole. Dhentaro found himself staring in awe at the full size of the beast. On his hind legs alone he'd be taller than the fortress itself, and that didn't include his tail. Zerrçainne had spoken almost fondly of Rahntamein's rival, Dehltas, who happened to be almost identical except he was jet black.

"We wait awhile," Zerrçainne replied nonchalantly, though she smiled with cruel satisfaction as she watched the massacre of the deer. "Ameldar is readying his army, and Rahntamein will shortly head to Aynfell. I have stalled Melkhar, but if she should discover our plan, it means she must unmask herself much too soon for the Nays' liking. They can't hide themselves from the world forever, so I'm giving them a little nudge."

She had told Adengeld's king about Rahntamein's refusal to escort his army, which certainly hadn't been a pleasant task. The foul-tempered monarch had thrown a fit of rage until Prince Rannvorn had stepped in and calmed him down. Zerrçainne secretly wished she could be rid of

Ameldar now rather than deal with him any longer, but it was still far too early. The army would have to take the safer paths through the mountains which would take longer, or risk becoming a banquet for the lesser dragons, wyverns and certain species of drake that dwelt there.

The ocean was a possible option for a portion of the army to invade Faltainyr Demura from Almenden and Newlen Southsea in the south of Sherne, but the weather was very changeable where the Eastern Aeuren met the Soreiden Sea, and the Sidel Channel wasn't much better. Ameldar was not one to rely on good winds and the absence of storms; his patience was almost non-existent. It was quicker, in his mind, to follow the River Aeiven up into the mountains. The passes tended to be narrow, weaving in a series of squiggles around the mountains which would prove arduous and time-consuming, but it was much safer than taking the valley's direct route.

Dhentaro smiled mirthlessly as he lazily scanned the craggy moorland. His clawed hands clasped the balcony rail while he studied the movements of the dragon intently. His lavender eyes locked on to the great beast, staring in gross fascination until Rahntamein snaked his head around to face him, his bloodied reptilian lips curling into a sneer, scaly brow creasing maliciously. There was something about him that held his attention, reminding him of the plan they were putting together and executing with each minute step.

Sudden realisation lit his face up as the answer revealed itself willingly as Rahntamein crunched and swallowed the last of the deer. Just like the dragon with his prey, they were taking steps toward their goal. They didn't rush, nor did they risk too much, but they tackled each obstacle singly and as a whole, and soon they would obliterate all obstacles in their path.

'Soon,' thought Dhentaro, 'but not soon enough. So near and yet so far.'

He spent some time thinking about when he would make his official entrance to the show. Zerrçainne had forbidden him to go to Aynfell before she was ready, nor to partake in the onslaught against the Archaenen. Perhaps the Nays and their Drahknyr had greater supplies of magica at their disposal due to their natural spiritual ties to Aevnatureis, but he would make sure Zerrçainne's plan came to fruition. Why should the world belong to *them*? Why should his kind be bound to the underworlds of Phandaerys?

It was only through Zerrçainne's help that he and a handful of his kin and other demons surrounding the Yahridican were able to break through the Dryft into the Netherworld, finally crossing the rift barrier into Aeldynn.

The only other way for a demon to access Aeldynn was through spiritual means when the Eidolon Ring contracted, and even then only certain types of demon were able to do it. Everything spawned by Phandaerys was contained within its realms beneath the Dryft, or *Dyr'Efna*, to call it by its original name. Some demonic races thrived there and thought it foolish to want to escape it. It was their home, it was where they belonged, and anything but that was unthinkable; except they still looked forward to the contractions of the Eidolon Ring so they might terrorise the mortal world.

Those who failed to return to the Eidolon Ring's area of effect before it expanded again did, of course, become trapped. As a consequence, in order to survive, sometimes a metamorphosis was required. When forced to roam in search of a body – whether living or dead – they were transformed into an entirely different kind of demon. The most malicious of these kinds of wraiths often found themselves drawn to ancient catacombs where they would possess and reanimate embalmed corpses; they tended to favour long dead sorcerers. It was they who became known as the Lich.

"Are you staying out here?" Zerrçainne asked as she made her way back inside. Dhentaro was now leaning on his elbow, his chin resting on his palm.

"For a while," the Fralh replied, mesmerised by the dragon's form and size. "I've never met a dragon before you know; only the wyverns tainted by Phandaerys. You once told me that all dragonkind, in general that is, fight alongside the Nays. It makes me wonder how a monster like that can possibly be tamed."

"They are never tame," the sorceress glanced over her shoulder at Rahntamein. The huge red dragon was slowly disappearing back into the cavern that had served as his prison, now a suitable lair. "Temperamental fire-breathing behemoths they may be, but they usually harbour great wisdom and cunning. There are those like Rahntamein, however, who take their superiority complex to an unjustifiable level." Dhentaro cocked his head, listening intently.

"They know the Drahknyr, particularly the Kaesan'Drahknyr, exist in part to make sure they do not step out of line if they wish to dwell upon Aeldynn rather than the Lhodha Drahvenaçym. If they step too far out of line, they are slain. Otherwise they are free to do as they please, but anyone picking a fight with them is fair game. Occasionally they'll take livestock, just as any other predator will, but if they attack settlements without good reason, they are branded as rogues and are marked for death. There are some, on the other hand, who are soul-bound to certain Drahknyr, but they are never tame. They are beasts but they are not animals, and may be no tamer than people; wouldn't you agree?"

"Are you telling me dragons actually decide to play fair, and even befriend the Drahknyr and the Nays?" Dhentaro pressed, his curiosity rising. Zerrçainne appeared thoughtful.

"That conjecture is sound, but you might also consider it a mutual respect for one another's power," she answered, smiling wryly. "Why would you think dragons incapable of being fair? Have you never heard of the Drahknyr being referred to as the *Children of Dragons*?"

"Not that I recall," he replied honestly, shrugging. "I suppose I wouldn't have thought such beasts would have cared to reason with beings they deem lesser than themselves, as Rahntamein clearly demonstrated."

"All Drahknyr have a dragon aspect, Dhentaro," Zerrçainne informed him.

"Which means...?"

"It means they are, in part, draconic in nature. They are related to both the Nays and the dragons as well as being ethereal in origin. It's a more complicated mix than most understand, and I suggest you do some reading on the subject if you are so interested in understanding them. Perhaps that kind of knowledge might assist you in your future endeavours for me." She disappeared back inside the fortress. "Who are the lesser beings though, I wonder? It's not always a matter of size, and strength."

Now that was an interesting thought. Building up his knowledge of the Nays and the Drahknyr would undoubtedly increase his chances of outsmarting them. He believed Zerrçainne was doing a good job of this already, but she was right; if he was going to be of more assistance to her then he'd need more knowledge.

The biggest problem was the Kaesan'Drahknyr who couldn't be permanently destroyed. Incapacitated though? Perhaps that might be an option? Zerrçainne's library wasn't extensive, he knew, but he guessed it still held a wealth of knowledge of which he couldn't pass up the advantage of exploring; that is, if he were able to read every relevant book and scroll. He had no understanding of the Nays language and alphabet, and asking Zerrçainne to translate would impact on her time. She intended for him to figure out the answers for himself, but she might be able to help him learn how to decipher it. That might make it more fun. Nothing could quite compare to having firsthand knowledge of your enemy's history, and their strengths and weaknesses.

Overhead, the skies over the Yahridican were growing dark as storm clouds began to settle in, and with them came the swift, strong winds of change. Dhentaro cast his eyes upward, noting the direction in which those ominous clouds were travelling. It was a south-westerly wind that would sweep across Armaran's south-eastern coastlines and up through Sherne.

"As black clouds and storms sweep across these lands," he mused aloud, "so do we follow in their wake as the Shadows of the Nahfellon." When morning finally came, Rahntamein would take to the skies and head for Aynfell.

III
Almadeira

Larkh rose to his feet and placed the brandy back in the cabinet. He approached his pipe bunk at the other end of the great cabin and stared down at the two black dragon ivory scimitars lying there. He'd released Arcaydia after his dizziness and nausea had passed. She'd told him she wanted to return to town to peruse the festival market stalls. He had some business to deal with on the ship, so he'd walked her back to the entrance to the harbour, telling her he'd catch up with her later in the afternoon to visit the gypsy campsite to discuss news with Arven.

He'd been right to have her with him while he bound himself to the scimitars. She was a good source of information, and sooner or later he would gain the means to bring his family justice. No punishment would be good enough for him. The monster ought to die as many times as the number of lives he had taken from the Savaldor family; all but one. He took a deep breath and picked up both scimitars at the same time.

The same rush of energy surged from his core and up through his arms, but it lacked the power it had previously. This time it was a cool energy that resonated through him, prompting the solneis and luneis stones to glow briefly. He sensed they were definitely his and his alone now. If what he suspected about his lineage were true, then he may be able to give up wearing the pendant sooner than he first thought. He sheathed the blades and left the great cabin, quite pleased with himself.

As he emerged on deck he was greeted by Larsan carrying a small crate into the ship. His eyes narrowed and his lips pressed into a thin line. "Not plannin' on smugglin' spirits on to my ship are we Laz?" The burly man swallowed hard. Larkh held his gaze, one brow lifting a fraction higher than the other.

"Oh don't look at me like that," Larsan snorted. He was on edge, but that was probably because he'd been trying to sneak his own stash of alcohol on board without him knowing.

"I'll let it slide if you let me in on it Larsan," Larkh smiled wryly, jutting his chin out a little. The corners of Larsan's mouth dropped. "Y'can put it in your chest an' leave the crate ashore so the others are none the wiser."

"And if I don't?"

"Don't test me. You wouldn't want to know. It ain't such a bad compromise really, is it?"

"Fine..."

Larkh peered into the crate and beamed. "Almadeira's finest liquors I see, good man. I look forward to havin' some o' that." He nudged Larsan playfully and went on his way.

Larsan stifled a sigh; he'd hoped to avoid sharing any of it. He found himself beginning to understand Zehn's frustrations with this man. Larkh had every reason to be smug about his position; he'd done well for himself and built himself back up from rock bottom, but damn was he far too clever. He was a young man who knew exactly how to get what he wanted, and it was that which had got him this far. Larsan told himself it could have been worse; Larkh was always known to play fair, but woe be to anyone who dared to violate his good nature.

"Captain!" Larkh heard Argwey call from across the deck as he emerged. The brown haired elf gave a casual salute as he approached. "Krallan tells me we may hav'ta leave at haste any time 'tween now an' tomorrow."

"Aye," Larkh confirmed. "Are the repairs finished?" He walked with the bosun across the length of the ship. Argwey nodded.

"Not much left. Just a bit of paintin' left to do an' tha's it for now. We're clear to leave any time. Shame about the festival if—"

"I'm just bein' cautious Argwey," Larkh assured him. "We're in an awkward situation whichever way you look at it, an' there's no point leavin' if we don't know the score."

"Tha's all we can be I s'pose," Argwey shrugged. He patted Larkh on the shoulder as he turned to walk away. "You comin' to the Mizzen Rest tonight? I assume it's still on; we're barely forty paces from it after all."

"You an' Krallan are so alike." Larkh forced himself to keep a straight face. "He asked me the same thing not two hours ago."

"An' you said?"

"I'll come, but I'll have no-one fallin' three sheets to the wind in case we need to beat a hasty retreat or I'll leave 'em behind."

"Wise plan, as disappointin' as it is," Argwey sniffed. "Later, Captain." He gave a little wave and trotted across the deck toward Krallan.

Larkh visited Arven's caravan to exchange news shortly after speaking with Argwey. He met with the minstrel privately. Arven spoke of how they performed for King Ameldar and his courtiers. They had met the fire dancer, Arieyta, there. She had joined their company to travel east to Almadeira for the spring festival. It was only when they'd reached Saldour they'd heard some troubling news and seen a few things they weren't supposed to. Arieyta had never been there before, so she wanted to look around the town for a while, but Arven and some of the other Ena Canei had noticed military activity around the largest estate in the area.

When they left Saldour later the next morning there were men carrying back sacks soaked with blood in several small carts pulled by mules. Further down the road there had been pools of blood scattered across the grass banks nearby. Arven said an entire small brigade had been annihilated, and the culprits were reported to the public to have been bandits. Bandits dismembering people out on the open fields? Surely not? They were murderous outlaws certainly – like most pirates in fact – but a group of bandits taking out an entire military unit by hacking half of them to pieces? He didn't buy it. Their strength would have to be unreal to achieve that, which led him to believe the killer was something else entirely, and he had his suspicions.

There was little point in suggesting otherwise to Arven. He wouldn't believe him if he told him who he suspected the killer was. "You've spent far too long at sea my friend," he would say. In truth, at sea, all that mattered was oneself, one's crew, and one's ship, but a travelling minstrel wasn't to know that. The man had never been on a ship in his life.

Regardless, the mention of military movement in Saldour troubled him. It was the duke who controlled Lonnfeir's forces, and just the thought of the man made his blood boil. When Arven almost spoke the duke's name aloud, Larkh flashed him such a fierce look the minstrel actually flinched. "A-are you truly sure it was him?" Arven had asked.

"I know it was him," Larkh muttered as Arven offered him a flask filled with some kind of spirits. He took a rather large swig of it and shut his eyes tight as he swallowed it. "Damn that's a good ol' strong one," he added as he quickly put the lid on. "What is it?"

"It's Merthen white brandy," Arven smiled. "I take it you needed that huh?"

"Only strong spirits'll quell my temper at the mention of the duke's name," Larkh grumbled, "but that's some fine brandy you've got there. Have you any bottles of that spare?"

"I might be able to spare a few," the minstrel chuckled. "It'll cost you though."

"What're you askin'?"

"Have you got any Tourenco Dark?"

Larkh sucked in a sharp breath through his teeth. "Oohh I d'know Arven. I'm quite fond of it," he winked. "I've not got much in the hold at the moment, but I'll be able to get more when we head back to Naredau anyhow. Three of one for three of the other?"

"Deal," Arven laughed, extending his hand. Larkh took hold of Arven's hand and shook it, grinning.

"Stop by the ship later today for the trade then," he suggested.

"I will do, if I can slip away early enough before we hav'ta get ready for the evenin's performances I'll stop by. Y'know though, that stuff I just told you..." Arven trailed off, thinking. If his expression were anything to go by, he was just as concerned about the movements in Lonnfeir. There had been no talk of war, and Faltainyr Demura was peaceful enough. It could mean one of several things, so making an assumption wasn't a wise plan, yet doing nothing was a risk.

Larkh watched his friend intently. After discovering he was being watched, he'd warned Mey, and he was taking action to make sure he and his own crew could get away with as little fuss as possible should the need arise. The border between Ennerth and Lonnfeir was literally right next door to Almadeira, and it was two to three days' walk from Saldour, including the necessity of moving around the northern section of the North Mazaryn Peaks. The other route would take longer as forces would need to make their way around the mountains and then cross the short mountain pass. This meant sending anyone to scout the area wasn't a good plan. All he could do was continue to be as cautious as possible and play it by ear.

"Don't worry about me, Arven," Larkh assured him. "It's a lot for me to think about when it concerns that murderous asscock, but whatever happens, you've my word that I'll be the one to send him where he belongs." The minstrel sighed, shaking his head. "Stop it Arven." Larkh's eyes narrowed. "Stop worryin'!" He leaned forward and patted the man on the shoulder. "C'mon, tell me how your journey from Adengeld went."

Arven bit down on his lower lip, twiddling the end of his goatee, and nodded. He explained all he'd seen along the road on the journey from Adengeld.

The narrow paths through the Valley of Daynallar were awkward as always, but at least those roads were small enough to prevent wyverns and dragons from attacking in force, and consequently destroying all travellers who attempted to pass through. Even drakes found it awkward fitting into such tight spaces, but they preferred to stay close to large bodies of water, and were generally quite docile so long as they were left alone. None could tell what the wyverns and dragons would do though. Some would respectfully leave travellers alone, but there were those who would see them as easy pickings, so traversing the quickest and most direct route was done at one's peril.

Eventually, they exhausted their conversation, and Larkh rose to his feet.

"Best you do get back then," Arven recommended. "You've been over here awhile now."

"Tellin' her I got lost won't work," Larkh winced. "She knows I'm a regular here an' I've shown her around town."

"Bugger off then!" Arven chuckled.

"See you later Arven," Larkh smirked as he jovially saluted and left the caravan, shutting the door quietly behind him.

CHAPTER 18

I
Almadeira

Wasting no time, Larkh submerged himself in the frothy bathtub suds and surfaced with a contented sigh. Feeling something brush against his arm, he groped for it, and lifted a painted wooden duck out of the bubbles. "Elsie..." he snorted in amusement, rolling his eyes and dropping the duck back into the water.

He closed his eyes and spent several minutes just enjoying the warmth; then he washed his hair and rinsed it using a jug and the pail of warm water sitting beside the bathtub. This done, he picked up the nearby sponge and scrubbed himself clean. Taking advantage of having a proper bath whenever possible was something he'd been drilling into his crew for a long time. His noble upbringing was certainly responsible for making him so particular about it; not that it was a bad thing.

Glancing at the floating wooden duck again, Larkh's eyes narrowed, a feeling of emptiness tugging at his sinking heart as he recalled another painful memory. Images once again flashed before his eyes; bath-time with Carina, his little sister. Ever since she was able to walk, his mother had insisted he helped give her a bath, but as soon as she'd started asking for him to join her, the trouble began. Their mother would wander out of the room for five minutes, and return to find the floor saturated with puddles of soapy water. There had been a wooden duck that was once his to play with in the bath, and there had also been a horse, but they soon became Carina's. She played with the duck while he was always left with the horse, protesting horses didn't swim like ducks. That never mattered to her though, she always insisted.

He took a deep breath, closed his eyes, trying to force the images out of his mind before he could succumb to the despair they brought. Reaching for a towel, he dried his face and took the excess moisture out of his hair. Standing up, he dropped the towel on to the floor and stood on it, absent-mindedly brushing his damp hair aside to reveal two small eagles tattooed either side of his neck, and a larger image of a phoenix in the centre, just below the nape. All three were of a tribal design originating from the native people of Enkaiyta.

A knock on the door disturbed his thoughts. "Yes?" he asked, picking up the heavy woven towel lying on the bed. The door opened, and Arcaydia walked in.

"I was wondering when you—" Arcaydia's cheeks suddenly turned pink.

"I didn't say come in!" he cried, quickly wrapping the towel around his waist, though it was clear she'd already seen more than she should have.

"I'm sorry!" she cried, turning to leave.

"Wait!" he called as she was about to shut the door. "I'm sorry, it's my fault. I didn't lock the door."

"No! I shouldn't have walked in, I—"

"I still forgot to lock the door, Arc," he sighed. "Anyone could've walked in. Sit down, I won't be long."

Arcaydia's brow lifted. "Don't you want to get dressed in private?" she asked.

Larkh shook his head as he turned away smirking to himself, dropping the towel to pull on his close-fitting trousers. "You ain't the first woman to see me naked y'know," he chuckled, "nor are you the first to have done so by accident." An awkward silence followed. "Anyhow, what'd you need me for?"

Arcaydia sat on the small chair beside the door and planted her hands on her knees, trying hard to avert her gaze, feeling her face flushing hot; but her eyes disobediently slid back to stare at his buttocks, even after they were covered.

"I... uh... wanted to ask if you'd like to go and take another wander around with me. Melkhar still hasn't returned, so I'm not sure what to do with myself," she stammered, continuing to watch as Larkh pulled on his boots. She tilted her head, noticing the tattoos on the base of his neck and shoulders. Her gaze glided over his bare chest as he turned to face her.

"Of course I'll tag along," he agreed with a friendly smile. Then he paused, frowning. "It does seem strange if she left just to undertake a mission an' hasn't returned. Could somethin' have gone wrong?"

"I don't know; possibly," Arcaydia frowned. "She wouldn't have disappeared deliberately; her orders were to return as soon as her mission was over. It was something to do with my training." Larkh stood, watching her intently. Arcaydia chewed anxiously on her lower lip, considering her thoughts.

"Like the Nays," she continued, "the Drahknyr are ageless and they are almost impossible to kill; when wounded their blood coagulates more quickly, and they are fast healers, but the Kaesan'Drahknyr are said to be indestructible. It's most likely something got in her way. If she is beyond a certain distance, she won't be able to contact me with mindspeech until she has recovered most of her full strength. Although Mount Dorne isn't that far from here, she should have been able to contact me, though I don't know if I'd be able to respond."

She considered the seikryth gem hidden in Melkhar's travelsack, but soon dismissed the thought, knowing she had no idea how to use it. The seikryths, she knew, were used to communicate over long distances without using mindspeech – especially for those whose minds didn't have an extensive reach like a Drahknyr at full strength – but there was a verbal command to activate them that she didn't know. Each one was marked with a small glyph. To contact another seikryth, the word or phrase for its glyph was required. If she knew how to use them, she could have contacted someone in an emergency.

"Until she contacts you," Larkh said, pulling on his shirt, "there's not much you can do except wait an' see if Marceau returns." Arcaydia stared at the floor wondering what could have happened. Then a hand suddenly appeared in front of her. "C'mon, let's see what's goin' on in town today. It's nearly time for lunch y'know." He winked, offering his hand. Arcaydia couldn't help but chuckle as she allowed him to pull her to her feet.

II
Almadeira

Almadeira's kathaedra, although smaller than its counterparts in other Nays' built cities, dominated the skyline like a shining beacon; built to honour Raiyah, known as the Lady of the Sun. Its whitestone had lost much of its original pearly lustre, and had faded to a more silvery hue. Without maintenance from the right kind of crystals and magic possessed by the Nays, whitestone lost its colour over the course of many generations.

Raeon brushed his white-silver cloak aside, striding through a towering arched doorway toward the altar at the far end of a great vaulted chamber, his footsteps echoing faintly. Sculptures lined every wall and arch; images ranged from the Aeva'Daeihn clergy and Galétriahn Highlords of ages past, to the Drahknyr and their dragons. Behind the altar stood a giant statue of the Sun Goddess herself, surrounded by the Kaesan'Drahknyr; the Adels perched on platforms above her.

Although Raiyah was the predominant deity of the Nays, her influence across Aeldynn had remained steadfast over the ages. Her temples were still revered as sacred sites by both humans and elves, and even new shrines and places of worship had been built in her honour. All such followers were known collectively as the *Tsolàr Fain*, meaning 'Followers of the Sun' or 'Those Who Gladly Follow the Sun', although it was rare to find any Cerenyr in their number, and neither Nays nor Kensaiyr could be found among them at all.

Standing before the altar, her head bowed to Raiyah's statue, stood a woman wearing ivory robes decorated with the finest of gold embroidery. Her mousy brown hair curled about her shoulders, the front strands braided all the way down and tied at the back of her head. On her back was a symbol of the sun bearing two Drahknyr figures supporting it either side, one arm high and the other low, their wings stretched out behind them.

The woman straightened and bowed as she turned to face him. Her faded glassy eyes searched longingly. She looked to be in her early thirties, though there were already visible streaks of grey in her hair.

"Raeon," she said softly, "your light is unmistakable, your spirit enriching. If only I could see what you look like in the flesh."

"Sister Nalane, you flatter me too much," Raeon replied, smiling. "It is good to meet with you again. How long has it been?"

"About four years, I think," Nalane smiled back.

Though blind to the material world, she had acquired the gift of spiritual sight in compensation. A person's expression was readable even in their spirit form. She was a silver mage like Raeon, but after her graduation she had taken a place offered to her as a priestess and healer of Thean Raiyah. It was common for silver mages with a faith to join the clergy of their respective religion, so long as they maintained their commitments to the Archaenen.

Nalane's eyes widened. "How do you do it?" she asked. "How has the taint not taken its hold on you yet?" Raeon shook his head and reached out to take hold of her hands.

"You forget," he said almost in a whisper, "I am half Cerenyr. It will take much longer for it to manifest in me;

though I don't know how long. I am the only half-elf in the Order of Silver, so I can only speculate on how long I have before it shows. Cerenyr formerly of our ranks reported the first signs in themselves between one and two hundred years after becoming Silver Mages. I'm still in my first century of life; I was still a boy sixteen years ago, so it is anyone's guess. If the elven part of me is stronger, I may yet have more time."

Nalane's expression hardened. "We made a choice knowing we couldn't escape the consequences," she sighed, "but are you still searching for a way?"

"I am," Raeon answered, watching her with a knowing sadness in his eyes. "We all knew what would happen to us when we made the choice to join the Order of Silver, but it does not mean we should not search for a way to stall or stop the taint. We chose this path to better protect our people. Even if we cannot stop it, we should still try to find a way to hold it back for as long as possible."

The priestess turned back to the statue of Raiyah where golden rays of sunlight flashed through high stained glass windows, bathing them in its pale light. She considered his words carefully, and then nodded slowly. "You are brave, Raeon Ayresborough," she said coolly. "You have my utmost respect for your endeavours. Now, what would you like to discuss?"

Raeon hesitated, glancing around the vast chamber. "Do you know where Lyte Warden Marceau has disappeared to?" he asked. "He must have informed someone."

Nalane fell silent for several moments before responding. "I am not really at liberty to say," the priestess replied. Raeon frowned.

"He sent a contract to Zehn Kahner, an elite mercenary who happens to be a friend of mine," he explained, looking to the stern, lofty female Kaesan'Drahknyr sculpture standing to Raiyah's left. "Marceau was Zehn's instructor in swordsmanship. In that contract was a request to hunt down a woman fitting the description of Kaesan'Drahknyr Melkhar Khesaiyde." Nalane stifled a gasp. "He was to meet Marceau here so he would enquire further about the contract, where the Lyte Warden would then explain the real reason he wished to speak to him," Raeon continued. "You see, Zehn is one of the two keys mentioned in the Taecade Medo; I have sensed it. I also believe the Mindseer Oracle candidate was supposed to be present at this meeting."

Quietly, Nalane approached the statue of Melkhar, appearing to gaze up at it despite being unable to see it. "He didn't mention any of that to me," she said, reaching out to touch it. Raeon wondered how the blind priestess could possibly know which one she stood in front of. His curiosity got the better of him.

"Excuse me Sister, but I'm interested to know—"

"How I know which statue is hers?" Nalane finished for him. "I can make out vague shapes or shadows of my surroundings once I know where they are, and each statue has a different kind of shape. My predecessor told me in which order they stand, but the most interesting fact is the shape I see of Melkhar's statue, very tall and slender, darker than any of the others." She turned to face Raeon again. "Marceau discovered a plot instigated by the Duke of Lonnfeir to take control of Almadeira in a bid to overthrow King Jaredh Faltain and to put the king of Adengeld on the throne instead. He left for Adner to warn the king. Though I suspect Duke Kradelow would rather take the throne for himself."

III
Almadeira

Numerous questions had been on Larkh's mind since he'd met Arcaydia, and one of them was his curiosity as to why she hadn't asked about why he favoured such a large ship. Perhaps she guessed it was merely that *Greshendier* was as much a family heirloom as she was a warship of the Faltain Navy, but the truth was there was more to it than that. Pirates typically favoured smaller vessels that were much faster, giving them a better chance of getting away, but *Greshendier* was a powerful warship built with an altirna system.

The altirna fluid inside *Greshendier* had been replaced by Yahtyliir, Larkh's mentor, with a purer variety, much more efficient than the human refined commodity. Granted, she couldn't outrun a brig or a clipper, but she was a man-o-war capable of matching the turning speed of a frigate with superior manoeuvrability, making her a monster not to be trifled with. The ship, coupled with his tactical capabilities, were what made Larkh such a devil at sea, and that pleased him.

He also wondered where Arcaydia came from within the Nays homeland of Ardeltaniah. He had seen ancient maps of the continent, but none of them had shown each region in great detail. Arcaydia was suffering with severe amnesia, so he was loathe to ask questions of her history.

Across the square, Larkh watched Arcaydia sorting through the wares of the festival stalls. The rough hiss of metal sliding against leather brought his scimitars flying from their scabbards as he pivoted on a heel and sank into a ready fighting stance; right arm extended, left arm arced over his head. Every civilian in the square scattered. All business ceased abruptly. Arcaydia had just placed a coin into a merchant's palm.

"Y'know you're really pushin' your luck this time," Larkh hissed. "Are you not aware of my status here?"

"Oh I know," Zehn sneered, "but I have written permission to pursue my quarry wherever it might go, and now I have permission from the mayor." He held out a letter. Larkh edged in closer to read it.

Frowning, he stepped back, shaking his head. "By my understandin', conflictin' permissions can only be resolved by the crown," he objected.

"The mayor is permitted to make a decision and then take it to the crown," Zehn retorted, "and if his actions are considered inappropriate he would lose his position. That's none of my concern though, *you are*."

Larkh tilted his head back disdainfully. "Oh I'm flattered you're so concerned wi' me," he sneered, his voice thick with sarcasm. "I'd believe it, were that truly the mayor's handwritin'. Did you even see the man?"

"I only needed the letter with his signature and seal, scum!" Zehn snapped.

"Cap'n!" two of his crew members ran out of the Silver Gull. It was Daron and Reys. "What is going on? This that *bastard* mercenary you were fightin' before?" Daron spat, scowling.

"Aye, but this ain't time for chitchat lads," Larkh replied, clenching his jaw. "Apparently the mayor takes full responsibility if the king should disapprove of him allowin' this one to attack me in our safe haven, an' he doesn't consider my crown-given position at all." He chewed his lip as he thought about it. "Make ready to leave would you? If it comes to it, get Gresh under away an' leave me a boat with a team to row me back. Don't worry about me for now."

"But—"

"I said GO!"

"Aye sir!"

Daron and Reys glowered at Zehn. Reys made a rude gesture with his fingers, his other hand resting on his flintlock. Daron's hand rested on his cutlass, a dangerous look in his eyes as they turned away, making their way briskly toward the harbour. Larkh considered the mercenary's claim again.

"Doesn't it strike you as at all odd?" he asked. "I thought a slave to the law would've known that was suspicious. It seems King Jaredh didn't think things through properly."

"He didn't think things through properly by givin' filth like you special privileges," Zehn snorted. "I've got my permission, and I'll see my contract through," he snarled, stuffing the letter into a side pocket on his tunic. He readied his sword, and lunged.

Larkh crossed his scimitars, blocking Zehn before his blade could make contact. "Tell me, do all royal ass-kissers like yourself bear such grudges on as grand a scale as you do?" Seeing Zehn's face turn red, he made a wry face. "An' I suppose ruinin' festivals is a part of the game as well!"

He danced to the left, sweeping his right arm at an angle, glancing across Zehn's shoulder as the mercenary twisted his body to block it. Larkh drove his weight into the right blade as he pushed the block to the side to strike at Zehn's side with his left. Zehn failed to fully avoid the strike as the blade glanced across his flesh, sending a second wave of stinging pain across his ribs. Larkh followed through with the motion, trapping the longsword between his scimitars.

Using his weight to drive himself forwards, Zehn forced Larkh to take a step backwards. Despite his efforts, he was met with considerable resistance as the pirate managed to retain the grip of his sword just a few seconds longer before sweeping the upper blade away, angling it upwards so that it glided effortlessly across Zehn's defending arm just above the elbow, slicing deep enough for blood to trickle freely down his arm.

Larkh skipped back and began flowering the scimitars in rapidly flowing figures of eight. Zehn realised getting too close to this windmill of steel would get him sliced to ribbons. Larkh had not done this in Senfirth, and he also hadn't witnessed the Kensaiyr use this move.

"Your turn bootlicker," Larkh scoffed. His brow knit, his bright blue eyes shining with keen ferocity. Blood streamed down Zehn's left arm and dripped from the fist that clenched the handle of his kite buckler. As he looked his quarry in the eyes, he saw no hint of amusement. There was a fierceness in the young captain's eyes Zehn recognised all too well.

Biting against the burning pain in his right arm, Zehn saw the chance to intercept the rapid swirling of metal ribbons and took it, knowing he was taking a risk. Larkh struck back at the same time, giving him a hard time parrying the next flurry of spinning blows. Using his recent encounter with Madukeyr as experience, Zehn launched himself back on the offensive. Where he found a gap, he struck, though he scarcely pierced the fibres of Larkh's shirt, only lightly scratching his skin.

'Seems he intends to kill me this time,' Larkh guessed, pulling his stomach back each time Zehn attempted to thrust his sword underneath his scimitars as his arms arced. The next time the mercenary thrust his sword forward, Larkh danced to the side and blocked it, but Zehn reached over with his other arm and punched him in the temple with the end of the kite buckler covering his hand.

Despite the sudden dull ache in his skull and the brief disorientation that followed, Larkh was quick to cross his blades when his balance faltered as Zehn bore down on him with enough momentum to knock him over. Larkh rolled back on to his feet as Zehn struck again, thrusting out his left foot as he ducked to the side, tripping the mercenary.

Zehn staggered and pitched forwards, banging his head on the cobblestones as he landed. He grimaced, but didn't have enough time to get back on his feet before Larkh kicked his injured left arm. Zehn howled in pain at the blow, blood further soaking his tunic. Larkh spat on the floor next to him, and turned away wiping his temple with the back of his right hand. He blinked at the red smears across it as his vision re-focussed after the blow he'd received. He heard

Arcaydia's voice calling him. She ran over and steadied him on his feet.

"You should go inside," he advised. "This is between him an' me."

"You're injured," she protested. "You—"

"It's just a few scratches an' I'll have a fucker of a headache, but other than that I'm fine," he countered. "The guards'll be here any second. If I kill him I won't have a leg to stand on here anymore." As Arcaydia opened her mouth to speak, Larkh's right scimitar flashed up. "Obviously I didn't kick you hard enough," he said dryly.

"Shut up and fight," Zehn snarled, gritting his teeth against the pain.

Arcaydia could do nothing but watch. Her eyes darted back and forth. They were both fast, but Larkh held an advantage in speed with his acrobatic skills. He used his surroundings effectively for assistance. Zehn was having a hard time fending off both blades at once with his injured arm, but he somehow managed to keep up. Larkh's movements, the strokes and flowering movements of his scimitars, were like a dance as he used them as perfect extensions of his arms.

Her vision flickered. What was that she just saw? She saw both their spirits; golden threads of energy weaved around and within both of them, and some strands began linking themselves together. She blinked. Her normal vision flashed back into focus, but this time she concentrated, and sure enough she witnessed the spectral forms again. It wasn't long before she lost it again, but she wondered if she might be able to start gaining control over it. *'I need to find out what this is,' she told herself. 'Melkhar where are you?'*

The continuous grating sound of grinding metal had drawn a crowd, and even Mrs. Menow came out of the Silver Gull to see what the commotion was all about. She was in the middle of polishing a tankard.

"What's he gotten himself into now?" she asked.

Arcaydia shook her head. "Larkh spoke of an elite mercenary who's been hunting him," she replied worriedly. "I'm guessing that's him." She pointed to Zehn. "He also said he has special permission in this town, so I don't understand any of this."

"The young captain does have a letter of marque for free movement within Ennerth's waters, but he can only moor his ship on a quayside in Almadeira," Elsie Menow confirmed. "Everywhere else along the coast of Ennerth he has to go to anchor and take a rowboat ashore. It isn't always a case of berths being too small for *Greshendier*, or her draft being too deep, it's also the authorities. He sometimes gets by with a bit of bribery though.

"So girlie, this is indeed his only safe haven in this area. Conflicts of permissions granted by the crown can only be resolved by the crown legally, and our mayor wouldn't allow something like this to go ahead without both men being taken before Faltainyr Demura's king. There's somethin' fishy going on." Tutting as she shook her head, Elsie wandered back into her tavern.

Arcaydia looked on, mesmerised by Larkh's sword-dancing. He parried and dodged Zehn's sword with lightning fast reflexes amidst spins, side rolls and skip steps that kept him light on his feet, and where his blades became engaged, he thrust out kicks that rarely missed their mark. He wasn't going to walk away unscathed though; his white shirt was in tatters and splashed with blood, and now he was bleeding from a cut on his forehead. Zehn wasn't any better off; in fact, his injuries were worse.

"Zehn!" a voice called from across the square. "Zehn, stop!" It was Raeon.

"Stay out of this!" Zehn snarled. "I will finish it!"

"You don't know when to quit do you? Arrogant son of a bitch!" Larkh spat, wiping blood from his forehead with his sleeve.

"There's going to be trouble here in Almadeira very soon Zehn, please stop!" Raeon pleaded desperately, stepping between the two regardless of the danger he placed himself in. The pair abruptly ceased fighting at his intervention. "I've also just received a telepathic message from the Archaenen that I must return immediately," he panted. "Larkh, please stand down and listen. You remember me, don't you?"

Reluctantly, Larkh stepped back. He nodded, recognising Raeon instantly. Though his eyes still burned with fury, he allowed the conversation to continue.

"What's going to happen here?" Zehn demanded. He lowered his sword, watching the tension in Raeon's shoulders relax.

"I just received a telepathic message from the Archaenen as I was leaving the Kathaedra," Raeon explained. "I need to get back to Aynfell as soon as possible. They only do this when there has been an omen or desperate message of some kind. And not only that, I have just spoken with Priestess Nalane. She informed me Marceau left Almadeira in a hurry because the Duke of Lonnfeir plots to overthrow King Jaredh, starting with this here town where he already has support. Since your instructor also doubles as a counsellor to the king, and he's left in such a hurry, it could only mean one thing..."

The shock on Larkh's face was enough to send chills up Arcaydia's spine. The colour drained from his face, and he swallowed hard. "Kradelow..." His voice was shallow and tense. His stomach turned to ice and shivers ran through his arms and shoulders. Slowly he took a deep breath. "So that's what it was all about. I lost everythin' because..." He rubbed his face, unable to finish his sentence. He gritted his teeth, hands gripping the scimitars tightly. "He's put this plan together over sixteen years. He must have known I was goin' to be here for the festival. He must've hired them to watch me."

Arcaydia watched helplessly at the look of dismay frozen on his handsome face as he stared down at the floor.

All she could do was put a hand on his shoulder to offer some form of comfort.

"It would seem his influence has spread over the course of that time," said Raeon. "And it would also seem he has unseated the mayor under all our noses." As he spoke, he regarded Zehn sternly. Sudden realisation swept over the mercenary's features as he remembered the letter in his pocket; the letter that gave him permission to attack Larkh here. It was in the side pocket of his tunic under his left arm, but he was barely able move his arm for the pain.

The townspeople suddenly erupted into panic, scattering for cover as thick black clouds of smoke billowed into the sky from the direction of the main gates, and screams rang out in abundance.

'And now it begins,' Larkh thought grimly.

"Into the Silver Gull," Raeon instructed all of them. "Zehn, I'll look at your arm while we're in there. We haven't got much time."

CHAPTER 19

I
Valamont Heights, Sherne

Melkhar awoke nestled within the craggy outcrops of the Valamont Heights; the lush moorlands of Sherne. She had travelled all day and half the night before stopping to rest as a storm swept overhead and unleashed its deluge. At least the crags had offered some shelter; though she'd had no bedroll, blanket nor any wood to start a fire. Now the rusty odour of damp, metallic stone hung thick in the air. She was no stranger to sleeping rough in the wilderness, but comfort was never to be sniffed at.

She opened her eyes, slowly blinking at the blinding light of the sun, already high in the sky. Frowning, she realised it was already nearing midday. Oversleeping meant lost time, but at least she'd gained a reasonable amount of rest, and for that she was grateful. Clambering out of her resting spot, she emerged on the grassy moor and stretched.

A brisk salty breeze blew inland from the south-eastern shores of Armaran, pushing clusters of woolly clouds northward. She closed her eyes again, focussing her energy on locating the dragon. Quite some distance still lay between them; his presence currently remained south-west of her position. She was unable to tell whether or not he'd already left the island of Ehyenn, but his presence was still far enough away to make drastic action on her part unnecessary. It was still a long way to Aynfell, but if she made good headway she could arrive by sunset. The probability that Rahntamein would attack today was uncertain; nevertheless she needed to reach Aynfell as soon as possible. It wasn't in her nature to take any unnecessary chances.

Gnawing hunger urged her to start moving in the hope of finding something edible to restore another fraction of the energy expended in her long flight. It was one of the banes of maintaining a physical existence, for spiritual energies were reserved for battle or long-term survival. Under normal circumstances, the Drahknyr experienced hunger and fatigue in the same way as everyone else. When excess spiritual energy had been utilised, however, those sensations became far more intense.

She didn't have time to move at a leisurely pace, so hunting for a meal was out of the question, and that wasn't counting preparation and cooking time. It wasn't effective to cook anything with magic except to assist in starting a natural fire. She remembered an attempt at cooking rabbit using her magica in a time long since passed; the meat had rapidly turned to little more than charcoal. Narrowing her eyes in disdain at the memory, she rose to her feet and began picking her way down the craggy path toward the River Nidhan, leaping across any even surfaces she could reach between intermittent gusts of wind blowing across the moors. Today the wind was giving in to its rougher nature.

After having travelled so far from the Len'athyr Sanctuary, one night sleeping rough on the moors wasn't enough to replenish her spiritual energy. Her location shift through Nira'Eléstara sapped more strength than it normally would, considering she was still recovering from an ancient, grievous wound.

Naturyth crystals didn't have the power to withdraw Phandaeric poisons completely. They regenerated the body, sending impulses to promote the quickest healing, but the root of the Phandaeric poison lingered. After waking from the long sleep, the body needed to do the rest of the work itself; and that could take months. If necessary, she could still fight for many hours, but the continued use of spiritual energies gradually took their toll on the physical aspect in a way akin to ordinary mortals losing hours if not days of sleep. Once she was fully healed, she would rapidly regain her full strength, and the drain on her energy levels would slow to the pace of an intermittently dripping tap rather than like one left to run freely.

At the river's edge, she knelt, cupped her hands in the cool water and drank deeply. Then she washed her face and neck. At the feel of the scar marking her right cheek, a stabbing pain knifed through her chest. That wound had been dealt generations ago, long before the War of the Eclipse, while she was still young. Even now, the memory of how and why it was done sometimes reminded her of what it meant.

'I want to find out what breaks a Kaesan'Drahknyr,' a male voice snarled inside her mind, spitting the word Kaesan'Drahknyr. *'Everything that has a physical existence must have a weakness, and you, as pitiful as you are, are no exception.'*

She stared fiercely at the palms of her hands while the last droplets of the cold highland water dripped on to the stone. Rising, she looked east, drying them on her tight leather trousers. The next best option to find a meal was to take to the skies and hope she found a small settlement along the way. After checking every direction for intruders, she released her wings. As they towered over her head, she spread them wide and now focussed her energy on her ascension into the sky until the wind rushed underneath, lifting her into the heavens.

II
Almadeira

"You don't know how to teleport, so you're only sure to get out by sea," Raeon countered as they fled inside the tavern. "Right now you and Larkh are on the same side, as much as you're both loathe to admit it! This is part of a coup staged by the Duke of Lonnfeir, and Rahntamein is intended to be

Adengeld's siege weapon against Aynfell, if not all of Faltainyr Demura."

Larkh shot Raeon a dangerous glare, understanding what he was suggesting, but before he could speak, the door to the Silver Gull slammed shut. Zehn rested his sword against a table and sat, pointing directly at Larkh using his good arm.

"You want me to go with *him*?" he snarled. The mercenary shook his head, glowering. "You must be bloody mad to think—"

"For crying out loud Zehn, swallow your pride for once!" Raeon snapped. "You need to get out of here! I can leave Almadeira undetected so—"

"Who the *fuck* do you think you are?" Larkh spat, shoving Raeon against the wall, scowling. He nodded in Zehn's direction. "You're suggestin' I let that piece of shit on board my ship?" he added in a harsh whisper. Grabbing the collar of Raeon's robes he pulled him closer. "We may've known each other once, Raeon, but in case you hadn't noticed, he an' I ain't exactly friends."

Elsie came out and began cutting away Zehn's sleeves to clean his wounds, gently pushing him back down as he attempted to rise to defend Raeon. "Stay out of it," she advised. "You're in no shape for another fight right now, and I won't have it in my tavern."   For the first time in a long while Zehn found himself too weary to argue, and he sank back to the chair, glowering at the pirate. His arm was wet and sticky with blood, and the ache and sting of the wound made him clench his jaw.

Arcaydia backed away and sat in a corner, her eyes fixed worriedly on Larkh, a sharp tension tugging at her heart at the sudden flare in his temper. The Lonnfeir soldiers were now storming the town, and she'd known it was going to happen. She knew! But Melkhar had told her to keep her mouth shut about it; this wasn't their fight, not right now anyway. What kind of level conflict was needed to attract the attention of the Nays, let alone the Drahknyr?

She considered trying to make a concentrated attempt at making a mental connection with Melkhar, but she dared not try here. She would need a calm situation in order to even try, though she was pretty sure she would fail; she was only a novice in mindspeech and she would never attain the Kaesan'Drahknyr's level of skill.

"I ask because he is my friend and so... you know what you did for me back then Larkh," Raeon reminded him. "You know why I don't reveal what I am to the public." Larkh tightened his grip on the mage's robes, staring into his eyes with a look that might kill. Then he sighed, releasing Raeon and stepping aside. He moved to lean against the wall by the door.

"Fine," Larkh shrugged in defeat, "but you'll owe me dearly for this. I'm not in the habit of doin' favours for free, an' certainly not for men who try to kill me."

"Alright," said Raeon, "besides what I need to live on, you can have the rest of what I've got with me as a down payment. You can have three months of my wages from the Archaenen minus my expenses when we next meet."

"Gods! Raeon are you insane?" Zehn protested. "I'm not going to—"

"If you don't go," Raeon interrupted, leaning to Zehn's ear as he knelt to assist the innkeeper in cleaning his friend's wounds, "I will be forced to put you to sleep, use an unnecessary amount of magica to get you on board that ship, and I will give him six months of my pay when we meet again rather than three."

Larkh mulled the offer over, folding his arms across his chest, watching as Zehn's expression turned from anger to dismay. He glanced at him, and smiled satisfactorily when the mercenary shot him a vicious look back.

"Alright, Silver Mage, we have a deal," Larkh said, rubbing his left shoulder. Raeon turned his head, nodding slowly.

"I'll fetch the money when I've finished sorting him out," he said, placing a hand over the more serious cut.

"Raeon don't do this! I should go with you," Zehn pleaded. Arcaydia watched closely as Raeon healed Zehn's arm, trying to put everything else out of her mind.

"Listen to him," Larkh hissed at Zehn, his eyes narrowing. "I don't really care what you think of me, or why 'cause frankly your attitude is enough to make me want to ram my fingers down my throat. You understand nothin' y'hear me! Justice isn't always on the side of the law!"

Snarling, Zehn began to shout in protest, but Larkh cut him off sharply. "I'm assumin' you'll want to protect your king? If Raeon so wishes it I'll get you out o' here, though I'd rather keel-haul you an' cut you loose to feed the sharks!"

Arcaydia saw soldiers wearing white, blue and gold patrolling the streets outside. Kradelow's men would not be forgiving if they were found. These men were now their enemies, and any resistance would likely ensure their execution. Since Larkh already had a personal history with this duke, it was more than likely he'd be executed without trial.

"Zehn, I'm going to patch you up, and then I'm leaving," Raeon said, wiping away the excess blood with a cloth and minimising the bleeding while he worked at closing the edges of the wound first. His hand glowed, faintly resonating white while the flesh slowly began to knit itself together. The mercenary winced, clenching his jaw tighter. "The gates will be swarming with soldiers loyal to Duke Kradelow," Raeon explained as the bleeding slowed and congealed. "I can teleport directly from here, beyond their line of sight. I cannot teleport you as well."

Reluctantly, Zehn met Larkh's gaze. He glared fiercely at the pirate, wincing at the pain as his wounds were forcibly closed, desperately resisting the urge to scratch as the itching became almost unbearable. Then he glanced at Raeon, who stared back at him long and hard, then back at Larkh.

"What will you ask?" he enquired, his expression doing nothing to hide his bitterness. Larkh's eyebrows arched so high they might as well have touched his hairline. He stifled laughter; his bruised ribs ached from the fight. He barely believed the man had to ask. "That you leave me the fuck alone, that's what!" he snapped. "Though I s'pose that's too much to ask ain't it?"

Zehn averted his sullen gaze from Larkh's blazing anger as Raeon removed his hand from the wound. Elsie directed him around the back of the taproom to wash his hands.

Restless, and seething, Larkh tapped his left foot repeatedly against the floor as he leaned against the counter. *'What a fine spring festival this turned out to be,'* he thought, frowning. Kradelow; it was all his doing. This plan had been sixteen years in the making. There was no other explanation for why the duke would have waited this long before making a move. He had to get under the skin of the entire kingdom first.

Apparently the first of his kin to have passed had succumbed to some unknown disease, but no-one else in the area had fallen ill and died. Kradelow had insisted afterwards that the family took *Greshendier* for her test voyage before she became the first fully fledged warship in Faltain's elite class ship-of-the-line, and the holiday would take their minds off the grief of their recent losses.

There was only one puzzle piece that seemed to fit in connection with his family's demise. Someone in the family, most likely his father, had somehow found out about the duke's plan. He, being a child at the time, couldn't have known any of the details. Now Kradelow's plans were complete, he had most likely waited for the spring festival when he knew he would be in port. Larkh drew the conclusion it was the duke who was behind him being watched.

Raeon returned a few minutes later with a coinpurse in his right hand. He stepped forward and offered it along with a small slip of paper.

"This is everything I have with me," he said, glaring over his shoulder at Zehn, who was about to protest yet again. When he returned his gaze to Larkh, he continued, "I won't need it to travel back. The rest will come later as agreed, and that piece of paper is a brief letter, written by my hand, detailing our deal."

Larkh accepted them, and unfolded the note. Nodding, he tucked it away in a pocket and tied the coinpurse to his belt. Raeon smiled meekly, then returned to Zehn and took a seat next to him.

"You will get on board that ship," the mage told him. "You can negotiate a release point once you are clear of Almadeira. I have written that condition into the note I gave him. The duke's forces are your enemies now, and your tunic marks you as loyal to the crown. I suggest you take it off and give it to me for now, and wear your regular traveller's gear. You may then get through Almadeira to the harbour appearing to be an ordinary mercenary, though I fear you will have to turn to deception in order to pull it off."

Zehn stared at the floor silently for several long moments before he spoke. "And what if he doesn't keep his word?" he asked. "What then?"

"Oh I think he will," Raeon returned confidently. "Even pirates don't like it when their deals are broken. And if he didn't, he wouldn't get paid. It's as simple as that really."

"Ah yes, you apparently know him," Zehn drawled. "Care to tell me how that came about?"

"That's a long story we don't really have time for right now," Raeon replied, "but I can tell you I was never involved in piracy. I know him from long before that ever occurred."

Zehn lifted his eyes as Elsie placed two mugs of water beside him, watching as she moved over to Larkh, handing one to him. His gaze hovered on the pirate longer than it ought to have, and Larkh returned his look with a scowl.

As a tankard of water was abruptly thrust into Larkh's hand, he jumped in surprise. Looking up, he saw Elsie staring at him earnestly. He nodded his thanks and drained it in one draught; glancing out of the window at the soldiers now standing on guard should anyone try their hand at rebelling. At least the Silver Gull was tucked away and inconspicuous enough to avoid being investigated immediately. It wouldn't take the soldiers long to settle in; soon they would swamp the taverns, expecting to be served.

His thoughts abruptly shifted to Mey. Where was she? Was she safe? His heart began to race. Pushing himself off the wall, he turned toward the group. He addressed Zehn first, anger still burning in his eyes while trying to block out the deafening noise of bellowing soldiers outside. "Head down to the docks as soon as you can an' go left when you arrive there. I'm sure you know which ship's mine." He looked to Arcaydia. "An' bring this lass wi' you."

This roused Arcaydia from her reverie of watching Raeon's healing magic and surgical skills. Her eyes shot to him as he made for the door. Elsie caught him by the arm. He flinched at her touch, the cuts on his skin stinging violently.

"Don't try to stop me Elsie," he warned. "I'm worried about Mey, an' I'm worried about my ship an' crew." The innkeeper took a hold of his belt and began tying a sealed pouch to it.

"Medicinal herbs lad," she said. "By the end of all this, I think you'll need them." She had given some to Zehn as well, he noticed. He was about to dig into his purse when she caught his hand and shook her head solemnly. "You've done more than enough," she assured him. Reluctantly, he withdrew his hand and gave her shoulder a squeeze.

"Thanks, Elsie," he said with a faint smile. "Take care of yourself."

"Please don't die Larkh," the innkeeper begged him.

"I'll try," he chuckled.

"Why can't I go with you now?" Arcaydia asked. Her eyes pleaded with him not to leave her. "I don't know this man, and he's—"

"I must find out if Mey is alright, an' get back to my ship to prepare for departure," Larkh interjected with a frown. He clenched his fists. "I won't be able to watch you. If this twat has any sense," he added, jabbing a thumb over his shoulder in Zehn's direction, "he'll do what'll keep him alive. Besides, he's still a lawful man. I'm not. He's not goin' to have swords an' guns aimed at him like I will till he boards the ship."

Larkh grabbed his scimitars leaning against the doorframe and looked over his shoulder. "I'll trust you to make up a good story to keep her safe," he winked, and then flew out of the door.

"What's with him?" Zehn snorted.

"You don't strike me as the type to give anyone much of a chance to tell you about who they are," Elsie remarked sharply, folding her arms across her chest. "Have you any idea what happened to that boy?"

Zehn growled under his breath. "I know he was from a noble family, and was the sole heir to his family fortune until he threw it all away to become a filthy pirate," he muttered irritably, his eyes cold and sullen. Elsie drew up a seat and planted her short, stout body upon it.

"You're right lad," she said matter-of-factly, "but that's a mere fraction of it. Did anyone in your family, or any townsfolk ever talk about a noble family being wiped out sixteen years ago?"

"I heard brief fragments, but back then my father..." Zehn began, then paused. "Wait...do you mean...?" Elsie gave him a knowing smile.

"You mean you never knew it was Larkh Savaldor's entire bloodline that was wiped out by the Duke of Lonnfeir?" the innkeeper asked. "He's the sole heir quite literally. I don't know all the details and he rarely says a word about it, but from what he did tell me, a few were subtly picked off first, then Kradelow suggested the rest of the family took *Greshendier* for its test voyage to Enkaiyta to *take a rest from the grief* of their recent losses. That lad treats me like I were his own mother."

Zehn's mouth fell open. He glanced across at Raeon who'd been silent throughout. "Did you know about this?" he demanded. "You mentioned something on the mountain..." Raeon's eyes lifted dispassionately to meet his. "I hope you understand why I did not tell you sooner," the silver mage said nonchalantly, wrapping a bandage around the wound on Zehn's arm. "You'd have snapped at me if I'd tried to tell you. When you're set on hating someone, there's no negotiating."

In seeing his friend about to protest, Raeon silenced him by lifting a hand. "Don't look at me like that. You know it's true. The incident occurred while we were away on the island of Ehyenn; and I know that's a memory you don't want dug up unnecessarily. I found out when I returned, but it seems knowledge of the family's identity was kept as a secret among the nobility. I never found out all the details. Anyway, I'm sorry that as things stand right now, there is no time to give you any more insight on Madukeyr's cryptic message."

Arcaydia's ears pricked up at the sound of Madukeyr's name, and though she said nothing, Raeon took notice.

"I am aware that you recognise both the names of Madukeyr and Marceau," Raeon acknowledged, looking to Arcaydia with a smile. "I also know who you are, Arcaydia Na'Sairdun." Reluctantly, she turned her head to him.

"H-how?" she stammered.

"There's no time to explain that either I'm afraid." Raeon picked up his own travel pack, and tilted his head toward the wooden rafters holding the ceiling, his body radiating a pale white light. "Farewell to you all."

"Raeon, w—"

The brightness expanded, flickered, and the silver mage was gone. Zehn held a pensive expression, finding himself suddenly unsure of anything he was thinking anymore. He scratched the back of his head with his left hand. "I'll have to muddle through I suppose," he shrugged, throwing his hands up. "Somehow I have a feeling some questions are soon to be answered anyway." He looked to Elsie. "Is there anything else I should know?"

Elsie rose to her feet and picked up the bowl of bloody water. "Try asking him yourself," she said, waving a hand dismissively, disappearing into the kitchen. She noticed Larkh had left the key to his room on the counter, and scooped it into the pocket of her apron as she went.

Zehn stood, bewildered. He swallowed hard, absent-mindedly ran a hand through his shock of hair, and adjusted his bandana.

Arcaydia watched him, her own expression despondent. "I'll go and get my belongings," she said eventually, thinking she may be just as confused as he was. "There is a lot considering my master is away on a mission, but I'm sure I can manage if you can fight your way through—"

"Don't be silly girl," the innkeeper objected. "Fit everything that's necessary into one bag and take that. I'll look after everything else until we meet again, and I'll make sure of the gypsies' safety as well."

Arcaydia cast her eyes to the floor worriedly. "Right," she agreed, looking to Zehn. "Give me just a few moments and I'll be there."

"I'm ready when you are," Zehn replied calmly – to his own surprise – watching her dash off into the back of the inn and up the stairs as Elsie once again addressed the mercenary, cloth in hand.

"Will you swallow that pride and board the *Greshendier* then?" she asked, wiping over a dark oaken table. This sounded more like a challenge than a question.

"What choice do I have?" Zehn muttered. "If Raeon's words are true, and I know they are, then that's my only guaranteed route out of here. Besides, he's effectively just sold me to a pirate. I could still be slaughtered by a large crew of barbarians. They'll not take kindly to me."

"Then you'll have to start eating some humble pie before you set foot on her decks lad," Elsie warned him. "I don't expect the Captain will go easy on you either." Zehn snorted disdainfully and moved over to wait by the door.

III
Aynfell

It was mid-afternoon by the time Melkhar came across a hamlet where a small church and mill were nestled in a cluster of trees. She spent little more than an hour there, concealing herself with a small amount of glámar this time; a black cloak with a hood, an eye-patch over her right eye to cover the scar, a slight rounding off of her ears, and lightening of the shadowy lines framing her eyes.

This allowed her to eat a decent meal quietly and in peace before she moved on. The locals had, as expected, stared at her stature and overall appearance; but those were things she was unable to mask; nor would she have the incentive to do so, were it even possible. Glámar was a skill only those of elven or fey blood could master; despite the level of magica the Drahknyr and Nays had at their disposal. Once she was a safe distance from the village, she dispelled the effects of the glámar, and once again took to the skies.

The Drahknyr were capable of fighting for many hours with a continuous stream of energy, yet maintaining long distance flight came with its drawbacks. Their high density energy was wasted on flying long distances when it was best put to use in combat; long flights drained their energy much faster. Once she had regained her full strength, this kind of setback would be more of a mere inconvenience than a debilitating problem.

By the time evening drew close, she was hungry again and needed to rest as long as possible in Aynfell before dragonfire engulfed the city. Rahntamein was on the move; his presence grew stronger by the minute, and the city lay just beyond the horizon.

The academic city of Aynfell was a welcome sight after she'd flown so far in such a short space of time. The first sights to come into view were the three Whitestone Sentinels; three great towers to the north, east and west, still standing and just as pristine as they had been aeons ago. They served as great lookout towers allowing Aynfell's watchmen to see further field across land and sea, but the Altirnathé shards perched at their peaks served a different purpose. The fact they were still intact pleased her.

Dotted about the sprawling half-timbered city were ruined whitestone walls and sealed off tombs where long dead Nays and humans alike rested. All other structures had been constructed around them, and expanded over the years to make the city what it was today.

In the centre of the Archaenen's courtyard on the northern side of the city was a Varleima, its tear shape supported by an ornate golden frame and arch, its pale jade glow accentuated by the warm glow of the sunlight dimming in the west. By melding with the coming darkness of night and redirecting the fading rays of the sun that touched her, she was able to conceal her approach.

Melkhar's first point of contact was the Archaenen, and she would need to speak with an archmage of the Order of Silver. As she dropped her invisibility glámar, she was quickly spotted by a group of acolytes who promptly pointed at her and bolted inside to inform their superiors.

The Archaenen itself mimicked the original baroque style architecture of the Nays, built and stylised by humans. The main building was hexagonal, and set apart from each seven hundred foot wall was a pentagonal outbuilding designed to be the living quarters and personal studies or laboratories of the students, tutors and faculties.

She landed beside the Varleima and folded her wings; as if by recognition of her presence, the strange mechanical resonance of the crystal momentarily increased dramatically before it resumed its steady rhythm. It was believed that such a reaction was a response to the level of power an individual wielded; so the greater the increase in resonance, the greater the power commanded.

It wasn't long before she was greeted by a high ranking member of the Order of Silver. To begin with she wasn't sure whether or not the man was an archmage or not, but it quickly became apparent to her he was suppressing a great deal of power for someone of his ilk. His hair was dark brown and tied back in a low ponytail, and his ears spoke of mixed blood between those of a human and an elf. The acolytes following him stopped close to the doorway.

"So, it really was you Marceau mentioned in his contract," Raeon breathed. He brought his right fist to rest over his heart and dropped to one knee. "Welcome to the Archaenen, Kaesan'Drahknyr Melkhar Khesaiyde. My name is Raeon Ayresborough; I am Second Archmage to the Order of Silver."

"E'verkéne, Arhcýn'Magían," [19] said Melkhar, bringing her right hand to her left shoulder. *"Éyn enlíhrnd vér'te zhaetsaren. Dauhs ye'n haeos al seikryth?"* [20]

"We do indeed have a seikryth," Raeon replied, "and we're so very glad you have learned of the situation and arrived so promptly."

"You understand Daeihn well," she acknowledged, shifting her wings. "I may need to use that seikryth later. I would have known of this sooner, but I was waylaid and forced to travel through Nira'Eléstara. I emerged at the Len'athyr Sanctuary."

"You have come far. What can we help with?" Raeon asked, masking his astonishment as best he could; though he suspected hiding it from her was impossible. Those eyes were as cold as stone and sent shards of ice knifing through

---

[19] Greetings, Archmage.
[20] I learned of the situation. Do you have a seikryth?

his gut. The acolytes behind him were equally awestruck and afraid. Melkhar eyed him intently.

"A sufficient meal and as much rest as I can achieve before the dragon arrives," she answered, straight and to the point. "At the rate Rahntamein is moving, he will arrive around the time the moon reaches its zenith. I suggest you evacuate as many as you can to the catacombs beneath the city before then. I'm quite surprised you hadn't thought of that already. With the number of people living here, the approximate death rate could easily reach twenty to thirty percent if you act now. If you delay much longer the city may well be lost entirely."

Raeon's eyes widened, "he's that close and you're not going to protect the city with a barrier!?"

Melkhar shot him a cold glare. "He is a dragon," she said matter-of-factly. "Dragons are not nimble creatures, but they can cover great distances swiftly; whereas we Drahknyr are built for speed and combat. Archmage, have you not studied long enough to know all this?" Raeon cast his eyes downward ashamedly.

"And no," she continued, "I am not going to protect the city with a barrier. Zerrçainne is behind this game, and if I know her, she has managed to gain Rahntamein's trust and will have him focus his attention on the Archaenen. Aynfell will be an added bonus for him. The wealth of knowledge within these walls is what she wants to destroy because the secrets to world restoration are shrouded in mystery, myth and legend, and ancient texts in the form of riddles. The city itself is intended to satisfy the dragon's appetite for destruction." She stared hard at him.

"From what I have learned since my awakening, that cannot be allowed to happen, for it may contain all the knowledge required to protect your world. By sealing off the Archaenen, there will be minimal damage and risk to its collapse and so I will fight him with a view to defend the city with skill alone. If I can minimise the death rate I have predicted, I will."

Raeon chewed his lower lip and stared at the ground, desperately trying to take the information on board, blaming himself for having not taken action sooner. But he too had only recently arrived. And that stare. That stare of hers was frightening! He'd had little rest since he'd left Zehn with Larkh – a pairing he was more than a little concerned about – only arriving in Aynfell a matter of a few hours ago. It was still no excuse; if they'd started making preparations sooner more lives would have been spared.

"You mentioned Marceau," Melkhar added, banishing her wings. "Perhaps you can explain that one to me at the table." Realisation washed over Raeon's face. *'That young woman...the coup!'*

"There is something else I must speak to you urgently about as well," he suddenly blurted as the Kaesan'Drahknyr nonchalantly passed by. "You weren't in Almadeira, so I fear it is important that you know of it." Melkhar's wolfish eyes narrowed suspiciously.

"Very well," she said, "but if you want the best I can offer from my current skill level, my requests must be fulfilled immediately."

"Understood ma'am."

'This isn't going to be easy,' Raeon told himself. *'How do I tell her about Marceau's whereabouts and what has happened in Almadeira since? I couldn't have brought the girl with me under such circumstances, even had I been aware Melkhar would come.'*

CHAPTER 20

I
Almadeira

Larkh emerged from the Silver Gull and peered around the corner. The streets were filling with thick, billowing smoke where a number of homes were ablaze, and the town square swarmed with soldiers. Townsfolk huddled into corners or fled into buildings that hadn't been set ablaze. Several dead guards lay strewn across the streets; evidently those who had resisted. Only someone like Kradelow would stoop so low as to slaughter civilians in a time of peace for refusing to bend to his will.

He covered his mouth as his chest constricted; he coughed violently against the smoke invading his lungs. Crouching low, he took his hand away from his face, bracing himself against a wall. His attention was drawn to an Aurentai man with wavy, mousy brown hair, dressed in black leathers, addressing the general. He recognised the way he was dressed; he was an assassin, and not just any kind of assassin. *'Noctae Venatora,'* he thought, squinting through the smoky haze.

"Have you seen our elusive pirate anywhere Einar?" he heard the Aurentai ask.
"No, but I know where his ship is," said the general. "It's the biggest one sitting in the harbour near the Mizzen Rest tavern. If he's in town, he'll probably be heading for the ship right now." Larkh frowned; the name Einar was familiar.

"Remember, the ship is not to be damaged," the Aurentai reminded him. "The Duke wants it without as much as a scratch, and don't touch any merchant ships either."

"Leyal, why would I want to destroy a Faltain Navy ship-of-the-line when I am a soldier in the Faltain Army? And why would I want to be rid of any merchant ships in that harbour?" Einar asked. "We may well stop others from docking to bring supplies in. The Duke wants the town under his firm control, and that is all."

"And what do you plan to do about the gypsies?" Leyal asked, glancing toward the hillside on the eastern side of the town.

"Ah yes, the gypsies," Einar forced a smile. "They may yet live if they bend their knee. Orders are orders after all."

"I thought you'd say that. It's unlikely, but I'll ask you not to kill them," he advised. "They are to remain unharmed, and not just because one of my kin is with them." Einar's brow arched as Leyal turned and walked away.

"Very well sir." Einar bowed his head, turning up the street leading to the grassy hill. "They will remain here under martial law until further notice."

"Fuck, damn and shit," Larkh muttered, bolting for the nearest alley. He dashed through the narrow backstreets, dodging paths blocked by fallen beams and collapsed rooftops, leaping over other obstacles lying in his path.

He couldn't be certain he hadn't already been spotted, but he was going to have to leave the restrictive alleyways anyway; the smouldering debris was slowing him down. At the next right turn, he pulled his scimitars from their scabbards and drove his right arm forward as one soldier confidently stepped into the alley, assisting him in burying his blade to the hilt. The man grunted, exhaled a mouthful of blood as the blade was yanked free, and crumpled to the ground.

Larkh broke into a run again, dancing to the side as another soldier ran at him head on. He spun on the balls of his feet, slashed through the man's side under the ribcage with his left blade, following through by plunging the right blade downward into his back as he fell. These men were light infantry; their minuscule amount of armour was made of leather.

Using his momentum, he blocked another sword swinging in from the side and swiftly swept his twin blade down at an angle, striking his assailant's knee with a nauseating crack; the man howled in agony as he went down. The pirate spun around to engage the fourth opponent.

Crossing left over right, he drove his weight against the attacker, who returned the pressure with equal force. Larkh kept his stance firm, allowing his spine to tilt backward from his hip before ducking out to the side, slashing across the soldier's back as he staggered forward, meeting the pavement face first with a heavy thud.

Two gunshots sounded behind him simultaneously. He turned to see two more soldiers fall to the ground with shots to the chest and neck. He caught sight of Mey crouching in an alley on the other side of the main street blowing smoke from her flintlocks. She winked, granting him a knowing smile, and made a dash for the harbour.

Glancing back up the street, another group of soldiers were charging to greet him. He stepped into the middle of the cobbled road, flicking the excess blood from his twin blades. There he took a deep breath, rotated his shoulders back and sank them as he lowered his right arm and arced the left over his head. As they drew closer, he began to flower them again, adding speed to their motion. With his eyes cold and fixed hard on his assailants, he registered their hesitation. He forced down laughter, knowing better than to allow his arrogance to take control.

"C'mon, he's only one man lads," said one, shrugging nonchalantly as he stepped forward. "This'd be *Captain* Savaldor wouldn't it? Yes, blond hair in layers, wields dual scimitars effortlessly. You're definitely him alright, *Sword Dancer*. Been a thorn in the Duke's side for too long, you 'ave."

"Believe me, the feelin's mutual," Larkh sneered.

"Try not to kill him lads," the soldier snorted disdainfully. "The duke wants a word before he hangs." Larkh arched a brow, but said nothing more.

Snarling, the man lunged at him. Larkh continued flowering the scimitars in figures of eight, dancing back a step at the final moment. As the soldier flew past him, the curved blades sliced into his flesh, blood sluicing as he sprawled across the cobblestones.

Larkh spun to meet the rest of the group, and launched himself without hesitation. His conscious thoughts had shut down; his movements had become entirely instinctual, yet he was always aware of the choices he made. Yahtyliir had taught him how to fight like this, but this time it felt somehow different. Maybe it was raw determination? Maybe it was his thirst for revenge against Kradelow? Maybe he couldn't allow them to get down to the harbour before Mey had a chance of getting away, but there was no way they were going to set foot on the gangway of his ship, let alone her decks. They'd have to face a number in the region of five hundred crew members first.

The scimitars arced and spun rapidly, independently of one another, his feet barely seeming to touch the ground, pirouetting with enviable grace. He jumped, rolled, kicked and slashed at his attackers with fluid swiftness and accuracy, somehow managing to stave off dizziness. It certainly hadn't been like this in the beginning. When he'd first begun training with Yahty, his head was spinning within moments.

He knew where all the openings were, and each well-placed strike saw another soldier fall, but the many bruises and cuts were enough evidence that he didn't always gauge his own defences successfully. He was smothered in them now, and while each cut stung viciously as dust and grit found their way under his skin, every bruise ached more and more. Each time he was knocked down, he used his momentum to get back to his feet.

With the last of that group taken care of, he stepped into an alley, taking a moment to catch his breath. He touched his hand to his left side and looked down to see it smeared with his own blood. The side of his shirt was soaked in it; there was a nasty gash underneath that would need stitches. So much for that long bath; he was now covered in grime, dust, smoke and blood. He looked up at the rising flames in the town centre, and then leaned out of the alley toward the harbour to see the *Duquesa de Estrellas* desperately endeavouring to make her way out to sea.

"You!" a male voice shouted. Larkh snapped his head round to see the Aurentai man dressed in black leather approaching. "You put on quite a show, don't you?"

"It seems you do as well," Larkh returned, a dangerous look in his eyes.
"Meaning?"

"Meanin' I know who the *Noctae Venatora* are."

"That saves me a bit of time then!"

"I think not!" another voice called out; it was Zehn. "I've been hunting this man for a long time now, and I'll be taking the bounty on him." Leyal turned to face him. Zehn locked eyes with Larkh in the hope he'd see through the ruse, but only for a brief moment. Larkh questioned him with as hard a look in return, but nevertheless took the opportunity to flee. He noticed Arcaydia standing behind a wall, keeping out of the Aurentai's sight.

"I have strict orders to—" Leyal began.

"Oh Duke Kradelow can have him when I catch him," Zehn interrupted with a shrug. "I've had the contract with the Hunter's Guild for several months now, but I'm sure the duke's reward would outmatch what they're offering."

Leyal observed the mercenary a moment, taking note of his sleeveless dark leather doublet, the shock of brown hair, and the striped bandana.

"Mercenaries," Leyal snorted, "always so damned greedy. Do you intend to pledge your allegiance to Duke Kradelow then?"

"Why don't we catch our quarry first?" Zehn suggested. "We can talk about that afterwards." Leyal turned. The pirate was gone.

"Damn!" he cursed, breaking into a sprint. "The soldiers will clear a path for us across the harbour. He can't have gotten far."

"I don't know about that," Zehn muttered, rolling his eyes. "He's given me the slip many times; his skill with those scimitars is nigh on inhuman, and the bastard can run." Glancing at the *Greshendier* making ready for departure, he narrowed his eyes, and followed after the assassin, beckoning Arcaydia to follow.

II
Foristead, the Fiveways

Kalthis arrived in the village of Foristead late in the afternoon, around the fifth hour. Like Melkhar he'd flown far from the Len'athyr Sanctuary, more than five hundred miles away, and now sought food and rest. He found a secluded spot off the road and out of sight of the villagers to banish his wings before returning to the road. Upon approaching the village, he saw a sign that read *Foristead, the Fiveways*.

His loose river of black hair casually danced back and forth in the cool evening breeze as he trudged up the dry gravel path, and while it seemed a calm and restful evening, a sickening knot of concern twisted in his gut, telling him this was the calm before the storm. He hadn't yet reached Almadeira, and who knew what was going on there now.

When Dreysdan had scried for Arcaydia's location, she had still been in Almadeira, but he would contact the Galétahr via a seikryth later to check again. It would be at least another week or two before he and the other Kaesan'Drahknyr were likely to reach their full strength, meaning their mindspeech abilities would soon extend to the farthest reaches of Aeldynn once more, but only a seikryth could project accurate visual images.

Foristead, as Dreysdan had informed him, was often called *The Fiveways* because five roads lead out from the village square. It was a small, quaint village situated near the border between Lonnfeir and Ennerth; made up of small wattle and daub cottages with thatched roofs. The pungent odours of horse, swine, hay and animal dung filled his nostrils, telling of a village that thrived off its farmland and livestock.

Of all the people to notice him, it was a pair of children playing with a small dog on a patch of dusty road leading into the village. He used glámar to hide the shape of his ears to appear inconspicuous. He would be recognised as one of the Yeudanikhda, but it was rare for even one of them to venture outside their strongholds in the Daynallar Mountains.

It saddened him there had been no time to visit his distant kin. They had dwelled there for thousands of years, but when the Nays withdrew into the homeland, only a small number decided to stay rather than move into the Ravhnar Canyon in Ardeltaniah. Since then, they had merged with the more numerous human tribes in the Daynallar region, and lost their immortality as the purebloods eventually grew tired of their long life in Aeldynn and crossed into Nalthenýn. Each subsequent generation became more human.

Regardless, they were still his relatives. The people of Marlinikhda favoured the forests, while the Yeudanikhda favoured the mountains, but both were part of the same tribal nation while also being born of the Nays. Only the Marlinikhda, and the Yeudanikhda now dwelling in the Ravhnar Canyon retained their Nays bloodline.

"Hallo!" said a ruddy-faced boy with cropped brown hair. "Not seen ye 'round 'ere before. Ye some sort of adventurer or somethin'?"

The boy could have only been about nine or ten years old. His shirt was smeared with dried soil and grass, and his grazed knees told of a young boy's misadventures in places he probably ought not to have ventured. Next to him stood a girl; she was perhaps seven years old. Her hair colour was the same as the boy's, but it was long and braided down to her waist; and she wore a pale blue dress with white frills along the hem, and short puffed sleeves. No doubt she was his sister, but her cheeks were merely rosy and there was no sign of an adventurous excursion upon her.

"Don't be silly! He's one of them tribal fellas from the mountains," said the girl, in a shrill little voice. "He wears the clothes an' has very long black hair. Where else could he come from?"

"Don't mind me sister," said the boy. "She don't know much." The girl stamped her feet.

"I do too!" she protested. Kalthis smiled faintly.

"Your sister is right," Kalthis nodded. "I am from the mountains, but I have not been here before. We do not leave the mountains much, but I am looking for someone who has travelled further north."

The girl cocked her head to the side. "I don't know anythin' about who comes by 'ere usually. Not seen many lately, an' certainly nobody from the mountains. By the way, I'm Lucie."

The boy planted both hands on his hips and puffed his chest up. "An' I'm Arron," he said confidently. Kalthis laughed and smiled again.

"It is good to meet you both," Kalthis said, bowing his head. The dog, now sitting at his feet, whined, wagging its tail. Leaning down, he laid a hand on its head and scratched behind its ears. "Could you show me where the inn is?"

Arron shook his head. "I know where it is," said the boy, "but you should come talk to ma first. She'd like you. But..."

"We'll get in trouble fer talkin' ta strangers," Lucie said sheepishly, shuffling her feet. "Ye seem nice 'nough though. I think she won't mind you."

"It would be wise not to—" he started, but before he knew it, both children were leading him by the hand down a nearby narrow trail where fields of crops grew either side. They stopped at a little cottage bordering on a small patch of woodland where smoke drifted lazily out of a chimney partially obscured by the trees.

He figured he was sure to be reprimanded by their parents for speaking to them, or at the very least asked to take his leave, but that wasn't the case at all. The mother came out to call them in for dinner, and spotted them pulling him down the path, one child grasping each hand.

She was a short, stout woman in both build and temperament, and wore a yellow dress with a patchy white apron that had seen better days. It was evident she'd spent many a long year tending the crops in the surrounding fields.

With her hands planted firmly on her hips she frowned and let out an exasperated sigh. "Who've ye brought home this time? You two seem to latch on to any weary ol' traveller wandering into the village these days."

"Not just any ol' traveller mam!" Arron protested. "This one's from the mountains, an' he's come a long way.....I think. He's awful nice too, but he's tired an'—"

"What's yer name stranger?" she asked, staring straight at Kalthis, though it sounded more like a demand.

"Kallas," he lied, "but you may call me Kal."

"Where are ye from?"

"The Daynallar Mountains," he replied. "I am one of the Yeudanikhda. I travel in search of someone."

A long moment of silence followed. She stared at him long and hard. There was a sternness about her that made him uncomfortable, and yet he sensed kindness, and bitter sorrow that told of recent loss. This woman was a widow.

"Come inside," she said eventually. "I always make too much for dinner. If we don't finish it off the pigs usually do." She went back inside the house, leaving him feeling baffled. Arron and Lucie stood in front of him grinning.

"We'll get told off when ye be gone," Arron chuckled. "Mam's always like that, even though she obviously likes ye."

Kalthis inclined his head toward the boy. "You think so?" he asked. Arron nodded quickly. Lucie copied.

"It'll go cold!" they all heard the mother yell. "Quickly now!"

"Comin' mam!" both of them cried. Kalthis watched them a moment, smiled meekly, and followed them inside.

Kalthis was glad the meal at the farmhouse was fairly plain. His intolerance for anything beyond mildly spicy was known to the majority of the Nays military, the Kensaiyr, and their acquaintances within the Cerenyr. It was a myth that the Drahknyr were impervious to any internal physical defects due to their ethereal origins; Kalthis was living proof it *was* possible.

Arron and Lucie peppered him with questions for much of the evening, despite his fatigue, so he was grateful when their mother – Fiana was her name – ushered them up to bed. Unfortunately, there wasn't enough room in the house, but there was an upstairs storage area in the barn he was permitted to use. It was that or a room at the inn, so he gladly accepted the use of the barn. He preferred to be closer to nature when possible, but when the sky darkened and the heavens opened during the meal, he was glad of having a roof over his head for at least one night.

He lay in his bedroll in the hayloft of the barn listening to the sound of rain battering the roof while he drifted in silent contemplation, wondering what the world was coming to. Balance was such a fragile thing to maintain, least of all when it came down to the very world itself. He never believed it could be achieved and last for long; this had been confirmed when Vharik explained it had begun to dissipate within the first century following that terrible war. It was a memory so clear to him and anyone who'd been involved who still drew breath today, more than three thousand years later.

Garoad's unquenchable thirst for power had led to the devastation of an already barren land where little life had settled since, and where distortions in nature were commonplace. It had become a vast mass graveyard for all races involved, and was a place Kalthis shuddered at the thought of returning to.

The Voice of Koborea, Anu Kobhoa, was reported to have fallen victim to dementia as a result. He was told its screams could be heard by anyone who dared set foot ashore on Koborea; a despairing wail faintly echoing at random across the vast expanse of land scorched by dragonfire and magica.

"When war is declared, there is little that can be done about it," Dreysdan had once said, "and wars must be fought somewhere." Anu Kobhoa's fragility, however, had been overlooked. That war had all but broken its mind. Many regions across Aeldynn had experienced cataclysmic events, but the climax of the War of the Eclipse had occurred on Koborea.

The Voices were spirits created by the Origin to act like nervous systems for landmasses, so their consciousness was spread across entire continents, feeling all that went on. Kalthis knew he was afraid of the eventual encounter he would have with Anu Kobhoa, though it wasn't necessary at the present time. It was a necessary part of his role as the Kaesan'Drahknyr of Balance.

He rolled over on to his side and pulled his hair from underneath him. Even though he was curled up in his bedroll, he'd still managed to get hay tangled in it. That was a task for the morning though; he was too tired to do anything about it now. When morning came, he would move on to Almadeira, at the end of another day's journey in flight using the celestial streams known as the Etherflow. It would take nigh on a week on foot. Letting out a long sigh of relief at having the chance to rest, he closed his eyes and was asleep within minutes.

III
Almadeira

Rows of soldiers blocked Larkh's path as he entered the harbour, sprinting toward *Greshendier*. His lungs burned, but his ongoing determination to thwart Kradelow spurred him on. Only a handful of soldiers held their position, certain they could take their aim and shoot him down, while the others scattered, realising he wasn't stopping for anyone. Blood spattered across the quayside as those who failed to move were sliced to ribbons as Larkh's scimitars spiralled back and forth, forging a path.

He ducked around the next corner, hiding behind a series of stacked barrels and crates, drawing ragged breaths as he sank against the wall, wincing at the biting and searing pain spreading across his body. His appetite had vanished, and now all he cared about was getting some rest. He suddenly wondered if Arven and his troupe were alright. After what he'd heard leaving the Silver Gull, he wasn't certain, but he knew he'd just have to wonder and hope they survived.

A shadow fell over him. Slowly he looked up, blinking wearily. A giant of a man stood over him, bald and bare-chested, tattoos marking his chest, arms and back. His skin was heavily tanned, and he looked down at him with such indifference that momentarily he had no idea whether he might have been friend or foe. Then he recognised the man's face; he was Harand Loftan's porter.

"Brahdor...?" he croaked, his throat dry and rough as sandpaper.

"I help you," the big man said, looking back across the harbour at the soldiers hurrying in their direction. "Harand say I need new life. Life with meaning. I help you now, you let me on ship?" Larkh slouched, trying to catch his breath.

"Aren't you goin' to help me anyway?" he breathed. Brahdor grinned.

"Yes, I get to crack heads of stupid men."

Larkh chuckled. He crept back around the cargo and followed Brahdor's gaze across the harbour. There he saw Zehn and the assassin followed by a pair of soldiers, ignoring the men he'd felled. He squinted, just making Arcaydia out as she followed them with their travel packs, staying out of the way as best she could.

He saw Brahdor's arm slowly reaching for something leaning against the crates beside him. Out of the corner of his eye, he saw the big man take hold of a bardiche. Lifting his head, Larkh looked him in the eyes. For a moment, Brahdor's face was serious, and then it broke into a goofy smile.

"Get to your ship," he said, serious again. "I take care of this. I meet you on board? You not answer before."

"Any friend of Harand's is a friend of mine," Larkh smiled, forcing himself to his feet. "See you on board lad; we could use your strength." He returned his scimitars to his side, replacing them with his flintlocks. He loaded them quickly with the paper cartridges he took from a pouch at his side. "Just let the girl and the mercenary through, but keep that assassin at bay as long as you can. When you hear the ship's bell, it's time to run." The big man nodded.

Larkh stepped out from behind Brahdor, carefully aiming at one of two soldiers accompanying Zehn and the assassin. There was a click, and the gunshot exploded from the pistol, hitting the soldier square in the chest, toppling him. The second of the two men ran straight into the following shot as Larkh aimed and fired again, staggering forwards, slumping to the ground.

Zehn spared a glance in his direction, to which he gave a casual albeit sarcastic salute, and dashed off down the western quay toward his ship where Argwey had linesmen already preparing her for departure. It was a convenient spot at the very end of the quay, meaning *Greshendier* could sail forward off the berth rather than having to be eased out sideways. She was a big girl, but once she gained momentum, the altirna system made a swift giant of her.

The gangway had already been removed, so, thrusting his pistols back into their holsters, he threw himself at the side of the ship, grasping hold of the rungs between her gun ports. He clambered up and almost fell on to the deck as exhaustion took its toll. It was Larsan and Krallan who caught him.

"Wait before throwing off the lines!" he bellowed, his chest heaving. "There're three more to come aboard yet, an' one of them you're all goin' to hate."

"What do ye mean?" asked Krallan, "we need to leave now ye're here!"

"I mean I'm doin' that silver mage Raeon a favour by lettin' that fuckin' mercenary on board!" Larkh spat. Krallan's face and the faces of several crew members darkened.

"Don't look at me like that!" Larkh snapped. "I didn't want to agree. He can have the brig to sleep in, an' he'll be put to fine use. You mark my words lads, Argwey'll give him all the *best* jobs he can think of." At this, the bosun's long, pointed ears pricked up, and he grinned devilishly, as did numerous others within earshot. "An' we're takin' the young lass an' Brahdor too."

"We can only give 'em a few minutes," Krallan warned.

"Aye, I know," Larkh breathed, resting his back against one of the twelve pounder cannons on the weather deck. "They'll not be long. The girl is with that asscock, an' good ol' Brahdor is buyin' them some time."

Larsan handed him his water-skin, and all too gladly Larkh swiped it and drank deeply.

"You look like shit," the warrior remarked. Larkh tossed the water-skin back, giving him his best unamused glare.

"An' you look like you're tryin' to grow a ferret on your face," Larkh retorted. "Kindly fetch the surgeon would you? I'm in need of a few stitches."

"At least I can grow a beard worth a damn," Larsan snorted, approaching the nearest hatch.

"I'm too good lookin' to need one anyway," Larkh smirked, managing to find a shred of humour despite the pain. Larsan regarded him as if he were a parent reprimanding an unruly child, then walked away laughing.

"You should watch this Cap'n!" Reys smirked.

"That good eh?" Larkh groaned as he forced himself on to his feet again, leaning on the deck rail. He squinted to see Brahdor standing guard over the western quay. The huge man hefted his bardiche and brought it down between Zehn and the assassin as the mercenary slipped past behind Arcaydia.

Leyal leapt back, whipping his blades from their scabbards. Zehn and Arcaydia shot around behind Brahdor and sprinted toward them. The assassin launched himself at the porter, his speed and agility outmatching him, but Brahdor's strength was also something to be reckoned with. As a curved, slender sword connected with the bardiche, the blade was embedded in the dense, hardy wood, giving Brahdor the opportunity he was looking for.

"Ring the bell, Reys," Larkh ordered. The boy did as he was told. "Throw off the lines now lads!" he shouted down to the linesmen ashore as Arcaydia and Zehn threw their bags up to the crew and climbed up the side of the ship.

The shaft of the bardiche creaked, and then snapped as the porter shoved him over the edge of the quayside. Leyal hit the water with a great splash just as the ship's bell rang out, and Brahdor lumbered toward her as more soldiers tailed him.

The lines were thrown off the bollards and *Greshendier* was on the move when the huge man connected with the side of the ship with a heavy thump. He climbed aboard effortlessly, and promptly sat down to lean comfortably against the main mast. He locked eyes with Larkh, grinning as the young captain turned away from the rail. "Long time I wanted to stand on your ship," he said.

Larkh found himself halfway into a waking dream when Brahdor spoke. He looked at the hulking figure sitting on the ground and smiled back faintly. There was sudden nausea and a faintness in his head as a flood of memories threatened to assault him.

"You could've asked," he shrugged, scanning the many faces of his crew on deck glaring daggers at Zehn. Others were simply leering at Arcaydia who stood next to him. "You're here now anyway. If you can make yourself useful, talk to Krallan." Brahdor nodded quickly. All around them gunshots sounded from the direction of the harbour as muskets were fired in the direction of the ship.

The forward hatch opened. Larsan returned promptly with the surgeon, a man named Thurne, who took one look at Larkh and said, "I can see there's more wrong wi' you than you let on. Let's get you down below so I can sort you out." Larkh rubbed his forehead while he fought to maintain his composure. Thurne's brushy brow wrinkled, staring hard at him, concern crossing his scarred and weathered face.

The surgeon had once served in the Faltain Navy, including on one of the ships Larkh's own father had served on as a midshipman. He was one of the few on board *Greshendier* who'd known him since he was a child. Larkh had met him in the Enkayitan city of Tourenco by chance. He'd been in his late thirties when he'd served, and now he was in his fifties with a greying ponytail and a straggly beard.

Thurne ushered him toward the bow of the ship and down the hatch toward the sickbay, glowering at Zehn as they passed. The mercenary averted his gaze, observing as the ship slowly turned, opening gun ports threateningly. Larkh stopped to regard his crew with fierce sincerity.

"Work him to the bone by all means," he said, nodding in Zehn's direction, "but he is NOT to be harmed without my sayin' so. He is *my* prisoner, an' he's under my safe charge as part of a deal settled between me an' a mutual friend. You harm him, *I* harm you. If you must have a fight over it, I'll gladly oblige later when I'm feelin' better. Argwey!" The elf shot him a wary look. "Get Zehn Kahner acquainted with the brig; he'll be sleepin' there for a while. You can give him a list of your best jobs in the morning. Arcaydia, follow me."

Argwey nodded, and pointed to two burly crew members standing behind Zehn, whose angry glowering at Larkh earned him a punch to the jaw from the bosun as his arms were seized. Hearing the blow, Arcaydia glanced back worriedly as she followed Larkh and the surgeon, then disappeared below deck.

"I thought he said not to harm me," the mercenary disputed, tasting blood. He winced as his injured arm was twisted behind his back.

"Trust me," Argwey said, sneering, "that doesn't count as harmin' you. What he means is beatin' you senseless or floggin' you. Now let's get you to your nice, cosy little cabin shall we?"

The elf met his sullen glare with a mocking smile. Zehn heard sniggering, but made no argument as he was shoved forward, gritting his teeth against the burning ache in his left arm.

AD INTERIM
The Imperial Council of Atialleia

Time and tide wait for no-one;
a dry river still runs its course.
Kensaiyr proverb

Arkkiennah's message to Madukeyr had been clear; hasten
to the Len'athyr Sanctuary, but not to be too concerned.
"Mekahn navhyst, Madukeyr, tseit dauhsna'the kaeursnh.
Vallh aeu'te veyushaér nir ye'n mhasaith," [21] she had said.
Considering the small amount of rest he and Avlashrenko
had managed to obtain, they were to split their journey in
half by stopping off in Cerendiyll if necessary.

 She now sat before the council, flanked by the five
Kaesan'Drahknyr remaining in Ardeltaniah, and each of the
awakened Galétriahn Highlords; except for Dreysdan in
Len'athyr, and Maiyah, who resided in Icina'Theniya. This
white-gold chamber with its vaulted ceiling and towering
windows appeared empty, even with so many present.

 Everyone in attendance in the palace conference room
sat in silence, waiting for someone else to speak up in
response to the matters at hand. Distinctly coloured and
embroidered uniform clearly depicted the class and rank of
its wearer.

 Lésos Taeren sat opposite the Atiathél. An unusually
tall white staff was propped up against his chair, a metal tip
about a foot long twisting into a coil at its tip. In the middle
of the coil was a marine-blue crystal, cut and polished to fit
the shape.

 Arkkiennah wasn't surprised to see so many faces lost
in thought, considering what had been discussed. Zerrçainne
was alive and orchestrating the impending war between
Adengeld and Faltainyr Demura. Melkhar had been stalled

---

[21] Make haste, Madukeyr, but do not worry. Halve the journey if
you must.

but was now on her way to Aynfell to battle one of the most dangerous renegade dragons to have ever existed; the chosen candidates of the Origin were still unaware of their purpose, and the Mindseer Oracle was alone in an unsafe city outside Ardeltaniah.

"I say we begin more intensive training for the apprentice Drahknyr and Galétriahn mages." The speaker was Rahkir Veskirahd, Kaesan'Drahknyr of the Order of Jade, who spoke. "We don't know what kind of stunts Zerrçainne will pull next."

The Atiathél inclined her head toward him. Tallest of the Kaesan'Drahknyr, he stood at six foot five in physical form, his unkempt brown hair swept back with the tip just reaching the top of his shoulder-blades. He was dressed in fine forest green and brown leathers.

"Considering she has already outsmarted the most astute among your ranks, I concur," Lésos agreed. "She knows how to pull strings we never knew we had."

"Can you not sense her, Lésos?" asked Daimra, Kaesan'Drahknyr of the Order of Crimson. Like Rahkir and her comrades, she wore the same kind of fine leather uniform, but hers was deep red and black. Her skin held a tan hue, and her raven hair rippled in waves down her back. Lésos shook his head.

"I'm afraid not, Daimra," the Astral Overseer replied. "The fact she is alive and I am unable to detect her presence suggests she has ventured into the depths of the phandaeric realms and spent far too long there; she will now be directly tethered to Phandaerys via Dyr'Efna."

"There is no way Melkhar can be wrong, is there?" Daimra frowned, balling her fists.

"As much as you would like her to be wrong," said Lésos, narrowing his striking aquamarine eyes, "there can be no doubt on the shoulders of Kaesan'Drahknyr Khesaiyde on something such as this."

"I know that," Daimra muttered between clenched teeth. "I just wish that somehow she'd be wrong."

"For the sake of all?" Zairen chimed in, leaning back in his seat. "Or just because you want her to be wrong?" His platinum-blond hair, perched neatly over his collar, and his pale skin and white-silver uniform, gave him an almost phantasmal appearance. He was Kaesan'Drahknyr of the Order of Alabaster, but it was not his title that had earned him the title of *Elaiythé the Ghost,* nor was it simply a reflection of his appearance. He regarded Daimra with an arched brow, an intense stare in his rich brown eyes.

"For the sake of all, Zairen," Daimra growled. "We should all want our comrades to be wrong when the wheels of fate are set in motion and the odds could be well stacked against us!"

Accepting her response, Zairen gave a solemn nod, and relaxed back into his seat folding his arms and crossing his knees.

Arkkiennah closed her eyes thoughtfully. If Zerrçainne really were seeking to revive Alymarn, she would be searching for each aspect of him that had been taken and sealed away, including the God Aspect that was cast beyond the depths of Phandaerys, where its peak pierced the barrier of the Abadhol, the true abyss, just as the peak of Aevnatureis once pierced the barrier to the realm where the Origin had first created Aeldynn. Not even the gods could remember its name. That barrier had been sealed long before the Drahknyr were first given physical form.

She hoped Madukeyr would reach the Len'athyr Sanctuary to install the new seikryth as quickly as possible, but he'd been travelling with Avlashrenko a lot recently. The wyvern needed rest as much as he did, but with Rahntamein set to execute an attack on Aynfell, the Mindseer Oracle at large and with the Origin's chosen still to realise themselves, it was going to prove a difficult feat.

'Nothing we haven't been able to set our minds to before,' she told herself. *'Nor is it anything we cannot triumph over.'* She took a deep breath, and breathed a heavy sigh.

"We may know more when Tseika'Drahknyr Saierkýn arrives at the Len'athyr Sanctuary and installs the new seikryth," the Atiathél explained. "If Madukeyr is as efficient as he usually is, it should be done by this evening. I suggest we all take a break to think about everything we've discussed, and return here when the clock strikes eight this evening. Hopefully by then the connection will have been established." All nodded in agreement. "No word of this shall be spoken outside these walls until we have agreed on a plan of action."

When the council resumed, Atiathél Arkkiennah confirmed Madukeyr's success in installing the new seikryth. He had sought to test the link a mere two hours after the first half of the meeting had drawn to a close, agreeing to connect again with Galétahr Dreysdan present during the second half.

Dreysdan confirmed Melkhar's arrival at the Len'athyr Sanctuary with the assistance of Lésos, having been forced to seek passage through the astral world of Nira'Eléstara, and told of her departure the moment she learned of Rahntamein's imminent release the following morning. Kalthis had then left in search of Arcaydia.

Arkkiennah sighed with relief. At least two of their dilemmas were being addressed. Still, she was concerned with how to combat the problem of the people of Armaran learning about their return to power so soon. She knew the people's fear would likely turn many against them, and with Melkhar now about to bear the brunt of it, Arkkiennah was suddenly very afraid. Nevertheless, Melkhar's unyielding relentlessness made her the perfect candidate for dealing with a monster such as Rahntamein.

Once the information had been conveyed to the council, she had the seikryth brought through and positioned on a pedestal at the end of the table. She proceeded to seek a new connection by touching the top of it, then drawing the glyph of the Len'athyr Sanctuary on it with her index finger as it began to glow.

'It won't make a difference to the people of Aeldynn even when we are ready to make our move,' she told herself. *'They would still be shocked, they would still be terrified, and many would still be resentful. Yet if we did nothing, the world would fall to ruin and Aeldynn would no longer exist as we know it.'*

Galétahr Dreysdan, along with Madukeyr, stood amidst a projected image of the communication chamber of the Len'athyr Sanctuary. The Galétriahn Highlord's arms were fully concealed beneath a jet black cloak that spilled across the floor. A trimmed red collar rested over a set of three ebony pauldrons perched on each shoulder, edged and decorated in gold. He stepped forward, brushing his cloak aside to bow before the Atiathél. Underneath, he wore matching black, red and gold robes. The design of the robes was identical to the finest regalia of the other Galétriahn Highlords. Next to him stood Madukeyr in his ebony leather armour, who stepped forward and bowed after the Galétahr.

'Dreysdan,' Arkkiennah thought ruefully. *'You're too much like Melkhar, though I suppose it is befitting of the Order of Ebony.'*

"Dreysdan, Madukeyr, we must get straight to the point. I am sorry, but we have no time for a more formal greeting than this," Arkkiennah apologised, bowing her head. Dreysdan returned the gesture.

"Worry not, Your Highness," he replied calmly. "Formalities aside, we have much to discuss and make sense of today. I inadvertently dismissed Kaesan'Drahknyr Ashkelleron's mention of the prophecies in question, and I was wrong to do so. For that I must apologise."

"You are not wrong, Dreysdan," Arkkiennah sighed. "These prophecies are indeed unclear to us; I remember having this discussion with you before. However, it is the mention of the Keys of the Origin that we must try to make as much sense of as we can. The promise of the Drahknyr and the Kaesan'Drahknyr was direct, but many others are obscure."

"What would you have us do, Your Highness?" Madukeyr asked, folding his arms. "As I mentioned recently, I have already met one of the two men Lésos located and duelled with him; he was already experiencing the dreams. The other has a well-guarded mind, and does not yet dream. Should I find them?"

Arkkiennah lowered her eyes from the seikryth to the table. Everyone in the room remained silent, watching and waiting.

"Not yet," the Atiathél replied. Noting Madukeyr's surprise, she continued; "Madukeyr, when you have had enough rest, I would like you to assist Galétahr Dreysdan in researching the Taecade Medo and the prophecies concerning the Keys of the Origin. I am sure the sage, Vharik, will be of use to you as well, as much as you both find him an annoyance. I ask that you operate out of the Len'athyr Sanctuary for a while, and travel when and where necessary for your tasks. I am certain you will uncover enough information to pursue them as a result. Lésos will be able to track their location on a regular basis."

Arkkiennah glanced around at the members of the council, who sat in respectful silence, then returned her attention to Dreysdan and Madukeyr.

"I am sure Avlashrenko would appreciate more time in the Valley of Daynallar," she added. "It also means you will be able to keep a closer eye on events between the two kingdoms there, especially considering Anu Amarey's words to Kalthis."

The Tseika'Drahknyr closed his eyes, bowing with his right hand resting over his heart. "As you wish, Your Highness," he said calmly in acknowledgement. "Might I ask, what about Melkhar? She is about to face Rahntamein."

Arkkiennah braced her left arm to support her right elbow, bringing her hand to her lips thoughtfully. "Someone should venture out there to find her," she replied. "Not one of the Kaesan'Drahknyr in this room has yet regained his or her full strength yet; neither Melkhar nor Kalthis are exceptions. As you know, it takes time after awakening from a long slumber for full capacity to be restored, let alone the regeneration from a fatality as they all suffered in the War of the Black Sun."

"I will go," said a smooth male voice to the left of the Atiathél. Arkkiennah turned her head to look upon Zairen. He looked even more ghostly in the dim flickering light of the conference room. "She will only confide in either Kalthis or myself after all," he added. "As Kalthis is now in pursuit of the Mindseer Oracle, I am confident I should be the one to investigate her whereabouts. She will be exhausted after the battle, and knowing her, she is more than likely to expend all her energy and will attempt to borrow more if necessary."

Arkkiennah considered the proposal carefully. She couldn't find a reason for Zairen not to go; in fact his idea would work to their advantage. As much as the people of Aynfell were likely to be shy and distrustful, the city would still be a likely target for some time, especially if an invasion were imminent.

"Zairen would also be able to provide some assistance in Aynfell's defence, should the need arise," Lésos suggested. There were murmurs among others in the room, particularly between the other Kaesan'Drahknyr, but no-one seemed to openly object. Then Lukien, Kaesan'Drahknyr of the Order of Sapphire, spoke up.

"If there really is a plot for invasion on Armaran, then is it really wise to send reinforcements there at this time?" he enquired. "We have covered our tracks so well most of the world considers us to be little more than a myth, and we'll be seen as an unwelcome interference." In agitation, he ran a hand through his ash-blond hair, cropped at his collar.

"Zairen's intention is only to provide Melkhar with some back-up," Rahkir argued. "Her Highness has just clarified that none of us are back at full strength yet, and we all know Melkhar will stop at nothing to accomplish her objectives. She would rather exhaust her energy and risk borrowing more in order to do so. That means she could easily remain unconscious for longer than she'd like under the circumstances."

Lukien glared at Rahkir, then rolled his eyes and groaned. "I'm saying we're not going to be welcome, and interfering is only likely to cause more problems at this point in time. Besides, don't you think you're underestimating Melkhar, knowing what she is capable of?"

"Nevertheless, someone still needs to go," Zairen interjected. "And unless I'm mistaken, we've already interfered." He leaned back and folded his arms. "Melkhar is just as aware as any of us here that the repercussions of this aren't going to be easy to deal with. Should she just ignore the warning of Rahntamein's release and allow an academic city to fall, along with the Archaenen? Once she engages him in combat, our cover will be blown."

"There is a way, Zairen," a female voice interjected. All heads turned to Kaellyn, Kaesan'Drahknyr of the Order of Ametrine, whose long frosty tresses fell across her face as she spoke. "We just don't like to use it." All present frowned.

"That's—"

"It's most likely the best option, Zairen," Rahkir interrupted.

"You cannot cover up damage," Zairen protested. "Blocking memories; what a fine way to earn their trust! The spell *will* wear off."

An uncomfortable silence fell across the room. The flames of the lanterns and braziers flickered and danced among the shadows. No-one spoke for several minutes, though wary glances were exchanged.

Eventually, Arkkiennah straightened and spoke. "The people of Aeldynn know the Nays still exist, but few know the Drahknyr are far from being a myth," she reasoned. "Until we know the full extent of what Zerrçainne is planning, and until we know how to combat the problem effectively, we will interfere as little as possible with their affairs. However, I do feel subduing their memories is our only reasonable option at this time, and under these circumstances, I will pray for assistance from Adel Nalaueii."

Zairen and Lukien shifted uncomfortably as the Atiathél went on to delegate tasks to each person in the room. Dreysdan and Madukeyr were to oversee the Valley of Daynallar and act according to their findings; Zairen was to travel to Aynfell to find Melkhar; Kalthis was already searching for the Mindseer Oracle; the remaining Kaesan'Drahknyr and Galétriahn Highlords were to train fledgling Drahknyr and mages; and Lésos would remain in Atialleia to maintain his role as Astral Overseer within the Kathaedra of Thean Raiyah.

The maintenance and restoration of gateways and Varleima crystals would also become a priority, and should it prove necessary, when more intelligence was available, Madukeyr would pursue the men believed to be the Keys of the Origin. Madukeyr followed up with his story of his encounter with one of the pair, but maintained that until they came to realise their purpose, there would be little chance in winning either of them over. Telling them the hidden truth of their lineage would change their lives forever – especially in terms of their longevity – would prove to be the hardest task.

PART II

"The law always claims justification for its actions when in fact it is far from the truth. Moral fibre is the crux on which justice pivots. The law does not have the right to claim justice for itself."

— Yahtyliir Matseavin.

CHAPTER 21

I
Almadeira

After scrambling to find a foothold against the slippery wall of the quay, Leyal was hauled up on to dry land with the assistance of two soldiers where he sank to his knees and spat out a mouthful of slimy seawater. Covered in grimy, pungent-smelling seaweed, he glared over his shoulder to scowl at the *Greshendier* as thirty-six guns ran out from the two gun decks on the port side.

No-one manned the cannons on the weather deck that granted her a three gun deck illusion, but the broadside of an elite class man-o-war bearing archana using the altirna system would be enough to render that entire section of the harbour unusable for a considerable amount of time.

"What are we going to do sir?" one soldier asked him.

Stiffly rising to his feet, Leyal balled his hands into fists, his teeth clenching. "Not much we can do right now," he growled, staring furiously at the ship as she made her departure. "The duke has another plan in place for that one anyway. Perhaps we can find something out about that mercenary though. I think he might have been after that pirate to begin with, though why he's escaped with him is anyone's guess. I also wouldn't mind finding out exactly how Savaldor managed to hold on to that ship." His lips pressed into a thin line as he turned about face and made his way back through the harbour, his mood soured further by the squelching of his boots.

By the time he made it back to the town square, the majority of the townspeople had been gathered, their solemn faces bent toward the ground as if ashamed. Some of the fires had been brought under control, but the dense smoke lingering in the air made him cough and gag. It even obscured the astronomical clock mounted over the entrance of Almadeira's Kathaedra. Commander Einar stood by the fountain.

"Have you made any progress?" Leyal asked as he approached.

"You look like you just crawled out of the sewer!" Einar sniffed. "And you stink like bilge water."

Leyal frowned. "Interesting you should say that," he said matter-of-factly, giving Einar a meek smile. "A giant brute of a man pushed me off the quayside. Anyway, kindly answer my question would you? I have a speech to make and a report to write."

Einar's eyes narrowed darkly. "The people know they don't have a choice if they want to live," the commander muttered, glancing around the square at the people disdainfully. "You need only to look at them to see that."

"Not going soft on me, are you?" Leyal asked, pulling stinking seaweed from his hair.

"Certainly not," Einar snorted dismissively.

"Good," Leyal muttered under his breath; "Let's get our little speech over with shall we? I'd like to have a bath as soon as possible."

By the door of the Silver Gull, Elsie Menow stood watching. There was little she could do except listen to what was said, and then make her way up on to the hillside to check on Arven and the other gypsy performers. She would take it upon herself to apologise on Larkh's behalf for his sudden departure, that is, if they still lived.

The gypsies were an easy target for anyone in authority to take advantage of in any way they saw fit, and considering it was no secret Larkh happened to be friends with their leader, they were likely to become targets in one way or another, and it was likelier still they'd be used against him.

Frowning, she turned, shutting the door behind her, wishing she could refuse to serve the soldiers. If it was one thing she could say Larkh had taught her, it was not to back down without a fight. "I'll never go quietly," he'd once told her. "I'll fight for what I've got till my last breath, an' I'll never hand over *Greshendier*. I'd rather she sink an' I go down with her than see her in the hands of Kradelow, or back in the navy for that matter."

II
Kasserin

King Ameldar stood in the murky, dimly lit conference room of Kasserin's keep leaning over a map of Armaran, his arms spread with his hands firmly planted on the table. The room was dusty, cloaked in cobwebs, and the strong odour of damp clung to the stale air. Apparently it hadn't been used in some time. Around the table stood Rannvorn, flanked by the first and second commanders, along with the third through to the sixth either side.

Ameldar plotted a route east through the Eyrlian Moors and east across the River Aeiven into the Daynallar Mountains. They would navigate through the winding passes of the Valley of Daynallar, assuring his men this was the best route for them to take without protection from a dragon. It was common knowledge the region belonged solely to dragonkind, so passing directly through the wide open valley meant you were fair game.

The dark voice at the back of Rannvorn's mind spoke often, advising him, giving him the best understanding of all that went on around them. He understood enough of battle tactics to get by, but to learn of each man's weaknesses, especially those of his father, was priceless knowledge. The entity could not tell him what a person's exact thoughts were, but he learned enough to know how to exploit them effectively to gain their trust. It was a gradual process that should not be rushed; he would have to learn to be more patient.

It had also asked him more and more questions, few of which he'd answered to begin with. Now they were becoming better acquainted, however, he had yielded a few secrets. The resulting amusement was not because of what he told it, but because it saw the fun in conducting the undoing of his enemies.

The Queen had been executed for treason while he was still a youth, and Ameldar hadn't married since, but he had repeatedly engaged in adultery with both unmarried and married women, noble and common, siring a handful of bastard siblings. She had learned of the plans made with Duke Kradelow of Lonnfeir early on in their development, and deemed her husband's ways uncouth and unbefitting of a king, let along the king of such a magnificent realm as Adengeld.

Ameldar had belittled him as a boy, calling him useless and pathetic because he had been a slow learner, but because he was royalty he was sent to the Kessford Academy in Faltainyr Demura anyway, and he *had* excelled there. He frequently reported his successes, which had pleased his father, except when he failed to rise to the top because of a more adept student, and a middle class commoner at that. The young man named Zehn had made him look a fool in front of everyone, and put him even more out of favour with his father. It was unforgivable.

He hated his father for what he'd done, taking his mother from him and for how he treated him as if were an imbecile. Ameldar had seen his prowess with a sword once he'd returned home, and thankfully he had been impressed enough to allow him to continue training, but he still looked on him disapprovingly for having lost to a commoner, and so he hated Zehn all the more. There was nothing left but for him to take matters into his own hands with the help of the demon within who still wouldn't reveal his true name.

The same black silhouette with glowing eyes and wings still haunted his mind, and though it terrified him it also made him feel special, it made him feel *chosen*. He'd been given the kind of purpose he'd sought from his father for years, except he wouldn't need his father's approval now. All he had to do was play along until the time was right.

"It will take us approximately ten days to travel to the Valley of Daynallar following the River Aeiven," King Ameldar explained, drawing a line with his index finger from Cathra to the valley's entrance. "The dragon has agreed to fight on our side, but he will not guide us. It seems he wishes to test our mettle. I expect Captain Falthen to meet us at the village of Hinshal, minus his brigade of course. I was informed by the sorceress that they were dismembered like cattle by one of the Kaesan'Drahknyr and strewn across the countryside after I'd sent them to investigate."

The third commander, a robust man with a rich tan and a shock of golden hair named Vellar, laughed. "With all due respect, Your Majesty, the being you speak of is a mythological wonder lost to the ages. Surely you don't trust that woman?"

"Vellar!" the first commander exclaimed. "Have some respect for your king!"

Ameldar raised a hand to silence him. "Let it go, Lokren," the King said all too calmly. "I would rather my men be outspoken and willing to express their beliefs and concerns. I didn't appoint any of you to the rank of commander so you could hide behind formalities." Lokren bowed his head, his dark, wispy hair falling across his bristly face.

"I apologise Your Highness," he said, taking a seat.

"I have respect for how you all feel," Ameldar assured them, "but I will ask that all of you take me seriously. The Kaesan'Drahknyr, indeed all Drahknyr, are very real and they pose a threat to our plans for Faltainyr Demura and beyond. They are not just statues, paintings or murals. The

Galétriahn Mages are also real, and I know this, for Lady Zerrçainne used to be one of their Highlords long ago."

Ameldar sensed the hackles rising distrustfully on his men; some had made brief contact with the sorceress and were already well aware of several such talents she possessed. The king smiled mirthlessly. "I will tell you now that I did not appoint her as an adviser on a whim," he continued. "She is able to see into the souls of men and women, and learn their true feelings and intentions. So far she has proven herself worthwhile." He paused, looked around at each of the commanders and Rannvorn, whose fists clenched beneath the table.

'Easy does it, calm down,' the voice whispered. *'Zerrçainne advised your mother to speak the truth. It was not her decision to have her executed.'* Rannvorn felt himself relax a little. *'That's better.'*

"We must take over Faltainyr Demura swiftly. Their army isn't quite as large as ours, but it is just as efficient. However, they do have a much larger and stronger navy. Duke Kradelow is working on the admiralty, and so long as we can take over with little bloodshed, we will integrate their army into ours, and almost double our size for when we take their ships to expand our territory beyond Armaran."

Rannvorn certainly approved of these ideas, and so did the entity within, except one way or another Ameldar wouldn't remain king, or even an emperor. He moved to the back of the room and leaned against the wall, casually resting his foot against it, folding his arms.

"And what do you plan to do once we have conquered Faltainyr Demura, father?" the prince enquired, lifting his gaze to meet his father's eyes. He made sure his smile was genuine. "What are your plans for the lands beyond Armaran?"

"One step at a time, my son," Ameldar laughed. "I have designs in progress for moving beyond the borders of Armaran. And if the Nays should dare to interfere, we will remind them they gave up their lands many generations ago and they may not reclaim them. We will send them back where they came from."

'He does like to talk doesn't he?' the voice chuckled. *'A little bit too much, I think.'* Rannvorn inclined his head to the side. "Most interesting, father," the prince replied. He bowed his head. "I feel privileged to be such an important part of your endeavours, and I look forward to uniting Armaran with you and every man standing in this room." He smiled warmly as Ameldar's chest swelled with pride.

"Truly, you do well by me Rannvorn," Ameldar brought his fist to his chest. "I expect you to get along with these men—" he gestured to the commanders, "and I expect results from you. The Lady Zerrçainne assures me that all of you can be trusted to fight wholeheartedly for the Kingdom of Adengeld."

'You are doing well, Prince Rannvorn.' Just the sound of the voice felt like it was coiling itself around his shoulders, its whispers in his ears like hissing of a wicked serpent. He could almost feel hands grasping his shoulders as it peered around the side of his head. *'Keep it up.'*

III
Sendero de Mercader

Later that evening, Larkh lay in his cot on the starboard side of his cabin drifting in and out of uncomfortable sleep. His body ached and stung all over, but Arcaydia's herbal remedy had helped to dull the pain. Thurne's stitches pulled tight on his skin as he shifted his position and groaned at the semi-conscious thought of wake up.

Both the surgeon and the cook had encouraged him to eat after he initially refused his evening meal. Under normal circumstances he would have been all to happy to – he'd been ravenous after all – but the events marking Kradelow's coup d'etat against Faltainyr Demura had quashed his appetite. Not even the persistent growling of his stomach compelled him to eat. He'd sat at the chart table cradling his jaw in his right hand, his weary eyes sliding down to stare at the food with morbid disinterest.

Still, Thurne had insisted, telling him it was for his own good *and* while the new stock of provisions was still fresh. Nathaniel followed up by reminding him of his vow not to let anything go to waste, so he grudgingly obliged. He would have informed the cook in advance if he wasn't feeling up to eating, but with so much on his mind he hadn't thought about it.

Arcaydia, who had visited him soon after, immediately surmised he wasn't feeling well. He'd been sitting at his desk charting the ship's course out of the Sendero de Mercader when she came in. His discomfort must have been written plainly across his face considering the comment she made, saying he looked as though he might want to be sick. Telling her it was merely indigestion induced by stress, and that it would soon pass, hadn't been good enough. She'd made a trip to the galley and brought back hot chamomile tea in a wooden mug, and refused to leave him until it was doing its job.

He stirred again, opened his eyes and blinked at the nearest window. The moon was high in the sky. He'd slept most of the evening away, and despite his fatigue he'd grown restless. Holding his left side tight to avoid tearing any stitches, he heaved himself out of the cot and pulled his boots on.

Arcaydia had attempted to use healing magic on him, but she was still a novice and hadn't achieved much. Still, her knowledge of herbs was already proving to be invaluable. He took his long red coat from its peg and slipped it on as he left the great cabin, locking the door behind him.

The berth the ship had been moored alongside in Almadeira was an easy one to sail from compared to some other ports, but he'd expected naval ships to be waiting for him in the Sendero de Mercader beyond Almadeira's sea wall. There had been none. The lookouts hadn't sighted a naval vessel anywhere nearby. After expressing his concerns to both Krallan and Argwey, they had posted additional men to keep a watchful eye this night.

The night sky was clear save for scattered wisps of cloud drifting east with a cool, crisp breeze sweeping down from the north-west. Thousands of stars glinted in the darkness, the black waters illuminated by the pearlescent light of the moon. The course sails, topsails and jibs were set, and the yards were braced to starboard. More sail would've been broken out, but he'd specifically instructed Krallan and Argwey to restrict *Greshendier's* speed so they wouldn't reach the Strait of Mabriltar until the afternoon if the current north-westerly winds persisted. That would give them more time to prepare for the kind of battle he anticipated, and they would be more likely to engage enemy ships during daylight hours rather than in the black of night, if his hunch proved to be correct.

He strode across the weather deck toward the bow and approached the rail, resting a hand against it as he watched a smaller ship a short distance ahead of them. Mey was obviously holding the *Duquesa de Estrellas* back to be safe; the brig wouldn't stand a chance against the broadside of a man-o-war, but with *Greshendier* there to defend her, she was in safer hands.

On the bridge Krallan stood beside the helm, overseeing the watch. He caught sight of his captain and nudged the other man standing beside him and pointed. Zehn regarded the quartermaster coldly. Krallan folded his thick, muscular arms and stared him down, his jaw set tight. He nodded in Larkh's direction. Zehn's eyes shifted to where Larkh stood on the forecastle. The mercenary couldn't take his eyes off him as a sudden coldness struck at his core. Frowning, he turned and made his way down to the quarterdeck, wandering over to Larkh, who watched a brig sailing a short distance ahead of them.

"That's close enough," Larkh warned, briefly glancing over his shoulder. "There are men on this ship who think I ought to kill you, an' some of them would gladly do the deed for me. Best not give them another reason eh?"

Zehn fixed a cold stare at his back. Larkh's long coat rippled softly in the light wind like the surface of an otherwise still lake. There was no mistaking the fierce tension between them was still very much alive, but Zehn felt a dark and brooding anger there, which he only played a small part in.

"Simply standing near to you is an offence?" Zehn asked.

Larkh snorted, trying hard not to laugh. "The fact that you walk on the very decks of my ship is an offence," he answered sternly, turning to face him. "It is only on Raeon's request that you are here at all, or else I'd have left you to the duke's wolves back there."

"Mind telling me how you know Raeon?" The question had been nagging at Zehn since Raeon had asked the pirate to help him escape.

Larkh licked his lower lip, relaxing his posture. "Raeon was raised an orphan in Kessford, as you probably know," the young captain explained, "but he was sent to a grammar school in Saldour."

"He went to the same school as you," Zehn guessed. Larkh nodded.

"Eventually he left to pursue the arts of magica at the Archaenen in Aynfell," Larkh continued. "Shortly after that, my life as I knew it was destroyed, an' I didn't have any further contact with Raeon until one day he showed up in Tourenco on a field trip organised by the Archaenen. We only met in passing."

"So that's what he was talking about," Zehn mumbled. "He dropped a hint about knowing you recently. I also heard from the innkeeper at the Silver Gull it was your family I'd heard about all those years ago."

Eyes widening, Larkh turned back to the side of the ship and leaned against the capping rail. "I'm surprised you didn't know," he grumbled.

Zehn ran his fingers through his hair, already tacky as salt began to settle into it. "I'd heard news about a family of the Lonnfeir nobility having been..." he hesitated.

"Slaughtered, wiped off the map, say what you want," Larkh muttered.

"The family name was withheld by the crown," Zehn added, "King Jaredh initiated an inquisition, but nothing more was said about it. The common people know little of the affairs of nobles. I was a boy myself at the time, and I was a long way from home when the tragedy occurred. I never knew, until today." Larkh grunted disdainfully.

Zehn took a deep breath, trying to control his frustration, though he could hardly blame Larkh for having such an attitude with him. He had repeatedly hunted him down, attempted to kill him, and allowed his anger toward outlaws to cloud his vision. His father had always taught him that all criminal activity was wrong, and should not be tolerated under any circumstances. Though he now found himself starting to think differently, he still couldn't bring himself to let go of his resentment. It was the wrong time to ask too many questions, and he knew Larkh's view of him wasn't likely to change any time soon, nor were the attitudes of his crew. He was all too aware he wasn't going to find it easy to think of Larkh differently either.

He remembered the quartermaster restraining a man called Laisner earlier, and in his anger Larkh had emerged from the sickbay after receiving stitches, hissing sharply in the man's ear; "I don't want him here any more'n you do, but his friend was an old friend o' mine an' I'm doin' him a favour. Your loyalty means a lot to me Laisner, but only on *my* word may *anyone* touch that mercenary! I made that clear when we left Almadeira!"

He'd then turned to all on the weather deck, snarling as he spat the words; "I'll say it again! The mercenary is only on this ship upon the request of an old friend! Now that he's in our midst he will learn many *valuable* lessons lads, but *anyone* who dares lay a hand on this man with ill intent without my consent will be flogged an' sent to do all the jobs meant for him! Do NOT make me repeat myself again!"

That had settled it. He was now trapped on a ship swarming with pirates where the odours of stale sweat, pitch, tar and gunpowder hung in the air despite the fact Larkh was meticulous about most areas of the ship being scrubbed clean every day. He could jump overboard, but would probably drown if he didn't die of hypothermia first. The Sendero de Mercader might have a warm climate, but on the open sea the water was far from warm.

After a long silence, he spoke up again. "Is there any reason why you aren't keeping me locked up except for when I sleep?"

Larkh rubbed at his eyes and yawned. The sound of the water lapping at the hull seemed to have brought back the fatigue. "What'll you learn in there?" he retorted. "The brig is where you'll be sleepin', but bein' cooped up in a cell just makes a man think too much, an' why the hell should I feed deadweight on my ship? You work for your meals, an' in your case you're also workin' for redemption as far as we're concerned, that is, if you happen to learn anythin'." He turned away from the rail and rested his back against it, noticing the fore course sail was under too much strain. Reys stood on lookout on the forecastle.

"Reys!" Larkh yelled. The boy's head snapped round. Larkh pointed up. "The fore course is too tight mate; give her a bit o' slack so the sail fills nicely." Reys nodded and promptly set to work. He turned his attention back to Zehn. "Argwey has the key to your cell, so when the watch changes, you can speak to him an' get some rest. You'll be seein' a lot of him, an' you may frequently hear him discussin' his sex life.....*or mine.*"

Much to his surprise, Zehn felt a tug at corners of his mouth. Still, he wasn't sure of how to further the conversation with this atmosphere. Larkh knew he could do whatever he wanted with him, but he was choosing not to keep him locked up on the basis he'd learn something, and that he didn't want to waste his provisions on an idle prisoner. He was also surprised his own anger toward Larkh had been strangely quelled – though it still lingered – and it frustrated him. The nagging resentment wasn't going to disappear overnight. He'd been forced into this position, he was surrounded by approximately five hundred hostile men, and Larkh *had* demanded payment for taking him on board.

Perhaps he was afraid? Or was it something else? Larkh watched him with amusement, though he too was wondering why Zehn's zealous hatred seemed to have dimmed.

The mercenary stepped over to the side of the ship and leaned on the rail, watching the brig Greshendier was tailing. "Who is it we're following? If you don't mind me asking."

Larkh gave another yawn. "My friend Mey," he replied. "She left shortly before us but waited nonetheless. I think she's probably as suspicious as I am."

"About what?"

"That there were no Faltain man-o-wars waitin' for us as we left the harbour," Larkh shrugged. "Why go to the trouble of tryin' to trap me in my safe haven an' not set up any precautions in case I got away? The murderous asscock callin' himself duke will no doubt have sent ships ahead to block me at the Ene Canal and the Strait of Mabriltar, an' Mey'll be stickin' close to me as there's no hope in all the hells below of her ship bein' able to take them on without sneakin' up on them. One broadside of a ship of *Greshendier's* calibre an' that'll be that."

Larkh pushed away from the rail and took a deep breath, relishing the brisk sea air filling his lungs as he turned on his heel and began making his way back to the great cabin. "I expect tomorrow will be another eventful day," he added wearily. "Keep your wits about you."

"Larkh?" Zehn called. Larkh stopped and glanced back at the mercenary. "Is that your real name?"

For a moment Larkh stood in silence, fighting down memories that threatened to rise to the surface. "Aye, it is," he answered ruefully. "Strictly speakin' it's the first half of it, but I dropped the rest." He continued on his way, disappearing through the doors behind the large helm wheels that weren't linked to the altirna system.

Zehn stood alone, wondering why Larkh had dropped the second half of his first name. He guessed it probably suited him better shortened, and surmised it was probably to do with blotting out his past. He considered the symbols he remembered seeing on the ship's flag and sterncastle; a phoenix flanked by two eagles.

'The phoenix; a symbol of new life,' he mused, glancing over his shoulder back at the brig they followed. *'What have I been thinking all this time?'* He turned his attention back toward the great cabin, narrowing his eyes in contemplation.

CHAPTER 22

I
Aynfell

Melkhar slouched in a low armchair in one of the Archaenen's luxurious guestrooms: a four poster bed swathed in blood red sheets dominated the space, oaken furniture lined every wall, and an ornate alchemical chandelier dangled from the ceiling. The smoky scent of sandalwood incense clung to every inch of fabric from curtains to bed-sheets; it was accompanied by the fresh, leafy smell of the potted plants occupying each section of wall that would have otherwise been bare.

After an ample meal she was ready for what rest she could manage before the impending battle, but Raeon's news had soured her mood and left her agitated. He had informed her of Marceau's disappearance, followed by Arcaydia becoming mixed up with unruly pirates, and to top it off, the account of the attack on Almadeira.

Fierce anger burned in her eyes on her otherwise impassive face. The captain of the troop she'd slain had been telling the truth, but she hadn't known the attack was imminent, and the phandaeric portal couldn't have been left. Nor could the circumstances have allowed Arcaydia to accompany her. Marceau's disappearance was also unexpected. He would answer to the Atiathél for abandoning his duty without so much as a word when he had been well aware Arcaydia was due to arrive.

The Second Archmage of Silver, however, was convinced Arcaydia was in reliable hands, despite the fact she was on board a pirate ship. Both young men the Nays were keeping track of were with her, one of them being the captain of that ship, and her abilities had drawn them both to her without them realising. Arcaydia's abilities as the Mindseer Oracle had not yet surfaced, but they had already set the wheels of fate in motion. Raeon's description of the energy circulating between the three of them when in close proximity to one another had involved an unusual and quite profound resonance.

Right now, nothing could be done about it. Kalthis had agreed to travel to Almadeira in search of her, but if she were no longer there, word would need to be sent to him. She would attempt to contact him using mindspeech after her battle with Rahntamein; by now she should be capable of reaching out a considerable distance, but had not yet thought to try. Arcaydia's mind wasn't yet strong enough to communicate in mindspeech across great distance, so she dared not attempt to contact her.

Melkhar glanced out of the arch of the large casement window, then back to the bed. With battle imminent, there would be no time to redress, and there was little point in bathing until afterwards. Her current physical condition was roughly sixty percent of what it ought to be for a battle with a greater hybrid such as Rahntamein, and combined with a lack of sleep and adequate nourishment, it was going to be a much more arduous undertaking.

With her knees bent up higher than the seat she sat upon, she was beginning to feel significant discomfort creeping up her thighs and spine. She pressed her hands down firmly on the armrests and levered herself out of the chair. She flung herself flat on her back against the silky covers, laced her fingers together and rested her hands on her stomach. After the long flight from the Daynallar Mountains, sleep came easily. Sometime during her rest, a deep, booming voice echoed in her mind:

'Have you located it?'
"The one some call the Nightshade? I'm not sure. Its presence never remains in one place."

'Yet it does remain in one place.'
"You know this?"
'It was never going to be an easy thing to find.'
"I did not experience a distortion like this last time."
'They now know what you are capable of doing with it.'
"I remember."
'Call it a test.'
"Are you the judge, or are they?"
*'You are already my Champion, Kaesan'Drahknyr
Khesaiyde.'*
"So I must win it."
'Correct.'

Melkhar's steely eyes flew open. She lay on the bed
staring at the ceiling, her chiselled features steeped in
contemplation. In her mind's eye she saw the smouldering
nostrils, the jet black scales, and a pair of enormous eyes
glowing like magma.

'Shaorodes.' She brushed her hair out of her face and
sat up. *'Might the Origin still linger within our reach?'* A
wry smile faintly crept on to her drawn lips. It might take
some time yet to accomplish her task, but if they were still
around in some inaccessible place, they would be watching.
Feeling the powerful aura of the dragon approaching, she
pushed to her feet, strapped her sword to her waist and
briskly left the room.

II
Aynfell

Just as she had predicted, the steady beating of leathery wings broke the silence of the skies over Aynfell shortly after the stroke of midnight. Melkhar stood waiting for the dragon's arrival atop the highest of the White Sentinels, clad in her shining black Drahknyr armour, towering wings partially extended to hold her balance on the spire of the tower. The pearlescent disc of the moon shone eerily out of the darkness in an almost cloudless sky, and as a strong wind blew in from the north-west, her flame red hair billowed proudly like a dignified banner.

The evacuation of the civilians into the ancient catacombs beneath the city had been smooth, until now. Her words had rung true. They were able to get a little over half the numbers underground before the dragon's arrival. She heard screams of terror in the streets below as the hulking shadow of the draconic behemoth swept over the city on a pair of gargantuan wings.

"Kaesan'Drahknyr Khesaiyde!" Rahntamein rumbled, his deep guttural voice resonating with anger. "I am surprised you made it after Zerrçainne's masterful trap. How does it *feel* to be fooled?"

"Refreshing!" Melkhar replied, a wry smile tugging at the corner of her lips. "Being right so often can be tiresome. It was a challenge making it here on time, but it will be well worth the effort."

The craving for battle was already surfacing in that stony stare, and not a moment later she was in the air, her Drahknyr helm covering the upper half of her face.

"Rahntamein ahzu me!" [22] the dragon roared in Drakaan. *"Kaesané, manaikh jheu'naa arlos!"* [23]

---

[22] I am Rahntamein!
[23] You are mine Kaesan'Drahknyr!

356

"Waé tsalen vaesyr!" [24] Melkhar spat back in Daeihn. Thrusting her left arm up into the air, she summoned a formidable black halberd, a red gemstone set into the base of the great axe blade poised at its tip.

Rahntamein's chest began to glow. With her halberd lowered, Melkhar brought her right hand over her mask in concentration. Searing heat blew past her as the dragonfire burst forth, momentarily engulfing her in flames as a wide, blinding beam of white hot light exploded from the Kaesan'Drahknyr's extended hand, screaming into the dragon's thorax. The beast roared in agony, the heat searing his scales, cooking the hide underneath.

In a fleeting shimmer of light Melkhar vanished, re-materialising above her adversary casting a series of crimson lightning bolts that flashed downward into the dragon's back, electrocuting the ridges on his spine, sending the shock surging throughout his body. Rahntamein shrieked, as much in anger as in pain, defiantly swinging his tail in a wide arc, snapping his jaws at the Kaesan'Drahknyr each time she closed in. With a brief swing of her halberd aimed at the dragon's face, she tore a bloody gash in the tough skin at the side of his head before diving under a giant leathery wing.

Again the dragon's chest glowed brightly, flames blazing out from the gaps between his monstrous teeth as he twisted in the air and banked in pursuit, screaming another jet of flame at her. Melkhar was still able to feel the intense heat of dragonfire despite the unseen natural barrier protecting her. Sweat streamed down her face. She ducked and swerved under the dragon's belly, avoiding claws and snapping teeth as she went.

Rahntamein swept over her and banked again, this time toward the Archaenen, firing a volley of concentrated balls of flame at the renowned magi-academy. Entire sections of the gardens instantly burst into flame, but the rooftops were merely scorched.

---

[24] We shall see!

"Kaesané nhatshas jheu'an!" [25] he growled. His wings made a steady whooshing sound as he paused to hover over the Archaenen. "How long can you keep up that barrier before you must drop it to concentrate your full strength on me I wonder? Is the city not protected then? Ah, you hold back because you've not yet regained your full strength. How interesting."

Melkhar cocked her head. *"Annharenas kaerus vhe dankreijhas,"* [26] she answered, showing no trace of concern. Instead a mirthless smile crossed her lips, telling him he would find no bluff here. His leathery lips curled back in a snarl, and with unthinkable speed for a creature of his size, the great hybrid swooped down over Aynfell with Melkhar in swift pursuit. Flames flickered out of the gaps between the dragon's teeth, growing larger and larger by the second. When black smoke came gushing out of his nostrils, Rahntamein screamed a flaming jet down on to the streets where fleeing victims were reduced to contorted blackened shapes, howling in agony as their flesh melted from their bones.

'He is mistaken if he believes this will faze me,' Melkhar thought callously, narrowing her eyes beneath her mask, drawing two arcane glyphs in the air one after the other with her right hand.

Dozens of blinding flashes of blue light exploded across the ridged crown atop Rahntamein's skull and along the full length of his back, followed by a shaft of crimson-black energy blasting into his cranium. With a deafening roar that reverberated across the city, the dragon twisted about-face in the air and charged at the Kaesan'Drahknyr. Melkhar responded, shifting back and forth across the sky, leaving split-second phantom images of herself in her wake.

The battle raged on until the early hours of the morning. No matter how often the dragon's searing fire engulfed her, no

---

[25] Damnation to you Kaesan'Drahknyr!
[26] Assumptions can be dangerous.

matter how many times she was slammed into buildings or into the ground, Melkhar rose to her feet again and again; though not unscathed.

If the history Raeon had learned was true, seeing the reality of it was even more incredible. The Nays could withstand several times more pressure than humans before their bones would break, but the Drahknyr could withstand inconceivable amounts. Despite that fact, they did still felt pain. While the shock of impact and resulting injury was naturally reduced, their barriers offered additional support to buffer them; though pain and injury would eventually begin to show just as it would for anyone else.

The Nays, and consequently the Drahknyr, were ageless beings, with the latter being nigh on impossible to vanquish as far as ordinary folk were concerned, but the Kaesan'Drahknyr were described as being infinite. Death could only ever be a temporary inconvenience for them. *'Or a temporary convenience,'* Raeon thought ruefully, watching the battle continue to unfold as more silver mages, battlemages and healers of the Archaenen filed out into the streets to control the damage to the city and to tend to casualties. He would only interfere if it became absolutely necessary; he was there to oversee the battle and to alter tactics if circumstances called for it.

"What must it be like?" he murmured, his eyes darting back and forth, trying to follow Melkhar's every movement. He couldn't fathom what it must be like to be truly incapable of dying; how could anyone hope to understand? The only record in history of the Kaesan'Drahknyr dying was in the legend of the War of the Eclipse, sometimes called the War of the Black Sun. It was said they regenerated and reawakened within the Naturyth they used for hibernation, often for centuries or millennia at a time.

He continued to watch in awe as Melkhar dived underneath Rahntamein's chest and drove the blade of the halberd upward, finally splitting through the dragon's tough hide as she began to create a fissure between his scales that she would eventually be made large enough to strike through. The hide of a dragon his size was tougher than any other creature known to the world, even to the Nays and the Drahknyr.

III
Aynfell

Below the city, in the musty darkness of the catacombs, the rush of the dragon's wings were heard overhead, the deafening roars and ear-piercing screams of white-hot flame reverberating through the ground. The heart-wrenching cries of those who didn't make it underground in time sent violent shivers of terror down the spines of all who huddled together among the city's entombed dead.

Young children grizzled, mothers and fathers wept, and family dogs cowered, their tails between their legs. All held one another tightly, wondering if this might be some kind of reckoning. They knew someone out there was fighting the beast, but no-one knew who save for the mages at the Archaenen; no mage in the history of humanity, or the elves, had ever been known take on a beast like that and survive to tell the tale.

On their way into the catacombs, some had claimed to have seen a red-haired woman bearing a pair of enormous white-feathered wings on her back, and suddenly all tales of the Drahknyr being little more than a myth gave way to shock, awe, and above all, fear. Many shook their heads in denial.

The fulminating sound of thunder and lightning above ground had nothing to do with a storm raging in the heavens; it was the sound of tremendous magic surging from the mind of the sublime being that fought the beast. All around them the foundations of the entire city were being shaken. Most were uncertain they would have a home to go back to.

A goodly percentage of Aynfell's populace were students studying at the language, alchemy and medical colleges, or the Archaenen if they were lucky enough to be accepted due to their displaying proof of magical aptitude.

Raeon, and other archmages of the Archaenen, had sent as many of the strongest mages as possible to see to the protection of the city in the hope of reducing the extent of damage, but keeping up with the pace of the battle was far more challenging than he'd anticipated. He hadn't expected it to last this long, and now the last group of competent magicians had gone out to relieve the group sent out before them, or at least those who survived.

Dragonfire and magica raged relentlessly across the sky, and dragon scales occasionally dropped on to the burning streets, followed by pools of dragon blood spattering the cobblestones and rooftops. Melkhar hadn't yet succeeded in creating the full opening she needed in order to pierce the dragon's heart, but she had succeeded in causing him a number of debilitating injuries that would make the job easier.

Rahntamein bled from a gash on his forehead that had narrowly missed his left eye, and from lacerations on his hide across his shoulders and flanks, all areas where the hide was invariably thinner than everywhere else on his body. Melkhar had gouged several holes in his hide through repeated strikes to loosen the scales, and torn part of the membrane on one of his wings. His strength for the fight was waning, but so was hers.

Melkhar drew heavy, ragged breaths, though the fervid pain of many dozens of bruises and bleeding gashes was barely readable in her body language. Nevertheless, her fatigue was becoming more noticeable. She, too, was saturated in blood, both hers and the dragon's. It clung to her tattered leather clothing, streamed down what could be seen of her face and matted her hair. Rahntamein perched awkwardly on the tower of Aynfell's alchemy college, his great chest heaving.

Raeon watched, awestruck. Both had stopped to recover what little of their strength they could before their final showdown. He certainly wasn't looking forward to the aftermath, nor the backlash that was sure to result. The warning hadn't come soon enough, barriers had not been cast in time, and the people had been forced to abandon their homes. The death count was almost certainly less than Melkhar had originally predicted, for she had paid a greater price in blood by defending Aynfell with skill alone, choosing instead to guard the wealth of knowledge within the Archaenen, and for a very good reason.

From what he could tell, most of the damage had befallen the city centre, and Melkhar's barrier had served to minimise the damage to the Archaenen's structure. He wondered if the Nays might now consider giving them the means to better defend themselves. Aynfell was not completely destroyed and the Archaenen still stood strong, but they had suffered a heavy blow this night with very little warning and barely any time to prepare.

Had Melkhar not come as quickly as she had, the destruction would have been nothing short of catastrophic. They had been incredibly lucky she had arrived when she did, but Raeon was uncertain of the reception she would receive. Fear all too often had an ugly habit of turning people against anything they didn't understand, especially if it involved great and unknown power. He brushed long dark strands of hair from his face, awaiting the next move.

Rahntamein's long sinuous tail uncoiled itself from around the tower he perched upon, and like a gigantic barbed whip, he lifted it and slammed it into the nearby buildings, shattering bricks, beams and roofing tiles that exploded in all directions. He opened his mouth and curled his lips back in a snarl, displaying his infernal maw of razor sharp fangs, once again summoning the fire and screaming it down upon the city in his rage.

It was an act of pure defiance only Melkhar understood. She spun the halberd backwards so the lower end rested against her left arm, her right arm extended with her palm facing the dragon.

"*Éynev en'uar ye'n Rahntamein!*" [27] the Kaesan'Drahknyr snarled. Rahntamein reared his head back, spreading his wings out wide; an invitation both bold and arrogant, but an unexpected interruption caught Melkhar off-guard as a surge of black lightning struck her full in the chest as she launched herself at the dragon, sending her crashing backwards into the building she'd just leapt from in a shower of debris. Watching from afar, Raeon felt his blood run cold.

"Sorry to interrupt," Zerrçainne intervened with mock disdain, now levitating at the dragon's side, a large tome tucked underneath her left arm. "You'll have to postpone your little showdown I'm afraid; I've got what I came for." She gently stroked the book's cover.

"You never meant for me to burn down the Archaenen?" Rahntamein snarled, his scaly brow narrowing.

"I did intend it, originally," Zerrçainne assured him, "but after you departed I had an epiphany. If you had burned the place down it wouldn't really have mattered as I'd have found another intact copy somewhere else despite there only being a few still in existence, but I realised that if my *favourite* Kaesan'Drahknyr *did* manage to make it here in time then she'd protect the font of knowledge stored here because there might be some key piece of information locked up somewhere. I then decided it might have information I too might be able to make use of, and guessed there was a chance that a copy may be lurking here." She smiled grimly, glancing at the cover of the book.

Melkhar forced herself to stand, gritting her teeth against the violent shocks of black energy exploding through every inch of her body. *'This is Phandaeric energy,'* she realised, gritting her teeth against the pain. *'So, she really has mastered it. I don't yet have enough resistance*

---

[27] I will end you Rahntamein!

to...' She stared at the book the sorceress held, her eyes narrowing. In her confidence, the sorceress laughed.

'You shall not laugh for long,' Melkhar chuckled mirthlessly to herself. With the paralytic shocks now dissipating, the Kaesan'Drahknyr ignored the surging waves of pain and launched herself into the sky again; her halberd now aimed at Zerrçainne.

Sudden shock struck Zerrçainne, cutting off her triumphant moment as Melkhar executed her attack. She had almost forgotten about the wound Dhentaro had helped to heal, and had once again ignored caution. A dark shape with a tail and red mane leapt across Melkhar's path, whisking Zerrçainne from harm's way muttering a string of unfamiliar words which summoned a swirling dark portal with a distorted image of the Yahridican Fortress rippling on the other side.

"Into the portal dragon!" Dhentaro yelled. "It will swell to accommodate you!" The Fralh warrior jumped from the next rooftop and through the portal with Zerrçainne.

A dense malignant aura emanated from within Melkhar as her fury boiled over. She began summoning additional power from another source. Rahntamein sensed from where power flowed, grudgingly acknowledging the Kaesan'Drahknyr could easily succeed in her mission if he did not escape now. He beat his wings and flew from the tower, slipping through the demonic portal as it began to fade, disgusted and ashamed that he must retreat. In a blink, the portal contracted and vanished, leaving Melkhar seething with anger, hovering over the burning city centre.

'Release it,' a voice echoed inside her mind. It was the same deep, guttural voice that had spoken to her while she slept. *'Your enemy has fled, and you need rest. It will not be much longer before you will be back to your full strength. Bide your time.'* Melkhar released the aura, quelled her anger and descended into the blazing main street where coal-black smoke choked the air despite the best efforts of the Archaenen mages and apprentices to quash it.

Despite the fact she knew Arkkiennah would have fully supported her decision to rush to the aid of Aynfell to fight the dragon, Melkhar was painfully aware there could never be a time in which the people would be ready to deal with beings such as herself, least of all now. Deep down she already knew what was certain to come.

Standing upright, she motioned to take a step forward but stopped as her head swam. *'I've gone too far,'* she realised, knowing that until her strength was fully recovered her energy stores would drain much faster. What an embarrassment; she was believed to be the one with the most endurance after all. She should be able to continue fighting. *'Patience,'* she told herself. *'Have patience. It will return.'*

Images of her past raced through her head. *"You'll never be good enough!"* a man's voice roared in her mind. *"You, one of the Kaesan'Drahknyr? Laughable!"* She felt herself losing consciousness. *"Your mother was chosen to bear me the greatest warrior that ever lived, but instead I got you. Aevnatureis made a grave mistake when it created you!"*

"Melkhar!" Raeon's voice called to her. Before she could think to respond, she collapsed, her wings splayed out beneath her. She drifted into unconscious, wondering what the real truth was.

Raeon ran to her side with no clue what to do with an unconscious Kaesan'Drahknyr lying at his feet. Melkhar was drenched in blood; it was spattered all over her brilliant white wings, her extravagant ebony armour, and her tight black leather clothing was in tatters. Her spectacular wingspan might stretch across the full width of the street if fully extended.

The magicians of the Archaenen held back the gathering crowd, but Raeon heard as many gasps of shock and awe as he did snarls of resentment. The city was rife with fear. Aynfell's survivors crept cautiously out of the catacombs to witness the entire city centre ablaze, thick smoke billowing up into the sky. Corpses littered the ground, their scorched flesh already dissipating to ash in the brisk wind that whipped through the streets. Only one thing about the dead here remained consistent; the sheer terror and agony written on their distorted, indistinguishable faces. None were recognisable.

'Archmages of the Archaenen, I require your assistance on the main street beneath the clock tower,' Raeon said using mindspeech. He gazed down at Melkhar. *'We have an unconscious Kaesan'Drahknyr to move, and her wings remain corporeal. Summon the healers.'*

'How are we going to move her?' asked one of the healers already present. *'We don't have a stretcher at the medical college large enough to accommodate her wings.'*

'I'm not sure yet,' Raeon replied, a touch of irritation in his voice, *'but I need some of you to bring in the watch and assist them in keeping the public at bay. I sense many mixed feelings floating about; the people are in turmoil and none are going to be thinking rationally.'*

CHAPTER 23

I
Sendero de Mercader

Zehn spent the next morning learning the "art" as Argwey called it, of caulking and paying the newly fitted planks on the weather deck with cotton and oakum before sealing them with pitch. When the job was done his clothes were spattered with the stuff and he had the burns to prove it. He stood up, and leaned against the foremast, wiping sweat from his brow with the back of his hand.

Looking up into the rigging, he noticed the ship was now under full sail. He absent-mindedly rubbed at his left arm. The work wasn't doing it much good; Larkh had given him quite a nasty gash. Though Raeon had used his healing arts on him, he always refused to attempt to heal a wound completely. It was necessary for the body to respond of its own accord, so he'd been told. Apparently it was something to do with the brain's response to trauma and shock. He didn't understand every detail, but a dull ache was now replacing the stabbing pain he'd experienced before.

Behind him, he heard a team singing as they hauled on the braces to bring the yards over to starboard with the wind having circled around to blow from the north:

> *There once was a young lad,*
> *His name, it was Jack!*
> *He's a rogue and a scoundrel,*
> *But I'll cut him some slack!*
> *He's a thief, he's a cutpurse*
> *—A swindler, a crook!*
> *He braved a mad storm,*

While other men shook
Larcener and prowler
—Spider and cheat
Who else but Jack, lads,
Would chase down the fleet?

Now Jack is a lover, a kind tender soul
The ladies they love him, they make his life whole
At times he is lonely, he just needs a friend
Yet by no single lady can his heart be mend.

O'er waves, o'er the waves
Riding the storm winds, Jack
Frees all the knaves
O'er the waves, o'er the waves
Through thunder an' lightning, Jack
Sends men to their graves.

Oh he'll slip an' he'll slide
An' he'll RUN and he'll HIDE!
Then returns with a swagger,
—Gets away with a bribe!
That scamp, that rapscallion
What clever bastard is he?
Who sails into tempests
—And calls himself free!
Oh Jack, he's a rascal
Sly through an' through
A high-spirited pirate
—An' a skilled sailor too!

Zehn watched the bounding waves of the Sendero de Mercader and the passing of a string of islands cloaked in dense woodland to the east of Gaieah. It was a place he'd wanted to return to for some time, but all of a sudden that no longer mattered as the increasing swell of the sea made the ship lurch, pitching her bow into the waves.

He instantly recognised the onset of an inherently evil, sickly sensation seizing the back of his throat, its influence quickly sinking, making his stomach clench. Paling, he lunged for the starboard rail, vomiting over the side of the ship.

A moment later, a hand dropped on to his shoulder. Staring wearily behind him, he saw Argwey. The elven bosun appeared more relaxed this morning, though there was still a cold and distrustful look in his eyes. Nevertheless, he was more tolerant than most others on the ship; many continued to glare, some spat at him, and others made threatening gestures. Argwey pointed over the port side to the islands.

"Focus on the horizon," the elf advised, smiling weakly, "but move your eyes a bit. Try not to worry or it'll take you longer to get over it." The mercenary gave a slow, weary nod.

"Why choose the life of an outlaw over your homeland?" Zehn eventually croaked.

"Long story, that one," Argwey shrugged. "Maybe I'll tell you should you somehow redeem yourself. Everyone here's got their reasons." He inclined his head toward the stern of the ship. "Anyhow, the Captain wants a word, but I'll get you some water an' tell him you'll be a few minutes while you get yourself together. Below deck, while feelin' seasick, ain't the place to be."

Zehn had never been able to find his sea legs and keep them, but at least he had been able to control the seasickness, at least for the moment. Taking a deep breath, he knocked on the door of the captain's cabin. He took the grunt he heard from the other side of the door as permission to enter. Opening it, he surveyed the room.

He noticed worn but expensive cherrywood furniture, a large hand-woven tribal rug, a pin-board covered with bits of paper, fragments of ancient maps, co-ordinates, and other scraps with notes scrawled on them. His attention however, was drawn to the coat of arms sitting on the plaque at the back of the cabin.

There was a variety of worldly scents he picked up on, including the musty smell of old books, and various fibres. The hand-woven rug seemed to give off an almost spicy aroma. Several windows were open on latches, allowing the fresh sea air in. This was perhaps the most pleasant area of the ship. Other scents across the ship ranged from the strong woody smell of the ship's oaken timbers, to paint, pitch and tar, iron, gunpowder, and to top it off, the overpowering acrid, sweaty odour of unwashed bodies.

Larkh sat at the chart table on the port side with a map of the Sendero de Mercader spread out before him, and a piece of worn paper beside it. He was using a magnifying glass to read the lines and numbers, tracing it with his right index finger as he studied it, periodically leaning over to write. The information he had uncovered that Larkh was naturally left-handed was certainly correct.

"See anythin' interestin'?" Larkh finally asked.

Zehn grunted, turning to face him. "You've got quite a collection, I'll give you that," he remarked. Larkh met the mercenary's gaze, then picked up his quill pen, wiped it on a piece of cloth and replaced the lid on the inkpot. He pointed to the fixed padded bench in front of him. That mischievous spark in the pirate's eyes grated on him. Zehn ground his teeth together. He sighed and took a seat. "Alright, what is it you wanted to talk to me about?"

"Feelin' better I see." Larkh laced his fingers and reclined. Stifling a smile, he watched the aggravation rise on Zehn's face with satisfaction. "I want you to tell me how I became the sole object of your attention," he shrugged. "To begin with I was probably just another job to net you a sizeable sum, but now you seem to bear some personal grudge against me."

"You're a criminal," Zehn grunted, rolling his eyes.

"Oh? Is that all?" Larkh let his gaze slide to the rolling ocean as he inclined his head toward a window. "I think that even were I a fellow mercenary it wouldn't make a difference. Let's face it, I just piss you off."

"Ha!" Zehn snorted. "Raeon said much the same thing."

"What did he say then?"

"Hmph, telling you would only feed your ego."

"Did he say I was clever?"

There it was again, that smirk, that infuriating spark of confidence that could only ever spell mischief. Zehn growled, refusing to answer. Larkh brushed sandy hair away from his face, his mouth quirking up at the corners.

"You'll never make any friends on this ship holdin' fast to that temper," Larkh commented, slipping out from the padded burgundy bench fixed under the window. He made his way to a cabinet by the door and opened it, taking out a bottle of brandy.

"Who said anything about making friends?" Zehn muttered. While he faced away from the mercenary, Larkh's brow arched as he opened the bottle. He stared at it a moment, then took a large swig that brought tears to his eyes as he fought down a cough.

"It was a figure o' speech," he croaked, turning back to face him, "but if you're happy with glares an' death threats, that's fine by me." He offered Zehn the bottle. Zehn almost refused, but decided he would accept, not to be polite but because he was under the impression he needed it. He took a generous swig and handed it back.

Larkh blinked and replaced the lid, returning the bottle to the cabinet. *'You make me want to drink myself unconscious.'* His eyes narrowed as he slipped back behind the chart table and put his feet upon it, crossing one ankle over the other. "Anyhow, have you ever thought that maybe some people are forced into a particular way of life?"

Zehn ran a hand through his shock of hair, and removed the bandana from around his head. "My father was of the mind that there are no excuses," he explained. "He said everyone is capable of living an honest life; that the only one who can change your situation is yourself."

"I did not ask for my family to be slaughtered," Larkh growled, frowning. "Granted, sittin' in a mansion behind a desk with mountains o' paperwork wasn't my idea of a good time, nor goin' to sea whenever I'm told, but that was the kind of life I was facin' if my life'd taken the course it was originally supposed to. I longed for freedom, but it sure came at one hell of a price." He saw a questioning look rising on Zehn's face, and decided to nip it in the bud. "You'd best go an' finish your tasks before lunch is served. If you're late, you'll go without. Save any further questions for later."

Zehn's brow arched. The conversation was closed, at least for now. He rose to his feet and made for the door. As he opened it he thought a moment, and considered a response. When no words came to mind, he stepped forward and shut the door behind him, not wishing to add fuel to the fire he'd accidentally set alight. Larkh snorted disdainfully, casting his eyes back to the map in front of him. With a heavy sigh, he opened the inkpot again and continued charting.

II
North Mazaryn Peaks

Kalthis had been about to say his goodbyes to Fiana and her children when Duke Kradelow of Lonnfeir and his forces paraded through Foristead on their way south, demanding provisions the village couldn't readily afford to give. He sorely wished he could have given them a piece of his mind, but his presence, even posing as one of the Yeudanikhda, would have given rise to too many questions.

He had returned to the barn and waited until the duke and his soldiers continued on their way. Fiana explained all he needed to know about Duke Kradelow in that time; the man was self-absorbed, interested only in his own gain, and if anything or anyone should stand in his way, they would be taken apart swiftly so as to not be an inconvenience for longer than he deemed necessary. It made him wonder why anyone would want to work for such a man.

Kalthis may have only spent a single night at Fiana's farm, but already he had grown fond of the small family, and now he was worried about them. Perhaps he might see them again one day, but as always, he could never quite shake the nagging fact that someday death would claim any mortal he befriended. He prayed it would not be too soon, for the impending war between Faltainyr Demura and Adengeld was certain to have devastating effects on small farms and villages like Foristead.

Atop a sweeping hillside away from the northern road leading to Saldour, he tied his hair back and adorned it with leather wrappings complete with dangling beads. Descending the other side, he searched for a secluded spot where his ascent into the heavens was unlikely to be noticed. Ten minutes later he was aloft, searching for thermals to carry him up into the Etherflow. If he reached Almadeira by nightfall, he would have made good time.

He recalled sensing the dragon the previous night as its presence flashed past, south of Foristead, heading for Aynfell. Rahntamein's energy trail lingered for hours afterward, but by the time the farmers were up and tending their crops, it had all but disappeared. When he focussed his senses, he could still faintly detect the greater hybrid. If the beast had died, his presence would have departed Aeldynn altogether. It could only mean Rahntamein had fled, but so far so quickly?

Kalthis considered the possibility his mental capacity for mindspeech had expanded enough to make contact with comrades across, at the very least, western Aeldynn. It was easy to forget that immediately after awakening, their abilities were significantly reduced despite still being many times stronger than ordinary folk. It was just as easily forgotten as there was no way to test their abilities without using them.

A few months following awakening they would typically be back at full strength, but the tactics used at the climax of the War of the Black Sun had left them with injuries that would take much longer than normal to heal. When Aevnatureis ruptured, all beings on Aeldynn and all planes of existence had been at great risk. Had it been functioning normally during the moments the Kaesan'Drahknyr were felled, the wounds would still have been grievous and taken longer to heal, but they would not have died so easily.

Kalthis decided he would make an attempt at contacting Melkhar, but the moment he did, he was immediately rebounded by her mental forcefield. *'She has either closed her mind, or she is unconscious,'* he guessed, a rueful expression crossing his face. *'Most likely the latter.'* A great amount of energy would have been necessary in fighting Rahntamein and she would be in need of rest. At least he now knew he would be able to make contact; she would know when she woke that he had tried.

When the Altirnathé atop the North Mazaryn Peaks rose out of the mountainside below him, he knew he'd found somewhere suitable to land and rest. He found the crystal's resonant hum followed a normal rhythm as he touched down only a few feet away from it; Madukeyr had finished the job swiftly and efficiently. Kalthis expected nothing less from him.

Having not stopped to rest since he'd left Foristead, he was ravenously hungry, and wasted no time in sitting down cross-legged to devour the packed lunch Fiana had given him. The meal was pleasantly basic and fresh from the farm, making it all the more enjoyable. At the time of the pig's slaughter, he had insisted that he thank the creature for its life, explaining it was in accordance with his people's customs.

Before looking for somewhere to spend the night, Kalthis decided to visit the shrine. Staring up at the collapsing walls, he reminisced of a time when the Nays made pilgrimages up the mountain to offer their most fervent prayers to Raiyah, and sometimes to implore the Kaesan'Drahknyr for their aid.

The musty smell of ancient stone filled his nostrils as he entered, and the sun's warmth, flowing in through every crack, mingled with the chill emanating from the interior walls. He laid his eyes on the statues at the far end of the room, wondering what it was like to be one of the ordinary folk praying earnestly to any symbol of faith, not just those like him. Perhaps he would find some sort of answer if he discovered a way to reach the Origin. Dismissing the thought, he turned his attention back to his search for Arcaydia.

'Dreysdan?' he called using his mental voice. *'Can you hear me?'*

A momentary silence followed.

'I hear you Kalthis,' the Galétahr replied. *'It is good to know your voice carries far enough without a seikryth now. Do you seek an update on the Mindseer's location?'*

'Yes.'

'She has gone to sea,' Dreysdan informed him, *'and Almadeira is under martial law, albeit not under the eyes of the crown. Be careful to conceal yourself as best you can if you choose to venture into town.'*

'I understand. Can you see what direction she sails in?' Kalthis folded his arms, relaxing his posture.

'East,' said Dreysdan, *'from what I can tell using my own abilities; Anu Amarey cannot show me her exact location unless she stands on Armaran's soil.'*

'Thank you Dreysdan.'

'You are most welcome, Kalthis.'

Kalthis pivoted on his heel, taking one last glance at the statues of Raiyah and the Kaesan'Drahknyr; his eyes lingered a moment longer on the statue of himself. He exited the shrine and began to make his way down the trail in search a secluded spot under a tree where he might rest for the remainder of the day. There was no need to hurry into town now that Arcaydia was no longer there. Despite the need to find her, he required rest. Though the distance was stretching between them, he had far better chance of success in finding her sooner rather than later if he took care of himself first.

Before long, he came across a row of trees lining the sheer cliffs overlooking the Sendero de Mercader where the Blue Emperor butterflies flitted among the flowers and long grasses. He dropped down beside the nearest tree, took one of two waterskins hanging at his hip, and drank deeply.

For some time he watched the rippling cerulean waves, dappled by the shadows of lazy tufts of cloud floating idly overhead. Fishing boats bobbed up and down at sea, and merchant ships sailed east and west, transporting cargo to support their livelihood. Somewhere north of the large island of Gaieah, just visible to the north, dwelled the white leviathan known as Albharenos the Ghost. Sooner or later, he was bound to intervene.

He would make a trip into Almadeira to the Kathaedra in the evening, though he suspected his physical appearance alone may startle the clergy of the Tsolàr Fain. They would not be expecting anyone of his ilk. He would leave attempting to make contact with Melkhar again until he was certain of the path he would be taking in pursuit of Arcaydia.

Lying down in the afternoon shade of the tree, Kalthis wondered how long it would be before the results would start appearing from all the research that had been done in trying to decipher the prophecy involving the so-called Keys of the Origin.

III
Sendero de Mercader

Conversation with Arcaydia and Larsan following lunch was cut short abruptly when a lookout cried, "sails off the starboard bow!" and the ship's bell rang. Larkh quickly ushered them both out of the great cabin, locking the door behind him.

With his long coat trailing behind him, he stepped out on to the quarterdeck, passing the manual double wheels and turning right, ascending the stairs to the altirna helm. He placed his hat upon his head and held out his hand for the spyglass. Krallan handed it over. Taking it, Larkh held it against his right eye, levelling the lens to the mass of white canvas in the distance. The ship's yards were braced to port. *Greshendier's* were braced starboard following the recent change of wind direction from north-westerly to northerly.

Carefully raising the spyglass to the top of the approaching ship's masts, he steadied his hands to glimpse a red and blue flag sporting an image of a white osprey. The colours of the flag were separated diagonally; red on the left, blue on the right, the osprey in the centre. The paintwork was almost identical to *Greshendier's*, except where *Greshendier* was painted red, the Faltain ship was royal blue, save for some of the rich detailing on the sterncastle. Larkh lowered the spyglass to study the figurehead; a griffon.

"SHIT! That's all I fuckin' need!" He cursed. At least a dozen pairs of eyes were aimed in his direction. "It's the *Allendrias*, Admiral Traven Wendale's flagship," he groaned.

"The man who got you the letter of marque from King Jaredh?" the quartermaster asked.

"Aye, an' my father's best friend," Larkh muttered. "I should've known that pissant would send someone like him. Kradelow's probably got him wrapped around his little finger. Traven is loyal to Faltain; always has been. He's just followin' orders. I dread to think what'd happen to him if he stood against the duke at this point."

Krallan's eyes narrowed. "She's barely fifteen nautical miles away," the quartermaster told him.

"Aye," Larkh frowned. "She'll be upon us in no time at this pace. Make ready for battle in thirty minutes; I want everyone ready. When we're a mile from her, run out the guns on the weather deck first and then bow to stern, stern to bow on the gun decks. Let's show them how organised we are eh?"

"Aye sir!" The burly quartermaster couldn't help but grin.

On the weather deck, Arcaydia absent-mindedly chewed on her index finger, nervously watching the approaching ship, an icy shard of fear stabbing into her gut. Zehn joined her, leaning on the rail next to her. She guessed he was feeling much the same judging from the grim look on his face. There hadn't been much of a chance to hold a conversation with him since fleeing Almadeira, and he didn't strike her as the easy-going type, so she'd avoided trying to start one.

"I hope Savaldor knows what he's doing," the elite mercenary muttered under his breath. "I've seen the kind of destruction wrought on ships in sea battles."

"Well," Arcaydia said, turning to face him, "he's earned himself quite a reputation, hasn't he? I don't think he would be able to command such a big ship at his age if he didn't know what he was doing."

Zehn blinked at her in surprise and returned his attention to the distant ship. "I can't argue with that," he mused aloud. "You're smarter than you look."

"And what's that supposed to mean?" the young woman snapped, her fists clenching.

'Ah crap,' Zehn winced. "I'm sorry, I meant no offence. I hadn't considered what you said before I spoke; your words made sense, and I felt a bit stupid I suppose." Arcaydia relaxed, following his gaze back to the enemy

vessel. She opened her mouth to speak again, but was interrupted by Larkh hurrying down the steps.

"Find Thurne in the sickbay," Larkh instructed. He'll need all the help he can get soon, especially from you Arcaydia." Pulling her wavy hair around the back of her neck to secure it against the bracing wind, Arcaydia nodded anxiously.

"I'll retrieve the supplies I have," she told him, "but I don't have much with me." Larkh shook his head, and with a wink he added; "just do what you can."

"Is there nothing else I can—" Zehn began.

Larkh offered him a faint smile. "Not this time," he interjected, "but if you somehow manage to help save a few lives, I might start thinkin' better of you."

"More sail!" another lookout shouted. Larkh raised his spyglass again, scanning the horizon to see more white flecks of white canvas dotted on the horizon, level with the towering Pharos of Tathynars on Pointer Isle. He couldn't make out the flags at this distance, but there was no question at least one of them was a naval vessel; merchant ships would likely have been prevented from entering or leaving the Sendero de Mercader by now. "Seems they're patrollin' the Mabriltar Strait!"

"Can you see how many?" Larkh called up to the man.

"One man-o-war and three smaller ships!" the lookout shouted back. "They look like mercenary brigs!"

Larkh closed the spyglass and placed it inside the inner pocket of his coat, his brows knitting. He returned to the helm, looking Krallan straight in the eye.

"Captain?" the quartermaster enquired. "Oh gods, I know that look."

"Do *not* approach the other man-o-war after this battle," Larkh ordered.

"Why—"

"We'll attack the brigs if it comes to it," Larkh interrupted. "If we go for the man-o-war, we'll be preoccupied with her, leavin' the brigs free to surround us.

They'll take the opportunity to rake us fore an' aft. Gresh may have hardened timbers, but she's still vulnerable in certain places just like any other ship. For all her strength an' endurance I'd love to believe she's indestructible, but that's simply not the case." He gave Krallan a long hard stare. "It's a trap; they expect us to go for the man-o-war. Until then, we take on *Allendrias*."

Mey reduced sail on the *Duquesa de Estrellas*, slowing her for *Greshendier* to draw alongside. Waving her arms, she shouted for Larkh, who promptly raced across to the port side and leaned over the side of the taffrail.

"Wha's the plaaan?" she yelled.

"We'll take on the *Allendrias* first, an' then plough through the brigs so they can't trap us," Larkh explained. "Trust me. Find somewhere behind one of these islets to hide where you can still get a good view. When we wear ship, move forward and cross astern of the *Allendrias* and take out her rudder. I'll cover you as best I can when we carve a path through whoever else wants to defy *Greshendier*!"

"Aye!" she shouted enthusiastically, and immediately began barking orders at her crew to manoeuvre around the forested islets north of their position.

Larkh fixed his gaze on the approaching ship. *Greshendier* was on a port tack; her yards braced to starboard to catch the wind sweeping south from the Nays homeland of Ardeltaniah. The *Allendrias* was on a starboard tack, catching the wind from the other side as she headed west toward them.

'So, Wendale desires a one on one without any assistance?' Larkh thought, hiding a smile. "Sorry Traven, fighting fair under these circumstances just isn't my style." Standing by the starboard rail, he bellowed; "run out the guns! Disable her, but do not destroy her! Use altirna powder, but use it sparingly!"

"Altirna powder?" he heard Zehn ask. The mercenary stood behind him, watching the *Allendrias* approach.

"Powder ground from altirna crystal, or *Altirnathé* to call it by the Nays term," Larkh replied nonchalantly, his eyes fixed on Wendale's ship. "It lends greater power to gunpowder without increasin' the recoil, but it's rare an' expensive stuff to come by. It'll increase the velocity of a thirty-two pounder cannon by about another half, just to give you an idea of its strength. You should get down below to assist Thurne now. There'll be spare buckets down there if you need to throw up." He didn't stop to take note of the look of dismay on Zehn's face, and before the man could speak again he was striding down the steps bellowing at the top of his lungs, storming across the deck; "stand by to wear ship!"

Chaos exploded above and below deck as the crew frantically darted back and forth, shouting at one another as they took up their positions, awaiting orders. While Argwey supervised the bracing and tacking manoeuvres, the master gunner was instructed by Krallan on which firing sequences to use. In what seemed like no time at all, the *Greshendier* and *Allendrias* were upon one another.

CHAPTER 24

I
Aynfell

In the infirmary of the Archaenen, Melkhar stirred into wakefulness. Something padded had been wedged between her wings; no doubt to prop her up so she didn't lie awkwardly on top of them, but they ached terribly, along with the rest of her body. Her wounds were already scabbing over, but were still sore and itching. Someone, however, was taking great liberties in examining her; treating her like a live specimen.

She seized the outstretched hand by the wrist with lightning speed as it reached to touch her again, her grip squeezing tightly enough to make the intruder scream. Blinking slowly, she sat up, quickly catching the sheet draping over her. Her brow furrowed; she was naked. Moreover, she was clean! It was an invasion of her privacy.

"Dhečna mhir qethahvt mhaer dzaemernas neghara," she warned him, *"Éynev kvaillth ye'n."* [28]

The young man didn't need to know her language to understand the meaning. Just the look in her fearsome eyes told the healer she would kill him if he dared lay a hand on her again without her permission. He backed away, trembling as she released him, shrinking down to his knees, clutching his wrist.

She rose from the bed, wrapping the sheet around her, stooping to accommodate her wings in the confined space. As the wings had also sustained damage, they ought to be given another hour or two to readjust, but she would have to

---

[28] Touch me without my permission again, I'll kill you.

bear the discomfort until time permitted. Reluctantly, she released them from their corporeal state, stifling a grimace at the burning ache that followed. Drahknyr wings regularly became uncomfortable when trapped in their incorporeal form – and therefore needed materialising regularly – but they would heal much faster that way. It was much like keeping a bird caged for any length of time without giving it any freedom to stretch. At the sound of the young apprentice healer fleeing the room, she gave a snort of disdain and surveyed her surroundings.

The room was plain; the walls and floors a constellation of different shades and colours of sandstone, the furniture made from dark pine. There was little else of interest to anyone save for the medical books falling over on the shelves. A mixture of faint scents hung in the air, ranging from healing herbs and old stone, to the less pleasant odours of illness and infection. Even if a room had been thoroughly cleaned, her far keener senses picked up faint traces mortals had left behind but would never notice.

To her right there was a screen where a pair of plain black trousers and a jerkin lay on a small chair. She would not be able to fly while wearing these, for they lacked the custom-made flaps that allowed the wings of a Drahknyr to expand without destroying their clothing.

Moving behind the screen, she dropped the sheet over the top of it to examine her wounds. The deeper gashes had all been stitched, and all minor scrapes were already little more than scabs or livid red lines. By the end of the day most of them would be barely noticeable. It would take at least a few more days for some of the larger wounds to fully disappear, but the stitches could be removed tomorrow.

She barely considered the scar that ran in a clean vertical line just beneath her navel; the healers would have been seen it, and that probably included Raeon, but all it would prove was legends told about phandaeric weapons being able to scar the Drahknyr were true. Come to think of it, the scar on her face would have already told them the truth.

As she dressed herself, she realised she was ravenously hungry again. After such a long and arduous battle, the Drahknyr required a considerable amount of rest and nourishment. The only way to replenish physical energy faster was to drink expensive distilled elixirs made from the nectar of *Aethyraeum* flowers, which only grew on warm highlands, and not always in abundant supply. Without it, more frequent meals and sleep were required for at least a day, depending on the extent of exertion. It was no surprise she ran out of energy during that battle; it was the result of her still being in the process of recovering her full strength.

At the sound of faint footsteps outside the room, she turned to face Raeon standing in the doorway.

"Ah, you're awake," said Raeon, entering the room.

"I take it my clothes are no longer fit for wear?" she enquired, stepping out from behind the screen. Raeon shook his head.

"They were in shreds," the young archmage told her. Raeon shrugged. "You were carried in on a stretcher, but it took six of us to move you with those wings of yours."

"Your generosity has been noted," she said with passive interest. "Your efforts are appreciated. Right now I am in need of food and rest again, so I must apologise—"

"No need to apologise," Raeon assured her with a smile. "It isn't any trouble. I'll show you to the mess hall."

"You have my gratitude," Melkhar returned, following as Raeon stepped back out of the room, his platinum robes rustling as they swept behind him.

"You seem to have given one of the apprentices a bit of a scare," the archmage said dryly as they started down the corridor. Melkhar's eyes narrowed darkly.

"That doesn't surprise me," she replied levelly. "I don't take well to people intruding on my privacy under any circumstances."

Raeon flashed a dubious look over his shoulder, which was ignored. "Turn right here," he said. "The mess hall is at the rear of the building. Usually I'd recommend taking the route through the central gardens but..." He looked out of the windows to see the beautiful gardens now reduced to blackened ash, and the statues shattered into dozens of pieces. The wreck of the Archaenen's garden was still smouldering, and some of the scattered fragments of statues were glowing. He swallowed hard. That meant Rahntamein really was a greater dragon, as Dehltas was rumoured to be.

It was said only greater dragons were able to breathe fire hot enough to superheat rock or stone, and Melkhar had held her position in its path more times than he was able to count with only streams of sweat soaking her hair and clothes to show for it. The city folk unfortunate enough to have been in its path were now distorted, charred corpses gradually disintegrating into ash, and others nearby had died from shock having been close enough for the fire to melt their flesh from their bones.

"So it will take an extra minute or two; hardly an inconvenience." Raeon heard the shrug in her voice though she hadn't moved a muscle. He blinked in surprise, anxiously running a hand through the sweeping fringe at the right side of his face.

'Straight to the point,' he thought. 'No beating about the bush.' He decided to change the topic. "Fair point," he admitted. "Might I make a request?" Melkhar briefly inclined her head toward him, and then focussed her attention ahead again.

"I was hoping it might be possible to establish more direct contact with Ardeltaniah. There has been little contact between the Order of Silver and the Nays for quite some time now," Raeon explained. "We received the message from Galétahr Dreysdan about the threat from the dragon, but we were ill-prepared for there was no warning of his actual release. We knew it could happen at any time, but we couldn't very well evacuate everyone from their homes or dorms when it might not have happened for another week or month."

"Galétahr Dreysdan could not have given you a warning with an exact timeframe if he did not know," Melkhar retorted. "You would also do well to ensure that you are *always* ready to defend your city. Rahntamein is not the only draconic threat out there, nor are they the only ones to be concerned with. As for the matter of little contact, do you realise the other Kaesan'Drahknyr and I were only awakened three months ago? Our first priorities do not involve updating the Silver Mages of new developments." Raeon opened his mouth, but before he could speak, she cut him off sharply.

"You were informed of an imminent threat the moment it was uncovered, and failed to take immediate action to safeguard the civilians of Aynfell." Her rich, stern voice echoed through the vaulted hallway. "I was forced to use an amount of energy inadvisable at my current level of strength to arrive before the dragon, and found I had to spend yet more to save as many mortal lives as possible as a result of precautions not having been undertaken. You are lucky more lives were not lost."

That stung. Raeon understood much about the Nays from ancient scriptures and other historical texts, but information about the Drahknyr was scarce. Learning all about their physiology and spirituality was among his greatest ambitions, but he would have to curb his enthusiasm and ensure his apprentices didn't go too far in their investigations.

"I'm sorry," he grimaced. "You have my sincere gratitude for your painstaking efforts to protect the city and the Archaenen."

Ignoring him, Melkhar turned into the mess hall. Feeling all eyes in the room turn in her direction, her jaw set tight. One sweeping stare at them all had them focussing their attention back on their meals, but mouths soon began to murmur and fleeting glances continued thereafter.

'Just a spectacle to be marvelled at.' She snorted at the thought. *'Like a performing animal in a cage. They're all the same.'*

The mess hall was more spacious than necessary, with chandeliers evenly spaced across the ceiling with towering arched casement windows. The floor was a mixture of both light and dark marble tiles with dozens of long pine tables arranged to create an aisle through the centre. There was even a stage at the far end with a pulpit positioned in the centre where there might have been entertainment on special occasions. Each faction within the Archaenen had its own building, as did the library, and the dormitories and mages' living quarters; only the mess hall was located in the main complex.

"So you're not back at full strength yet?" Raeon enquired, leading Melkhar to the far end. He gestured for her to take a seat. Sitting down, she scanned the room. It wasn't yet midday, she realised, so there were few mages and apprentices eating at this time. She decided it was for the best; crowded places always set her on edge. Taking his own seat, Raeon waved over a member of the kitchen staff.

Melkhar resisted the urge to roll her eyes at the question. It wasn't a problem to discuss such matters with the mages of the Silver Order; they were in direct alliance with the Nays after all. The majority studying within the Archaenen's grounds, however, were not aware of all the studies the Silver Mages undertook. Reluctant as she was to discuss it, this half-elf *was* the Second Archmage of Silver; denying him the information would only postpone him finding out from someone else eventually.

"Under normal circumstances it would take approximately three months," the Kaesan'Drahknyr explained, "but assuming you know about the climax of the War of the Black Sun, our mortal wounds of the time were caused by Phandaeric weaponry, which has delayed the final stages of healing following our awakening." Seeing the next question already on his face, she decided to pre-empt him.

"If you were to evaluate the full strength of a Kaesan'Drahknyr, last night's output would have been akin to about one quarter of my true ability. My current levels of stamina and endurance were diminished before the battle began as a result of my long flight from the Valley of Daynallar."

Raeon's eyes widened. *'Such unbridled power at its full capacity would be unstoppable,'* he concluded, desperately trying to quell his childlike curiosity. As two meals were brought over by a serving maid approaching them cautiously, Melkhar considered the words of the old sage generations ago. He had spoken of his intention to create the Silver Order, and how he intended to achieve it.

~ *"They will be a supportive order to the Nays," Vharik explained in the Council of Atialleia. "There is a silver lining to every cloud, and that is what I want them to be."*

"Do you understand what the consequences are?" the Atiathél asked him. Vharik, a young man bearing faint physical and mental traits of the Nays, gave a bleak smile and nodded. His hair was mousy brown, and framing his jaw was a neatly trimmed beard.

"The continued use of greater magica will eventually sap all the strength from the individual," he said calmly. "That is why the initiates into the Silver Order will understand all consequences and make an educated choice for themselves. Not only that, but all who study within the academy will swear an oath of secrecy to the Nays, lest they be hunted down."

"You suggest the initiates of the Silver Order sacrifice themselves?" Arkkiennah enquired. Lowering his head, the Sage sighed and shook his head.

"It is not a case of wanting them to sacrifice themselves, Your Highness," he said. "It's a case of those wishing to support their people and the world they live in so that they may not have to rely entirely upon the Nays for support in sustaining their existence. Mortals may be a

fickle lot, and they may have a habit of resorting to folly, but they are proud and do not want to be seen or believed to be weak." ~

'Yet how did Vharik propose to deal with dragons?' Melkhar wondered. *'Without the Drahknyr, even the Nays have limited abilities in combating them; they have no choice but to have us take the lead.'*

II
Sendero de Mercader

Admiral Traven Wendale peered through his spyglass at the ship the *Allendrias* approached, noting the red flag atop her mainmast sporting two eagles facing each another with a phoenix in the centre depicted in gold. There was no mistaking the elaborate paintwork on her broadside and sterncastle. It was definitely the *Greshendier*.

'How long has it been Master Savaldor?' Traven wondered solemnly as the crew of the Allendrias frantically prepared for battle. "I wish I didn't have to open fire on you," he muttered to himself, *'especially when you're supposed have an agreement in these waters on account of my efforts for my best man's son.'*

What he witnessed next was most theatrical; *Greshendier's* gun ports opened in near perfect synchronisation, bow to stern on the upper gun deck, and stern to bow on the lower, but...he looked again. The guns on the weather deck had already been aligned! It was a clever display of control; a warning, telling foes Larkh Savaldor knew exactly what he was doing, and was not to be taken lightly.

"Run out the guns! RUN OUT THE GUNS!" Traven heard Captain Westley screaming.

Traven spotted Larkh standing by the main helm instructing the helmsman; the white plumes of his hat dancing in the wind and his long red military type coat billowing. His arms were neatly folded across his chest with the same natural authority his father had possessed. The admiral hastily tucked the spyglass into the inside pocket of his dark blue jacket, complete with red and burgundy lapels and gold embroidery. He tightened the tiny bob of a silvering blond ponytail and rushed down on to the quarterdeck screaming orders.

"Remember men we're to disable her, not sink her!" Traven yelled. "And try to avoid Savaldor, the duke wants him alive!"

He glanced over his shoulder to glimpse the young captain staring directly at him, tipping the brim of his hat. Traven gritted his teeth, rubbing at the thick stubble on his chin, suddenly aware that he was quite possibly annoyed. He'd never faced Halven's son in battle before, but he'd certainly heard the rumours of the young man's formidable prowess both at sea and in melee combat, and his knack for thwarting his opponents almost effortlessly. *'What will Alirene have to say to this?'* he wondered.

"Maintain course," Larkh instructed the helmsman, his smooth voice holding a strict and authoritative tone. Then, at the top of his lungs he bellowed; "hold, HOLD! ...FIRE!"

In a series of deafening explosions *Greshendier* fired her broadside. Cannonballs exploded from her guns, mercilessly pummelling the hull of the *Allendrias,* punching through her timbers easily with the increased velocity provided by the altirna dust, sending splintering shards of wood erupting in all directions. Larkh glanced sideways at his enemy, re-focussed his eyes forward and shouted; "get down! Brace yourselves!"

The timbers beneath his feet reverberated as the *Allendrias* returned fire. As her broadside hammered into them, the screams of casualties resounded above and below deck.   Though *Greshendier's* altirna-soaked timbers resisted the worst of the impact, she was not totally impervious to damage.

Larkh strode down the steps again, making his way across the deck.

"Upper guns! Chain shot, on the upward roll!" he shouted, listening as the order was repeated across the ship. Counting almost a minute, he waited for the ship's starboard side to lift out of the water. *'One, two, three...'* "FIRE!"

The booming sound of cannon-fire echoed across the water as the chain shot was fired; the shot slammed into the *Allendrias*, shredding her capping rail and biting into the timbers of her mainmast. *'Lucky, but not quite enough,'* Larkh thought.

He pushed the thought of more repairs and paintwork out of his mind, subtly watching the movements of the enemy, squinting through the roiling gun-smoke. She was about to tack. Traven might disable the rudder if he managed to align his broadside with *Greshendier's* stern to rake her, but Larkh knew he could get astern of the *Allendrias* first.

It was time to wear ship; a slower manoeuvre than tacking, but it would give the ship a dead run downwind. It needed to be done now, and as quickly as possible.

"WEAR SHIP!" Larkh yelled. "Up mainsail an' mizzen, brace in the after yards!" He turned to the helmsman. "Up helm," he ordered.

The helm was eased to starboard while the main course sail and spanker were taken in to avoid countering the turn. Larkh kept a watchful eye on the activity on deck as *Greshendier* began to round behind the *Allendrias*.

"Main an' mizzen, let go an' haul!" The main and mizzen yards were braced to port, forcing their sails to flutter briskly in the wind.

"How the bloody blazes did he ever get that many pirates to follow him let alone train them that well?" Captain Westley wheezed, coughing through the smoke. He was a man of about the same age as Traven, though his untidy mop of brown hair was noticeably greyer. Through the gun-smoke, he bellowed, "stations for stays!"

Traven stared across a mangled deck strewn with blood, gore, maimed corpses and dying men, shards and splinters of wood protruding from limbs and torsos. He ground his teeth, hearing the screams of agony echoing across the ship. One dead midshipman lay flat on his back, his face a bloody ruin, a long thin shard of timber wedged into his right eye. Another lay close to him, a long sliver piercing his sternum.

Below in the sickbay, the surgeon and his assistants were desperately tending the wounded, some of whom would be missing limbs later, if they survived. One broadside from a ship-of-the-line could cause devastating damage to almost any ship, but the power *Greshendier* had just demonstrated was unheard of – until now.

The chaos seemed endless as the *Allendrias* began her manoeuvre on to a port tack, and the gun crews readied themselves to fire again. *Greshendier* was turning much faster than even the *Allendrias* was able, especially given wearing ship was typically a slower manoeuvre than tacking; it appeared her ability to utilise the altirna system was much more efficient. If that were the case, it was a safe bet she would be more efficient than all her sisters as well. This would have to go into his report to Duke Kradelow; he couldn't risk anyone else informing him if he lied about noticing anything unusual.

"Standby to tack!" the bosun roared. Frantically all seamen scrambled for their bracing stations, the men manning the forecastle rushing to the jibs and fore staysails above the bowsprit.

"His father was perhaps the best tactician I've ever known," Traven replied hoarsely, "often managing to end one on one sea battles almost as quickly as they began. Ansaren Savaldor was the boy's grandfather for crying out bloody loud, and he designed that ship before the boy was even born. With all due respect, Larkhalven spent an awful lot of time in the shipyard while she was still being built.

He's learned about ships since he was very young, picking up everything almost instantly; he's nothing short of a prodigy."

"He's that clever you say?" Westley's brow knitted thoughtfully. *'I wonder.'* "Duke Kradelow was right wasn't he? That ship does have secrets, and I think we've now got a few ideas on what at least one of them might be."

"Helm's a'lee! Ready about!" The jibs and fore staysails began to flap in the breeze as their sheets were eased, assisting the ship's turn.

"I think there might be something in the gunpowder," Traven mused.

"Something mixed in with it?" Westley enquired. Traven nodded.

"If he tried to carry more heavy guns than he already has, he'd over-balance her," the admiral observed, speaking quickly. "So, if he's using his thirty-twos and twenty-fours on his gun decks, the only possible explanation would be something in the gunpowder, and I'm interested to know what."

"By the gods!" Westley, staring through the smoke as it began to clear, saw the *Greshendier* was beginning to cross astern of the *Allendrias*. "He's already astern of us!"

Traven felt a stab of pain in his chest as stark realisation gripped him, and wasted no time in barking his next set of orders, sending men scurrying in all directions. *'Too late,'* he sighed, closing his eyes as *Greshendier's* guns ran out again. Raking cannon-fire exploded, smashing through the sterncastle windows and across the length of the *Allendrias*, slaughtering and mutilating dozens of her crew.

III
Sendero de Mercader

When the battle was finally won, and the thick, choking cloak of gun-smoke starting to clear, Larkh tossed hair away from his face and raised a brass speaking trumpet to his lips as the helmsman put the *Greshendier* alongside the *Allendrias*, while the yards of her mainmast were braced square.

"Clew up the main course!" Argwey yelled.

Traven struggled to prop himself up against the edge of *Allendrias'* taffrail, blood running in rivulets down the right side of his face and left arm as he wearily watched the corners of *Greshendier's* main course sail lift as she manoeuvred to slow to a halt. The *Allendrias* was motionless in the water, her rudder dashed to pieces.

"Afternoon old friend!" Larkh hollered. "Fine day to get caught up in a skirmish that makes no bloody sense! Kradelow's got you right where he wants you hasn't he? Give it a few more years an' you'll be wipin' his arse for him an' all!"

"Don't you dare speak ill of the duke!" Captain Westley spat, grimacing, clutching at his thigh, a shard of wood jutting out of it.

"Hold your tongue Westley!" Traven growled, staring up at the young man standing on the ship opposite, his vision blurred. "Someone get the captain to the sickbay!"

"Want me to come over there an' pull that out for you *Captain*?" Larkh sneered. "Though, I think twenty or thirty minutes'd be more'n you deserve! It's a shame your surgeon has to stitch the likes o' you up."

Two midshipmen approached the snarling Westley, wrapping his arms around their shoulders and hauling him away. Traven's head was pounding from a blow to the skull. He squinted, slowly bringing the billowing red coat into focus.

The admiral forced himself to shout, "I must do as the duke commands, if only for Alirene's sake..." Traven closed his eyes, shaking his head.

"Liri...?" Larkh whispered. "What about her? She had better be alright!"

"I'm sure you can figure the circumstances out yourself," the admiral retorted. "Another of Greshendier's sisters waits for you along with three brigs at the Strait of Mabriltar. Two other man-o-wars have been positioned at the Ene canal just in case. Do you really think you can get past them?"

Larkh chuckled under his breath, and then laughed aloud; "he's sent all of you just to take care of me!? Well now, I really must be somethin' then mustn't I? You must thank the fat old son of a bitch for me when you see him for my pride an' ego swell nicely!"

"Captain get down!" Argwey yelled, but Larkh's attention was fixed on Admiral Wendale. Someone on board the *Allendrias* loaded a musket, their eyes fixed on him. Before the bosun could shout again, Laisner bolted for the stern deck and launched himself at Larkh, colliding headlong into him the moment the marksman fired.

Larkh crashed into the deck on his left side, dropping the speaking trumpet, groaning as he clutched at his ribs, only faintly aware of what had happened. He heard Laisner howling in pain behind him, and Traven bellowing at the musketeer; "we're not to kill him you bloody fool!" Larkh withdrew his hand from his side, now smeared with blood. His wound would probably need re-stitching now. Krallan rushed to his side as Argwey tended to Laisner.

"Will he be alright?" Larkh winced. Krallan glanced over to where Laisner lay next to him as he began helping Larkh to his feet.

"I think the bullet hit his shoulder," the quartermaster replied. "I can't say, but I don't *think* he's been hit anywhere vital."

"Get him to Thurne," Larkh said between gritted teeth, drawing a pistol from the holster at his right side. "We're gettin' out o' here." Rising to his feet, he fixed an angry glare upon the man – now being restrained – who'd fired at him. He cocked the pistol, aimed it, and returned fire. The man cried out once, and slumped against the officer restraining him.

"Stop it Larkhalven!!" Traven bellowed, wiping the blood from his brow.

"Don't ever refer to me by that name!" Larkh snapped. "It's just Larkh now."

"I will do my job, Larkh," Traven coughed, his voice trembling. "Cruel fate has brought us here, but I will do my job for the sake of my daughter."

"You're in one hell of a position, Traven," Larkh shrugged, thunder in his eyes. "I hope you find some way out of it. Kradelow will do everythin' he can to get to me, an' you know it, but for now I'll just wait until the next time we meet in battle. Would you mind doin' me one favour though?"

"What's that?"

"Tell Liri *faint memories drift on a distant breeze, but true friendship is forged from ancient stone, and there it will remain'*. She'll know what it means."

"What does it mean?"

Larkh gave him a knowing smile. "I'm sure you can figure it out for yourself."

IV
Aynfell

The Archaenen was home to many different kinds of magician, but only the Order of Silver extensively studied the Nays. Melkhar knew what the Silver Mages stood for, and she was all too aware of their secret. There was something they couldn't speak of to the rest of the world;

something that affected and controlled their very lives they were forced to conceal.

Raeon was taken aback by her stern retort after he mentioned the most recent efforts of the Silver Order to search for a means of staving off what they had named the Taint. She stared at him sharply, watching as fear filled his eyes and chills ran down his spine.

They sat in the Silver Order's private lounge, adorned in a similar fashion to the guestroom she currently used, except it was several times larger. Melkhar slouched on one of the crimson cabriole sofas, her legs crossed, arms folded. Raeon sat up, leaning on the arm of another opposite her, across a low oaken table.

"I fail to understand what drives you people to give up your lives so easily," Melkhar remarked, her expression impassive as usual. "It is folly to compare yourselves to those of my ilk; you cannot possibly hope to defend Aeldynn against forces that are beyond your reckoning. Vharik is a fool; his ideas are beyond reason."

"You're wrong," Raeon protested. The passion for his work was clear in his pale green eyes. "It gives the people of Aeldynn hope that we can defend ourselves. The Order of Silver knows it cannot reach the level of magica held by the Nays, let alone the Drahknyr, but at least we have something to offer. We protected what we could of the city—"

"Human lives are short enough without shortening them further," Melkhar interrupted. "Even the long-lived have limited time available to them before they must move on."

'Except your kind,' Raeon mused. "That is our choice to make," he argued, his brow knitting, his hands balling into fists.

"As you wish." Melkhar rose from her seat and strode out of the lounge, an aura of such magnitude emanating from her all other mages in the corridor stiffened or froze on the spot. Raeon sagged and hung his head, his forearms resting on his lap.

'She's right,' he sighed, *'but she doesn't understand why we do it. Men become soldiers to fight for their countries; they lay down their lives just as easily, always knowing there's a high chance they won't return alive. Are we really any different from them?'*

On her way back to the room she had been allocated, Melkhar sensed the growing uneasiness within the city. Before long, the Archaenen would know the wrath of the people, and the air would be rife with animosity. Anyone who had seen her would either think of her as their saviour, or a threat they wanted rid of. Knowing what humans were like, there would be more of the latter than the former, and she wondered why she bothered to protect such ungrateful beings; not that her opinion mattered of course. After all, she was a weapon to be used in the defence of Aeldynn to restore and maintain balance. The corner of her lips twitched, her brow creasing at the thought.

Reporting to Empress Arkkiennah was her next priority after another short rest, though she ought to attempt to reach Kalthis as well. After arduous battles, it could take days to fully recover depending on the extent of exhaustion and injury. Once at full strength however, if *all* energies were expended it could take longer, though it was such a rare thing to occur it wasn't worth thinking about. Moments after she had bathed and climbed into bed, she was asleep.

'Nemàres mélern, Kaesan'Drahknyr Khesaiyde.' [29]
"Remain calm? I am not sure that is possible."
'Aesčev émitas ye'n garàiel feorlàidhir.' [30]
"Stronger each time am I? I disagree."
'Patience and anger do not go hand in hand.'
"I know this."
'You allow your emotions to rule you. You always have.'
"I do not understand emotion."

---

[29] Remain calm
[30] Each time you grow stronger.

'They still rule who you are and what you have become.'
"That may be so, but they do not get in my way."
'The turmoil of the people will.'
"Mortals are weak and selfish."
'They fear what they do not understand.'
"They never have, and they never will."
'But some do make an effort to try, including your own kin...'

~ Ancient memories return in the form of dreams; sometimes one long dream, sometimes many short ones strung together in quick succession. The little girl in the arms of a woman with long dark brown hair, set down on the ground, came running towards her, her arms wide open, her cropped hair of the same colour as her mother's, dancing in the brisk wind of the golden plains within the Keilah Deylta Basin south of Aier'Nairohn in Ardeltaniah. Those small arms wrapped around her legs, barely higher than her knees, the beaming face of the child gazing up at her with bright green eyes.

Melkhar pictured her own surprised expression as the girl giggled, telling her in Daeihn that she looked like she'd seen a ghost, but that she wasn't so surprised because she'd already seen her from miles away, because high torches were easily visible. When Melkhar arched a brow at this, the girl explained; "well, you're really tall aren't you? And your hair is like fire, so you're really hard to miss. Little torches can't be seen very well from a long way away, but tall ones like you always stand out."

"I see," said Melkhar, bending to one knee as her legs were released. "What about seeing them up close?" The child considered this question carefully, cocking her head to one side, then the other.

"Well," the girl thought, fondly staring Melkhar directly in the eyes, "up real close fire is very hot and can be scary, but it also keeps you warm, you know?" Now it was Melkhar's turn to look thoughtful, but before she could think of a response, the girl launched herself at her,

wrapping her arms around her torso, making her topple
backwards. "I've missed you!" she laughed.

"Areianne stop that!" the dark-haired woman barked;
"your aunt has travelled a long way to see you, so she's
probably tired." The girl hung her head apologetically.~

"Karséi arkéthas..." [31]

Melkhar awoke misty-eyed, staring up at the canopy of the
bed, hearing the rattling of the wind against the window.
Heaving a sigh, she blinked and sat up. Glancing outside at
the dimming glow of a coral sky, she realised it was long
past the time she should have made contact with the Atiathél.
It was going to be a long evening.

---

[31] That's enough...

CHAPTER 25

I

Almadeira

To better conceal his appearance, Kalthis entered Almadeira after nightfall, a black cloak draped over his shoulders with the hood pulled over his face. He had, after all, slipped into town over a secluded and unguarded section of wall; entry and exit from the town being heavily restricted. Access was only permitted to certain individuals such as Lonnfeir soldiers, and anyone with confirmed healing abilities.

Sensing two auras of an origin greatly disfavoured by most Nays, he clenched his teeth, frowning; the Aurentai. *'There are two of them here,'* he realised. *'One male, one female, and both are powerful. If they are wise they will not engage me here; I would rather not be responsible for further destruction of this town. They must be working for someone.'*

A number of buildings were now smouldering ruins. The air was thick with the combined stink of damp and burning following the recent downpour, and the stench of sewage was beginning to rise from the drains. He only faintly remembered how the town had once looked thousands of years earlier, and how the Nays had built sophisticated sewer networks underground, which many of Aeldynn's more recent settlements still lacked, save for its larger towns and cities. With proper care and attention Nays architecture would endure for many millennia, but without, it would tarnish and eventually fall to ruin. All that remained of the Nays here in Almadeira was the Kathaedra and the sewerage system.

The Nays had removed themselves from much of the world, leaving it to its own devices long before the War of the Black Sun, and it seemed for the most part Aeldynn had done well for itself; except many of the world's rulers had again fallen to corruption and greed, harbouring a well fed lack of tolerance.

Now he wandered the rain-soaked city streets searching for any sign of Arcaydia. The rain sweeping north-west through Ennerth the previous night had doused most of the fires, though roiling smoke still drifted out of the embers of destroyed furniture and broken beams of half-timbered houses. Rubble was scattered everywhere; collapsed buildings blocked the streets, and debris mixed with swirling black water washed through the gutters and drains.

At the town square he turned left, feeling drawn toward the tavern located around the back, out of the way. The building was intact but had not come away from the assault unscathed; the roof was missing a number of tiles and half the windows of the upper level were smashed together with some of the timber beams, but otherwise it still stood strong. The battered looking sign depicted a silver seagull with a ship in the background; it bore the name The Silver Gull.

Arcaydia's spirit trail was everywhere about the town. He sensed she had spent time at the Silver Gull, but traces of her presence lingered all over Almadeira, finally vanishing at the far end of the harbour where there could be no question she had boarded a ship and gone to sea. Entangled with her presence, however, were traces of two other individuals; both harbouring potent spiritual strength. Although Arcaydia had yet to develop her abilities as the Mindseer, it was clear she had met the two believed to be the Keys, but someone else had also been involved.

Kalthis closed his eyes, thinking. *'A half-elven male,'* he surmised, *'and he's a silver mage...'* The spiritual residue led down the main street in the direction of the harbour, then veered to the right toward the Kathaedra. Glancing up at the sound of thunder overhead, Kalthis felt the cool wet splash of raindrops on his face.

'*Yet another storm,*' he mused. '*It's all starting to come true.*' He hurried down the street to the towering Kathaedra and hurried inside, looking over his shoulder to see the next downpour crashing down on the cobblestones.

"Can I help you?" a soft female voice asked from across the vast candlelit hall. A woman in ivory robes decorated with gold embroidery rose from the pews by the altar. He noted how the front strands of her grey-streaked brown hair were braided in the traditional fashion of the Aeva'Daeihn priestesses in Ardeltaniah.

Facing him, a gasp escaped her lips. Covering her eyes with one hand, she grasped for something to steady herself with the other, missed and toppled forwards. Kalthis swiftly caught her by the shoulders and held her still. Slowly she took her hand away from her face to stare up at him with sightless eyes. Kalthis guessed her to be no more than thirty despite the ribbons of grey in her hair. His expression soured in realisation that she too was a silver mage.

"A—Am I...dreaming?" she stammered, reaching up to touch the side of his face. "I never thought I'd live long enough to— but it's true isn't it, you're one of them..."

"You can see me?" Kalthis enquired, gently easing her into a seat. He brushed the hood of his cloak back, watching her glassy eyes scan him.

"For what you truly are," she said shakily, "yes. I am Sister Nalane; I was born blind, but was gifted with spiritual sight instead. Your light is almost too bright to look upon Kaesan'Drahknyr, so much like the sun. Tell me...why have you come?"

Nalane searched his ethereal face as if for something specific. All Thean races were said to have some kind of otherworldly beauty, but that certainly wasn't what she was thinking about.

"I'm looking for someone," Kalthis replied. "Traces of her spirit are all over this town, but they vanish at the harbour. I am told she fled to sea after the recent attack on this place."

"Are you the one known as Kalthis?" she asked.

"Yes, I am. How do you know?"

"You speak as a tribesman and behave like a soldier," the priestess smiled. "I see the endless conflict between them in you. And, believe it or not, your appearance is quite clear to me, even in your empyrean form. There is much I can tell about an individual just by looking at their spirit. But please, tell me about the person you are looking for."

Following Kalthis' explanation, Nalane explained in turn the details of the conversation she'd had with Raeon, which had later included a brief mention of Arcaydia, the spring festival, and the assault by Lonnfeir that had followed. Zehn and Larkh's names also surfaced.

Kalthis sat in quiet contemplation considering his next move. Unless he could find out in which direction Arcaydia was travelling, he didn't have much hope of quickly finding her. Even if he contacted her using mindspeech, she hadn't been trained to use it herself, and she certainly wouldn't be able to reach him at such a distance.

"Is something the matter?" Nalane asked. Kalthis snapped his attention back to the priestess, lifting his eyes to meet hers. Despite the fact she was blind, he could see the relief in her face, as if something she had longed for had finally come true. He swallowed hard; he'd seen others wear this expression many times over the course of his long, endless life. It was a look people wore when they believed they had found salvation and no longer feared death.

"No, I was thinking about how I'm going to find her." He sighed. "If she has gone to sea, it may prove to be difficult."

"You should at least get some rest before you continue your search," Nalane advised. "And I must tell the others—"

"No!" Kalthis objected sharply. "No, do not tell anyone about who I am. It would draw too much attention. Tell them my name is Kallas; tell them I am from one of the

Yeudanikhda tribes in the Daynallar Mountains, and I am searching for someone. It is too soon for the people to know. Please, keep my identity to yourself for now."

Silently, Nalane nodded her agreement. The disappointment was clear on her face, but at least she understood. Whether or not he could trust her to keep it to herself for long, he wasn't sure; he couldn't have known a blind priestess would be able to see his true ethereal form.

Kalthis considered the option of staying the night to be a sensible idea to boost his strength for continuing his search. He didn't know how long it was going to take. Tracing a spiritual essence across land was difficult yet possible, but across the sea, one could not place a footprint to leave any spiritual impression. Of all the Kaesan'Drahknyr, he was the only one with the ability to track the exact movements of a person's spirit. The biggest drawback was that he had to have at least met the person in question, and it was easier if he knew them well.

"I will stay the night and resume my search tomorrow," he said, his expression softening. The passive look on Nalane's face brightened, her lips breaking into a beaming smile.

"Thank you so much for accepting our hospitality," she said excitedly. "I will show you to the guest quarters of the clergy house immediately, and make sure there is a hot meal for you...if you'd like one?"

"As long as it isn't spicy, that would be very welcome," Kalthis replied, bowing his head. At this, the priestess cocked her head to one side as she beckoned for him to follow her. He stifled a sigh. "I'll explain later." With a fleeting glimpse at the statues behind the altar, he followed her through the vaulted corridor to the far right of the nave behind the chancel.

II
Almadeira

The mayor's estate was situated at the apex of a gentle slope, ten minutes walk up the left hand path from the mountain pass entrance of Almadeira. The street gradually wound around to the right before veering left again, leading up a gravel path lined with trees. At the front of the manor was a large fountain decorated with Drahknyr sculptures.

Leyal frowned. These people didn't care one whit for the Nays in this day and age, and yet they still decorated their homes with images and statues of them. *'Hypocrites,'* he thought. *'They may be my enemy, but if I were them I'd be pretty pissed off if I saw this and knew they despised the idea of my return.'*

He turned toward the house, then looked over his shoulder. *'I sense him. His aura is incredible. How I would love to go and meet him. Alas, I cannot risk my life against one of the Kaesan'Drahknyr right now.'* Leyal smiled to himself and made his way inside the manor. "It's a shame it has to be this way," he muttered under his breath. "I wonder what you're here for."

The next few days were going to be busy, though he suspected Duke Kradelow would have some task for him to undertake he wasn't going to be pleased about. The mayor's usurper would likely have received details of Kradelow's orders by now. He told himself it was necessary if he was going to work in accordance with Zerrçainne's plans. Assisting the humans? What a farce that was already turning out to be, and it wasn't about to end any time soon.

Arieyta was staying with the gypsies for the time being. She would travel with them, gathering information, and then wreak havoc wherever and whenever necessary. Adner was the next likely target. It was Faltainyr Demura's capital after all. The gypsies didn't like the idea of keeping her on board, but what choice did they have? Arieyta was permitted to punish anyone who resisted her authority, even though the troupe weren't expected to do her dirty work. How fragile morality could turn out to be when one's own life and the lives of one's family and friends were at stake.

Leyal entered the main reception room and dropped on to one of the soft, dark green armchairs. There was a small open fire within an elaborately decorated hearth, below an equally showy mantelpiece. He laced his fingers around the back of his head and slouched, crossing his legs.

'I feel almost like a king sitting here,' he mused. *'Perhaps that's what these people like to mimic. Yes, they like to think they're important, don't they...'* An expression of boredom crossed his face. *'I could never live in a place like this.'*

When the maidservant walked in, he looked up to see her offering him a sealed letter from the duke. Taking it, he nodded, and waved her away. Opening the letter, he scanned Kradelow's scrawled handwriting. *'For a learned man, he writes like a child.'*

Leyal,
You are to return to Saldour and meet with Admiral Traven Wendale when the Allendrias is brought back into port. Relay to me everything he tells you about his battle with Savaldor. I will then write to you again with your next orders.

Sincerely,
Jarlen Kradelow, Duke of Lonnfeir.

Snarling, Leyal crushed the letter. *'May Velhana have his hide! I am not a private investigator. When the Noctae Venatora find out about this...'* Grudgingly he folded the letter and replaced it in its envelope. He tucked it into a pocket, seething. Drumming his fingers on the arm of the chair, he glowered into the flames of the crackling fire. Hopefully this would lead him to a target soon, for if not, alternative payment would have to be arranged.

III
Yahridican Fortress

Zerrçainne spread open the book she'd stolen from the Archaenen's library. It was a perfect replica of the original Taecade Medo written thousands of years ago; a replica that was an antique in its own right, more than five centuries old.

Rahntamein's agreement to assist her in uncovering Aymarn's Dragon Aspect was still in effect, but the dragon had retreated into his former prison to heal the savage wounds sustained at the hands of the Kaesan'Drahknyr. Despite her strength not yet being fully restored, Melkhar had nevertheless come dangerously close to destroying him, and her for a second time, for that matter. There could be no doubt the Nays would send out the Drahknyr before long, for Rahntamein would soon find supporters among his kind, but so long as he behaved and honoured her wishes, believing he had something to gain from allying himself with her, she had no reason to undermine his own mission.

There wouldn't be enough time for her to study the entire book at length, so she skimmed the pages, searching for anything relevant to the prophecies surrounding the so-called Keys of the Origin. As one page caught her eye, she read aloud:

> *"When mortal folly passes the threshold of power,*
> *the seven shall awaken and bide their time.*
> *When mortal folly passes the threshold of greed,*
> *the centre of balance will shift.*
> *When mortal folly passes the threshold of malice,*
> *the Keys of the Origin shall rise.*
>
> *Awakening the Keys brings light to the shadow,*
> *And the Mindseer Oracle stirs, drawing them closer.*
> *Watch for storms wreaking havoc o'er their bearings.*

Lock and Key work together as one;
doors unlock above and below,
Shifting all paths in space and time."

"Well now, that's interesting," Zerrçainne mused. "A pity they need the Nays to tell them what they are."

Dhentaro's ears pricked up. He lay by the blazing fireplace in his mistress' quarters. Lazily he rolled over on to his back, folding his arms around the back of his head. "Found something interesting?" he enquired, smiling up at the ceiling.

"There is a reason why certain events happen at certain times," Zerrçainne replied absent-mindedly, resting her chin on her palm. "Everything is as it is meant to be; choices simply shape the paths we walk so we arrive at any one conclusion or destination of our making."

"Do you intend to pursue them?" Dhentaro propped himself up on his elbows, eagerness glinting in his lavender eyes.

"Their part in the show hasn't yet reached its peak," Zerrçainne drawled, marking the page with her thumb while idly scanning each page searching for further shreds of information. "It would put us in closer contact with the Nays than we'd like right now."

'She is definitely afraid of the Kaesan'Drahknyr,' Dhentaro surmised. *'The power that emanated from that one was astonishing, and her magica wasn't even fully restored!'* A dangerous grin spread across his pitch dark face, flashing his sharp, silvery teeth. *'I would love nothing more than to engage her in combat.'*

"Ah! Here we are," Zerrçainne thought aloud. "There is more information on this so-called Mindseer Oracle. She is capable of entering a person's memories, and is able to explore the environment for a short period of time. She is only able to bear witness to the events of the past, but views the memories as if she were there as a spectator. It says the Mindseer Oracle is also linked to the wisdom of those deemed to be the *Guardians of Elemanthei*. Elementals, and not the *Wardens* of Lyte; interesting."

Dhentaro scrambled to his feet and padded around the side of the desk to peer over Zerrçainne's shoulder. "I'm guessing this Mindseer Oracle is closely linked to these Keys?"

"Oh yes," Zerrçainne smiled mirthlessly, lifting her head. "It would appear, in this prophecy, she acts as a kind of guide."

"You keep saying she," Dhentaro pointed out, spinning around and walking toward the window, folding his arms. "Why is that?"

"Because the Mindseer Oracle is only referred to as a she in the Taecade Medo," Zerrçainne answered thoughtfully. "I am assuming the chosen individual is always a female." The Fralh warrior rolled his eyes.

"But you don't intend to intercept them?" Dhentaro asked. "Surely if they were removed from the picture you would have nothing to worry about?"

"There is enough information here to confuse anyone without the correct understanding," Zerrçainne informed him. "There is much more to this than those who are supposedly intended to restore balance to Aeldynn, Dhentaro. I have other designs for them, for when they come to understand who and what they really are, they will quite literally have the ability to unlock a number of doors; some of which I may want to open myself."

Dhentaro planted his hands down and leaned forward on the sill of the casement window. "What kinds of doors?" he asked excitedly, watching the menagerie of demonic sentinels arguing with one another out in the courtyard. Zerrçainne smiled secretly; his eagerness pleased her.

"Doors relevant to the elevation of the Eidolon Ring, for one," the sorceress replied coolly. "And then, there is the Stairway. I'm not certain which kinds of doors these Keys are capable of opening directly, but we will find out. Patience is a virtue."

Dhentaro's eyes narrowed thoughtfully. Dusk was falling over Ehyenn, and more rainclouds were moving in for the night. "Is the army's delay going to cause us many problems?" he enquired, looking over his shoulder. "Rahntamein made it quite clear he would not guide them; not that anyone can control a dragon—"

"The Drahknyr can," Zerrçainne cut in. "That is one of the primary reasons they exist. Were it truly up to the dragons to decide, they would do entirely as they pleased, as we do, and if that were the case it would mean civilisation as we know it might not exist, not without them. For rogues like Rahntamein, however, there is but only one outcome, and that is to be destroyed."

"And you intend to let that be so?" Dhentaro asked, his tail flicking back and forth. Zerrçainne had quickly learned to read when this meant agitation or excitement; it was clearly agitation this time.

"If it is one force that should not be taken lightly Dhentaro, it is the Drahknyr; particularly the Kaesan'Drahknyr," she reminded him. "Rahntamein pleases only himself, but he is lending us his aid because he is in agreement with Alymarn's creed. So long as he lives long enough to serve his purpose, I do not care what the Drahknyr do with him, just as I do not care what becomes of the Prince of Adengeld once Alymarn claims him."

Dhentaro turned his head back to the window. He stared at the outcrop of crags just south-east of the fortress to the Dragon's Gaol. For one who had been cooped up in there for so long, sealed in a deep slumber, Rahntamein had oddly claimed it as his lair. He found himself wondering why the beast had been put to sleep rather than slain all those generations ago.

Another matter weighing on his mind was Zerrçainne's true goal. He knew enough to go by, but there was something else lurking at the back of her mind she refused to let go of. It was the source of her motivation. It was something to do with Alymarn, he was sure of that, but there was a fierce bitterness surrounding her, an unquenchable thirst for revenge he couldn't quite pinpoint. What or who was Alymarn to her exactly?

Dhentaro knew the demons of Dhavenkos Mhal, including the Fralh, considered him to be some kind of a god, and they weren't wrong. He definitely wasn't a legitimate god, but he certainly held the power of one. Perhaps it was time he did some more research on Aeldynn's history in the library. Myths and legends always held at least some truth, and he wanted to find out where they would lead him.

"The prince will die, won't he?" he finally asked. He frowned at the silence that followed. "He is human and has no natural tether to Aevnatureis, if my understanding serves me correctly. Surely having a being of Alymarn's power within him would ultimately cause his demise?"

Zerrçainne's brow creased as she sifted through the pages of the Taecade Medo. "Yes, but it won't happen in the manner you may be thinking. It doesn't matter what kind of being the host is, so long it is strong-willed, and one who has both the motivation to succeed and the motivation for vengeance." She sat back in her chair, staring intently at a particular page in the book as she tried to decipher its meaning. "Essentially, Rannvorn DeaCathra is the cocoon a caterpillar wraps itself in before it transforms into a butterfly, or perhaps a moth. You know what those are, don't you?"

Dhentaro wasn't certain, but he knew of demonic beings that evolved in the manner the sorceress was describing. "I think so; your description reminds me of a species I have come across in the depths of Dhavenkos Mhal. I will look up the creatures you have described when I next go into the library."

"You mean the Lanokh, don't you?" Zerrçainne asked, her mouth curling into a wry smile. "Yes, there is a great similarity between them; except butterflies and moths tend to be small and harmless."

Dhentaro whirled around and strode back over to Zerrçainne's seat. The sorceress' brow softened, a satisfied smirk crossing her finely chiselled features as she scanned another page. Dhentaro's enthusiasm had returned; the tip of his tail flickering across the floor in anticipation.

"What have you found?" he asked, eyes gleaming.

"I don't know just yet," Zerrçainne smiled. "Leave it with me. We have plenty of time on our hands at the moment. Let's sit back and bide our time. Within the next month or two, Adengeld and Faltainyr Demura will be at war."

"Shall I—" Dhentaro began.

"Yes," said Zerrçainne. "Go to Cathra, and give the runes to the Prince of Adengeld. Remember to cast a Thannyc seal, and always report to me using the seikryth I gave you if there are any problems, or if we are unable to meet for any reason. You do remember how to use it?"

"I do," said Dhentaro; "it's simple enough. They're not unlike the *Athokra* we have in Dhavenkos Mhal."

"Very good," Zerrçainne nodded. She relaxed into her seat, propping her head up as she rested her elbow on the armrest. "In the meantime I shall investigate a means of sabotaging the barrier that keeps the Eidolon Ring at bay. Just remember to tell me all about his screams." Dhentaro shot her a satisfied smirk, which she returned gratuitously.

IV
Cathra

"Is this absolutely necessary?" Rannvorn stared anxiously at the minuscule amount of bubbling black liquid in the small cast iron pot Dhentaro had set over the hearth in his quarters. "They'll certainly notice the—"

"I'd keep them covered if I were you," Dhentaro warned him, flashing a sly look. "Your subordinates must not know about the runes until the right moment, not until you are able to wield your power – or rather Alymarn's power – successfully." With the tip of his tail gently brushing the floor, he stepped toward the centre of the room speaking clearly; *"Thannyc o majon saejos nata Fandares-o do aofah zhes ramo-a."* [32]

Swirling tendrils of purple mist crept stealthily into the room, curling on a random path toward the Prince of Adengeld before expanding, illuminating the room in an eerie indigo glow. Chills ran down Rannvorn's spine, gripping his chest and turning his stomach to ice. If any part of him questioned this, it was far too late now. Each time he doubted himself, the voice in the back of his mind laughed, urging him to remember his purpose.

'There is no going back,' he told himself, taking a seat at the table in his chambers. *'After this, the pact will be solidified.'*

"Correct," said the voice, *"but you are already mine, and my power is yours. We are one."*

'What about the runes?' Rannvorn asked.

"They will allow you to utilise my power," the voice replied, thick with malice and amusement. *"The pain will be excruciating, but once it settles down you will be able to draw upon my power naturally as if you'd been anchored to the source all along."*

---

[32] Magica of Thannyc bring forth of Phandaerys the bound cloak of silence.

'*The source? You mean the Foundation, Aevnatureis?*'

Cruel laughter echoed in Rannvorn's mind.

"*Aevnatureis?*" the voice spat. "*Hardly. You, my friend, will harness the truly black magica of entropy from the darkness of Phandaerys.*"

The prince swallowed hard; he held little knowledge of magic, and hoped the abilities truly would come naturally. Until now, he had never cared to learn save for basic alchemy with his private tutor.

"Hold your hands out, palms down on the table," Dhentaro instructed him. Rannvorn took a deep, shaky breath and placed his hands on the table, his eyes fixed on the glyph irons as the Fralh demon dipped them in the boiling black liquid.

'*I am not afraid.*' The prince clenched his jaw and closed his eyes. '*I am not afraid. Adengeld...no! All of Armaran will be mine!*'

"*Yes that's right...*"

As both glyph irons were pressed firmly on to the bare flesh of his hands, white hot agony surged through Rannvorn's hands and he screamed, arching his back and grinding his teeth while the tar-like fluid hissed black smoke, searing his flesh. If the room had not been prepared with a Thannyc seal, the entire castle would have heard.

"*When Armaran is conquered, I will call forth the demons and the dead, and I shall take the fight to the Nays,*" the voice sneered. "*You are my vessel, Prince Rannvorn, and the more you use those runes, the closer you come to fulfilling your destiny.*"

"Alymarn, the deceiver," Rannvorn breathed through clenched teeth. Despite the terrible pain, the prince felt a grin tugging at the corners of his mouth. "I know you now."

Dhentaro folded his arms, flashing a fanged grin in his direction, and Rannvorn heard Alymarn's maniacal laughter echo not just in his mind, but around the entire room.

LORE
The War of the Eclipse

Follow your chosen path with conviction,
and you will learn who you are.
Kensaiyr Proverb

The month of Arenun, 947 AN Aerétas Nehkúridas, the Era of Guardians

It was the Aurentai, the highest ranking of the fey races, who declared war on the Nays. The reason their emperor, Garoad, made such a fateful choice is one few understand or even know the full truth leading to it. Perhaps it was down to his sheer jealousy of the Nays and the Kensaiyr, naturally more powerful than all other races existing on Aeldynn. There is a well-known trait among the leaders of nations and races; many of them covet power, and will stop at nothing in their attempts to obtain it.

The greatest of all battles fought in the War of the Black Sun, otherwise known as the War of the Eclipse, took place in the vast expanse of barren moorlands of Koborea, a continent strangely shaped like an eye in the middle of the Aeurenial Ocean. This ocean lies to the west of Ardeltaniah, and east of Zaern'Kairnell. It has a north and south divide, so called because of the angle and shape of Koborea itself, through which one of the three ocean ridges runs from north-east to south-west. The Aeurenial Ridge was also known as the Middal Ridge because it stretches across the centre of the Aeurenial Ocean.

A swarming conglomeration of different races had fought in the war; the Kensaiyr, Cerenyr, and Thényr were among those fighting alongside the Nays, the Drahknyr and their Dragons. The Aurentai were joined by the Shäada, the Vhaeoul, and even the demonic Fralh. Humans simply took one side or the other. And, in an attempt to match the power of the Drahknyr and the Dragons, the Aurentai, Shäada and

Fralh used their own magi to summon the Elemanthei, known in the Armen common language as Elementals.

Koborea was consequently reduced to less than the natural barren landscape it once was. The very soil was scorched and blackened by dragonfire and rent asunder by the explosive clash of magica that thundered ceaselessly across land and sky. As a result, nature itself was distorted, and Koborea has never been the same since. In some areas a weightlessness reduces gravity's pull, allowing denser objects to drift and bounce on air so thick it feels as if one is walking underwater. The fact the weightlessness is accompanied by a heavy sensation is a phenomenon few understand. In some areas, the collision of magica was enough to create pockets of swirling distortions, amplifying or nullifying certain types of arcane energy.

It was due to the unnatural power residing within the devil known as Alymarn, the great unholy harbinger, that Aevnatureis suffered a severe rupture. Volcanoes erupted, tidal waves surged, tornadoes spiralled down from the heavens, and severe earthquakes shook the land. One such earthquake had been powerful enough to tear a ravine in the region known known as Ennerth in the kingdom of Faltainyr Demura, resulting in a major shift within the geological strata that caused the volcano Mount Dorne to lose its source of magma. When this ravine filled with seawater, it became known as the Ene Canal.

At the same time, the sky became dark as the sun turned black. This was an ominous time for a solar eclipse to have occurred, and it is how the war acquired its name. During this eclipse, all natural magica and function of life was lost. Had it lasted a greater length of time, all life on Aeldynn would have been wiped out. It was then the Drahknyr, including the Kaesan'Drahknyr, were rendered mortal. Their natural anchorage to Aevnatureis was severed, and their mentality distorted. This allowed their enemies to strike them down with little but their physical prowess to be concerned with. It was foolish of them, however, to think the Kaesan'Drahknyr would remain deceased.

Aevnatureis restored its power within an hour of its rupture, but it would be many generations later the Kaesan'Drahknyr reawakened. Perhaps they could have been reawakened sooner, perhaps not. It is said their hearts began to beat again soon after Aevnatureis was once again stable, but they were to be incapacitated for some time, and were overdue for a long rest. While their bodies regenerated, they slept within the Naturyth in suspended animation, during which time their spirits returned to ethereal Valdysthar.

CHAPTER 26

I
Sendero de Mercader

Little over an hour had passed since the *Allendrias* was left stranded with a shattered rudder and weakened mainmast in the northern territories of the Sendero de Mercader. Larkh stood on *Greshendier's* forecastle, his spyglass fixed on the pirate hunter brigs in the distance. Straight ahead was the colossal Pharos of Tathynars, an ancient Nays beacon built on Pointer Isle, a small island shaped like an arrowhead pointing east toward Enkaiyta.

Though no longer manned by the Nays, the pharos was still in use. Pointer Isle was known for its sharp rocky outcrops, many of which were concealed beneath the ocean's surface. Each night a great alchemical brazier was lit and kept in rotation by an altirna system.

The sails had been trimmed to allow for recovery while Larkh plotted a course of action. It had given Thurne enough time to re-stitch the gash at his side, torn open when he'd crashed to the deck following Laisner's collision with him, ultimately saving his life. The wound stung and ached terribly, but he was otherwise no worse for wear.

The brigs were on the move, but as far as he could tell, they were sailing south around the other side of the island, most likely to make themselves appear inconspicuous. Greshendier had already been spotted, and the pirate hunters were likely trying to position themselves to surround her.

'If I were them,' he mused, *'I'd choose one to bring up the rear and one to remain ahead to attempt raking fire, and another on standby as back-up.'* He scanned the horizon

again. The man-o-war was nowhere to be seen. *'Lying in wait,'* he surmised.

Three pirate hunting brigs wouldn't be a match for *Greshendier* unless they were fast enough to manoeuvre into a position to rake her. Although the damage would be somewhat lessened, altirna-soaked timbers wouldn't stop windows from shattering. With another of *Greshendier's* sister ships in the party as well, matters could prove problematic. He knew he was an excellent tactician, but he was struggling to deny Kradelow had certainly put his plan together well.

'The wind is shifting to the west,' he mused; *'that means they'll need to tack to engage me, so could we perhaps navigate a path to give us more of an advantage?'* Lowering the spyglass, he frowned, scratching the back of his neck, maintaining a pensive expression. Today, the warmth of the sun and its glittering light on the surface of the water held a kind of unsettling serenity, and not because of the danger that lay before him and everyone else on board. No matter how much he tried to put the thought aside, it refused to let go, and instead tightened its iron grip on his heart. Well, at least the weather wasn't foul and stormy; it was fine weather for sailing. The conditions could be a damn sight worse.

"Captain?" a voice called. He turned to see Argwey leaning against the foremast, eyes fixed on him. "I think I might have a solution to our problem."

Larkh cocked his head as he took a coin from his pocket and began turning it over in his right palm. "Alright Argwey, go ahead an' spit it out. The sooner the better." The elf averted his gaze.

"Argwey...?" Larkh pressed, suspicion growing in his tone. Argwey sighed heavily.

"I'm sorry Captain, I couldn't tell you before as it's a secret among the Cerenyr," he began. "There's a hidden channel not shown on any chart; none that I've ever seen anyway. It's not far east of here an' it splits east an' west.

East leads out beyond the Mabriltar Strait, an' west...well it comes out in the north of the Sendero de Mercader between Nays an' Cerenyr lands."

"Hidden, you say?"

"Aye, with glámar. I'm sorry I—" Larkh took a step forward and gripped Argwey's shoulders.

"Where exactly?"

Argwey felt his shoulders stiffen. He pulled his head back, nervously staring into Larkh's fierce azure gaze. *'Is he not going to punish me?'*

"It's almost directly east of Pointer Isle," the bosun explained, avoiding eye contact with Larkh. "It's where the land starts to curve to the south like a hook, or the beak of a bird, an' further up the channel forks east and west." He felt guilty he'd never told him about it before despite having been loyal to his kin by keeping it a secret, until now. "If we head east we'll come out on the Wahren Sea just beyond the Mabriltar Strait."

"Can you dispel the glámar?" Larkh enquired, arching a brow.

"Aye, I think so," Argwey shrugged. "It should work long enough for us to pass through. I'll warn you though, the channel is quite narrow. The Duquesa de Estrellas won't have much of a problem, but we'll need to be more careful. We'll need to be braced sharp up most of the way."

"That's not a problem, is it? Gresh has squeezed through tight spaces before, even if she doesn't much like it." Larkh gave him a meek smile. "Thank you Argwey." He turned, briskly making his way aft to the helm.

"Captain! Aren't you—" Argwey shouted after him, but Larkh waved a hand in the air.

"If you must explain yourself Argwey, do it when this is over alright?"

The elf opened his mouth to speak, but quickly shut it again. Larkh was good at reading people, which could sometimes be annoying, but at least he understood. He was fair, and he didn't discriminate; it took Argwey back to the day Larkh saved him from the gallows in the city of Aiedar on the island of Anjeania.

"Krallan!" Larkh hollered. "Set a course to follow Ardeltaniah's southern coastline!"

"Captain?" Krallan enquired, eyeing him suspiciously.

"Argwey informs me there's a shortcut we should be able to use so we can bypass the rest of the trouble Kradelow has set up for us," Larkh smiled, restraining his aggravation. Krallan shot him a puzzled look.

"Why didn't he—"

"Say so before?" Larkh cut in, shrugging. "My guess is he had his reasons as one of the Cerenyr; I'll talk to him later about it." The quartermaster pursed his lips, glancing at Argwey from the corner of his eye.

"What are we looking for?"

Larkh scanned the jagged coastline off the port side of the ship. "He said the entrance is almost directly east of Pointer Isle where the land protrudes like a hook or a beak," he replied dubiously. "I suppose we'll know it when we see it, though the channel itself is apparently hidden with the use of glámar. My guess is we'll be headin' into Nays territories, or somethin' of the like. The north of the Sendero de Mercader is full of it apparently. The Nays do like to keep to themselves. We'll follow the coast an' hope we can slip through before the man-o-war and brigs know what's happened."

"What about the *Ghost Leviathan*?" Krallan reminded him.

"Albharenos..." Larkh reflected on the legend of the white leviathan, eyes narrowing. "Aye, he's said to guard the misty waters north of the Isles of Cerendiyll. I doubt a creature of his size would be able to fit in this channel we're headin' into though, an' we intend to head east, not west. We know for certain there's trouble ahead at the Mabriltar Strait, but we don't know that he'll bother us even if we did find ourselves in those waters. I've not heard any reports lately of any ships havin' been attacked for enterin' the area."

"Tha's 'cause none go there except the folk who live there!" Krallan protested. "The legends say the monster is Ardeltaniah's southern sentinel."

"Well, a fight with a giant sea serpent sounds like it'd make a good legend," Larkh said dryly. "Nevertheless it's the lesser of two evils as far as I'm concerned."

"Careful Cap'n, you're startin' to sound just a bit mad," Krallan sighed, giving Larkh a pointed look. "If that beast is real then—"

"Since when have I ever been completely sane, Krallan?" Larkh shrugged, flashing Krallan a wry smile.

"True enough," Krallan yielded, sighing and rolling his eyes, reconciling himself to his fate in remembrance of the number of foolhardy voyages he and Larkh had already been through together. Turning his attention to the helmsman, he gave his order; "twenty degrees to port; we're changin' course; seems Argwey's given us a way out o' this mess – we hope."

"Aye sir," said the helmsman, giving them both a dubious look. Larkh winked at him; the man was a long-serving member of the crew, and he too knew the measure of his captain's daring lust for adventure.

Arcaydia's clothes and hair were spattered with blood from assisting Thurne with the injured men in the sickbay. Her heart was still racing, and the roar of cannon-fire persistently thrummed in her ears even long after it had ended. She wasn't sure how long it would take for her to calm down after the battle with the *Allendrias*, but it had already been about an hour.

She sat, quietly staring at her quaking hands. If she was going to spend any length of time on board a ship, she knew she was just going to have to get used to it. It was a good thing *Greshendier's* timbers were strengthened; a lot more damage would've been done if that hadn't been the case, and as a consequence, a lot more casualties. It was one thing seeing Melkhar ruthlessly taking her foes apart, but it was quite another being in the midst of any kind of barbaric chaos.

Zehn sat across from her, his face covered by a bloody cloth he held to the side of his head. When the barrage of the *Allendrias'* broadside pounded *Greshendier's* hull, he'd fallen against one of the bulkheads, bashing his head and slicing a gash open on the left side of his face from forehead to ear as he went down. Thurne had stitched him up, but it was no surprise that the mercenary was suffering from a merciless headache. Much to Arcaydia's surprise, Zehn had willingly assisted the injured men as they came in; even when it had meant fighting to restrain them while the surgeon did his work. Looking up, she saw Thurne approaching.

"You two should go get cleaned up," Thurne told them, breaking the silence. "Many thanks for the help; s'appreciated." He dropped two buckets beside Zehn and threw in two cloths. Turning away from them, he added; "you'll have to get some rope an' lower the buckets into the water. Sadly we don't have any salthen crystals on hand to purify the seawater right now. Damned expensive things."

"You don't need any more help?" Arcaydia asked, glancing around the room. The floor and tables were slick with blood, along with Thurne's surgical utensils. The surgeon shook his head.

"Nah lass," he said. "All the livin' are now accounted for, an' my usual assistant's gone to get some water an' scrubbing brushes already. Go sort yourself out. I expect the captain'll want a word sooner or later anyway."

Groaning, Zehn rose, steadying himself against the nearest bulkhead. Arcaydia jumped to her feet, motioning to assist him, only to be waved off.

"I'll be fine," he grimaced, "though I'd appreciate it if you'd carry the buckets up for us. I'm starting to feel sick again, and this headache is making it worse." He stumbled out of the sickbay toward the nearest hatch leading out on to the weather deck. Sighing, Arcaydia watched him go.

"You alright lass?" Thurne queried.

"I'm alright," Arcaydia responded quietly, picking up the buckets. "It looks like he doesn't know who he is anymore either." The surgeon harrumphed.

"That *elite* mercenary doesn't know who he is now 'cause his eyes've been opened a bit, an' the truth is startin' to get to 'im." Thurne set to work cleaning the sickbay floor. "If anyone around 'ere knows what it's really like not to know who he is, it's the captain."

Arcaydia stared after him, questions suddenly buzzing around in her mind like frantic, trapped insects. She opened her mouth to speak, but it was clear the surgeon was done talking. With a puzzled expression, she turned and made her way out on to deck.

II
Sendero de Mercader

Sweeping his hat from his head, Larkh bowed graciously to Mey who stood on the bow of the *Duquesa de Estrellas*, before striding away to join Arcaydia and Zehn at the starboard capping rail, doing a poor job of hiding a satisfied smile.

"Not feelin' well again I see," he remarked, stretching his arms over his head. He leaned against the rail, watching the white froth of the waves rebounding off the ship's hull, averting his gaze while Zehn threw up noisily over the side.

"Why the hell do you care?" Zehn croaked. "I was below deck.....where you wanted me, an' if you haven't noticed I took a nasty knock to the head helpin' your damn crew."

"An' it's very much appreciated," Larkh returned levelly. He glanced at Arcaydia, who was still cleaning blood off her face and arms. Pushing off the rail he turned toward the forecastle where Argwey stood waiting. "We'll turn north into a hidden channel shortly, I hope."

Arcaydia dropped the cloth back into the bucket. "A hidden channel?" she asked, giving him a quizzical look.

"Aye," Larkh confirmed, "seems there's a channel hidden by some sort of Nays or elven glámar Argwey's known about for a long time. He's from Cerendiyll after all; the city of Eldoviir on the island of Gaieah to be precise."

"But that would mean you'd be heading into Nays lands!" Arcaydia blurted. "Aye, that's also true," Larkh admitted, "but it'll avoid a lot of damage to my crew an' my ship. There're three pirate hunting brigs out there, an' another man-o-war. I was ready to engage the brigs in battle earlier, but now this option has arisen, an' forgive me for sayin' so but I don't give a fuck whether the Nays or the Cerenyr have a problem with it."

Arcaydia felt her stomach turn to ice. She fought the urge to warn him about what might happen, but kept her mouth shut, realising she'd been the one to betray Nays secrets to a pirate. Picking up her bucket, she slung the bloody water over the side and began to lower it into the sea again. *'Best let that one go,'* she told herself. *'I won't exactly be in their good books myself.'*

Stepping up behind Larkh, Larsan snatched his hat and placed it down on his own head, though he found it slightly too tight. "I've always wanted to go to Ardeltaniah," he said, attempting to wedge the hat over the width of his skull. "I hear the spirits there are good." Larkh snatched the hat back and held it tightly like it were a priceless family heirloom. Wordlessly, he placed it back upon his own head and glanced down toward the bow.

"You break it, you buy me a new one," he growled. "Besides Laz, those voices you hear tell you the spirits are good everywhere." Larsan gave a snort of amusement and wandered down the length of the ship to join Argwey.

Lacing his fingers and flexing them, Larkh rested his back against the rail and took a deep breath. "Havin' fun yet?" he asked, knowing full well the reaction he was going to get. The look in Zehn's eyes as he glared back at him might have been dangerous were the man not feeling like a warmed up corpse – and looking like one for that matter.

"I suppose you're finding this funny," Zehn groaned.

Larkh's brow perked up. "I'd say I find your sufferin' quite satisfyin'," he admitted, "but not funny. Most sailors experience seasickness either a little or a lot, an' I'm no exception. In that regard, I actually sympathise."

"You're kidding me? It's hard to believe someone like you would—" he leaned over the side and retched again.

"We feel tired, we sleep; we feel hungry, we eat; we fall, an' we damn well get back up again," Larkh frowned. He turned to face the ocean again. "We all function the same way, Zehn. No man or woman who steps on board a ship is exempt from the possibility of succumbin' to it. It disturbs our natural balance, an' some are luckier than others. I still fall victim to it every once in a while."

"Are you trying to console me?"

"Hah! No."

"Then why are you—"

"Call it a lesson. We ain't so different from you."

Larkh whirled around and made his way toward the forecastle, leaving Zehn speechless. The mercenary wore such a bemused expression that Arcaydia, still standing nearby, had to turn away to hide her amusement.

For the remainder of the afternoon they followed Ardeltaniah's southern coastline as Larkh took them eastward. The *Duquesa de Estrellas* followed in their wake. During that time, Larkh took the opportunity to visit Laisner in the sickbay. Arcaydia joined him, if only to watch and listen while the loyal crewmember reminded his captain of a time when he had been hit. He murmured something about how they'd not been in possession of any laudanum at the time and how he'd barely been able to stand the screams as the surgeon searched desperately for the bullet.

"I don't know what kind o' strength ye possess Cap'n," Laisner had groaned, "but that weren't a light wound. I was there y'know. Thurne had quite bit o' trouble gettin' that damn thing out o' ye. Seems like yer guts are made of steel or somethin'." He winced.

Larkh stared despondently down at the deck of the sickbay all the while Laisner spoke before meeting the man's gaze and finally speaking up; "I probably should've died that day if I were any normal run of the mill lad," he mused, "but—"

"I know, I know," Laisner smiled. "You ain't like the rest of us 'ere. There's always been somethin' about ye, but I still can't pin what. Doesn't mean I can't take a bullet for my cap'n though does it?"

"Laisner, you're a fool," Larkh chuckled. "I'm thankful, an' glad to see you still alive."

III
The Veiled Channel

Apparently, the hidden channel Argwey had spoken of was just ahead. Zehn scanned the horizon for anything unusual, but saw nothing useful. All he saw were the sharp, serrated cliffs of a sealed continent.

Larkh was supervising the helmsman while Krallan and Argwey mustered the crew ready for bracing the yards to port as the channel wasn't just narrow, it was as jagged as the coast that lay in front of him, as if a giant beast had ripped a scar across the land with its claws. They would have to brace the yards back and forth, trimming the sails as and when necessary.

On Larkh's orders, nobody was to sleep a wink until they were at anchor somewhere safe, or back out on the open sea. When called, Zehn too was instructed to assist in the manoeuvres. As for what was to be done at nightfall when visibility would be diminished, he wasn't sure.

He noticed Arcaydia making her way out on to the deck using the hatch next to the ship's forecastle. She approached Larsan, who stood by the starboard bow staring up in awe at the colossal Pharos of Tathynars to the south, a sight Zehn had seen almost every day while growing up in Faltainyr Demura's capital city, Adner. It was a glimpse into the enigmatic history of the Nays and their phenomenal architectural endeavours, but Zehn's heart lay elsewhere as he followed their gaze, trailing upwards to the lofty spire at its peak. Never did he expect to see the day he'd come to sail on board a pirate ship.

Memories of his father's stringent beliefs all criminals deserved death flooded his mind as the pharos loomed over the ship, a brisk crosswind rattling through the rigging like a prisoner shaking the chains that bound him to a cell wall. He realised there were some prisoners in those exact circumstances who might have been starving, and so desperate for a meal they'd resorted to theft. *'Does someone like that deserve death, father? Really?'*

"Argwey!" he heard Larkh shout from astern. The young captain's voice certainly carried well across the full length of the ship. "When you're ready!" Argwey flinched at the sound of his captain's voice, every muscle in his body tensing. He rubbed his forehead and took a deep breath.

"Em Argwey Fal Ceren, Cerendiyll Prionas hwen." [33] The bosun spoke loudly and clearly in the language of the Cerenyr, his voice focussed toward the land.

A moment later, a monumental white arch unveiled itself from the base up. An enormous statue of a dragon was revealed, perching on its apex, wings spread wide and snarling mouth agape. It clutched a red spherical crystal in one clawed hand, holding it up for all to see, while the other was firmly planted on the arch. A glistening watery film rippled in the centre of the arch.

---

[33] I am Argwey Fal Ceren, Prince of Cerendiyll.

"Mie velaidh enwffa Aeithyl, lethayn-se!" [34] Argwey commanded, and with a sound like shattering glass, the jewel in the dragon's raised claw changed colour, slowly morphing to purple before brightening to royal blue. The rippling film quickly dissipated, revealing the channel beyond.

With avid interest twinkling in his eyes, Larkh ran down to the bowsprit to peer through the arch with his spyglass. "You weren't kiddin', that is bloody tight through there," he conceded in serious tones, though his interest in what lay beyond was more than a little obvious. "Still, we've tackled worse, an' I prefer this over our other choice."

"We'll need to keep teams on deck ready to brace at all times," Argwey advised. "Some of the turns in there are sharp, an' bracin'll need to be done very quickly."

Larkh smiled meekly at him. "Then I'll trust you to give the word at the correct times. The riggin' an' canvas is in your care after all." Argwey smiled nervously in return.

On the other side of the ship, Arcaydia swallowed hard as *Greshendier* approached the arch. The ship's masts had little more than a metre's clearance, and her yards approximately three metres either side, but it was a relief nonetheless. If the ship couldn't have fit through the gap, they'd have been getting ready for battle again.

Something else was bothering her though. A strange, uneasy sensation gripped her throat, and began to coil itself around her insides, tightening as it went. She'd read legends about the great white leviathan Albharenos in Atialleia's extensive library, and though they weren't heading west into his territory, she felt herself being drawn westward. According to Melkhar, that leviathan was one of Ardeltaniah's sentinels, and she prayed to Raiyah that whatever this dreadful feeling was, it would go away.

---

[34] My voice in the ether opens the way.

IV
Aynfell

The seikryth orb sat on a pedestal similar to the one in the conference room of the Atialleia's palace, except it was in a much smaller room designed only for a small cluster of people to gather around it. Some existed in rooms like this back in Ardeltaniah for more private conversations; those in much larger rooms were only used for meetings and conferences.

Raeon had requested to stay, insisting as the Second Archmage of the Silver Order, he was still a part of the alliance with the Nays. He was keen to maintain that relationship, but found it difficult when useful Nays glyph codes had been withheld.

"Using a seikryth requires little magica," Raeon told her. "It doesn't affect Silver Mages in that way."

"Of that I am aware, but I am disinclined to bestow you any glyph for the Atialléane Palace, nor any others unless Her Highness the Atiathél wishes it," Melkhar retorted, flashing him a dangerous look. "The system has been abused before; we do not want too much contact from lands beyond Ardeltaniah, which is why there are barriers surrounding the continent. You may stay while I make contact, but if Atiathél Arkkiennah wishes your absence, you will leave." Shivers ran down Raeon's spine at the passive intensity of her stare.

"I understand," he replied reluctantly. Why did he suddenly feel like he was a novice again? He hadn't felt like this since he'd begun his training. Vharik hadn't been his only master, but the other archmages he had studied under were nothing to do with the Order of Silver. At the Archaenen, an individual was obliged to study particular disciplines in magic to become eligible to join certain orders within its walls. There was one man who had always made him nervous, however, and he knew Zehn hated him as well.

Alleran Jorical was bad news, and to make matters worse, he was also one of King Faltain's advisers.

From what he could tell of Melkhar, on the other hand, her loyalty to her homeland was intense, and her dedication to the purpose of her existence was profound. He remembered reading historical texts and legends about her, but all those facts and tales fell short. She was far more terrifying in reality. After witnessing her engage an ancient greater dragon in combat, he was beginning to realise truly how much she and her kind were necessary. There had been something other than malice in her cold, steely eyes though. He sensed a great deal of sorrow lay buried deep in her primordial past, but knew it unwise to speak of it.

"Mirveidr vér'te tsolàiyh," [35] Melkhar chanted before the seikryth, drawing a glyph over a mirror-like disc beneath the base of the blood red seikryth with her index finger. The glyph somewhat resembled an image of the sun; *"revsllaidhir mhaer vesphrévens tsai'te aethyr."* [36]

The glyph manifested in gold on the disc, shimmering once as Melkhar brought her hand over the top of it. Sensing the direction of her energy, the glyph sank into the mirror, and once every third second the seikryth resonated with a sound likened to the single ring of a tiny bell.

Raeon moved to stand beside the Kaesan'Drahknyr as the call was answered within five chimes. Mesmerised by the Atiathél's beauty when her image appeared, he took a long, rigid breath. He bowed his head respectfully while Melkhar saluted by bringing her right hand to rest on the left side of her chest. She made a brief query in Daeihn, the language of the Nays, and turned to him briefly when she had her answer. "Did you understand?" she asked.

"Only some of it," Raeon admitted.

"You may stay for this meeting, but you may speak only if spoken to," Melkhar instructed. "You may not understand the full extent of our conversation, but I will

---

[35] Mirror of the sun
[36] reflect my presence through the ether.

432

relay what is necessary. How much of our language do you understand?"

Raeon stiffened. "I know enough to get by, and I have studied it in texts for many years, but I would not be so bold as to say I could read or speak it fluently," he replied nervously. Melkhar gave a subtle nod, and turned back to Arkkiennah.

"Aeu'te aeghavéadh drahkouen Rahntamein heuas vahreatna," she began. *"Éyn al'hest seiroçedh, tseit Zerrçainne enytreillandi mhét neghara."* [37]

Raeon understood enough to know the bulk of the conversation was about how Melkhar had fought the dragon known as Rahntamein. She relayed to Atiathél Arkkiennah that the dragon had retreated, and she had almost succeeded in defeating him before Zerrçainne had intervened yet again.

He knew the name all too well. It was the name of the sorceress he'd encountered sixteen years ago when he'd followed Vharik and stowed away on the same ship as Zehn. The old sage had claimed he had no way of contacting the Nays over the matter; a truth he now understood some of the reasons for, but still disagreed with. If the Nays had only given him a means to contact them, they might have been able to stop Zerrçainne years ago. Melkhar told him they wanted to restrict contact, not cut it off entirely, but she and the other Kaesan'Drahknyr had only recently been awakened. Either way, it wasn't going to change anything; those years were long gone now. He looked up, watching and listening as the discussion progressed entirely in Daeihn.

"You are sending Zairen to Aynfell?" Melkhar enquired. "What purpose would his presence here serve?"

"First you'll be supplied with fresh clothing," Arkkiennah replied. "My guess is your specialised clothing was either destroyed in the battle with the dragon, or been

---

[37] The renegade dragon Rahntamein has retreated. I almost succeeded, but Zerrçainne intervened yet again.

left behind in Almadeira. Secondly, I must inform you Zairen will be stationed in Aynfell in the short term to assist the Archaenen in reinforcing its defences, including the city. Furthermore, Galétahr Dreysdan has already updated me on military movements in Adengeld; her army is amassing for war on Faltainyr Demura, and their magi-academy, the Magicista Akadema has been developing new archana weaponry, with which only we may be able to contend."

"We are to intervene further then?" Melkhar enquired, her stoicism unwavering.

"Not directly, but there are a few strings we can pull behind the scenes for now," Arkkiennah replied. "The longer we can keep a low profile the better."

Melkhar folded her arms, frowning thoughtfully. "I've already been seen, Your Highness, what do you plan on— no, surely can't mean to—"

"Adel Nalaueii will see to the problem," the Atiathél assured her. "As the Adel of wisdom, logic and philosophy, she will do only what is necessary to blot out your presence in the affair. Were Lesos to perform the task, as you well know, we could be subject to more unfavourable consequences."

"Understood."

"You have more than one mission Melkhar, and I would speak to you in person on how we will move forward now our plans have been manipulated by your cousin. Kalthis is searching for the new Mindseer Oracle, so when Zairen arrives, return to Atialleia as soon as possible." The Kaesan'Drahknyr nodded once, saluting again.

Arkkiennah regarded Melkhar knowingly, suggesting she knew something Raeon did not. The silver mage suddenly felt uneasy. Was this simply confidential information, or was there something else to it? Either way, more of her kind were on their way. Reluctantly, he accepted the fact without them there would be no hope of saving the Archaenen, or Aynfell, or perhaps even all of Faltainyr Demura. What was most worrisome was the talk of Adengeld developing new archana weaponry. *'Gods, are we as powerless as this?'*

CHAPTER 27

I
Saldour

The *Allendrias* was listing badly, her port side sagging into the water as she was towed into Saldour's harbour behind the *Solarias*; another elite ship-of-the-line like the *Greshendier*. It had been patrolling the entrance to the Ene Canal in case Larkh had attempted to flee through there. Reports had already been made to the shipyard that the *Allendrias'* rudder was shattered and her broadsides a splintering mess. Despite the mainmast having not fallen, it had sustained enough damage for it to need replacing. Once she was secured in the dry dock, Admiral Wendale and the survivors of his crew disembarked.

Traven took a good look at the harbour as he descended the steps on to the quayside, though his vision was somewhat blurred still from the blow to his head. Despite Adner being Faltainyr Demura's capital city, Saldour, with its sprawling harbour, was unquestionably its capital port, boasting the largest naval dockyard on the continent with enormous sea walls and huge, tiered plazas stretching all the way up to the top of the cliff and beyond. Every street and building was constructed from the purest whitestone; its grandeur kept untainted with regular maintenance overseen by the Archaenen.

A spear of icy dread lanced into his gut at the sight of the Aurentai assassin waiting for him, leaning against the wall outside The Siren, a dockside tavern built into the base of the cliff.

"What went wrong, Admiral?" Leyal asked, nodding

toward the shattered mess of the Allendrias' hull before Traven could even step on to the quay.

Traven clenched his jaw, careful not to let his temper get the better of him. "Savaldor is a very talented young man, as you can see," he replied amicably, gritting his teeth as he attempted to adjust the sling supporting his left arm. "That would be what happened. Oh! And as he departed, a brig followed him."

Leyal considered the admiral's words thoughtfully; then turned and laid a hand on the man's shoulder, gesturing forward. "Did you perchance see the name of this brig?" he enquired while they walked. Traven moved his hand to scratch the side of his head, but thought better of it. Merely touching the bandage around his skull was painful enough. He was lucky not to have suffered a concussion, and luckier still not to have broken any bones.

"I believe it was the *Duquesa de Estrellas*," Traven winced, gingerly rubbing at his head instead. "I believe I've seen that ship before; it's a registered merchant vessel."

Leyal smiled broadly. *'Perhaps the duke's plan for me to meet this man wasn't such a bad idea after all.'* "Oh is it now?" The assassin's face brightened, suddenly intrigued. "So the Savaldor bastard has a friend who is supposedly a 'merchant' now does he? What do you think of that Admiral?"

"They're most definitely smugglers," said Traven, ignoring the insult directed at his friend's son.

"I think so too," Leyal agreed. "I think there's something to be done in tracking this ship down and see if we can't give Savaldor a hand in making a few tough decisions," he added with a cruel smile. "What I'd like to know is, how in the world did he get past the hunter brigs and your other elite ship? What was it called, the *Madranier*?"

Traven shook his head. "I'm afraid I don't know anything more," he replied honestly, shrugging. "Why, did something happen?"

"Well," said Leyal, considering his next words carefully, "a contact of mine within the *Noctae Venatora* is on board one of those brigs – though I won't say who – and she tells me the *Greshendier* turned north at the Pharos of Tathynars, and vanished beyond a great stone arch. After investigating the area, no such arch was to be found."

The dubious – or perhaps perplexed – look on the admiral's face told Leyal the man was baffled, and wasn't going to be any help on the matter. At least that eliminated him as an accomplice. He gave Traven a soft pat on the back. "My guess is he's got someone who knows their glámar magic on board, and they knew there was a hidden exit there," he added. "There's nothing we can do about it at the moment, but that doesn't mean we give up. I don't think your duke would want us to give up, would he?"

"You certainly know the way his mind works," Traven commented, cautious not to say anything that might give Duke Kradelow a reason to question his loyalty. After all, his daughter's life was at stake.

Leyal simpered. "If a man wishes to rule anything, he should make sure he knows how to rule himself first," the assassin pointed out as they walked slowly along the quayside. "Duke Kradelow knows what he wants, and he'll stop at nothing to get it. If he really wants Savaldor neutralised, and we both know he's obsessive about it, he will either succeed or die trying. I wonder which it'll be. Nevertheless, he is an exceedingly patient man, though I fear that patience is now wearing thin."

"Get to the point," Traven snapped, his own patience thinning.

Leyal shrugged. "Your daughter was asking about you," he said. "I informed her you'd be docking in Saldour shortly."

Traven frowned. *'Why is he bringing my daughter into this?'* he wondered. *'If he intends to use her to gain an advantage over Larkh I swear I'll...'* "What has this got to do with my daughter?" he demanded.

"I know you disapprove, Traven, but the duke sent word to her you were going to be doing battle with her dear childhood friend out there," Leyal warned him. "It's understandable, don't you think, that she would be asking after you? I went to your manor to make sure she was safe, and while she pestered me to tag along, I persuaded her to stay home and wait until I returned with you."

Traven took in a deep breath and nodded. "Thank you, I'm glad she agreed to wait," the admiral replied.

"Now," Leyal said, coming to a halt and gesturing to a carriage in front of him, "I will finally get to the point once we're inside." Giving Leyal a wary glance out of the corner of his eye, the admiral stepped inside.

The carriage crossed the main city plaza and turned west, rolling around a path sweeping around the edge of the city and climbing a gentle paved slope that had been sculpted out of the cliff-face. Saldour's tiers were accessed via large steps with ramps positioned in-between for small carts, too narrow for carriages.

Leyal followed up by bringing matters into discussion to ensure Traven's hands remained tied for the sake of his family. Deep in his heart, however, Traven knew he wouldn't be able to lie to himself till the end of his days. King Jaredh was failing his people, having undermined the court in his endeavours to increase his own authority, and jeopardising his allegiance with Adengeld by denying its people access to the continent's greatest academies and increasing prices on materials only found in Faltainyr Demura, which had ultimately earned Ameldar's hatred. It was no wonder King Ameldar DeaCathra now sought revenge by conquest.

What Traven didn't agree with was selling out the country to Adengeld from under Jaredh's nose. It would be better to replace him with his son, which made him question why Duke Kradelow was so determined to give the crown to Ameldar. He followed Kradelow's orders only to keep his family safe, especially Alirene, his daughter.

Leyal then asked about what the encounter had been like; he wanted to know every minute detail Traven could remember of it. Reluctantly, Traven told him of how the young man's resolve had led to his determination to succeed. He'd seen much of Halven Savaldor in him, but with much greater aptitude. He made it clear to the assassin, Larkh's intelligence was well above average, and his crew were so well trained he'd had them open all the gun ports in a synchronised pattern.

"So what you're saying Admiral, is that he was effectively toying with you?" Leyal enquired, a crude smile crossing his face.

Traven pursed his lips. "He was certainly showing off; that much was obvious," he shrugged, refusing to play the assassin's game. "I suppose he might have been; he's certainly very confident in his own abilities, and those of his crew and ship."

"And arrogant," Leyal sniffed. "I ran into him in Almadeira. I was about to duel with him when a mercenary showed up claiming to have been hunting him for some time with an extended contract granted by the Hunters' Guild. Savaldor fled at that moment, and we pursued him together. What I didn't expect was for the mercenary to be in league with the pirate, and escape with him on the ship."

Traven kept his mouth shut on this occasion. After what he'd been put through, he was far from surprised at the kind of attitude Larkh had adopted. He wasn't going to tell Leyal that though, and he certainly wasn't going to tell him he'd briefly exchanged words with Larkh that included a message to Alirene. It was the mention of the mercenary that got his mind racing.

"Did the mercenary give you his name?" Traven asked, puzzled.

Leyal shook his head. "No. He looked like any ordinary sellsword wearing leather gear not unlike my own. He had a shock of wavy brown hair held back by a purple-striped bandana though. It was my intention to settle business with him once Savaldor was caught; damned mercenary seemed to think he'd get his bounty from the guild and then some from the duke, or so I was led to believe. The *Noctae Venatora* won't be happy with me for having been so careless, but you understand, we rarely work out in the open like this."

Traven's brow furrowed in thought. "I think," he said, still mulling the thought over, "you might have been dealing with an elite mercenary who wasn't wearing his uniform."

"One of King Jaredh's Elite Mercenary Guard?" Leyal enquired, his funnel-shaped ears pricking up. "You think he might have been undercover?"

"Members of the EMG are usually required to wear their uniforms to be distinguishable from ordinary mercenaries, which tends to earn them a fair amount of contempt considering they tend to get the better paid jobs," Traven explained; "however, under certain circumstances they are permitted to go undercover if they feel the circumstances require it. I believe the man you crossed paths with was none other than Zehn Kahner; his appearance and skills are quite distinct."

Leyal's eyes flashed with intrigue. "I believe I have heard of him," he said with avid interest. "He would be the son of Rajan Kahner, correct?" Reluctantly, Traven nodded. The assassin leaned back, an impish grin curling the corners of his lips. "Well now, this gets even more interesting the more I hear!"

Traven felt as though he'd just been knifed in the gut, and the blade was being wrenched. He was serving the duke's hired assassin as an accomplice against his will, and there was nothing he could do about it, at least not for now. Larkh's message still rang clear in his mind; "tell Liri this; *'faint memories may drift on a distant breeze, but true friendship is forged from ancient stone, and there it will remain.'* She'll know what it means."

He intended to pass the message on, but it would have to be when he and Alirene were well and truly alone.

II
Aynfell

Most of the damage was in the commercial and academic districts in Aynfell. Melkhar had at least managed to keep Rahntamein's attention within those areas while the magi of the Archaenen warded off the residential districts as best they could. Many survivors despondently picked through rubble and smouldering debris for lost possessions, wares and resources, while families gathered to mourn their losses. Following a public meeting, all missing individuals were presumed dead, for the charred remains of the dragon's victims were unidentifiable.

The people now clamoured outside the Archaenen demanding answers. Raeon and the other Archmages were responsible for quietening the crowd and sending them on their way. Raeon entered the building; intent on making his way outside to meet with the people of Aynfell, only to be blocked by his most hated mentor, Alleran Jorical.

Jorical was a tall, gangly man with high cheekbones, a thin face and greying mousy brown hair. He wore a slate grey set of robes with a bluish tint embroidered in gold. Faltainyr Demura's white osprey insignia was pinned at his left shoulder, marking him as a member of King Jaredh's Royal Council. He held a gnarled black staff in his right hand with a polished solneis crystal set with gold perched at the top.

"I'll deal with them," he said coldly, his deep, nasally voice carrying tones of disdain. Pushing his way past Raeon, he made his way through the Archaenen's main block and out toward the tall black gates at the end of the charred boulevard, once lined with healthy trees. Raeon agreed Jorical might be better suited to calming the masses. He was, after all, one of the first-ranking archmages, while Raeon belonged to the second rank.

The arguing and gossiping of the city folk ceased as soon as the older man approached the gates. "People of Aynfell," Alleran spoke soundly, "I am the Archaenen's First Archmage in the Order of Ash. We are prepared to answer what questions we can about events relating to the dragon's attack, but we ask that you remain calm while survivors are tended and the city cleared of rubble and debris."

"To the hells with being calm!" shouted one man, a scholar from Aynfell's Royal Library. "I've not just lost all the books that were in my office, I've lost friends and family to that abomination, and I want to know who, or *what* was fighting the damned beast!"

"That's right, we have a right to know who that was!" someone else shouted from further back. "Are the legends of the Drahknyr true?" another asked.

"I definitely saw something shaped like a person with huge feathered wings as I fled into the catacombs!" a young woman called out.

"Whatever or whoever it was, they failed to defend the city!" an older man snapped. "Why did they have to interfere anyway!?" a young man sneered. "We should protect our own. If those legends are true, I say to the hells with them. They have no right to meddle in our affairs."

"Magic as tremendous as what the Nays possess should not be allowed to exist! It's too powerful!" the young man's father added.

"Are you an idiot? How would you stop a dragon without it?" a scholar challenged.

"How dare you!" the father snapped. "Where there's a will there's a way, weren't you ever told that?"

"ENOUGH!" Jorical roared. "We will discuss this amicably like reasonable folk, is that understood?" The crowd fell into awkward silence as the First Archmage of

Ash continued to speak.

Melkhar stood in the charred central gardens of the Archaenen with her arms folded, her towering wings stretching high over her head. Her expression remained impassive, but Raeon saw the fury burning in her eyes. She wasn't even looking in his direction, but he still felt as though he ought to fall to his knees and beg for his life. He stood at her side, his dark brown hair tied back neatly, his long fringe tidily swept to one side. Despite the gardens being out of view of the public, they were still close enough to hear the people of the city shouting at Jorical.

The Atiathél had explained Adel Nalaueii would distil the memories of the city folk, along with strict instructions no-one was to leave the city until after the deed was done, which would follow shortly after Zairen's imminent arrival. Anyone having left the city before those instructions had been given would be tracked down by the Astral Overseer, Lésos Taeren.

Raeon knew Melkhar had been dubious as to whether or not it was such a good idea, but it was only a temporary measure. The concern was it would give the people more reason to distrust the Nays. Many of them were already rejecting her intervention, though if it had not been for her, Aynfell would likely have been completely destroyed.

The people would remember the dragon after the Adel had suppressed their memories, but it would still mean the Archaenen would have a lot of explaining to do. Atiathél Arkkiennah reassured Melkhar the distillation would be relevant only to her own participation, depending on how many civilians had witnessed her engaging Rahntamein in combat. She would be remembered little more than a vague image in a fragmented dream.

A thin veil of mist slowly descended from the heavens as the skies began to cloud over. The choice to send Zairen had been a good one, for he shared the title of Ghost with the great white leviathan Albharenos who dwelt in the waters in the northern area of the Sendero de Mercader. Like the leviathan, he had the ability to merge with mist and fog, becoming almost invisible. It was similar to Melkhar's own ability where she would meld with darkness. There was no better way of making a subtle entrance, though from where the sudden mist appeared would undoubtedly be called into question; a story about an atmospheric experiment would sort that one out.

Zairen Elaiythé descended from the skies into the central gardens, wings spread and arched to catch the wind like a parachute. As he planted both feet on the ground, the fog slowly began to lift, and his ghostly glámar vanished. He brought his right palm over his left shoulder sharply and bowed his head in salute. Melkhar followed by returning the gesture in kind.

Raeon remembered learning about this in his training; the Drahknyr were only able to use basic forms of glámar, masking aspects such as the black lines framing their eyes, the shape of their ears, the colour of their skin if necessary, and melding with major elements for the purpose of stealth. Elves, on the other hand, could use more advanced forms of glámar, but only for short bursts of time. Keeping it up for several hours was easy enough, but it was necessary to take a rest in-between should there be a need for its continued use.

"E'verkéne Melkhar," [38] Zairen greeted her. His resonant voice was strong, yet soft and alluring. *"Ye'n arth laekhilna whiale."* [39]

"Yíhde, kharun ye'n," Melkhar replied. *"Éyn yaerst kalanétha nhaisa."* [40]

Zairen's platinum-blond hair fluttered about his shoulders in the faint breeze like a cluster of feathers. His ivory complexion even made him look like a ghost in the pearlescent morning light. Raeon noticed there was an

---

[38] Greetings
[39] You are looking well.
[40] Yes, thank you. I just needed rest.

unmistakeable balanced energy flowing between the two; a mutual understanding few could hope to make sense of. They were also of matching height, but while Zairen's energy was warm and impartial, Melkhar's was icy and foreboding. Nevertheless, they gazed at one another with intimate familiarity. Raeon wondered if the other Kaesan'Drahknyr shared such harmony, for here there was definitely a rare kind of bond.

Melkhar regarded him with the same stony expression, but she bowed her head respectfully in turn. Zairen smiled knowingly. He was always able to sense her tension despite her passive, unfeeling demeanour. There was a conflict in her so strong that one day, he was sure the threads of control would snap, and he wouldn't blame her. He was surprised it hadn't happened thousands of years in the past.

Alleran was trapped rebuking the people's arguments for longer than anticipated. He listened to them, taking in all they had to say, or at least he made it appear that way. Some desired to meet their saviour in person to thank her, but many more were resentful and angry. Raeon understood all too well why these people didn't want to rely on a higher race to protect them. They wanted to remain independent, feeling races such as the Nays wished only to control and rule them as though they were children incapable of defending themselves. The facts, however, were much more complicated. Mortals were never meant to understand the higher truths of the world, nor contend with their complexities.

It had been proven from one generation to the next that mortals could not hope to engage a greater dragon and survive. A lesser dragon could be taken down by humans, but it took an army to accomplish such a task, and hundreds if not thousands would die in the process. Teams of two or three Drahknyr could bring down a lesser dragon turned rogue, but for a beast like Rahntamein, it could take several, or perhaps, a single Kaesan'Drahknyr.

Alleran Jorical called for silence. "I think that is quite enough," he said, spreading his arms. "Remember, people of Aynfell, you are not equipped with the expertise or gifted with the skill or magica to fight a dragon such as the one that attacked this city." He paused, scanning their faces.

"Heed my words," the archmage continued, "the Archaenen did its best to shelter you and fight the dragon on your behalf last night. The winged being some of you saw was a memory from aeons past when the Drahknyr played a predominant role across all of Aeldynn. Cities and landscapes may hold ancestral memories should significant events take place, and sometimes those memories can be witnessed, not unlike the recollection of a dream. This is not the first time Aynfell has been attacked; it was attacked long before it was even called Aynfell. The dragon's attack was a warning."

The crowd looked puzzled. "A warning against what?" a middle-aged woman called.

"Rubbish! I know what I saw!" the young man who'd spoken earlier snapped, turning on his heel, stamping away irritably. "The truth will out..." As the congregation began to murmur and discuss the archmage's words, Alleran Jorical interrupted again.

"People of Aynfell," he said, "do not be troubled. We will seek help for the city, and call for aid in re-building the damaged and the destroyed. Do what you can to help one another; there is much for the Archaenen to organise and implement at this time, so we will be grateful for your patience." He paused for a moment to think, and then continued once more. "The magi of the Archaenen will assist in any way we possibly can, just as we did our best to minimise the destruction and saved as many lives as we could. Had we been better prepared, we might have been able to save everyone. We are not the Nays, and we are certainly not the Drahknyr, but we do our best to learn from what they have left us so that we may continue to build on our knowledge to protect our people. Most of you know this already, and I thank you for your understanding and support. Healers will be tending to the wounded shortly."

As Jorical finished his speech, Melkhar turned from the charred remains of the Archaenen's garden and dissolved her wings, striding back inside the main building with haste, heading for the library. Zairen flicked a glance in her direction. The senses of the Drahknyr were incredibly keen; both of them could hear the voices of Aynfell's civilians from where they'd been standing. Their callous words were shamefully misspent. Melkhar remembered much, forgot little, and rarely forgave. He understood her all too well; more so than the other Kaesan'Drahknyr, save for Kalthis. On this occasion, however, he sensed the reactions of the townsfolk weren't the primary reason she had chosen to make such a brisk exit.

Melkhar picked up her pace, suddenly curious about the book Zerrçainne had been in possession of when she'd intercepted her battle with Rahntamein. The corridors of the Archaenen were almost devoid of life; most of the students and graduates were at work in their laboratories or engaging in research and developing theories. She pushed open a door set into a tall, arched wooden doorway made of polished oak and black iron, and strode into the great library.

A great vaulted ceiling soared over her, a domed roof at its peak adorned with gold friezes of the Nays, the Drahknyr, and their draconic allies. Vast columns stretched up to the ceiling and numerous tiers were set out along each niche. Quadrangles of tables were arranged in the centre of the hall, and smaller desks were dotted about in each department, with a reception to the right of the entryway.

At the far side of the room was a door, which she suspected might lead to the rarest as well as the most dangerous books in existence. As she approached, a glyph seal flashed up in front of her. Wasting no time, she hurried over to it. The archivist's attention shifted in her direction as she reached for it. "What do you think you're—"

The archivist, who also served as the chief librarian, felt a shiver race down his spine that sharply turned to ice as Melkhar's merciless eyes fixed on to him. If he didn't know any better, the wisps of grey on the cropped brown hair on top of his head might well have been standing on end. His face was thin like the rest of his body, but it was a shrewd kind of face, telling of a well-educated man.

Melkhar turned her attention back to the glyph, and reached out. The moment her hand touched the glyph, it glowed, resonated once, and faded. The door clicked open. When a pair of bells either side of the door began to ring, the archivist quickly flipped a switch both sides.

"How is it that you have not reported the loss of one of your most treasured books?" Melkhar asked in icy tones.

"I-I have n-no idea what you are talking about," the archivist stammered. Despite the shakiness in his voice, he was otherwise an eloquent and well-spoken man. His fear was painfully obvious, and all in the room now stared at them. "What book are you referring to?"

Melkhar pushed the door open and stepped inside the sealed room. "Do you perchance carry an intact copy of the Taecade Medo?" she enquired, glancing back and forth across the chamber at the few dozen bookshelves along with a series of decorative glass cabinets lined up alongside one another.

"Y-yes we do have a copy," said the archivist. "That one was kept in a small wooden chest, also locked with a glyph. I assure you nobody has been in here."

"That you are aware of," Melkhar added, shooting him another frosty glare. "Where is that chest?"

"It's in the locked cabinet at the back of the room," he told her. "Let me fetch the key." He shuffled around to the desk at the back of the room and fumbled in one of the drawers until he drew out a key and proceeded to the cabinet in question. "By the way, I am Tanshel, in case you need to refer to me by name."

"What has suddenly brought about this investigation?" he asked worriedly. "No-one but myself and my assistant have keys to this library, for I am also the librarian. The facility is also locked with a glyph when neither of us is around, and the pass code is changed every week. The glyph for this restricted area is changed every day. Lessons were cancelled yesterday and this place was locked down the night of the dragon's attack. There is always someone in authority in here when the place is open."

"No-one guards the door?"

"There has never been a need to post a sentry on the door; if anyone tries to enter without the proper instruction, the alarm bells beside the doors ring, as you just heard."

Melkhar lifted her chin. *'A clever system, that one,'* she admitted silently. Tanshel's answer was adequate enough; even if the library had been guarded, Zerrçainne would have silenced or disposed of them before they could blink. She might have been able to teleport inside the library, but considering glyph seals encased the surrounding area, she would have set off the alarm bells merely by passing the barrier. Unless she knew how to dispel the glyphs using the methods by which they were set up, there was only one other way she could have gained access. Someone must have let her in.

"Please accept my apologies Master Tanshel; mild amnesia sometimes follows for a day or two when we Drahknyr fall unconscious after exceeding our energy limits, especially when not fully restored from their long sleep," Melkhar explained. "The former Galétyr Zerrçainne was in possession of a large tome the night she intercepted my battle with the dragon. She claimed the battle was a welcome distraction, and must have entered the Archaenen, somehow disguising her presence. Breaking through the seals on these doors would prove to be a cinch for her, as it was for me, but unless she knew the proper sequence for dispelling the glyphs, the alarm would have sounded. It can only be that someone let her in."

Tanshel blanched as he laid the chest down on the desk. "I can't think of anyone who could have let her in," he swallowed nervously. Beads of sweat were forming on his brow. "It's still locked," he added, a dubious expression crossing his gaunt features as he examined it.

"Open it," Melkhar ordered, her eyes narrowing on the chest. The chief librarian did as he was told. He dispelled the glyph on the lock, and used another key he procured from the drawer at the desk. The gasp that escaped the man's lips as he lifted the lid told Melkhar all she needed to know.

III
Sherne

Following the coast road south, Duke Kradelow's party approached the edge of the Elkinwood. The option to cut across the north side of the forest to follow the river, which would have meant taking the horses cross country, was dismissed. The ground was far too soft and marshy in places where the Nidhan River flooded after torrential downpours. In the next few days they would reach Almenden, and once plans had been put in place there, they would tie up any loose ends in Newlen Southsea.

Without considering the interests of the men who rode behind him, Jarlen reflected on the troops he'd positioned around Foristead and the surrounding area, wondering whether or not they would really be enough to patrol Lonnfeir's borders. How he was going to persuade Duke Anthwell to join him in his cause was another dubious matter weighing on his mind. If the man had to be silenced, how then would he persuade Sherne's forces to join him?

Lord Verden on the other hand, despite his youth, was likely to be the more difficult of the two to win over. The young man was wise beyond his years, but if Anthwell's loyalty could be won, Verden would find himself outnumbered should he refuse to pledge his allegiance. Just to be cautious, he'd arranged for additional members of the *Noctae Venatora* put in place to deal with any troublemakers. Either way, he would take control of Sherne's forces.

Thinking of troublemakers, he wondered how Leyal's plans were going to finally bring down Captain Savaldor. By now the *Allendrias* should be back in Saldour, and the assassin should be in talks with Admiral Wendale. He was confident word would arrive soon enough. Rather than trusting a courier with such sensitive information, he was using his own men to relay his messages.

It was likely to be at least a month if not more before Ameldar's army arrived, so long as they didn't end up as dragon fodder while crossing the Valley of Daynallar. The development of the new archana was still in progress at the Magicista Akadema the last he'd heard, and he hoped Mahtaio, god of war and government, would look upon the new developments with favour. Numerous alchemists had already been seriously injured, or died as a result of their research for the project, but that was only because they hadn't been careful enough. They knew their experiments were going to be far more dangerous than anything they'd set their minds to before, and hadn't taken the necessary precautions to safeguard themselves against failure.

Looking up at the sky, Kradelow studied the hazy outline of the sun behind a curtain of thickening grey cloud; it was well past its zenith. The cool wind blowing up from the south smelled strongly of rain. Casting his eyes southward, he saw the nebulous gloom of storm clouds gathering in the distance.

"Make camp here!" he ordered his men. "It's already the middle of the afternoon and there's a storm brewing over the Soreiden Sea. I want to be dry inside my tent by the time it arrives."

The resulting sound of the soldiers sighing with relief behind him made Kradelow roll his eyes. And these men were supposed to be seasoned soldiers? He could laugh at them and call them a bunch of girls, though if he did it would only breed contempt; he needed their loyalty. *'Let them have their rest,'* he told himself. *'There will soon come a day when they cannot afford such luxuries until every piece of the puzzle has fallen into place.'*

CHAPTER 28

I
The Veiled Channel

Zehn sat on one of the cannons, a wooden beaker of water in his hands. He was still pale from seasickness, but appeared to be faring better now the rolling of the ship had slowed to a gentle lilting sway in the quiet, sheltered vale. Arcaydia hesitantly made her way over to him and leaned against the rail.

"How are you feeling now?" she asked, brushing aside the cascading blonde waves of her hair; tacky now the salt in the air had seeped into it, and full of tangles – those would be a nightmare to get out later.

"Oh, I ah... I'm better than I was," Zehn stammered, snapping out of his trance. Rubbing his forehead, he looked up. "Argwey gave me a little water to help, and insisted I try chewing on a bit of ginger root."

"That's good," Arcaydia smiled. Her expression became rueful on seeing Zehn's sombre expression while he absent-mindedly watched the landscape rolling by; thick clusters of trees multiplied, rising up high along the sloping banks of the river and up into the hills beyond. "What's wrong?"

"I've been forced to work on a pirate ship under the command of a man I've hunted along these coastlines for longer than I care to recall," he grumbled. "If someone else got the bounty on him that'd be that, but whenever I hear his name mentioned by the Hunters' Guild, I continue my pursuit as per the contract if I've no other pressing job to do. Everything has just—"

"He could have refused Raeon's request you know," Arcaydia pointed out. "He could have just left you back in Almadeira where you might have been killed, but he chose to allow you on board his ship knowing his crew would disapprove, which could have cost him their respect and trust, *and* despite the fact you've been trying to kill him." Suddenly Zehn was lost for words. He looked up to where she stood.

"You know," she continued, "I bumped into him when I was struggling into Almadeira with two sets of luggage. My master had to leave on an errand, and he very kindly gave me a hand with getting the luggage to my room at the inn. He showed me around town, and took me to Marceau's home. That's when we found Marceau had suddenly left town—"

"Marceau..." Zehn's brow creased. "How do you know him?"

"I don't know him, but my master does," Arcaydia told him. "I think she wanted me to train under him; something about the abilities I was supposedly born with. What about you? How do you know him?"

"He was my instructor in swordsmanship at the Kessford Academy, near Senfirth," he replied. "I graduated about four years ago. Who is your master?"

"Ah, I'm not really supp—"

Arcaydia doubled over, a sudden pain seizing her chest. Clutching it tightly, she grabbed the rail with her other hand to steady herself. Zehn jumped up and, taking a hold of her, eased her gently down to the deck.

"Arc! What is it? What's the matter?" he pressed urgently. Arcaydia looked up. The very same golden threads of light she'd seen previously wove about Zehn's spirit, just as she had seen in Larkh, and when the two of them had fought in Almadeira's town square. Reaching for him, she touched his cheek.

"I don't know why—"

A sudden surge of energy sparked between them, and she fell unconscious.

"Arcaydia!"

Larkh emerged on deck to get a view of their heading, but instead rushed to Arcaydia's side as Zehn braced her against his chest. "What happened?" he asked, laying a hand on the young woman's forehead.

Zehn shook his head in dismay. "I-I don't know," he hesitated. "It seemed like she had a pain in her chest, and then when she touched me I felt an electric shock." He stared down anxiously at her unconscious form. "That's when she lost consciousness. It happened moments before you came out."

Frowning, Larkh stood upright. "Keep her there for the moment," he instructed. "For the safety of the ship I must keep my attention fixed on our navigation of this channel, an' we must round the upcomin' turn quickly. If it's as narrow as Argwey says it is, we're in danger of runnin' her aground if we don't keep our wits about us. If she doesn't wake up in a few minutes, take her down to Thurne. Stay with her; you're excused from duty till we know she's alright."

With a hard expression, Larkh turned and began barking orders to his men to prepare the ship for bracing again. Zehn could still hardly believe what he was experiencing; first the dreams, then the so-called trial with Madukeyr on the mountain, and Raeon forcing him to board the *Greshendier*. That, and the number of storms occurring during the past few days in these parts was most unusual. In the summer they were a fairly frequent occurrence, but not like this, and certainly not in the spring. His emotions roiled like those tumultuous skies, especially now he found himself beginning to see the world from an entirely new perspective; and part of him hated it.

~There was a boy with brown hair clambering on board a three-masted ship. He hid amongst the cargo in the ship's

hold, quickly finding barrels of potatoes to squeeze behind. He was small; perhaps ten years old. As the ship swayed back and forth on a tumultuous sea, he was throwing up on the deck soon enough.

Behind him was another boy; he was somewhat older with dark hair cut neatly at the collar, wearing what had once been a white robe. It was now covered with a copious amount of dirt and grime. The older boy's ears were distinctly pointed, though the tips were angled toward the back of his head; so he couldn't be an elf.

Their words were somehow inaudible. The dark-haired boy offered the other something, perhaps it might be something to help with the seasickness? Reluctantly, the offer was accepted, and a question posed. What was he doing there? An answer, and then the same question asked in return. The image flickered.

Next there was an island, lush and green with rolling moorlands, and yet there was a chill wind in the air. Before them was an enormous fortress, its walls blackened as though it had been burned. Numerous foul beasts occupied its walls and the surrounding sky, some of them quite obviously gargoyles. The heavens were dark and grey, and thunder rolled overhead. The boys quietly made their way through the gates and into the courtyard. The boy in the white robes cloaked them with basic glámar to hide them from the vicious beasts that would otherwise tear them limb from limb.

Inside, there was an old man wearing smart red robes decorated with gold embroidery, and a dark-haired man with a trim moustache and goatee, wielding a familiar-looking sword of exquisite design and quality. The woman they fought against wore a long black cloak with matching pauldrons curving upward into sharp points. Blonde hair fell long and freely down her back, and her eyes were framed as if they'd been outlined in black ink. Her right eye was milky white. She bore a fairly close resemblance to—

The scene shifted again as magica exploded across the hall. The bearded warrior was on his knees, gasping. Then his eyes bulged in shock as he was suddenly poised above the sorceress, blood frothing at his mouth, his limp form held in the air, impaled upon a sword without a wielder. The sorceress stood, her right arm extended and the palm of her hand facing the ceiling. Her hands were armoured in gauntlets with long talons extending from the tips of the fingers.

In the entrance hall, the boy with the lighter brown hair screamed. It was obvious what he was screaming; "FATHER!!!" The old mage snapped at the white-robed boy, and with one desperate shout of apology and farewell to the dying warrior, conjured a portal for the boys to flee through before teleporting himself out of the fortress once they had made their exit, leaving the warrior lying in a pool of his own blood; his last sight the sorceress' smug expression of satisfaction.

"Father!" the boy sobbed outside on the moors. The old mage and white-robed boy stood despondently by his side. "Father, why?"~

Arcaydia stirred later that afternoon, waking in the sickbay. To her stronger senses, the iron stench of blood and the sickly reek of infection lingered long after the sources were gone, despite the efforts the crew went to scrubbing the place clean. Yawning, she sat up in the hammock. Blinking fast, her head swimming, she lay back down and took a deep breath.

"How are you doing?" asked a voice from beside her. Arcaydia turned her head to see Zehn standing there, his eyes fixed on her with concern.

"Oh, I'm alright," she smiled. She felt her pulse was quicker than normal, but the dream she had just experienced would account for that. "Just a little dizzy, but it'll soon pass, I'm sure."

"Do you know what happened?"

"I possess some abilities I don't yet understand, so I'm not sure, but I had a dream and I think it might have been about you."

"Me?"

Arcaydia looked down at her lap. "When I touched you, I had a dream. I saw a brown-haired boy stowing away in the cargo hold of a ship. Then another boy with darker hair wearing white robes arrived. The younger boy looked maybe ten years old, the older one, perhaps thirteen. There was a dark fortress guarded by demons, a sorceress inside who impaled a man on a sword, commanding it with her mind. She had long blonde hair, and one white eye."

Zehn shivered, swallowing hard as a lump formed in his throat. The rolling of the ship below deck didn't help matters. He turned away from her to hide the shock on his face. "You're right," he said all too calmly. Taking a deep breath, he looked back at her. There was a different kind of sincerity in his russet brown eyes. "You're one of the Nays aren't you?"

Reluctantly, Arcaydia nodded once. "Yes," she sighed, feeling her anxiety rising as her worries over her people's reactions grew. "I am— well half at least. You probably noticed my eye marking isn't as dark as theirs. You probably wouldn't notice much of a difference with my ears..."

"I thought so from the look of you," Zehn mumbled, folding his arms. "A long time ago Raeon explained much to me about them, and who the Kaesan'Drahknyr are, though I always dismissed his ramblings as mere myth, or at best ancient history. Does *he* know?" His eyes angled in Larkh's direction.

"I think he knew the moment he met me," she admitted. "He had that knowing look about him, and he has also studied the Nays for a long time apparently—"

"Listen well all o' you!" Larkh shouted above deck, standing by the open hatch closest to the sickbay. "From now until we're back out on the open sea, everyone on deck is on lookout as well as those aloft unless we're bracin'. Only the helmsman keeps his eyes on the bow!"

Zehn told himself that at some point before they emerged on the Wahren Sea, he needed to ask Larkh if he would consider stopping off at Adner, Faltainyr Demura's capital, so he could disembark and seek an audience with his king. Raeon had made him aware Marceau had left Almadeira in a hurry to warn King Jaredh, but that didn't mean he'd actually succeeded in arriving and delivering the message.

At this point, Arcaydia said nothing. Her mind raced as she began to worry about the possible consequences of these people trespassing in Nays lands. Her presence on board wouldn't matter. She had seen maps of the Nays continent of Ardeltaniah, and this was almost certainly the southern region of Kalthis' homeland, Marlinikhda. It was said no-one could make landfall anywhere along the coastlines of Ardeltaniah unless they were invited into its territories, and now it made sense why Argwey hadn't mentioned the channel to Larkh sooner.

The Cerenyr were responsible for sealing off entrances into Ardeltaniah on the southern coastlines where the continent's barrier split to allow for watercourses to function naturally. Nays ships, however, were impervious to such boundaries, and could pass through untroubled with no need for spoken word to dispel it.

Minutes later, Arcaydia emerged on deck, assisted by Zehn. Larkh stormed back across the deck from the forecastle, seemingly not noticing them. "Helm, north-east by north, an' keep her steady!"

"North-east by north, aye!" the helmsman repeated, gently easing the wheel to starboard.

It was going to be a long evening trying to navigate through this passage; Arcaydia could see Larkh's weariness was giving way to irritability. He had no map of this channel; only Argwey's memory to rely on. Their progress had slowed to a crawl; the sails were trimmed to allow for no more than three knots of speed out of the ship, not that the wind was currently favourable. As she wondered if they were going to be in a position to anchor before sunset, Larkh spoke to Argwey.

"Are there any small coves where we might be able to anchor for the night?" Larkh asked the bosun, standing by the mainmast. "At this rate we won't be out of here before sundown tomorrow unless the wind changes; an' I don't fancy the idea of tryin' to navigate this passage in the pitch dark. The *Duquesa de Estrellas* isn't far behind either."

"If my memory serves right," said Argwey, "there's a small bay a little further north where the channel divides east and west, but there are still a good few miles in it."

Larkh inclined his head toward the elf. "If we can make it there by the time the moon rises," he sighed with a smile, "I'll be able to rest."

II
Saldour

Alirene hurriedly placed her cup of tea down on the low rectangular table in the vast drawing room, and leapt to her feet, almost tripping over the hem of her embroidered lilac dress to fling her arms around her father's neck as he entered.

"Whoa Ali! Careful," he grimaced.

"Oh!" she gasped, suddenly taking notice of her father's injuries. "I'm sorry father. Was that—"

"A result of the battle?" he regarded her solemnly. "Yes dear, it was."

She brushed her fingers under the curling waves of her chestnut hair, sighing and turning away in a vain attempt to hide the sadness in her hazel eyes. Resolving herself, she whirled back to face him. "What was he like then?"

Leyal rested a hand on Traven's shoulder. "Sorry to interrupt, Lord Wendale, but if I may, I shall retire to the nearest inn." He nodded toward the main front door. "I shall leave you two to talk. It is best our differing feelings do not get stirred up again at the moment."

Traven glanced over his shoulder at Leyal. Despite wishing not to have an assassin staying in the manor, it would seem rude if he did not extend an offer. "You would be most welcome to use one of our guestrooms," he suggested.

Leyal smiled humbly, watching Traven's distrustful expression with interest and judgement. "You have my gratitude Admiral," the assassin bowed his head graciously, "but I am much more accustomed to the ways of a traveller and would rather enjoy an evening alone to relax for a change." Out of the corner of his eye, Leyal saw Alirene eyeing him suspiciously. Traven nodded.

"Very well, Leyal," the admiral agreed. "Enjoy your free time; you deserve it. I suspect Duke Kradelow has kept you exceptionally busy lately."

Leyal bowed his head again. "My thanks," he said with gratitude. "I shall call on you in the next few days to see how you are faring, and no doubt the duke will have another message for me all too soon." With that, he turned and briskly left the manor, escorted by the doorman.

"Now where were we?" Traven turned his attention back to his daughter. "Larkhalven, or rather *Larkh*, has done very well for himself, despite his lawlessness. He has gathered quite a following of cutthroats. Who knew one young man could achieve what he has done. It would seem many are drawn to him."

Alirene gripped the sides of her dress, stiffening. "And what does he look like?" she asked, quietly telling herself to relax.

"He's grown into a very handsome young man," Traven replied, his expression rueful. He went on to give her a detailed description of her childhood friend's adult appearance.   Alirene smiled as she tried to picture him. "I've heard he's remarkably clever," she thought aloud. "Shame he hasn't found any means to send a letter to me all these years. As soon as it was reported he was alive and had somehow kept possession of the *Greshendier*, I've so longed for word from him."

Traven approached her and rested his hands on her shoulders. "I know, Ali," he said calmly, "but bear in mind the kind of life he leads. It wouldn't be easy for him to send a letter to anyone, and he purposefully avoids Saldour's waters for good reason. I was lucky enough to receive a message from him for you though."

Alirene pressed her lips into a thin line and waited. When her father said nothing, she swallowed hard. "Go on..." she urged him.

"He said; *'faint memories may drift on a distant breeze, but true friendship is forged from ancient stone, and there it will remain.'* He said you'd know what it meant." The young woman stared across the room wide-eyed for several moments. Unable to contain herself, her eyes welled up and she burst into tears, covering her face with her hands.

"He told me that one day after we'd been playing in the meadows," she sobbed. "Our mothers called to us; we were about to head home when I told him I was scared we'd drift apart as we grew up. He stopped to look at one of the blue roses his mother loved so much, and that's when he said it. I don't know where he learned of such a saying, but I've *never* forgotten it."

"Come here," said Traven, lightly touching her shoulder. Alirene turned around and wasted no time in burying her face against her father's chest.

III
Aynfell

"If you're certain there's no other way she could have entered, then someone within the Archaenen is to blame." Zairen paced the Silver Order's private lounge, contemplating how Zerrçainne managed to steal the Archaenen's copy of the Taecade Medo without sounding the alarm. "Have you any idea who?"

Melkhar's eyes narrowed darkly. "I have yet to be formally introduced to anyone of significant rank besides Lord Ayresborough," she replied, glancing in Raeon's direction. "Most have been busy clearing debris from the city or healing the wounded, but I understand Archmage Jorical arrived during the evening while I slept in preparation for the attack."

Raeon shot her an accusing stare. "Are you accusing Lord Jorical of allowing the sorceress entry to the library's vault?" he demanded. Melkhar regarded him coldly, arching a thin brow. The corner of her pressed cinnamon-tinted lips quirked into a wry smile. "Come now, is it that obvious?" Her rich voice was thick with sarcasm. "I need not have met the man to have sensed the ill intent behind his presence, and I'll wager he is far from being a popular entity within these walls."

Raeon grunted in disapproval. "You might be right that he is far from being a popular man, but I feel such rash judgement is unbecoming of the Nays," he growled. "Alleran Jorical is still an Archmage of the Archaenen; we must tread carefully."

"You forget your place Lord Ayresborough!" Zairen snapped, his dusky brown eyes flashing angrily. "Had Melkhar's *rash* judgement that Rahntamein be put to death aeons ago been heeded, there would not have been a cause for her to fight him for the benefit of you and your people in the present day! It is because of her quick thinking many worse disasters have not occurred!"

"I am sorry to have offended you," Raeon apologised. Frowning, he pushed to his feet and made his way to the door. "I will speak with Lord Jorical, and the other Archmages who are present," he said, a vexed expression crossing his face. "An investigation must be conducted though; it is protocol after all. I can only assume such procedures are also undertaken where you come from."

Zairen started forward with his fists clenched as Raeon left the room, only for Melkhar's arm to stay his path. *"Élh séi al hraeisthés havné,"* [41] she counselled him, returning her attention to the window. *"Yaellt élhir dauhs kenahr élh mhasaith."* [42] Zairen relaxed, following her gaze to the window where rain began to patter softly against the glass.

"A righteous man he might be," he said, "but the way he spoke to you was—"

"To his credit, he is honest and loyal to his cause," Melkhar finished. "As I said, let him do what he must. He is right; despite what our senses may tell us, we cannot go by feelings alone in situations such as this."

"That's rich, coming from you," Zairen remarked lightly, folding his arms and dropping on to one of the cabriole sofas. He felt himself flinch after he'd spoken; he didn't need to see her face to know the kind of expression she wore.

"Need I remind you, Zairen, even in Ardeltaniah these kinds of problems are addressed in exactly the same way?" she countered, narrowing her eyes at the worsening weather. "Do not back me up if you are intent on changing your tune afterwards."

That was it, now he'd dug himself a nice hole and jumped straight into it. Zairen tilted his head back. There was only one thing for it now. "You know I didn't mean it like that," he sighed. "I know you too well; your heart is ruled by instinct and intuition. If more people listened to you, perhaps they would care to avoid throwing caution to

---

[41] He is a righteous man.
[42] Let him do what he must.

the wind more often. I know your judgement of this Alleran Jorical was to ensure Raeon kept him firmly in mind."

When Melkhar didn't answer, he knew not to speak another word on the matter. He knew what she believed, and he knew all too well how she'd been treated. Long ago she had given up trying to convince others of ill-advised courses of action should they refuse to acknowledge her counsel and expertise. It only had to happen once for her to turn her back and walk away.

As an adviser in the king's court, Alleran Jorical often travelled back and forth between Aynfell and Adner. Sometimes he would stay for days or weeks in either location, depending on where he was most needed. Considering the Archaenen had just been attacked by the dragon, it was no surprise he arrived so swiftly. Raeon took care to remember he had received the same urgent call.

He suspected, under the current circumstances surrounding the threat from Adengeld, Jorical would need to return to Adner in the next few days if Marceau had managed to get word to King Jaredh. Knowing what he knew about Marceau, it was highly unlikely the renowned swordmaster would have failed in delivering such dire news.

One other thing kept nagging at him from the back of his mind; something he had neglected to tell Melkhar when she had woken after the battle. He knew he wouldn't be able to keep it from her – or Zairen for that matter – much longer. If they didn't discover he'd encountered Zerrçainne once before, albeit briefly, the chances were his old mentor Vharik would spill the beans sooner rather than later. He doubted he would be reprimanded for having kept the matter to himself, but then these *were* two members of the Kaesan'Drahknyr he was consorting with.

Arriving at the door to Archmage Jorical's quarters on the north side of the Archaenen's grounds, Raeon took a deep breath, and knocked. The cold, harsh glare that greeted him when the door opened paled in comparison to Melkhar's intense, icy stare.

"What is it, *Lord* Ayresborough?" The disdain in Alleran's voice was enough to make Raeon's blood boil, and when the man looked down his long nose like that it made him feel incredibly small. "You know full well I'm *busy* when I'm not present in the communal lounge."

"Please accept my apologies, Lord Jorical," Raeon bowed his head; "I wished to ask that you and the other Archmages, along with Lord Tanshel, meet tomorrow to further the plans for the restoration of the city, and also to discuss the rather serious matter surrounding the theft of a very ancient tome that was locked in the library's vault. Since the alarm bells were not triggered, there's some cause for concern someone who knows how to dispel the glyphs may have allowed a powerful sorceress inside to gain access and to steal it."

Alleran's mouth twisted in irritation, though it was more like the look of disgust someone wore when an offensive smell struck their nostrils. "Did I not warn the Mage's Council years ago such glyphs would prove ineffective should someone one day learn how to dispel them?"

Raeon eyed him suspiciously. "That you did," he replied, "and that is why the doors were also locked with keys, should it ever occur. Only someone highly skilled within the Archaenen would have the capability of dispelling those glyphs, and it would also have to be someone who knows where Tanshel keeps the keys to the library."

Jorical's steely gaze hardened on Raeon as he leaned forward. "I will ensure afternoon lessons tomorrow are cancelled, but be warned, Lord Ayresborough, the Lady Madoveska will hear of this when she returns," he threatened.

"I don't think that will be a problem," Raeon countered with a smile. "Lord Tanshel has already consulted with the

Premier via seikryth, and she has agreed to allow the meeting to take place in her absence considering our only copy of the Taecade Medo was stolen, and it happened to disappear while secured under magica as well as lock and key." He watched unwaveringly as fury blazed in Jorical's eyes. The man positively hated being crossed, let alone outwitted, and if Raeon didn't know any better, he was definitely hiding something sinister. "That's also bearing in mind she isn't due back from her trip to meet Duke Anthwell in Almenden for at least another week. I'll ask Lord Tanshel to arrange the meeting for the second bell of the afternoon tomorrow. That way we have the morning to get lessons over with and homework set."

"Very well," Jorical grumbled, turning back into his room, "but I do hope you have a feasible means of proving someone else besides Lord Tanshel and his assistant has the knowledge to dispel those glyphs, as well as the necessary keys." As the door closed, he added; "perhaps it might be an idea to arrange a social audience with the two Kaesan'Drahknyr. I'd like nothing more than to meet with such fables." Then it clicked shut.

Realisation gripped Raeon's heart like the hand of a powerful giant; Lord Jorical was right, how could he hope to prove that it was anyone but the librarians? A shiver ran up his spine. Despite his fear, he betrayed no hint of it to the First Archmage of Ash. Straightening, he whirled around and strode off down the vaulted corridor, sunlight glinting off his white-silver robes through the tall arched windows.

IV
The Veiled Channel

A vibrant terracotta sky streaked with cerise clouds cloaked the channel and its surrounding vale in dusky shadow, gradually making the steep banks more difficult to see as the sun sank below the western hills. Much to Larkh's surprise, however, they'd reached the fork sooner than expected.

Argwey had been sure it was further ahead, and believed they were going to have to make an attempt at anchoring in the middle of the channel. His estimation had been pleasantly incorrect.

Greshendier now sat quietly in the middle of the channel fork, both her bow and stern anchors holding her fast in the water, ensuring she didn't swivel and damage her hull. It was a short row ashore in the longboat, but trying to set foot on solid ground here was barely worth the trouble. The riverbanks were accessible for as little as ten metres before individuals found themselves walking back in the direction of the ship. Several times a scouting party wandered into the forest, only to blink seconds later to find themselves at the edge of the trees, facing the wrong direction.

Puzzled, Larkh sent Argwey ahead with a small party to check their route for fear of the ship being trapped in this channel where the magic of the Nays was clearly keeping them at bay. He climbed up on the bowsprit for a better view of the longboat's position. They rowed east, disappearing behind the trees along the opposite riverbank from where *Greshendier* sat, only to row back mere moments later. After making the attempt three times and still mysteriously returning to the ship, Argwey called to him, insisting they test the western route. Reluctantly, he agreed. He didn't want to sail west, he wanted to sail east back to Enkaiyta. Much as he feared, Argwey's party rowed down the western section of the channel and were not seen again until the sun had disappeared altogether, leaving behind a dim, fading glow.

"Did you know about this?" Larkh asked when the bosun climbed back on board. Argwey shook his head.

"I knew about the channel entrances, an' I knew about the barriers turnin' outsiders away," he answered honestly. "I didn't bet on there bein' any barriers in the channel. What I can tell you is I don't think that's normally the case."

Larkh shot him a suspicious glare. "Meaning?" he pressed.

"Meanin', sir, it seems we ain't *allowed* to sail east." Argwey swallowed nervously, waiting while his captain digested this information.

"You're tellin' me *they* know we're here," Larkh guessed. "If they didn't, we'd be clear to sail east an' wouldn't be doublin' back on ourselves; is that right?"

"Aye, I think that's the nature of it."

"Could such a phenomenon have caused us to arrive here sooner than we expected?"

"Can't be sure," Argwey shrugged, "but I'd say it's a possibility. The only Nays I ever met 'fore I met you were traders; though on occasion I saw one of their ivory naval ships docked in Eldoviir or Celait. It was never the done thing to ask about their magica; if they told you, it was of their own accord an' 'cause they wanted to."

"It's just as the legends say," Larkh mused, staring up at the dusky sky now sparsely sprinkled with stars. "Even their most subtle magic isn't to be taken lightly." Glancing south, he frowned at the ominous black clouds looming over the horizon, threatening to mar the tranquil view of the glittering heavens. *'Another storm?'* he wondered. *'The weather sure has been strange lately.'*

"I'm sorry," Argwey said ruefully, running a hand through his dark hair. He scratched the back of his head. "I should've thought twice 'bout bringin' her up 'ere."

Larkh shook his head and pointed a finger at him. "No Argwey, better we're here than potentially havin' seven sorts of shit blown out o' the hull in the Mabriltar Strait. If the Nays have any sense they'll understand—"

"An' if they recognise us as pirates?" Argwey interrupted just as the bell rang for first sitting of the evening meal.

Larkh rolled his eyes. "Argwey, we're already up to our necks in shit as it is; there were risks whichever way we went," he shrugged. "Let's see if we can work a little magic of our own an' conjure up some optimism eh?" The elf shot him a wary look. Larkh smiled meekly and clapped him on the shoulder. "Go an' eat; we'll figure out what comes next when we're fed an' rested." With a reluctant sigh, the bosun nodded and made his way toward the nearest hatch. Hearing thunder in the distance, Larkh briskly strode aft and disappeared into the sterncastle, heading for the great cabin.

CHAPTER 29

I
Almadeira

'Why are you here, Kaesan'Drahknyr?' a woman's voice purred inside Kalthis' mind. *'We are not friends, you and I.'*

Kalthis was roused from sleep by the voice; one he did not recognise. The words were unmistakably those of the Aurentai woman whose aura descended from the grassy hillside on the eastern side of the town. The other Aurentai he had sensed had recently vanished, and he wondered why. Unless they had become a much more sociable race outside their own niche societies – and he doubted that was the case – there were definitely other reasons they would choose to abide in countries like Faltainyr Demura.

'I am not here to challenge you,' Kalthis answered coolly opening his eyes, folding the covers back. He flicked a glance at the open window where the pale blue glow of dawn began to creep over the horizon. The chill of the early morning air danced gracefully into the room, brushing against his bare arms and chest. He took a long, deep breath.

'A Kaesan'Drahknyr who thinks himself a gentleman; how interesting...' Her mocking reply flowed like honey. An image of her was revealed in his mind's eye; wavy black hair, skin the colour of caramel, and striking dark brown eyes. She lay on her bed inside one of the gypsy caravans, propped up on one elbow. Her magenta shawl barely obscured her shoulders and breasts, though her lower half was covered by a light fur blanket. *'You're looking for a young woman are you not?'*

'How could you know that?' Kalthis demanded, feeling the rise of anger. 'And why ask why I am here if you already know the answer?'

The faint sound of tutting clicked at the back of his mind. 'My my, you should calm down,' she advised him. 'I thought you were a gentleman. I asked to be sure that you were not hunting me, and I know because I saw her during the spring faire the day before she fled the city with a most handsome pirate... Now there's one I wouldn't mind slipping under the covers with.'

'You know more than you let on,' Kalthis guessed. 'What do you want?'

'She doesn't even know how powerful she is,' the dancer chortled. 'Isn't that cute?'

'I am waiting.'

'Very well...'

Kalthis knew she pouted before she sent another image of herself. 'I am Arieyta Ei Nazashan, a high priestess and seer of the Lady of Flames, Adjeeah,' the Aurentai woman told him. 'I saw the ship your oracle boarded turn north into the forest lands east of the Isles of Cerendiyll, only to vanish.'

Shivers raced up Kalthis' spine at the news. That meant they had entered the Veiled Channel! But how? Arcaydia certainly didn't have the level of power needed to reveal glámar yet, much less open a gateway of any kind, but someone on board certainly had such an ability. The magica defending the Nays boundaries was cast and maintained by the Aeva'Daeihn; so if Arcaydia was on those waters with the two believed to be the Keys, they were more than likely being guided toward Atialleia. If what Arieyta said were true, it would mean he would be returning to Ardeltaniah sooner than anticipated.

'Why tell me this?' Kalthis asked. 'As you say, we are not friends.'

'I have my reasons,' Arieyta taunted, though there was an edge of disdain in her voice. 'All I will tell you is this... I

*experience many things, Kalthis of the Ashkelleron tribe. I
have woken from prophetic nightmares in cold sweats on
many occasions. What I do, I do for my people, but you must
understand one thing, and that is I am no friend to any of
your kind, not even Zerrçainne. Her plans do not work in
unison with mine, though I do not begrudge Leyal's
allegiance to her.'* Then she was gone before he could
pursue the conversation further.

Kalthis decided it was best not to attempt making
another connection. Arieyta's words rang clear enough, but
even if she didn't agree with Zerrçainne's plans, why did
she choose to inform him of Arcaydia's location? It was
unlikely she knew anything about the Veiled Channel,
meaning she had given him a description that couldn't
possibly be false. His brow furrowed.

Taking another deep breath, he sat up. There was no
way he would be going back to sleep again, and for such a
short amount of time it wasn't worth trying. Sister Nalane
would likely be calling soon to tell him breakfast was
available.

After a simple breakfast, Kalthis took it upon himself to
assist the kitchen staff in cleaning up before packing away
his meagre handful of belongings. He hadn't long returned
to the musty guestroom before he was interrupted by
Dreysdan seeking a mind-link.

'Hello Drey; what news?' he asked.

'Good morning Kalthis,' Dreysdan replied. Kalthis
could hear the fatigue in his voice. *'I have scryed again for
the oracle's location, and as unlikely as it seems, she is
within the borders of your homeland.'*

'So, she was telling the truth,' Kalthis mused aloud.

'I'm sorry, who was telling the truth?' Dreysdan
pressed.

It took Kalthis several moments to think of a response.
It wasn't going to sound good that he'd held a conversation
with an Aurentai. That she had chosen to speak to him – and

tell him the truth for that matter – concerned him. There was something more to it than Zerrçainne's interference with the world's affairs, but the information had nevertheless been of help to him; not that Arieyta could have known Dreysdan was going to call to tell him the same thing.

'*An Aurentai woman who is in this town spoke to me using mindspeech,*' he eventually replied. Immediately he felt Dreysdan's disapproving – and defensive – reaction. '*She is a priestess of Adjeeah, who travels with a troupe of gypsies; though I do not know why. During the Vàreia she claimed to have seen Arcaydia, and informed me at dawn this morning of her location. It matches what you have just told me.*'

Dreysdan considered these words. Little known to the Galétahr, his emotions carried a little too strongly across mind-link; so Kalthis was able to guess what he was going to say next.

'*And you trusted her?*' he growled.

'*Mind yourself, Drey,*' Kalthis warned. '*I respect your feelings, and I expect you to respect mine in return. I had reason to believe her only because she told me where the ship turned north and simply vanished; besides you have just confirmed she was telling the truth. I doubt the Aurentai of this day would know much, if anything, of the Veiled Channel. It has never been drawn on any maps and has remained hidden for millennia. That aside, there are matters concerning this encounter requiring further discussion, but not here and not now.*'

'*And what if she did know about the channel?*' Dreysdan growled.

'*Have faith our barriers and defences are still as strong as they were many generations ago,*' Kalthis assured him. '*The Aurentai woman exposed herself by speaking to me. She took a great risk in making contact, including what she told me of her not being in league with Zerrçainne.*'

'*You may well be right,*' Dreysdan conceded. '*I trust your judgement of course, but there is something else you seem to have forgotten, and it does not concern this woman.'*

Kalthis slung his backpack over his shoulder and stopped to think as he reached for the door handle. What could he have forgotten? Now he thought about it, something was indeed eluding him. His hand gripped the door handle, and he frowned. Dreysdan waited patiently.

Arcaydia was on a ship that had turned north into the Veiled Channel, therefore she was within Ardeltaniah's boundaries. Those who managed to pass through any barriers uninvited were repelled from the shore as they attempted to make landfall, and sometimes the barriers would shift, propelling them along their way, sometimes guiding them in a particular direction. The channel forked to the east and west. East would take them beyond the Sendero de Mercader, west would.....

'Albharenos!' Kalthis realised. *'Arcaydia has missed the necessary training with Marceau, but even if the training had taken place she still wouldn't be ready for the leviathan's test!'*

'Hurry back to Atialleia, Kalthis,' Dreysdan urged him, *'but don't underestimate Arcaydia; she may yet surprise us all. We cannot know for certain, but if she has the two Keys in tow as the Atiathél believes, then she has already saved us a great deal of time. I must go now; take care.'*

'You too Drey,' Kalthis replied, his heart racing. Albharenos was the guardian of Ardeltaniah's southern waters; so regardless of whether or not Arcaydia was on board that ship, he would perform his duty if he so much as sensed ill intent in the air. The fact Arcaydia was sailing on board a ship run by pirates didn't exactly place her in an ideal position, but perhaps the threads of fate weaving about her were a cause for him to trust in her abilities; even if she were not yet aware of what they meant.

Shaking his head, he opened the door and hurried toward the Kathaedra to bid farewell to Sister Nalane. What he wasn't sure of, was how he was going to get out of

Almadeira without being seen. Unless... Suddenly an idea struck him. He couldn't be certain whether or not one still existed within the Kathaedra's walls, but if anyone would know, it would be Nalane. He doubled his pace.

II
Atialleia

Adel Nalaueii had done her work overnight, visiting both Melkhar and Zairen in their dreams to inform them. The silencing had been completed; the scan stretched two hundred and fifty miles in diameter from the centre of Aynfell to ensure anyone who might have left the city since the dragon's attack would be affected. Those who had witnessed Melkhar would now only remember her as little more than a vague shadow of a figure whose existence could not be confirmed.

All students and mages of the Archaenen were withheld from speaking of what they knew of the Nays to anyone outside the academy the moment their oaths were sworn. Such restrictions were put in place either by an archmage of the Order of Silver, or by the Premier – Lady Madoveska – at the behest of the Atiathél. It was enough to keep tongues from wagging where they shouldn't.

Melkhar made her departure from Aynfell during the early hours of the morning, much to Archmage Jorical's frustration. Raeon had endeavoured to keep her from leaving long enough for proper introductions to be made, at Jorical's request, but the Atiathél's orders that she return to Atialleia swiftly were paramount. It would be Zairen who would have the misfortune of dealing with the surly bastard of an archmage; though he need only stay long enough to strengthen Aynfell's magical defences, especially with the knowledge of Adengeld developing new archana with which to launch an attack on Faltainyr Demura.

Once Melkhar had climbed to the peak of the nearest White Sentinel, Zairen called the clouds down from the overcast sky to allow her to spread her wings to fly up into the fog without being seen. As the temperature plummeted on her ascent, her etheric barrier flickered into life, following the contours of her lithe body as it sank into her skin, protecting her from the chilling atmosphere of the heavens.

It was mid-morning when she reached the peak of the nearest mountain where a black wyvern known as Savhastrak awaited her arrival.

"Kaesané Khesaiyde, wuten eth," the wyvern rumbled, bowing his head. His amber eyes glittered in fond remembrance. *"Azjonha ez'at vann."* [43] Melkhar brought her right hand to rest below her left shoulder in salute.

"Savhastrak, zo svjehr jheu'an ez'es khaade," [44] Melkhar replied respectfully in the draconic tongue. The wyvern nodded slowly in approval. She stepped forward and began unravelling two lengths of strong leather rope from around the wyvern's hind legs. She followed up by wrapping them around the ridges on his shoulders, from which his wings extended underneath. When she was finished, he stooped to allow a quick mount.

"Ayónhe, vhar Atialleia," [45] Melkhar instructed in Daeihn as she mounted.

"Kaesané, jheu'naa mekh nahvek wes," [46] Savhastrak answered, spreading his gleaming obsidian wings and leaping from the summit.

Melkhar strode into the throne room of the Atialléane palace late that afternoon, and knelt before the Atiathél. Her great towering wings trailed behind her, almost touching the palace floor in front as she lowered her head. Despite the resplendent rays of sunlight breaking through the narrow vaulted windows, the tall braziers behind the throne were lit,

---

[43] Well met, Kaesan'Drahknyr Khesaiyde. It has been aeons.
[44] It is good to see you.
[45] Home, to Atialleia.
[46] My service is yours, Kaesan'Drahknyr.

478

illuminating the statues of the three Adels and the grand sculpture of the Dragons of Origin entwined around Aevnatureis.

"Venildhráin ayónhe, Melkhar." Arkkiennah's voice was smooth and calm as she welcomed her home. *"Ye'n arth al dalhé nearihn."* [47]

"Kharun Ye'nah Atiathél," [48] Melkhar answered with grace. "I came to you as soon as I arrived bec—"

"I know you far too well, Melkhar," Arkkiennah interrupted, smiling warmly. "You must know your future plans or complete a task before you can even think about relaxing. The way you conduct yourself can be quite predictable, even if everything else about you is an enigma."

Melkhar's wolfish eyes narrowed. "I see," she hesitated. "—Then may I ask a personal question?"

Arkkiennah tilted her head, her brow lifting. "You may," she answered gently.

"Have my habits in the field of my sworn fealty pleased you over the ages?" Melkhar enquired, her low, resonant voice betraying no shred of doubt.

The Atiathél slowly rose from the throne and approached the Kaesan'Drahknyr. Melkhar closed her eyes, awaiting a break in the silence. The Atiathél came to stand before the arc of her wings and spoke softly. "Stand, Melkhar."

Obediently, Melkhar pushed to her feet and rose to stand straight. She stood the better part of a foot taller than Arkkiennah, but their eyes met easily where mutual respect was wordlessly exchanged.

"Your professional conduct is what makes you the ideal warrior, Melkhar," Arkkiennah said assuredly. "Your loyalty is unquestionable. Your methods can be extreme, but are often necessary. You take on each task assigned to you without question, and you do what must be done. You are

---

[47] Welcome home. You are a day early.
[48] Thank you Empress.

always one step ahead. Why in all of Aeldynn would that displease me?"

Melkhar's stone cold stare remained steadfast as she looked into the Atiathél's eyes. "If anyone can defeat me with words, it is you, Your Highness," she said, her expression static, "but I fear I am unable to express the appropriate level of gratitude."

"You have already expressed enough." Arkkiennah's voice was almost a whisper. "You still won't talk about it though, will you? What was done to you..."

Melkhar stiffened; her jaw clenching. "There is no need to speak of it. Zairen and Kalthis told that story aeons ago," she answered, her tone impassive. "It is done, and it cannot be changed. I became what I was destined to become; it is my belief that is all that matters. I sincerely apologise, but I will not speak of it."

Arkkiennah kept her eyes fixed on Melkhar's steely gaze, desperately searching those deep emerald eyes so many found intimidating. Underneath that harsh, ruthless exterior she saw enough pain and sorrow to turn her own blood to tears. Melkhar was, without a doubt, a closed book; a walking, breathing statue. There were only two things that seemed to truly animate her, combat, and taking the lives of her enemies. It might be possible to predict her general behaviour as a warrior, but every other door into her life was shut and barred tight.

"Very well," Arkkiennah sighed in disappointment. Sweeping her long dress back, she returned to the throne. She sat, crossed her legs and folded her hands across her lap. "Adel Manahveria expressed that you exhausted your power when you fought Rahntamein recently. You did not mention it in your discussion with me over the seikryth. You have done this before, at times when your power has not yet been fully restored after having sustained either terrible injuries or awoken from the long sleep – perhaps both. It is related to the reason you will not speak of what was done to you, is it not? What runs through your mind in those moments, Melkhar? Can you at least tell me that?"

The Kaesan'Drahknyr stood for several long moments staring. What went through her mind? Her blood boiled just thinking about it; though no break in her composure could be measured, not at this level of anger.

"You will never be good enough!" a male voice bellowed inside her mind. *"You will never be strong enough to best any of them; you're a woman! You are PATHETIC!"* Memories of unbearable physical pain jarred all her senses at once. *"As far as prophecies are concerned,"* the voice spat, *"your conception and birth were apparently a necessary evil for me to have to bear, but mark my words you will never be adequate. You will always be a failure!"*

"Unpleasant memories," Melkhar replied, her brow furrowing. Arkkiennah saw her fists clenching. "With all due respect, Your Highness, I will go into no more detail. My magica is almost fully restored now. It will be a matter of two to four weeks at the most. However, had Zerrçainne and her sycophant not interfered, Rahntamein would finally be dead, as he should have been millennia ago."

"Her sycophant?" Arkkiennah's brow perked up. "Tell me more about him; and what of Zerrçainne herself? I am still troubled knowing she yet lives."

"I saw but a glimpse of him," Melkhar admitted, "but there was no mistaking the race he belonged to. He was Fralh, and definitely a warrior; perhaps even a prince. He cleared her of my path before I could slay her or the dragon, and opened a Thannyc portal through which they escaped – Rahntamein included. Had I not used—"

"Do not blame yourself," Arkkiennah told her. "I agree Rahntamein should have been slain aeons ago, but it was that one act the majority of the royal council considered to be redeeming. His life was spared, but he was sentenced to binding for an indefinite amount of time as punishment for his previous sins. That binding was supposed to keep him slumbering for much longer, but Zerrçainne somehow learned how to dispel it. Dragons may heal swiftly – though not as swiftly as you do – but remember it can take years for new scales to harden. There will be time enough for you to claim his life."

'Time enough?' Melkhar wondered, 'what does Her Highness have in mind?'

"I see that look in your eyes," Arkkiennah smiled again. "How different you look when you're uncertain." The Atiathél sat upright. "I will put this to you plainly; unless they interfere further with your objectives I'd like you to hold back in making any moves against Zerrçainne or Rahntamein until we have more information."

At first, Melkhar thought her anger might get the better of her, but she quickly resolved herself to listen to Arkkiennah's unspoken words. Fixing her eyes on the Atiathél, she read her expression and understood.

"You believe Zerrçainne knows our actions too well," she surmised. "You wish to wait to see what she and the dragon have planned next."

Arkkiennah nodded. "As you know, your forebears were once fertile, yet their breeding was forbidden for the sake of the world's safety, and the story of Alymarn's birth is no fable. Let us go back to the beginning..." Melkhar stood silently, listening as Arkkiennah recited what she felt necessary.

"Despite knowing the reasons why Alymarn was bound and suspended in animation, Zerrçainne still fell in love with him and sought a means to release him; she eventually succeeded. When the Lyte E'varis once again bound him with the help of the Tseika'Drahknyr, we know his soul and spirit were divided into four, and then sealed and scattered across all realms of existence. Until now, Zerrçainne was believed to have perished, and from your description and that of Lésos, we know she has become a creature of Phandaerys. What are your thoughts on this, Melkhar?"

Melkhar relaxed her stance and folded her arms. The answer was obvious; Zerrçainne's preliminary goal was likely to find all the aspects of Alymarn's soul and spirit, to unite them, and resurrect him, but her involvement with Adengeld was ambiguous, and why should she require Rahntamein's support?

"It is without question she seeks Alymarn's resurrection," Melkhar discerned, "and as to her alliance with Adengeld's king and Rahntamein, I can only speculate she has far more planned for Alymarn's return than we may be aware of. No such ideas would cross her mind if she did not think she could *weave her own designs into stolen fabric.*"

"I fear you are right Melkhar." Arkkiennah reclined, a thoughtful expression crossing her porcelain countenance. "My reason for asking you to hold back unless absolutely necessary is the knowledge Zerrçainne has proved she can throw our plans into disarray simply by reading our moves with such accuracy she has been successful in implementing countermoves to thwart us. We have been far too predictable."

"You suggest we bide our time then?" Melkhar enquired, cocking her head to one side. Arkkiennah nodded slowly. The Kaesan'Drahknyr continued; "we must consider all tactics and then discern which changes need to take place in each given situation. Whatever she decides to do next, we must rethink our most natural course of action."

Arkkiennah was glad it was Melkhar she was discussing this matter privately with. The other Kaesan'Drahknyr would also see the sense in this course of action, but Melkhar was headstrong given the opportunity, and her solutions were almost always straight to the point. There was no beating about the bush with her.

"Are you able to communicate in mindspeech at a greater distance yet?" Arkkiennah enquired.

"I believe so," Melkhar surmised. "Kalthis attempted to contact me while I was unconscious, but I never found the time to respond to the call. I suspect he hasn't had the chance to try again either."

The Atiathél nodded. "We will discuss these matters further in the next few days," she said assuredly, her expression softening, "for we are expecting company." How she loved that bemused expression on Melkhar's face. Her left eyebrow always arched suspiciously while the rest of her features remained perfectly static. Arkkiennah chuckled. "It would seem our original plans to lure the two Keys here weren't necessary. The Mindseer Oracle is guiding them here of her own volition; though I suspect she isn't the least bit aware of it."

"What of Marceau?" Melkhar enquired. "It was he who abandoned his post, forcing these circumstances in the first place."

"Marceau would have had his reasons," Arkkiennah sighed, "but you are right. The Mindseer Oracle was put in danger because of him, even though matters have worked out in our favour in that regard. I may ask Madukeyr to fetch him, if he isn't too busy assisting Galétahr Dreysdan in determining the movements of Adengeld's army."

"Might I suggest Nelraido instead?" Melkhar offered with a wry smile. "He has as quick a tongue on him as any, and given Madukeyr is already indisposed, I recommend him as the most ideal candidate." Giving her a sly look, the Atiathél smiled back in approval.

III
Aynfell

Zairen still couldn't believe what he had heard, or could he? All Archmages of the Archaenen who were present, save for Raeon, had reached the conclusion no solid proof could be obtained to point the finger at the one who had committed the crime of allowing such a dangerous sorceress to steal the facility's only copy of the Taecade Medo.

As Melkhar had rightly said, they couldn't go by intuition alone to place the blame, and it was true it would be too difficult to prove who had the knowledge to do such a thing. Short of transporting every adept magician in the Archaenen to Atialleia for mindreading – which could be an exceptionally dangerous practice – there was very little that could be done. The culprit had covered their tracks well.

It still left the problem of what to do about the stolen copy, but if it was in Zerrçainne's hands, there was little that could be done at present without the Archaenen waging war in a vain attempt to reclaim it. It would only result in their deaths, and pending further meetings on the matter, he knew he was hard pressed to find an effective means of encouraging them to see sense.

As far as the Nays were concerned, the Taecade Medo was never a book intended to be understood by mortals, but a renegade of their own race intent on using its secrets to bring about malice and destruction would soon prove to be a far greater threat. Humans had forever been seekers of knowledge, and never ceased in their attempts to drink in more of it, heedless of the fact one day it might prove to be their undoing. They were rarely satisfied with what they had; but he had to admit he admired them for always being prepared to strive to better themselves. Nevertheless, all things came with a price – especially forbidden knowledge.

"Kaesan'Drahknyr Elaiythé?" Raeon called. "Are you alright?"

Zairen snapped out of his reverie and regarded Raeon across the carved pine table in the Archmage's lavishly furnished quarters, as much adorned with ornate decoration as the rest of the Archaenen's main buildings. He looked down at the fork in his hand, then at his half empty porcelain plate of pulled poultry meat and braised vegetables. "I'm sorry," he muttered, "I was thinking about this morning's meeting." He then added; "oh, and forget the formalities; just Zairen is fine."

"Alright, Zairen," Raeon replied with a meek smile. "Shall we finish dinner and then discuss it further over a glass of Felanshia wine? It might be a good idea to share your concerns with another, especially one who is trapped in the same boat."

Zairen took a moment to gather his thoughts. "Fine," he agreed, nodding, "though I want to add Archmage Jorical's interest in Melkhar to the discussion. I'd like to know why he was so vexed she was to leave so urgently on the Atiathél's orders."

A shiver knifed its way down Raeon's back just thinking about it. He had spoken to both of them immediately after he'd disturbed Alleran Jorical in his chambers, asking for a chance for himself and the other Archmages to meet the two Kaesan'Drahknyr formally in person. Melkhar had only declined on the basis her orders to return to Atialleia took priority, but when Jorical learned she had left during the early hours of the morning, the archmage had looked as though he were about to explode. Raeon steeled himself for a long evening of intense discussion, and quite possibly a sleepless night.

Whether or not Zerrçainne had planned to earn the Archaenen's wrath was irrelevant. The truth was, they wanted their copy of the book back and they might just think themselves strong enough to overpower her – and they would be wrong. Zairen had to admit, that copy of the book had long been safe hidden in the library's vault, and it wouldn't have taken much for her to learn of its location. It would only take a magically adept accomplice who was also of a high enough rank to know every detail of the library's inventory.

Despite the fact humanity was a race with no natural anchorage to Aevnatureis, those who proved to be adept in anchoring themselves had nothing to stop them from training their minds to withstand greater amounts of magica over time. They would never be able to harness it as the Nays, elves or fey could, and it would drain them far more quickly, but rare exceptions to the usual rules of nature did sometimes occur. Forcing one's spirit to accept an unnatural connection to the source, however, was far more detrimental, which was why the Silver Mages were signing their death warrants by willingly injecting Nays blood into their veins when they had not been born with it.

Was it even possible to defeat not just a Galétriahn Mage, but a Galétriahn Highlord – though her title had long been revoked – with a small army of highly trained Archaenen magicians? Even if it were, no-one could be spared if Adengeld marched on Faltainyr Demura. The kingdom would need as many magically adept fighters as it could get.

The knot forming in Zairen's gut tightened, telling him there was more to all of this than Zerrçainne's desire to revive Alymarn; far more, and not knowing what, bothered him.

"They aren't going to listen," Raeon warned, reclining in his armchair by the fireplace; "they don't realise the threat from Adengeld is imminent, and they covet that book. I agree it should not be in Zerrçainne's hands, but it should only ever be in our hands if the Nays agree to let us have it, which they have for centuries now."

"Just as Vharik didn't listen when he was told what creating *silver* mages would do?" Zairen reminded him as he sat across from the Second Archmage of Silver. The Kaesan'Drahknyr leaned forward. "Just as you and your kind ignore the perils of taking powerful blood into your own bodies when you were not created to withstand it?"

Raeon rolled his eyes, his shoulder sagging. "I've already been through this with Melkhar," he sighed, "but yes, if you want to look at it that way, it is much the same sort of predicament getting the stubborn council of archmages to agree to anything other than what their hearts are set upon."

Zairen regarded Raeon sternly, though it wasn't half as intense as Melkhar's inexorable gaze, and with his ethereal features illuminated by the crackling flames that danced in the hearth, he had the look of an apparition. His nickname suited him well.

"Though I agree with her, I also appreciate it is your way of seeking to protect your own, for only the most adept of mortal mages may accomplish drawing upon a higher level of magica," Zairen affirmed, clasping his hands and resting them on his stomach. "So why don't you tell me how you met Vharik, and what made you decide to become a silver mage in the first place? Because I believe a certain incident that happened sixteen years ago had something to do with it, and it links with one of the Keys we're searching for." For a moment, Raeon thought his heart had stopped. How could he have—

"I see you're surprised," Zairen continued. "Melkhar told me that when Zerrçainne left her no choice but to flee the Dorne Shaft by using a rift into Nira'Eléstara, she re-emerged again at the Len'athyr Sanctuary, where Kalthis was staying, along with Vharik himself. There was a meeting between them and Galétahr Dreysdan. It would seem they divulged at least some of that old story."

Burying his face in his palm, Raeon groaned. It was a long story, and one he preferred remain buried in his past, but a Kaesan'Drahknyr was asking him. Being marked as uncooperative might eventually have consequences. If it helped to unravel the story behind Zerrçainne's return, then who was he to deny the Nays that kind of information? One way or another, as history had already proved, the Nays always got their answers.

"I was born in Eldoviir, though I was conceived in the port town of Celait," Raeon began. "As you know, I am half human and half elven. The Cerenyr nobility, as you will already know, have long looked down upon unions between elves and humans, but for a Cerenyr noble to engage in such a union was unthinkable. I never learned the reason for it, though it was always my guess that like human society, nobility must remain pure of blood." He glanced at Zairen, who remained silent but attentive.

"I know not what happened to my parents," Raeon continued, "for I was too young, but it was decided if a guardian did not claim me and take me into exile, I was to be taken into the forest for the fey to decide what to do with me. Vharik, as it turns out, was visiting Eldoviir at the time. I think you can guess the rest. As for how I decided to become a silver mage, that's a much longer story you might want to save for another day."

Zairen glanced out of the window to see the moon was almost at its zenith. Looking back to Raeon he nodded. "Very well," he agreed. "We will postpone the rest of your story. And Raeon, I do apologise for having asked you to revive old memories. I know all too well how painful they can be."

With a meek smile, Raeon rose to his feet. "No need to apologise Zairen, some stories need unravelling before others can follow suit." He turned toward the hearth, gesturing toward the kettle sitting beside it. "Is it too late for tea, do you think?"

Zairen shook his head. "Almost, but not quite. Besides, the kettle has just reminded me of a funny tale that is one of many, and you will be surprised by who they involve." At Raeon's bemused expression, Zairen couldn't help but let out a chuckle.

CHAPTER 30

I
The Veiled Channel

Arcaydia leaned against the capping rail the following morning, tracing the splintered edges with her index finger, staring down at the restless saltwater sloshing against the ship's hull. She was nervous; all too aware of where they were heading. Whenever one of their barriers was breached, the Nays knew. They would rise to high alert when such a breach was unexpected, and were able to tell what manner of being it was. She wasn't aware of how it was done, and she suspected she probably wasn't meant to. It seemed only certain individuals and ordinary wildlife could pass through freely as if no barrier existed.

On the northern banks of the channel, she noticed the trees stood far taller, rising over two hundred, perhaps even three hundred feet into the sky, and their trunks were up to thirty feet wide. *'These must be the giant redwoods of Marlinikhda Kalthis told me about,'* she surmised. *'What was their name again? Cheréqua...'*

Her tranquil thoughts were abruptly interrupted by a thunderous voice echoing through her mind; *'Mhenda'zee Onakrehde, drehdas jheu'naa naza'ot. Ghiivadan zo mhazai kjaza'vrehn jheu'an cahza'ot.'* [49]

Despite having never heard the language spoken before, she understood the words came from none other than the language of dragons, and somehow she fathomed their meaning. As she wondered to whom the voice belonged, an

---

[49] You are not ready, Mindseer Oracle. You cannot bind to me right now.

image rippled in her mind's eye, settling on that of an enormous white serpent with the head of a dragon, uncoiling itself from its resting place in an undersea cavern.

'Albharenos!' The realisation shook Arcaydia to the core. The great ghost leviathan was speaking to her, but why? She questioned its words. *'I am not ready. What is the Mindseer Oracle? And what does he mean that I am not being able to bind to him right now? That doesn't make any sense.'*

Having sailed all day with a reasonably favourable wind behind her, it was only a matter of hours before the *Greshendier* would reach the mouth of the channel that opened out into the northern waters of the Sendero de Mercader. Up ahead, the channel was gradually widening.

Trembling, Arcaydia made an attempt at projecting her mindvoice, hoping she would be heard; *'I don't understand. Please tell me what this means.'*

'Drehdas jheu'naa naza'ot,' the leviathan replied levelly. *'Drehdas jheu'an ylln'va wohn ikheedaz ahta hestorva jheu'an cahza zee.'* [50]

'I will be ready when I can willingly see the past?' Arcaydia enquired. *'I have seen something of the past in dreams that have happened upon me suddenly, but I don't understand this power...'*

'That you can already understand my tongue without training is remarkable, young one,' Albharenos acknowledged, switching to Armen, *'but you should not be venturing into my domain at such low strength.'*

'We didn't have a choice!' Arcaydia protested, sagging to her knees. *'And how was I to know I would be tested here? There has been no mention of this! I don't know who I am!'* An intolerable silence followed. What was little more than a few minutes felt like hours. *'Albharenos?'*

---

[50] You will be ready when you can willingly see the past.

'You must nevertheless be tested before you can be guided into the capital,' Albharenos answered, and then he was gone.

Larsan rushed to Arcaydia's side as she cried out; "but why? I don't understand! What's happening to me?" The big man knelt, putting an arm around her shoulders, ignoring the crew's suspicious stares as they went about their work scrubbing the deck, splicing ropes and retouching damaged paintwork.

"What's the matter?" he asked, looking intently at the quivering young woman. Beads of sweat and tears slid down her cheeks. "What happened to you?" She shook her head, her mind lost in thought.

Moments later, Larkh burst out on deck making straight for Larsan and Arcaydia. "What's goin' on?" he demanded.

"Albharenos.....he..." Arcaydia hesitated. "He spoke.....he wants to test me! Raiyah help me I... I don't know anything!"

Larkh inhaled sharply, cold fear twisting like a knife to the gut. "We're in trouble," he muttered under his breath. "Laz, bring her with you. She needs someplace quiet to calm down an' rest. The great cabin is where she'll get it."

As the warrior scooped her up into his arms, Arcaydia made no move to resist him. She stared off into space as if in some kind of trance. Larkh fixed his gaze ahead of the ship's bow. While the channel had widened enough to allow for the yards to be braced without risk of collision, it was still too narrow for Ito be turned around, and even if it were possible, it was likely they would encounter the same phenomenon as before.

He wished Mey were still with them. The *Duquesa de Estrellas* was small enough to continue sailing through the night; so Mey had said her farewells and turned east at the fork in the channel. Somehow she hadn't been affected by the same phenomenon he and his crew had experienced – not that he was aware of at least. Had they stayed alongside one another and returned to Enkaiyta together, Mey might have jeopardised her position as a black market trader. The longer she delayed getting her contraband to its buyers, the more impatient and angry they were likely to become. He hoped she and her crew were well, for there was no telling what would happen if any of them were caught in this place.

The last thing Arcaydia expected when she woke was to find herself lying in Larkh's cot. She sat bolt upright, her heart racing, wondering what had happened. She was certain she hadn't fallen asleep, but she didn't remember being brought in here, so she must have blacked out. Her mind started to wander in inappropriate directions just as Larkh made his way into the room carrying two steaming mugs of what her keen sense of smell recognised as camomile tea.

"Ah you're awake," he said, handing one to her as she stood up. "How're you feelin'?"

At first, Arcaydia didn't know what he was talking about. As she made her way over to the chart table, it struck her like a blow to the skull. *The leviathan!'* Gasping, she quickly put the mug down and sat on the nearest seat, fleeting faintness clouding her mind.

"Al-Albharenos," she stammered, "the ghost leviathan; h-h-he spoke to me!"

"Calm down," Larkh said, leaning toward her, putting his own mug down. "Take slow, deep breaths an' try to think carefully. What did he say?"

Larkh couldn't deny knowing that the great white leviathan was aware of Arcaydia's presence worried him. It didn't bode well for his plan to attempt slipping past the beast undetected. Though some of the world's dragons were greater in size and bulk overall, a fully grown leviathan made up for it with length upon monstrous length of serpent extending from a narrow torso that might have otherwise belonged to a wyvern; for these beasts also boasted wings adapted for what one might call underwater flight.

As he recalled, it was even possible for them to burst up above the surface of the water into the air and fly; though only a short distance. Leviathans could also move on land, albeit clumsily, but their aquatic scales would eventually begin to dry out as with any other marine creature. Like most reptiles, they occasionally liked to bask where they could; so long as the weather wasn't too hot, and where there was a quiet, vacant spot of coastline available – such as on an uninhabited island.

It took several minutes for Arcaydia to calm herself enough to speak. "He said I must undergo some kind of challenge," she explained, "but that I am not ready for it. Despite knowing that, he still means to test me." With tears in her eyes, she gave Larkh a bleak look of apology and shook her head. "I don't know what he's talking about, and I'm sorry I didn't know... If I had known—"

"But you didn't," Larkh interrupted. He took a seat and leaned on the table with his cheek resting on his fist, feathery blond hair spilling across his arm. "I might have somethin' that could give you an idea though." The resulting dubious expression on her face made him smile wryly.

From the bench built into the ship's bulkheads, he lifted a large tome bound with thick reptilian leather and gilded leaf and vine patterns on the cover. In the centre of the cover was a title written in the Daeihn alphabet. As he laid it on the table and pushed it in front of her, Arcaydia's eyes widened.

"Where in Aeldynn did you get this?" she gasped, running a hand over the cover. "Few copies were ever made, and fewer still exist!"

"My dear Arcaydia," Larkh chuckled, "there are many things I've found in the course o' my travels, an' most of them I probably shouldn't have. As it so happens, I have them anyway." He gave her a sly look. "Are you able to read it?"

Arcaydia stared at the book in disbelief; this was the Taecade Medo, a book filled with ancient Nays lore, scripture and prophecy. Opening it carefully, she studied the contents page. "I've only been back with the Nays for about half a year, so I don't yet know much, but I can read bits of it," she admitted. Then she looked at him, confused. "Why are you showing me this?"

Larkh shrugged, pushing against the table as he stood. "I don't know, perhaps I thought it might help you decipher somethin' about that leviathan," he suggested. "I sure as seven hells don't like the idea of the beast crushin' my ship in its coils an' draggin' us all down into the depths with it; an' after your little episode earlier I thought I'd dig the book out on the off-chance it might give us a clue."

Smiling, Arcaydia looked up and nodded. "Thank you," she said quietly, taking the mug of hot tea into her hands. "I'll see what I can make of it."

With a wink, Larkh slid around to the far side of the table and sat down on the bench, taking his own mug with him. "I'll be lookin' over my charts if you need anythin'," he offered. "I've never sailed the northern waters of the Sendero de Mercader, so I might as well learn a bit about it while I've got the chance."

"Good idea," Arcaydia agreed, her hand stopping over a string of Nays letters on the first page of the book. She began flicking through the pages. "I think I might have found something already."

II
Almadeira

Sister Nalane was inside the Kathaedra as Kalthis had suspected. She knelt in prayer before the statues of the Kaesan'Drahknyr beneath the much larger one of Raiyah positioned directly behind them. Glittering rays of sunlight danced in the silent air of the Kathaedra through the high-reaching windows, casting a serene atmosphere around the building, befitting its purpose.

Kalthis maintained his distance, allowing her to finish before he approached. Though she did not speak her prayer aloud, and she was not contacting him directly via a mind-link, he felt the words of her plea.

Prayer was a complicated matter for his kind; how and when they were answered, and in what fashion, was first heard and always determined by Raiyah herself and conveyed to the respective individual if necessary. The Kaesan'Drahknyr were only able hear prayers directed toward them if they stood within close proximity to the person praying.

During long sleep, physical responses were suspended. Aeons ago they may have occasionally answered Raiyah's followers in person depending on the nature of the request, the identity of the asker, and what was occupying them at any given time – but even back then it was an uncommon occurrence. Today, it only tended to concern those dwelling within the borders of Ardeltaniah, and the Tsolàr Fain.

Feeling his presence, Nalane concluded her prayer and stood. Turning to face him, she smiled warmly, though her face was a picture of sadness. "It is time for you to go, isn't it?" she asked, approaching slowly.

"Yes, I'm sorry," Kalthis replied solemnly, feeling her disappointment. "I came to thank you for your kindness, and to say farewell, but I must also ask you something about the Kathaedra." When Nalane inclined her head, he continued; "I believe there is a gateway. I need you to take me to it; it might be my only way out of Almadeira during daylight hours. I know the location of the one I am looking for, and under the circumstances I cannot delay."

Straightening herself, Nalane bowed her head and started in the direction of the Kathaedra's cloisters. "This way," she said. "I can't say if it will work, but if anyone can tell it will be someone like yourself."

Kalthis followed quickly after her, and no more than two minutes later, he emerged from the cloisters into the central courtyard. The whitestone gateway stretched upwards at least thirty feet into the air, though some of its ornate masonry was chipped and crumbling. Nalane explained it had been left alone for fear of tampering with something that harnessed powerful magica; even the Order of Silver avoided attempting the repair of such an artefact. It had, on the other hand, been kept clean and untarnished.

"Forgive me for asking, but how come you didn't know where to find it?" Nalane asked curiously. "You've been around for generations after all—"

"Many Kathaedra were built across the world," Kalthis replied, approaching the gateway. "Not all have a gateway, but in those that do, the location varies, and memories are often vague – especially for an immortal." He gave her a knowing smile, hoping she would notice with her spiritual vision. "That, and with its power depleted, it would be difficult to detect."

Resting a hand against the snow white stone, he extended his senses a little over a hundred feet in all directions, making sure it was only himself and Nalane present. Despite the Tsolàr Fain's loyalties to Raiyah, he thought it best his identity remain a secret for the time being.

Scarcely feeling a faint thrum beneath his fingers, he looked up at the crystalline red orb built into the apex of the arch, and spoke softly; *"Éyn anovhiir déhl mhaer strahvar."*

[51] He clenched his teeth as the surge of energy tore from his solar plexus and flowed down his arm as it was siphoned out of his body into the stone. *'What can Nalane see of this?'* he wondered. The look on the woman's face was more surprise than anything else, and now she was standing far too close.

"Stand back," he warned her. "This gate has not been used for many generations; we don't know how it will react to the energy I give it."

Obediently, the blind priestess backed away and stood aside, her hands clasped tight to her chest. Kalthis didn't blame her for her fear; it was only natural. And yet, he recognised Nalane's aura as one belonging to one of Vharik's silver mages, so there could be no doubt she could sense the true strength of the magica her kind so avidly sought to wield. The ribbons of grey in her hair marked the price mortals inevitably paid for seeking to master a power beyond that which one's soul was capable of enduring.

"You sense it don't you?" Kalthis asked, closing his eyes while he fed magica into the gateway. Nalane turned her head away ashamedly.

"I accepted the fate that came with such abilities," the priestess told him. "I was never a strong enough healer by myself, something I always wanted to be. I have saved many lives through being able to use stronger magic, so I do not mind."

"I respect that," Kalthis replied coolly, though she detected a hint of sorrow in his voice. When the orb atop the gateway glowed fiercely and began its steady resonance, he withdrew his hand and turned to face her, opening his eyes. "I won't lecture you; I just want you to think about something, and remember it."

"What is it?"

"Ask yourself what the disadvantages might be to having eternal life."

---

[51] I offer up my strength.

Kalthis' words struck home sooner than expected. Nalane took a deep breath, and slowly nodded her acknowledgement. She was aware she had never possessed the strongest of spirits, nor had she adequately trained herself to shield her spirit against the steady drain of energy that would inevitably end her life.

Smiling, Kalthis turned to the gateway and drew the glyph for Atialleia before the gap. Judging by Nalane's reaction, she could now hear the rhythm of the magica's resonance within the gateway as its power increased, for she closed her sightless eyes to listen attentively to the long, steady hum that came with its every ebb and flow.

"What a beautiful sound," she said dreamily as Kalthis watched the orb reflect the glyph. The arch filled from top to bottom like a theatre curtain with a clear, rippling image of Atialleia at the end of a wide boulevard lined with trees leading from the gateway straight into the palace district. Feeling strong arms touching her shoulders, Nalane opened her eyes again to look up at the towering, sublime spiritual form of Kalthis.

"It is," he agreed, gripping her right hand in both of his. "Thank you, Nalane, for your hospitality. It will not be forgotten. I hope we meet again one day." Giving him a gentle smile, Nalane planted her left hand on top of his.

"To have been graced with your presence has been the greatest honour," she told him earnestly. "I will look forward to the next time we meet." Kalthis returned her smile, though he knew not how much she could discern of his expression, and then released his grip on her hand. "Farewell, Kalthis," Nalane added as he turned away and approached the gateway.

"Farewell, Sister Nalane," Kalthis replied, glancing over his shoulder once to see her wave. With one circular wave of his hand he entered the gate and was gone, and with him the film of energy projecting the image of Atialleia.

Nalane wanted to cry. She wished she could have gone with him. There was something about him that made all her worries fade away; a sensation that made her feel almost invincible, that nothing could harm her while he was close. His energy had been so level and rational. *'Will we meet again?'* she wondered. *'Maybe, if I live long enough...'*

III
Sendero de Mercader

"Albharenos called me *Mindseer Oracle* in Drakaan," Arcaydia explained, sifting through the pages of the Taecade Medo trying to find any shred of text she could read. "I'm sure I would have had some idea of what that is if Marceau hadn't disappeared when he was supposed to train me."

"Ah yes, the famous swordmaster," Larkh drawled. "How pissed off are your Nays friends goin' to be after all this eh? What'll they do when they find out it was a pirate who helped you, an' what'll happen to poor Marceau, I wonder?"

Arcaydia shuddered at the thought. "I don't know," she shivered, "but I don't think he'll get away with it; even if he was going to warn King Jaredh. It makes me wonder who he really is."

"I happen to know who, or rather *what* he is," Larkh grinned, rising from the table. Arcaydia looked up from the book, one brow arched. "Sorry lass, I can't say. You'll have to find that one out for yourself. Y'see, my mentor swore me to secrecy, an' I don't want to cross the lady who trained me to fight, if I've a choice in the matter." Her eyes followed him as he stepped behind her, placing both hands on the back of the seat.

"And what about you?" Arcaydia asked, looking up at him. Her fine features were a picture of innocence. "Can you tell me more about who you really are?"

With a cheeky smile, Larkh leaned over and seized her, albeit gently, by the jaw, and kissed her firmly on the lips. For a moment Arcaydia was about to pull away, but instead she felt herself relax in the moment and closed her eyes, returning the gesture. When they parted, she added, "I didn't mean quite like that—"

"You enjoyed it though," Larkh interjected, shrugging. "In answer to your question though, who I really am is exactly what you see. My past is who I *was*, an' as I told you before, a lot of that is too painful to talk about."

Turning away, he felt Arcaydia grasp his arm. Looking over his shoulder, he saw her about to speak when a bolt of energy sparked between them. A short, shrill scream escaped her lips before she fell limp over the arm of the chair.

"Arc!" Larkh cried, dropping to his knees, holding her hand in his own. Examining her face, he saw she was vaguely semi-conscious; her eyelids sagged and she blinked only occasionally, but remained still as though paralysed. *'This must be what happened before,'* he speculated.

A loud bang on the door made him jump. "Captain?" he heard Krallan shout. "What's happened?"

"Come in, the door's unlocked!" Larkh called. When the door clicked open, he gave the quartermaster a sidelong glance, worry etched into his crystal blue eyes. "It's much the same as afore."

"Y'mean what happened wi' that mercenary when she collapsed before?" Krallan asked.

Looking bleakly at the barely conscious young woman, Larkh nodded. "I think it's got somethin' to do with her bein' what the Nays call the *Mindseer Oracle*." He briefly turned his attention back to Krallan. "Make preparations for battle; we don't know what we may be up against when we exit the channel."

~ Arcaydia found herself drifting through what she was certain was a series of Larkh's fragmented memories, and this time she was fully aware of where she was. Her consciousness was in a strange state of limbo, but she was fully aware of her surroundings.   There was a beautiful

white manor house surrounded by meadows of all colours and a long boulevard lined with tall trees; the view from the cliffs there was breathtaking. A little girl with wavy brown hair chased after a slightly older boy with sandy blond hair cropped under his jaw-line. Both were dressed in finery only worn by children of the nobility.

At the front door of the manor stood a man with hair matching the colour of the girl's tresses; he wore it swept back behind his ears. He was dressed in a Faltain admiral's uniform. Beside him was a woman adorned in a white dress, her own hair the same sandy-colour as the boy. Together they smiled at the two children running toward them.

"We have something to tell you two," said the lady. This time she was able to hear what was being said. The man gripped the woman's left hand as she placed the other on her belly. "At the end of the year, you're going to have a new brother or sister."

Shock plunged through Arcaydia's heart like a lance. 'No, say it isn't true...'

Images shifted through a series of funerals in what she guessed to be the following few weeks, and soon the family were boarding a ship. She recognised the masts and the designs on the hull; except the stripes were royal blue instead of cardinal red, and black. Under the sterncastle read the name she'd come to know since she'd met Larkh in Almadeira; the name of the ship she was sailing on, Greshendier.

So, the ship had been repainted when Larkh became her captain. Why were the children on board though? In seeing the solemn face of the admiral and his unusually beautiful wife in tears, she guessed it wasn't long after the funerals. Could it be a journey to alleviate their grief? She could only guess.

Then realisation washed over her. Larkh had told her he lost his entire family, but how? Duke Kradelow was the one responsible, of that Larkh was certain, but in what manner? How many of his family were on board? There were so many questions she wanted to ask him, but she dared not. It would prove too painful for him to even think about it.

In a spark of white energy, the scene disappeared and was replaced by one of a tropical island. The ship was at anchor in a small bay. Those on board were awaiting the return of a shore party; they had been waiting a long time – a very long time. The scenes then shifted so rapidly Arcaydia barely had time to consider each one in turn.

Out of the jungle a smaller group eventually emerged from the trees; less than half the original number, which had included most of the Savaldor family. "Why aren't they with them?" the boy asked worriedly. "They went to scout before and said the island was safe... Why have they got father tied up? Mum!" He tugged sharply on his mother's dress, but she already held a face like thunder, staring at the men who dragged her husband back to the ship a hostage.

"Why is my husband bound and gagged?" she demanded. "Release him at once!"   The admiral was bound by the wrists around his back and around his chest, a filthy rag between his teeth, fastened around the back of his neck. The men shoved him into the longboat waiting on the beach. They and their prisoner were soaked; their faces and arms smeared red with blood.

"The rudder's gone sir! The chain's broken!" Arcaydia heard one of the crew members shout to an older man perhaps in his late sixties who emerged on deck.

"What's going on here? Where is my son, Admiral Halven?" the older man snapped. "How did the rudder get broken when we're at anchor? Never mind, see that it's repaired."

A gunshot stopped the crewman in his tracks as he moved to act on his orders, and as dark red blood bubbled from his lips, he fell to the deck. The little girl began screaming and the boy stood trembling, grasping a hold of *his sister's hand and pulling her closer to their mother. The older man had no time to respond to the death of the man he'd just instructed to repair the rudder as a sabre abruptly sank into his back and emerged bloodstained from his chest.*

"Sorry, Ansaren," said the captain, a man with dark hair and short ponytail with a matching uniform save for the badges he wore to mark his rank. "The Duke can't afford to 'ave his plans found out now can he?"

"Grandaaaaad!!!" the boy screamed, struggling against his mother's desperate grip as he fought to reach his grandfather.

More gunshots resounded across the ship, and the clashing of steel suddenly became deafening. "Only Halven, the woman an' those blasted kids left now."

"Bran—dall..." Ansaren sputtered, crumpling to the floor, blood pooling beneath him.

"We really 'ave to kill 'em as well?"

"The Duke said no survivors."

"Surely we can 'ave a bit o' fun wi' the woman first eh?"

The little girl wailed and screamed. Stiff with fear, the mother spoke quickly to the boy, telling him to go and hide with his sister. Quaking violently, the boy nodded, grabbed his sister by the hand and ran, moving as quickly as they could to the hold of the ship.

"Wait here," he said when they reached the hold. His smooth young voice was strangely steady. His bright blue eyes were wild with terror, his face as wet with tears as his sister's. "Don't make a sound. I'm going to help Mum."

"Don't go," the girl whimpered.

"Cari, I must," he said, shakily. "Mum needs my help, ok? I'll be back, I promise."

"Ok...I'll try..."

Stealthily, the boy made his way back up on to the ship's weather deck, hiding where he needed to, stepping over the bodies of all loyal crew members, men he knew, along the way. He tried desperately to be quiet, even when he gagged and paused to vomit on the deck, recoiling at the iron stench of blood. Occasionally his feet slipped in gore as he was forced to pick his way around the dead. Somewhere nearby he heard the shouts of the men who were searching for him.

Eventually he found his way back to the weather deck, bloodstained and dishevelled, and froze as he approached the great double wheels of the ship's traditional helm. His father was on his knees, his hands still tied behind his back, with a sword poised over his back in the hands of the man who had killed his grandfather. His mother, a noose around her neck, was blindfolded and bound, and held tightly by her sandy tresses by another goon on the first platform of the mainmast.

"We found the brat squealin' down in the hold," said another of the thugs as Cari was brought out shrieking like a banshee.

'Cari no!' The boy's frantic thoughts resonated within her mind. 'I told you to be quiet!' Tears flowed down his cheeks and into his gaping mouth in salty rivulets; as much as he wanted to scream, he daren't. How could he help them if he was caught?

"Not my children! Please not my children!" the mother begged. Halven, the father, struggled furiously against his bonds, screaming for his daughter's release heedless of the rag in his mouth muffling his speech. The boy hid behind the wheels, trying in vain to think of a way of saving them.

"Shut up you fuckin' brat!" The man holding Cari snapped. As she continued to bawl and flail, he lost his temper and dumped her over the side. Halven, with murder in his eyes, battled to free himself, snarling with rage and writhing furiously in his desperation against the ropes shredding his flesh.

"Larkhalven! Wherever you are, please live!" his mother cried, whimpering through her tears. "This world *needs you! Whenever you see a blue rose, my son, remember me!" Halven's head was painfully yanked back as his beloved wife was kicked from the mast platform before his eyes, then he choked, spluttered, and saw no more.*

On the other side of the bay, white sails drifted into view, but the boy called Larkhalven had suddenly disappeared somewhere into the depths of the ship where he remained for longer than he could remember, like a soulless doll without purpose. As Arcaydia regained wakefulness, she heard the boy's thoughts once more; 'I didn't know what to do, I was too late, so I failed... I failed to save them. I'm a coward.' Or were they the boy's? No, the voice was young, but much more mature.

'So that's what he really thinks of himself...' Arcaydia mused as her tear-streaked eyes re-focussed. ~

Arcaydia was staring into Larkh's bright azure eyes as she came to from her trance. He wiped the tears from under her eyes and regarded her with concern; yet there was a defensive look in his expression she couldn't ignore.

"Arc?" he called softly. "How do you feel? Is there anyth—"

"You're not a coward!" she blurted without thinking. "How could you have fought and won when you were only a small boy?"

It was as if the bottom of his stomach had dropped out. Larkh stepped back, taking a long, shaky breath, his chest constricting, his heart suddenly pounding. "Laz, I think you'd better take Arcaydia out on deck for some fresh air," he recommended firmly, swallowing against the dryness in his throat. "I need a little time alone."

In realisation of what she had just said, Arcaydia leapt to her feet, almost collapsing as her head swam, her vision briefly darkening. Larsan caught her in his arms as her ankles buckled beneath her. "I'm so sorry!" she cried, but Larkh turned his back.

506

"Give him some space," Larsan whispered, guiding her toward the door. "Trust me, trying to force anything on him now won't end well." Looking over her shoulder, Arcaydia saw how Larkh stood facing away from her; there was fragile tension in his hunched shoulders. Taking a deep breath, she nodded slowly, allowing the big warrior to usher her outside.

AD INTERIM
Movement in Len'athyr

*A traitor seeks to weave their own designs
into stolen fabric.*
Nays Proverb

The Voice of a continent confides only in the Centre of
Balance for fear of misinterpretation and bias. Kalthis,
considered to be the Centre of Balance, possesses the ability
to reserve judgement in order to weigh up all sides of a story
before acting upon it. Communication with any other was
minimal and only possible for the high-ranking Drahknyr
and Galétriahn Mages.

Dreysdan stood on the circular mirror within the
Chamber of the Voice; Madukeyr stood next to him, his
arms folded. The room was filled with the presence of Anu
Amarey, emanating from the mirror. The Voice of Armaran
was bound by oath to show Dreysdan visualisations of
locations around the continent in real time whether she liked
it or not; even if she refused to discuss anything more with
him.

"What do you wish to see?" Anu Amarey's voice
resonated. Dreysdan stood firm and fixed his gaze ahead.

"The city of Cathra and the surrounding areas," the
Galétahr replied.

At once the Chamber of the Voice vanished as
Dreysdan and Madukeyr appeared to be standing on the
mirror in mid-air, poised over the undulating hills of Eyrlian
Moors in central Adengeld; behind them was the dense
Varllan Forest where the small village of Aurenil could be
glimpsed at its edge. The military town of Kasserin lay to
the south-west of the great city of Cathra itself.

Dreysdan witnessed the army amassing around
Kasserin; steady streams of battalions were already
marching up the highroad toward the pass into the Daynallar
Mountains, via the trail alongside the River Aeiven. The

main bulk of the forces seemed to be centred around Kasserin, which had always been a tradition in the region.

The Nays had always constructed settlements specifically for military use. This particular town had been rebuilt from the decimated ruins of a town once destroyed by one of the Kaesan'Drahknyr, since it had become infected by a demonic parasite that had originated in the depths of the Phandaeric underworld of Dhavenkos Mhal. The townsfolk had pleaded for their lives, but the parasite had spread fast and hidden itself among the people. No chances were taken. There had been no survivors.

There were no ships in Tarvon Bay waiting to depart, so it appeared they were more than likely going to brave the mountains. Taking ships from Cathra would mean gambling on the weather, and the unpredictable waters where the Eastern Aeuren and Soreiden Seas clashed. The waves there were often tumultuous. Even ships arriving in or departing from Gaventon were forced to wait for the brightest of skies before making or leaving port, regularly having no choice but to anchor off Aeiven Bay or the Aeuren Coast.

Venturing north to the Sendero de Mercader via the Tarynes Strait also bore troubles. The leviathan inhabiting those waters was rumoured to have the ability to sense unwelcome threats across a greater distance than most of his kin, simply by being attuned to the water surrounding it, especially since the beast had dwelt there for countless generations. It wasn't worth the risk whether it was true or merely a myth. There was also more distance to cover than by the mountain route, and Ameldar wasn't going to risk so many of his men against any of those seas – though he was quite prepared to pit them against drakes, wyverns, and quite possibly dragons. Taking the mountain passes was sure to get the majority across Daynallar's treacherous terrain; the cliffs would shelter them from the worst of draconic predators.

Dreysdan angled his head in the direction of Kasserin. "You remember that place, don't you Madukeyr?" he asked.

"Or rather, the place it *used* to be." The Tseika'Drahknyr followed his gaze, frowning.

"How could I forget what happened there?" Madukeyr closed his eyes as he spoke. "Conscience is a powerful thing, but it can weigh too heavily upon some when a vile deed is necessary. Only one out of the seven accepts such missions unquestioningly and without complaint in order to do what must be done."

"You and I understand better than most," said Dreysdan, "that is why we will support her cause. As Shaorodes' chosen champion, she holds the raw destructive power for wiping the slate clean."

Madukeyr thought for a long moment, watching the activity of the massing army of Adengeld in and around Cathra and Kasserin. "Do you think it will come to that?" he asked, his bright aquamarine eyes falling despondent. "The prophecy of the Keys of the Origin only gives us a hint of what to expect, but it is also laid out in the Taecade Medo that Shaorodes and Quaetihs choose their own champions to test the Keys in their endeavours to bring about the reckoning."

"The champions chosen by the Dragons of Origin will clash, that much is inevitable." Dreysdan spoke in such an indifferent tone of voice it was hard to tell what he was really thinking. "The outcome is unknown, and in what form the Keys unlock their prophecy is up to them. Fate is not entirely set in stone as some believe. The primordial scrolls state the Origin never believed in the idea of a world's future being fixed before it has happened."

As Anu Amarey brought the vision back to the Len'athyr Sanctuary, Madukeyr regarded Dreysdan quizzically. "You've read them?"

"Now you know something new about me." Dreysdan smiled thinly. "A few of the Galétriahn Highlords can read them, but there aren't many of us. I am one of the three currently awake who can; the other two are asleep. As for the others, the only one I know of is Lésos."

"None of the Kaesan'Drahknyr can read them?" Madukeyr pressed, relaxing his stance, dropping his arms to his sides. Dreysdan shook his head.

"Not that I am aware of," he said, turning. "Anu Amarey, please accept my humble thanks for the vision. I will return again soon. I won't expend more energy today."

"A pleasure, Galétahr," Anu Amarey said softly, the sound of her voice fading into the mirror.

Dreysdan swept out of the Chamber of the Voice and down the long corridor with Madukeyr at his side. There was much to discuss before they could seek another audience with the Voice of Armaran for visions of other locations on the continent, and to enquire information about her siblings. He was certain Anu Amarey would refuse to speak much of her brothers and sisters to him; it was one of those subjects she would speak of only to Kalthis. All the other Voices were the same. They would show visions to almost anyone capable of expending the amount of magica required, but delving into their very thoughts and feelings was for Kalthis alone.

It was decided between the two of them Madukeyr would set out for the brume of Daynallar's highest mountain later that afternoon to meet with Dehltas. The great peak lay a short distance north of the Len'athyr Sanctuary and the Dragon's Gate like the apex of a triangle between the two.

Despite the great dragon's words that he would not get involved unless the fight was taken to him, they still had to try to win his support in the hope of avoiding being seen to be interfering in mortal affairs sooner than necessary. The whole mess was Zerrçainne's doing – without a doubt – but something had to be done to at least stall Adengeld's army, to buy time. Dreysdan had already sought and received approval for the mission from the Atiathél.

It wasn't going to be an easy task; like any dragon, Dehltas drove a very hard bargain, but convincing him to renounce his own oath to Adengeld would be even more taxing to say the least. Madukeyr was, therefore, to take a seikryth with him in case of the need for further negotiations. If neither Madukeyr nor Dreysdan could reason with him – and Madukeyr was the more likely of the two to succeed than one who was not of the Drahknyr – then they would need to seek the counsel of a Kaesan'Drahknyr, and who could be better than the partner of Dehltas' own father?

While Avlashrenko was on his way back to the sanctuary, Madukeyr packed his belongings into a leather rucksack. The wyvern would sleep out on the landing pad extending from the sanctuary's rear garden when he arrived. Until then, he would bide his time before the evening meal was served, then bathe and retire for the night to be ready for departure shortly after dawn.

CHAPTER 31

I
Adner

With tiers of wide steps leading up to its gates, Castle Faltain stood poised over the half-timbered city of Adner like a watchful guardian over the Coast of Eresta. Surrounding it, boasting extravagant gardens were the mansions of the local noble families.

The castle was of Nays origin like Castle DeaCathra in Adengeld; fashioned from whitestone but displaying the same slow tarnish; turning greyer the longer it was improperly maintained by humans rather than the Nays. Both inside and out, it was still an impressive structure, sitting perched on the tip of Ennerth, overlooking the Wahren Sea.

Adner was well-known for its canals, winding around the city like entangled serpents dissecting the city into island districts linked by bridges. It was possible to hop into a longliner or local gondola to travel between them if one so desired; even if it were for nothing more than a romantic evening out. It was home to the second largest port in all of Faltainyr Demura, but the second station of the Faltain Navy, Port Rovany, was further south across the water on the shores of the island of Nirskay.

Having re-cloaked himself with glámar to appear as a human man in his early fifties with speckles of grey in brown hair, Marceau strode into the audience chamber. The hall was lit by large alchemical wall sconces with a pair of towering brass braziers burning either side of the throne. There were hidden rungs on the back of them, which allowed a servant to climb up in order to clean and refill them. The alchemical oil burned very slowly, so the job didn't need doing often.

He sniffed. The entire room smelled of some kind of musky incense; a different one from usual. The King sat on his throne seemingly relaxed, but the expression he wore was vexed. Jaredh was a strong-willed king who would sooner give up his own life than relinquish control over Faltainyr Demura.

To Marceau, it appeared Duke Kradelow's intention had been to destroy Jaredh's foundations from beneath him, so King Ameldar DeaCathra would have less trouble conquering the kingdom. He didn't believe for one minute the Duke had executed his scheme in such a manner as to avoid too much bloodshed. He had enough blood on his hands already from wiping out one of Lonnfeir's noble families to cover his tracks, and Marceau knew the bastard had used the most feared guild of assassins around, the *Noctae Venatora*.

Jaredh sat on the throne, his left elbow resting against the armrest and his legs casually crossed. His wispy blond hair hung to his collar, and he wore a moustache and short goatee, giving his stern face greater authority. He was in his mid forties, though he could have easily passed for late thirties. He was dressed in the typical Faltain colours of white, blue and a small amount of red. The long white cloak, lined in royal blue, spilled across the floor like trickling water, and at his right side was a Nays-forged single-handed longsword. The design was different to the one Rajan had left to his son, but the hilt and handle were still made from white dragon ivory.

"Has there been word from Aynfell?" the King enquired as Marceau knelt on one knee and bowed his head.

"The chancellor has confirmed the threat has been dealt with by one of the fabled Kaesan'Drahknyr sire, and then another showed up not two days later," Marceau answered truthfully. "It appears, however, the sorceress of Ehyenn has made off with the Archaenen's copy of the Taecade Medo."

Jaredh leaned on his right elbow, propping his chin against his palm, his fingers closed. "So, they have made their existence known at last," he mused aloud. "What are the chances we can use them to our advantage in this war against Adengeld?"

Fortunately, Marceau had already prepared an answer for such a question as this. "I fear they will not get directly involved; their endeavours have always been to avoid engaging in the affairs of our kind unless absolutely necessary, and by that, I mean if there is a threat we as mortals cannot hope to overcome on our own."

"Like the dragon, you mean?" Jaredh suggested.

'Yes, like the dragon,' Marceau thought. *'I don't like where this is going.'* He replied quickly; "indeed sire."

"So, what if the dragon attacks again?"

"The Second Archmage of Silver is already negotiating terms of defence with the Nays," Marceau replied swiftly, hoping it would be enough to buy him some time, "but sire, I urge you to keep the matter of the Kaesan'Drahknyr private for now. The people of Aynfell had to be quelled; the historical records state the Nays have powers at work to safeguard themselves against too much information getting out. Chancellor Jorical will confirm this when he returns to Adner."

King Jaredh gave a solemn nod; "you have my word Swordmaster Marceau," he said, smiling meekly. "Now, I'd like to discuss the matter of Duke Kradelow's betrayal further, and how we are going to make him think we are unaware of his plot. Thanks to you, we have a small amount of time to prepare."

The conversation lasted long into the evening. At each mention of Chancellor Jorical's name, Marceau felt himself tense. There was no way he could mention it to Jaredh; he knew he wouldn't listen. The king trusted Jorical, and that was that. Alleran Jorical was bad news; he felt it deep in his gut like a freezing shard of ice that just wouldn't melt, but without evidence, he couldn't accuse the archmage of any crime, much less a crime in which he couldn't yet prove he was involved. He expected to remain in Adner for a short while longer; so perhaps he'd have a better chance of learning more about the chancellor when he returned.

Marceau took the chance of putting in a request to go to Aynfell, but King Jaredh had offered him a more important job to do – as if anything could be more important than securing as many of Faltainyr Demura's defences as possible! He was free to decline, he knew, but it would do him well to accept in order to maintain his relationship with the man who had been his king for many years now. He had become renowned as a swordmaster and the head instructor at the Kessford Academy, and that in turn had eventually earned him a place in the king's court as an adviser.

He left the audience chamber in a sombre mood and made his way to his allocated guestroom. Once inside, he approached the window to stare out into the clear evening sky, wondering whether he had any other part to play in the prophecy of the Keys of the Origin. But there was something else that didn't sit right with him. He sensed something was guiding these events; something, or perhaps someone, was acting as a catalyst.

II
The Valley of Daynallar

Avlashrenko banked and swooped down, dropping Madukeyr off on a wide section of the craggy path. It was as close as the wyvern dared get to the fog-enshrouded mountain looming ahead of them without rousing the dragon's anger. Large dragons tended to be far more territorial than lesser dragons, and generally disliked sharing their domain. The central valleys and mountains could be considered to be communal areas, but taller or more remote peaks were private, intimate sanctuaries. As was usually the case, the taller the mountain, the larger the dragon.

Madukeyr had made Avlashrenko aware of the meeting he and Kalthis had chanced upon with Dehltas several days before. The great black dragon had managed to quell his rage for a time to speak with them respectfully, but Adengeld's betrayal had stung him to the core. Even here they could feel his seething bitterness. It would come as no surprise if he refused to make another pact with mortals.

It was a long trek up the winding jagged path, and Madukeyr could only use his wings here in short bursts to make the ascent quicker in such dense fog. The Tseika'Drahknyr's wings were a slightly different shape to those of the other Drahknyr, being of the Kensaiyr rather than the Nays. His were more like those of a swallow, whereas those of a Nays-born Drahknyr were more like an eagle's.

The biting chill of the brisk mountain wind sank its teeth into his pale flesh as he climbed higher. Silently Madukeyr willed his etheric barrier into effect. Long before he reached the dragon's eyrie, he both felt and heard Dehltas' disapproval of being disturbed; yet he gave no warning of taking any action against it. *'There may be some chance of getting through to him yet, then,'* Madukeyr hoped, pushing onward. Dragons were never easy to negotiate with, but he had to admit, Dehltas was perhaps the most reasonable he'd ever known.

When at last he reached the summit, a colossal monument to the Thean deities loomed before him, depicting Raiyah at the top in the centre, Lyte to the left, and Velhana to the right. Between, them at the rear of the plaza, was an altar. It was Madukeyr's guess no-one but Dehltas had been to this shrine for centuries, and in all his long years, it was the first time he had been to this particular one.

From a slope on the north side of the shrine the dragon came, climbing easily up on to the plaza. Approaching Madukeyr, Dehltas growled in annoyance; a deep, guttural sound that was frightening irrespective of its intent. "Explain to me why you have come, Tseikané," he rumbled, "though I think I must already know what you shall ask. Did I not make the terms of my involvement clear before?"

Madukeyr knelt on one knee, feeling strangely nervous despite Dehltas having been a long-term friend of the Nays and Kensaiyr. "You did indeed tell Kalthis and me that you would only involve yourself if the humans' war was brought to you," he conceded, "but should the war make it to Faltainyr Demura, we fear the repercussions of allowing it to happen will be grave."

Dehltas' huge claws clung fast to the crags as he crawled up on to pinnacle of the mountain behind the shrine, the gargantuan length of his tail following him like a prodigious serpent. The upper edge of his leathery lips, lined with long, sharp fangs, curled into a sneer. "After Adengeld's betrayal I care nothing for their kind," he snarled, "but nonetheless I shall listen."

Madukeyr took a deep breath. He explained everything he knew of Zerrçainne's involvement, including: Rahntamein's release and his battle with Melkhar; the knowledge imparted on to Kalthis from Anu Amarey; and the movement of Adengeld's army, right down to the foreboding aura that now emanated from the Magicista Akadema within Cathra's walls.

"I fear the consequences will be disastrous if use of such unbridled magica becomes widespread, especially in the hands of humans," he continued. "Now we are aware Zerrçainne is behind it, we must give much more forethought to the situation. We have already been thwarted; the sorceress' Nays origins, especially as a former Galétriahn Highlord, have given her extensive tactical knowledge."

The ridge of Dehltas' scaly brow creased into a frown. Due to the musculature of a dragon's face being expressively restricted compared to that of a person, it was sometimes difficult to discern whether this look was one of anger or puzzlement.

"Leave now, Tseikané, it is time I was alone with my thoughts on this," he advised, his deep, gravelly voice now carrying thoughtful tones. "You shall know my answer when the time comes."

Though at first he felt the constrictions of dread grip his chest, Madukeyr admitted he was lucky Dehltas had been prepared to listen to him at all. It was a decision requiring a lot of thought, and it would mean the dragon would have to break an oath he had kept for generations. Resolving himself to make sure the issue would be settled no matter the cost, he chose to believe Dehltas would make the right decision and take action when Adengeld's army advanced through the Valley of Daynallar.

Bowing in salute, Madukeyr gave the dragon his gratitude, and leapt from the mountain summit to join Avlashrenko once he'd left the chilling mist behind. After watching him leave, Dehltas growled deep in the back of his throat as he turned his head south-west, in the direction of Adengeld.

III
Yahridican Fortress

It was late in the evening when Zerrçainne's eyes flashed in delight. She placed a marker on the page, and closed the Taecade Medo with a wicked smile. Finally, she'd found something she could act on immediately! Rising, she lifted the book and cradled it against her chest.

Moving toward a door left of the tall arched windows on the far side of the room, she glanced over her shoulder at where Dhentaro slept on a fur rug laid out by the roaring fireplace. With a quiet snort of amusement, she swept out of her spacious study, deciding she would allow him to sleep for now. With his first task of bestowing the runes on Prince Rannvorn complete, he would need all the rest he could get for all the work to come.

She cared nothing for Ameldar's war with Faltainyr Demura; it was merely a means to a far superior purpose, and now Leyal had finally made contact via the seikryth she'd given to him, she planned on paying him a visit in a tavern called The Siren on the other side of the continent in Saldour. First of all, she would need a bath, and have Dhentaro cook their evening meal before opening another Thannyc portal to take her there.

Just the very thought of what was to come excited her; she would discover what Leyal had learned from his encounters with – dare she think it – the *chosen ones*, the so-called Keys of the Origin, and then she would plot how she would use them to assist her in breaking the astral tethers holding the Eidolon Ring in place.

"The *Eléstolaiyn Aneiro*," she thought aloud; "who would have thought it had the potential to prove so useful?" She chuckled wickedly to herself. *'Time is on my side; Alymarn shall have his army soon enough, but Rahntamein needs access to the Lhodha Drahvenaçym to locate the Dragon Aspect. Who cares if Ameldar gets a dragon to fight for him or not? It really doesn't make any difference to me.'*

As the thought of Alymarn's army crossed her mind, she gave the thought it might be time to get back in touch with her acquaintances in the far north-east of Zaern'Kairnell some consideration. It had been quite a long time since she had last been in touch with Commander Karneyl and Queen Emnueraillé of the Shäada. She had of course warned them her plans for Armaran were going to be extensive, but she was still obliged to inform them of the latest developments. They were going to be delighted with the news everything was going according to plan, and how the occasional setback might actually serve as an advantage if manipulated correctly.

She decided she would give it at least a few more days, or perhaps a week, before contacting them. By then Ameldar's – or rather Rannvorn's – forces should be almost ready to begin the trek towards the Valley of Daynallar.

Anything could go wrong between now and then, of course, but she was confident there was always a way to recover from a minor slip-up. If only there were a way to keep the Drahknyr off her back. Perhaps there might be a clue in her distant memories that might help her uncover a solution.

An ear-piercing shriek outside caught her attention, directing her to the window. Peering through the latticed glass, she saw the climax of a fight between two of Dhentaro's gargoyles. One of the larger beasts had a taloned hand buried in the chest of a smaller individual, and, with its fanged maw clamped around its victim's throat, crushed its heart. Releasing its jaws, dripping with blood, the victorious creature bellowed in triumph and cast the corpse to the ground, still holding the gory remains of the dead one's heart in its claws.

High as the level at which she stood was, Zerrçainne still heard the sickening crunch as the felled gargoyle hit the paved stone courtyard below, followed by the thankful cries of other ravenous fiends lurking below. Rolling her eyes, she turned away and continued down the cold, tarnished corridor toward her chambers. She would have words with Dhentaro about the unruly behaviour of his pets later, though she was quite certain their tactics would one day come in useful.

IV
Sendero de Mercader

Arcaydia spent the following few hours up on the forecastle racking her brains over what the leviathan could possibly provide for her test. She dared not speak to Larkh until he was ready to speak to her; the way he reacted had shocked her initially, but she had spent time thinking about it. Truthfully, it wasn't at all surprising his reaction was so severe. Under those circumstances, she would probably have reacted the same way.

As time wore on, she wished the copy of the Taecade Medo wasn't still sitting on the chart table in the great cabin. Larsan had gone to ask Larkh if she could bring it outside to study it, but the answer was a very firm "no". It wasn't because he didn't trust her, Larsan told her, it was because the book was so old and so few copies existed. Larkh didn't want to risk anything happening to it if he could have any hand in preventing it, and there were few on board who actually knew he possessed a copy. If word got out, even at the idle slip of the tongue from a crew member, he could be hounded for it by the god's knew who.

A sudden tremor lasting several moments rocked the ship out of her steady rhythm. A murky blanket of cloud lay thick across the sky, but the wind was fair, the swell of the sea barely breaking waves. From where she sat with her back against a carronade, Arcaydia felt as though her heart was trying to climb up into her throat. 'Is he here?' she wondered, the onset of panic setting her pulse racing.

"What in the blazes was that?" one crew member shouted.

"Fuck me that shadow's bleedin' huge!" a lookout cried.

"It's 'im lads!" declared Laisner, sitting by the foremast, his arm in a sling to support his wounded shoulder. He cast a knowing glance in Arcaydia's direction. "The sea monster's 'ere. Best we start prayin' it ends quick."

With a shiver, Arcaydia rose to her feet and peered over the rail. They were now back in the Sendero de Mercader, so they had entered the white leviathan's domain. When several minutes had passed, the shockwave reverberated through *Greshendier's* timbers again as a titanic shadow, sinuous and lithe, passed beneath the ship once more. She swore her heart stilled in that moment. This time, Larkh flew out on to the quarterdeck to witness the beast emerge.

In a fountain of saltwater jetting skyward like a geyser, Albharenos erupted from the depths, arcing over *Greshendier*, clearing her mast-height of more than sixty metres with ease. His brilliant white scales gleamed in spite of the heavens being overcast; the membrane of his aquatic wings reflecting the small amount sunlight that did manage to squeeze in-between clusters of the nebulous haze.

The crew on deck fell into silence, frozen with terror. Even Larkh became rigid as stone with only his eyes following the immense arc of the great serpent's vast body. Zehn crouched beside a cannon, and Larsan's expression, as he stood by the large wheels of the traditional helm, could only be described as dumbfounded. With a thunderous roar, Albharenos plunged beneath the waves.

As the vicious barbed tip of his tail disappeared, the ship's crew allowed their breath to escape their lungs, though many dared not move from where they stood. Others crept slowly to somewhere that looked to be safer; though on board a wooden ship faced with such a tremendous being, all sense seemed to have fled the men.

Seizing a moment to make a move, Larkh rushed over to Arcaydia, followed quickly by Zehn and Larsan. Arcaydia leaned against the carronade, trembling once more. She fought to keep her breathing under control, but her expression was calculating.

"There is something," she mumbled; "something I have never known, yet something I must remember. It's like trying to remember a dream you quickly forget soon after you wake."

"Sir, should we ready the—" Krallan began.

"No." The quartermaster gave Larkh a sidelong glance as if to question if his captain were mad. "Just make sure we stay on course Krallan. I don't want the helmsman runnin' her aground 'cause he's distracted."

"Even if you did attack Albharenos you wouldn't stand a chance!" Arcaydia interjected. "He is not here to fight you. He is here to test me, and all I need to do is pass. He is not our enemy."

"What a load o' shit that is," Laisner spat. Arcaydia stared up at the man sitting by the foremast. "That fuckin' monster's about to smash us to smithereens an' us along with it! We're done for—!"

"No, we're not," Larkh interrupted, feigning bravery. Just the sight of the beast had knotted his guts, and judging by the pallor on the mercenary's face he guessed he felt the same. "If it wanted us dead I think we'd already *be* dead. Albharenos was giving us a display of the least he could do. If we attack him, it *will* be the end of us, though perhaps not Arcaydia."

"Wise words, young captain," the granite voice of the leviathan rolled as its imposing draconic face slowly lifted out of the water. This time he was not using mindspeech. "However, you and one other beside the Mindseer Oracle are also of great importance."

"Me?" Larkh questioned, bemused. Quickly looking around, his gaze fell upon Zehn and fixed upon him. "Me and...?"

"Yes, the one with the bandana." Albharenos angled his head toward Zehn, whose chest heaved nervously, exchanging wary glances with Larkh. The leviathan continued; "you must remove all on deck who are not at this time needed, but you and he must remain."

"Why?" Larkh asked defensively.

"For my test." Arcaydia rose unsteadily to her feet as she spoke. Behind her, Laisner and numerous other crew members were glaring.

Larkh swallowed hard and licked his lips. "GO!" he ordered. Stricken with terror, many of the men failed to move. A low growl rumbled at the back of the leviathan's throat. At once, all idle hands fled below deck, quickly dropping the hatches behind them.

Little did they all realise, the wind had suddenly died, slowing the ship to a barely noticeable drift. All was still in the following moments as Arcaydia stood before Albharenos. The moment their eyes locked, both were surrounded by a pale, ghostly luminescence.

"The deepest truth that lies in the hearts of all..."
"...is the will to be recognised."
"The highest power..."
"...bears the seed to future creation."
"Honour is the undying foundation..."
"...on which dignity finds its cause."
"Trust is the eternal burden..."
"...of all who seek contentment."
"Loyalty tests the chains of fate..."
"...which binds all in everlasting comradeship."

The luminescence between them dimmed and vanished, leaving Arcaydia stunned. With her mouth agape, she stared into the defiant eyes of Albharenos. Utterly speechless, she wondered where the words had come from. As far as she knew there had been nothing in her memory, even before her amnesia had robbed her of her most recent memories.

"You may proceed, Mindseer Oracle, you have passed," Albharenos declared. "Go with my blessing in your mind, heart and soul."

"But how?" Arcaydia stammered. "I've never heard those words before in my life!"

Albharenos held his stare against hers. "The answers were there all along," he told her. "You are indeed the very embodiment of she whose destiny was destroyed."

"She? She who? Who do you speak of?" Arcaydia demanded, her eyes brimming with tears. Zehn and Larkh each placed a hand on her shoulders. "I don't know who I am! Tell me!"

"It is not my place to say," the white leviathan answered solemnly. "You will understand in time. We shall meet again, farewell."

Before another word could escape her lips, Albharenos sank beneath the waves. Shocked and dismayed Arcaydia buried her face in her hands and wept. Moments later, Albharenos burst out of the water again some distance ahead of the ship, his twisting, undulating form rising and falling between air and sea until eventually he disappeared from sight altogether into the early evening mists slowly beginning to creep across the surface of the water.

The two young men standing either side of Arcaydia remained in stark silence, conscious of their absence of comprehensible thought. Looking at one another incredulously, they soon realised their immediate feelings were mutual. That silence was broken by Larsan approaching them from behind as he spoke; "I don't know about you guys, but after *that*, I think I need a drink – and a lot of it."

Startled, Arcaydia shrieked in surprise; Zehn and Larkh were similarly alarmed. A flintlock barrel was being aimed at Larsan's chest. "Do that again Laz," Larkh warned, "an' I might just let my finger slip over the trigger."

"Easy!" Larsan flinched. "It was an accident. To be fair, you were all away with the fairies just then." Hands flattened against his chest, palms facing outwards defensively, the warrior took a step backward.

"By our rights we were," said Zehn, "my brain is still telling me none of that was real, though I'm well aware it was. Your idea of a good hard drink sounds like a grand idea."

A puzzled expression crossed Larkh's face as he turned to face Zehn. "Well you've certainly changed your bloody tune, you feelin' alright Mr Elite? You're startin' to sound like one o' the crew."

"Seems like he's started to loosen up a bit," Larsan chuckled.

Zehn snorted. "The situation doesn't look like it's going to change any time soon," he observed with a shrug. "I'm stuck on a ship with a crew of filthy, thieving pirates in largely unknown and closely guarded waters – and that's that."

"I'd watch your tongue if I were you," Larkh advised, pulling a wry smile. "You're grossly outnumbered an' there are an awful lot of ears on this ship."

"Hmph," Zehn grunted.

Taking a deep breath, Arcaydia whirled around to face the group. "Let's go and have a drink then shall we? I could do with something to take my mind off what just happened. Larkh, sorry about earlier by the way; I was shaken and worried, like I am now, you understand right? I do hope—"

"Arcaydia?" Larkh called in a placid voice.

"Yes?"

"Don't worry about it." He took her hand. "We'll find a secluded spot and go to anchor for the night. An' we'll all have a drink. I'm sure Larsan'll be happy to go an' fetch a few bottles of the spirits he tried to smuggle on to my ship without me noticin'."

"You bastard," Larsan said through clenched teeth, his stare fixed on the ever familiar impish glint of satisfaction twinkling in Larkh's eyes.

"Alright," Arcaydia sighed inwardly. "Wait, he did what?"

"Doesn't matter!" Larkh linked his arm with hers, leading her toward the great cabin. "Nothing matters between now an' what happens next."

Zehn rolled his eyes, wishing he hadn't perpetuated the idea. *'Still, he's got a point,'* he admitted. Inside he mentally kicked himself. *'What in the world is wrong with me?'*

CHAPTER 32

I
Sendero de Mercader

Greshendier went to anchor off the coast of Isla Narvierr late in the afternoon, sheltered by a small cove where no settlements were in sight. If there were any, they would likely be Nays or Cerenyr, and the chances of them being welcome in dock were uncertain; even with Arcaydia in their midst.

As Larkh had promised, there was an evening of merriment with the ship lit up by alchemical deck lanterns. The crew took turns in singing shanties and tavern songs; the bawdy ones earning a raised brow from Arcaydia. Much to everyone's surprise, even Zehn made an effort to join in upon hearing songs with which he was familiar.

Late into the evening Arcaydia found Larkh perched on the end of the bowsprit, where he sat gazing up at the stars in the midst of a clear sky, the cloudy gloom lost to the spectacle of every tiny light blinking in the darkness. The waning moon was still full enough to shower *Greshendier* with its opalescent glow, casting her as a magnificent silhouette where only the inhabitants of Isla Narvierr might catch a glimpse of her.

Arcaydia decided it couldn't be put off any longer. "I uh..." she faltered, failing to find the right words, nervously tugging at the fabric of her blue gypsy skirt. Larkh shifted his position to regard her, his expression unreadable. "I didn't want to disturb your quiet moment," she eventually continued, "but I wanted to apologise. I was so shocked by what I'd seen I didn't think of how you would feel."

Despite himself, Larkh smiled meekly. Facing the bowsprit, he climbed down wordlessly. It wasn't until his feet were planted firmly back on the forecastle deck he responded; "I think no less of you lass," he shrugged, "but I was taken aback by what you said. Someone all of a sudden screamin' your own thoughts into your face ain't exactly an easy thing to deal with."

"I'm so sorry." Her eyes brimmed with tears. "Are you still angry with me?"

"No."

"Then—"

"Arcaydia," Larkh said, taking a deep breath of the fresh sea air, the tang of salt mixed with the rich earthy scent of dense forest. He placed his hands on her shoulders, glancing briefly at the joviality and debauchery going on behind them. Some members of the crew were now playing musical instruments, from violins and guitars to drums and tambourines. "Stop worryin'," he continued, "I *just* can't face any of it; I told you so in Almadeira. Even now, the very thought of it makes my stomach turn. If I let it run away wi' me there's a good chance it'll make me sick. It's somethin' few of the crew know an' I'd rather it stayed that way, you understand?"

"Why?" she asked.

"They need a strong captain," Larkh informed her, looking her firmly in the eye. "People lose faith if they feel they can't rely on someone. If I show too much weakness, someone'll seek to take my place an' try to rally as many of the others as possible to mutiny."

Arcaydia shivered at the thought. "What do you do if you feel like you did earlier?" She searched his eyes earnestly, wondering what he truly thought of her; especially now her power had begun to surface.

Larkh chuckled. He released her shoulders and motioned to the starboard side rail. "I lock myself away till I feel better. I let one of the mates know, like Krallan or Argwey, an' then I'm left alone to deal with it without havin' to show my face – unless we have an emergency o' course." He studied the puzzled expression now crossing Arcaydia's face. "Is that so strange? You've an odd look about you."

Arcaydia folded her arms, her eyes downcast toward the deck in speculation, her brows knitting. "No, just something you said made me think of someone else I know. You may have just helped me understand something, that's all."

"Cap'n!" a man with a scruffy beard yelled from across the weather deck. Larkh tilted his chin, looking up. "Why don'ya go'n get that ol' flute o' yers ye coggy-'anded bastard? We ain't 'eard ye play fer ages like!"

"Ah, now there's a good reason to cheer up." Larkh clapped Arcaydia on the back as he stepped past. "C'mon, come an' have another drink. We can afford to be a bit more relaxed when we're at anchor."

"Wait!" she caught him by the wrist, her mouth agape. "You play the flute?"

Larkh covered his mouth to avoid spitting as he stifled his laughter. "Your expression Arc, I'm so sorry, it's priceless. I do indeed play the flute; though not often enough apparently." Rotating his wrist to grasp hers, he pulled her back across the deck toward the merrymaking where Larsan was dancing in drunken circles, arm in arm with Argwey.

Squinting at them in amusement, Larkh leaned in toward Arcaydia's ear. "Give it a few more drinks an' Laz'll be a right exhibitionist." Giggling, she jabbed him lightly in the ribs. With a smirk, he added; "I'm goin' to get my flute; won't be a minute."

It was that look she found so intoxicating. A smirk it might be, but it held such irresistible mirth; and on a face like his, it was so captivating! But, she told herself he was a pirate, and nothing would stop him from getting what he wanted. There was also something else about him that unquestionably refused to be tied down. What was it she felt then?

Larkh played a selection of tunes for them all on his small brass flute; some solo and some within a group. To Arcaydia, he appeared contented as if his pain and worries had mysteriously vanished, but the look in his eyes when he lifted them to her told a different story. His men all clapped and cheered, and out of the corner of her eye she saw Larsan chatting with Argwey. Then, another shanty broke out:

> *Never were the ladies there,*
> *Never – ever –*
> *Never in Tourenco fair!*

> *Cut loose from a tops'l yard*
> *Her canvas flyin' free*
> *Cor blast she drives a bargain hard!*
> *Sendin' men listin' back to the sea*

> *Never were the ladies there,*
> *Never – ever –*
> *Never in Tourenco fair!*

> *Her sheets are flappin', free like a bird*
> *Sly like a vixen in heat*
> *A man's cry for freedom never was heard*
> *Those ladies, they do like to cheat*

> *Never were the ladies there,*
> *Never – ever –*
> *Never in Tourenco fair!*

> *Beware those bold ladies, rigged in disguise!*
> *Held fast by seductive deceit*
> *T'is easy for men to fall for such beautiful lies*
> *But my lads she's a wonderful treat!*

> *Never were those ladies there,*
> *Not were they ever*

Never – EVER –
Never in Tourenco fair!

Eventually Larkh came to sit beside her as she sipped at a cup of Felanshia wine while discussing with Zehn his work as an elite mercenary. It turned out ordinary sellswords weren't all that keen on the elites for the sole reason they tended to get the higher paid jobs. Zehn shrugged it off by draining his mug, claiming he was in the better position, and that he really couldn't care for their hostility.

Arcaydia wondered if her cheeks weren't already pink with the effects of the wine, they certainly were now as the wily young captain casually put an arm around her, only to burst out laughing at Larsan, who, just as predicted, made an exhibition of himself. When he'd been plied with enough drink, the man became subject to a number of dares before finally tearing off his shirt and swinging it around his head six times before slinging it over the side of the ship into the sea. In declaring himself triumphant, he plopped down beside a cannon and was snoring against it in moments.

Arcaydia couldn't help but laugh, but it was all made so much worse by Argwey's jokes and stories. She soon found herself cackling in tears of hysterics as every embarrassing tale in recent months of the northern sellsword poured out in abundance, much like the flow of alcohol this very evening. Several of those stories also happened to include Larkh, which left him fidgeting throughout the entertaining discourse, rubbing his eyes and forehead.

Rising from his seat abruptly at the mention of another humiliating story, Larkh held out his hand to Arcaydia; "let's go an' have a dance lass, so Sir Fancy Pants can laugh at my expense." She stared open-mouthed at him for a moment, then beamed and rose, lifting her skirts to join him.

"Fancy Pants?" Zehn frowned. "Look in the mirror! Where did you come up with *that one*?"

Larkh flashed him a sidelong glance accompanied by a playful grin. "I don't need a mirror!" he announced. "An' last I recall, you worked directly under royalty. For what it's worth, I meant nothin' by it. I'm havin' too much fun to be givin' a damn. Besides, your face looks warm enough to fry an egg; go take a breather." With a wink in Zehn's direction, he led Arcaydia out into a clear space on the weather deck as another lively tune commenced.

"Damn him!" Zehn growled under his breath; though he realised his words were without their usual venom. He touched his cheek, realising he did feel rather warm. Argwey dropped down beside him, his fair elven skin also flushed.

"Y'know, he threw himself off a cliff into the sea once – after his hat," the bosun said, almost too casually.

Zehn's eyes widened incredulously. "He what?"

"His hat blew right off. It wasn't that big of a cliff mind you," Argwey continued. "He took off that priceless coat o' his beforehand an' entrusted it to Krallan, then jumped feet first. Took him the rest of the day to walk back to the ship mind you. He was nearly dry by then, but his boots still squelched."

The mercenary snorted in amusement as he removed his bandana to run a hand through his shock of hair. "What a pillock," he muttered, shaking his head.

After the dance, Arcaydia looked up at the sky to see the moon was past its zenith. Despite how tired she had been after the trial, she somehow felt invigorated, and she could feel her face glowing with the effects of the wine. Feeling relaxed, she waited while Larkh gave the final round of night orders to his crew. Men who were designated lookouts stood either side at the fore and aft ends of the ship, while two others climbed aloft into the rigging.

When he returned, he invited her into the great cabin to get something for supper to sober them up before going to bed. He informed her drunken men manning any ship, least of all one well in excess of three thousand tons, was asking for trouble. With this in mind, his crew tended to behave;

unless of course *they* happened to be Larsan, who still lay curled up next to a twelve pounder cannon.

Some time after they'd eaten a little bread washed down with water, Arcaydia stood, and was reaching for the door when Larkh placed a hand on the door before she could open it. "There's somethin' I've not told you yet," he said, his voice almost a whisper, "somethin' I ought to have said earlier."

Lowering her arm, she turned to face him. "And what's that?" she asked, gazing up into those bright azure eyes. She realised then she was holding her breath, increasingly aware of her own heartbeat.

With a shaky sigh, his words fell with relief; "thanks for tellin' me I'm not a coward. I can't say I believe it's the truth, but I thank you all the same."

"But it is the tr—"

"Shut up."

Seizing her by the shoulders, he planted a kiss full on her lips, and, bearing no resistance, she relaxed into his arms, gratuitously returning the gesture. Pulling her close against his chest, he freed one hand and quietly locked the door.

II
Almadeira

"When do you think we'll be able to leave this town?"
Arven muttered, sitting in Arieyta's caravan that evening.
"It's been several days, an' there's been no hint of a word.
Seems the merchant ships don't want to dock for fear of not
bein' able to leave again. There's so little comin' through
from the farms too. We'll end up starvin' at this rate. What a
grand Váreia this turned out to be."

As Arieyta brought her hand to her mouth, yawning, the
jewels around her wrist jingled. "Oh Arven, do quit your
whining," she drawled. "You know what the score is;
though I've a mind to carry out my threat on you, and you
alone if you keep this up. Remember, it's for the money.
You and your troupe need to make ends meet, and if it
wasn't for our little arrangement you'd be wallowing in
poverty by now."

"An' for that we're grateful, Arieyta," Arven sighed,
stroking his goatee while reclining against the back of the
dancer's caravan. "No-one likes threats, an' I just wish I
didn't have to keep so much from Larkh."

"If you'd told him everything, our position would've
been compromised," she reminded him. There was a
mischievous flicker of amusement in her rich brown eyes.
"Still, you needed to tell him enough of the truth to maintain
your friendship. You think he will go back to Enkaiyta when
he leaves the Nays' homeland?"

Arven shrugged, picking up a bottle of the Tourenco
Dark one of Larkh's deckhands had brought him before the
coup. Examining it closely, he smiled. *'A good age, this
one,'* he thought. "If he has his own way when he leaves – if
he leaves – that'll almost certainly be his headin'. He's got
black market deals comin' out of his ears. What is it you're
really after anyhow?"

An unwilling smile tugged at the corners of Arieyta's
voluptuous lips; "that doesn't concern you or your friends

and family in this wondrous band of yours, Arven," she said, gesturing a circle with her hand, gems and gold flashing in the candlelight. "Just be content you're being well looked after."

There was something about it all Arven found unsettling. He knew very little of Aurentai history; gathering from what he did know, it had a lot to do with their ancient grudge against the Nays. What it spelled for him and his troupe, he couldn't hope to know at this stage of her game, but for the time being, they were indeed being well-rewarded for accepting Arieyta's service as an additional performer. What deals she had struck with Zerrçainne or King Ameldar were known only to her, and no amount of pleading would make her talk. What worried him most was what would become of them when her plan finally did come to light.

"I will tell you one thing about what happens next, Arven," Arieyta purred, her eyes drawing his attention toward her like a powerful magnet; "once we're able to secure a private ship to take us to Enkaiyta, we will by then have a means to leave Almadeira, for Leyal shall arrange it for us. We will play our part as innocent victims of Kradelow's coup till then, and try to lift the people's spirits. When we reach Adner, we will begin Act Two by performing for the unsuspecting king."

Arven's breath caught in his throat as he realised what Arieyta meant to do. How could he possibly go along with this? She was testing him now; he saw the devious twitch in her smile. If he betrayed her, that would mean instant death for him, and probably the entire troupe as well.

"What's the matter, minstrel?" she chortled. "You look as though you've seen a ghost. You've nothing to worry about; the deed isn't yours to commit, it's mine. You're just a distraction. Remember the welfare of your entire company or—"

"I know!" Arven snapped. "I know. Gods, damn it all, please stop remindin' me. You know I'll go along with it."

Arieyta sat up. She slipped down on to the caravan floor on her knees, and brushed the side of Arven's face with the side of her hand, her soft breasts pressing against his arm. "Poor Arven," she cooed, "so loyal." The minstrel knew he was being seduced by her, but he was in her thrall. He was powerless to resist her.

III
Kasserin

Prince Rannvorn sat on a tall black stallion before the vast army of Adengeld, the dark curls of his hair fluttering in the fresh, early morning coastal breeze, heavy with the promise of more rain. It had proved to be another wet spring, but that was to be expected with the continent's awkward position; the great ocean ridges disturbed both aerial and oceanic currents, and according to ancient maps, there were also some great mountain ranges in the Nays homeland similar to the Valley of Daynallar.

Cold winds blew down from the north, warm winds swept up from the south, and the ocean currents of the Eastern Aeuren, the Aeurenial Ocean and the Soreiden Sea all collided. The kingdom's landscapes were nevertheless lush, but its temperate climate could be unpredictable.

The sorceress had also informed him there were other forces at work across Aeldynn that were rumoured to play a part in the seasons; one being a particular area lost to the ages; the Azaeras, known as the Unseen Isles. The region was heavily cloaked with glámar, rendering the islands invisible. No sailor who had ventured out into those waters in search of them ever returned alive. She had been adamant, however, there was a mystery to be uncovered there, but even she and her Nays kin had been unsuccessful in unravelling its secrets.

Rannvorn smiled a rather knowing smile as he thought of King Ameldar DeaCathra lying on his sickbed. It meant he would no longer be playing any part in commanding the army marching on Faltainyr Demura. It had all fallen to him, and with fierce determination in his eyes, he had sworn to make his father recognise his worth at any cost. That cost had ultimately been his own soul, and sooner or later, it would cost Ameldar his own life.

Upon his request, Zerrçainne had infiltrated Castle DeaCathra swiftly and silently, and manipulated one of the king's servants with her nefarious magica. The poison was designed to keep Ameldar ill, rather than kill him, for as long as was necessary. Rannvorn desired to make sure his father knew his every effort and deed to win his favour before he died, and he hadn't yet decided on a method of execution. He would consider that in due course. First he had to get an army across the Valley of Daynallar and win a war – though with Duke Kradelow's plan now in full swing it should prove easy enough.

Sadly it wasn't possible for ordinary folk to make the crossing using a Thannyc portal. The Phandaeric Magica would kill or mutilate any being incapable of withstanding its corruption. *'Pitiable weaklings,'* thought the prince, *'to think I was once so weak like them. Were it not for their weakness we could be across there in minutes.'*

'Patience is a virtue.' Alymarn's devious voice echoed inside his mind as if he spoke within a vast cavern. The only way he knew no-one else could hear it was because no heads turned to search for a disembodied voice when it spoke. *'These things cannot be rushed; besides, now that my magica has allowed your voice to brainwash your army, none of them will have cause to doubt you when you use it to defend them against the draconic beasts of Daynallar.'*

Alymarn was right of course. The most difficult task at the present moment was resisting the urge to scream at the agony that burned through the runes into the backs of his hands, winding its way into the muscles of his forearms. Even though Adengeld's army would not now question his use of phandaeric magica, their eyes could still be opened to the truth if they discovered his means of obtaining it. It was a fundamental loophole existing even in magic; deceit could be maintained unless the deceived should discover the truth, no matter how the deception was orchestrated.

'What about the dragon?' Rannvorn asked. *'Do we still need him, and will he still fight for us?'*

'Rahntamein is an old friend,' Alymarn drawled, *'he will not give you protection, but he will be true to his word if he is needed. When my power is under your control, you will be able to use mindspeech to call on him when he has rested enough, but bear in mind he is required in the search for my Dragon Aspect.'*

'And the Kaesan'Drahknyr?'

'They will always be a problem, that is, so long as Aevnatureis functions...'

That confirmed everything for Rannvorn. He knew enough about history and mythology to be aware of what Alymarn was referring to. The very thought made him smile wickedly; Alymarn revelled in it. If his last days panned out as he hoped they would, he would go down in history, leaving his father an insignificant king whom nobody would discuss in the ages to come.

IV
Sendero de Mercader

The swirling mists of the ghost leviathan's domain had thickened to linger as a dense fog over the water, and drifted lazily among the trees along the coast of Isla Narvierr for the better part of the morning. All was deathly silent above deck save for the deckhands going about their daily tasks of swabbing, painting or repairing ropes and rigging.

The cool air seemed to tingle with the ghostly promise of something unknown, a sensation that roused Arcaydia from her sleep. She found herself lying curled up in Larkh's cot with him, and almost gasped in realisation. *'What happened?'* she asked herself worriedly. Until her mind cleared, the majority of the night's events would elude her.

'*Raiyah preserve me,*' she prayed, tentatively attempting to extricate herself without disturbing Larkh. '*Let this remain a secret, at least for now...*'

The abrupt ringing of a bell and frantic shouts from above deck startled her as Larkh erupted from his cot and began dressing himself hastily. He'd just pulled his trousers on when someone banged furiously at the door. He pulled a screen in front of Arcaydia where she stood, and quickly unlocked it. He opened it to see the swarthy form of Daron.

"They're coming out of the fog Captain," said Daron, "the ivory ships of the Nays; at least three of them. They've got us surrounded."

Larkh swallowed hard. "You're sure it's *them*?"

Daron nodded. "One is close enough to see, and she will shortly come alongside. Krallan is preparing to weigh anchor. I am sorry captain, nobody saw them coming."

"It wasn't as if the Nays were goin' to just let us pass quietly by now was it?" Larkh shrugged. "We were forced in this direction by whatever forces of magica they used back in the Veiled Channel; so it's safe to assume they meant to bring us in." He shot a wary glance at Arcaydia, whose head shrank toward her shoulders. Looking back toward Daron, he added; "tell Krallan I'm on my way an' get *everyone* to their stations."

Bowing his head, Daron turned and hastened his way back out on deck calling to the quartermaster. Shutting the door behind him, Larkh resumed dressing. He put on his boots and scanned the room for wherever he'd left his shirt. "Sorry I made you jump," he said to Arcaydia, noticing the shirt lying across his desk at the back of the cabin. "Ringin' of the ship's bell means there's an emergency, or a warnin' to other ships of danger."

Arcaydia shook her head, holding her defensive position. "Don't worry about it," she replied sheepishly. "It's just...I'm sorry about all this."

Larkh stopped to regard her suspiciously, his brow furrowing. "Sorry about what?" he asked. "I wasn't aware you'd done anythin' wrong."

"Neither was I," Arcaydia murmured absent-mindedly, "but I can't help but feel I'm partially responsible. I just hope everything will be alright..."

"Now that *does* sound worryin'," Larkh remarked, buttoning his shirt and reaching for his coat. "Perhaps you can elaborate a bit later when this is over. C'mon, let's go an' see what your kin have to say. They've not blasted the hell out o' my ship yet an' your leviathan friend thought me an' Zehn were somehow valuable; so they certainly can't mean to kill us." Stepping through the door, he tossed the key to her, adding, "lock the door behind you an' pass the key back to me when you come out."

'That's not what worries me,' Arcaydia thought as the cabin door closed. She took a deep breath and began putting on some clothes. 'It's what comes next.'

When leaving the great cabin, she locked the door, hurried to her tiny cabin, swapped her gypsy skirt for her travellers' leggings, and hesitantly crept out into the open air to witness the ship mentioned by Daron drawing alongside the *Greshendier*. There were two reasons Nays ships were called the *Ivory Ships*; one was the colour of their immaculate paintwork over wan oak and albequa timbers, the other because every inch of carved detail, including the ram was fashioned from white dragon ivory; though some details, such as on those on the sterncastle, shimmered gold.

Arcaydia didn't need to see the name on the ship's stern to know who commanded it. It was the As *Nehkúridas Càraellna* [52] , the flagship of Kherindal Valan – the Nàvamier – a Nays admiral, who also happened to be a Galétriahn Highlord. Knowing what she knew, she was certain he would be someone Larkh might find troublesome to get along with.

---

[52] Atiathél's Ship (svhíde) Guardian Crest.

Kherindal stepped across the gangplank on to the Greshendier once the ship was safely alongside, wisps of wavy blond hair dancing in the breeze having escaped the bonds that tied rest of his thick locks at the nape of his neck. What he wore on his head was an elaborate metal circlet, matching the colours of a midnight blue coat embroidered in gold that hung to his mid-thigh and tapered into a point at the back. The winged shapes at the temples were reminiscent of a leviathan's aquatic wings, and beneath those, behind his softly pointed Nays ears, were long, mottled plumes.

"E'verkéne mhaer vesaujr," [53] he nodded politely toward Larkh, who stood rigid. The hunched postures of the crew told of their readiness to fight. Some were already brandishing weapons. Then Kherindal's stern, chiselled Nays features softened into a knowing smile as his cobalt eyes fell upon Arcaydia. "I am pleased to see you have treated my cousin well."

---

[53] Greetings my friend.

CHAPTER 33

I
Auréial Varthalédas
The Imperial Passage

Zehn was observing the passing scenery with enthusiasm when the most colourful forest he'd ever seen burst into view as the veil lifted for Greshendier to follow Kherindal's ship through an archway almost identical to those governing entry and exit to the Veiled Channel. Clusters of cerise blossoms swayed high on the boughs of their trees, dancing in the dainty breeze, complemented by myriads of rhododendrons and carpets of flowering bulbs and lavender. Sweet floral aromas and the earthy musk of the woodland filled the air, loose petals fluttered idly across the channel, some landing on the recently swept deck.

'What must you think of me now, father?' he wondered, feeling content despite the uncertainty of what lay ahead. *'I was never cut out to take over mother's business; if only the rest of our family could have understood that.'*

His eyes slid over to Larkh, who stood in tense conversation with Kherindal by the mainmast. To his amusement, the young captain wore the petulant look of an impatient teen as the Navàmier's egocentric confidence dug its claws into his nerves. A satisfied smile tugged at the corner of Zehn's lips. By the time the unsettling news of Kherindal being Arcaydia's cousin had sunk in, he'd begun to believe it would prove to be the least shocking of any surprise waiting for them in Atialleia.

The mercenary then considered the loss of Larkh's family. Though most of his own family still lived, he was dead to them. The moment he'd decided to follow in his father's footsteps that fact had been guaranteed. They had always disapproved of King Jaredh's *Elite Mercenary Guard*, thinking them no better than glorified sellswords, robbing others of the right to undertake higher paid jobs and contracts of utmost importance. Most nobility didn't trust the average run of the mill mercenary; so their kind only managed to land the sort of work they offered if an elite happened to be unavailable. But that wasn't the only reason his family hated him.

He sighed, thinking of his aunt's humiliating words, accusing him of dishonouring his mother by renouncing his claim to her business; "you disgrace this family Zehn!" she spat, "when your mother inherited your grandfather's business, the first thing she did was write you as its next heir into her Will! But no, you decide to chase after death just like your despicable father who preferred gallivanting across the world instead of looking after his family. And look where that got him! You are *no* nephew of *mine*!"

His mind flashed back to the present as Larkh swept past him up the stairs to the helm. "Bear north-west by west a couple of degrees when the signal is given," he heard him instruct Krallan. "Accordin' to the Navàmier," he added derisively, "we'll need the space to turn into the northern channel. He said we should reach Atialleia by sundown."

"I don't like this Larkh," the quartermaster grumbled. "We're bein' treated like ruddy prisoners."

Larkh shrugged half-heartedly, placing his hands in his pockets. "If they wanted us dead, don't you think we'd already be so?" he reasoned. "We'll have to be on our best behaviour for now I reckon. Breakin' too many rules in a land we know nothin' about, an' with a race so well known for both their physical and magical strength, would be suicide." Turning, he looked over his shoulder. "Besides, we're goin' where nobody's been in centuries! Remember what we found in the Lost City of Velantiir?" He winked. "Think of the possibilities!"

There was no arguing with that. In fact, Krallan felt himself beaming at the thought. Whether they would be given any freedom remained to be seen, and tales of great feats made for grand legends. *Greshendier* was already feared for her superior firepower and manoeuvrability, having brought down dozens of ships of varying sizes that dared confront her. She had sailed through the *Maidhrég*, the Maw of Elinda of all places, a deadly feat for any ship, let alone one of her size. Larkh had a fair idea of what the quartermaster was thinking, and so left him to mull over the prospects. He took out his spyglass and made his way to the forecastle for a better view of the approaching fork in the channel.

It was late afternoon with at least another hour or more to go before they reached Atialleia. Their convoy sailed with an easterly wind on a starboard tack, following the curving channel arcing around to the north-west. If the wind remained favourable, he had no doubt Kherindal's prediction of their arrival time would prove accurate.

"Something botherin' you?" Larkh enquired as he stepped up on to the forecastle deck, idly leaning against the rail as he lifted the spyglass to his right eye. Zehn sat with his back to a cannon, his gloomy mood reflected by his cheerless face as he pulled apart lengths of worn out rope for use as oakum; his fingers red and blistering.

Zehn flicked a glance in his direction. "There's a lot that's the matter, pirate," he muttered, "and you're one of them." Larkh rolled his eyes as he closed the spyglass, returning it to its pouch at his side. He bent to examine a section of the capping rail that had been smashed by a cannonball during the battle with the *Allendrias*, but before he could think of a response, the mercenary continued; "but seriously, I'm thinking of what might have been if I'd made different decisions. Would I still have ended up on my way to the heart of the Nays homeland on board your ship? If I'd chosen differently, I'd have had the respect of my family, but my heart wasn't in the world of trade."

Larkh reconsidered using the witty response that had come to mind, but instead chuckled, brushing the sandy hair from his eyes. This earned him a fixed stare from Zehn, to which he held up an index finger and returned the look.

"I sometimes wonder the same thing," he admitted, "but the past has already happened, so *what ifs* don't matter. One thing you must remember is while you're in the employ of the king, you're still a sellsword, an' that *was* your choice."

"And you're still a pirate; how ironic!" Zehn countered, gritting his teeth.

"Aye," said Larkh, his eyes wandering over the multicoloured forest he somehow found captivating. It was like one of the finely detailed watercolour paintings of his mother's. "The difference is I've never denied that fact."

"You think I have?" Zehn snorted. "You must have a *heart of solid gold* to be doling out that kind of advice."

"A pirate with a heart of gold?" Larkh mused, grinning. His eyes flashed dangerously, giving Zehn a rather pointed look. "What a fancy an' most fictional idea. If you ever come across one, do let me know eh? I'm willin' to wager they'd fetch quite a handsome price on the black market." His expression hardened. "Don't ever mistake me for a high seas philanthropist; they don't exist."

"Ah, so there are your *true colours*," Zehn scoffed, dropping another length of dismembered rope into the bucket beside him. "I was waiting for those to show."

"Bravo! It's good to know your sense of humour is improvin'," Larkh retorted, pushing away from the rail. "You must have been deep cut last night 'cause I'd say you were havin' rather a good time."

Zehn paused, hesitating. He looked up to see Larkh already making his way aft where Kherindal and Arcaydia followed him up the steps to the helm. Whether or not the captain had truly been offended, or if he simply chose to find amusement in his words, he was unable to tell. Either way, the response baffled him. There were more angles to the man than he could count.

At the sound of orders being barked at the stern of the ship, Argwey came striding up to him; "leave the oakum for now an' stand by to brace the yards square," he instructed. "Take the foremast wi' Daron's team."

Zehn dropped another piece of unravelled rope into the bucket and stood, biting his lip and hissing at the stinging pain in his fingers. His hands may have been toughened through swordsmanship, but his skin was unused to such painstaking work on board a ship, making him wonder how anyone could possibly choose to lead such a laborious, unsettled, and moreover uncomfortable existence.

"What's happening?" he asked the elf.

Argwey gave him a dubious look. "We've reached the fork in the channel, an' the wind's shiftin' around to the south; so we need to brace the yards square," the bosun explained. "Just as Kherindal said, we'll reach the Nays capital by sundown."

II
Adner

Marceau hurried down a spiral staircase to a lift powered by an altirna system operated by a lever. He stepped inside, shutting the cage door with the device behind him and pulled on the handle. The lift made a loud clanking noise and slowly dropped, the sound of its gears clinking and grinding all the way down the shaft. The acrid tang of copper and rust hung heavy in the air, suggesting maintenance had been neglected for some time.

Eventually he arrived at a dock beneath the castle where the king's flagship, the *Rapheillas*, sat dormant under a towering ceiling of vaulted stone. He strode along a narrow path and down a steep set of stairs before reaching the bottom, where the ocean lapped at the hulking hull of the ship and the stone walls of the dock.

The *Rapheillas* was a three gun-deck first rate man-o-war, and carried in excess of one hundred guns. A full altirna system had been debated for use within ships of this size, but it had eventually been decided it would require too much altirna fluid and cost far too much to replace should the ship be lost or damaged.

The altirna mine beneath the North Mazaryn Peaks had been running dry for some time, and thanks to Madukeyr, was now starting to recover. Smaller ships didn't appear to need the system, and so the result of a majority vote at a naval conference several years before had been that the system was most efficient in the elite class ships-of-the-line, designed specifically for such a purpose, already combined with other classes of ship. It was possible to make a ship too easily manoeuvrable, for it made them unsteady and far more difficult to handle; and the elite class ships already required extensive training in how to sail them properly.

As he passed the hulking form of the ship, he took care to check no crew on board were in a position where he might be spotted. Few crew remained on board to keep watch, and as yet there were no preparations to sail a fleet to Adengeld. There was nobody on deck; so he was able to slip by unseen.

It was superstition about the ghost leviathan that deterred Adengeld from sailing into the Sendero de Mercader via the Tarynes Strait, and the turbulent waters of the south made moving a fleet dangerous in an area where three bodies of water met. King Jaredh had no such worries taking the Tarynes Strait route, and he hadn't yet ruled the idea out; he was simply biding his time.

Nelraido stood on the crags just outside the enormous rocky entrance of the cove; his loosely braided blond ponytail hovering on the wind, accompanied by a handful of flyaway strands that otherwise framed his handsomely chiselled countenance. His framed Nays eyes, the colour of slate, told more of trouble than he could discuss in the short space of time they had to make use of, but Marceau knew exactly why he had come.

"E'verkéne, Marceau Saiyinn," said Nelraido, his voice carrying high authority even when he spoke at low volume. *"Ye'n arth aràenora vér'mhaer svréhmar, arth ye'n na'the?"* [54]

"You too, Arhcýn'Drahknyr Valan," Marceau replied, picking his way over the slippery rocks plastered with seaweed. "Indeed, I am well aware of why you have come; though I have no doubt you understand my reasons. But nevertheless, I must be held accountable for the grave situation I have caused."

"Grave is the least of what it is, Lyte E'varis," Nelraido insisted, his flinty stare hardening. "Did you by any chance know Arcaydia, my cousin, is the Mindseer Oracle finally reborn?"

Shock struck through Marceau's core like a spear of ice, though his aquatic stare remained unwavering. Nelraido's lip curled. "You *would* have known," Nelraido continued, "had Arcaydia been able to pass on the letter Melkhar carried and entrusted to her before departing for the Dorne Shaft. You thought the idea was simply to train her as a fledgling Galétriahn in partnership with your former student, who happens to be one of the two keys identified by Lésos. You knew the full details were yet to come, and you knew it was a vitally important task."

The following silence was broken only by the sloshing of waves echoing around the mouth of the cove. Marceau could hardly believe what he had heard. Arcaydia was the reincarnated Mindseer Oracle? He had fulfilled his task of ensuring Zehn received his swordsmanship training, but as far as he had been aware, Arcaydia was a new Galétriahn in need of physical combat training. Though the Galétriahns were mages by nature, they were required to become battlemages, meaning they were obliged to learn enough physical combat to defend themselves rather than always having to rely upon their magica.

---

[54] You are aware of my purpose, are you not?

"Raiyah and Lyte forgive me!" Marceau breathed. "I had to warn King Jaredh about the plot against him. Had I not done so—"

"You are a Warden of Lyte before you are an adviser to a mortal king of another country, Marceau," Nelraido reminded him. "You have become far too accustomed to living among their kind and have forgotten your true loyalty. You can explain yourself to the Atiathél upon your return to Ardeltaniah, and only then will you learn how grave the situation truly is, for the coming war between Faltainyr Demura and Adengeld is but the smallest ripple resulting from a far greater impact."

Marceau didn't like the sound of this. He wished to ask the Arhcýtar of the Order of Ebony for the details now, but he couldn't spare more than a scant handful of minutes. If he should be summoned to the king and he was nowhere to be found, he would have a great deal more explaining to do. King Jaredh already expected him to accompany him when Faltainyr Demura marched to the Valamont Heights to engage Adengeld on the battlefield. How was he going to get out of this to return to Atialleia? The Atiathél would be most displeased if he caused further delay in returning.

"Then I must forge a lie for me to get away from here for any length of time," the swordmaster explained. "Would you be able to linger in Adner until I am able to obtain leave?"

Nelraido eyed him suspiciously, folding his arms. "I am here to take you back, Marceau. I won't be leaving without you, if that's what you mean. What are you suggesting, and how long do you need?"

Marceau shrugged in exasperation. "If you're able to write a letter in Armen addressed to me detailing a family crisis in Celait, and get it into the royal courier's bag before morning, there's a good chance King Jaredh will grant me leave," he offered. "He believes I have family living there, which is neither true nor completely false, but he has already tasked me with accompanying him to the battlefield.

We don't know when Adengeld's army will arrive, and the Duke of Lonnfeir has already made his first move on Almadeira, so we have his traitorous troops to deal with as well."

"You've certainly spread yourself rather thin this time haven't you?" Nelraido smiled wryly. "Are you hoping to kill two drakes with one stroke again, or do you not mind pulling a disappearing act on your beloved mortal king as well?" he added scathingly.

"Nelraido, please!" Marceau protested, his anger flaring. "I have kept up the glámar for many years now, and I am growing tired of it. It *is* time I let this facade go, but I cannot just yet."

"So you can betray the Nays and your kin, but you will not betray the king of this country?" the Arhcýtar snapped.

"Of course not!"

"Then what, Marceau? Explain!"

"Not here and not now," Marceau growled, regarding Nelraido levelly. "Your anger toward me is understandable given the circumstances, but you are a kind-hearted and understanding man beneath that Arhcýn'Drahknyr temper of yours. The situation is far more complex than you know, but I promise you now all of this has been a part of my mission here. I will explain it to you when we have more time. Now, I must go before my absence is suspected. Get the letter to me, and I will return to Atialleia with you the instant I am granted leave."

Nelraido rested his back against the cliff face, folding his arms impatiently. The greater the delay, the more likely Zerrçainne was to succeed in whatever moves she was planning next. She had already managed to manipulate enough circumstances that had forced Melkhar into situations according to her designs, and now with a copy of the Taecade Medo in her possession, it was only a matter of time before she discovered something useful to her purposes.

"Alright Marceau," Nelraido agreed, staring up at a blue sky blotched with downy clouds gliding lazily northward. "Supposing I find the ink and paper; where should I wait for you?"

"The *Singing Mermaid* inn on Adner's seafront," Marceau replied. "It's on the Marthel Quay, and it's where the passenger ships dock. If King Jaredh believes I will be going to Celait, he will expect me to take a ship from there."

"I see," Nelraido speculated. "If you're seen wandering anywhere else, it'll be suspicious, and with the Duke of Lonnfeir already at work to overthrow Jaredh, your loyalty to him will be called into question."

"You have the right of it," Marceau confirmed, turning away. "I am the *only* Lyte E'varis on this continent, and as far as I am aware, the only one with a government standing among the mortals," he added. "My situation here is a very complicated one; so I can only apologise for my behaviour having been construed as being unfaithful. Please think on it and try to understand. I shall await your letter, and if you should get bored waiting, use mindspeech to tell me where you're going."

III
Dragon's Gaol, Ehyenn

The meeting with Leyal had gone as expected; the Aurentai assassin of the *Noctae Venatora* was now in receipt of his next set of objectives, and he would soon release the gypsies, along with the Adjen priestess, Arieyta Ei Nazashan, to fulfil their end of the deal. Next, Zerrçainne needed to discuss the plan of action for uncovering Alymarn's dragon aspect with Rahntamein.

It had only been a matter of days since the great red dragon's nigh on fatal encounter with Melkhar, but his wounds were already almost healed. If a dragon could find a safe haven in which to recuperate, they were able to enter a state of deep meditation to speed up their healing processes, an ability the Drahknyr also possessed besides their natural ability to heal swiftly. The difference was the Drahknyr could not sleep during the process, whereas a dragon could.

One huge blazing eye opened as Zerrçainne swept into the dragon's lair, the ground vibrating beneath the sorceress' feet at the sound of the growl rumbling deep in his throat. "Do you know where it is?" Rahntamein sneered, slowly raising his head.

Zerrçainne smiled mirthlessly. "Not exactly," she answered smoothly. Sensing the dragon's anger, she held up a hand. "I have previously explored the Netherworld of Ne'Vedanhyr, I have travelled the Dryft, and I have been into the very depths of Phandaerys to the Abadhol, where I found the God Aspect. I found the Fey Aspect, which Rannvorn now carries within him, in Caran D'aerken where I met with the Shäada."

"Your point?" Rahntamein grunted, pretending to be disinterested.

"The Fey Aspect sat in the depths of a seemingly bottomless ravine known as the *Scar of the Fallen God*, caused by the cataclysmic events of the War of the Eclipse," the sorceress continued. "It is my guess if the other two aspects of Alymarn are anywhere, they are buried deep where no-one would ever find them. Were I truly dead as the Nays have believed for millennia, they would have remained lost. I can think of two such places in this realm, and only one of them can we reach at this point."

Rahntamein considered Zerrçainne's words carefully, intrigued by her intelligent string of thoughts. But like all dragons, he was impatient. "Get to the point," he rumbled. "Your riddles are just as frustrating as they are boring." He laid his head back down, closing his eyes.

Zerrçainne sighed in exasperation. "The first of those locations is the *Cave of Whispers* on the forgotten continent of Koborea. The second is the *Throat of Elinda*, which will be the more difficult of the two to approach because it is, dare I repeat myself? A *seemingly bottomless* pit beneath the sea guarded by a leviathan."

"Koborea? The land in which the climax of War of the Black Sun was fought?" Rahntamein yawned. "You think the Dragon Aspect is there?"

"I think either one of the two that remain could be there," Zerrçainne corrected, folding her arms beneath her cloak. "I sense something useful is out there at any rate, and I would consider that part of your oath fulfilled if you would simply venture there with me, whether or not we find one of Alymarn's *aspects*."

"My oath?" the dragon snorted in amusement, lifting and angling his head almost quizzically. "Bah! It is only because you promised me access to the *Drah'kanos o'va Harkjuun* I assist you sorceress!"

"You are incorrect, Rahntamein," Zerrçainne grinned wickedly. "I told you I knew of a way you might rival them, and while I said I knew the resting place of the Dragons of Origin was located beyond the Lhodha Drahvenaçym, I did not say I knew how to get there."

"Tell me how!" the red dragon demanded, rising, his lips curling into a snarl filled with fangs. The ever familiar glow of fire began to radiate from within his chest. Zerrçainne rolled her eyes, sighing as she vanished into thin air the moment he screamed his flames in her direction.

"You will know how to match them, Rahntamein, when you fulfil thine oath!" The sorceress' voice echoed throughout the chamber, her laughter following like the shrieking cackles of a woman gone insane.

With a deafening roar that shook rocks from the roof of the cavern, Rahntamein stormed out of his lair, his gargantuan body followed by his great meandering tail, and took to the skies, bellowing again from the depths of his lungs, alerting every village and hamlet along the Sidel's Coast to his anger.

IV
Atialleia

The moment *Greshendier* passed beneath the final grand arch, the illusory veil surrounding the city shimmered and vanished, revealing the vast metropolis in all its otherworldly glory; clusters of great white turrets tipped with gold struck up at a vermillion sky like colossal lances raised in triumph against a backdrop of cinnamon-hued mountains.

Awestruck, Zehn felt his jaw slacken. Staring, mouth agape at the splendour of it, he felt a shiver run down his spine as something of a memory flickered in his mind, as if he'd been here before. He ventured a quick glance at Larkh, whose stunned expression told him he probably felt much the same. He averted his gaze as Arcaydia approached the pirate.

A massive crystal shaped like a tear and glowing with a soft jade hue loomed before them, positioned at the end of a protruding section of the quayside. It was supported by an elegant golden frame with an equally elaborate arch over the top. Though it certainly wasn't as large as the Altirnathé Zehn had seen on the mountain summit near Almadeira, it was still a sight to behold against all other phenomenal feats of architecture in this place of transcendence.

"Behold the capital city of the Nays homeland!" the Navàmier announced, standing at Larkh's side by the helm. "Atialleia."

The ship's crew almost forgot their work as the expanse of the scene before them stretched into a broad panoramic landscape, gradually melting into the distance.

The moment was interrupted as Larkh noticed the apprehension in Arcaydia's eyes. It was clear she harboured some kind of fear he suspected related to the business of her being the Mindseer Oracle the leviathan had spoken of. Did she even have a choice in the matter? It was one thing escaping the bonds of fealty to one's society as he had –

albeit under tragic circumstances he dared not think about – but it was quite another being born into a predetermined role.

"What happened between us," Arcaydia hesitated, her voice almost a whisper, "keep it a secret from them; particularly Kherindal and Nelraido, but especially Melkhar. Did we actually—"

Larkh shook his head, giving her a wary look. "We'll talk another time. For now, best you tell Argwey not to gossip. An' remember, Daron was the one who saw you in my cabin," he advised. "When your bloody arrogant cousin has gone, I'll make it known no word of it is to be breathed while we're here. Rumours spread like wildfire on a ship, no matter its size. Mark my words. But that's not the reason for the look on your face, is it?"

Arcaydia nodded, her fingers lacing into the curling locks of her hair nervously. "There's another thing," she added. Larkh inclined his head, listening. "I will have to leave the ship when we are in the port, and on top of that, I can feel her presence already." Unease wrapped itself around her like a cold, oppressive blanket.

"By *her* you mean—"

"...Melkhar."

Larkh regarded her with a dubious expression. "Is that—"

"Why I've been so quiet since Kherindal found us?" she finished quietly. "Yes."

He averted his gaze, but found his right hand clasped in both of hers as she tried to reassure him; "don't worry; there will be more to come. Nays culture is different from what you and your men are used to, but there are some similarities. Just follow the rules you're given and you should be fine."

Larkh's eyes flickered to Kherindal, whose stately appearance alone commanded respect from all around him, and he glared, knowing full well even his own crew were cowed by his presence.

Sensing eyes on him, the Navàmier turned his attention to them and pointed toward the crystal. "That is a Varleima," he explained, shooting a knowing glance at the pendant hanging below the gold locket around Larkh's neck. "It is the kind of artefact ordinary mortals ought to leave well alone; but of course you already knew that." At the contempt he saw blazing in Larkh's eyes, he smiled politely. "Not that *you* are in any way ordinary."

Arcaydia stiffened, her brow creasing. "Rin, I don't think—"

"How about you stop patronisin' me an' tell me where I'm to berth my ship?" Larkh snapped, stepping in front of Arcaydia, "for in case you'd forgotten, I am her captain whether you stand on board or not."

Arcaydia winced, rubbing her eyes with both hands. *'Wonderful...'*

Kherindal's eyes widened in surprise, and then he burst out laughing. "My, aren't you valiant! What made you think I was trying to take over your beloved ship? Please accept my apologies Captain Savaldor; planting such thoughts in your head was not my intention." His unfamiliar accent sounded ever more peculiar in his mirth as he spoke Armen. He gestured theatrically to the left. "Feel free to find a suitable berth anywhere along the western side of the harbour, but you must understand, we cannot allow too many unsavoury misdemeanours in Atialleia; so while your personal access to the city will be closely supervised, your crew's will be limited to the dockside areas. We are very wary of strangers; pirates especially. I am quite sure you will agree it is a necessary precaution."

Larkh's jaw clenched, his posture rigid. Forcing a smile, he replied with an edge of sarcasm; "that's perfectly understandable, Navàmier – I do hope I pronounced your title correctly – but while I'll endeavour to put your rules across to my men who only follow orders given on this ship, don't expect perfection from them. I wager your harbour'll become just a tad livelier for a while."

"I admire your spirit Captain," Kherindal chuckled, giving Larkh a measuring look. He turned and strode past, clapping him on the back as he went. "I think I'm going to enjoy working with you."

Larkh's brow arched incredulously. "I beg your pardon?"

Kherindal remained with his back turned, hiding a smirk. "Don't concern yourself at the moment; it's nothing to worry about."

In his frustration Larkh started down the steps towards him. Arcaydia grasped a hold of his arm and shook her head. "Leave it," she told him, releasing her grip. "He's like this with everyone, especially those he can get a rise out of."

"Annoying isn't it?" Zehn called from the quarterdeck.

"Go fuck yourself Zehn," Larkh muttered, diverting his attention to the helmsman, ordering him to guide *Greshendier* around to the western side of the harbour as the Nays ship ahead of them made its way east. Satisfied his former quarry had been put in his place for once, Zehn grinned to himself.

Aureate rays of declining sunlight cast Atialleia in gleaming honey-gold luminescence, causing the golden rooftops of the city's major buildings to glitter with dazzling radiance as *Greshendier* was moored along the whitestone quayside. The resplendent light was accentuated by the terracotta peaks of the *Tsolàiyh'unsyld Kelntnéial*, the Sunset Frontier.

Crowding the dockside were dozens of elegantly chiselled faces with bright and inquisitive eyes outlined in black. They were drawn to the unfamiliar warship as it had been escorted into the harbour. Some pointed and conversed over the orb clutched in the talons of the eagle figurehead. As yet, no-one appeared to show any hostility, but all were as curious as they were circumspect. However, there was one individual in particular who caught the attention of all standing on deck, Arcaydia most of all. That chilling stare made her spine freeze.

Melkhar stood on the quay with domineering authority in her typical tight-fitting black leathers. She stood upright; shoulders held back, arms folded, long legs parted.

"Navàmier Valan!" she called out, her strong, vibrant voice enough to cause those standing nearby to step back.

"Arcaydia séi vhar kamen qeth mhir narh! Tselndés selhé durnh emýhràndhllr!" [55]

Kherindal gave Arcaydia a stern look, indicating his head toward Melkhar. "You'd better do as she says," he told her firmly. "I will catch up with you later."

"You won't be leaving?" Arcaydia asked.

The Navàmier shook his head. "I'll be here for a while yet; there is work to be done concerning these new friends of yours."

Arcaydia nodded, sighing inwardly. She approached Larkh and Zehn – who were once more speaking peaceably – both of them conferring, their eyes locked on Melkhar. Following her hasty explanation that she must disembark immediately, Larkh gave her a solemn nod of approval, and pulled her into a friendly embrace. To Zehn's surprise, she then turned to him and gave him a quick peck on the cheek before hurrying below deck to retrieve her belongings.

Ten minutes later she hurried down the gangway to join the striking flame-haired warrior waiting on the quay. The two men watched keenly as the lofty stranger's callous stare softened, albeit scarcely, as she looked upon Arcaydia. Few words were exchanged before the pair set off, soon vanishing beyond the city's main gate.

Side by side, Larkh and Zehn watched them go, and for a brief moment, something invisible and alien arced between them in the cool evening air as a bracing wind swept down from the high-rising russet slopes that cradled Atialleia in its lap.

---

[55] Arcaydia is to come with me now! Send her down immediately!

"By all the gods," Zehn murmured, suppressing the shock of stark realisation, fixing his eyes on the gate, "she really is the one Marceau mentioned in the contract he sent to me. Even the statues of her bear her likeness! And I didn't take Raeon seriously..."

"You mean you never believed the Drahknyr actually existed?" Larkh asked, surveying their surroundings, eventually shifting his line of sight to the Varleima.

"I believe there is always some truth to every legend," Zehn admitted, adjusting his bandana, "but how much? That's another question entirely."

LORE
The Legend of the Koborean Eclipse

Live strong in hope and faith.
Kensaiyr Proverb

The month of Arenun, 947 AN Aerétas Nehkúridas, the Era of Guardians

The time at which the moon blotted out the sun over the skies of Koborea during the War of the Black Sun was only moments after Aevnatureis suffered the rupture, and lasted as each of the seven Kaesan'Drahknyr fell. It passed mere seconds after the last of the seven to fall drew his last breath, before the storm clouds rolled in and the heavens opened, saturating all of blood-soaked Koborea for a full hour until bright sunlight washed over the desolate landscape once more.

Raiyah, Goddess of the Sun, was believed to close her eyes in sorrow at the fall of her greatest warriors as eclipse darkened the sky. The following storm was, therefore, representative of her anger, pain and tears. In the rarest of all events that the Kaesan'Drahknyr died, as they did in the War of the Black Sun, such a death was only temporary. It mattered not they were immortal and would rise to life again. Their amaranthine existence is believed to be the very reason for the goddess' despair. They had died mortal deaths protecting their charge, but their peace would not last. They are her generals, her protectors, and they are Aeldynn's guardians, but unlike other Drahknyr who could at least die in battle and be reborn in a cycle, the Kaesan'Drahknyr would always remain as they were. They could rest for many long years in deep slumber that could span months, centuries or even millennia, but that was the best they could ever hope for. Eventually they would be woken for a purpose and could remain active for an indefinite amount of time, from years to many centuries.

The war was won in those moments except for the continued existence of the menace of Alymarn and the woman who loved him. Alymarn's unnatural gift that defied all laws of magica stemmed Aevnatureis' own outward flow of power, causing it to swell and explode, resulting in the rupture. It is unknown how Alymarn was able to access the Aevanythra, the static realm in which Aevnatureis itself exists; but it is believed to be due to the instability Aevnatureis suffered when he was first given life as a result of the joining of a fertile Drahknyr and an Aurentai magician. He and his demon allies had been weakened by the Kaesan'Drahknyr, and it had been in their final moments the Lyte E'varis and the Lyterané finished him and divided his spirit into four; the Nays Aspect, the Dragon Aspect, the Fey Aspect, and the God Aspect – his soul. They were sealed and dispersed into far off realms, with the God Aspect having been cast into the Abadhol beneath the tip of Phandaerys.

EPILOGUE

I
The Stairway

The Stairway sat atop a series of steep high-climbing crags, forming sheer cliffs on each side except south. The stone steps running up the centre of the edifice, timeworn and slick with moss, appeared to have been sculpted from the very crags themselves. Near the summit, where an imposing, weathered gateway stood, was an open air shrine not unlike the one perched on top of Dehltas' mountain; except there was no great statue to be seen here.

Located on an unnamed island west of Baen, this remote place was more ancient than even the Drahknyr, and in the quiet of the fading evening light, one could just hear the faint thrum of its power.

Zerrçainne ascended the final set of steps leading up to the ancient monument; the keen wind rippled her long blonde hair and the cascading black cloak wrapped around her shoulders. She regarded the gate with avid curiosity and determination to unlock its secrets. According to the Taecade Medo, the Stairway could only be activated under certain phases of the sun or moon depending on the location sought. There were even realms only reachable during much rarer events, such as a full solar or lunar eclipse. It was designed to unlock locations only accessible to those capable of enduring the otherworldly environments that lay beyond.

"So, why is this gate not connected to Dhavenkos Mhal?" Dhentaro enquired, standing at the side of the great arch. He ran his ebony fingers over the smooth whitestone, now grey as slate, tarnished with age and lack of maintenance. His talons barely made a faint scratch as he raked them across its finely sculpted surface. "Why was the gate in the Dryft so much easier to open?"

"It wasn't easy to open in the slightest," Zerrçainne replied, examining the pedestal, "but the truth of why no phandaeric realms open from here is we are in Aeldynn, a realm of Aevnatureis. We are only able to utilise the magica of Phandaerys here because we are tethered to it."

"Huh," Dhentaro grunted, curiously examining the artefact further. "And this thing has some kind of device that makes it work I suppose, and we don't know where it is? Am I right?"

Zerrçainne's white eye flashed as her gaze flickered to Dhentaro; she was smiling wickedly. "That doesn't matter," she purred. "The Taecade Medo mentions little of the Stairway, but I know of a tome which can tell me all I need to know; the *Mahktas vér'te Lunéiyhr*, which means 'Book of the Moon'. It is one of a number of heavily guarded volumes, and by all rights, the Taecade Medo is one of them, but in the hands of mortals, you can be sure the guard will never be sufficient to hide something so valuable from prying eyes."

Dhentaro plopped down cross-legged by the gate, cocking his head in contemplation. "Have you any idea where a copy might be found?"

Zerrçainne smiled thinly. "The Archaenen may have one of the few copies ever made; though I suspect they will not be so careless as to risk another infiltration so soon. My contact there, however, might just be able to help me with that one."

II
Atialleia

The silence was deafening in the small whitestone villa on the estate of the Kaesan'Drahknyr. Each of the seven lived in one, and all were built on a single, wide plot of land on the Zephyr Gallery, an aerial garden on the slopes of the nearest mountain, rising above the plateau where the Atialléane Palace stood. In the Daeihn tongue, it translated to *Zaphraeys Ghàleyr*.

Arcaydia had no idea how long the silence lasted; it could have been five minutes or half an hour for all she knew, but it was growing too uncomfortable to bear. Her heart was thumping so hard she could hear it. Melkhar had barely said a word to her since they'd left the harbour, and now she said nothing.

Unable to put up with it any longer, she lifted her eyes to the tall, commanding figure standing in the doorway of the living room and snapped; "aren't you going to say anything?" She stepped toward her. "Normally you'd come out with some kind of sarcastic remark, or lecture me for being stupid! If you hadn't abandoned me then—"

Hot pain lashed into the side of Arcaydia's face. Trembling, she brought a hand to her cheek. It throbbed and stung madly, making her eyes water. "I—I'm so sorry," she stammered, "I didn't mean that. Honestly, I—"

"I see how it would seem that way to you," Melkhar muttered, turning on her heel. "But the truth matters not. If you have not yet eaten this evening, do let me know." She planted two silver coins on to a small wooden table standing by the arched doorframe, and strode out of the room.

Arcaydia's mouth fell open, gazing up from the floor at the vacant doorway. Pushing to her feet, she approached the table. Examining the coins for several moments, she puzzled over what Melkhar could have meant by leaving them there. Thinking hard on Melkhar's words, she reached a conclusion. *'She can't mean... she wants to eat out with me?'*

she ruminated on the thought, her eyes widening in realisation. *'Why didn't she just ask? Thinking about it, I don't know anything about her; she won't say anything about her past, and I couldn't get much conversation out of her when we travelled to Almadeira.'*

Reaching out, Arcaydia took the coins and examined them; an image of the goddess Raiyah in the centre of the sun was on one side, with a wyvern on the other. That made thirty fal; enough for two. She sighed inwardly.

'One of the seven greatest warriors and leaders to ever exist, but unable ask someone out to dinner? By the gods, what happened to her to make her like this?' she wondered. Clasping the coins tightly, she left the room to look for her.

Finding her nowhere inside, or in the small courtyard at the back of the premises, she approached the staircase at the end of the hall on the upper level. It was hidden behind an arch, leading out on to the terrace. There the Kaesan'Drahknyr stood, her great wings spread wide; a silhouette to marvel at against the backdrop of the setting sun as it cast a honey-gold glow over the breezy mountain meadow.

"I uh—" Arcaydia faltered, swallowing hard as her heart attempted to leap into her throat as Melkhar folded her wings and spun to face her. "I'd like to; I... haven't eaten this evening yet. I don't think I'll look decent with a burning red face though..."

"You may use my aluren crystal," Melkhar suggested. "It will calm the skin."

"Th-thank you," Arcaydia faltered.

Releasing her wings from their corporeal form, Melkhar approached the staircase. She paused, listening as Arcaydia continued; "you know... I really didn't mean what I said. I was just angry you didn't say anything. I always thought there would be a good reason why you didn't come back."

Melkhar shrugged half-heartedly. "Forget about it," she insisted, starting toward the stairs again. "Use the aluren, and be ready in half an hour."

The matter was closed; Arcaydia knew as much, but what did it say about how Melkhar felt? If she didn't care about what was said, she wouldn't have struck her, would she? Did she forgive her for saying such a stupid thing or not? Other questions whirred around in her mind on top of the conglomeration of puzzles surrounding the enigmatic figure of her guardian. Why was Melkhar her mentor, and also her guardian? Why was it not a Galétriahn Highlord with knowledge of seers, or perhaps even a seer like Lésos? There was something almost familiar about her, and then she began to sense loneliness so bitter and so profound it sent a chilling wave of despair through her heart. And what about the words of Albharenos? There was a link between the words of the leviathan, not only to herself, but also to Melkhar; she was sure of it. "Can I just ask something?" she blurted.

Melkhar stopped again, arching a brow at her and folding her arms. Clearly she didn't appreciate being delayed. "Go on."

Arcaydia shrunk back sheepishly. "Why were you the one chosen to be my mentor and guardian?" she enquired. "And the white leviathan, Albharenos, said I was *the very embodiment of she whose destiny was destroyed.* What does that mean? Did you ever know the one who was supposed to be the previous Mindseer Oracle?"

Melkhar stiffened. Drawing in a deep breath, her fingers tightened around her arms. "It is too soon for these questions," she told her. "I am as yet without the liberty to discuss them. The answer has not yet been confirmed; only suspected. There is much work to be done this next week, for your new friends – Zehn and Larkh – have a test to complete."

"A test?" Arcaydia gasped; "what kind of test?"

There was a dangerous flash in Melkhar's steely emerald eyes as she inclined her head towards her. "A test that will determine if they truly are the Keys of the Origin."

KEYS OF THE ORIGIN GLOSSARY

Adels, the – Raiyah's guardian trinity: *Manahveria* (courage/valour), *Nalaueii* (wisdom/logic), *Varuneiwa* (harmony/peace).

Adjeeah (ad-jey-ah) – the goddess of fire. She is the patron goddess of the Adjen cult.

Aeldynn (ayl-dinn) – the name of the physical realm and also the planet.

Aethyraeum (ay-tih-ray-um) – *Ethereal flower*. Brought to Aeldynn long ago by the Drahknyr for their restorative properties, they were adapted to grow on earthly soil; though only in warm highland regions. Due to differences between their native habitat and the earthly realms, they do not always grow well.

Aeva'Daeihn (ay-fa' day-een) – meaning '*of Aevnatureis*' and '*to call into being*'. It is the name given to the Nays priesthood, who are in service to the Sun Goddess, Raiyah.

Aevanythra (ay-fa-neeth-ra) – the realm in which Aevnatureis exists.

Aevnatureis (ayf-na-tu-rey) – mortals usually refer to it as the *Foundation, or World Crystal*. It upholds all that may be considered natural, and it is the original source of *spiritus* and magica. The words *Aeva* and *Aevan* refer to anything relating directly to Aevnatureis itself.

Albequa (al-beh-kwa) – a giant tree with off-white/grey bark (albino sequoia).

Albharenos (al-vah-re-nos) – the white leviathan (nicknamed 'the ghost') dwelling in the northern waters of the Sendero de Mercader. He is a guardian of Ardeltaniah, and is oath-bound to the Mindseer Oracle.

Altirnathé (al-tir-nah-tey) – enormous shards of turquoise/aquamarine coloured crystals protruding from the ground, usually in highland areas such as mountains. *Altirna* energy flows through them, which can be mined as a fluid known simply as altirna. It has a variety of properties, including: hardening and cleaning structures, and powering archana.

Aluren (al-uhr-en) – a translucent crystal of ivory colour, similar to the volcanic Alum crystal. It reduces swelling and calms the skin.

Anjeania (an-jey-ah-ni-ah) – one of the larger islands surrounding Enkaiyta.

Anu (ah-noo) – the spirit of a continent. **Amarey** (am-ah-ray) and **Kobhoa** (koh-voh-ah) are two of them.

Archana (ar-cah-na) – mechanical devices powered by altirna or other forms of magica – predominantly Nays magi-technology.

Ardeltaniah (ar-del-ta-ni-ah) – the Nays homeland.

Arhcýn'Drahknyr (ah' seen-drahk-neer) – either a prodigal Drahknyr, or an ancient Drahknyr of exceptional skill, usually also an Arhcýtar.

Arhcýtar (ahc'sih-tar) – any Drahknyr military commander with an additional rank level 1-5: *A'retiasr* (1st rank), *Te'ltiasr* (2nd rank), *Dretiasr* (3rd rank), *Vaytiasr* (4th rank), *Čihltiasr* (5th rank).

Arkkiennah [ar-kee-en-nah] – the Atiathél of the Nays.

Atialleia (ah-tee-ah-leya) – the Nays capital city.

Atiathas (m) / Atiathél (f) – (ah-tee-ah-thas / theyl) the emperor/empress of the Nays.

Avamont – a port city in Lorhnia in the central region of Zaern'Kairnell. Produces fine wine.

Caran D'aerken (cah-ran d'air-ken) – the lands of the Shäada; located in the north of Zaern'Kairnell to the east of Icetaihn. Black canyons and deep pine forests can be found there.

Cerenyr (seh-re-neer) – the forest-dwelling elves of Cerendiyll and Nirskay; they are typically fair-skinned with either blond/blonde, black or brown hair.

Cheréqua – giant redwood tree (sequoia).

Daeihn (dahy-een) – the language of the Nays. The word itself means "to call into being".

Daynallar (Valley of) [day-nal-lar] – the great valley of dragons/dragonkind dividing Armaran into two countries, running north-west to south-east.

Dehltas [dairl-tas] – a greater hybrid dragon [black] living in the Valley of Daynallar. Long ago he swore an oath to protect the kingdom of Adengeld.

Dhakar Miúhrer [dah-kar mih-yoo-rair] – the capital city of the Shäada, sheltered within a naturally protected canyon in Caran D'aerken.

Dhavenkos Mhal (dah-ven-kohs mahl) – a series of underworlds, and home to a large variety of demonic species, including the Fralh.

Drahknyr (drah-k-neer) – ethereal winged warriors born into physical form into the Nays race.

Dragon's Gate – Drahkouenýs Kahgathis (drah-koo-en-ees kah-ga-this) in Daeihn. A teleportation gate large enough for dragons to fly through.

Drakaan (dra-kahn) – the language of dragonkind; "*kaan*" being the draconic word for *speech*.

Dyr'Efna (dir' eff-na) – The Dryft; the mirror plane that separates the realms of Aevnatureis from those of Phandaerys.

Eidolon Ring – *Eléstolaiyn Aneiro* (el-eys-to-layn ah-ney-ro) in Daeihn. A colossal band of spiritual energy circling the planet where the souls of the lost and damned dwell in purgatory, which occasionally converges with Aeldynn, causing the physical and astral realms to overlap unnaturally.

Enkaiyta (en-kai-ih-ta) – a very large island pinned between Ardeltaniah and Manlakhedran. It's typically tropical climate is influenced by a number of factors: the Wahren Sea, and Eutheniar and Athacas Oceans, as well as the Eutheniar, Soreiden and Elindas Ridges, and the mountain ranges of eastern Ardeltaniah.

Felanshia – a region in the centre of the continent of Zaern'Kairnell well-known for its wine.

Fralh (frahl) – an ebony-skinned demonic race; tribal in nature with shaggy flame-red hair, who adorn themselves with red tattoos for a number of purposes. They are beast-like in appearance, somewhat resembling lions with long tails and violet/lavender-coloured eyes.

Galétriahn (ga-leh-tri-ahn) – Nays individuals harbouring a greater amount of magica than average train and eventually become this kind of mage. The word comes from an amalgamation of the Nays words galé'de (gal-ey-deh - grand), and triahnsjýr (tri-ahn-s-yir - thaumaturge). Highlords are known as Galétahr (m), and Galétyr (f).

Icetaihn (*ee-seh-tayn*) – an icy region to the far north of Zaern'Kairnell.

Kaesan'Drahknyr (kay-san-drahk-neer) – the seven highest ranking and most powerful Drahknyr; second only to the gods. Some mortals have referred to them as Dragonmasters.

Kathaedra (kah-tay-dra) – an enormous place of worship built by the Nays; a cathedral.

Kensaiyr (ken-say-ir) – the white-silver elves. Their hair is pure white or silver, their eyes aquamarine in colour, and their skin like porcelain. Their bond with the Nays has long stood the test of time. They, like all elven races, are the people of the Moon God, Lyte, but they were the first of the elves to come into being.

Koborea (ko-bo-rey-ah) – a continent shaped like an eye with a largely barren landscape, and the location where the climax of the War of the Eclipse/Black Sun was fought.

Lhodha Drahvenaçym (loh-dh-ah drah-ven-ah-sim) – a parallel physical world from which dragonkind originate.

Lyte (lite) – the elven god representing the Moon; particularly the patron deity of the Kensaiyr.

Lyte E'varis (lite-eh' vah-ree) – the Wardens of Lyte, each is a member of the Kensaiyr.

Lyterané (lite-eh-rah-nay) – the three members of the Nays who became *Lyte E'varis.*

Macea (ma-shay) – one of the islands surrounding Enkaiyta. *Maceani Rum* is produced here.

Magica (ma-jih-ca) – a collective or plural term for magic.

Manlakhedran (man-la-keh-dran) – a continent in the centre of the map bearing tropical and barren/desert landscapes.

Marlinikhda (mar-lin-ik-da) – the forested lands of southern Ardeltaniah, Kalthis' homeland, and also the name of the forest-dwelling tribes in the area.

Nairéilln – the native language of the Kensaiyr and the Cerenyr elves.

Nalthenýn (nal-the-neen) – the realm in which the Nays, Kensaiyr, and Cerenyr move on to when their time in Aeldynn draws to a close; their place of afterlife. Those who die while in Aeldynn (referring to the physical plane of that name), or on another plane of existence, are sent to a far region in this plane.

Naredau (na-reh-daw) – a free settlement close to Enkaiyta ruled by pirates/smugglers.

Naturyth (na-tuh-rith) – also naturyn. Pale ice-blue crystals capable of inducing stasis/hibernation.

Nays – known as the guardian race, they are the people of the Sun Goddess, Raiyah. They are the only race with the physical capability of bringing the Drahknyr into physical form, and as such, were chosen.

Ne'Vedanhyr (ne' veh-danh-ir) – the Netherworld that lay between the physical world of Aeldynn, and Dyr'Efna, the Dryft.

Nira'Eléstara (ny-ra' el-ey-sta-ra) – the astral realm. It is the spirit world where the living are tethered until they die before moving on to their respective afterlife, and it is also the realm in which people dream.

Noctae Venatora [noc-tahy ve-na-to-ra] – literally, *Night Hunters*. They are the largest and most renowned organisation of professional assassins in all Aeldynn.

Origin, the – the creators of Aeldynn who vanished generations before any Drahknyr were born into the physical world, now lost to history and mythology.

Phandaerys (fahn-day-ris) – the inverted/opposite counterpart of Aevnatureis. It is the *world crystal* of the underworlds.

Rahntamein [rahn-ta-mayn] – a tyrannical greater hybrid dragon [red]; put into long sleep and chained in the Dragon's Gaol beneath the island of Ehyenn south of Armaran.

Raiyah (rahy-ah) – patron goddess of the Nays, representing the Sun.

Shäada (shah-ah-da) – the shadow elves; grey-skinned, black-haired and amber-eyed. The race that bridges the gap between elves and fey. They are known to be reclusive and aggressive.

Tourenco (toor-en-co) – the capital city of Enkaiyta. Produces *Tourenco* Dark (rum).

Tseika'Drahknyr (sai-ka-drah-k-neer) – the three members of the Kensaiyr who became Drahknyr, and specifically provide auxiliary support to the Kaesan'Drahknyr.

Valdysthar (val-dis-thah) – the ethereal realm in which Raiyah resides; also the place where the Drahknyr originate.

Vandro-en (van-droh –en) – the language of the demonic Fralh.

Vàreia (vah-rey-ah) – the Spring Festival in Armaran and Ardeltaniah; Nays origin.

Varleima (var- ley(lai)-ma) – a large, jade-coloured crystal shaped like a tear. They have a number of uses, such as soul-binding particular types of armour and weaponry to users, and casting barriers. Varlenstones (Varlen Artefacts) are small chunks of Varleima to be turned into jewellery for portable use and to bind items to those who may have no access to a Varleima, or who are less adept at using magica.

Velhana (vel-ha-na) – the patron goddess of the Fey races.

Yeudanikhda (yu-da-nik-da) – the mountain/plains-dwelling cousins of the Marlinikhda. One group left Ardeltaniah, and consequently thinned their tribal Nays bloodline by merging with the human tribes of Daynallar in Armaran.

Zaern'Kairnell (zay-ern'kair-nel) – the largest continent in Aeldynn, on the eastern side of the map.

NAYS (DAEIHN) PRONUNCIATION

à – ah
á – ou (as in house)
ae – ay (like the letter a)
au – aw (as in jaw)
bh – v (soft)
é – ey
eu – u (like the letter u)
gh – g (*soft*, like genre, h is lifted)
č – ch (as in child)
ç – s (as in Français)
í – e (like the letter e)
ii – ih (like it and in but *longer*)
j – y (as in yarn)
ll – y, sometimes ll (as in Versailles and villa)
ph – p*h* (drop the h)
š – sh (as in shoe).
th – t*h* (drop the h)
ú – *y*oo
v – *v*f (sounds like an f, the v is almost silent)
w – v (hard)
ý – ee (*long* as in keen)
zh – j (as in sojourn)
' – (indicates a pause in a word)

NAYS NUMBERS

1. A'ren
2. Te'les
3. Dren
4. Vayen
5. Čihlt
6. Seias
7. Zaven
8. Aiyeth
9. Naere
10. Threln

Niathenica Ocean
(West)

Aeurenial Ridge

ARDELTANIAH

Western Aeuren
(West Aeuren Sea)

Sendero de Mercader

KOBOREA

Wa

Eastern Aeuren
(East Aeuren Sea)

ARMARAN

Soreiden Sea

Aeurenial Ocean

Soreiden Ridge

LANDS
OF ELINI

AZAERAS
THE UNSEEN ISLES

Inèts Channel

AIECE

N
W   E
S

MAP OF AELDYNN

Niathenica Ocean
(East)
thenica Ridge
Icetaihn
Eutheniar Ridge
Zhenathos
Sea
Eutheniar Ocean
Senetheren Sea
Enkaiyta
Zaern'Kairnell
Manlakhedran
Medean Sea
Athacas Ocean
Mithrans Channel
Elindas Ridge
Inètathica Ocean

ABOUT THE AUTHOR

Melissa A. Joy is a new fantasy author who challenges the conventional expectations of fantasy and takes them to a whole new level. It is no secret that she believes in the existence of all things fantastical, and that *anything* is possible.

She began building the world of Aeldynn and started writing seriously aged approximately 13, and has since developed it into something truly magical worth sharing. From the glorious winged Drahknyr and wise and fearsome dragons to pirates of the high seas and a world rich with history and lore, her imagination could be said to be limitless.

When she isn't locked in a reverie about what's going on in the world of Aeldynn, she's probably out sailing the high seas on a tall ship, or perhaps dressed up in costume at an anime convention.

Connect with her on:
Facebook: /DefineImagineMJ
Twitter: @DefineImagineMJ
Websites: www.aeldynnlore.com
https://definitiveimagination.wordpress.com/

Lightning Source UK Ltd.
Milton Keynes UK
UKHW01f0746051018
330054UK00001B/365/P